The Dangerous Flood

By the same author:

THE BLUE RIBAND
WITH MAGIC IN HER EYES
HEIRS TO ADVENTURE

The Dangerous Flood

DEREK NICHOLLS

LITTLE, BROWN AND COMPANY

A *Little, Brown* Book

First published in Great Britain by
Little, Brown and Company in 1994

All characters in this publication are fictitious and any resemblance to real persons, living or dead, is purely coincidental

A CIP catalogue record for this book
is available from the British Library

ISBN 0 316 91025 2

Typeset by Solidus (Bristol) Limited
Printed and bound in Great Britain by
Mackays of Chatham PLC, Kent

Little, Brown and Company (UK) Limited
Brettenham House
Lancaster Place
London WC2E 7EN

For
Janice and Graeme Webster
Dear friends and stalwart encouragers

Author's Note

This is a work of fiction and all the principal characters are imaginary. I emphasise this particularly in respect of the Archduchess Annaliese von Habsburg, who is presented as a member of a very real and distinguished family. The Habsburgs ruled Austria uninterruptedly from 1273 until their enforced exile in 1919 and they still exist. The present head of the family, Dr Otto von Habsburg, eldest son of the last Emperor, is a member of the European Parliament and has many living relatives. But Annaliese, her parents Joseph and Elsa, and her brother Leopold are products of my imagination.

However, since the story takes place against the backdrop of events in Europe and Great Britain, my characters do tend to have contact with real people, individuals whose place in history puts them in the public domain.

My thanks go to Lisa Eveleigh, my agent, and Alice Wood, my editor, both of whom contributed ideas and encouragement.

Derek Nicholls

THE BOOTHBY-GRAFFOE FAMILY
1914–1925

Edmund Boothby-Graffoe
7th Duke of Lincolnshire

William,
8th Duke of Lincolnshire
(1855–1921)

Ralph
9th Duke
(1890–1925)
marries
=
Celia Jameson
(1903–)

Gerald
(1892–1916)

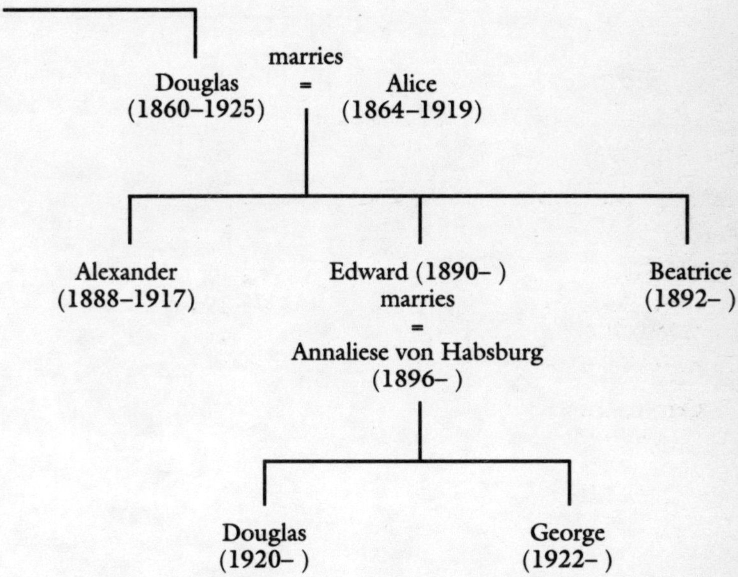
marries
Douglas
(1860–1925)
=
Alice
(1864–1919)
Alexander
(1888–1917)
Edward (1890–)
marries
=
Annaliese von Habsburg
(1896–)
Beatrice
(1892–)
Douglas
(1920–)
George
(1922–)

1

28 May 1914
The Double-Headed Eagle

Edward Boothby-Graffoe leaned out of a carriage window, surveying the scene on the platform as the special train pulled out of the Deli Payaudvar, Budapest's gateway to Europe. On the whole, the Hungarians had done rather well, entering into the spirit of the three-day visit with a sort of manic enthusiasm, finding the half-hearted attempts to humour them a rich source of cynical merriment. But now it was over, they couldn't wait to get back to what passed for normal in this strange, febrile city – a seething hotch-potch of ideas which owed more to Constantinople than Paris or Vienna. Magyar extravagance, alternating between feverish joy and deep depression, completed the volatile brew that was Budapest.

The guard of honour stood itself at ease before the three coaches conveying the members of the Imperial Family had cleared the platform. Every bit as eager to be done with the pomp, the civilian dignitaries were removing top hats and mopping brows: bandsmen were grounding their instruments: acting on orders, two boys began to roll up the red carpet. Looking back, Edward smiled wryly.

In one of those moments that seem to last a disturbingly long time, he realised that the girl standing slightly apart from a group of officials probably thought he was smiling at her. Obviously the daughter of someone important, she was both beautiful and contemptuous, sneering openly at the whole charade. Then, her mood changed. She stared directly at Edward, appraising and challenging. Making no secret of her findings, she smiled and waved, conveying blatant invitation and regret in a single fraction of a second. Deeply embarrassed, Edward drew back and closed the window.

The Dual Monarchy of Austro-Hungary, so powerful and grand to the casual observer, was, in reality, the uneasiest, least likely of alliances. The thirty-odd years between 1867 and 1900 had seen a level of disagreement that was low enough to allow the advocates of the partnership to paper over the cracks to produce a semblance of harmony. Since the turn of the century, however, friction had increased relentlessly, with Vienna forced to make concessions. In 1902, the Hungarian Army had been granted the right to its own flag and language; in 1908, a specifically Hungarian national bank was established; there were dozens of other contentious issues. But Austria, sniffing at every opportunity for war with Serbia, was desperate to boost the illusion of unity.

The visit to Budapest of the one-hundred-strong delegation had been a cynical attempt to patronise and placate what was, to most Austrian eyes, the lesser part of the Dual Monarchy. A handful of cabinet ministers – rumoured to be losers in a lottery – together with their senior civil servants, a motley collection of experts in every conceivable problem; and a token fragment of the Imperial Family were bundled off to Budapest and told to be charming and useful. When ordering the expedition, von Berchtold, the Foreign Minister, had stated that the scheme was entirely the idea of the Emperor himself. No one believed Franz Joseph remotely capable of such stupidity.

On the surface, Edward Boothby-Graffoe, an official at the British Embassy in Vienna, was an improbable member of the mission. Much as he would have liked an excuse to visit Budapest, the chance of an invitation seemed remote. But, after a whisper from one of his Hungarian contacts, Count Gustav Altendorff, the civil servant who ran the Austrian Foreign Ministry, virtually demanded Edward's presence. It seemed that the Budapest municipal authorities were anxious to increase the amount of electricity available to the city. There were undoubtedly men from the University on Ringstrasse who would pontificate impressively, but Altendorff had little time for academics. In any case, no one knew more about steam turbines, the up-and-coming method of driving generators, than young Boothby-Graffoe, the man in charge of the Trade Bureau at the British Embassy.

In the sanctuary of his reserved compartment, Edward regained the composure that had been shattered by the bewitching girl on the platform. Self-consciously, he gazed into a mirror, rearranging his sleek, fair hair after the slip-stream outside the window. Although everyone said that he was very handsome, Edward was never entirely sure about himself: the pale blue eyes and chiselled features were fine enough, he supposed, but he always thought his face was a shade too long and narrow, curiously rectangular and emphasising the prominent jaw. The girl with the fiercely expressive eyes had found him attractive enough – and shown it. He cringed at the memory of his reaction to her searingly suggestive look and wondered if he would ever conquer the distressing weakness. A combination of background and education had left him, at the age of twenty-four, a complete fool with girls.

Boothby-Graffoe men had been educated at Winchester since the year dot. After that, their paths parted: most joined the Army, the brighter ones went to Oxford. None had ever measured up to Edward's brilliant double first in Classics and Philosophy. His tutor, a man with many friends in high places, had written a letter of recommendation to the Foreign Secretary, Sir Edward Grey. Having sailed effortlessly through the selection board, Edward found himself taken to a large private house in the depths of Dorset to be quizzed about his willingness for 'special duties'. It sounded interesting, so he agreed, submitting to an intensive six-month indoctrination period with the promise of several immediate steps up the promotion ladder and a plum posting to Vienna.

Early on in the training, Edward was told to select a façade behind which he could hide. Inspired by an article in an illustrated paper, he had chosen turbines and generators, half-expecting to be laughed out of court. Instead, he had been packed off to Manchester to receive intensive instruction in the factory set up by Sir Charles Parsons, the steam turbine's inventor. After two years in Vienna, Edward no longer worried about being considered strange; with their overweening self-esteem, the Viennese with whom he came into contact simply regarded him as yet another eccentric Englishman. If anything, the rumours of his aristocratic connections added to the whimsical smiles that often came close to expressing pity.

The crews of the two Austrian locomotives hauling the train were making their intentions clear: the 170 miles to Vienna were to be covered as quickly as possible. With speed already up to fifty miles an hour, the suburbs of Budapest were giving way to the beauties of the Danube valley. Soon, when the track turned away from the river, heading west towards Bicske, there would almost certainly be views in which Edward should take an interest. Checking the readiness of his miniature binoculars, he settled down to assess what he had learned during three days in the Hungarian capital.

But before he had time to compose his thoughts, the compartment door was sliding open: with a conspiratorial wink, Count Altendorff joined Edward.

'You don't mind, do you, Boothby-Graffoe?' he asked, his English virtually free of accent. 'The politicians are becoming unbearable.'

'I'm honoured, Herr Graf,' Edward replied and waved at the empty seats. 'Make yourself comfortable.'

The Count did so, feigning total exhaustion. He was a man of sixty with aesthetic features that wore an almost permanent world-weary expression. A diplomat to his fingertips, Altendorff wielded immense power without the slightest show of self-importance or arrogance. He came from a family with strong liberal and artistic leanings: his grandfather was an early patron of Beethoven, a younger brother had mounted a spirited defence of Mahler in a brave but vain attempt to save him from the anti-Semitic hatred of the clique who dominated Vienna's musical life. Count Altendorff liked to give the impression that dealing with affairs of state and controlling the hysterical vagaries of politicians was a poor way for a man of his intellect and tastes to earn a living.

But behind the mask of bored disdain was the shrewdest brain Edward had yet encountered. Altendorff was a calculator, a man who dealt with percentages and probabilities, always producing an answer that would work in practice. He was a master of *realpolitik*, the venal science of Metternich and Bismarck, where morals and ideals counted for nothing in the face of material needs. Any man – whether he was an altruistic politician, or the editor of a socialist news-sheet – had his price, and Altendorff always knew what it was.

Despite their difference in age and outlook, Altendorff and Edward had become friends through their shared passion for card games, especially bridge. Finding a club where the standard of play matched his talents was one of Edward's first tasks when he arrived in Vienna. At the same time he was welcomed into Frau Schindler's circle, the man who had partnered Altendorff for nearly thirty years died. After watching Edward play a couple of rubbers in an ill-matched combination, the Count took him to supper in a private booth at the Altwienerhof. The bridge-playing alliance that resulted was rarely beaten.

It was not long before the relationship went much deeper than that which passed across the card-tables. Already determined to build a career that would take him to the highest levels in the Foreign Office, Edward appreciated that Altendorff's tuition might save him years of study and painful experience. Whenever the Count chose to speak about the problems of his job, Edward listened attentively. As soon as Altendorff was sure of his young friend's discretion, the advice flowed freely.

'Well, what did you make of the great visit?' Edward asked after allowing Altendorff time to settle himself and stretch out into the languid pose he adopted at every opportunity.

Briefly, the Count's eyes sparkled with a mischief that was almost sly. Were they going to play games or get straight down to brass tacks? Altendorff decided on the latter.

'It wasn't the fiasco I'd feared. Not *quite*.'

'You think some good may come out of it?' Edward asked.

Altendorff sighed. 'My dear Edward, I was seeking to imply that no harm had been done. *Good* is an entirely different matter!'

According to their code, the use of Christian names meant that Altendorff was prepared to be totally frank. Edward waited.

When he finally spoke, Altendorff switched to French, the

language of diplomacy. It was a device to emphasise the strict confidentiality of what was to follow. 'There are times when I could be persuaded that von Berchtold wants a republic.'

To Edward, the hidden message was clear. 'You think our Royal figure-heads were less than useful?'

'The Habsburgs are the oldest ruling family in Europe,' Altendorff replied. 'Seven hundred years is a long time, a very long time indeed. Naturally there is great respect.'

'Especially for His Majesty, the Emperor,' Edward prompted.

'Of course.' Altendorff paused, weighing his words even more carefully. 'But it's no good pretending that there isn't criticism. The chief complaint seems to be that there are too many of them . . . all with the "Imperial and Royal Highness" tag.'

'And we were saddled with one of the less able ones,' Edward was bold enough to suggest.

'You do the Archduke Joseph an injustice!' Altendorff said with a sardonic smile. 'I can't think of a better man to command the suppression of a street riot. After all, why settle for a handful of arrests when you could have a massacre?'

'And he isn't famous for his Hungarian sympathies.'

'Hardly! Strangely enough, however, his wife and son may have eased matters. *They* went down very well with our Hungarian friends.'

Edward was baffled. 'Why?' he asked.

'Budapest seems to have decided that it likes Germany,' Altendorff said with monumental disapproval. In common with many Austrians of his class, distrust was the kindest emotion he could bring to bear on Berlin.

'Yes, I see. The Archduchess Elsa was a Wittlesbach, wasn't she?' Edward allowed himself a small measure of pride at his background knowledge.

'I expect she still is.' Altendorff smiled. 'Bismarck may have displaced them by unification, but I'm certain they continue to consider themselves rulers of Bavaria.'

'And haven't I heard things about the son?' Edward asked.

Altendorff glowered. 'The Archduke Leopold is an idiot! He

believes that Kaiser Wilhelm will save civilisation.' The very idea was clearly beneath contempt.

'Why have the Hungarians become so fond of Germany?' Edward asked.

'Because they know we don't like them.'

'As simple as that?'

'Yes, as simple and childish as that. The Germans are making the most of it, of course. How do you think you got on with Szabo?'

Zoltan Szabo, Budapest's city engineer, had picked Edward's brains mercilessly on the subject of power generation. Their meeting, originally scheduled to last three hours, had gone on for two days and half a night. 'Reasonably well,' Edward replied, conscious of the need for caution.

'You gave him full details of the London Electricity Company?' Altendorff asked.

'Yes . . . he was very keen.'

'Let me tell you what I learned from Horvath over dinner last night.' Altendorff paused to add effect. 'Salesmen from Siemens have been fawning over Szabo for the past two months. Money has been no object. You understand?'

Edward nodded, pretending to be downcast. 'Siemens have been blinding Szabo with science and grossly exaggerating the scale of the task. Now I've given him an honest assessment of what's needed, he can beat them at their own game. Naturally, Siemens will win the contract.'

'And?' Altendorff asked.

'Szabo will be given a bribe.'

'A very big one, according to my information,' Altendorff said.

'I let you down,' Edward said contritely.

'My dear fellow, you did no such thing! All that I wanted was to show them that we could produce the right sort of technical advice, and you did that splendidly.' Altendorff smiled grimly. 'As it happens, there *are* a few honest men in Budapest . . . I was able to have a word with one of them. Szabo will find his finances under scrutiny after the contract has been awarded.'

Suitably gratified, Edward wanted to return the conversation to the

Archduke Joseph's family. 'The daughter,' he said. 'What about her?'

'Ah!' Altendorff waved a hand airily. 'The fair Annaliese. What can one say? She broke another two dozen hearts at the ball last night . . . much to her father's disgust, I might add.'

'Isn't she supposed to be rather . . .' Edward searched for the right word '. . . *individual*? Something of a nonconformist?'

'So it's said.' Altendorff was not interested in the views of a young female member of the Habsburg hierarchy. Instead, he turned his attention to the scene outside the compartment window. Almost at once, there was something to irritate him. Breaking into open country from dense woodland, the train was running close to a detachment of Hungarian artillery engaged in firing practice.

'Do you see those guns?' Altendorff asked, sitting bolt upright and showing considerable animation.

'Yes,' Edward replied, making it sound like a question.

'One hundred and thirty millimetre field pieces,' Altendorff confided. 'Purchased from Krupp only six months ago. What do you think of them?'

'Well . . .' Edward seemed to be at a loss for words. 'They look pretty effective.'

'They *were*,' Altendorff said. 'Twelve, fifteen years ago, they were the last word. Now . . .' He shrugged.

'Obsolete?' Edward inquired.

'Totally. That model has a range of about seven thousand metres. The new Mark Six fires a heavier shell nearly *ten* thousand metres. The Hungarians, however, refuse to believe it . . . they're convinced that they have the very latest thing. So the Germans aren't exactly *sincere* friends.'

'No, I see what you mean!' After looking shocked, Edward craned his neck for a last glimpse of the guns, pretending a layman's curiosity. He had known about their inadequacies since they were delivered. It was time for one of his periodic pangs of guilt at the way he habitually deceived Altendorff: as usual, the remorse was slight and brief.

'Is a unit like that any good to you?' he asked. 'Are they to be relied on?'

'Whose opinion do you want?' Altendorff asked. 'Mine, or Conrad von Hotzendorff's?'

Aware of the antipathy between the two men, Edward said, 'What does the Chief of Staff think?'

'That they're next to useless.'

'And you?'

'That they *are* useless.'

As they laughed, Altendorff produced a hip-flask. Drink was one of his infrequent weaknesses; the other, Edward knew, was women. Not that the Count was ever in serious danger of making a fool of himself with either. The way in which he divided his life into hermetically sealed cells of work and pleasure was something that occasionally earned Edward's grudging admiration. But perhaps his vices accounted for Altendorff's curious blind spot regarding his right-hand man. After allowing him to savour the Cognac, Edward said, 'My Ambassador is worrying about war.'

'Again?' Altendorff murmured. 'Sir Lionel must be a very nervous man.'

'Oh, no, I don't think so,' Edward replied. 'He dined at the French Embassy last Friday.'

'Where they talked of nothing else?' Altendorff suggested, smiling at Edward's confirming nod. 'Well, for once, the French may be right. The pressure *is* becoming intolerable. Frankly, I don't know why Berchtold and Hotzendorff didn't drag us into it months ago. They've persuaded the Emperor that it's inevitable.'

Edward needed no telling that the trouble was Serbia: loud-mouthed, belligerent, and, perhaps worst of all, advocating a rabid nationalism that was anathema to the Austrian Empire with its patchwork assortment of races held in an unenlightened, vice-like grip. For nearly a decade, the high-office holders of Vienna had viewed Serbia as the deadliest threat to Habsburg dominion for more than two centuries.

'To be honest,' Altendorff said after another swig from the flask, 'it's becoming a case of the sooner the better. There *must* be social reforms – even the reactionaries admit it from behind their barricaded doors – and it's best if we're seen to act from a position of victorious strength. Magnanimity instead of panic, you appreciate.'

'You subscribe to the view that Serbia can be thrashed in a few days?' Edward said.

'No, I do not! I think it will take eight to ten weeks.'

'*That* long?' Edward was surprised.

'Oh, yes, definitely. Belgrade is three hundred kilometres from our borders, Edward. And the terrain isn't favourable: there are at least ten places on the route where a few hundred competent defenders could delay us for days. No, all this talk about shelling Belgrade into submission within forty-eight hours of mobilisation is so much hot air.'

Altendorff's realism gave Edward the chance to find out what he thought about the issue that was exercising minds all over Europe. 'But surely, the longer the campaign, the greater the risk of another country joining in?'

'Don't tell me that you believe in this "Slavic Brotherhood" nonsense!' In one of the extremely rare departures from his customary suavity, Altendorff was close to derision. 'You imagine that Russia will come to Serbia's aid?'

'I believe it would be imprudent to rule the possibility out,' Edward replied.

'Don't you think Russia's in a big enough mess without getting into an argument that doesn't concern it?'

'What *I* think is irrelevant,' Edward pointed out. 'It's what Moscow decides to do. The Tsar seems very taken by the idea of being Serbia's guardian angel. Put Russia into the game and all hell could be let loose.'

'I know the scenario that the prophets of doom paint,' Altendorff agreed indulgently. 'Once Russia moves, so, by treaty, does France. Consequently, Germany declares war on France and Russia. Anything else? Do you want England in?'

'God forbid!' Edward said with genuine depth of feeling. 'Isn't it bad enough without us?'

'Yes . . . on paper.' Altendorff took another drink, glanced at his watch and grimaced. The sealing of the flask and its return to his pocket was a sign that a sense of duty was calling him back to his political masters at the rear of the train. 'But it can't happen, my dear fellow . . . not in a million years.'

'Why not?'

'Oh, there are dozens of reasons.' For a moment it seemed that a strangely expansive Altendorff was about to recite them, but time was pressing and he thought better of it. 'Germany is the key, yes?' Edward nodded. 'The whole world knows what the Kaiser has been *saying* these last few years – and very belligerent it all sounds. I understand that the man in the street reacts very strongly. Now, let me tell you something, Edward – the people who matter don't believe a word of it. Wilhelm is an immature mountebank with delusions of grandeur and a big mouth. He struts and makes noises, but that's all. Show him a *real* crisis, a point at which he has to take *action* and you won't hear a peep from him. I promise you, on the day that the first whiff of serious trouble drifts down *Unter den Linden*, Kaiser Wilhelm will take to his bed with a mysterious illness that refuses to be cured.'

'What about his mental condition?' Edward asked.

'Not what you and I would call sound. But does that make him mad enough to fight a war on two fronts?' Altendorff shook his head. 'No, my friend, not even the Kaiser is *that* demented! In any case, his generals would never allow it . . . they're quite a cautious bunch when you study their careers. And what of France? Do they want a repetition of eighteen seventy-one?' Edward inclined his head to concede the point. 'As to Russia . . . well!' Leaning forward, Altendorff lowered his voice. 'Our latest intelligence reports suggest that the whole ramshackle mess is on the brink of revolution and starvation . . . You toss a coin to decide which comes first. The Tsar is in no better position to go to war than fly to the moon. No, our quarrel with Serbia is just and we shall be allowed to solve it in our own way.' He stood up. 'I must leave you. Frau Schindler's tomorrow evening?'

'Nine o'clock sharp,' Edward smiled.

'*Excellent!*' Altendorff paused in the doorway of the compartment. An entirely new line of thought had come to him. 'By the way, my deputy minister and some of his friends were talking about you when I left them.'

'Oh?' Edward was mildly curious.

'They've decided that you're a very suspicious young man,' Altendorff said. A slight twinkle in his eyes made the pause bearable. 'The suggestion is that you're a clandestine salesman for this fellow who makes the turbines . . . I can't remember his name.'

'Parsons,' Edward replied calmly. 'Sir Charles Parsons.'

'Of course. *That* would be totally incompatible with your status as a member of an embassy.' Altendorff winked. 'Don't worry, they have at least three idiotic ideas every day. I expect they're off on another wild-goose chase by now.'

He was gone and Edward breathed out heavily. The increase in his covert activities over the past month had courted disaster on several nerve-wracking occasions. Yet it seemed that all was still well: the secret police were far too busy hounding Liberals to worry about the notoriously eccentric Englishman.

Automatically, while his mind was starting to assess the significance of Altendorff's attitude towards punitive action against Serbia, Edward scanned the horizon on both sides of the train. To the north, about two miles away, an infantry unit of at least brigade strength was on the march with cavalry protecting its flanks. The train had passed half a dozen similar exercises during the conversation with Count Altendorff. It all added up to what his contact in Budapest had told him over a brief meeting in a café: the country *was* preparing for war. Four weeks at the most, Karoly Puskas had said. Astonishingly, the normally cautious Altendorff, famous for leaving no stone unturned in search of pitfalls, subscribed to the belief that the campaign would be nothing more than a 'small local difficulty'.

Blessed from childhood with immense powers of concentration, Edward was unaware of the passage of time as he began to think out the report he would send to London that evening. Half an hour passed, at the end of which he consulted his watch. Assuming an arrival in Vienna at two o'clock, the document would be in the diplomatic bag by five. Then, he had to prepare for the evening's engagement. The prospect filled him with gloom: after three exhausting days, putting up with Edith Rathbone seemed more daunting than ever. Edward was preparing to feel sorry for himself when the compartment door slid open again.

Irritated, and intending to insist on his privacy, he turned to confront the intruder.

Not only was the girl quite dazzlingly lovely, she radiated *joie de vivre* and warmth of spirit. And, with a benign assurance that stemmed from personal strength, rather than privilege, she was smiling at Edward's state of shock.

Three months ago, a ball had been held at the Belvedere to celebrate her eighteenth birthday. The Archduke Franz Ferdinand, heir to the throne and her father's cousin, had done her proud, inviting nearly one thousand guests to his magnificent baroque palace. During the supper interval, Edward had stood in line to be presented to her.

Since then, they had been within a few paces of each other half a dozen times. However formal the occasion, she usually managed to give Edward a quick smile of recognition. Now, Her Imperial and Royal Highness, the Archduchess Annaliese von Habsburg, had left what should have been a sealed, heavily guarded section of the train and was entering his compartment.

'Hello, Mr Boothby-Graffoe,' she said as he pulled himself together and rose to his feet. 'I'm very bored. May I talk to you for a while?'

Edward's mind was in turmoil, leaving him incapable of speech. Assuming that he had ever been aware of it, he had forgotten that the Archduchess Annaliese was so tall. With her crown of shining, golden hair, she matched his height of six feet. Allowing for her exceptionally upright bearing, and assuming that she was wearing shoes with high heels, he guessed that she was five feet nine. The second surprise was her cornflower-blue eyes, the brilliance of which was unnerving.

'Are you feeling unwell?' she asked. 'You look as though you've seen a ghost.' Her impeccable English was coloured by mock concern.

'No.' He shook his head vigorously, hoping to clear it. 'You surprised me. I'm terribly sorry, Your Imperial Highness . . . yes . . . please, sit down.'

She did so, taking the seat opposite the one he was using. With her feet now visible below the hem of the long white and pink dress, he saw that her shoes had a two-inch heel. Looking up at him, her smile became mischievous, emphasising the generous mouth and wonderful cheek bones. 'I think you'd better call me "Fräulein Habsburg", Mr Boothby-Graffoe,' she said. 'All that "Highness" stuff is a dreadful bore. Are you going to stand there all day?'

Experiencing a mixture of elation and resentment at her bantering tone, Edward subsided into his seat. She saw that he had no intention of starting the conversation.

'Did you know that you have the whole carriage to yourself?'

'Er . . . no, I didn't.'

'I'm told that you're a close friend of Count Altendorff,' she said. Despite – or was it because of – her desire to appear controversial, Edward found himself warming to the young Archduchess. Later, he realised that he immediately began to think of her as 'Annaliese'; it was as though all her titles had ceased to exist.

'I partner him at bridge,' Edward said. 'But I didn't expect such special treatment for it. Perhaps it's because I'm the odd man out.'

'Yes.' She gave him a searching look. 'Why *have* you been to Budapest?'

'To tell them about electricity generation.'

Annaliese's uncontrollable laughter showed that Edward's assumption was correct: she *did* have a delightfully musical, soprano voice. 'What on *earth* do you know about electricity?' she spluttered.

'Quite a lot, as a matter of fact. It's a hobby.'

'A *hobby*?' She stared at him in amazement, shook her head and gave up. 'What did you think of the trip?' she asked.

'It was very useful.'

'In what way?'

'Well, most of the Hungarians I spoke to believed it had achieved something.'

'What might that have been?'

'I think . . .' Under her steady gaze, Edward saw the futility of tying himself in knots and gave up. 'Useful window-dressing, perhaps?'

'Not even that. For a start, they couldn't have chosen a more unsuitable delegation leader than my father – he *detests* Hungarians! He blames them for everything.'

'Why did he have to do it?' Edward asked.

'I mustn't say.' Annaliese laughed at the expression on Edward's face. 'No, honestly, my lips have to stay sealed about anything to do with politicians . . . I get into trouble too easily!' Briefly, her veil of maturity and assurance parted to reveal a deliciously naughty child. 'I don't suppose it's the slightest consolation to the beastly Hungarians, but Father hated every minute of it. He's like a bear with a sore head and Mama is ignoring him. Now, Mr Boothby-Graffoe, I want to know your life story . . . is it true that you're part of the English aristocracy?'

Edward blinked. 'Really, Fräulein Habsburg, what makes you think that?'

'My maid, Eva, tells me *everything.*'

'Where does she get her information from?'

'It comes with the morning papers and milk . . . Vienna is a hotbed of gossip, Mr Boothby-Graffoe, even for those of us who are virtually prisoners in Schönbrunn. Tell me all.'

'My uncle is a duke,' Edward said. 'I'm an ordinary "mister".'

'That's very unfair.'

'It's what happens,' Edward replied.

'What's your uncle's title?'

'He's the Duke of Lincolnshire.' To forestall the other questions she was bound to ask, Edward provided further information. 'The title was established in seventeen-sixteen and my uncle is the eighth holder. His second title, Marquess of Axholme, is assumed by his eldest son – that's my cousin Ralph. Because he's the son of a duke, my father is entitled to be *Lord* Douglas Boothby-Graffoe, but I'm nothing at all.'

'How disappointing,' Annaliese said, turning her beautiful face into a picture of misery. 'Are you furious about that?'

'Good gracious, no! I couldn't stand being trapped in our English class system . . . I intend doing something with my life.'

'What?'

'I'm going to be really big and important at the Foreign Office by the time I'm fifty,' Edward declared. As soon as the words were out, he realised that they made him sound both immature and pompous. Annaliese, however, was downcast.

'*I* want a job,' she said.

'You!' Edward was feeling so much at ease that he made no attempt to conceal his amused disbelief. 'What could you do?'

Apparently eager to poke fun at herself, Annaliese ignored the implication that status rendered her useless. 'I've been *terribly* well educated . . . Mama believes in it and Father was always too busy to bother arguing.'

'But you didn't go to *school*, surely?'

'I did.' Annaliese's chin tilted defiantly and her eyes flashed. 'When the private tutors had finished with me, I went to schools in Switzerland and Paris. I speak all sorts of languages and I'm good enough for university.'

'All right, I believe you,' Edward laughed, holding his hands up in a gesture of surrender. Beneath the veneer of the woman, he was certain that Annaliese was no more than a child: was that why he felt so comfortable with her?

'I've joined the Musikfreunde,' Annaliese said. 'And the Singverein. We're performing Verdi's *Requiem* at the Sophien-Saal next month.'

Although woefully ignorant of the arts in general and music in particular, Edward knew that this was more than amateur posturing. The Association of Friends of Music and their choral society were institutions with a high reputation.

'And I know about art,' Annaliese went on. 'Paintings and sculpture. Katerina Leinsdorf would let me work in her gallery on Walfisch Gasse if only Father weren't so stuffy.'

Edward knew Frau Leinsdorf's establishment, a combination of showcase and auction-rooms. 'As it happens, my family owns a similar establishment. Father runs it.'

'Where is it?'

'In Bond Street. It's called "Boothby's" – the shortened version of our name.'

'Is it like Sotheby's?'

'Oh, no, nothing like as grand or famous,' Edward replied, beginning to see that Annaliese *was* well-informed. 'To be honest with you, I know next to nothing about the place. I'm rather a philistine.'

For a moment or two he was half-afraid that she was about to take him to task, but her plunge into deadly earnestness was caused by far more dramatic thoughts. 'I *must* find something useful to do,' Annaliese said, leaning forward intently. 'Quite apart from what I feel is right, I'm sure I shall have to earn my own living.'

Although the idea struck him as absurd, Edward managed not to laugh. 'Surely that won't be necessary,' he said cautiously. 'Your husband will see to things like that.'

The crushing look she gave him could only have come from a fully mature woman. 'They've been queuing up since I was sixteen,' she said. 'You can't imagine what toads they are – especially the one from Spain – ugh!' Confusingly, the gruesome face and exaggerated revulsion were childish. 'Everyone says that you're very clever, Mr Boothby-Graffoe . . . Will you answer a question for me?'

'If I'm able to.'

'How long do you think the Empire will last?'

'Which one?' Thrown by the sudden reappearance of the mature Annaliese, Edward was at a loss.

'*This* one . . . the Austrian Empire, of course! How much longer can it go on?'

'What a strange question. I don't see any reason why it shouldn't last indefinitely, assuming that a programme of gradual reforms could be implemented.'

Looking exasperated, Annaliese sank back into the upholstery of the seat. 'Really, Mr Boothby-Graffoe, what *have* you been doing for the last few months?' she demanded. Fortunately, she did not wait for his response. 'Austria is controlled by the secret police, split from top to bottom by Nationalistic unrest, and is about to make a complete fool of itself by going to war. How can you possibly sit there and tell me that everything will just carry on?'

'You said you weren't allowed to talk about politics,' Edward replied, sure that he had found a way out.

'I'm concerned about the safety of my family, not politics,' was the heated retort. 'Would it help you to be honest if I told you that my father is very worried?'

'Well . . . yes . . . perhaps there *are* difficulties,' Edward confessed.

'Do you think that the present system can survive the death of the Emperor?' Annaliese asked.

'I don't see why not.'

Edward squirmed at the way she looked at him. Bad though it was for his self-esteem, it was better that she thought him an idiot than suspect the truth.

'Franz Joseph will be eighty-four in a few months,' Annaliese went on, giving the impression that she had decided it would be better to talk to herself. 'I'm not sure whether he's loved, or loathed and pitied. His son committed suicide over an actress and his wife was stabbed by a madman at Geneva.' She looked directly at Edward. 'The Empress Elisabeth was Mama's aunt.' He murmured a sympathetic banality. 'They say that Franz Joseph works eighteen hours a day in a dull room right at the top of the Hofburg. Do you believe that?'

'I have no way of judging, Fräulein Habsburg,' Edward said. 'Surely you know? You're part of his family.'

She shook her head. 'Guess how many times I've met him.'

'I can't.'

'Twice.' She smiled at his disbelief. 'The first time was at my christening. I don't remember much about that.'

'And the second time?' Edward prompted.

'New Year's Eve, eighteen ninety-nine. The family gathered in the Domed Chamber at the Hofburg to celebrate the new century. I was nearly four.'

'Do you remember that?'

'Very clearly. Franz Joseph reeked of cigar and he ignored the heir to the throne.'

'One *has* heard stories,' Edward murmured, as if he were letting out a great secret. In fact, the antipathy between the Emperor and his nephew was common knowledge. 'And you haven't seen him since?'

'Only on state occasions and from a distance. I've never been in the same room as him.' Annaliese paused reflectively and Edward made no attempt to speak. 'It's the secrecy that's so very bad,' she continued. 'No one has any idea what he does or how he does it. People are starting to object to that. The trouble is, the Emperor still believes that he's an absolute ruler, yet Father says he'll sign anything that dreadful man von Berchtold puts in front of him.'

This, from inside the Imperial Family, was damning confirmation of the conclusion Edward had reached a month ago. The dangers of the situation were appalling. Changing the subject abruptly, Annaliese seemed to be hinting at them.

'What sort of war do you think it will be?'

'There is definitely going to be one?' Edward asked as a formality and delaying tactic.

'Please don't play games,' Annaliese said impatiently. 'The British Foreign Office must have the whole thing worked out.'

'You may be right, Fräulein Habsburg, but they're hardly likely to take me into their confidence; I'm very unimportant.'

Her face registered a spectrum of emotions. The initial anger had an alarmingly imperious edge to it; the subsequent disappointment seemed fatalistic; finally, she burst into life, brimming with energy and moving forward so that their knees almost touched. 'No one ever tells me the truth about things like this,' she said. 'Father says it's none of my business, Mama pretends she doesn't care, and Leopold thinks I wouldn't understand it. All the other people I meet just bow and scrape and spout polite rubbish. I have a feeling that you know a great deal.' The look in her eyes was both frightening and intoxicating: Edward felt that she was staring straight into his mind. 'I *need* someone who will be honest with me,' Annaliese went on, her voice little more than a whisper. 'Please be my friend, Mr Boothby-Graffoe.'

Edward was light-headed. Blind to the very real possibility that this lovely girl, an Imperial and Royal Archduchess, had seen through him to discover what his real occupation was, he wanted to kiss her. As if to guard against such a disaster, he clamped his hands together, cleared his throat, and scowled.

'Well?' Annaliese smiled, totally unmoved by the display.

'Yes.' He nodded furiously. 'Yes, of course. I expect . . .' She remained frozen in the attitude caused by her energetic eagerness, very close, and staring at him expectantly. Deciding that he must find a way of ignoring her eyes, he began again. 'I expect you are aware of the theory that Austria will be able to wage a punitive war against Serbia while every other nation turns its back?'

'Yes . . . and I don't believe it.'

'Neither do I.' Now he was committed, Edward knew that the rest was going to be easy. He spoke with flowing confidence. 'Everything that we hear suggests that your government is convinced that no one else will intervene. In my view, that is a dangerously flawed position. Austro-Hungary got away with Bosnia only by the skin of its teeth, but it won't be allowed such latitude the next time.'

Annaliese's eyes signalled her comprehension. Six years ago, in 1908, acting in flagrant contravention of the 1878 Treaty of Berlin, Austria had annexed the Balkan provinces of Bosnia-Herzegovina. With one exception, European opinion was bitterly opposed to the move and a conference was demanded. Vociferously supported by the Kaiser, Franz Joseph had refused to discuss the matter and the uproar eventually died down.

'There are two factors,' Edward went on. 'No one was prepared for war in nineteen-o-eight – not even Germany. Things are very different now. Germany *is* ready, France soon will be. Secondly, Russia must have control of Serbia if she is ever to reach the Dardanelles to acquire an ice-free port. That's why she became involved in that fiasco against Japan. She can't go through Persia to get at the Gulf because of her friendship with Great Britain, so it's the Dardanelles or nothing. Russia will fight if Austria attacks Serbia.'

'Is she ready to?' Annaliese asked.

'No. I can't imagine a country being *less* able to go to war, but that doesn't matter. The moment Russia moves against Austria, Germany will jump in and France has to follow. The treaties make it inescapable and everyone is armed to the teeth.'

'What about your country?'

'In the very strictest confidence, Fräulein Habsburg?'

'Yes. Trust me.'

'*If* all that were to happen, my impression is that Great Britain would do her utmost to stay out of it.'

Annaliese's gaze became quizzical. 'Do I gather that you don't approve of that attitude, Mr Boothby-Graffoe?'

'No, I don't. We're a member of the Triple Entente and we should fight our corner if the worst happens.'

'Against Austria?'

'I'm afraid that's the way it's arranged,' Edward sighed.

They looked at each other in sombre silence for a few moments. 'So it will be a *big* war?' Annaliese asked.

'*I* think so.'

'But not everyone agrees with you?'

'No,' Edward said unhappily. 'Hardly anyone, in fact. People seem blind to the destructive power that will be unleashed. I find it doesn't bear thinking about.'

The silence became charged with his distress and her sympathy for it. Spontaneously, Annaliese leaned closer to Edward, placing a hand on his. 'Don't upset yourself,' she said. 'Perhaps it won't ever happen. What if we can't find an excuse to go to war? I mean, there has to be a reason, doesn't there? If the Serbs keep calm and refrain from provocation, it will blow over.'

'That's right.' But Edward's optimism faded quickly into a despondency that caused Annaliese to draw away from him. In the event, it was as well that she did: barely had they adopted postures that were proper and conventional when the Archduke Leopold appeared, obviously searching for his errant sister.

At twenty, he was a young man who didn't quite know what to make of himself. Much darker than Annaliese, with brown hair and eyes, and a suggestion of the over-fleshy lower lip that was a Habsburg trait, Leopold was well on the way to being arrogantly self-satisfied, yet he fell short, apparently unsure how to carry it off. The result was brashness tempered by nagging uncertainty. He was clearly ill-at-ease in the military uniform which protocol demanded for the occasion: the maroon trousers and white jacket, complete with a selection of decorations that must have been loaned by his father. The uniform was splendid enough, but not on the Archduke Leopold, who contrived to look like a slightly shifty turkeycock. Edward, who had a nodding acquaintance with Leopold through casual encounters at the house in which Frau Schindler's bridge club met, was suddenly taken with the idea that the Archduke would turn into a man with a clever nose for the way the wind of expediency was blowing.

Standing up, Edward bowed quickly and said, 'Good-day, Highness.'

'Hello, Boothby-Graffoe. I hope my little sister hasn't been making *too* much of a nuisance of herself.'

His tone was lofty enough to bring an edge to Edward's reply. 'On the contrary, sir, she has been a most entertaining companion.'

'What a relief!' Leopold turned to Annaliese. 'You are the limit, Liese,' he said good-humouredly. 'Are you trying to get Major Zuckmayer shot?'

'He gave me permission to go for a walk,' she replied. Turning to Edward, she explained, 'The good Major is in charge of the guard for our part of the train. He's hopelessly in love with me, so I can do as I like.'

Was she joking, or was this the re-emergence of the child? Edward had no idea. In the midst of his confusion, he longed to knock the indulgent smirk off her brother's face.

'Come along, Liese,' Leopold said firmly. 'Father will be waking up soon and asking where you are.'

On her feet and ready, Annaliese was not intending to argue. She was collecting her thoughts for a gracious little speech of farewell to Edward when the train, which had been crawling for some time, came to a grinding halt. Automatically, Edward held out a hand towards Annaliese and she grabbed it to maintain her balance against the final jolt. More than that, she held on to it for longer than was strictly necessary, blushing faintly when she saw that Edward understood what she was doing. Even so, she returned the pressure of his final squeeze and there was a conspiratorial gleam in her eyes. Leopold was too busy making sure that he aired his knowledge to notice the incident.

'There's a train with a faulty locomotive in front of us. I hope it hasn't given up the ghost altogether.'

'Oh, look, we're in a station,' Annaliese cried and moved to the window to read the sign. 'Eggenkirchen . . . we're back in Austria, thank God.'

Peering over her shoulder, Edward saw that there was a small crowd of about fifty people milling around on the platform, a strange sight at a minor stopping-place where only two or three trains a day called. Dressed in what were obviously their best clothes, the adults seemed at a loss, whereas the children were in excited, gala mood. Suddenly, one of the youngsters was inspired to begin waving a small flag on a stick. As the rest followed his example, Annaliese and Edward understood what was happening. No doubt ordered to do so by whoever controlled this delightful part of the country, the villagers had turned out to pay their respects to the Imperial portion of the train as it passed. But, instead of being a roaring blur, the special express had ground to a standstill. Uncertain whether they should stare or be stared at, and not liking the choice, the grown-ups were disconcerted, wondering whether their children's chaotic exuberance was right and proper.

Leopold was standing in the corridor, on the side of the carriage furthest from the platform, striking a pose that was meant to convey long-suffering elegance to anyone who had the good fortune to catch a glimpse of him. He was in no position either to read his sister's mind, or stop her once she had made it up. Moving swiftly to the large window, Annaliese lowered it and leaned out.

'Good-morning, everyone,' Annaliese said, speaking in her native German. 'Have you been waiting long?'

There was a good deal of shuffling and muttering before the answer came. It was from a boldly good-looking lad of eighteen or so. Very smitten by Annaliese, he was bursting to make a favourable impression on her. 'Not really . . . only a couple of hours.'

'We were late leaving Budapest,' Annaliese told him. 'They found lots of extra things for us to inspect.'

While the lad smiled and nodded, implying that he knew what it was like, some of his companions were exchanging worried looks and whispers. Edward heard the words '. . . the Archduchess Annaliese . . .' in a snatch of otherwise unintelligible conversation. It spread rapidly. The children, thinking it was tremendous fun to be so close to a member of the Imperial Family, were all grinning from ear to ear and waving little flags; the men were removing their hats and bowing; the good-looking lad was praying for the ground to swallow him.

'It's very good of you to be here,' Annaliese said. 'I'm glad we stopped.'

Leopold, having woken up to the situation, was furious: his sister's unorthodox behaviour might be tolerable within the confines of Schönbrunn Palace, but *this* was totally unacceptable. He was, however, incapable of doing anything about it. Was it weakness, or a fear of exposing himself to the common herd by pulling her away from the window? A mixture of both, Edward decided.

An old man had detached himself from the main group on the platform and strode right up to the window. He had the fearless eye and upright bearing of an ex-soldier. Strangely, the posy of wild flowers in his gnarled fist didn't seem in the least incongruous. 'For you, Highness,' he said, holding up the gift.

'*Thank* you! They're beautiful.'

She took the flowers in her left hand, holding out the other to the old man. Bowing as low as his back would allow, he kissed it. Behind him, his fellow villagers murmured and smiled their approval. The astoundingly fortuitous encounter between graciousness and gallantry was one of the most moving scenes Edward had ever witnessed. Despite the Nationalists with their wild, mostly impractical ideas, love and loyalty for the House of Habsburg was still a potent force. Nor had the old man finished.

'When you see the Emperor, tell him that Hans Albrecht, who used to be in the Third Imperial Guard, sends his best respects.'

'I will, Herr Albrecht,' Annaliese said. 'And thank you again for the lovely flowers.' With a radiant smile, she held them aloft and the crowd applauded her.

Half-turning to Edward, who was close enough to detect her perfume, she whispered, in English, 'When I see the Emperor! What am I supposed to say to the poor man?' The happy expression on her face was unchanged and not even Leopold could have heard her bitterness.

Before Edward had a chance to savour the intense companionship of the moment, the train lurched forward, jerking and clanging as the slack was taken out of the couplings and buffers clashed together. Annaliese continued to lean out of the window, waving, until the platform had fallen behind the carriage.

'May we go back *now?*' Leopold asked with heavily overdone patience.

'Yes, of course, my dear,' Annaliese said. 'Thank you for our talk, Mr Boothby-Graffoe . . . it was *most* instructive. Perhaps . . .' Her attention was caught by what was happening at a signal box. Two men were leaning out of the windows with the Imperial flag spread out between them. At the centre of the large, yellow rectangle was the famous black silhouette of the eagle with two heads that looked in opposite directions to denote constant vigilance and readiness. 'Ooh, look!' Annaliese pointed. 'The Double-Headed Eagle! Its power and influence is *everywhere.*' The final twist to what was cynicism disguised as childishness was delivered with almost coquettish levity. 'Perhaps we don't need to worry about those beastly Serbs.'

After Annaliese, smiling angelically, had allowed herself to be pushed towards the front of the train by an irritated Leopold, Edward collapsed into a seat. The notion that his life had undergone a dramatic change did not seem all that fanciful.

Forty minutes later, however, at the Sudbahnhof in Vienna, his mental state was very different. Keen to get on with his work, Edward was first off the train. He dodged several fellow passengers who seemed anxious to speak to him and spared only the briefest of glances for the Imperial carriages as he hurried past in search of a taxi. The windows were heavily curtained against public gawping, the doors guarded by soldiers. In the fullness of time, when the crowd had dispersed, Their Highnesses would be taken back to Schönbrunn to resume a life of cocooned luxury, and the wayward Archduchess Annaliese would forget her encounter with the man whose bizarre hobby was electricity generation. As his cab headed along the Landstrasser,

Edward himself was half-convinced that it had been a dream.

The British Embassy was on Mayrhofer Gasse, close to its junction with Rennweg. Behind the grandiose building, once the headquarters of Maria Theresa's favourite field marshal, was a four-acre garden protected by a high wall. In common with the other three unmarried men who worked at the Embassy, Edward had a flat in a converted stable-block at the bottom of the garden. There was a big sitting-room, a monk's cell of a bedroom, and a bathroom which he shared with Archie Shackleton. Except on Sundays when they had to fend for themselves, they took their meals in a staff dining-room next to the kitchens in the basement of the Embassy.

Leaving his bags at the reception desk with instructions that they should be taken to his rooms, Edward climbed up to his bureau on the second floor, using the back stairs to avoid the main offices and ambassadorial apartments on the lower floors. The building was quiet, basking in a post-lunch lassitude that was unlikely to be disturbed until the preparations for the evening's function began. Beyond the last turn of the stairs it was also hot and stuffy, a taste of the unbearable conditions to come if the summer turned out to be the scorcher that the experts were predicting.

Naturally, those Austrian businessmen who wished to learn about Great Britain's trade did not have to climb up here: whenever a visitor arrived, he would be shepherded into one of the high-ceilinged rooms along the front of the ground floor and Edward or Archie descended from on high. Even so, the outer part of what lay behind the door marked TRADE BUREAU was a passable attempt at respectability: it *looked* as though it was the workplace for two diligent civil servants who could lay their hands on every import and export possibility. It was, as usual, deserted.

Crossing the office, Edward opened a semi-concealed door into another world. The fifteen-feet-square room was packed with filing-cabinets and steel cupboards. At its centre was a table covered by a large-scale map of Austria and its neighbours. The young man who was poring over it had a magnifying glass in one hand and a sheaf of papers in the other, both of which he abandoned in his exuberance at Edward's return.

Because his academic performance at Cambridge had turned out rather below average, Archie Shackleton considered himself lucky to be with the Foreign Office – especially as Edward's assistant. Archie had the sort of cheerfully philosophical disposition that classified all the good things in his life as luck, while the others were unhesitatingly attributed to his own damned silly fault. As he jumped to his feet in greeting, grinning hugely, and with his light-brown hair in its customary tousled mess, his formidable physique became evident. Archie may have had difficulty with his final examinations, but his prowess on the rugby field and in two winning boat-race crews had been a legend. He was the same age as Edward and the two men had become firm friends.

'My God, it's good to see you!' Archie said. 'How was it?'

'Damned exhausting,' Edward replied, removing his jacket and giving serious thought to getting rid of his starched collar. 'All quiet here?'

'More or less,' Archie replied. 'That shifty devil Egon Beckmann wants to see you.' He handed Edward a sheet of paper on which all the necessary details were logged.

'Thanks, Archie. I wouldn't say "no" to a pot of tea and a sandwich. There was no lunch on that blasted train . . . at least, not for the likes of me. Do you think you could . . .?'

Archie was already on his way, not to use the internal telephone, but to race down to the kitchen to fetch the much-needed refreshment. Studying the details of Beckmann's message, Edward stood up again and moved to the open window and a draught of cooler air. Less than half a mile away, beyond the tree tops in the Belvedere Gardens, the steeply pitched roofs of the palace were clearly visible. It all seemed so normal, so *permanent*, yet if those whispers in Budapest were to be believed – whispers that Edward's intuition told him Beckmann's story would strengthen – time was running out.

Not in the least out of breath from his dash, Archie was back in minutes, spreading a napkin as a makeshift tablecloth over the south-eastern corner of the map. 'Did you make contact with Puskas?'

Edward, already wolfing a beef sandwich, nodded and reached eagerly for the cup that Archie was filling with tea from a silver pot.

'He told me an amazing story,' Edward said, after swallowing hurriedly. 'We're asked to believe that the Austrian Government is giving money to the Black Hand.'

Archie was so taken aback that his look of disbelief was comical in its pop-eyed intensity. The Black Hand was a Serbian Nationalist group who had sworn that they would murder the Emperor if they were ever given the merest fraction of a chance.

'Durotovic and his henchmen don't know this, of course,' Edward went on. 'They think the funds are coming from a wealthy sympathiser in Odessa, via a bank in Bucharest.' He held up a hand to restrain the scepticism that Archie was bursting to unleash. 'This *may* not be as far-fetched as it sounds. Austria wants war with Serbia. But what happens if Serbia doesn't do anything to justify such drastic action? If they start without some vestige of justification, Russia will be down on them like a ton of bricks.'

'Oh, yes, I appreciate that,' Archie said. 'But surely even *this* lot wouldn't go that far?'

'Berchtold would,' Edward replied grimly. 'He's a thorough wrong 'un. Altendorff never misses a chance to debunk the Black Hand mob – which is a sure sign that his department is taking them seriously. No, it bears thinking about, Archie.'

They chatted until Edward had eaten the sandwiches and a lump of fruit cake, then began work on the dispatch to London. Edward wrote in a firm, flowing hand, pausing only occasionally to think or make a correction. Archie took each sheet as it was finished and typed it on a machine in the main office, displaying a surprising level of skill. There was one pause while Archie clarified a complicated passage concerning the disposition of Hungarian army units. Edward's point, that the Army was looking tremendously busy, but was totally unprepared for anything serious, was slightly garbled. Apart from that, they worked steadily for nearly two hours, at the end of which Edward sealed the result of their efforts into a special, linen-reinforced envelope with the instruction: FOR THE PERSONAL ATTENTION OF SIR EDWARD GREY printed on it in red capital letters.

'I'll take this down,' Edward said. 'Have a bit of a clear up, will you, Archie. I have an idea that we're due for one of His Excellency's visits . . . It makes him nervous if we leave too much evidence lying around.'

They grinned irreverently at each other and Edward was off, still without his jacket.

The ceremony of sealing the diplomatic bag took place each day on the stroke of five o'clock in the Duty Office, an uninviting cubby-hole tucked away behind the reception desk. Edging in through the door, which never opened fully because of the clutter, Edward groaned inwardly; as well as the senior messenger who oversaw the loading of the bag before taking it to the 7p.m. train for Munich, JDT Lomax himself had decided to keep an eye on the operation.

Lomax, a sour-faced martinet of about sixty, never let anyone forget that, after the Ambassador, *he* was the most senior member of the staff at His Britannic Majesty's Embassy in Vienna. His official title was 'Counsellor, Consul General and Head of Chancery', a throw-back to diplomacy's arcane past. Although no one pretended to know what it meant, Lomax made the most of it. Edward suspected that the man's authoritarian airs and graces stemmed from his realisation that he would never attain the coveted ambassadorial rank.

'I see,' Lomax snapped. 'Another one of *those*.' He was glaring at the envelope in Edward's hand.

'Yes, sir, I'm afraid so,' Edward replied, apparently contrite. The continuing muddle surrounding the infant, very special Foreign Office department for which Edward and Archie worked, meant that Lomax had no jurisdiction over them. But, from childhood, Edward had gone out of his way to avoid making enemies, an activity that had always struck him as a waste of useful time and energy. Therefore, he showed respect whenever it seemed appropriate.

Lomax hated it. Snatching at the envelope, he flung it into the bag. Then, as he stared at Edward, his eyes lit up with spite. 'I am aware that you and your friend Shackleton are laws unto yourselves, Mr Boothby-Graffoe,' he said. 'I wonder, however, if I could prevail upon you to respect the dress conventions of this establishment?'

'Of course, sir. I'm sorry.' There was nothing Edward could do about his flagrant display of shirt sleeves, but he made a show of buttoning up his waistcoat, conscious of the messenger's embarrassed sympathy.

The last word had to be with Lomax. 'These little touches are necessary to those of us who do the mundane work down here. Some of our visitors are so sensitive, you see. Were they to gain the impression that we allowed *labourers* to wander around at will, things could become difficult.'

Edward bowed his head obediently and escaped. Trudging back upstairs, he felt an ironic pity for the Counsellor, Consul General and Head of Chancery. It was those pre-printed envelopes that did the greatest damage to Lomax's self-esteem: the very idea of an upstart having direct access to Sir Edward Grey was an abomination. The truth was that the envelopes, like everything else about the Trade Bureau, were a deception. The hand-picked men in Whitehall who opened diplomatic bags passed the special packages to someone called Mr Amery. He had an imposing office close to the Foreign Secretary's suite, but no one in London had the faintest idea what he did.

Reaching the outer office, Edward discovered that his premonition had been accurate. Archie, totally out of his depth, was trying to cope with the Ambassador Extraordinary and Plenipotentiary to the Imperial and Catholic Court of His Majesty Franz Joseph von Habsburg-Lothringen, His Excellency Sir Lionel Rathbone. Not that it should have been difficult: anyone less of a chump than Archie must surely have spotted that Sir Lionel was so out of his depth that he was incapable of frightening a mouse.

Tall, with lush silver hair and the healthy glow of a young boy, Sir Lionel was an imposing figure in his everyday dress of black frock-coat, grey double-breasted waistcoat, and striped trousers. In less than two years he would retire from a career that had begun in 1872 during the first of Gladstone's four terms of office. He was knowledgeable, urbane, much more shrewd than he looked, and a gentleman in the finest tradition. If anything, he was more relieved than Archie at Edward's return.

'Hello, Boothby-Graffoe,' he beamed. 'How was Budapest?'

'Very hot and noisy, Your Excellency,' Edward replied.

Sir Lionel nodded sagely, inferring that he'd guessed as much. 'Good trip?' he asked airily.

'Reasonably satisfactory, sir,' Edward said. There was an air of finality about the uninformative answer that caused the Ambassador to relax visibly. He was the only person in Vienna who knew what Edward and Archie were up to. That was more than enough for a man who revered the time-honoured channels of diplomacy: the thought of discovering any of the sordid details filled him with dread.

'Well done!' Sir Lionel smiled, looked round the office, and was immediately less comfortable. 'I . . . ah . . . I thought I'd come up to see how you were getting along . . . and to remind you about this evening. You're not too tired after all that dashing about, I hope?'

'Not at all, sir,' Edward replied cheerfully. 'I'm looking forward to it.'

'Capital!' Sir Lionel cheered up again. 'Look here, my boy, Edith's dying to see you.' He made a joke of it. 'Wants to be sure that the Hungarians didn't do you any harm, I suppose. Come to us for a drink first, eh? Seven-thirty, say? We needn't go down until eight, so that should satisfy her, what?'

'Thank you, sir. I'll be there.'

'That's the spirit! Well . . .' Sir Lionel looked round, vague and bewildered. 'I must be off. Nice to talk to you again . . . er . . .' He gave up the attempt to remember Archie's name and went.

'Well I'm damned!' Archie said, a slow grin spreading across his face.

'Yes?' Edward asked.

'I do believe I've seen the light. That poor old buffer was as nervous as a kitten.'

'Wouldn't you be if you were in his shoes?' Edward asked.

'Sorry, not with you.' Archie's insight had evaporated.

Edward sighed. 'Poor Sir Lionel is near the end of a very distinguished career. He gets a first-rate posting to represent Great Britain at what's arguably the finest court in the world – other than our own, of course; everything looks marvellous for him until it emerges that he's probably in the very place where the balloon is most likely to go up. That must be dashed unpleasant.' Archie nodded sympathetically. 'Then, when he's adjusted to that, he gets a couple of *spies* billeted on him.'

'You don't think he approves?' Archie asked.

'It's not a question of him approving or disapproving,' Edward replied. 'He's *upset*. Our way of doing things isn't the way a gentleman would conduct himself. It isn't cricket. I expect it leaves a nasty taste in the mouth of a chap like Sir Lionel.'

'Hmm . . . yes . . . see what you mean,' Archie said. 'It's always struck me as odd that we have to be here, pretending to be part of the Embassy. In fact, it's more than odd . . . I often think that miserable old devil Lomax is more of a danger than the secret police.'

Edward nodded. 'It could blow up in everyone's face, but there isn't an alternative until they stop arguing in London. Give it another ten or twenty years and they'll have thought of something better. In the meantime . . .' Edward shrugged. 'What are you doing this evening?'

'A few drinks with Frobisher, I think.'

'I'd better start getting ready. A bath is the first priority.' Edward paused in the doorway. 'Tomorrow morning we must decide what to do about Beckmann.'

'Right you are.' As a cheeky afterthought, Archie added, 'Good luck with the delightful Edith.'

Although Edward knew it was a joke, his parting look was angry enough to wipe the smile from Archie's face.

Lady Rathbone, eighteen years younger than Sir Lionel, was an ambitious woman. The fact that her husband, once a confirmed bachelor of nearly forty, had done what was expected of him was no reason for her to relax. The future had to be secured.

By all accounts, the Rathbone's son was a tearaway. In fact, he was no more than an exceptionally intelligent and independent-minded boy. On leaving Eton, he decided that his mother was a domineering pain-in-the-neck who would regulate and ruin his life if allowed to do so. Realising that total separation was his only chance of success, he went to Australia. Now twenty-five, he managed a 100,000-acre sheep station, was engaged to the young woman who owned it, and communicated with his parents only when absolutely necessary.

But Sir Lionel and Lady Rathbone's daughter, Edith, was at one with her mother. Or almost. Four years ago, when she was eighteen, Edith had come to the conclusion that there was no need to be a martyr to ambition. Of course marriage to a successful man was essential, but if, as in her mother's case, it involved union with an ineffectual bore, there was no obligation to stretch fidelity to ridiculous extremes. To the best of Edith's knowledge, her mother had never taken a lover, despite the endless propositions inspired by her charm and Junoesque beauty. Determined not to allow such misguided sentiments to interfere with *her* enjoyment of life, Edith had spent the two years before her twentieth birthday encouraging the aspirations of half a dozen powerful men, every one of them over fifty.

Then Edward Boothby-Graffoe appeared.

For the first time in her life, Edith Rathbone was genuinely attracted to a man. Allowing her emotions to overrule tactics, she made a bad start. Only three days after Edward's arrival in Vienna, she monopolised him at an informal reception, attempting a pre-emptive claim to his affections. Picking up the pieces afterwards, Lady Rathbone was of the opinion that Edward's abrupt departure had been the result of ineptitude, not rudeness: he was, she insisted, painfully shy of women. Already suspecting that he was an an eminently suitable prospect, Lady Rathbone wrote letters to friends in England and paid careful attention to what Embassy gossips had to say about the handsome young man who had made impressive progress up the promotion ladder.

A month later, she was certain that Edward would make a splendid son-in-law. His family connections and achievements at Oxford actually took second place to Lady Rathbone's sixth-sense perception that Edward Boothby-Graffoe was destined for the very highest echelons of the Foreign Office. Edith was given precise instructions.

By now anxious to make amends for his gaucherie, Edward fell in with the plan. Proceeding with soft-footed caution, Edith spent nearly a year turning them into friends. Thereafter, it became accepted fact that an 'understanding' was developing.

Two months ago, Edward had woken up to the fact that it was getting out of hand. Dressing after his bath, he realised that the evening ahead was littered with pitfalls. The dinner-party was for six Viennese worthies and their wives, and was a purely social event, without a shred of diplomatic significance. There was no earthly reason why he should be present – except as the permanent escort of Edith Rathbone. But at this late stage there was no escape, and he presented himself at Sir Lionel's private quarters on the second floor of the Embassy on the stroke of seven-thirty.

Edith met him at the door. She was, Edward admitted to himself, very attractive, with her long, brown hair cascading down to bare shoulders, and an intimate look of welcome in her eyes. The green, straight-skirted silk dress that drew attention to her figure had a daringly low-cut neck, which was alluring, but somehow purposeful.

'You survived Budapest?' she asked.

'Yes. The heat was the main problem.'

'Don't ask him anything else, darling,' Lady Rathbone said, smiling archly to imply complete knowledge of Edward's activities. Edith assumed a knowing air that was even more irritating, and Sir Lionel launched into a monologue about how well Surrey were doing in the County Cricket Championship, carrying on until it was time to join the guests in the antechamber of the ground-floor room that was always used for semi-official dinners.

Edward found the meal tedious. The six men had been chosen to avoid the faintest hint of controversy, so they were dull and self-important. The elephantine conversation rumbled on, each attempt at a new topic foundering sooner or later – usually sooner – in a quagmire of platitudes. Although not attempting to take part herself, Edith watched all the moves with a politely attentive half-smile on her full lips. A banker made a hesitant reference to the possibility of war, but Sir Lionel, supported by two other men, changed the subject abruptly.

Strangely, when they all left the dining-room at a few minutes to ten, the evening showed promise of coming to life. Some of the men were keen to play cards, the others, accompanied by two of the wives, asked about Sir Lionel's snooker table, a popular talking-point in Vienna. There was also rumour to be raked over: the banker's wife, much more interesting than her husband, was bursting to spread the latest scurrilous stories about the heir to the throne and his much-maligned wife. Before taking the scandal-mongers to her private sitting-room, Lady Rathbone hurried to Edith's side.

'Why don't you and Edward slip away?' she whispered. 'This will go on for *ages* . . . Frau Schwarz is *bursting* with gossip and you know what your father's like when he gets a cue in his hand. Enjoy yourselves.'

Rather taken aback by Lady Rathbone's latest demonstration of the lengths to which she would go to foster her designs, Edward followed Edith into the garden. They walked in silence for a while, enjoying the cooling breeze that had come with dusk.

'Father's in one of his *bland* moods tonight,' Edith said eventually. It sounded inconsequential enough, but Edward knew that it was meant as a criticism.

'In what way?' he asked.

'War,' Edith replied. 'Did you see how he stuck his head in the sand when that man with the funny eyebrows tried to talk about it?'

'It isn't the best of topics for small-talk,' Edward pointed out. 'Least of all *here*, in Vienna.'

Recognising a mild reproof, Edith allowed a few moments to pass before asking, '*Is* there going to be a war?' She looked and sounded much more serious than normal.

Edward found himself suppressing irritation. It was clear that he was expected to give an answer based on the special knowledge of espionage, an unpardonable presumption on Edith's part. Yet, struggling to find the right words, Edward suddenly saw the difficulties and dangers of Austria's unreasoning hatred of Serbia in an entirely new light.

'Yes,' he said. 'I'm very much of the opinion that there will be a war.'

'A big one?'

'In all probability.'

'With England and Austria on opposite sides?' Edith asked after working out what Edward meant.

'That's the way the treaties are arranged.'

'So we shall all have to go back home?'

'I'm afraid so.' Edward's face gave no clue to his innermost thoughts. A return to England, especially in crisis conditions, would irrevocably separate him from the Rathbones, springing the trap that Edith and her mother had worked on so relentlessly.

'Well, we shall just have to put up with it,' Edith said, with a stoicism that was patently insincere. 'Come along, let's walk all the way round, then we can creep back indoors and find a cosy little place.'

Although the suggestion dismayed Edward, it was something else that stopped him dead in his tracks.

If war did come to free him from the nuisance of Edith Rathbone, it would also take him away from the Archduchess Annaliese von Habsburg. That the thought had occurred to him at all was a surprise: its intensity was horrifying.

'I'm sorry, Edith, you must excuse me,' Edward snapped. 'That trip to Budapest has exhausted me . . . I'm going to bed.'

She was tempted to chase after him as he strode off towards the old stable-block. Instead, Edith cursed under her breath and went back indoors to wonder what on earth *would* persuade the exasperating Mr Boothby-Graffoe that he should marry her.

Edward was tired, very tired indeed.

Nevertheless, he lay awake until nearly three o'clock thinking about the dazzlingly beautiful but unattainable girl with golden hair and cornflower-blue eyes.

2

June 1914
'They say that Serbia is responsible'

Edward's existence during the next ten days was devoted to tracking down Egon Beckmann. Normally, this was an extremely tiresome chore, sapping patience and energy, fraying nerves. For once, however, Edward welcomed the task. It was a wonderful excuse for having nothing to do with Edith. There was also a chance that it would obliterate thoughts of Annaliese.

Archie had found Beckmann about a year ago. He played the piano in a café on the corner of Reisner Strasse, opposite the main entrance to the Botanical Gardens. Between four and five o'clock on most afternoons, a group of officers from the Schwarzenberg Barracks made loud-mouthed attempts to impress a pretty waitress. Eavesdropping was ridiculously easy and it yielded snippets of information about troop movements, all useful for the jig-saw intelligence picture being assembled in the Trade Bureau's inner office. As he pretended to study the newspapers, Archie was uncomfortably aware of the pianist's increasing interest in him: there was something profoundly disturbing about the deathly pale youth's dark eyes. They seemed to be windows into a world where misery rubbed shoulders with a corrupt elation.

Then, on an afternoon when high winds and torrential rain had deterred all other customers, Egon Beckmann left the piano, approached the solitary occupant of the café and offered to sell him secret information.

Archie's response proved that he had an infinitely better brain than he gave himself credit for. While expressing innocent bewilderment that anyone should think him interested in such a proposal, he did not reject it. Making a virtue of his less than fluent command of German, Archie coaxed the musician into revealing far more than he had intended in that first discussion.

Egon Beckmann was a homosexual. Until he was seventeen, he had drifted through a series of liaisons with semi-important men who were on the fringes of public life. For the past year, however, he had been involved with someone whose need for total secrecy made him extremely generous. Kept in the style of a royal mistress, Beckmann lived in an apartment at Dobling, one of the city's most fashionable districts. In addition to material gifts, there was a reasonable amount of pocket-money, but not enough to satisfy Beckmann's ambition. With the right teacher, he was certain that he could gain international fame as a pianist. Consequently, he intended to spend three years in Berlin as a pupil at the *Hochschule* and was determined to go in September, disappearing from Vienna suddenly, without trace.

The man responsible for the luxurious decadence at Dobling was respected, influential, and universally believed to be happily married. He was also ruthlessly vicious: not all that long ago, a youth foolish enough to attempt blackmail had 'accidentally' fallen to his death from a train. Acutely aware of the perils, Beckmann searched for a safe method of converting his relationship with Anton Leitner into money. The answer was so glaringly obvious that it eluded him for months. During their periods of intimacy, Beckmann's warped lover liked to boast about his work, often providing a wealth of detail in order to draw attention to his status.

Leitner was the second most senior civil servant at the Austrian Foreign Ministry: he was Count Altendorff's deputy.

Edward's initial reaction was annoyance at being expected to believe what struck him as a complete cock-and-bull story. It took three weeks to convince him that Beckmann was not lying, that Altendorff knew nothing about his assistant's proclivities, and that there was no possibility of a trap. Having double-checked everything himself, Edward asked Archie to organise a meeting with Beckmann.

For a while, it seemed that farce and frustration were likely to be the only results. Beckmann's understandable caution was combined with an obsession for the theatrical that manifested itself in excessively complicated arrangements. Long journeys to out-of-the-way spots, with instructions for continual changes of route to thwart every conceivable chance of detection, were either cancelled at the last minute, or led to a fruitless wait at the rendezvous. When Beckmann finally did turn up, Edward found him thoroughly distasteful. He was grasping, demanding payment in Swiss francs; he spouted Marxism as justification for his action and was obviously unstable; and Edward was extremely disturbed by the mere thought of being within touching distance of a homosexual. The arrangement very nearly came to grief before it started.

But Beckmann's information was sufficiently interesting to compel tolerance of his repulsive presence. It was all concerned with the clandestine efforts of the Austrian Government to incite an atrocity by Serbian extremists, a deed vile enough to justify extreme retribution. Although Anton Leitner was the man charged with seeing the plan through, Beckmann was always adamant that someone else had hatched it. Privately, Edward agreed, sensing the hand of Leitner's fellow Freemason, von Berchtold, the Foreign Minister. As the months passed and the evidence accumulated, Edward wondered how much – if anything – Count Altendorff knew of his deputy's efforts to provoke a serious international incident.

Attempting to follow up the message Archie had given him on his return from Budapest, Edward found his efforts blocked by an increase in Beckmann's elusiveness. It emerged that he was fascinated by a flautist in an Italian orchestra paying a two-week visit to the Imperial Opera, but terrified of Leitner's potential jealousy. When, after ten days of wild-goose chase, he condescended to appear at the agreed place and time, it was with a story so outlandish that Edward felt a fool for handing over good money to hear it.

At some time between 26 June and 3 July, the Archduke Franz Ferdinand was to be assassinated. Using a chain of double agents that had been operational for several years, Leitner had provided the Black Hand organisation with several suggestions as to how they might go about it. On the journey back to the centre of the city, an irritated Edward promised himself that he would never use Beckmann again.

But, that evening, the wretch's nuisance value presented itself in a new light. As he was leaving the Embassy for an important bridge game, Edward caught a glimpse of Edith at an upstairs window. She was frowning petulantly. Ten days of watching the man she was attempting to snare come and go like a will-o'-the-wisp had left her lonely and baffled. Smiling to himself, Edward hurried on his way, grateful for Beckmann's deviousness.

The air of complacent well-being lasted for five hours, until just after midnight.

Alone in the spacious smoking-saloon of Frau Schindler's house, Edward and Count Altendorff were savouring their victory in a knock-out tournament, Altendorff sniffing appreciatively at a large measure of fifty-year-old brandy. Suddenly, as though he had jumped out of a reverie into unpalatable reality, he was regarding Edward with a look of melancholy.

'We may not be meeting like this for very much longer,' he said quietly.

'Why on earth not?' Surprise raised Edward's voice.

The Count remained softly spoken, chillingly so. 'Because everything is about to change. I shall be far too busy for playing cards.' As though it hardly needed saying, he added, 'You will be back in England, of course.' After looking round the ornately luxurious room in a way suggesting valediction, he provided the unasked-for detail. 'Early in July, I think.'

Edward was very still, listening to the sound of his own breathing. Altendorff, making a great show of inspecting the ash on his cigar, smiled sardonically. 'No one will ever believe I said that,' he murmured.

Nodding acceptance of the disclaimer, Edward gazed into space, concealing the ferment in his mind as Beckmann's seemingly far-fetched story began to acquire a frightening plausibility.

Altendorff yawned, stretched, and was on the point of heaving himself out of the deep armchair when they heard the sounds of a very late arrival. After a flutter of activity and discreetly muted conversation, footsteps sounded on the tiled floor of the entrance-hall and the Archduke Leopold was framed in the saloon's open door. Despite the warmth of the night, he wore a long cloak over evening dress, an obvious attempt to mask his identity. Taken aback to see two acquaintances, he used arrogance as a substitute for self-confidence. Drawing himself up, he nodded curtly, and headed towards the imposing staircase.

The observers exchanged eloquent looks. As well as providing facilities for cards in the setting of a gentlemen's club, Frau Schindler ran what was allegedly Vienna's best brothel. Edward harboured a strait-laced disapproval for what happened on the first floor, but, like many compulsive bridge players, he was prepared to put up with virtually anything for a game of the right quality. Altendorff, a fairly regular patron of the establishment's more exotic facilities, smiled, expressing cynical amusement at both the strutting young Habsburg and Edward's censure. The only good to come out of the embarrassing scene was that Altendorff began to consider going upstairs himself, allowing his companion to slip away.

In the grip of urgency to prepare a report for Mr Amery, Edward ran most of the way back to the British Embassy. It was four o'clock and the first signs of dawn were in the sky before he was satisfied with what he had written, then, free from the need for fierce concentration, his thoughts returned to Leopold von Habsburg. Inevitably, it was a short step to his sister, Annaliese. At once, all the benefits of Beckmann's disruptive distractions evaporated.

At half past six, Edward abandoned the idea of sleep and went to the bathroom.

Ten hours later, on the warmest day that an exceptional summer had yet produced, he was dropping with exhaustion and barely capable of understanding the note that came by a special messenger. It was from the Archduchess Elsa, asking him to have lunch with her at Schönbrunn Palace on Friday 12 June, the day after tomorrow.

JDT Lomax was disgusted. The invitation itself was bad enough; that the Ambassador should bless the venture to the extent of making his motor car available to that upstart Boothby-Graffoe was intolerable.

Archie predicted a poisonous atmosphere for at least a week.

Still mystified by the motive behind the summons, Edward was more or less at ease during the three-mile journey to Heitzing, Vienna's most beautiful suburb. But his fragile composure faded at the first sight of Schönbrunn. Seeing it in a new light, Edward discovered that it was very much larger than he had realised. Built between 1696 and 1730 in an attempt to rival Versailles, the cream-stuccoed Palace extended for well over half a mile and was reputed to have 1400 rooms. Afflicted by an uncharacteristic attack of panic, Edward imagined that he would never find the Archduchess Elsa – even if he were allowed inside. Worse, as the main entrance loomed ahead of the car, it was obvious that Sir Lionel's black-humoured Austrian chauffeur was looking forward to seeing his passenger humiliated.

There was, however, a miracle lying in wait. Outside the guardhouse, wonderful in a blue riding-skirt and crisp white blouse, was Annaliese. When she spotted Edward among the flurry of arrivals that were a regular occurrence at this time of day, her face registered undisguised relief as she hurried towards the car. After that, her manner was briskly cordial.

'May I give your man instructions?' she asked, sitting down beside Edward. 'You can get sore feet walking to our quarters!' He nodded and she leaned forward to fire orders at the driver.

'Now!' Turning her full attention on Edward, Annaliese gave him a glowing smile. 'You're looking tired, Mr Boothby-Graffoe. Too much work?'

'I *have* been busy,' Edward replied and awarded himself a pat on the back for not blurting out that she struck him as several times lovelier than he remembered. To be sure of suppressing his feelings, he took an exaggerated interest in the Palace as they cruised sedately towards its western extremity.

'Isn't it huge,' Annaliese laughed. 'There are hundreds of people hidden away inside – including *twenty-three* Imperial and Royal Highnesses . . . we hardly ever see each other. Are you wondering why you were invited?' Edward nodded. 'I told Mama all about our interesting talk on the way back from Budapest, so she decided to have a look at you.' Edward's smile was weak. 'There's no need to worry, she won't eat you and we're alone: Father's lunching at the Hofburg and Leopold's gone to Munich to practise being *German*.' She sounded disapproving, but her eyes sparkled with fun. Giving up the struggle to decide what sort of mood she was in, Edward feigned calmness while Annaliese directed the chauffeur through a maze of arches and courtyards.

They eventually came to what looked like a tradesmen's entrance, a door that was open to show a hallway littered with boots and coats. Annaliese took charge. She dismissed the driver, informing him that arrangements would be made for her guest's safe return, grabbed Edward's hand, and led him indoors. Beyond the untidy passage, there was a broad corridor, sumptuously carpeted. Between innumerable doors, a veritable art gallery decorated the lofty walls. Fortunately, there was no time to be overawed: a forty-four-year-old double of Annaliese emerged from one of the rooms. The resemblance – including the angle at which the Archduchess Elsa carried her head – was close enough to make Edward blink.

'Here he is, Mama,' Annaliese said in English, deftly establishing the rules. 'Mr Boothby-Graffoe of the British Embassy.'

Edward bowed over the hand that was extended to him. 'A great honour, Your Imperial Highness,' he murmured.

'You are most welcome,' she replied. 'My daughter has told me all about you.' Her eyes displayed gentle amusement at his discomfort. 'Please, in here, and we shall begin.' The voice, with undertones of her native Bavaria, was warm and slightly husky.

It was a small room, made fragrant by a profusion of freshly cut flowers. A circular table, set with three places, stood close to wide-open French windows; outside, beyond an alpine garden, the famous Schönbrunn Park stretched away to the Gloriette, a classical arcade built in 1775 to commemorate the victory of Maria Theresa's troops over the Prussian army of Frederick the Great at the Battle of Kolin.

'Yes, it is beautiful,' the Archduchess Elsa said, reading Edward's thoughts. 'We are lucky here. This is the part of the *Schloss* where they hide the nonentities – but it's so peaceful and lovely. Would you take that chair, please, Mr Boothby-Graffoe?'

At a secret, unseen signal, the serving of what was to prove a relatively simple meal began. A clear soup was followed by a delicious morsel of baked sole; the main course was a wafer-thin steak with asparagus. Surprisingly, instead of being a local or German vintage, the wine was a white Bordeaux in unlabelled bottles. Exceptionally good though it was, Edward drank as little as possible in order to keep alert. It proved to be a wise decision.

The Archduchess Elsa cross-examined him with a persistence that was concealed by courtesy and something akin to sorcery. After disarming Edward by asking permission to use his Christian name, she went on to display a subtle but powerful sensuality. Mesmerised to the extent that he did not experience any of the unease that usually paralysed him in the company of a fascinating woman, Edward answered all her questions, feeling honoured at being able to satisfy her curiosity. He had no grasp of the way the conversation ebbed and flowed, or where it was leading; he simply coped, praying that he would avoid gaffes and resolutely ignoring Annaliese's dancing eyes.

Then, after nearly an hour, just as he was beginning to relax, it came to an abrupt end. 'You must excuse me,' the Archduchess said. 'I have an official engagement this afternoon.'

Fearing that he was being sent packing, Edward struggled to his feet, muttering a jumbled mixture of thanks and apology.

'You don't have to go,' Annaliese said. 'We can walk in the Park.'

Her mother was all smiles and encouragement. 'You must! It's far too nice a day to be stuck in your Trade Bureau. In any case, you said you had nothing to do this afternoon.'

Edward looked sheepish, took formal leave of the Archduchess, and followed Annaliese through the French windows. At the end of the private garden, a gate took them into one of the Park's magnificent yew-alleys.

'Do you like my mother?' Annaliese asked with blunt simplicity.

'Of course. She's very . . .' Edward floundered as his reflex response ran out of steam.

'Nice,' Annaliese said firmly. 'Very nice indeed. That's because she's more *royal* than any of them except the Emperor. They say she could have done much better for herself than Father . . . but she's happy enough. She likes you, by the way.'

Not prepared to contemplate a response to any of the astounding statements, Edward created the silence that enveloped them as they strolled towards the Neptune Brunnen, the biggest of the three fountains. When they reached it, Annaliese perched on the parapet of the wall surrounding the pool and asked, 'Has anything exciting happened to you since Budapest?'

'No . . . I don't think so.' Edward was disconcerted by the candid gaze of the unnervingly blue eyes: could she possibly know about his hectic pursuit of Egon Beckmann? 'It's been rather dull, as a matter of fact. How about you?'

'Aha!' Her face lit up triumphantly. 'Big developments. I'm starting work at Katerina Leinsdorf's on Monday.'

Edward was astounded. 'I understood that your father was very much against it.'

Shrugging elaborately, Annaliese made a face that pulled the corners of her mouth into a doleful grimace. It was a uniquely Viennese gesture to indicate that she was turning her back on the problem: therefore, it would cease to exist. 'Mama will arrange it,' she said in a way that combined boredom with finality.

'I'm sure she will,' Edward replied, convinced that the Archduchess Elsa could organise *anything*. 'But it's a very big step for you. Aren't you a little nervous about it?'

'I suppose so.' The effort of deciding to reveal the whole truth was visible. 'I'm not being paid . . . not at first, anyway. And it's only for three afternoons a week.'

'What's expected of you?'

'I'm a curiosity to get people into the gallery. Once they're inside and I've charmed them, Frau Leinsdorf will relieve them of money.'

'You'll do much better than that,' Edward said.

She rewarded his loyalty with her warmest smile. 'I intend to. The trouble is, Father's threatening to take us away on holiday for the whole of July and August. Frau Leinsdorf isn't going to like that.'

'Where are you going?'

'Switzerland.' Annaliese was so annoyed that she failed to notice Edward's dismay. 'Archduke Franz Ferdinand has taken a villa on Lake

Lucerne and he's insisting that we join him. *He's* leaving next week, if you please!'

The news that the heir to the throne was proposing to spend the summer well away from his future empire got the better of Edward's professional instincts and training. '*Is* he, really?'

'You sound relieved.'

'I am.'

'So you've heard the rumours about assassination?'

Edward nodded. 'We pick up all sorts of things in the Trade Bureau.' It was near enough to the truth to leave his conscience untroubled. 'Does his Imperial Highness take the stories seriously?'

'He has to,' Annaliese replied. 'Any Habsburg is a sitting duck, but most of us aren't important enough to bother with.' She rested a hand on Edward's shoulder as she eased herself off the fountain's parapet. At once, she began to walk. 'Do you think Cousin Franz will be safe in Switzerland?'

'In theory, yes,' Edward said, falling into step beside her. 'But a madman who thinks he has a cause will operate anywhere. There's no guaranteed defence.'

'The Empress Elisabeth was murdered in Switzerland,' Annaliese pointed out, voicing the thought that Edward had avoided.

After that, they were silent for a long time, wrapped in a companionship that transcended the countless differences that should have kept them in separate worlds.

As they turned back towards the Palace, Annaliese appeared to tighten the bond. Taking Edward's arm, she talked about ways in which she might evade going to Switzerland. She was thinking aloud, plotting, searching for the excuse that would allow her to be more than a two-week wonder at the Gallery Leinsdorf. Her chatter included a wealth of personal detail about the uncles, aunts, and remote cousins who might prove useful. Edward learned that the Archduke Karl Johann's habit of *never* being without a loaded gun ruled him out of the reckoning; and, although Great Aunt Eugenia was terribly sweet, she spent most of her time in an attic at the Belvedere, unwilling to face the servants.

The irreverent recitation of the Imperial Family's foibles was so enthralling that Edward was startled to discover they had reached the mews where coaches and motors were kept. Before he knew it, he was being bundled into a car with only the most perfunctory of farewells. Then, as the vehicle began to move, Annaliese unleashed one of her thunderbolts.

'Monday, Wednesday, and Friday afternoons,' she called. 'Remember!' And, as if to be sure of leaving his mind in tatters, she blew him an extravagantly cheeky kiss.

Archie was all agog, wanting to know all the details of the visit to Schönbrunn. Satisfying his curiosity proved to be a useful exercise, forcing Edward to make a rational assessment of an episode that had taken place in a cocoon of unreality.

Suddenly, there was a pattern to the interrogation over lunch. The Archduchess Elsa had asked about his work and prospects, but hindsight revealed that her interest had been cursory. The real objective of her persistent probing had been to unearth as much as possible about Edward's family background, especially his aristocratic connections. After they had stared at each other in disbelief, it was Archie who blurted out the most likely explanation. 'If you ask me, old man, she was digging to find out if you were suitable for the delightful Annaliese.'

'Don't be absurd,' Edward protested, trying to heap ridicule on the idea.

'What else could it be?'

'I don't know . . . the whole thing's beyond me.' Edward decided on an abrupt change of subject to head off the dangerous question of his own feelings. 'One thing, though – perhaps we needn't lose sleep over Franz Ferdinand.'

'You think they won't be able to get at him in Switzerland?' Archie asked.

'It isn't that simple,' Edward replied. 'They *could*, but I don't think they will. Murdering the heir while he's on holiday in a country that prides itself on its neutrality wouldn't give them anything like the political *coup* they need.'

'Hmm . . . I see.' Archie scratched the back of his neck, a sure sign of unease. It was always the same when Edward became calculating, viewing the most complex and sensitive issues with a detachment that seemed ruthless. Sensing his friend's mild disapproval, Edward started to search for a file, unwilling to bother with an explanation. Archie was a first-class chap, but awfully naïve about the harsher realities of European politics.

Frau Leinsdorf's gallery was on Dorotheer Strasse, between the Hofburg and St Stephen's Cathedral. Even without the magnet of a beautiful young Archduchess, it was ideally situated to act as a focal point for the cream of Viennese society. When Edward peered through the window of the main showroom at about four o'clock on Annaliese's first Monday afternoon, the place was seething. After what seemed an eternity, there was a glimpse of her distinctive golden hair in the centre of the largest group, but the thrill was spoiled by the knowledge that passers-by were giving him strange looks. Cursing his feeble-mindedness, Edward retreated.

Wednesday was the same. Archie, who had tagged along to bolster the myth that the casual saunter along Dorotheer Strasse was taking them to the Ministry of Commerce in search of export statistics, made the mistake of suggesting that Edith Rathbone was surely a much easier proposition. It was two days before he dared speak to Edward again, and that only in the euphoric aftermath of Friday afternoon.

Approaching the gallery on the opposite pavement, Edward's attempt at nonchalance was destroyed by the sight of Annaliese grinning at him from the window. She watched his pantomime of feigned surprise with mocking amusement, then beckoned him across.

'I saw you the other day,' she said, meeting him at the door. 'You should have come in?'

'How could I? You were swamped by customers.' Painfully conscious of the very few people who were taking a weary interest in what was on display, Edward found himself whispering.

'Not today!' Annaliese retorted. 'It's hopeless. They've all gone to the country to get away from this heat. You could take me to the

Prater . . . I've never been on the Ferris wheel.'

There was no need to worry about framing a tactful reply: a quick glance at the formidable Frau Leinsdorf was enough to squash even Annaliese's wilfulness. 'That woman is a tyrant,' she said in German, wanting to be overheard.

'Are you enjoying yourself and learning things?' Edward asked.

'Naturally.' Annaliese dismissed the question. 'I'm glad you called in. Listen.' She moved closer to him, her voice and manner warmly confiding. 'Father would like to meet you.'

Edward was aghast. 'Why?' he spluttered.

'Mama has been talking to him.' In deference to his state of shock, Annaliese tried to be serious.

'Good Lord!' Edward was at a loss, his brain refusing to contemplate the implications. 'What should I do?'

'It's very easy. You must come to dinner tomorrow evening. Seven-thirty. I'm afraid you'll have to dress up very grand . . . Father insists on it. He'd wear medals if Mama didn't laugh at him.'

'But I can't. I promised to go to the theatre with Archie and Frobisher.' It was the blethering of a half-wit, frantic for an excuse to escape.

'Don't be so silly.' Annaliese softened the rebuke with a smile. 'Father is *much* more important than some third-rate play. A car will pick you up at seven.'

Edward gazed into her eyes and was done for. 'I'll be ready,' he promised, flushed with a courage that was quite irrational.

'Good boy.' Conscious of Frau Leinsdorf's continuing glare, Annaliese was steering Edward towards the door. He was outside before he knew it, light-headed and far from certain that his feet were in contact with the ground.

The preparations for Saturday evening degenerated into chaos. Edward cut himself while shaving and was unable to find a single one of his half-dozen white bow ties. Dragged in to help, Archie saw the need for a steadying influence.

'This is a damned rum do,' Edward grumbled when they had finally stemmed the flow of blood from his chin. 'God alone knows why the Archduke Joseph wants to meet *me*!'

'I take it that you haven't made advances to his daughter?' Archie said.

'Certainly not!' Far too tense to detect the flippancy, Edward was deeply offended.

'All right, keep your shirt on,' Archie laughed. 'Especially while I'm doing this.' He was wrestling with Edward's starched collar. 'They seem to be courting you, so there's no need to be nervous.'

'Do you think it's that simple?'

Archie chuckled. 'I'd hardly call it *simple*, old man. The most beautiful girl in Vienna has taken a shine to you and her parents are—' Noticing that Edward had assumed his detached, calculating look, Archie broke off to ask, 'What's up?'

'Well . . .' There was a sign of hesitation before Edward took the plunge. 'I wonder if they suspect I'm a spy?'

'What the devil makes you say that?'

'I sometimes have the feeling that Annaliese is looking straight *into* me,' Edward said, awkward at expressing such a sentiment.

Archie shook his head sadly. 'All the chaps I know would give an arm for a second look from her, but you complain.'

'Men talk about her?' Edward asked sharply.

'My dear fellow, what do you expect? A corker like the Archduchess Annaliese is bound to cause excitement. You're a lucky dog. As to them suspecting you, I'd say you were way off beam.'

Edward spared a morsel of attention from his work on the tie. 'Go on,' he ordered.

'The Archduke Joseph is an out-and-out reactionary *and* he's on good terms with Willauer.'

'I didn't know that.' Edward was intrigued. Xavier Willauer was the nebulous individual believed to be at the head of the Secret Police.

'It's common knowledge,' Archie replied airily. 'You see the point? If Joseph had the slightest grounds for suspicion, you'd be up to your neck in trouble, not being asked to dinner, so sit back and enjoy yourself. Nothing can come of it, of course, but that doesn't stop you basking in a spot of glory.'

Making no attempt to reply, Edward masked his feelings behind an over-elaborate study of his efforts with the bow tie.

Annaliese was waiting at the 'tradesmen's entrance'. Her full-length dress was pale cream, dramatically complemented by a crimson sash and diamond-encrusted Imperial order. Even though she carried it with unaffected ease, Edward found himself acutely aware of her status.

'Leopold is still in Germany,' was her opening remark, made in a way suggesting that she knew it was good news. Reassured, Edward followed her into the long, picture-gallery corridor.

Someone was playing a piano. Both the music and the performance were striking enough to kindle Edward's interest.

'Schubert,' Annaliese said. 'The E-flat impromptu. Do you know it?'

'Er . . . no . . . not this *particular* piece,' Edward replied, hoping to conceal the extent of his ignorance. Smiling archly, Annaliese made for the door from which the sound was flowing.

The drawing-room, startling with its ultra-modern furniture and fabrics, presented Edward with a jolting reminder that hearsay could be widely inaccurate. It was not, as he had supposed, the Archduchess Elsa seated at the superb grand piano, but her husband. The man widely depicted as an arch-reactionary had a sensitive, finely drawn face and hair much longer than the current, German-influenced fashion. Instead of the ceremonial uniform that Edward had been expecting, Annaliese's father wore ordinary evening dress without decorations.

There was, however, an abrupt rectitude in the way the Archduke Joseph stopped playing and stood up. Briefly, Edward felt out of his depth. The Archduchess Elsa, regal in a dark green dress, yet still with that teasing hint of sensuality, moved expertly into the daunting vacuum.

'Edward! How nice to see you again. Joseph, my dear, this is Mr Boothby-Graffoe, a nephew of the Duke of Lincolnshire.'

The language was to be German this evening. Adjusting his mind to that and concentrating on the obeisance necessary for a male

Habsburg, Edward had no time to be irked at the way he had been introduced.

The Archduke's handshake was firm, his eyes friendly but astute. Although he was sixty-one, seventeen years his wife's senior, he looked no more than an energetic fifty. Having delivered the effusively formal welcome that the occasion demanded, he unbent and guided Edward to the sideboard on which drinks were arrayed.

After the small-talk on the inescapable topic of the warm weather had exhausted itself, the Archduke looked for details of Edward's aristocratic connections.

'Does your uncle have large estates?'

'Yes . . . at least, they're big by British standards,' Edward replied, hoping that he would not be pressed for further details. He was an infrequent and disinterested visitor to Compton Allardyce, and knew only that Glengrantach's 40,000 acres were somewhere between Perth and Fort William.

'And he takes part in government?'

'He sits in the House of Lords, but I don't think he does much.'

Sensing Edward's lack of enthusiasm for the topic, Annaliese started a diversion. 'Not like you, eh, Papa? You're into everything you can get your hands on.'

Far from receiving the rebuke it deserved, her impudence brought a gentle smile to the Archduke's face. 'I like to think I have useful talents,' he said mildly, showing that he thought the world of his capricious daughter.

'I'll believe you,' Annaliese laughed. 'Lots don't, though. They say you're a meddler who'd like to be a despot.'

To judge by his expression, the Archduke's response would have been worth hearing, but at that precise moment the major-domo flung open the doors of the adjoining room to announce dinner. In a manner grand enough to suggest parody, Archduke Joseph offered an arm to his wife and they executed the short walk in dashing style. Not to be outdone, Annaliese attached herself to Edward.

'Why do you care so little about your uncle?' she whispered, granting him a breath of her perfume.

'I want to be judged on merit, not my relatives,' he replied, then almost exploded into laughter at the look she gave him.

The conversation during the first part of the meal made it obvious that Annaliese and her father had not had an opportunity to talk to each other for several days. The Archduke Joseph, who listened indulgently to an account of life at Frau Leinsdorf's gallery, showed genuine interest in Annaliese's progress with the Singverein and preparations for the Verdi *Requiem*.

A deep knowledge and love of music was a strong family trait. The Archduchess Elsa began to recount her early memories of Wagner's special theatre at Bayreuth. As she did so, Edward became fully aware of the tiara nestling in her luxuriant flaxen hair. At first sight, it had seemed no more than a piece of costume frippery, a skeletal framework of silver acting as a setting for a collection of undistinguished stones that were probably sham. Then, a shaft of evening sunlight produced a revelation. The gems came to life with a cool viridescence that was followed by flashes of fire. They were emeralds, the palest of greens, like a shallow sea seen from cliff tops. All ten of them were large, the four biggest measured more than an inch across. Inasmuch as they possessed a finite value, it was enough to ransom every Habsburg in Vienna.

Aware that his keen interest had been observed, Edward smiled self-consciously. 'Your emeralds are magnificent, Highness,' he murmured. 'Quite magnificent.'

The Archduchess Elsa smiled her thanks.

'They're a family heirloom,' Annaliese said. 'Wittelsbach, naturally . . . The Habsburgs have never been able to thieve *that* sort of quality. They're at least five hundred years old and soaked in blood! Are you going to spirit them back to London to break up and sell through your business?' She turned to her father who was clearing his throat in a way that betrayed irritation. 'It's true! Edward's family own an auction-house that's nearly as famous as Sotheby's. They could dispose of our treasure as easily as falling off a log!'

'Hush, Liese,' the Archduke said with just enough edge in his voice to make her contrite. After that, there was slight tension during the remainder of the meal; it was almost a relief when Annaliese and her mother withdrew, leaving the men to their brandy and cigars.

The Archduke moved his chair from the head of the table to sit closer to his guest. 'May I abuse my position to ask you something desperately serious, Mr Boothby-Graffoe?' he said.

'Please do, Highness,' Edward replied with a calm that was entirely bogus. This was the prelude to being ordered to steer clear of Annaliese.

When it came, after a hesitation that was diffident, the question caught Edward off-guard. 'Could you possibly tell me what the British Government thinks of the European situation?'

Collecting himself, Edward said, 'It would have to be in the strictest confidence, sir.'

The Archduke nodded. 'Not even my wife and daughter must know that we've talked about it.'

'Of course.' Edward decided to be blunt and succinct. 'War is regarded as virtually inevitable within the next year, but His Majesty's Government is expecting to be able to keep Great Britain out of it.'

'Will they succeed?'

'No,' Edward said with total assurance. 'It's Russia, I'm afraid. Everyone thinks of the Kaiser as the rogue elephant, but I don't see it that way. The assumption that Tsar Nicholas and his advisors will behave logically is pure fantasy. If Austria lifts a finger against Serbia, Russia will mobilise. You can work the rest out for yourself, sir.'

'I already have done.' The Archduke frowned thoughtfully, making up his mind whether to go on. 'I'm concerned about the standing of my family,' he said. There was another pause before he came out with the whole truth. 'To be frank, Mr Boothby-Graffoe, if the world does get turned upside-down, I would fear for our safety. What do you think? Should I be looking for a bolt-hole?'

Edward was in his element: it never occurred to him that this was an extraordinary and highly irregular conversation to be having with a member of the Imperial Family of a potential enemy. 'May I make a suggestion?' he asked.

'I'd be grateful if you did.'

'I gather that you are about to set off for a long holiday in Switzerland. That would seem . . .'

The Archduke shook his head strenuously. 'That's all off. We were to share a villa my cousin had rented, but he's changed his mind.'

'I see.' Edward's voice and manner hardened. 'Why did His Imperial Highness change his plans?'

The Archduke did not mind the forcefully direct query. 'There is a rumour that the Emperor is unwell . . . at his age, perhaps the heir shouldn't be away.'

'So His Highness intends staying in Vienna?'

The Archduke's long, calculating look was a compliment to Edward's shrewdness. 'Actually, I believe he has it in mind to join the Army manoeuvres . . . They're mounting a major exercise.'

'In Bosnia?'

'Precisely.'

The ensuing silence was rich in implication, including the Archduke's realisation that his young friend knew immeasurably more than was necessary for the execution of his mundane-sounding job.

'In your place,' Edward said quietly, 'I would be inclined to make my own way to Switzerland. After that, you may care to consider Portugal. It's non-aligned, it *will* stay out of any war, and I've heard good reports from our Embassy in Lisbon.'

'Thank you, I'm grateful.' Joseph von Habsburg swallowed the last of his brandy and sighed. 'What a mess.'

'It will be . . . and far worse than most people appreciate.'

'Most people don't appreciate *anything*,' the Archduke retorted, suddenly angry and bitter. 'Especially here, in Vienna. All they think about is impressing each other.' The resentment disappeared as quickly as it had come. 'I hear that you're an excellent bridge player.'

Edward blinked at the abrupt change of tack. 'I like a game, sir.'

'I suppose you've seen my boy, Leopold, at Frau Schindler's place?'

'Yes.'

'He doesn't go there for cards, of course. He's infatuated with all this pan-German nonsense, too.' Having implied that allegiance to Kaiser Wilhelm's ambitious ideals was a natural adjunct to a weakness for prostitutes, the Archduke stood up. 'Time to rejoin the ladies,' he said.

As they moved towards the door, the oddest thing happened. In a way that combined anxiety and confidence, the Archduke said, 'Look, Edward, I can see that you're a good fellow . . . You will look after Annaliese, won't you?'

'Oh . . . yes, sir . . . I will,' Edward stammered.

It made no sense whatsoever. Nevertheless, they shook hands on it.

Half an hour later, Annaliese was gaily unrepentant as they left the garden and walked into the yew-alley.

'Don't be silly! What makes you think I gave the wrong picture of Father?'

'You implied that he was a frightful old die-hard.'

'So he is . . . deep down.'

'Rubbish!' Edward laughed. 'He's one of the most sensitive and perceptive men I've ever met.'

'But he *hates* Hungarians,' Annaliese protested, determined to struggle on. 'And he keeps well in with that wretch Willauer . . . He's in charge of the Secret Police.'

'Perhaps there's a reason for that?' Edward suggested.

In a twinkling, Annaliese was serious. 'Yes. He gets worried about safety. And there's Leopold.'

'Oh?' Edward sounded barely interested.

'To be frank, we're afraid that Leopold is involved with some unsavoury and dangerous people. I think Willauer maintains a special watch on him.'

'To keep him out of trouble?'

'Something like that.' With another mercurial change of mood, Annaliese was vivacious again. 'We aren't going to beastly Switzerland!'

'Your father mentioned it.'

'It's marvellous! I shall be able to carry on at Frau Leinsdorf's and she'll have to give me a proper job.'

'Very good,' Edward said, monumentally expressionless.

'Also, it means that *we* shan't be parted,' Annaliese added, her eyes dancing.

Secretly, Edward despaired, convinced that he was somehow being drawn into the Viennese quagmire of pretence and insincerity. It was the only possible explanation for the game Annaliese appeared to be playing.

Or was it? Back indoors, her parents were genuinely pleased when she began to suggest occasions when she and Edward could meet. Then, in the car returning him to the British Embassy, Edward remembered that he had entered into a pact with the Archduke Joseph. He had no idea what the arrangement entailed – but already that seemed destined to have no effect on its binding validity.

Although it was Sunday, Edward and Archie spent most of the following day in the Trade Bureau's concealed inner office, racking their brains over the heir presumptive's decision to join the Army manoeuvres.

His motive for doing so was easy enough to deduce. As all Vienna knew, the Emperor was coldly indifferent towards the Archduke Franz Ferdinand, allowing him few official duties or access to state papers. Moreover, the heir had made things worse for himself by marrying for love. His wife, Sophie Chotek, once a lady-in-waiting at the Hofburg, was a commoner. Eventually, and very grudgingly, she had been awarded a title: she was Duchess of Hohenburg, a worthless cipher since mere Duchesses were ten-a-penny in Austro-Hungary. The marriage was declared morganatic, allowing the children no claim to the throne or any Habsburg property. At official functions, Sophie suffered the indignity of having to walk behind the least important women of the royal blood and was always seated at the remotest corner of the Imperial table.

In only one sphere did Franz Ferdinand enjoy unhindered prestige: he was Inspector General of the Army, in which post he was rumoured to enjoy the respect and confidence of the High Command.

'Playing soldiers must be a sight more fun than twiddling his thumbs in the Belvedere,' Archie said.

'What worries me is where he's gone for his fun and games,' Edward replied.

'Bosnia, isn't it?'

'Yes. I've no idea of the exact location, though.' Edward scowled at the map for a few moments. '*That's* what bothers me,' he said, stabbing a finger at the region to the south-east of Zagreb. 'Croatia!'

Archie groaned to himself at the prospect of yet another lecture on Balkan imponderables. To his relief, however, it was fairly straightforward, with Edward basing his argument on Franz Ferdinand's well-known desire for constitutional reform. The present dual Empire was to be turned into a triple Austro-Hungarian-Slavic monarchy in the expectation that sharing power would both unite and pacify the Slavs. Edward listed the objectors, ranging from a clique of tin-pot officials in Budapest, through the Austrian Foreign Ministry, to Kaiser Wilhelm and the Tsar.

'As if that isn't enough,' Edward concluded, 'Franz Ferdinand wants to see the Croats taking the lead in the Slavic Union.'

'Even I know that Serbia hates Croatia's guts,' Archie said.

'Exactly.' Edward returned his attention to the map. 'Our man is very popular in Croatia . . . I wonder if he's planning a quick visit? Zagreb must be tempting. And Split . . . he keeps a yacht there.'

'You're afraid he'll do something to stir the Serbs up?'

Edward shook his head. 'I don't know what I'm afraid of, Archie. The only thing I'm sure of is that it stinks!'

And that was where the matter lay six hours later when they had finished scouring every file in the office. Edward was far from happy with the string of vague spectres that made up most of his memorandum to Mr Amery and agonised over it for much longer than usual. It was the insufferable temperature in the airless cubby-hole that forced the final decision.

'Come on, old man,' Archie chided. 'We need a breather and some food. Either send the damned thing or burn it.'

Edward sent it. A last-minute postscript stated that he expected an attempt to be made on the Archduke Franz Ferdinand's life if he set foot on Croatian soil.

On Wednesday evening, Edward obeyed the instructions relayed to him by a private secretary at Schönbrunn. At ten minutes to eight, he presented himself at the Altweinerhof restaurant, murmured a password to the head waiter, and was whisked into a private room. Soon afterwards, Annaliese joined him. She had been to a Singverein rehearsal and they were to have supper together.

She was in a bad mood. Apparently, Vienna was abuzz with spiteful stories about the Duchess of Hohenburg's attempts to cope with the rigours of life with the Army. Several members of the choir, presuming too much on their tenuous friendship with Annaliese, had added to the gossip.

'They won't dare speak to me again,' Annaliese said with grim relish. 'You wouldn't believe the things poor Sophie has to endure.'

'You sound fond of her,' Edward said, overawed by the anger that was flashing from his companion's blue eyes.

'Yes, I am. She's very sweet . . . She loves Cousin Franz with all her heart and look how they reward her.'

'I *have* heard stories,' Edward murmured sympathetically. 'What on earth will happen when His Highness becomes Emperor?'

Annaliese shrugged. 'I presume he'll insist on big changes.'

'Do you know if Their Royal Highnesses are with the Army all the time?' Edward asked with what sounded like idle curiosity.

'Of course not.' Annaliese's bad humour evaporated into a broad grin. 'They're with friends at Visoko . . . Count von Stolzing and his wife. It's a lovely house.'

'Are they intending to stay in that area?'

'Yes, I think so. They're returning to Vienna next Tuesday.' Annaliese cocked her head quizzically. 'You seem concerned.'

'I am,' Edward admitted. 'The fact is, I'd prefer it if they stayed out of Croatia.'

'But how extraordinary – Father said the same thing.' Annaliese gave him one of those looks that seemed to delve into his most secret thoughts. 'You have a wide range of interests, Edward.'

Confronted by the Annaliese who was a mature, shrewd woman, he decided to be bold. 'They coincide with yours, Fräulein Habsburg.'

'I'm sure they do. No, don't worry, Cousin Franz will be staying in Bosnia, surrounded by loyal troops. Now, let's talk about something else. Would you like to hear some of the scandal

I'm discovering at Frau Leinsdorf's?'

'No, thank you.' Edward laughed.

'In that case, tell me all about British democracy. How does it work?'

That, with the diversions introduced by Annaliese, kept them talking until eleven o'clock, when Edward was permitted the honour of paying for Her Imperial Highness's meal. A motor car was waiting outside, a commonplace sort of vehicle without crests, and the chauffeur was accompanied by a man forbidding enough to deter most villains.

'They're taking care of you,' Edward remarked.

'I told you, Father fears for our safety . . . He's more nervous than ever this week.' Confirming that the slight stress in her voice was real, she took Edward's hand, clasping it tightly until they reached the Embassy.

'You're to visit us on Sunday afternoon,' she said. 'Mama is arranging afternoon tea . . . very polite and English!'

Edward took refuge in polite gratitude. 'That's extremely good of her.'

'Isn't it just.' Annaliese smiled. 'You'll be collected at two o'clock sharp . . . Be a good boy!'

As the car chugged off into the sultry darkness, she blew another of her outrageous kisses.

Sunday 28 June dawned warmer than ever, but the sky was full of leaden cloud by midday. On the way to Schönbrunn, Edward noticed that the plane trees along Mariahilfer Strasse were stirring in a freshening breeze and felt certain that a thunderstorm was imminent.

He was out of sorts after an alarming discovery. The previous evening, Count Altendorff had cancelled an appointment for bridge because of pressure of work. The note explained that the difficulty was exacerbated by his deputy's absence on holiday. Soon afterwards, Archie turned up with news from a drinking pal at the French Embassy. Anton Leitner, complete with wife and children was in the Tyrol. 'The French are pretty annoyed,' Archie added.

'Why?'

'They were expecting important things from him this week, but he didn't turn up at the meeting on Wednesday. No warning, no apology!'

'Are you saying that Leitner cleared off on the spur of the moment?' Edward demanded.

'Sounds like it,' Archie replied.

'The Tyrol,' Edward muttered. 'That's as far as you can get from Vienna and still be in Austria.'

After a restless night, he was convinced that Leitner's absence had sinister implications: travelling to Schönbrunn, his annoyance at not being able to deduce what they were was mounting.

Annaliese, at her most effervescent, soon lifted his spirits. She had found a spot in the garden where the benefit of the breeze was greatest, but was surrounded by umbrellas for the expected deluge. Sitting down at her side, Edward found that her infectious glee was at its most irreverent. Two evenings ago, there had been a banquet at the Hofburg for a group of important Germans. According to Annaliese, the visitors had behaved so badly that the Emperor had stalked away from the table in disgust.

To Edward's surprise, when the Archduchess Elsa joined them she made no attempt to stop the flow of gossip. On the contrary, she added to it.

'It was a shambles . . . quite a disgrace. What can you expect, though . . . they were *Prussians*.' The wealth of meaning with which she embroidered the word reduced the concept of German unity to shreds.

'Is it true that two of them turned up with mistresses?' Annaliese asked.

'Yes. As you might imagine, they were even worse than the men.' With an effort, the Bavarian-born Archduchess regained her composure and said, 'I'm afraid that some of my so-called compatriots have a way of upsetting me, Edward. They're starting to believe that they own Austria.'

'It's causing a great deal of concern, Highness,' Edward said quietly.

'Internationally?'

'Yes.'

They drifted into a discussion of the problem and its ramifications, becoming so engrossed that they lost track of the time. Nor did they notice the change in the weather.

Inside the apartment, a clock struck four. As it did so, the three people in the garden realised that the breeze had vanished: there was not a breath of air and the sky was a terrible colour.

'Goodness, the time,' the Archduchess Elsa said. 'I must organise tea.'

She was in the act of standing up when they heard her husband's voice. His tone was deeply disturbing: was it anger? The glances that Edward and Annaliese exchanged agreed on something far more alarming.

It was impossible to hear and understand all that was being said. One thing *was* certain: a servant was being put through the mill. As the exchange drew to an end, Edward did manage to pick up a snatch.

'No, Highness, I'm afraid this *is* true. Look – that's His Majesty's signature.' Exasperation was intruding on respect.

The ensuing silence had a malevolent quality that made Annaliese and her mother stare at each other in near-panic. Yet they were incapable of movement and, despite the heat, Edward had to suppress an urge to shiver.

At last, the Archduke Joseph appeared through the French windows. He looked utterly crushed.

'It's Franz and Sophie, isn't it?' the Archduchess Elsa asked in a voice that was nightmarishly matter-of-fact.

'Yes. I'm afraid they've been murdered.'

'Where?'

'Sarajevo.'

A shared sense of horror produced absolute, frozen stillness. Edward, suddenly very much the outsider, watched Annaliese, who had turned into a wax effigy of herself. Even the brilliant eyes were clouded.

'When?' the Archduchess Elsa asked.

'This morning . . . four hours ago.' The Archduke shook his head as if trying to come to terms with it. 'They were on their way to lunch at the Town Hall.'

'What happened?'

'They were shot. It's all very confused . . . but it seems that Serbia is responsible. The Government says it has evidence.'

In his own detached world, Edward felt a twinge of morose satisfaction. Serbia was to carry the blame: by early evening, every café in Vienna would be full of talk about the Black Hand.

Apart from the need to remove himself from private grief, Edward had work to do. As he cleared his throat to express sympathy and beg leave to be excused, a sheet of lightning threw the whole of Schönbrunn's great park into a ghastly, bluish relief. The storm was breaking.

3

July 1914
'It will split us . . . probably forever'

The so-called facts surrounding Franz Ferdinand's fateful visit to the Bosnian capital were sketchy and posed far more questions than they answered. The decision to go to Sarajevo seemed to have been a spur-of-the-moment affair. This explained why the military presence in the town was so small, but made Gavril Princip's role in the catastrophe still more remarkable. Even after the procession of motor cars had been fragmented into three parts – all taking different, improvised routes – the desperate young student was in precisely the right place to use his gun at point-blank range.

Unable to resist the mystery, Edward yielded to his inevitable weakness. His otherwise brilliant mind could be thrown off-course by a desire to get to the bottom of things that the tide of events had rendered insignificant. Consigning Annaliese to a past that seemed part of a dream, he began to scour Vienna for clues.

Information was non-existent. In two days of hunting, Edward's solitary discovery was that the city was in a strange mood. After the initial shock of the assassination, café talk was suggesting that perhaps it was all for the best: Franz Ferdinand might not have made all that good an Emperor and as for his wife, well . . .

As always when he was in this frame of mind, Edward was doggedly thorough, careless of his own comfort. Consequently, he was at the Sudbahnhof at four o'clock in the morning on 30 June. That was when the special train bringing back the bodies of the murdered couple slunk into Vienna. One of the coffins was draped with an Imperial flag, the other was covered by a plain, black sheet. The insults were to go to the grave with Sophie.

Late on the evening of Wednesday 1 July, Edward instructed Archie to continue the search and disappeared, not returning until breakfast on Saturday. After what Archie correctly suspected was an expedition to Sarajevo which must have broken every rule in the book, Edward looked smugly pleased with himself. The note that had come in the previous day's diplomatic bag soon changed his attitude. Ruefully, Edward handed the terse message to Archie.

Never mind Sarajevo! Mr Amery had written. *What the hell is the Austrian Government playing at?*

'Yes, I've been worrying about that,' Archie said.

Edward, still preoccupied with the details of the assassination plot, looked blank. 'They aren't doing anything.'

'That's the whole point,' Archie replied, delighted at being ahead for once. 'Tomorrow, it will be a week since poor old Franz Ferdinand was bumped off, yet they haven't made a move. Practically everybody in Vienna believes that the Serbs were behind it, so there's the excuse they've been looking for.'

'But nothing's happened,' Edward said.

'Not a sausage!'

'You're right.' Edward shook himself. 'We must find out what's going on.'

He was, Archie saw, in one of those grim moods that were often the prelude to ruthlessness. To make up for the time wasted in Sarajevo, someone was going to cop it.

Vienna was unnaturally quiet on the Sunday evening of 5 July. The café on Reisner Strasse had only two customers, a couple so intensely involved with each other that they were oblivious to the musical feast on offer. Egon Beckmann was excelling himself.

For several days after the assassination and his consequent recall from holiday, Anton Leitner had been in a foul mood. His temper, terrifying enough in itself, had driven his sexual voracity to new and unpleasant heights. Now, however, he was in Budapest with other Foreign Ministry officials. During the grumbling discontent of his departure, he had indicated that he expected to be away for at least a week. Free of all care, Beckmann was playing brilliantly enough to justify his ambitious self-esteem.

At a few minutes to eight, he paused halfway through Chopin's 24 *Preludes* and glanced into the dim alcove that concealed his minuscule audience. Smiling sardonically at the couple's obviously illicit passion for each other, Beckmann reached for a glass of wine. Before he could raise it to his lips, Edward and Archie came into the café.

Edward reached the piano in a few resolute strides. 'I want to talk to you,' he told Beckmann. 'Outside! Now!'

The look on Edward's face prohibited argument. Archie seemed uneasily apologetic, as if alarmed by his companion's manner. Beckmann went, terrified by the man he had hitherto regarded as an ineffectual English snob. Firm hands on his elbows bustled him across to the Botanical Gardens. Escorted into a deserted glasshouse, densely packed with ferns, Beckmann found himself confronted by a cold, deadly fury.

'I have neither the time nor the inclination to argue,' Edward said. 'If you don't provide the information I need, I'll expose you – tonight! The way this damned city is behaving, you'd be shot out of hand.'

'I know nothing,' Beckmann gibbered. 'Nothing at all!'

'Let me be the judge of that,' Edward retorted. 'Why is Leitner in Budapest?'

'The Hungarians are being difficult over the note to Serbia,' his relief at being able to provide an answer was pathetically apparent.

'Note? What do you mean?' Edward's eyes were piercing. 'Is that an ultimatum?'

'Yes, I think so.'

'Why the delay?'

'Leitner said that Austria must make unreasonable demands that Belgrade can't possibly accept. The Hungarians aren't so sure.'

Edward was prepared to accept this: it was in accord with what he knew of the leading figures in the Hungarian Council of Ministers. 'Is there any other reason for delay?' he demanded.

Beckmann nodded furiously. 'The Army. There are terrible

arguments. That vile creature von Hotzendorff is trying to save his skin by blaming the generals.'

'What for?' Edward asked, irritated by Beckmann's lack of clarity.

'The Army isn't ready. Imagine that, after all the planning.'

'How long do they need?'

'You can't expect *me* to know things like that,' Beckmann protested. He was starting to sweat.

After a whispered conversation with Archie, Edward was satisfied. 'Right, clear off!' he said and Beckmann took to his heels.

'Typical, don't you think?' Edward said. 'We've had the conspiracy, now it's time for the botch-up and the villains falling out.'

'Is that all there is to it?' Archie asked.

'I'm not sure.'

In fact, the report to Mr Amery hinted that there was almost certainly another factor delaying the ultimatum. While it continued to do so, Europe settled into complacency.

It was Archie, scouting round on the off-chance of stumbling across something interesting, who found the answer. On Tuesday 7 July, a group of cabinet ministers, accompanied by Count Altendorff and three other senior civil servants, left Vienna in a special carriage attached to the mid-morning train for Berlin. Seizing on the probable significance of the mission, Edward instituted a rota for himself and Archie to keep the city's northern railway terminus under observation for twelve hours a day, looking for the delegation's return and other significant movements.

Trudging back from a fruitless vigil on Thursday night, Edward noticed the limousine parked near the British Embassy when he turned the corner from Rennweg. As he approached, the man concealed in the depths of the passenger compartment leaned forward to beckon. It was the Archduke Joseph.

'I thought I'd wait,' he said after Edward had crossed the road. 'You've been a long time.'

'Is there something I can do for you, Highness?' Edward asked, stiffly polite and ignoring the implied question.

'Yes, there is. I would like you to visit us on Saturday. *Please* come.'

There was a moment or two of painful indecision before Edward threw caution to the winds. 'Very well.'

'Good. Thank you. *You* may be able to make them see sense and reason. Four o'clock.' The Archduke tapped the glass partition with the handle of his cane and slid back into hiding as the chauffeur set the vehicle in motion.

Totally immersed in problems that he knew would dictate the future of Europe, Edward gave no further thought to the invitation. He was, therefore, unprepared for the strained atmosphere that confronted him at Schönbrunn on Saturday afternoon. The situation was made worse by Leopold's peevish presence.

Annaliese's truculent greeting intensified Edward's disquiet. 'If Father has brought you here to make Mama and I change our minds, don't bother wasting your breath!'

'Hush, my dear,' the Archduke said. 'The poor man has come in all innocence and good faith.' Wearily, he turned to Edward. 'In view of what I fear is about to become of Austria, I have suggested that we remove ourselves to Switzerland.' He gave a thin, rueful smile. 'I'm *very* unpopular!'

'I think it's a good idea,' Leopold muttered sulkily, but no one paid any attention.

Despite the restraining hand that the Archduchess Elsa placed on her shoulder, Annaliese let fly. 'Father, you're suggesting that we run away! How *could* you? This is *our* country! Our family has ruled it for six hundred years. If there is to be trouble, we have a duty to stay here and do all we can to help. But *is* there going to be trouble? Franz and Sophie have been dead for nearly two weeks and no action has been taken. *I* think it's appalling, but maybe it's for the best.'

In the ensuing silence, while everyone shuffled and avoided looking at each other, Edward experienced something close to shock at the vehemence of the young woman who had given him the impression that she cared nothing for Habsburg authority and traditions.

Clearing his throat with what sounded like explosive force, Edward told the truth as he saw it. 'This delay is no cause for optimism. I believe that we are on the brink of war. You should give Switzerland every consideration.'

While Annaliese looked as though she had been betrayed, the Archduchess Elsa attempted to introduce calm. 'I can see that you feel deeply for us, Edward,' she said. 'It's very kind of you.' The Archduke Joseph nodded in agreement. 'To be honest with you, I wish we could leave, but my conscience would never allow it. We can't behave like rats, leaving a ship that hasn't even started to sink. We recognise our obligations.'

'I don't!' Leopold's tone, a mixture of petulance and panic, brought anger from Annaliese and a look of cold contempt from Edward. 'All this talk of duty is clap-trap – absolute rubbish!'

'Where are you going?' the Archduke Joseph asked as Leopold stormed towards the door.

'Out! Away!' Leopold shouted. 'To find people who still have the sense they were born with.'

'Your German friends would laugh if they knew how spineless you were,' his sister taunted. 'Good riddance!'

Although the outburst was Annaliese at her most childish, it went some way towards converting Leopold's boorish behaviour into a much-needed joke. Determined to obliterate the incident, the Archduchess Elsa steered Annaliese towards the French windows.

Edward and the Archduke Joseph exchanged the looks of men who consider themselves the victims of female temperament.

'Why *are* they dithering over the ultimatum?' Joseph asked, waving Edward to a chair.

There was no point in playing games, pretending that such imponderables were far removed from a minor Embassy official. Edward's reply was immediate. 'The Hungarians are making difficulties.'

'They always do!'

'This is different,' Edward replied. 'They appear to be wary of Serbia – and her protector. There's something else, too. Incredible though it may seem, the military aren't ready for war.'

'I'm not surprised. I always suspected that they'd start producing excuses if anyone mentioned *real* action.' The Archduke thought for a few moments, his eyes searching and astute. 'Is that all?' he asked.

'No, it isn't. Your Government seems anxious to talk to the Kaiser.'

'To be sure of his help?'

'Not necessarily . . . they may only be looking for his blessing,' Edward said. 'That might be a valuable weapon in facing down Russia. Unfortunately, His Majesty is on holiday – cruising round the Baltic – and is refusing to deal with affairs of state. The Emperor's representatives have been told to talk to the German Chancellor.'

'Hah!' The Archduke's explosive response hovered between exasperation and sarcasm. 'Theobald Bethmann-Hollweg wouldn't tell you the time unless Wilhelm had given him permission – in writing, mind you!'

'That's what we're expected to believe,' Edward said quietly.

'So, we await the whim of an unstable war-monger?'

Edward inclined his head in agreement. 'The Russian Ambassador left for St Petersburg yesterday evening,' he said, making it sound like an inconsequential observation.

'Ah, I see.' A minor mystery had been cleared up for the Archduke. 'Hence the cancellation of Monday's reception?'

'Undoubtedly.'

'And you think this is a step on the road to war?'

'It's difficult to place any other interpretation on it,' Edward replied. 'We have information suggesting that there are powerful factions inside Russia who would welcome war. They see it as a means of rallying support for the Tsar and distracting the masses from revolution.'

'Yes, I can see that,' the Archduke said. 'It wouldn't surprise me if the same idiotic thoughts weren't exercising some minds here, in Vienna.' He stood up to take a turn round the room. 'The world becomes more extraordinary by the day, does it not? Look at me! I'm a member of one of Europe's most privileged families, yet I know nothing. Fortunately, I have the confidence of a *singularly* well-informed young gentleman who could be my enemy in a few days.'

Edward, his face impassive, made no reply. At first, he thought that the surprising change of direction in the Archduke's next remark was a symptom of unease. 'A wife and children are a great comfort, of course. Do you have any plans in that direction, Edward?'

'No, sir, I don't.'

'There isn't a beautiful girl fretting for you in England?' Not waiting for a reply, the Archduke wandered into even stranger territory. 'I worry about Annaliese. As you'd expect, we've been swamped by offers of marriage, but she wouldn't give one of them a second thought. In some cases, she was very outspoken . . . rude, in fact.' He paused to smile in admiration of his daughter's spirit. 'She's a funny creature, you know. What on earth am I to make of her lectures on duty and tradition when she spends so much time poking fun at the family and all it stands for? Six months ago, I came to the conclusion that it would be to everyone's advantage if she were to settle down outside Austria.'

'Did you have anywhere in particular in mind?' Edward found himself asking.

'Oddly enough, I thought she might do well in England.' Joseph von Habsburg spread his hands in a gesture of hopelessness. 'It's too late now, of course.'

Until he returned to what seemed like the safe, rational haven of his room at the Embassy, Edward was unable to rid himself of the notion that he was an unwilling guest in a madhouse. Failing to respond to her mother's attempts at pacification, Annaliese was churlishly distant, speaking only to criticise most of what anyone said to her. At nine o'clock, after one of the least enjoyable dinners he had ever known, Edward made little pretence at concealing his relief at being able to escape. There was, he presumed, no possibility that he and Annaliese would ever meet again. By the time he fell asleep, Edward had reached the conclusion that this was for the best.

Annaliese's note, delivered just before lunch the following day, killed that idea stone-dead in two seconds.

It was wrong of me to be so despicable yesterday. Father and Mama did not need to point this out to me – but they did, of course. Will you forgive me, Edward? To show that you have, be at the Altweinerhof at 8 o'clock.
Your own, very contrite,
Fräulein Habsburg.

'Er . . . something wrong, old man?' Archie asked with tongue-in-cheek nonchalance as Edward remained engrossed by the crisp sheet of notepaper.

'No . . . nothing . . . well . . .' Edward shuffled and mumbled nervously. Was he ever going to recover from the shock of seeing those two devastating words, *Your own*? 'No, everything is in order,' he announced with consummate pomposity.

'Her Imperial Highness is keeping well, I hope?' Archie asked roguishly.

'Perfectly, thank you. She's a splendid young lady, quite splendid – a trifle feather-brained at times, though.'

Archie's face was a picture.

Far from being feather-brained, Annaliese was tenaciously businesslike when they were together in a private room at the restaurant.

'We must make the most of whatever time we have left,' she said. 'Father believes that you will be recalled to London at any moment.'

Too surprised to argue, Edward listened to her plans for the next week, pretending not to be amazed.

'That all sounds wonderful,' he said when she had finished. 'Unfortunately, I have work to do.'

'Oh!' For once, she seemed nonplussed. 'Father thought that there'd be nothing left for you.'

'I'm afraid he's mistaken,' Edward said. 'We're up to our necks.'

'*We!*' Annaliese's eyes were alight as she pounced. 'Make your assistant do it all. See, it's easy!'

With Archie's generous co-operation, a compromise was reached. Edward, who could manage with very little sleep when the need arose, worked from midnight until ten each morning; Archie did the rest. On afternoons when Annaliese was not at Frau Leinsdorf's gallery and every evening, she and Edward were together.

Quickly realising that Vienna was far too preoccupied with war – or the disappointment of its waning prospect – to recognise one of its most famous beauties, they moved about freely, like ordinary citizens. Annaliese achieved her ambition of a ride on the Ferris wheel and pulled hideous faces at Edward when he reminded her that it had been built by a British engineer. They took a steamer trip on the

Danube, went to the Musikverein to hear the Philharmonic play Bruckner's monumental Seventh Symphony – which impressed even Edward – and saw Hugo von Hofmannsthal's morality play, *Jedermann*, at the Burgtheater.

On Sunday 19 July, there was supper at Schönbrunn. Elsa, who served the cold meal herself so that they could talk without the constant interruption of servants, apologised for the absence of both her husband and son. 'Joseph was summoned to the Hofburg,' she said. 'His Majesty wanted company.'

'Perhaps he knows something,' Annaliese said eagerly.

'I very much doubt it.' The Archduchess suddenly betrayed the cynicism she felt towards the way Austria was being run during these critical weeks. 'And even if he does, he's *most* unlikely to take your father into his confidence.'

Noticing that no excuse was offered for Leopold, Edward waited for the comment he was sure Annaliese was dying to make. She did not disappoint him.

'Another week has gone by and *still* nothing is being done about Serbia. I told you that there wouldn't be a war.'

Edward's self-deprecating smile persuaded her that she had scored a point. 'May I ask you to pass a message to His Highness, your father?' he said mildly.

'What is it?'

'Tell him that Kaiser Wilhelm has given his blessing. To the best of our knowledge, it happened yesterday.'

'I don't understand,' Annaliese said, clearly expecting details.

'I do,' the Archduchess Elsa said grimly.

For the moment, that was the end of the matter, but while Annaliese and Edward were walking in the park during his visit to Schönbrunn on Wednesday evening, she made it plain that the Archduke Joseph had taken her into his confidence.

'But no ultimatum,' she said. 'It's twenty-four days since Franz and Sophie were killed, you're saying that the Kaiser has given Austria *carte blanche* to deal with Serbia, yet they do nothing. Why?'

'I don't know,' Edward admitted, strongly tempted to add that he had given up caring. As was the custom in these few days that seemed to be lasting forever, Annaliese had linked arms with him. Stopping to stare into her eyes, Edward Boothby-Graffoe finally yielded to the temptation to jettison all his instincts and professional training. The crisis *would* pass and the summer would continue for ever, allowing him to continue enjoying the company of this delectable creature.

The rumour began to galvanise Vienna into chauvinistic excitement at about two-thirty the following afternoon, Thursday 23 July. Every café in the old inner city had a customer who boasted of his or her exclusive, fully authenticated right to the news. Total strangers began congratulating each other.

At four o'clock, special couriers hurried from a side entrance of the Foreign Ministry, heading towards the elegant, tree-lined streets of the diplomatic quarter. Ten minutes later, Sir Lionel Rathbone was taking his first appalled look at the ultimatum that had gone to Belgrade soon after breakfast. Not bothering to read all five pages, he asked a messenger to fetch Edward from the Trade Bureau. JDT Lomax, hanging around outside the suite of ambassadorial offices, was left quivering with rage at his exclusion from what should have been the most momentous discussion of his career.

Badly shaken though he was, Sir Lionel displayed the qualities that had earned him his position: he remained seated behind his desk, apparently quite composed, while Edward spent a full five minutes studying the convoluted text of the ultimatum.

'Good God!' Edward said at last.

'That bad?' Sir Lionel asked mildly.

'Yes, Your Excellency.' Edward collected his thoughts. 'As you will have appreciated, the Austrian Government is making sixteen demands on the Serbs. Two of them are directly connected with assassination of the heir presumptive and are perfectly reasonable. The others are preposterous . . . they seem to have been designed to humiliate Serbia and turn her into an Austro-Hungarian puppet.'

'You don't think it will be acceptable in Belgrade?'

'Absolutely not, sir.' Edward's sense of outrage was so great that his emotions got the better of him: briefly, his face flushed with anger. 'This has been drafted by someone hell-bent on war.'

'And the reply must be made within forty-eight hours,' Sir Lionel murmured, as if thinking aloud. 'Very well, my boy, thank you. In the light of all this, I expect you have things demanding your attention.'

'Yes, sir.'

'Don't let me delay you.'

Edward took the stairs three at a time on his way back to the Trade Bureau, collected Archie, and was out of the building before the livid JDT Lomax had summoned the courage to face Sir Lionel.

'Where are we going?' Archie asked plaintively after he had been bundled into a cab.

'Everywhere,' Edward snapped. 'The ultimatum has gone to Belgrade. It's the most unreasonable thing imaginable.'

If Archie was astounded by the recitation of what was being demanded of Serbia, it was nothing compared to the revelations of the next few hours. It emerged that Edward had a string of contacts of whom Archie knew nothing. Their progress through the tenements along the west bank of the Danube Canal was nerve-racking – especially for the six men and two women who found themselves confronted by Edward at his most implacable. Not understanding a word of what was going on, and given no explanation, Archie soon cottoned on to the part he was meant to play. By puffing himself up to look even bigger and stronger than usual, he was helping to get answers, though God alone knew where they were leading.

At eight o'clock, Edward was looking for another cab. Archie heard the words, 'Hummel Gasse', and 'Liechtenstein Park' in the instructions to the driver and suppressed a cheeky smile. One couldn't expect a chap like Edward to know such things, but that was the road in which one of Vienna's most famous and expensive tarts lived. The Irish girl, Siobhan O'Mara, undaunted by her failure as an actress, had put her stunning looks to lucrative use in other directions. According to Archie's drinking pal at the French Embassy, the ravishing Siobhan was beyond the pocket of mere mortals. Once, after a little too much to drink, Archie and Claude Aurillac had gone to Hummel Gasse to spend a disrespectful ten minutes goggling at the splendid residence that Siobhan's small clique of admirers provided for her.

It was the house at which the driver stopped the cab.

Edward was in a tearing hurry. 'Wait here,' he told Archie. 'This is likely to be damned ticklish, so I'd rather do it on my own.' Tense to the point of being overwrought, Edward failed to notice his companion's expression, nor, as he strode towards the front door, fighting dread with bravado, did he see the look that Archie and the driver exchanged.

The maid who answered the bell was distressed and in no mood to listen to what Edward was trying to say. For a few moments, it seemed that the door was about to be slammed in his face. Then Siobhan O'Mara herself appeared, dressed for travel. When she nodded at Edward and beckoned him indoors, the fleeting glimpse of the entrance hall as the door was opened wide showed stacks of cabin trunks and hat boxes.

To the driver's vastly exaggerated surprise, Edward reappeared in a matter of minutes. His step was jaunty, his eyes gleamed with satisfaction. Having ordered the driver to take them back to the British Embassy and quelled Archie with a look, Edward plunged into deep thought.

Only when they were inside the Embassy did he speak. 'Miss O'Mara numbers the Foreign Minister among her clients. She is leaving Vienna tonight because he told her to.'

'Why?' Archie dutifully asked.

'Because, no matter what Serbia says to that ultimatum, there is going to be war,' Edward said, strangely triumphant. 'Whatever happens, that devil Berchtold will find an excuse. Miss O'Mara is being sent packing – allegedly for her own safety.'

'I take it that she wasn't too pleased?' Archie ventured.

'She was not! Come on, let's get cracking. We can still get this to London in time for it to be useful.'

What promised to be a straightforward memorandum proved to be exceptionally difficult. It was well past midnight before the papers were sealed in the special envelope and ready for the diplomatic bag.

'You're an amazing fellow,' Archie said admiringly. 'Fancy tracking Siobhan O'Mara down.'

'I suppose you're going to tell me that you knew all about her?'

'Yes, afraid so,' Archie grinned sheepishly. 'It's the bad company I keep. Mind you, I had no idea that she was Berchtold's playmate.'

'Ah! The advantages of being a prude,' Edward said self-mockingly. He stretched his arms high above his head, then slumped forward, elbows on the desk and placed his hands over his face.

'Me, too,' Archie said ruefully.

They enjoyed the silence and the feeling of a job well done – even though it had unearthed such a dire conclusion. Suddenly, however, Archie came to with a start.

'I say, weren't you supposed to be seeing your lovely Archduchess this evening?' he asked.

Briefly, as Edward lifted his head to stare across the desk, his face was a picture of desolation. 'Yes, I was,' he said. 'It hardly matters now, does it?' He stood up, forcing his shoulders back. 'It's all over.' Picking up the envelope for London, he held it aloft. 'Unless I'm very much mistaken, Archie, this is our last effort for Mr Amery.'

Saturday morning's news was dramatic. Serbia had accepted Austria's demands. Or very nearly. She could not accede to one of the sixteen points, but was willing to submit it to international arbitration and be bound by the verdict.

The silence from the Foreign Ministry was deafening. During the afternoon, there was news that led Edward to hope that the ground had been shot from beneath Berchtold's feet. Reuter's agency was quoting Kaiser Wilhelm as saying: 'It is a most satisfactory outcome. With it, every cause for war disappears.' The British Ambassador in Berlin telephoned Sir Lionel to confirm the statement.

Although not consciously sceptical of the air of euphoria that was settling over Vienna, Edward was restless, looking for something with which to occupy himself. He considered and quickly rejected the idea of going to Schönbrunn: without an invitation, or Annaliese waiting at the gate to vouch for him, his chances of gaining entry were slight. Eventually, acting on a timely premonition, he roped Archie in to help tidy up the Trade Bureau's inner office.

'What ought we to do with this lot?' Archie asked, as they began to discover how much paper of a highly confidential and potentially embarrassing nature they had allowed to accumulate.

'No idea,' Edward replied. 'But let's have it all out in the open.'

With frequent pauses to drift out for a walk to the nearest café, they spent Sunday and Monday sorting documents into related piles. Tuesday was going the same tedious way when Sir Lionel Rathbone wandered in, smiling nervously and wafting a handkerchief at the clouds of dust being stirred up.

'Good-morning, sir,' Edward said eagerly. 'Has something happened? Any reaction from the Austrian Government?'

'Eh?' Sir Lionel was baffled by the question. 'Oh, you mean that business with Serbia? No, it's all quiet. If you ask me, we've heard the last of that. I always knew that common sense would prevail. No, I thought I'd pop in to remind you about this evening.'

'I beg your pardon, sir?' Edward was at a loss.

'You're our guest at the ball – surely you remember, my boy. It's the annual diplomatic shindig at the Hofburg.' Sir Lionel beamed indulgently.

Edward gaped at him. 'Hasn't that been cancelled?'

'Good Lord, no!' Sir Lionel found the idea amusing. 'It takes more than a vague threat of war to put the Viennese off a ball. You really will have to make more of an effort to understand these people, my dear fellow! Seven o'clock, if you please. Don't be late.' He wagged an admonishing finger. 'It would upset Edith.'

For once, Archie stopped his face letting him down. After Sir Lionel's departure, he assumed an expression of doleful sympathy. Deprived of an excuse to vent his exasperation, Edward set to work on yet another pile of paper.

In the event, Edith, who looked lovely with a new hairstyle and a white dress, was subtly different. On the surface, her manner was exactly as normal, but Edward felt more at ease with her: she seemed far less blatant, content to treat him as an escort, rather than a conquest.

The ball was being held in the Grand Chamber of the Alte Burg, the oldest part of the palace. At the magnificent entrance, an unexpected honour awaited the guests: the new heir presumptive and his wife were greeting everyone individually. The Archduke Karl and

Archduchess Zita, both aged twenty-seven, were an attractive, slightly earnest couple. She, a princess of Bourbon-Parma, had already produced the son who would be the next Emperor but one. A concentrated campaign by the press had, in next to no time, made them far more popular than the increasingly unlamented Franz Ferdinand and Sophie.

'Well, what do you think of them?' Edith asked when they were safely clear of the Imperial couple.

Edward shrugged. 'I've no idea.'

'Really?' Edith's expression became teasing. 'I felt sure that you'd have an opinion . . . after all, aren't you virtually a member of the family?'

'Certainly not,' Edward retorted, much more angrily than he had intended. 'The Archduchess Annaliese and I are merely acquaintances – and not particularly close ones, I might add.'

'Oh, I see.' Edith was serious. 'You sound disappointed. Oh dear, I'm sorry, Edward. Have I put my foot in it?'

'It's quite all right,' he said stiffly.

'Can you forgive me enough to help me this evening?' Edith asked.

'In what way?'

'Since you aren't in the least bit interested in me, I've made friends with a gentleman from the American Embassy,' Edith said. 'Would you mind if he danced with me occasionally?'

'Of course not.' Edward was barely able to contain his relief. 'Is there anything I might do to distract your parents?'

'Edward, that *is* good of you,' Edith said. 'Perhaps if I were to introduce you to Chester, we could make up our own tiny party?'

It worked reasonably well. Chester Warren proved to be an amiable enough fellow – albeit nervously determined to seduce Edith at the very earliest opportunity. Feeling light-headed and detached from what was going on around him, Edward experienced an urge to tell the American not to worry: Edith was anxious to *be* seduced.

The three hundred guests made much of a rumour that the evening was to be graced with an appearance by the Emperor. Edward doubted it even before nine-thirty: later, he knew that the social aspirants were doomed to disappointment.

Following several days of more comfortable weather, the temperature had climbed back into the eighties and the Grand Chamber was almost unbearable. Leaving Edith and Chester to whisper sweet nothings to each other, Edward strolled into the antechamber and made his way towards the Heldenplatz entrance to the palace. He was intending to go outside to search for a breeze and smoke a cigarette.

Without warning, the deserted peace of the lobby was shattered by a flurry of palace aides. It seemed that they had appeared without purpose from nowhere, but a Daimler-Benz motor car drew up and Leopold von Berchtold sprang from it. Chin thrust forward, grim resolve stamped on his face, he ploughed through the officials who attempted to flock round him. He knew exactly where he was going and no minor bureaucrat would delay him for a fraction of a second. There was one small hesitation: he was unsure how to operate the thing, so one of his pursuers was allowed into the small lift that was famous throughout Vienna. It went directly to the Emperor's study on the remote top floor.

After the lift had clanked out of sight, Edward remained stock-still. The Foreign Minister was grasping a single sheet of paper, folded in half. The matter was so urgent that there had been no time to bother with a document case.

Returning to the Grand Chamber, Edward maintained a discreet watch on the heir and his wife. They danced a waltz together, made polite small-talk with the French and Italian Ambassadors, then found themselves in the centre of a group of Scandinavians. The Archduchess Zita was starting to show signs of boredom, glancing round the crowded room in search of interest or rescue.

Edward spotted the man bringing relief long before she did. The military equerry slipped unobtrusively through a door that was being used by waiters as they replenished the buffet. Casual though his movements seemed, he reached the Imperial couple quickly, delivering his message with undemonstrative efficiency. The Archduke Karl, smiling apologetically to those around him, guided his wife to the service-door and was gone. Apart from the crestfallen

Scandinavians, only Edward had noticed it.

He strolled round the chamber to exchange civilities with half a dozen friends, partnered Edith in a dance, and accepted an invitation to join the New Zealand High Commissioner's party for supper.

After the supper, Edward mooched around, allowing himself to be inveigled into dancing with a sensational Romanian countess who, although almost old enough to be his mother, had visions of a relationship. It would, she promised him, be highly educational as well as pleasurable. Beating a retreat with as much dignity as he could muster, Edward considered leaving the ball. It was, however, only ten-thirty and protocol demanded that he should display his loyalty to Sir Lionel by staying until midnight.

Inspiration came with the realisation that the huge windows along one side of the chamber were now open to provide much-needed ventilation. Ducking behind one of the curtains that hung from ceiling to floor, Edward found himself on a long, glass-covered terrace. For the summer season of social events, thousands of potted plants and shrubs had transformed the arcade into an exotic miniature forest that extended along the entire length of the Alte Hofburg's immense north-western arm. The light from the ballroom windows, given a greenish hue by the mass of foliage, was just strong enough to show Edward that he was completely alone. Lighting the cigarette that had been denied him an hour ago, he sat on a window-ledge and considered Berchtold's visit to the Emperor.

There was only one possible reason for such aggressive urgency. Out of control, the tide had run to the point Edward had always dreaded: the fate of Europe rested on whether Franz Joseph, desperately old and worn down by more than sixty years of overwork and personal tragedy, could stand up to Berchtold, a reckless bully whose only policy for Austria was expansionism whatever the cost.

Looking for a solution to the impossible problem, Edward stared into the darkness of the courtyard beyond the slender wrought-iron pillars that supported the glass arcade. Twice, he was certain that he saw the shadows move: twice, he was equally sure that his imagination was playing tricks. But the third occurrence of the phantasm was accompanied by a footstep – the crunch of fine gravel beneath a delicate shoe. Treading on the butt of his cigarette, Edward moved to the edge of the terrace, making himself visible. Immediately, there was a gleam of golden hair in a sliver of light and Annaliese rushed at him.

'What are you doing here?' he gasped.

'To see you, of course.' The suggestion that she was talking to an idiot was banished by the way she clasped his hands. 'We are declaring war on Serbia.'

'How do you know?'

'Never mind, I do. It will be tomorrow.'

'The Emperor has signed it this evening,' Edward said, bowing to the inevitability of what he had seen. 'Berchtold was here,' he added. 'Soon after he arrived, the Archduke Karl was summoned.'

'I wonder why they bothered to tell him,' Annaliese said bitterly. 'Oh, Edward, what will happen?'

He was in no doubt. 'Russia will be furious. One has to assume that it was they who made the Serbs kowtow to that ultimatum. You can imagine . . .' He left the sentence unfinished, distracted by the expression in her eyes.

'This is terrible for my country,' she whispered. 'But what about *us* – you and me? We shall be enemies. It will split us . . . probably forever.'

'I'm afraid you're right.' Edward's disbelief of what she had said made him sound downright prosaic.

'Don't you understand anything important?' Annaliese asked, tightening her hold on his hands. 'I love you, you silly, pompous Englishman. I love you with all my heart.'

Edward's head spun as they were drawn to close what was left of the gap between them so that their lips met. For a few moments, with Annaliese still clutching his hands, the kiss remained chastely ethereal. But when she flung her arms round him, Edward embraced her with an ardour that was unlike anything he had ever known and the full extent of their feelings for each other flared into passionate incandescence.

Eventually, lack of breath forced them to break off. As if seeking support against faintness, they continued to hold each other.

Struggling to say the most important four words of his life, Edward was conscious of agitated voices to his left: they were no longer alone on the terrace.

'Annaliese, I love you,' he blurted out.

'I know.' Her smile was radiant with bitter-sweet sadness. 'Do you think that . . .'

There were two interruptions, from different directions. Along the terrace, an agitated man was asking, 'Are you sure you saw Boothby-Graffoe come out here?'

In the courtyard, hurried footsteps were followed by the voice of a woman. 'Liese! Come quickly! Her Highness, your mama, is asking for you. His Majesty has summoned his family to an audience.'

'Who's that?' Edward whispered.

'Eva, my maid.'

'She sounds frightened.'

'Yes . . . what about that man calling your name?'

Turning to peer through the fronds of the plants that were screening them, Edward was able to see without being seen. 'Oh, Lord, it's Sir Lionel,' he said. 'My Ambassador.'

Annaliese nodded. The fever that would have the whole of Vienna in its febrile grip by morning was taking root here, in the Alte Hofburg, home of the Habsburgs for over six centuries.

'*Liese!*' The maid's voice was full of panic.

Annaliese gathered up her courage with an effort that was painfully visible. '*Auf Wiedersehen, Liebste,*' she said. In the act of turning away from Edward, she changed her mind and pulled his head towards her for a last, fleeting kiss. 'I shall never forget you. *Never!*' This time, she did go, resolutely and quickly. When all else had merged into the darkness, the golden hair remained. Closing his eyes tightly, Edward willed the picture of the shining orb on to the retina of his memory: he tried to superimpose the cornflower-blue eyes. Then, he emerged from the mass of shrubs and flowers.

Sir Lionel, who was twenty yards away, saw him at once. Dismissing the people who had gathered around him, he hurried towards Edward, affable now that the mystery was solved.

'I'm sorry about this, my dear fellow,' Sir Lionel said. 'There's the most awful flap on. It seems that Austria *is* going to war and London has ordered me to prepare the Embassy for closure.'

'I understand, sir,' Edward said.

'I say, are you all right?' Sir Lionel was concerned. 'You look a touch off-colour.'

'A shock,' Edward replied honestly. 'I've had a bit of a shock.'

'Don't blame you,' Sir Lionel said. 'It's upset me, I don't mind telling you. Look here, I've received special instructions about you and young Shackleton from a chap called Amery.'

'That doesn't surprise me, sir,' Edward said, realising that Sir Lionel's ability to remember Archie's name underlined the extreme gravity of the situation.

'You two are to leave as soon as possible,' Sir Lionel went on. 'It's likely that things will get damned unpleasant over the next few days and all sorts of questions might be asked.'

'I quite understand, sir,' Edward replied. 'To be on the safe side, we'd better avoid Germany. There's a train to Zurich at five tomorrow morning.'

'Will you be able to catch it?'

'We should be cleared up in time,' Edward said, answering the question Sir Lionel had wanted to ask. 'There'll be nothing left when I've finished.'

The Ambassador nodded gratefully. 'I'm sorry to drop this on you,' he said. 'Er . . . am I right in assuming that your evening was in trouble already?' He lowered his voice to convey sympathy. 'You know, Edith and that American chap.'

'Yes.' Edward smiled bravely. 'She and Mr Warren *do* seem to be hitting it off well, don't they? If you'll excuse me, sir, I'll get on.'

'Well done. My car's at your disposal . . . It's waiting in the Balhausplatz.'

Given that assistance, Edward was at the Embassy inside ten minutes and found himself in the middle of hectic activity, most of it well-organised. Although everyone was preparing to leave, it soon became apparent that obliterating all trace of the Trade Bureau was the first priority, with the main effort directed towards feeding the fire in the garden incinerator. Archie, dishevelled, sweating profusely, and grinning like a madman, was wielding a huge, ornamental poker to ensure complete combustion.

'Congratulations, old chap!' he bellowed. 'Sorting all our rubbish out was a brilliant idea. We're getting through it at a tremendous rate.'

Edward's response was swamped by the shock of seeing JDT Lomax emerging from the smoky darkness. The Counsellor, Consul General and Head of Chancery, wearing a porter's overall, and without his eternal winged collar, was struggling under the weight of a load of papers for the fire. After dumping his burden at Archie's feet, he turned to Edward.

'Let me know if there is anything else we can do for you, Mr Boothby-Graffoe,' he said and was gone.

Edward's attempts to regain the power of speech produced nothing more than a splutter that sounded like, 'Well?'

'I rather think that His Excellency has had a word with him,' Archie said. 'Set him straight about us.'

'When?'

'About an hour ago. Sir Lionel came back from the ball when the flap started. Rum do, isn't it?'

Having decided not to be annoyed about the disclosure of their secret, Edward slid into an almost devil-may-care mood. 'Yes, Archie, it is a rum do,' he said. 'Get used to it, though. This is the night the world begins to go stark, staring mad!' He treated himself to another cigarette, lighting it from the bonfire with a top-secret document twisted into a makeshift taper.

Despite the weekend's preparations, the night was perilously short with a last-minute problem. Packing up all their personal belongings proved excessively time-consuming and would, in any case, produce an unmanageable millstone for two men in a hurry. It was left to Archie to suggest that they took no more than was necessary for the journey, leaving the bulk to be shipped home with the Embassy baggage.

Finally, when all seemed to be as ready as it was ever likely to be and the Ambassador's motor car had its engine running, ready to take them to the train, Archie asked Edward how far he intended travelling in the evening clothes he had worn for the ball. It was the final straw, and it turned the goodbyes into a rushed travesty of what they should have been. There was, Edward managed to notice, no sign of Edith: had she and Chester Warren shut themselves away from the ever-growing hysteria?

As soon as the train was on its way and they had regained their breath, the strange bubble of elation which had seen them through the night burst. Edward, who had never travelled from the Westbahnhof, was driven further into depression by an unexpected view of Schönbrunn Palace as they cleared the sidings and marshalling yards alongside Felber Strasse. The huge building looked more beautiful than ever in the first rays of the newly risen sun: presumably, she was inside. Was she asleep, or lying awake in the grip of fear? Sensing the mood, Archie resigned himself to a long silence.

It was nearly three hours before it broke. Breakfast was served between Linz and Salzburg and Edward felt bound to make conversation once they were sitting opposite each other in the dining-car.

'I suppose this creates problems for you,' he said, recalling that Archie had no immediate family. 'Where will you stay when we get to England?'

'I have a choice,' Archie replied jauntily. 'There's Aunt Elspeth in Perth, or Second Cousin Albert in Truro – he's a stinker.' The cheerfulness faded. 'I shall have to find digs in London.'

'You'll do no such thing!' Edward retorted with his old spirit. 'I won't hear of it. My parents would never forgive me if I turned you loose. Until we know what's what, you'll stay with us.'

'I say, that's awfully decent of you!' Archie's relief was on a par with his very considerable gratitude. 'Do I remember you saying that your father had a house in Cadogan Square?'

Edward nodded. 'Yes. Actually, I wouldn't mind betting that they're down at the other house, in Sussex.'

'I wonder if we're going to be stuck at the Foreign Office, twiddling our thumbs,' Archie said, viewing the prospect with grave misgiving.

'Over my dead body!' Edward replied. 'If Britain is dragged into the mess that Berchtold and his cronies are going to create, we'd better be given something useful to do.'

'I second that,' Archie declared.

At four o'clock in the afternoon, eleven hours after leaving Vienna, the train crossed the border between Austria and Switzerland and began the descent to Lake Constance and Zurich. Numb bleakness enveloped Edward. Archie, who sensed that it was connected with the wondrously beautiful Archduchess Annaliese, took an over-studious interest in a three-week-old London newspaper that he had grabbed just before leaving the Embassy.

Edward stared out of the window. The railway line was following a river that cascaded down the floor of a long valley, alternating short stretches of comparative serenity with the turbulence of frequent, boulder-strewn cataracts. The hills, rising only to about 3,000 feet in this corner of Switzerland, were green and lush under a cloudless sky, looking for all the world like impossibly steep bowling-greens. Occasionally, there was a glimpse of a farm, always with the distinctively high-pitched roof and wide eaves that somehow suggested a cuckoo clock. From a meadow near one of the quaint homesteads, a group of children jumped for joy and waved at the speeding train, but Edward barely saw them.

He was struggling to recreate an image of Annaliese on the terrace at the Hofburg. The hair and eyes were engraved on his soul. So was that last look, a haunting mixture of infinite sadness and a sensuality that, Edward now realised, suggested the Archduchess Elsa. But it was not enough: suddenly, the man who often failed to notice a woman's clothes was desperately anxious to recall what Annaliese had been wearing. Initially, he was at a loss, knowing only that she had created an impression of incongruously elegant grandeur – she was not, after all, attending the ball. Yes, that was it! Beneath her dark cape, Annaliese wore what seemed to be a ball-gown. It had been pink, the palest pink, with an austere, high neck. However, after clinging to her hips, the long skirt was straight, quite unsuitable for dancing. It was probably the type of dress prescribed for audiences with the Emperor. Although her maid implied that the Imperial

Family gathering was an unexpected act of near-panic, Annaliese must have had advance warning of Franz Joseph's summons.

Lastly, Edward remembered the gossamer silkiness of the gown. In the embrace of their long, breathless kiss, his hands had gone inside Annaliese's cloak, caressing the fabric, feeling the vibrant firmness of her body. Perhaps, if the circumstances had been different . . .

Appalled by what his mind was doing, Edward shook himself, letting out a grunt of self-disgust. Startled into anxiety, Archie abandoned the newspaper. 'Are you all right, old man?' he asked.

'Yes.' Edward sat up very straight, attempting to take refuge behind a statesmanlike façade. 'Thoughts, you know.'

'What about?'

'Oh . . . this and that.' Edward cleared his throat portentously. 'I was wondering about Russia . . . whether they might behave sensibly.'

Archie, good chap that he was, believed him.

At Zurich, where there was a three-hour wait for a train to Paris, a single topic had turned the crowded railway station into a bedlam of speculation below which undercurrents of fear were gaining strength. Austria had declared war on Serbia at midday. Queuing for sleeper tickets, Edward memorised the day and date.

It was Tuesday 28 July 1914.

4

August 1914
'This isn't for the faint-hearted'

The train was an hour late leaving Zurich. It travelled ten miles, came to an abrupt halt in the middle of nowhere and stayed there for half the night. Already, on the basis of nothing more than newspaper headlines, Europe's transport system was losing its nerve. When they finally reached London at seven o'clock on the evening of 31 July, Edward and Archie felt ridiculously proud of themselves for taking only three days over the journey.

At Victoria station, the cries of the boys selling the late editions of the *News* and *Standard* carried the message that Edward had feared for weeks: Russia was mobilising against Austria.

'Is this it?' Archie asked.

'It all depends,' Edward grunted.

Correctly attributing his friend's taciturn attitude to a combination of exhaustion and thoughts of Annaliese, Archie made no attempt to pursue the matter and they set out to walk to Cadogan Square.

The house, currently the property of Edward's father, Lord Douglas Boothby-Graffoe, had been in the family for over two hundred years. For much of that time it had served as a London residence for successive Dukes of Lincolnshire. Archie, somewhat overawed by its imposing façade, thought that it was well-suited to such a role. At least twice the size of any other house in the square, its grandeur was softened by elegance and an indefinable air of contentment. There was, however, no sign of occupation: the windows had a blank, lifeless look.

Sure enough, when the door was opened by an immaculately attired manservant, it was the dust-sheets that caught the eye first. It was some time before Archie appreciated that the entrance hall boasted a chandelier and graceful staircase as fine as anything in Vienna.

'Mister Edward, sir, this *is* a pleasure,' the man at the door said. 'Very unexpected, too.'

'Hello, Franklin,' Edward replied, his spirits soaring. 'I take it that everyone's down in Sussex?'

'Since Tuesday, sir.'

'We'll go down tomorrow. Now, Franklin, this is my very good friend and partner in crime, Archie Shackleton. We shall be looking after him until he finds a place of his own.'

'How do you do, sir?' said Franklin, a paragon of welcoming courtesy.

'Evening, Franklin,' Archie replied breezily. 'We're deuced glad to be here!'

'Franklin is my father's butler,' Edward explained. 'He's a gem and he rules this place with a rod of iron.'

It was meant to be a joke, yet Archie was inclined to take it as literal truth. There was something disturbing about Franklin and in Edward's almost sycophantic reaction to him. Fresh-faced, tall, and in reasonable condition, Franklin was probably aged about fifty. Superficially, he looked a model butler, but his eyes were a touch too shrewd for Archie's liking; there seemed to be a calculating mind behind them that gave the lie to his polite affability. It was entirely possible that apart from Edward – and Lord Douglas himself, presumably – there were few people who could count Franklin as a friend, or even cared much for him.

'We need baths, grub, and beds,' Edward said. 'And clean clothes, for God's sake.'

'Certainly, sir.' Franklin studied Archie appraisingly and said, 'A sixteen-inch collar, I fancy, sir?'

'Bang on,' Archie said.

'It will be attended to,' Franklin murmured.

'One other thing,' Edward said. 'Has my father had the sense to have the telephone put into Upper Overs yet?'

'I fear not, sir. His Lordship continues to regard the instrument as an intrusion that has no place outside London.'

'Tchah!' Edward's exasperation was affectionate. 'Be a good chap, Franklin, get a telegram off, will you? Tell Father that Archie and I will be down tomorrow . . . in time for lunch, I hope.'

Without further ado, Edward led the way to the stairs. Picking his way over the dust-sheets, Archie was sure that beds would have been made up in freshly cleaned rooms by the time they had finished their baths: for Edward, Franklin would move heaven and earth.

Although the following day was Saturday, Edward was convinced that the Foreign Office would be working at full stretch. He was right, but finding sense and reason proved impossible.

Faced with what was rapidly assuming the nightmarish proportions of the greatest crisis in the history of Europe, no one had any time for the two young men who turned up at half past eight, eager for instructions. Edward and Archie spent an hour waiting in cavernous corridors and another half-hour trekking hundreds of yards round the rambling edifice, passed from one department to another like unwanted relatives. At long last, in an office on the third floor at the back of the building, they found someone who recognised their names.

'Aren't you part of Mr Amery's lot?'

'Yes,' Edward replied, perking up.

'Hang on.' The man was ransacking a pile of papers. 'Yes, here we are. Hmm . . . as I thought. Amery went to Paris on Thursday. He isn't expected back for at least a week. You can clear off.'

'There *must* be something we can do!' Edward protested.

'Only get in the way,' was the ungracious response. 'You've both got masses of leave owing – take it!'

Edward glanced out of the window, studying the view of St James's Park, where nannies were pushing the morning procession of perambulators round the lake. Would the ritual survive the next seven days? 'Come on, Archie,' he said. 'We'd better do as we're told.'

Back at Cadogan Square, they had coffee, packed their few

belongings – all impeccably laundered or cleaned since the previous evening – and went to the garage at the rear of the house. Acting on Franklin's advice, Edward chose a gleaming, brand-new Sunbeam from the impressive range of vehicles available and they set off.

Through Southwark, Lambeth, and the more pleasant streets of Merton and Sutton, Edward was uncommunicative, saying little except that he feared there would be another declaration of war before the day was out. Archie, who enjoyed motoring, was content to watch the passing sights, waving cheerfully at those people who interrupted whatever they were doing to admire the Sunbeam. At the top of Box Hill, where he stopped to admire the views across the Weald, a change came over Edward. His feelings for this lovely part of England enabled him to take the first steps towards consigning Annaliese to a sealed episode in his life that was over and done with. He relaxed enough to begin telling Archie what lay ahead.

'As you've gathered, this house we're going to is called Upper Overs. Father bought it when he and Mother married, whereas he didn't get Cadogan Square until ten years ago after it was released from entail in the Lincolnshire estate.'

'The Duke of Lincolnshire is your father's brother?' Archie said, wanting to double-check.

'Yes.'

'So, how should I address him?' Archie was anxious to have the niceties of etiquette resolved in advance.

'"Lord Douglas",' Edward replied.

'Or "sir"?'

'Just as good, yes.'

'And your mother?'

Edward smiled fondly. 'She's "Lady Alice" – but only because she had a title before she married Father. She was the Duke of Laverstoke's daughter.' The look on Archie's face prompted Edward to complicate the issue. 'If she hadn't had her own title in the first place, they'd still be Lord and Lady Douglas Boothby-Graffoe, but Mother couldn't be addressed as "Lady Alice". It's like a chap with a knighthood – he and his wife are Sir Fred and Lady Brown, but she can't call herself "Lady Phoebe". Father's title isn't hereditary, so it can't be used to ennoble the unworthy hangers-on!'

'Like you?' Archie suggested.

'Exactly!' Edward laughed.

'Right. If I keep my wits about me, I think I might cope with that,' Archie said. 'This road's a different matter, though.'

The surface over which they were travelling had left a great deal to be desired since East Grinstead. Now that they had entered thick woodland, Edward was coping with an unmetalled track that was mostly ruts and pot-holes. 'The motor car has made hardly any impression down here,' he said. 'This is the start of the Ashdown Forest. The road's better from Crowborough, but I like to come this way. You should see it in autumn.'

'It's not so bad at the moment,' Archie said, gazing round admiringly.

After rattling and bouncing along for three miles, they reached a fork at which Edward took the turn that descended sharply into a small valley, passing a group of three houses as it did so.

'They're decent places,' Archie said, craning his neck to get a good look.

'All retired grandees from the City,' Edward replied. 'I think there's enough money hidden away there to buy Oxford Street. Here we are . . . hang on tight, this corner's a beast!'

The Sunbeam complained noisily – especially after Edward made a ham-fisted gear change halfway through the turn. Largely thanks to the tarmac surface of the private drive, they came through it without mishap.

It was another two hundred yards before the house, screened by beech trees, came into view, causing Archie to exclaim, 'I say, what a topping set-up!'

Upper Overs looked exactly what it was, a delightful maze of a place, originally constructed in 1740 and extended incessantly throughout the following century. What made it so very pleasing was that, although successive builders had wilfully avoided architectural consistency, they had always used the same bricks and tiles. The mellow orange – the tiles were a shade darker than the bricks – produced a harmony that transcended the extraordinary, higgledy-piggledy structure.

Alerted by Edward's fanfare on the horn, three people came hurrying from the front door. The merest glance at them was sufficient to tell Archie that Edward was a member of a close-knit, loving family. Lord Douglas Boothby-Graffoe, a strikingly handsome man in his mid-fifties, could obviously be a terrific swell when the occasion demanded, but the arrival of his second son after an eight-month absence had him acting like a schoolboy on a treat. Lady Alice, a few years his junior and with her fresh beauty of thirty years ago still powerfully in evidence, was almost as excited. As befitted an elder brother who was a captain in the Coldstream Guards, Alexander attempted a show of po-faced dignity before hauling Edward out of the Sunbeam and clasping him in a bear-like embrace.

In the ensuing chaos, Archie somehow got himself introduced: Lord Douglas and Alexander were cordial, but much more interested in Edward's views on the international crisis. It was left to Lady Alice to welcome Archie, a task she performed with warm sincerity.

'It's a great pleasure to meet you, Mr Shackleton,' she said. 'Edward has mentioned you frequently in his letters. I have the impression that there were dozens of times when he would have been quite lost without you.'

'Oh, no, Lady Alice,' Archie stammered. 'That can't be right . . . apart from a spot of bag-carrying, I'm not much good.'

'Lesson number one,' she smiled. 'When you get praise from Edward, cherish it. It's a very rare commodity and he's given you a good deal. I feel I know you so well that I shall call you Archie – you don't mind, I hope?'

'Not at all, Lady Alice.' Totally overcome, Archie was about to make a complete ass of himself by saying that he felt honoured when another member of the family appeared.

The brothers and their father, embroiled in European affairs and the reasons for Edward's sudden departure from Vienna, were unaware of her presence. So was Lady Alice until she saw that Archie's confusion had taken a marked turn for the worse: the poor man was poleaxed, rooted to the ground.

'Ah, there you are, darling,' Archie heard Lady Alice say, her voice sounding as if it were coming to him from on high. 'This is Edward's friend, Mr Shackleton, who's been helping him in Vienna. Archie, may I introduce you to my daughter Beatrice?'

The older members of Society always swore that there was something uncanny about it. 'Do you want to know what Alice Boothby-Graffoe looked like at twenty-one?' Lady Torksey, the doyenne of gossips would say. 'That's easy . . . take a look at that daughter of hers. Two peas in a pod! Quite amazing when you think that the Boothby-Graffoe men nearly always look the same, regardless of the mother. But Beatrice is the spitten image of Alice in her coming-out year.'

The chestnut hair, brown eyes, and classic features were identical, with the mother as living proof that, no, it most definitely was not too good to last.

Lady Alice saw that Beatrice, like Archie, was frozen into total immobility – except for her face, which showed a tiny smile of pure enchantment. The moment passed, but not before Beatrice had bemused her mother: nearing the end of a debutante season that had seen the rejection of more potential suitors than it was wise to count, this *was* a bolt from the blue.

'How do you do, Mr Shackleton?' Beatrice had recovered her composure and was ensuring that their handshake was firm and drawn out a fraction longer than strict good manners dictated.

'How do you do, Miss Boothby-Graffoe?' Archie replied. He coped very well, then reduced Beatrice to helpless mirth with his explosive, 'Gosh, I say!'

The sound of his sister's laughter extracted Edward from the intense discussion with Lord Douglas and Alexander.

'Hello, Bee!' he said, hurrying towards her.

'Hello, fish-face,' Beatrice responded, wrapping her arms round his neck. 'Have you been chucked out of Vienna?'

'Yes.'

'Serve you right – I expect you've been a terrible nuisance. I'm glad, though. It's lovely to see you.'

'Darlings, may we go in and continue this uproar over lunch?' Lady Alice said, and was rewarded with instant obedience. Archie, furiously telling himself that it was ludicrous to be jealous of Edward for embracing his own sister, found Beatrice falling into step beside him. Nothing was said, but the companionship in her smile was worth more than words.

Inside, Upper Overs had an aura that promised everything a visitor might need, be it soothing, or serious mental stimulation, with laughter never far away. It was a house that seemed to pay the most careful attention to the creaking of its beams and the ticking of its many clocks, a house of beeswax polish and appetising kitchen smells. Lady Alice, helped by a cook and three maids, ran Upper Overs as a benign dictatorship, always at pains to ensure that it was the antithesis of Cadogan Square's rather aloof grandeur.

Lunch was a buffet of cold meats and poultry, salad, and diced potatoes with a delicious dressing. In addition, the sideboard contained jugs of beer, cider, and apple juice, together with enough freshly baked bread rolls to satisfy a small army.

'I'd advise against the cider,' Beatrice whispered to Archie while they stood aside, allowing Lord Douglas, Alexander, and Edward to load their plates, never ceasing their argument over the prospects for war.

'Why?' Archie whispered back.

'Father makes it!' Beatrice's eyes were saucer-wide with mock horror. 'It's Mother's fault – she said he ought to have a hobby. It's *ghastly*! I'm sure it rots socks.'

Keeping an unobtrusive watch on the pair in the corner, Lady Alice saw that Archie Shackleton was being comprehensively bowled over by the most remarkable young woman he had ever had the amazing good fortune to meet.

After lunch, while Alexander drove Lady Alice and Beatrice into Crowborough for shopping and social calls, Lord Douglas disappeared for a nap and Edward took Archie on a tour of the gardens and grounds, 300 acres of woodland that was virtually identical to the surrounding forest.

'I gather your brother hopes that we shall be involved in a war,' Archie said tentatively.

'He's a professional soldier,' Edward replied. 'So's my cousin,

Gerald. He's in the same regiment. Chaps like that see things differently.' There was an edge to his voice that warned Archie off the subject for the rest of the afternoon.

Dinner was a pleasantly informal affair, with conversation limited to the gossip and anecdotes picked up by Lady Alice and Beatrice in the village. When the meal was over, Lord Douglas challenged Edward to a game of chess and Beatrice dragooned the others into a rubber of whist, making it plain that she and Archie were to be partners. But they got no further than setting up the table and hunting for the cards: one of the maids appeared with a late edition of the *London Evening News*, brought in by her gentleman friend who was a guard on the railway and had come down with the six o'clock train from Victoria.

Germany had declared war on Russia.

'What does this mean?' Lord Douglas asked Edward.

'Go on, Archie, they won't believe me.' Edward seemed to be washing his hands of it.

Conscious that Beatrice was willing him on, Archie was far more self-assured than usual. 'We shall be at war within forty-eight hours,' he said. 'Seventy-two if things are delayed.'

'How do you make that out?' Alexander asked.

'France is bound to help Russia. That means war between France and Germany which will suit Kaiser Wilhelm down to the ground. To get at France, the Germans will take the short-cut through Belgium and that's when Britain gets dragged in.'

'Why?'

'We are guarantors of Belgian neutrality,' Archie replied. 'Treaty of London, eighteen-thirty.'

Beatrice was quick to spot the flicker of approval on Edward's face.

'Knowing that, won't the Huns leave Belgium alone?' Alexander asked.

'I doubt it. They have a plan hatched up by a chap called Schlieffen and the Germans worship plans. They won't change it.'

'What's this plan supposed to achieve?'

'Flattening France in four weeks,' Archie replied.

'Three,' Edward interjected quietly.

'That's ridiculous!' Alexander scoffed. 'You're sure about this Belgian caper?'

'Definitely!' Archie said. 'The Germans will stick to the plan. That may be the only thing you can rely on during the next few weeks.'

'Fine.' Alexander stood up, rubbing his hands. 'I hereby declare that my leave is over. Would you excuse me, please, Mother? I must prepare my kit.' Lady Alice nodded weakly, not understanding what was happening. 'I tell you what,' Alexander said on his way to the door. 'I reckon it *will* be over in three weeks, but not in the way the Kaiser thinks.'

His departure left a slightly awkward silence. Lord Douglas cleared his throat and held up the newspaper. 'These chaps seem to think that it won't last long,' he said, clearly hoping for Edward's agreement.

'Father, Germany can put *two million* men in the field – and that's today, not next month, or next year.'

Beatrice's half-hearted endeavour to resurrect the idea of whist was doomed to failure. Instead, an uneasy discussion of what war might mean to Britain and her Empire ebbed and flowed sporadically until Lady Alice suggested that it was time for bed.

Alexander's original idea was that he should leave at six the following morning. It was, however, a Sunday, which meant that the first train to London did not leave Crowborough until nine-thirty. The disenchantment this caused put everyone out of sorts and, at nine o'clock, when there was scarcely time for such luxuries, Lord Douglas and Edward were grumbling at each other in an attempt to decide who should drive Alexander to the station. In the event, none of it was necessary: a tooting in the drive heralded the arrival of a young man in a bright red Morris Oxford motor. He was wearing the uniform of a second lieutenant.

Following Alexander outside at a more leisurely pace, Edward stood back while the two soldiers enjoyed a boisterous reunion. When the exuberance had subsided, he greeted the new arrival with obvious affection.

Still lingering over breakfast in a room with windows that gave a good view of the scene outside, Archie had Beatrice to tell him what was going on.

'That's our cousin, Gerald,' she said. 'He's been on leave, too – visiting people in Worthing, I think. I expect he's called in for Alexander on his way back to Wellington Barracks.'

'He must be the Duke of Lincolnshire's son,' Archie said.

'One of them, yes. Not the heir.' A preoccupation with working out what was happening outside made Beatrice sound brusque.

In fact, Lady Alice was nipping the idea of an immediate departure in the bud. 'Have you had breakfast, Gerald?' she asked.

Second Lieutenant Lord Gerald Boothby-Graffoe, the mainstay of the Coldstream Guards' Rugby XV and an irrepressible destroyer of furniture on bachelor mess nights, wilted sheepishly. 'Actually, Aunt Alice, no. There wasn't time.'

'Well you can jolly well make time now! I'm not having you going off to kill Germans on an empty stomach.'

He was twenty-two, four years younger than his hero, Alexander. The blond hair and rectangular face were, Archie realised, the hallmarks of a very distinctive family.

After staving off the inevitable for well over an hour, Lady Alice accepted that Alexander and Gerald must be on their way. Not wishing to get in the way of what was likely to be an emotional parting, Archie said his piece quickly and wandered round to the garden at the back of the house. To his surprise, Beatrice joined him almost at once.

'I can't bear this,' she confessed. 'Both Alexander and Gerald think they're off on some sort of outing.'

'They're quite wrong,' Archie replied. 'I don't believe they'll be going anywhere.'

'Really?' Beatrice indicated a rustic bench. To make sure that Archie understood her meaning, she took his arm and guided him towards it. 'Can you explain why you think that, Archie?'

It was very nearly too much for him: she was touching him and using his Christian name! Archie had to play for time to compose himself, waiting until they were settled on the seat before attempting to answer the question.

'Assuming there is going to be a scrap, it will be in France or Belgium, won't it? Our chaps can't march across, can they? Getting them there will take a fair bit of planning, so I'm sure you'll see them again while it's all being organised.' Apparently comforted, Beatrice fell silent, staring round the garden. Becoming uneasy at her abstraction, Archie asked, 'What about your other cousin . . . Lord Gerald's brother?'

Beatrice was miles away, so engrossed in a group of magnificent beech trees that Archie began to wonder if he had said something wrong. 'Ralph is the only person I know who makes Mother angry,' Beatrice said at last.

This, Archie realised, was damning criticism. 'Oh, dear. Is he a bit of a stinker?'

'Very much so!' Beatrice replied. 'He wasn't *so* bad until Aunt Honoria died three years ago. She was a tartar! Poor Uncle William misses her terribly and can't be bothered trying to control Ralph. He gets into *the* most awful scrapes. There's bound to be a really big scandal one day.'

'And he's the next Duke of Lincolnshire?'

Beatrice shuddered. 'Don't mention it! I've heard Father say that he hopes he doesn't live to see it.'

'How old is Ralph?' Archie asked.

'Twenty-four, the same as Edward.'

'And your uncle?'

'About sixty, I think.'

'Your father's far too young to be . . .'

But Archie's opinion was cut short by Lady Alice's cry. 'All right, you two, it's safe to come out now! The brave boys have gone and we shall be late for church if we don't get a move on!'

So ended their last short period alone together for two weeks. At four o'clock, following a late, leisurely lunch, Lord Douglas announced his attention of returning to London. Beatrice, who was his assistant at Boothby's in Bond Street, wanted to go with him. That set Edward off.

'It's no good being stuck down here,' he muttered, half to himself, half to Archie. 'Especially without the telephone.' He gave his father a suggestive look. 'I need to know what's happening.'

'You're dealing with this crisis all alone, are you, darling?' Lady Alice asked, using straight-faced humour in an attempt to soothe her son's nerves.

'Archie and I need jobs,' Edward said, doggedly missing the point. 'I know we're supposed to be on leave, but we must keep in touch.'

'Very well,' Lady Alice sighed. 'I don't particularly want to be here on my own, so I'd better join you all.'

She went with Beatrice and Lord Douglas in the Rolls. Bouncing along behind with Edward at the wheel of the Sunbeam, Archie mulled his last exchange with Beatrice before they parted.

She said, 'Cadogan Square isn't like this place. I suppose you met Franklin?'

'Yes, I did.'

The slight narrowing of her eyes indicated that she had picked up the inflexion in his voice. 'He never comes down here, thank God! It's beneath his dignity to be seen south of Sloane Square. Father won't hear a word against him.'

'I guessed as much,' Archie said.

The catastrophe unfolded exactly as Edward and Archie had predicted.

On 3 August, Germany declared war on France and issued an ultimatum to Belgium, demanding unrestricted passage for its troops. The Belgians refused. Twenty-four hours of futile diplomacy followed, during which the vanguard of the Kaiser's army began violating Belgium's borders. Great Britain declared war on Germany on the evening of 4 August. Hanging around in a Foreign Office corridor at the time, Edward and Archie heard talk of plans to start sending men across to Ostend within two days. On Lord Kitchener's orders, the enterprise was to be known as the British Expeditionary Force.

Walking down Victoria Street on their way back to Cadogan Square, Archie noticed that passers-by were in a greater hurry than usual, their faces fearful and alert. 'This lot don't have all that much to worry them,' he said. 'What must it be like in Europe?'

Edward nodded grimly. 'I wonder if Berchtold is pleased with his handiwork. Vienna didn't deserve this.'

'No, by George!' Without pausing to think, Archie put his foot straight in it. 'What do you think will happen over there? You must worry about your lovely Archduchess.'

'Look here, let's have one thing clear once and for all.' Edward stopped walking to confront Archie. 'She is not *my* Archduchess. It was always out of the question that she ever could be and I don't want to hear that sort of talk again. And while we're on the subject, I'll thank you to keep your mouth shut in front of my family – I don't want them worried by silly stories. Do you understand?'

'Of course, old man. Look here, I'm frightfully sorry.'

'Hmm . . . Right.' Embarrassed by Archie's totally abject apology, Edward walked on abruptly, but found it impossible to let go of the subject. 'We don't need to worry about Annaliese. She's part of a clan that's made a damned good job of looking after itself for six hundred years. They won't let *anything* come between them and their self-interest.'

The most remarkable facet of the outburst was its patent untruth. Back in Vienna, Edward had spoken frequently of the increasing precariousness of the Habsburgs's hold on power and status. The probability of their downfall and the consequent destabilisation of a dangerous region had been the subject of several long memoranda to Mr Amery.

Edward's tense mood persisted throughout dinner in the grandest of Cadogan Square's two dining-rooms. His parents and Beatrice naturally attributed it to the fact that Britain was at war, news that bewildered and appalled them. Lord Douglas and Beatrice were, in any case, distracted by a problem that had cropped up at Boothby's in the course of the day's business. From what Archie could gather, there were grounds for doubting the authenticity of a painting that a much-respected peer wished to sell.

As at Upper Overs, family unity overrode the convention of the ladies withdrawing while the men drank port and smoked. Lady Alice decided to have one of Edward's cigarettes and Franklin was at her side, holding what proved to be the latest type of petrol-lighter. Seeing the novelty, Edward held out his hand and Franklin passed it over.

'This is rather clever,' Edward said after testing the ignition mechanism several times.

'Would you like one, sir?' Franklin asked.

'Yes. Where did you get it?'

'Leave it to me, sir. It will be dealt with first thing tomorrow.'

'You are a good fellow, Franklin,' Edward said. Briefly, he was like a small, spoilt boy, basking in the latest treat. Pleased with himself, Franklin left the room and Edward launched into a description of the pandemonium at the Foreign Office.

Archie intercepted Beatrice's disturbingly eloquent look. 'Do you see that I mean about that *wretched* man,' she seemed to be saying.

Edward's impatience ensured that the next ten days were a purgatory of suspense and frustration. Mr Amery resolutely failed to appear, so other officials were pestered within an inch of their frantically busy lives. Evicting Edward and the far less troublesome Archie from the Foreign Office became an all too common event. On exceptionally bad days, they were thrown out twice.

Hasty letters from Alexander and Gerald indicated that, contrary to Archie's reassurances to Beatrice, they had sailed for Belgium on 7 August as part of the British Expeditionary Force's second wave. The newspapers spoke glowingly of the liaison between Belgian and British forces, which was proving most effective in stemming the German advance. It was Edward, armed with copies of the same day's *Times*, *Morning Post*, *Mail*, and *Graphic*, who pointed out that their reports were absolutely identical, right down to the last comma.

'This isn't *news*,' he said. 'They're printing bulletins from the War Office. I'd be very surprised if this was anything like the truth.'

Lord Douglas and Lady Alice pointedly avoided asking Edward for his version of what was happening across the English Channel.

Then, on Friday 14 August, Mr Amery was not only in the Foreign Office, he had left orders with the doorkeepers at every entrance that Edward and Archie were to be delivered to him the moment they showed their faces.

Mr Amery was a slight man of about forty with bright, inquisitive eyes and a youthful pinkness that was at odds with his prematurely grey hair. Some people thought he looked rather like a university don – which is exactly what he had been until about twelve months ago. Sir Edward Grey had enlisted the help of Mr Asquith himself to persuade Cambridge's Trinity College to lend their best mathematical mind for nearly a century to an unspecified department in the Foreign Office. There was, however, nothing remotely donnish in Mr Amery's greeting.

'You two seem to have been making a hell of a damned nuisance of yourselves. What do you mean by it, eh?'

'We're tremendously keen to get fixed up with something useful, sir,' Edward replied.

'So are several thousand others, but they don't go round creating problems for chaps who don't know which way to turn. Another thing, Boothby-Graffoe, you're losing your grip!'

'In what way, sir?'

'Your assessment was that Franz Ferdinand would get himself assassinated if he went into Croatia. He did no such thing! It was Bosnia.'

'I'm sorry about that, sir,' Edward said, the beginnings of a smile at one corner of his mouth.

There was a twinkle in Mr Amery's eyes as he said, 'Keep your wits about you, Edward. I must have information that is *totally* accurate.'

'Of course, sir.'

'By the way, that last report of yours about Berchtold wanting war at any price was useful . . . at least, it would have been if I'd managed to find anyone prepared to believe it. They do now.' He gave a short, barking laugh. 'Right, sit down.'

Edward and Archie did so, expectant as Mr Amery shuffled through the papers on his blotter.

'Do you two scoundrels want to carry on working for me?'

'Yes, sir!' came out in perfect unison.

'I've been given special responsibilities and powers.' Mr Amery paused to squint at them. 'That was a warning,' he added. 'This isn't for the faint-hearted.'

'Please carry on, sir,' Edward said after a quick glance at Archie.

'Let me put you in the picture about how things are likely to develop in Europe,' Mr Amery said. 'I do so in the utmost confidentiality. Not a breath of this must get out. Is that clear?' The two young men nodded solemnly. 'As some of us knew they would, the Germans are deploying the Schlieffen plan. They're making a complete mess of it.'

'Oh!' Edward was surprised. 'They're usually good with plans.'

'Not this time. Two things appear to have gone wrong. Russia got cracking quicker than anyone expected. Last night, they had half a million men within ten miles of the border with East Prussia. The Germans are pulling men back from the west to deal with them. However, even before that, the High Command had started playing silly buggers with the plan. We believe that von Moltke has reinforced his left wing at the expense of the right. Another twenty thousand men facing him could turn his flank and start a rout.'

'But the men aren't there?' Edward said.

'No. If only the French had got off their backsides in time . . . if only!' Mr Amery shook himself. 'Sooner or later, the German advance is going to grind to a standstill because of logistics problems and infirmity of purpose. The best crystal ball we've got says that this will leave a million men strung out along a line from approximately Amiens to Nancy.'

'Will the French be out in force by the time this happens?' Edward asked.

'Presumably. So shall we.' Mr Amery leaned back in his deep chair. 'Your observations, if you please.'

Archie blurted out, 'The machine-gun', startling himself. Catching Edward's eye and gaining in confidence, he carried on. 'They can hardly stand out in the open and slaughter each other, so they'll dig in. That could lead to stalemate.'

'It could indeed,' Mr Amery said with a smile of approval. 'Artillery will bolster the tendency to start digging. You won't find a military man to agree with this idea, but it's going to happen, as sure as eggs is eggs! This business *won't* be over by Christmas – or by next Christmas. As you've often said, Edward, it's going to be a long and bloody war. I've been told to come up with plans for making a useful contribution behind the scenes.'

'What are we going to be doing, sir?' Edward asked.

A sorrowful expression stole over Mr Amery's face: he hated having to douse Edward's enthusiasm in cold water. 'I promise that you will be the first to hear about it – when I've worked it out. At the moment, I haven't the faintest idea.' Smiling apologetically at the crushed disappointment on the other side of his massive desk, Mr Amery changed tack. 'Until such time as the muse condescends to alight upon me, you are to go away and behave yourselves. I don't want to see you until I send for you. Nor do I wish to hear further reports of your nuisance – is that clear?'

'Yes, sir,' Archie said. Edward glowered and nodded.

'Haven't your parents got rather a nice place down in Sussex?' Mr Amery asked Edward.

'Yes, they have.'

'May I suggest that you go there and *stay* there?'

'That isn't an awfully good idea,' Edward said. 'It *is* a nice house, but it isn't connected to the telephone.'

'In that case, I shall have to be content with the telegram service,' Mr Amery said. 'I know that you could find this difficult to accept, Edward, but I can't see us losing the war simply because of a few hours' delay in getting you here. Kindly write down your address.' While Edward was doing so, Mr Amery asked Archie, 'Are you staying with him?'

'Yes, sir.'

'If need be, sit on his head. I would like those within these hallowed halls to forget that you two exist.'

'Right you are, sir,' Archie said, grinning at a mournfully resigned Edward.

'If you persist in upsetting people, you could be putting my plans at risk,' Mr Amery said. 'Now clear off!'

After spending the previous weekend in London, everyone went to Upper Overs that Friday afternoon, escaping from the heat, noise, and ever-mounting tension of the city. Accompanying Edward in the

Sunbeam, Archie spent most of the journey screwing up his courage to ask a question and trying to work the conversation round to a point at which he might slip it in. The latter proved impossible. Edward, his teeth gritted, was doing his utmost to overtake, a hopeless task in view of the way Lord Douglas handled the more powerful Rolls: he was far too involved to respond to hints. Eventually, Archie was left with no alternative to coming out with it when the last few miles through the Ashdown Forest had imposed a drastic reduction in speed.

'Look here, old man, would you have any objection to me speaking to your parents about Beatrice?'

'Bee?' Edward was mystified. 'What's wrong with her?'

'Damn it, man, there's nothing wrong with her.' Archie had wound himself into such a state that his nervousness boiled over into what sounded like anger. 'She's wonderful. I think . . . well . . . er . . . that is . . . oh, dash it!'

Bereft of speech, Archie had to endure the additional discomfort of watching the truth dawn on his companion with painful slowness. At long last, Edward's face broke into a smile. 'You're sweet on her?'

'Yes!' It was a full-blooded shout.

'You and Bee, eh?' Edward mulled it over. 'Yes, I could give that my vote.'

'Thank you,' Archie babbled.

'A word of caution, though.' Edward said, his inherent wariness asserting itself. 'Don't build your hopes up too much.'

'Why?' Archie was ashen.

'She's been coming out this Season,' Edward explained. 'From what I can gather, it's been murder. The chaps flocked round, but she gave every single one of them his marching orders the instant he dared to suggest another meeting. Father's calling it "The Massacre of the Swains". As a matter of fact, I think the Season's still going on, but Mother said that Bee should give it up about a month before we arrived.'

'Oh, my Lord!' Conjuring up images of the men who had been sent packing, all of them infinitely more suitable and attractive than him, Archie became desperate. 'I draw nearly a thousand a year from a pile of investments my grandfather left me.'

Edward assumed his statesmanlike expression. 'If I were you, I wouldn't mention that, Archie. Bee's the sort of girl who gets uppity if she thinks a chap is trying to bamboozle her with money. That's probably how half the lounge lizards she met on the circuit blotted their copy-books. No, talk to Mother and Father by all means . . . they like you. Come to think of it, so does Bee. Have a go!'

Archie was given no time to consider it. The moment they reached Upper Overs, Lady Alice said that she would die without a cup of tea and asked for a large pot to be brought into the drawing-room. While Lord Douglas was collapsing into his favourite armchair and agreeing with her, Edward concocted a pretext for taking Beatrice into the garden. Stranded on the hearthrug, Archie was horrified to see that his hosts were gazing at him expectantly. He plunged in.

'Er . . . Lord Douglas, sir, I wonder if I may have permission to pay court to Beatrice.' Much to the relief of Archie and his audience, it came out right.

Lady Alice clapped her hands delightedly. 'How charming,' she said. 'Jolly well done, Archie.' She turned to her husband. 'Well, Douglas, what thinkest thou?'

'Blessed if I know.' Lord Douglas rubbed his chin and gave a convincing imitation of a man in the toils of perplexity. 'What do you say, my dear?'

'I think our young friend has spoken up in the nick of time.' Lady Alice gave Archie her warmest smile. 'There's a strong possibility that Beatrice is on the verge of speaking to you about this very matter. My impression is that she's running out of patience.'

'Oh.' Archie was flabbergasted.

'So, unless you can face up to being brow-beaten by a self-willed female, I suggest you get cracking, Archie.' As an afterthought, Lady Alice added, 'With our full blessing, of course.'

'Absolutely!' Having made his enthusiastic contribution, Lord Douglas turned to look out of a window. In the garden, Beatrice was displaying signs of irritation with Edward. 'She's twigged that something's afoot. I think you should go out to her, my boy.'

*

Edward parted with his precious Sunbeam so that Beatrice and Archie could spend most of the following day at the seaside. They had a picnic lunch in Pevensey Bay, paddled in the sea, then decided to take tea at Eastbourne's Grand Hotel. The conversation in the crowded Palm Court was dominated by the war news, but Beatrice and Archie, insulated in a private world of earnest confidences, were ten thousand miles away. Afterwards, at Beatrice's suggestion, they drove up to Beachy Head. There, high above the Channel they exchanged their first kisses. With even Beatrice's nerve failing at the crucial moment, it was a bashful, slightly awkward venture, yet it touched them with a rare magic.

Arriving at Upper Overs two hours later, they remained permeated with sufficient enchantment to stop Edward in his tracks. He hurried outside, intending a few pleasantries about the extended duration of their absence: he also had it in mind to make a mock inspection of the Sunbeam, as if checking for scratches and dents. One look at his sister and Archie, however, changed Edward's mind. He grinned foolishly, scuffed at the gravel, made a noise that sounded like, 'Harrumph!' and shot back indoors.

Lord Douglas returned to London alone on Sunday evening. Archie was insisting on obeying Mr Amery's orders to stay in Sussex and Beatrice decided it was high time she took a holiday. Lady Alice was only too pleased to be able to keep them company. Officially, she was a chaperone: in reality, this was no more than an excuse to keep her out of London. Beatrice and Archie came and went as they pleased. Their only difficulty was avoiding Edward as he prowled round waiting for the telegram.

It arrived on the evening of 26 August. A six o'clock departure from Upper Overs the following morning left Edward and Archie kicking their heels for nearly an hour before Mr Amery reached his office on the stroke of nine.

Curiously, he was in no hurry to get down to business. The usually brisk Mr Amery spent ten minutes wandering round the room, studying the bookshelves as if the contents were a complete surprise to him, staring out of the window, talking about the weather, his sister's dahlias, and a baffling host of other trivialities. When he finally sat down behind the desk, there were a few moments of complete stillness that seemed slightly ominous.

'Dieter Hoffmann,' Mr Amery said at last.

'Yes?' Edward's manner was guarded.

'Discuss.'

'I take it that you're referring to the chap who was up at Oxford with me?' Edward asked and received a nod. 'He was more or less my best friend.'

If Mr Amery felt any irritation at the brevity of the response, he concealed it. 'Would you consider him sound?' he asked.

'Yes.' Edward's response was immediate and wholehearted. 'I know that we're meant to hate all Germans, but Dieter's one of the best.' There was a pause accompanied by a wry smile. 'I don't know whether *you* would regard him as sound, though.'

'Explain.' Mr Amery's face assumed the benign glow of a man whose patience was going to last all day.

'Dieter comes from what you'd call a humble sort of background,' Edward replied. 'When he was ten, he won a scholarship to a *Gymnasium* – one of the top schools in Germany, equivalent to our . . .' Mr Amery waved the unnecessary explanation away. 'The pupils at this place were mostly the sons of Prussian *Junkers* or Army officers. Dieter suffered persistent bullying until he was fourteen.'

'Why did it stop?' Mr Amery asked.

'They broke Dieter's arm . . . the right one. The doctor made a mess of setting it. One complication led to another and it ended up paralysed. I think they damned nearly amputated it. The upshot is that Dieter isn't too fond of his country's ruling class. To be frank, he had socialist leanings.'

'Do you keep in touch with him?'

'We used to write, but it petered out a year ago. He'd just got himself a job with a newspaper in Berlin.' Edward's willingness to continue the strange dialogue suddenly disappeared into frowning suspicion. 'May I ask what this is about, sir?'

'We've had a letter from your friend, Hoffmann,' Mr Amery said, smiling nonchalantly.

'How?' Edward was astounded. 'The authorities in Germany surely aren't allowing people to send letters *here*?'

'No, they aren't. It was forwarded by a a bank in Zurich with which we – the Government that is – does business. Hoffmann claims to be very disillusioned and angry at Germany's part in starting this war. He says that he expects to have access to information that would help us shorten the hostilities, thus getting rid of the Kaiser and his clique. To put none too fine a point on it, Edward, Dieter Hoffmann wants to commit treason.'

It took Archie to break the rather pained silence that ensued. 'Why us, sir? What's wrong with the French?'

'Dieter doesn't like them,' Edward said. 'Most Germans don't.'

'We're at war with them, too,' Archie insisted.

'There's a feeling in Germany that Britain is – or ought to be – a natural ally,' Edward replied. He was assuming that hard, calculating expression that always made Archie uncomfortable. 'What's the official view, sir? Do we want to do anything about this?'

'There is no official view,' Mr Amery replied. 'I have a free hand.' While he and Edward gazed at each other speculatively, Archie kept quiet.

'That fracas at Mons,' Edward said, referring to the battle which the British Expeditionary Force had been involved in five days previously. 'An heroic failure?'

'Yes.' In one of his rare displays of emotion, Mr Amery shook his head sadly. 'We held the German advance up for twelve hours, apparently. They're into France now, of course.'

'Still trying to execute the plan?'

'That's what we're meant to believe.'

'If the French can hold them on the Marne, that will be the beginning of the stalemate,' Edward mused. Archie could feel the calculation and guessing that was going on across the desk. At last, Edward said, 'I think we should find out what Dieter Hoffmann has to offer.'

'I was hoping you would,' Mr Amery murmured. 'Have you any idea how we might set about it?'

'There is only one way – I shall have to go to Berlin.'

Edward sounded so matter of fact that Archie almost burst into nervous laughter. It was the most ridiculous idea he'd ever heard. Then he woke up to the fact that Mr Amery and Edward were studying him.

'I suppose I'd better come with you,' Archie said. It was a loyal, reflex action that rode roughshod over practicalities and moral scruple. 'You need someone to look after you. Dash it all, old man, you aren't fit to be let out on your own – especially on a job like *this.*'

'What about the language?' Mr Amery asked. 'I don't wish to be unduly harsh, but you aren't exactly fluent, are you?'

'I shall have to knuckle down and make a proper job of learning it,' Archie declared stoutly.

An hour later he was on his way to Putney to meet a German-speaking lady who had once worked with Mr Amery at Cambridge.

5

8 December 1916
'At times, he's such a cold fish'

Two years, three months and one week later, Edward and Archie came ashore from a Royal Navy destroyer at three o'clock on a Friday afternoon that was losing the battle with a dusk made dismal by sleet showers. After spending the last hour on deck, straining for a sight of England after an absence of six weeks, they were rigid with cold. The captain, a morosely preoccupied man with whom they had not travelled before, was glad to be rid of them at Portsmouth. Climbing into the motor car that was waiting to take them to the railway station, Edward and Archie exchanged glances signifying that the feeling was mutual.

That single, minimal display of friendship and understanding was their only attempt to communicate until they reached Cadogan Square nearly three hours later. Throughout the train journey up to London, Edward and Archie sat in opposite corners of the reserved compartment, staring at the darkness beyond the windows. Deep in thoughts that were best left unsaid, they were fearful of what discoveries lay in store for them after a mission that had lasted twice as long as any of the previous trips. Their disquiet was not only for the family which now regarded Archie as one of its members, but for the whole country. What everyone called the Great War was proving to be awful, beyond description or comprehension. The War dominated everything.

In the early weeks, while Germany's intention to crush France in a swift, pre-emptive onslaught was degenerating into stalemate,

Russia had suffered a military disaster of the first magnitude. At Tannenburg in East Prussia, two German generals called Hindenburg and Ludendorff had overseen what amounted to the destruction of the Tsar's army. Two years on, although the Russians continued to fight, they were offering little more than token resistance, a minor distraction from the Western Front.

Deadlock, foul and bloody, was unfolding its ghastly course in and between an incredible maze of trenches in north-eastern France. A strip of land 500 yards deep and a few miles wide would be gained by one side at a cost of ten, twenty, or thirty thousand men: two weeks later, the other side took it back with identical slaughter. It had been bad enough in 1915, when the tactics were random, lacking in overall purpose. The summer of the year now nearing its end had produced something even more frightful.

An all-out German assault on the historic fortress town of Verdun was launched in February 1916. The initial tactic was to open up an alternative route to Paris, but General Petain's decision to defend the town at all costs provided an alternative objective. Petain's cry of, 'They shall not pass' made Verdun a talisman of French honour: it also presented an opportunity to bleed the country to death.

The losses on both sides were appalling. In Berlin during May, Edward and Archie had learned that the true scale of the carnage was being concealed from the German people. The French Government was doing the same. It was, however, pleading with the British to launch a massive attack in the trenches of the north to relieve the pressure on Verdun.

The offensive began with an artillery barrage of unprecedented ferocity. For seven days and nights, 3,000 guns pounded the German defences. On two of the nights, a light breeze from the south-east carried the distant rumble of hell nearly one hundred miles to Upper Overs. The people of the Weald thought that a great sea battle was being fought in the Channel. Later, they were puzzled by the absence of newspaper reports telling of a famous victory, something to remove the unease at the inconclusive engagement off Jutland three weeks previously.

On the morning of 1 July, the barrage was lifted. Lord Kitchener's

Army, the greatest volunteer force ever assembled, clambered out of their trenches and moved forward to deal with the remnants of the enemy. They walked into the disaster of miscalculation: a week of continuous bombardment had left the German Army virtually unscathed.

The Battle of the Somme dragged on until the middle of November. It was the last straw for Europe's sanity: the Somme and Verdun made sure that nothing could ever be the same again. Those with access to the real casualty figures drew consolation from the fact that the daily butcher's bill for Britain was never quite as bad as during that first Saturday: on 1 July 1916, 19,000 men were killed and 57,000 wounded.

To all intents and purposes, nothing had been gained. The press dutifully trumpeted the territorial gains – such as they were – but failed to point out that the strategic position was unchanged. Albeit in private, and only among those who were much better informed than most members of Asquith's Government, questions were being asked: there *had* to be an alternative to the horrific waste of life.

In a strange, gruesome way, Edward and Archie were bringing good news back to London. In three weeks of wandering round Berlin more or less at will, they and Dieter Hoffmann had gathered enough information to calculate that Germany had lost half a million men on the Somme. Even for a nation schooled from the cradle to believe in the ethic of war and conquest, it was a grievous blow, bringing the first signs of unrest. There were people in Whitehall who would be cheered by that news.

Now that they knew the full enormity of what one side had suffered, Edward and Archie were racked with worry over the British position. In particular, how was the fight to be continued? Most of those who had flocked to the colours in response to the slogan *Your Country Needs YOU* were dead, scattered across Picardy in shell holes and hastily dug pits. How could they be replaced?

Lady Alice joined Franklin at the front door of the house in Cadogan Square. Edward more or less ignored her manner, ascribing it to the all-pervading conditions. It was commonplace to blame the War for everything.

'My dears, you cannot imagine how glad I am to see you!' Lady Alice cried, looking them up and down in an obvious check for injuries, or signs of ill health. 'Have you come straight from Portsmouth?'

'Yes, Mother.' Edward kissed her, then stood aside so that Archie could do likewise. 'We'll report to Mr Amery tomorrow morning.'

'You've been away for a long time.' There was reproach as well as anxiety in Lady Alice's voice: the knowledge that it was impossible for Edward to send word of their safe progress and expected return did not make the absences easier to bear.

'There was a great deal to do,' Edward said. He was perfunctory, concentrating most of his attention on shaking hands and exchanging warm smiles with Franklin.

'We've been very worried,' Lady Alice said. 'I know it's frightfully weak of us, but . . .'

She stopped as the group came into the entrance hall from the sitting-room. Beatrice and Lord Douglas were with another man: she was between them, her arms linked through theirs. Archie's urge to rush to Beatrice was stifled by the grave expressions on their faces and the presence of a stranger. Aided by the familiar, distinctively characteristic features, Archie guessed at once who the man must be.

'Uncle William!' Edward hurried towards him. 'What's wrong?'

'Damned bad luck, I'm afraid, my boy,' the man said, extending a hand to his nephew. 'I'm sorry to say that poor old Gerald's been killed in action. Happened on October the tenth, apparently, but I didn't get to hear of it until the other day. It was at a place called Beaumont Hamel – is that something to do with the Somme business?'

'It was right in the thick of it,' Edward replied. 'Look, Uncle, I'm . . .' He found himself at a loss for words.

'I know, it's a devil, isn't it? Shook me, I can tell you. Look here, Edward, you know a thing or two – what the blazes is going on out there? Back in 'fourteen, twenty-three of my chaps from the estate volunteered. Do you know how many of them are left? *Seven*. What do you make of that?'

Edward spread his hands. 'I don't. There's nothing I can say. About Gerald, I . . .' Inarticulate and close to tears, he embraced his uncle. It was a bad moment, especially for Beatrice, who felt the first terrible shock of grief of an hour ago coming back at her. Lord Douglas put an arm round her, Lady Alice and Archie were frozen.

For a few seemingly interminable moments, William Edgar Sleaford Boothby-Graffoe set aside his own feelings to comfort his nephew. Then, Archie found himself being examined by a pair of eyes in which a wry humour mingled with shrewdness. 'You must be Archie Shackleton,' the Duke of Lincolnshire said.

'Yes, sir . . . Your Grace. May I offer my deepest sympathy for your loss.'

'Thank you.' The Duke detached himself from Edward and advanced to shake Archie's hand. 'I've been hearing a lot about you over the past couple of years. Am I right in assuming that you and Edward are getting up to some pretty hair-raising stunts?'

Archie shuffled self-consciously. 'Actually, Your Grace, most of it's rather dull. There are times when we get very bored.'

'Hmm . . . That's not the impression that Alice and Douglas have been giving me. Look here, young man, I believe you're nearly one of us . . .' He smiled at Beatrice '. . .so you'd better drop this "Your Grace" nonsense. Be a good fellow and call me "Uncle William", eh?'

While Archie debated whether he would ever come to terms with this, Edward realised that the Duke was wearing formal evening dress. 'Where are you off to?' he asked.

'My presence is required at the Carlton Club,' the Duke said with a flourish of mock grandeur.

'The Carlton Club?' Edward's curiosity was aroused by mention of the Conservative Party's bastion. 'What *have* you got mixed up with?'

'Ridiculous though it may seem, my opinion on all this political upheaval is considered important.'

'Political upheaval?' Edward's curiosity was immediately at fever pitch. 'What's happening?'

'Asquith's gone,' Lord Douglas said. 'Lloyd George became Prime Minister yesterday evening. We're going to have a National Coalition Government.'

'And I'm to be asked for my blessing,' the Duke chuckled. 'Makes you think, what?' In a flash, he was desperately serious again. 'Gerald thought he was in a madhouse, you know – told me all about it on his last leave. I wonder what he'd make of all this.'

'I think Lloyd George is the right man for the job,' Edward said.

'Can he control the generals?' the Duke asked. 'That's the crux of it. We need someone who can whip those pig-headed lunatics into line . . . Dash it, that's what went wrong on the Somme, isn't it? Asquith just sat back and let them get our chaps killed.' After a furious shake of the head, there was an abrupt change of mood. 'I mustn't keep these fellows waiting – where's my cab, Franklin?'

'At the kerb, Your Grace.' Franklin, who had been hovering at the front door, bowed magisterially. Suspecting that the butler was in his element with a peer of the highest rank, Archie was startled to find that the Duke had a last word for him.

'I may see you tomorrow, Shackleton. On the other hand, I shall probably scuttle back to Wiltshire as soon as I've done my duty. You must come down to Compton Allardyce . . . It's a marvellous place for a honeymoon!'

After encompassing a mortified Beatrice in his astonishingly cheeky smile, William, eighth Duke of Lincolnshire strode towards the front door. His gait had a jaunty bravado and, Archie thought, a suggestion of vanity. One of the wealthiest men in the country, he was sixty-one, looked a good ten years younger, and, despite his pretence at being something of a backwoodsman, tremendously influential. On this occasion, Archie suspected that he was better-informed than Edward: the grandfather who had raised him after the death of his parents had been a leading light in the Carlton Club. It was, the young Archie had soon learned, a place where critical issues were decided by men who wielded great but unseen power.

As they continued to stand in the hall while Franklin accompanied the Duke to his cab, Beatrice decided to break the bemused silence.

'Alexander came through all right,' she said to Edward. 'We had a letter from him last week. He's at a rest-camp near Calais.'

'Good.' Edward's reply was absent-minded and he appeared not to hear Lady Alice when she said that Alexander was hoping to be home for Christmas. Instead, he was peering anxiously into the Square, watching Franklin's every move. When the butler came inside, Edward accompanied him towards his pantry at the back of the house.

'Gone to talk about Gerald, I expect,' Lord Douglas murmured. 'He often turns to Franklin when there's trouble.'

Beatrice, in the midst of her delayed welcome to Archie, was reminded of a problem that she felt ought to be faced.

'Do you think Archie and I ought to stay in this evening?' she asked her mother.

'Why, darling?'

'Well . . .' Beatrice was not entirely sure. 'As a sort of sign of respect for Gerald, I suppose.'

Lady Alice thought quickly. On Archie's first evening back from Berlin, he and Beatrice went out to dinner at a restaurant near the Victoria and Albert Museum, a discreet, highly respectable establishment in which a young couple could spend a pleasant hour or two without setting tongues wagging. It was a tradition that had, over two desperately difficult years, become almost inviolate.

'Isn't it rather late to be worrying about that sort of thing?' Lady Alice said. 'Poor Gerald has been dead – and buried – for over two months. In any case, we must do our best to carry on as normal. Thousands and thousands of families are having to do it – most of them without any of our advantages. We have to avoid turning sorrow into self-pity. That sort of indulgence is no good to man or beast, let alone Gerald.'

Beatrice had always respected the secrecy surrounding the trips that Edward and Archie made to Berlin. For two nerve-racking years, she had somehow avoided asking a single question. On that December evening in 1916, however, her stoicism was destined to collapse under the agonising pressure of needing to know something of how the man she loved spent his time during the mysterious missions. The last six weeks of waiting and praying, with no idea where Archie was, or what dangers he might be facing, had been too much. But first, as soon as they were settled at their favourite table in the restaurant, there was a matter that had to be tidied up.

'You mustn't take Uncle William too seriously,' Beatrice said. 'What you saw was all an act – he's *terribly* upset about Gerald.'

Archie shook his head. 'I never thought anything else, old thing.'

'Do you know what I heard him telling Father?' Beatrice went on. 'He said that if one of his sons *had* to go, it should have been Ralph . . . it would have saved everyone a great deal of trouble. Imagine that!'

Archie tried to. 'Does that mean that the Marquess of Axholme is still misbehaving?' he said.

'*Misbehaving!*' Beatrice exploded. 'That doesn't begin to describe it . . . At the moment, he's having an affair with *two* married women.' Responding to Archie's look of alarm, she lowered her voice. 'He and Violet Weeford are boasting about the fact that they're spending Christmas together at Biarritz. They've done everything except put an announcement in *The Times*.'

Mrs Weeford was a famous beauty who repeatedly triumphed over the hostility of the women who controlled London Society. The news that Mrs Weeford had been cut dead yet again by Lady Something-or-other invariably boosted rather than damaged her reputation. 'That's a bad show,' Archie said. 'What about Mr Weeford? Hasn't he got any say in this?'

'The man's an idiot,' Beatrice retorted. 'He spends all his time drinking and gambling. He's much older than *her*, of course.'

'Isn't your cousin, Ralph, doing anything towards the War?' Archie ventured, immediately regretting it.

'He's never had a day's illness in his life, yet he has medical certificates signed by half of Harley Street.' Beatrice was attracting the attention of other diners again. 'He even bamboozled the Army medical board into saying that he was unfit for service. Goodness only knows how he wangled *that*.'

'There are plenty of other things to be done.' Archie grinned facetiously. 'He could count blankets – or something equally exciting.'

'The wretch refuses to do *anything*. Uncle William has turned part of Allardyce Castle into a convalescent home, but Ralph won't go near the poor men in it.' Quieter now that her anger had spent itself, Beatrice was dejected as she added, 'Mother blames Uncle William for most of it and I'm afraid that she does have a point.'

'In what way?'

'He gives Ralph a tremendous allowance. It's something totally ridiculous like ten thousand a year.'

Archie was shaken. 'Aren't the aristocracy normally pretty stingy with their sons?' he asked.

'Yes – and you can jolly well see why when you look at Ralph. He should be under constraint, not roaming round with more money than he knows what to do with.'

'Why is your uncle so lax?' Archie asked.

'I think it's so that Ralph *will* roam around,' Beatrice replied. 'Given the money to be here, there, and everywhere, he doesn't spend very much time at Compton Allardyce. Uncle William prefers that.'

Archie would very much have liked to know more about Ralph's character and personal qualities, suspecting that ten thousand a year, formidable though it was, might not be enough to turn the head of a woman with Mrs Weeford's notorious tastes. While he was pondering what questions he might risk asking, Beatrice's mood changed.

'Look, my dear, I want you to let me into a few secrets.'

'I'll do whatever I can,' Archie promised.

'It really is beastly while you're away, Archie. Can you imagine what it's like for me? I don't want to know what you and Edward are doing – I realise it's all secret – but aren't there *some* things you can tell me?'

'Such as?' Although willing to oblige, Archie was guarded.

'Well . . .' Beatrice stopped eating to tie her fingers in a knot. 'Promise you won't think I'm silly?'

'I'll never do that,' Archie said.

'The greatest difficulty I have is imagining how you can possibly get into a place like Berlin,' Beatrice said.

'Sorry, I'm not with you,' Archie replied.

'Isn't it sort of sealed off?'

'London isn't,' Archie pointed out.

'It is *really*,' Beatrice said. 'We're surrounded by sea.'

'And you won't find me complaining about that.' Archie paused reflectively. 'Yes, now I come to think about it, I suppose it is a touch difficult to grasp. You see, most of Europe is carrying on as normal. As far as most Germans are concerned, the fighting is on another planet. To threaten Berlin, our troops would have to advance four hundred miles.'

'That sounds impossible,' Beatrice said.

'It is.' Archie pressed on quickly, not wanting to dwell on the strategic futility of the Western Front. 'Anyway, the upshot is that Berlin is wide open and we just go in on the train. We have documents that prove we're Swiss journalists.'

'Surely, though, you can't go straight there,' Beatrice said, struggling to come to terms with the idea of catching a train to an enemy capital. 'Not by the direct route.'

'Good Lord, no! The War Zone is in the way and you can't expect the Hun to let anyone through that. No, the travelling is the worst part of it. We have to go all round the houses.'

'Tell me,' Beatrice urged. '*Please*, Archie. I won't say a word to a soul . . . not even Mother. She never mentions it, anyway, so I won't even be tempted.'

'It's Edward you mustn't tell,' Archie replied, very serious. 'He'd be livid if he found out that you knew.'

'Cross my heart and hope to die,' Beatrice promised.

'All right.' Archie was satisfied. 'The Navy takes us from Portsmouth or Devonport down to Bordeaux. Then we make our own way across France to Lyon. That can take three days and it's a pain in the neck. I'm a terrible nuisance because of the language.' Archie grinned ruefully. 'It took me ages to scrape enough German together and I don't stand a chance with French.'

'Why don't you tell them you're British?' Beatrice asked.

Archie shook his head vehemently. 'That's absolutely *verboten*! Mr Amery goes on blind about it. He insists that we mustn't trust a living soul – apart from our special contacts.'

Beatrice was glad to hear it. 'How do you manage?' she asked.

'When it's necessary, Edward tells people that I'm a deaf and dumb idiot. I pull faces and dribble.'

'How awful!' Beatrice laughed. 'Do you get sympathy?'

'Blessed if I know,' Archie replied. 'I wouldn't be surprised if they weren't making fun of me half the time. They're a peculiar bunch.'

'What happens in Lyon?' Beatrice asked when she had stopped laughing.

'We lodge with a lawyer. Going out, it's usually only for one night. On the way back we stay until we know when we're going to be picked up at Bordeaux or La Rochelle.'

'Is this lawyer in contact with the Admiralty?'

'More likely to be Mr Amery,' Archie said. 'It's always seemed polite not to ask. From Lyon we go to Geneva, then Basle, Frankfurt, Leipzig, and Berlin. When we started going, the borders were still wide-open, but they've gradually tightened things up. That's a funny thing . . . it actually makes it easier for us . . . the more often our documents get stamped, the more genuine we look. It takes us at least a week each way – it can be much longer coming back if we have to wait for a ship.'

Archie thought he had finished until he found Beatrice looking at him quizzically. 'Can you tell me anything about what goes on in Berlin?' she asked.

'Well, the fact is, old girl, we spy. We have a chap who acts as our guide. Amazing thing . . . Edward was up at Oxford with him.'

'What, Dieter Hoffmann?' Beatrice reacted as though an old, rather dear friend had popped up at her side. 'He and Edward were very close. Dieter visited us at Upper Overs. How on *earth* did you find him?'

'Mr Amery.' Archie uttered the magic words that could be used to explain practically everything.

'How is Dieter?' Beatrice asked.

'Well enough,' Archie replied. 'I fancy that his ideas have changed a great deal since you knew him.'

'In what way?'

'He has socialist sympathies.' Archie was choosing his words with care: Hoffmann was an out-and-out communist. 'I assume that he wasn't like that when you knew him?'

'Certainly not!' Beatrice's indignation made Archie realise how naive and badly informed she, the most intelligent and perceptive of women, was. An appreciation of the Western Front's horrors was one thing, understanding what they would do to the way Europe thought and behaved in the years ahead was a very different matter.

'I shouldn't have told you about Hoffmann,' Archie said.

'Why not?'

'It makes it easier for you to put your foot in it with Edward.'

'You're right.' Beatrice frowned resolutely. 'I shall be extra careful – and you mustn't tell me any more.'

'I wasn't going to,' Archie said with his big, gentle smile. 'It's best if you don't know about the rum things that are going on in Berlin.'

'And here,' Beatrice retorted. 'Conscription.'

'A bad business,' Archie agreed. 'But what's the alternative?'

'There isn't one. That doesn't make it any less unpleasant – and the consequences don't bear thinking about.'

'Sorry, I'm not with you.'

Quite out of the blue, Beatrice produced a look as keen and far-seeing as Edward at his most calculating. 'The Government has empowered itself to *order* men to their deaths,' she said. 'That's what it boils down to. No one will worry too much while the War lasts, but as soon as it's over, there'll be a clamour for the *quid pro quo*.'

'Do you mean this Welfare State idea?' Archie asked.

'I do.'

'Lloyd George believes in it.'

'He may do,' Beatrice said. 'On the other hand, he may not. When we've beaten Germany, he won't have any choice in the matter.'

'You surely aren't saying that his ideas are bad?'

'Certainly not. From what I've heard, they don't go far enough. No, my dear, the difficulty I see is that expectations are building up – quietly, in the background – but no one is thinking about how they can be satisfied. Look at what women are doing – working in factories, driving lorries and ambulances – yet they *still* can't vote.'

Archie was beginning to wonder how wrong he had been to assume that Beatrice lacked perspective when she lost him by shooting off at an astonishing tangent.

'Do you think that Edward would do well in politics?'

'Good gracious!' Archie blinked. 'The idea's never occurred to me. After all, why should it?'

'Why shouldn't it?' Beatrice countered.

'Dear girl, he's dead-set on going to the very top of the Foreign Office. You know what he's like when he puts his mind to something.'

'I do indeed.' Beatrice nodded with great feeling. 'I expect he'll succeed, too. That doesn't mean he wouldn't be good at politics as well. Much as I adore him, I have to say that my dear brother can be a schemer. At times, he's such a cold fish.'

'I know,' Archie agreed.

'He sees things that most of us miss completely and he can be *frighteningly* detached about the most awful problems.'

'I know that, too,' Archie said. 'The thing is – and this is strictly between the two of us – I've an idea that Edward believes he'll be *running* the Foreign Office thirty years from now.'

'Of course he does.' Beatrice laughed. 'Mother cottoned on to that ages ago. What's wrong with him being Foreign Secretary?' She studied the various shades of amused scepticism and tenderness that crossed Archie's face. 'All right, I agree. It's a daft idea.'

'Very daft,' Archie grinned. 'Let's leave him to do it his own way.'

'We have no choice,' Beatrice replied. 'Have you ever tried telling him anything?' They pulled faces at each other to signify the utter hopelessness of attempting to interfere with Edward's stubborn ambition.

'Your uncle had an interesting idea,' Archie said, valiantly trying to sound casual.

'Oh? I don't remember.'

'About Compton Allardyce being a good place for a honeymoon.'

'Ah, yes.' Beatrice's feigned disapproval lasted all of two seconds. 'He's quite right. It's beautiful. Mother and Father spent a week there after they were married.'

'There you are, then.'

'Archie, is this another of your undercover proposals?'

''Fraid so, old girl.'

There was one small potato left on Beatrice's plate. After prodding it with her fork, she spent an eternity frowning at it in furious concentration. 'Where are you expecting to spend Christmas?' she asked, continuing to study the potato.

'We're seeing Mr Amery tomorrow morning,' Archie said. 'It's *almost* certain that he won't expect us to go back to Berlin until the middle of January.'

'That would be a big improvement,' Beatrice murmured. Edward and Archie had been away for Christmas in both 1914 and 1915.

'There's every hope,' Archie went on. 'We've found out all there is to know for the time being.'

'So you'll be with us at Upper Overs?'

'If I'm invited.' Archie was growing nervous.

'You will be.' At last, Beatrice raised her head to meet his gaze. Her eyes were shining. 'Can I recommend that Christmas would be a good time for you to talk to Father?'

'Do you mean . . .?' Archie stopped, gaped, and decided that he was probably suffering from hallucination. 'I say . . . do I understand you correctly? Dash it, I don't want to jump to the wrong conclusion . . .'

'Yes, Archie, I *will* marry you.' Beatrice laughed.

Her voice, slightly louder than she had intended, was projected into one of those moments of sudden, inexplicable quiet that can descend on a public place. Archie's soaring elation received a terrible jolt when he realised that twenty-odd total strangers were goggling at him, manifesting emotions that were enough to make a chap dive under the table.

The War was producing one beneficial effect: everyone was more friendly. They were also eager to snatch at anything that could be treated as good news. When the hubbub of congratulations broke out, several men were competing for the wine waiter's attention. The winner, a man wearing the uniform of a Royal Artillery major, delivered the bottle of Bollinger himself. Between them, Archie and the gunner made a hash of opening the champagne, causing shrieks from the ladies as the cork ricocheted wildly off the ceiling. Beatrice clapped her hands in pure delight. To rousing cheers, she and Archie declared themselves the happiest couple alive and promised to marry the day after the War ended.

6

12 April 1918
'Confession is good for the soul'

Edward's nerves were on a razor's edge. The very last thing he wanted was to be spending an evening being polite to three total strangers and a woman of whom he disapproved strongly. Only his loyalty to Beatrice restrained Edward from walking out of the drawing-room to seek refuge in Franklin's pantry. For the last three months, Beatrice had been running Boothby's, virtually on her own, and she deserved the fullest possible support. That meant putting up with Nancy Shenstone and her latest 'discovery', Jackson O'Malley.

The brother of the sixth Duke of Lincolnshire had founded Boothby's in 1835, almost as an afterthought. Lord Jeremy Boothby-Graffoe had been providing a tactful service to aristocrats in financial straits for ten years before he decided to make a proper business of it and took premises in Bond Street. Although shunning publicity, the auction house had flourished, evolving its own distinctive traditions.

Of these, the major feature was that control of the firm was vested in the second sons of successive Dukes. In this way, Lord Douglas had eventually become the third owner, after an upbringing and education devoted to that end. His stewardship had begun in 1898 and contained only one error of judgement: despite the flood of indications to the contrary, Lord Douglas had steadfastly clung to the belief that his nephew, Gerald, would follow in his footsteps. The boy grew up without showing the slightest interest in fine art or business: when compelled, at the age of seventeen, to spend two days with his uncle to observe how Boothby's functioned, the impeccably polite Gerald did his level best to convey his dislike of what he saw.

To everyone's astonishment, Lord Douglas also insisted on ignoring Gerald's decision to become a professional soldier. Of course the Army had its attractions, it was conceded, but Gerald would tire of it and come to see where his true duty lay. Lady Alice was convinced that her husband clung to that hope until the news of Gerald's death on the Somme.

It was Lady Alice who began the debate to nominate a replacement, someone who *would* take Boothby's forward when the time came. Continually stressing the need to begin preparing a successor, Lady Alice eventually persuaded Lord Douglas to treat the matter seriously. That was when the real difficulties emerged.

For a man of liberal views who admired his daughter as well as loving her dearly, Lord Douglas displayed an unaccountable intransigence to accept that Beatrice was the natural choice. Indeed, for nearly twelve months, he refused to acknowledge that she was the *only* candidate. Asserting that the job was far too demanding for a woman, and knowing that Edward would never give up the Foreign Office, Lord Douglas attempted to persuade Alexander to resign his commission when the War was over.

Alexander never treated the argument seriously. Understandably concerned to make the most of his precious periods of home leave, Alexander was whimsically evasive, never quite ruling the idea out with sufficient firmness to squash it once and for all. On the contrary, in October 1917, he wrote a letter from the Front which contained the hint that he was, after all, warming to the idea of running Boothby's.

'I wish he'd stop teasing,' Lady Alice said to Beatrice. 'Your poor father thinks he means it . . . The wretched boy is simply wasting time.'

Only ten days later, they heard from Alexander's commanding officer. Alexander was missing, presumed dead, in the hideousness that eclipsed all that had gone before – the mud of Passchendaele. As well as mind-numbing grief, the dreadful news sowed a seed of doubt: had Alexander, finally sickened by three years of horror, been serious about giving up the Army?

Weeks afterwards, Lord Douglas admitted that he had always thought of Alexander as being invincibly lucky. 'I was certain that he'd come out of it without a scratch,' he said, inadvertently explaining why his son's loss had laid him so dreadfully low.

Swamped by sadness, Lord Douglas became forgetful. In December 1917, Beatrice conducted an auction for the first time after her father had simply failed to appear. He apologised, but missed another important appointment three days later. By the middle of January, Beatrice was in charge of Boothby's. No announcement had been made, but staff and clients deferred to her.

Now, with Lord Douglas permanently isolated at Upper Overs, Beatrice had also taken charge of the house in Cadogan Square. When Nancy Shenstone suggested that the O'Malleys were worth cultivating, the invitation to dinner was duly issued.

It was perfectly natural that Edward should be expected to lend his assistance.

Jackson O'Malley's grandfather, a Waterford grocer, had sold up and emigrated to America in 1847 when the inescapable consequences of the famine were becoming apparent. Six weeks after arriving in New York, he married a Brooklyn girl and opened a minuscule provisions store on West 42nd Street in Manhattan's Garment District. Nearly seventy years on, O'Malley's Stores had a coast-to-coast network that ranked third in America's retail food trade.

Ignoring the submarine menace that had finally forced President Woodrow Wilson to declare war on Germany in April 1917, Jackson O'Malley had crossed the Atlantic to investigate the British food distribution system. When Edward, purely out of courtesy, had inquired what he had in mind, O'Malley had made no secret of his intention to buy any organisation which took his fancy.

'And with things over here the way they are right now, maybe that won't cost me too much,' he chuckled.

His wife, a Bostonian who continued to harbour fears that she had married unwisely nearly thirty years ago, attempted to repair the damage. 'Jackson, you must remember that these good people have been at war for a long time. I'm certain that you don't *mean* to give the impression that you're out to take advantage of their misfortune. We should have been helping them out long ago, you know. A lot of folks blame the President for waiting.'

'Oh, sure!' O'Malley sketched a grandiloquent gesture designed to make amends. 'I'm here to help . . . just like our boys in France. They'll soon fix those German bums. Another three months at most – you'll see.'

Beginning to feel decidedly guilty at having introduced O'Malley to Beatrice, Nancy Shenstone decided that it was time to curtail his bombast.

'It's a nice idea, Jackson, but the facts seem to be against you. These advances that the Germans have been making are *extremely* worrying. They've overrun our front line and gone straight through – forty miles in some cases. That strikes me as one hell of a way of getting beaten!'

O'Malley was at a loss. He side-stepped. 'I couldn't agree more, Lady Shenstone,' he said. 'It's a dangerous situation. Hey, didn't I say so this morning, Marigold?'

While Mrs O'Malley was pretending to search her memory, Edward felt a stab of admiration for Nancy Shenstone. It was the first time he had ever thought kindly of her. But, even as he did so, he resolved not to soften his disapproval of the attractive American.

By all accounts, Nancy Hagen had travelled from Philadelphia to London in 1909 merely to spend a few weeks on the periphery of the Season. Those gentlemen fortunate enough to make her acquaintance were not meant to attach too much importance to Nancy's winsome disposition: they were supposed to be blind to her superb figure, copper-coloured hair, green eyes and sensuous mouth – and stories of a six-figure dowry were pure hogwash. Incredibly, what *was* widely believed was the whisper that Nancy was acting as a scout for her mother. Amelia Hagen – a Vanderbilt before she eloped with Fred Hagen, a clerk on the Baltimore and Ohio Railroad – was alleged to be hunting for a young lover. Devoted to Fred, who now owned the Baltimore and Ohio – as well as the Acheson Topeka and Santa Fe – Nancy's mother did just enough to fan the flames of rumour while attending to the real purpose of the visit, which was to arrange for

Nancy to be absorbed by the English aristocracy.

Viscount Shenstone, a leading light of the House of Lords and Jockey Club, was smitten by Nancy, then aged twenty-two. A widower, thirty years her senior, Shenstone needed £250,000 for his run-down Norfolk estate. It was paid into his bank the day after Nancy became Viscountess Shenstone.

Soon after returning from a honeymoon that had done nothing for Harold Shenstone's self-esteem, the couple began to embark on a life style that was, to be euphemistic, unconventional. After a brief inspection of her husband's ancestral home near Thetford, Nancy returned to London, swearing that she would never set foot inside the place again. The house in Westminster received equally short shrift: it was handy for the House of Lords, but quite unsuitable for a young woman of Nancy's taste and mettle. A week later, using her own money, she purchased a house in Upper Belgrave Street, spending another small fortune on a top-to-bottom renovation.

As if to draw maximum attention to her abode, Nancy called it 'Martha's Vineyard', a commemoration of the island resort at which she had spent idyllic childhood holidays. In what was tantamount to a public statement, Nancy let it be known that she would be living there alone, leading a life apart from her husband. There was, however, no question of marital difficulty and Viscount Shenstone would always be a welcome – albeit somewhat infrequent – visitor. Martha's Vineyard, initially so promising, quickly turned into a gossip-writer's nightmare. It was a busy house, with incessant comings and goings, but the men and women who became Nancy's friends were unknowns – even though most of them looked and acted as if they ought to be famous. They were a glamorous bunch, apparently from a wide range of professions and social backgrounds, and that was as much as any outsider ever discovered. Nancy Shenstone constructed her own society that was completely self-contained and independent of the Mayfair set.

Cornelius Markham, the uncrowned king of Fleet Street's scandal-merchants, was furious with Nancy. 'It's five pounds to a penny that Martha's Vineyard is a seething hot bed of sin,' he would tell colleagues over a lunchtime drink. 'I guarantee it. But it isn't news, so help me! In the first place, Lady S has as good as told everyone that she's leading the life of Riley and in the second place, the people she's doing it with are of no interest to our *dear* readers. I tell you, it's a bloody tragedy!'

Now thirty-one and more beautiful than ever, Nancy was a focal point for visiting Americans. The O'Malleys had been granted an invitation to afternoon tea at Martha's Vineyard, blithely ignorant of how unimportant Nancy thought they were. To avoid disrupting an otherwise useful and pleasurable day, they were made to coincide with one of Viscount Shenstone's rare visits. In the course of the painfully stilted conversation, it emerged that Jackson O'Malley was looking to spend a great deal of money on *objets d'art* for his latest acquisition, a Long Island mansion.

While he was enjoying O'Malley's discomfort at Nancy's intervention, Edward wondered yet again how Beatrice and the notorious American had become such firm friends. Nancy had started looking in at Boothby's during the summer of 1916, apparently eager to learn about the furniture of Sheraton and his contemporaries. There was no harm in that – especially since the trouble taken to provide Nancy with information was rewarded with a string of introductions to people who spent a lot of money at Boothby's. Four months ago, however, Beatrice had begun to visit Nancy in Upper Belgrave Street, spending hours at the house with the exotically ostentatious name. Edward was thinking it was time to warn Beatrice to steer clear of Nancy.

Not this evening, though. Once the O'Malleys were out of the way, Edward intended blotting the world out with two of the sleeping-tablets recommended by Franklin.

Irritating as he was, Jackson O'Malley did not pose any sort of threat. His daughter, Irene, was a different matter.

At first sight, she had seemed no more than a curiously handsome girl of about twenty-two who was desperately eager to be seen as a spiritual and intellectual counterbalance to her father's cheerful crassness. Nancy knew otherwise: Irene O'Malley was looking for a husband and Edward Boothby-Graffoe struck her as a splendid possibility.

As the evening progressed, Nancy was forced into grudging admiration of Irene. The girl horrified Edward by using his Christian name. Consequently, she received one rebuff after another, all delivered in a way calculated to freeze the wine. Undeterred, Irene ploughed on, stubbornly unresponsive to remarks that came close to insult. Nancy found it difficult to keep a straight face through some of the exchanges.

'And you work for the Foreign Office, Edward?'

'I do.'

'That must be tremendously interesting.'

'I find it so, *Miss O'Malley.*'

'Are you very important?'

'No.'

'Edward, I think you suffer from chronic modesty. Why don't you tell me what you do, then *I'll* judge if you're important.'

'That's quite impossible, Miss O'Malley.'

'Why?' Moving so that she made Edward a visual present of her audacious *décolletage*, Irene's full lips remained slightly apart and her eyes had a sparkle that went far beyond mere curiosity.

After he had flinched away from her, embarrassment reduced Edward's reply to gruff politeness. 'My work is secret, I'm afraid.'

'You're afraid!' Irene clapped her hands. 'You see, you *are* important.' She turned to O'Malley. 'Now, Pop, can you understand what I'm trying to tell you? It's all very well for you to keep saying that I should marry someone who's rich, but I want a man who's important because he's clever – up here.' She tapped her forehead.

O'Malley took up the challenge to indulge in robustly good-natured banter with his daughter, somehow imagining that this would re-establish him as the life and soul of the party. While they traded affectionate insults, Nancy arrived at a conclusion with which she had been toying all evening: Irene O'Malley was ready to do *anything* to impress Edward. It was a damned shame that he was incapable of seeing that and taking advantage of it. Her face *did* have a slightly masculine look, but her body was voluptuous enough and Irene was not without experience. It would do Edward good to let his hair down once in a while. Briefly, Nancy and Beatrice exchanged knowing looks: just as telepathy might have been about to play fascinating tricks, Irene O'Malley spotted the flash of the diamond ring on Beatrice's left hand.

'Beatrice, you're engaged to be married! Is *he* clever and important? I'll bet a thousand dollars he is.'

'I don't know about that,' Beatrice said. 'He was *the* most enchanting man and I always thought that was more important than brains or prestige.'

'*Was?*' Irene's voice dropped apprehensively.

'He was killed a couple of weeks before Christmas.' Beatrice's serenity was ethereal even though she could sense the anguish enveloping Edward.

'The War?' Irene ventured.

'Yes.'

'I *am* sorry,' Irene whispered. Her mother and father nodded earnestly, hoping that they were helping to dispel an awkward moment.

'I'm very lucky,' Beatrice said. 'Far luckier than most of the women who've lost their men. Mine died on the way home, so I got him back. He's buried quite near to Upper Overs – that's Father's house in Sussex. It's a big comfort. All the soldiers are in graves on the battlefield, you see . . . I think that makes it much worse for their loved ones. Edward and I have lost a brother and cousin like that.' As a tender afterthought, Beatrice added, 'My fiancé's name was Archie Shackleton.' She made it sound like a benediction.

Ignoring the unease of the O'Malleys, Nancy was watching Edward. White as a sheet, he was staring into space, bleakly vacant. He would have been horrified to learn that Beatrice had told Nancy everything, not only about Archie's death, but the work that he and Edward had been doing. As a result, Nancy felt great pity for the man who so disliked her: she was very much afraid that Edward might never forgive himself for Archie – even though he was blameless.

When Edward and Archie had reached Berlin on the evening of 28 November 1917, they sensed the change of mood immediately. On their previous visit, in September, the city had been persisting with the illusion that the War was a distant myth. Now, even on the short journey from the Friedrichstrasse railway station to their regular lodgings in the Luisenstadt district, the slump in morale was shockingly visible. The people on the streets had become shrivelled and afraid, working hard at minding their own business.

Frau Schmidt, the landlady who always looked after them so well, soon abandoned the struggle to be her usual cheerful self. Yes, things were bad, she said, very bad and getting worse by the day. However, when asked for details, she did no more than complain about politicians and food shortages. As expected, Dieter Hoffmann was able to provide much more.

The scarcity of food, now brought to a crisis by the effectiveness of the Allied blockade on German imports, was the least of the problems. Belatedly, the public was waking up to the fact that the Western Front was exacting a terrible price to maintain its deadlock. It was common knowledge that over one and a half million men had died and outrage was replacing national loyalty. Increasingly and openly, the Kaiser was the object of scathing criticism. Allegedly in thrall to Hindenburg and Ludendorff, Wilhelm was close to letting them impose a military dictatorship over what was supposedly parliamentary democracy. The Social Democrats in the Reichstag were, Hoffmann alleged, behaving like mesmerised puppets, but there were breakaway groups struggling to bring Germany to its senses before disaster struck.

It was apparent that Hoffmann's sympathies lay with a group calling themselves the Spartacists – apparently after the slave who had led the successful rebellion against the might and excesses of ancient Rome. The driving-force of the movement was a man called Karl Liebknecht, once a Reichstag deputy, now an inmate of Luckau Prison on charges of attempted treason. Liebknecht was in constant touch with Rosa Luxemburg: together, they would organise the German revolution. With manic fervour, Hoffmann indicated that he was helping Rosa Luxemburg.

'You don't like this, do you?' Archie said to Edward as they hurried back to Frau Schmidt's after the meeting with Hoffmann.

'Definitely not. That woman, Luxemburg, is poison. The Germans are idiots to let a creature like her wander round as she pleases.'

'What's her game?' Archie asked.

'She's a communist. Used to be quite close to Lenin until they fell out over some abstruse theoretical point.'

Archie whistled. Lenin's revolution, barely a few weeks old, had already taken Russia out of the War. 'So, what does all this mean?'

'God alone knows.' Edward was bitter. 'It's turning into a bigger mess than I ever imagined.' Then, after they had walked fifty yards in thoughtful silence, he came out with the conclusion that Archie had been half expecting. 'I'll tell you what it means, old man. Berlin is a very dangerous place. We must take extra care. And Dieter isn't reliable any more – the poor devil's losing his senses.'

Throughout the ensuing ten days, they carried their Webley automatic pistols with them. The weapons, issued at Mr Amery's insistence, were normally locked in a stout case under Edward's bed.

In addition to reporting on Germany's political and social state, Edward and Archie had been charged with attempting to discover how many army divisions were being moved to the Western Front now that Russia had collapsed. It emerged that the High Command, fearful its troops would be infected with Communism if they were allowed the merest contact with the broken enemy, was carrying out the transfer in unseemly, badly organised haste. Berlin's febrile state, far from endangering Edward and Archie, made their task rather easier than they had anticipated. While the police hounded suspected communists and sympathisers, the railway chaos caused by moving 300,000 men from east to west during the first four days of December was open to unhindered inspection. Leaving Hoffmann to his frantic plotting, Edward and Archie did the job, presented Frau Schmidt with a Swiss watch as an early Christmas present, and slipped away from Berlin on 6 December.

They reached Lyon the following evening. During the morning of 8 December, Pierre Flammarion, the lawyer who provided the safe house, made a series of telephone calls from his office. It emerged that there would not be a passage on a warship from Bordeaux until 23 December. Edward was dismayed. They had never experienced such a delay: what were they supposed to do for two weeks? Flammarion said that there was an alternative. An armoured freighter, commandeered by the Royal Navy was leaving Marseilles for Plymouth at midnight on 10 December. Edward jumped at the chance. As he and Archie made an immediate start on the journey south, Pierre Flammarion returned to his office to notify the network of contacts and go-betweens of the decision.

Anxious to ensure that they spent no more time than was strictly necessary in the infamous port, Edward introduced several delays into the journey. His endeavours were crowned by a slice of good luck. At six o'clock on the evening of 10 December, having left the stopping train from Nimes, they had a meal at a café only three miles from the outskirts of Marseilles. In response to the *patron*'s friendly interest and obvious loathing of Germans, Edward was unusually frank. 'It doesn't matter,' he whispered to an astonished and worried Archie. 'This is bound to be our last trip. Let's make it easy for ourselves, eh?'

By happy chance, the café owner's brother was about to take the village's eggs and cream into Marseilles in his lorry: providing a lift for two English allies would be an honour.

The man went out of his way to take Edward and Archie to the docks, driving round until they found a sign of the rendezvous. Turning a corner in the rabbit-warren of warehouses and mean, narrow streets, they finally saw a Royal Navy lieutenant and two ratings on the quayside. They were no more than one hundred yards away, and Edward told their benefactor that they would walk, thus relieving him of the need to manoeuvre the lorry round what looked like an impossibly tight corner. Jumping down from the cab, Edward waved: the lieutenant raised a hand in acknowledgement and spoke to the sailors who stiffened alertly. For the first time since their arrival in Bordeaux over two weeks ago, Edward relaxed.

He was vaguely aware of the uproar coming from the alley to the left. As they drew level with it, three people were visible in the shadows, a woman – who was screaming blue murder – and two oafs who were attempting to rip her clothes off. The result was by no means a foregone conclusion: the woman's defence was viciously determined and her assailants were obviously the worse for drink.

Averting his eyes, Edward walked on.

Almost at once, a sixth sense warned him that he was alone. Archie had stopped, glowering at the unsavoury spectacle. 'What's the matter with you?' Edward hissed after retracing his steps. 'Come on!'

'I'm damned if that's any sort of way to treat a lady!' Archie retorted.

'I doubt very much if she's a "lady",' Edward said wearily. 'Don't be a chump, Archie. We're not here to get involved with filth like them.'

Outraged, Archie shook his head. 'Sorry, old man, it isn't on. I'm not having this.' Throwing caution to the winds, he bawled at the men in the alley. 'Oi! Pack it in, you blighters! Stop it, I say!'

Understanding his meaning if not the words, the men paused to stare at Archie, their faces befuddled. Taking advantage of the interruption, the woman slammed a knee into the groin of one of her tormentors, then, with unaccountable stupidity, instead of taking to her heels, began to screech abuse at the other. With a punch that brought the sound of cracking bone from her face, the man who was still standing knocked her flat.

Afterwards, Edward was tortured by the thought that one of the sailors had been more alert than he. As Archie strode purposefully into the alley, Able Seaman Briggs left his post on the quay and was pounding down the street. Edward, gripped by disbelief and indecision, lost track of events. He never saw the stevedore's fear at Archie's muscular bulk and intention, nor did he glimpse the evil-looking knife that was whipped from the inside pocket of a donkey jacket.

Edward was still rooted to the spot three seconds later as Archie sank to his knees and his attacker made off into the depths of the alley. The other man, clutching his groin, followed less nimbly.

Briggs was at Archie's side. 'Your friend's been stabbed, sir!' he shouted, and Edward finally came to life. By the time he had crossed the street, Archie was back on his feet, smiling sheepishly.

'That will teach me!' he said.

'Where did he get you?' Edward asked.

'Stomach. Here.'

Pulling his coat aside, Archie indicated a point on the left of his abdomen, slightly above the trouser waistline. There were ragged threads of wool surrounding a puncture in the grey sweater, but no other sign of damage. 'Flesh wound, that's all,' Archie said. 'It must have been the shock that put me on the floor.'

'Let me give you a hand,' Briggs urged.

After watching Archie set off confidently and steadily enough, Edward crossed the street to collect their bags. Apart from the stifled sobs of the injured woman, an unnatural silence had fallen on the area. Hurrying to catch up, Edward experienced a moment of fear.

A motor launch had been sent from the freighter that was standing off in the deep water of the main navigation channel. Archie negotiated the slippery steps down to the boat without difficulty, and joked about the rough, ten-minute dash to the final safety of a British ship under Royal Navy control. It was the ascent of the rope ladder against the side of the pitching vessel that seemed to do the damage. Archie had to be pushed and dragged up the last few rungs, only to collapse in a dead faint when he finally reached the deck.

While Edward and Able Seaman Briggs toiled to get Archie down to a cabin, they discovered that he was losing blood. The ship, a supply vessel under orders to avoid action, had a medical orderly, but no naval doctor.

Edward was never able to decide whether the orderly, a quietly spoken, unruffled man from the Scottish Highlands, worked a near-miracle, or prolonged Archie's suffering unnecessarily. Even though the knife-thrust had done damage that called for surgery if there were to be any hope, it took Archie fifteen hours to die.

On a fine afternoon, with the ship passing the island of Menorca in light sea conditions, Archie raised himself from a morphine-induced stupor and gazed up at Edward in a way that was earnest enough to be almost comical.

'Beatrice isn't going to be too pleased about this,' Archie said. 'Will you tell her that I'm sorry I was such a silly ass? I love her very much . . . Do you think you could let her know that, old man?'

Archie died before Edward was able to force a reassuring response through the emotional paralysis that gripped him.

Later, however, he was able to do something that was to prove of great comfort to Beatrice. The captain – possibly interested in avoiding paperwork and delay at Devonport – suggested that Archie should be buried at sea. Edward persuaded him against it.

The evening would probably have survived the consequences of Irene O'Malley noticing Beatrice's engagement ring had it not been for Edward. His morose brooding affected even Irene's thick-skinned father. It was Jackson O'Malley, in a rare flash of sensitivity, who brought the evening to a close at the first opportunity.

'We were down at Windsor, this morning,' he told Beatrice. 'It's been a long day.'

'I quite understand, Mr O'Malley. We've so enjoyed meeting you.' Beatrice was shrugging off the strain to present herself as the perfect hostess. 'If you would care to visit our premises in Bond Street, I'm sure you'll find a few knick-knacks that appeal to you.'

'Great! Say, how about tomorrow morning? Do you folks operate on Saturdays?'

'For someone of your standing, we operate at *any* time,' Beatrice replied, the breadth of her smile admitting that she was indulging in pure flattery.

'I appreciate that, Miss Boothby-Graffoe. We'll call by at eleven o'clock.'

To Beatrice's great relief, Edward took the trouble to accompany the O'Malleys to the front door, joining in the farewells. It was no more than a last-ditch display of good manners, a dutiful response to social obligation. The instant Jackson O'Malley ushered his wife and daughter across the threshold, Edward turned on his heel and headed for the stairs, beckoning Franklin to follow him. Nancy Shenstone, who had correctly interpreted Beatrice's signal to stay for a chat, watched him with a heavy heart.

Beatrice led the way to the small sitting-room that was Lady Alice's private domain when she was in London.

'Is your brother going to destroy himself over Archie Shackleton?' Nancy asked when they were settled.

'I don't think so,' Beatrice replied. 'It looks bad at the moment, but Edward's tougher than he seems. He'll get over it. Eventually.'

Nancy was anxious to explore a topic that had been bothering her all evening. 'Just before the O'Malleys got here, did I hear you say that Edward had been to Berlin again?'

'Yes. He came back on Tuesday.'

'He went on his own?'

'Yes.' Beatrice smiled sadly. 'There's no one to look after him these days. He won't be going again, though. That's absolutely definite.'

'You mean Germany *is* going to win?' Nancy was alarmed.

'Good gracious, no!' Beatrice was suddenly animated. 'They're well on the way to defeat.'

Nancy studied her friend in puzzled silence for a few moments. 'Like I told O'Malley, they're going a hell of a way about it,' she said quietly. 'From what I hear, the Germans have broken out all over the Western Front. How does that square with getting beat?'

'They've advanced too far, too quickly,' Beatrice replied, 'and unevenly. That means their supply lines are over-stretched, their flanks are exposed, and they're out in the open. Edward volunteered to go to Berlin on his own to look for information to help confirm all this.' She nodded in response to the expression of amused scepticism on Nancy's face. 'It made perfect sense when Edward explained it. He says that when it comes to a *proper* fight, we shall be able to finish them off. And the Americans *are* making a big difference now enough of them are there.'

'Surely,' Nancy agreed. 'But I wasn't going to let that loud-mouth O'Malley get away with what he was trying to say. So, Edward doesn't *need* to go back – is that how it is?'

'Well, actually, no, not really.' Beatrice was uncomfortable. 'The fact is, he had to kill a man while he was in Germany – some sort of official, I think.'

As a rule, Nancy worked hard to avoid sounding too American. This, however, was beyond her. 'Jesus Christ!' she exploded. 'Why?'

'Berlin is very unstable and dangerous,' Beatrice said. 'There's talk of deposing the Kaiser, setting up a communist regime and heaven knows what. Everyone's very highly strung and suspicious. I think one of the security police found something wrong with Edward's papers.'

'And how did Edward kill him?' Nancy asked.

'He carries a gun when he's in Germany.'

'So, he's a wanted man, eh?' Nancy seemed impressed. 'Yes, staying away makes a lot of sense. Do you know, Beatrice, a lot of people just wouldn't believe that your brother had it in him.'

'It didn't surprise me,' Beatrice said. '*Mentally*, Edward has always been ruthless. Given that and the terrible conditions, I suppose pulling a trigger isn't all that big a step. To be honest, I have an idea he enjoyed it. He may feel that he was doing something to help avenge Gerald and Alexander. And Archie, of course.'

Nancy allowed a pause before asking, 'How are your parents?'

'Oh, not so bad!' Beatrice's bravery was wafer-thin. 'Father is dreadfully upset about Alexander, but Mother will pull him through. At least, I hope she will.' She laughed nervously. 'Father *still* doesn't like the idea of me running Boothby's.'

Nancy shrugged. 'I sort of sympathise with him. He's not like most men, remember – *they* think women are too stupid to do anything except sit at home.'

'Yes, I know that,' Beatrice said. 'Father believes that running a business is demeaning for a lady of breeding and delicacy. I shall have to show him how wrong he is.'

'You are doing, my dear. One day, when he comes back to the real world, he'll see that.' Nancy's tone remained confident and reassuring as she came to the most difficult question of all. 'How are you deep down?'

'It's getting better.' Beatrice sighed, guilty that she was shaking off the grief of Archie's miserably tragic death. 'I've started sleeping again. Actually it's quite peculiar. Part of me has come to terms with it, but I'm almost certain that I shall never find anyone who'll *quite* take his place. Silly, isn't it?'

'Not at all. I guess there are at least a hundred thousand women who feel exactly the same way.'

'There's one thing I regret,' Beatrice said, then looked as if she regretted speaking.

'Yes?' Nancy asked gently. 'Go on.'

After a short hesitation, Beatrice blurted it out. 'I wish that Archie and I had been lovers!'

'Presumably you had chance enough?' The revelation had left Nancy completely unmoved.

'Goodness me, yes! Especially when we were at Upper Overs.'

'And Archie wanted to?'

Beatrice's smile was wistful. 'I don't know. He was the perfect gentleman – even more so than Edward. It's how the silly man got himself killed.'

'And you were never able to show him how you felt?'

'No.' Beatrice was raking over memories that were disturbing. 'I tried a few times, but I suppose I wasn't very good and he didn't seem to understand.'

'Your English public schools have a lot to answer for,' Nancy said, applying a touch of humour. 'Look at Edward. Did you see how he froze on Irene O'Malley when she gave him the sign?'

'I think Edward had a bad experience while he was at Oxford,' Beatrice replied. 'He was very taken with Frank Morgan's sister, but she let him down. He never was very happy with women, but he's been ten times worse since that.'

'Irene wanted to show him the way,' Nancy said. 'And I could name two *very* experienced ladies who'd give anything to have Edward Boothby-Graffoe to themselves for a night.'

Nancy's quiet authority pulled Beatrice up short. 'These women are friends of yours?' she asked. 'At your house, I mean?'

'They are.'

'Does this mean that Martha's Vineyard *is* a palace of sin?' Beatrice asked, attempting to inject a tone of facetious bravado into her desperate nervousness.

'It certainly is,' Nancy replied proudly. 'You wouldn't believe the hard work that's gone into making it so.' Nancy's expressive smile faded, leaving her intensely serious. 'You deserve a good time, Beatrice. Say the word, and I could introduce you to a guy who'd look after you. All my men know what it takes to please a woman – otherwise they don't get through the door.'

Beatrice rose from her seat, walked to the window, and parted the curtains. She remained there, staring out into the darkness of the square for so long, that Nancy began to fear she had committed a terrible blunder. When Beatrice turned back to the room, her face was drained of expression, giving no clue to her thoughts.

'May I ask you something, Nancy?' she said.

'Sure.'

'Now that I've lost Archie, I have the feeling that I shall never marry. It's early yet, I know, and I might change my mind. But I don't think so.' She paused, examining her thoughts carefully. Nancy waited, patient and comforting. 'I must have companionship, though. And I need love. Does this sound ridiculous?'

'Not in the least,' Nancy said.

'Love is very important,' Beatrice went on. 'And I mean your sort of love . . . do you understand?'

'Sex,' Nancy said gently.

'Yes. I have this awful feeling that I would enjoy it.'

Nancy was full of admiration for Beatrice's courage. '*I* certainly do,' she said. 'If they but knew it – and *if* they had the chance – most women would.'

'I thought so,' Beatrice said, nodding to herself.

'Like I said, any time you like.'

'Right. Give me time to think about it.'

Nancy left fifteen minutes later and Beatrice went straight up to Edward's bedroom. Wearing pyjamas and a dressing-gown, he was slumped in an armchair in front of a dying fire. He was nursing a glass of brandy. The decanter was within easy reach, as were two magenta-coloured tablets on a small silver tray.

'What are they for?' Beatrice asked.

'To make me sleep.' Edward was morose, his eyes fixed on the embers.

'Where did you get them? Doctor Murdoch?'

'That man's no damned good.'

Beatrice sighed. 'I suppose that means Franklin, then?'

'Yes.' Edward raised his eyes to hers defiantly. 'I know you don't approve of him, Bee. There's no need to labour the point.'

'I don't *dis*approve of him.' Beatrice was bending over backwards to avoid an argument. 'Just be careful, my dear. Strange pills and brandy may not be a sensible mixture.'

'All right.' Mollified by the brevity of the lecture, Edward smiled weakly. Immediately, however, he seemed determined to be cantankerous. 'The O'Malleys were pretty awful.'

'I didn't think they were *that* bad,' Beatrice said firmly. 'In any case, business is business.'

'Can't we manage without their sort of money?' Edward asked peevishly.

'*We* can,' Beatrice retorted. 'But Lord Hammerwich isn't nearly so fortunate! He needs the best possible price for half a dozen paintings so that he can provide for his grandchildren who are orphans thanks to the War. Their father went on the Somme and their mother was killed by one of those abominable Zeppelin things. If I can squeeze another thousand out of O'Malley, so much the better for poor little Vicky and Peter. For them I shall probably waive our commission.'

'Oh!' Edward was taken back by the strength of Beatrice's feeling. 'I'm afraid I didn't know that you were trying to help Hammerwich.'

'Frankly, Edward, I don't know how you have the gall to say that. You heard Father and I talking about it less than two weeks ago. As to the O'Malleys, they *are* rather insensitive, which is just as well. With any luck, they may not have noticed exactly how rude you were to Irene.'

'Women like her make me sick!' Edward seethed. 'The wretched creature damned nearly propositioned me.'

Respecting her brother's mood, Beatrice allowed a few moments to pass before she continued in a more conciliatory tone. 'Edward, my dear, I'm sometimes afraid that *all* women make you sick. Isn't it time you stopped feeling sorry for yourself over Daphne Morgan?'

'How do you know about her?'

'Because I've always taken an interest in you. I want you to be happy.'

'Well you don't have to worry about Miss Morgan.' Edward was standing on his dignity. 'It's ages since I thought about her.'

'Good. Maybe it's time you were thinking about someone else, though.'

'Bee, I'm only twenty-eight.'

'That's no sort of reason,' Beatrice said. 'It isn't even an excuse. You *need* a wife, Edward.'

'Why? I heard you telling Mother that you'd probably stay single now old Archie's gone.'

'I've got Boothby's. That hardly leaves time for a husband – even if I could find one who would put up with my doing a full-time job, and that isn't very likely.'

'And I've got the Foreign Office!' For a moment, Edward believed he had scored the winning hit.

'How far will you go without the right sort of wife?' Beatrice asked gently.

Edward considered the point, grunted, and reached for the brandy. As he sipped, his mood changed. To Beatrice's surprise, he looked like a little boy who was lost and frightened.

'As a matter of fact, Bee, there is someone,' he said. 'Is? I don't know. Was. Yes, that's it, there *was* a girl.'

'Who?' Beatrice asked, wonder making her voice no more than a whisper.

'Her name was Annaliese,' Edward said tonelessly. He squinted into his glass and Beatrice waited, hardly daring to breathe. *Annaliese.* It sounded German. A girl in Berlin, perhaps? What had become of her? Not killed, surely?

Edward raised his glass in a mock toast. 'Her Imperial and Royal Highness, Annaliese von Habsburg, Archduchess of Austria.'

'You're making this up,' Beatrice accused, certain that Edward was well on the way to being drunk.

'I'm not, I promise. It seems like a fairy-tale, but I'm afraid it's true.' Suddenly, he was his normal self and as sober as a judge.

Beatrice had remained standing since entering the room: it gave her the necessary advantage to administer a ticking-off. Now, she sank to a stool at Edward's side, overcome by amazement. 'Would you like to tell me about it?' she asked.

He shook his head.

Untroubled, Beatrice remained quiet and motionless. A coal shifted in the grate, throwing up a last flicker of flame; the clock on the church in Beauchamp Place struck the half-hour past eleven; a gang of rowdies was ejected from a party in Sloane Street, complaining bitterly until there was a threat to send for a policeman.

Startlingly, Edward sat bolt upright, his face illuminated by an expression the like of which Beatrice had never seen before. The man who made a fetish of aloof calm was in the grip of a wild joy.

'Yes, perhaps I should,' he said.

During the time it took him to assemble his thoughts, Edward's elation left him. When he spoke, it was in a voice drained of all feeling.

Beginning with their meeting on the special train from Budapest, Edward recounted virtually every minute he had spent with Annaliese, absorbed and completely unaware of his sister's mounting perplexity. Not only did the story beggar belief, Edward's narrative sprang from a part of him that he had never revealed previously. The man who had always displayed complete indifference to the way women looked and dressed was lavish with his descriptions. Although he interrupted himself repeatedly to remember what Annaliese had been wearing on a particular occasion, his most extravagant words were used in an attempt to portray her blue eyes and golden hair.

Finally, at long last, Edward came to the final meeting on the terrace of the Hofburg. 'I told Annaliese that I loved her,' he concluded.

Beatrice gaped. 'You loved her and you actually *said* so?'

'Yes.' Edward was defiant. 'I still do. She said she'd never forget me.'

'This was three years ago,' Beatrice pointed out. 'It's nearly four, actually.'

'What difference does that make? There hasn't been a day when I haven't thought of her – not even when Archie died.'

'But . . .' Beatrice was distraught, struggling to bring sense to bear on something that appeared to have no contact with reality. 'Nothing can ever come of it, my dear. Isn't she some sort of princess?'

'Yes – a minor one, though. She never attached any importance to status.'

'It wouldn't be up to her, would it?' Beatrice said. 'And even if you could find a way round that and she *hasn't* forgotten you, what's happening in Vienna? We hardly hear from Austria.'

'Things are almost certainly very bad,' Edward replied. 'The Army hasn't exactly distinguished itself and the Italians have been settling old scores. I imagine that the Habsburgs are in serious trouble.'

'Why?'

'The old Emperor died eighteen months ago. Franz Joseph was the only man with any hope of holding Austro-Hungary together – but that was before the poor fool let himself be duped into declaring war on Serbia. The new man – Karl – doesn't stand a snowball's chance in hell. As a matter of fact, Annaliese's father wanted to get out *before* Franz Ferdinand was assassinated.'

'Why didn't he?'

'Annaliese and her mother opposed it – very strongly.' Edward grimaced at a memory that was now exceedingly painful. 'That may have changed, of course. From what I've been able to find out about things in Vienna, being part of the old order is not recommended.'

'So, this girl, Annaliese, may be anywhere?' Beatrice said.

'Or dead.' Edward appeared to derive a strange, morose solace from his own bluntness. 'Even if she's still in Austria, the future could be worse than whatever she's suffered during the War.'

'In what way?'

'Nationalism will run amok,' Edward said disapprovingly. 'I'm afraid the Americans are going to push an idea called self-determination. If it's put into practice, it will create all sorts of trouble in the Habsburg territories.'

Not understanding what he meant, Beatrice was certain of one thing. 'It sounds hopeless – you and the Archduchess Annaliese.'

'Ye . . . es.' Edward drew the word out, pondering its finality. 'I don't know where she is and there's no hope of finding her.'

'She could trace you through the Foreign Office,' Beatrice said with an optimism that was entirely false.

'No, she couldn't,' Edward replied. 'Her status doesn't alter the fact that she's an enemy alien. Whatever she tried, she'd find herself up against a brick wall. Europe's changed out of all recognition, Bee. There are barriers all over the place – and they aren't necessarily tangible ones that you can climb over.'

It was true enough. King George was not the only Englishman who had bowed to pressure to get rid of his German-sounding family name. Nearly four years of organised patriotism had introduced many unpleasant side-effects.

'There's no hope, then?' Beatrice asked.

'None whatsoever.' Edward's resolve disintegrated and he was desolate.

Fearing that he was close to tears, Beatrice was overwhelmed by pity. Perching on the arm of his chair, she stroked his sleek hair. 'You poor old boy,' she soothed. 'Behind that brave face, you've been having a terrible time.'

'Everyone has,' Edward muttered. It was the closest he would go to conceding the point. 'Incidentally, don't mention Annaliese to Mother and Father. They have more than enough to worry about.'

'Of course.' Beatrice was thoughtful. 'Did Archie know about this girl in Vienna?'

'Yes.'

'He never breathed a word to me,' Beatrice said. 'Perhaps he didn't think it was all that serious.'

'Oh, he knew,' Edward said. 'I forbade him to mention it.'

'Why?'

'I didn't want anyone to think I was a fool.' Edward smiled ruefully. 'But I'm glad I've told you, Bee – it might make me feel better.'

'Confession is good for the soul,' Beatrice smiled. After kissing his forehead affectionately, she frowned at the sleeping-tablets, garish against the silver tray. 'You don't really want those horrible things, do you?' she asked in a wheedling tone that evoked echoes of their childhood.

'All right, I give in.'

'What a plucky old fish face you are!' Beatrice reached across, grabbed the pills, and tossed them into the fire.

*

In the sanctuary of her own bedroom, Beatrice succumbed to depression. The revelation of Edward's love for Annaliese emphasised the far-reaching havoc wrought by the War. Archie, Alexander, and Gerald were gone; Lord Douglas was showing signs of being permanently broken; now, it emerged that Edward had lost what might prove to be the only woman he was capable of loving. How was anyone ever going to find happiness again?

Tossing and turning in search of sleep as the Beauchamp Place church clock struck two, Beatrice became convinced that something new was called for: a radical and fearless approach to life that would carve a way through misery and uncertainty. Her mind was drawn inexorably back to what Nancy Shenstone had said so compellingly.

You deserve a good time . . .

7

November 1918–January 1919
'What are you proposing to do with this Archduchess?'

As expected, Edward did not go back to Berlin. Instead, he occupied a corner of Mr Amery's office, sifting and analysing intelligence reports. The position papers he drafted went to Lloyd George and Marshal Foch, the man leading a reorganised Allied Command in preference to Sir Douglas Haig, with whom Lloyd George was at daggers-drawn. It was fascinating work and Edward immersed himself in it, often supplementing the twelve-hour days of the normal week with extra work on Saturday and Sunday. Gradually, as the summer of 1918 passed, he began to lose the oppressive sense of guilt for Archie's death.

Although there were one or two alarming setbacks, the War news was consistently good from April onwards. This, together with the repeated requests of old and valued clients, drew Lord Douglas away from his grief-stricken isolation at Upper Overs. He refused to spend a night in London, but his appearances at Boothby's became more frequent. Each time he visited the firm that had played such an important part in his life, he seemed to gain a little in strength and confidence.

Beatrice was cautiously hopeful. To bolster her spirits further, she had a new friend. From their first meeting, she was sure that Charles Templeton was destined to put her life on a better, happier course.

Charles was thirty-four, nine years older than Beatrice. Fair-haired, tall, and obviously strong, he had more than a passing resemblance to

Archie. Although invalided out of the Army in 1915, he appeared perfectly fit and played a useful game of cricket whenever the opportunity arose. Behind the courteously bland exterior that was the badge of his profession, Charles Templeton concealed a shrewd business mind and considerable artistic flair. In the fullness of time, when his father stepped aside, Charles would take up the reins of the merchant bank established by his great-great-grandfather in 1796. Until that happened, he was learning about the more obscure points of interest in every nook and cranny of the City of London, dabbling in water-colours, and enduring a wretchedly unsatisfactory marriage.

Charles, an occasional but as yet uncommitted member of Nancy's circle, was not at Martha's Vineyard on the August evening when Beatrice moved from being a casual visitor into the select group. There were a dozen men and women in a sitting-room that was set well away from the public part of the house, a party that represented about one third of Nancy's closest friends. When Beatrice was settled, they continued with the conversation that her introduction had interrupted. It was all about Penelope Templeton and how Charles managed to put up with her: more to the point, *why* did he bother?

Assimilated into the coterie with undemonstrative warmth, Beatrice was expected to know what was being discussed. It was impossible to deduce anything beyond generalities. They were a subtle, sophisticated bunch, conversing in hints and understatements to create an atmosphere of innuendo that was both tantalising and frustrating. Not that it lasted long: at seven-thirty, the party fragmented as men and women paired off and drifted away. Their purpose was plain, but it was all done with a calm confidence that gave Beatrice her first glimpse into the secrets of Martha's Vineyard. Eventually alone with Nancy and another woman – both of whom were unconcerned at not having a partner – Beatrice was able to ask questions.

Nancy described Charles, then launched into a scathing condemnation of his wife. 'She married Charles for his money . . . don't ask me why the poor sap couldn't see it, but he didn't! She gave him a son, then kicked him out of her bed.'

'Oh dear,' Beatrice was dismayed.

'Too right.' Nancy retorted. 'Women like that make me sick. Personally, I could understand it if she was involved with another man . . . I mean, you either live with good old-fashioned adultery, or you do something about it. That ain't good enough for Penelope, though! *She* has to get mixed up with a load of cranks who have religion. It's *bad*.'

'What sort of religion?' Beatrice asked.

'God knows.' Nancy thought about it and laughed. 'Hell, he probably doesn't.'

The other woman had something to offer. 'I think it's a movement dedicated to meditation and the condemnation of bodily lusts.' Since her very presence in Nancy's inner sanctum made her sentiments plain, there was no need for any other comment beyond the whimsically raised eyebrows.

'Isn't divorce possible in a case like this?' Beatrice wondered.

'Only with the greatest difficulty,' Nancy said. 'In any case, Charles's old man won't hear of it. Whisper the word "scandal" to him and he's out of his skull. He's threatened to disinherit Charles in favour of a cousin if he doesn't keep quiet and put up with it.'

'The poor man.' The sympathy that Beatrice felt for someone she had yet to meet did not strike her as at all strange. Nor did Nancy's next remark.

'Beatrice, you and Charles might be right for each other.' Their companion was nodding. 'He comes here looking lost every so often, but he never seems to find a partner who can make him feel comfortable.'

'He sounds a most deserving case,' Beatrice said, her voice over-bright with recklessness.

The meeting took place the following week. Nancy arranged a special evening at which she, Beatrice, Charles Templeton, and a barrister called Michael Richardson dined together. Beatrice and Charles established a quiet rapport from the outset. At the end of the meal, when Nancy announced that she was taking Michael Richardson upstairs, the two new friends sat in the well-stocked library at the back of the house and told each other their life stories.

They met twice a week throughout September and October, often as part of a gathering of the select group. Untroubled by the procession towards bedrooms that always began at around half past seven, they exchanged confidences. Charles explained that his domestic problems were compounded by the existence of his seven-year-old son, Nigel. Charles's father and wife were ruthless in their exploitation of his love for the boy. It was all part of the incessant war of nerves designed to maintain appearances at what was supposed to be the matrimonial home in Twickenham. In return, Beatrice told Charles about the man whose engagement ring she would always wear.

Unobtrusively, Nancy watched the friendship deepen, certain that it would soon flower into something that would do the two participants a power of much-needed good.

The Armistice on 11 November was a blessed relief. It sparked a festival of national rejoicing that, for a few hours, threatened to be as ferocious as the fighting it replaced. In Trafalgar Square, a huge crowd lit a bonfire round the plinth of Nelson's Column; men and women who didn't know each other from Adam copulated on the pavements; shops in surrounding streets were smashed up and looted. The police tactfully made themselves scarce. The land fit for heroes promised by David Lloyd George was ushered in by a near-riot.

The stay-at-homes, especially those of a more thoughtful nature, were inclined to be surprised by the sudden, unexpected cave-in of Germany. Not so Edward and Mr Amery: they knew that secret negotiations had been in progress since 7 October.

Using a Swiss intermediary, the German Government had addressed itself personally to President Wilson of the United States, asking him to organise a cessation of hostilities on the basis of his so-called Fourteen Points. No one in Britain or France had ever taken Woodrow Wilson's high-sounding rhetoric seriously. Now, unless the killing was to continue, the arrogant intellectual who had set himself up as the world's moral conscience was on the way to becoming a Messiah.

Three days after the Armistice came into effect, a letter from

Dieter Hoffmann reached Edward after travelling from Stockholm in a diplomatic bag. The first few paragraphs were devoted to a point that was self-evident: whatever the German Government thought, the High Command would attempt to use the breathing space of the Armistice – which was not an unconditional surrender – to regroup with a view to launching a new offensive in the spring of 1919.

A wealth of interesting detail about the confusion and tragicomedy of the Kaiser's abdication and flight to Holland followed.

'What a shambles,' Mr Amery muttered as they studied the letter, heads close together.

'Yes . . . but look at this.' Edward, who had been reading ahead, stabbed a finger on to a new topic.

Hoffmann warned that a dangerous myth was going the rounds in Germany. Far from being defeated, the Army was in finer condition than at any time since August 1914; the ignominy of defeat had been engineered by left-wing politicians, all of whom, it was being said in some circles, were cowards and traitors. Within the first twelve hours of its currency, the story had won the support of at least a quarter of the population.

'Hmm . . . yes,' Mr Amery said. 'What with that *and* Woodrow Wilson, life looks like being full of interest.'

'I fancy I can add to that,' Edward said. 'Don't be surprised if Lloyd George decides to have a general election before Christmas.'

Mr Amery deplored displays of emotion. During their years of working together, Edward had watched his superior maintain a straight face at everything except Archie's death. Now, however, he goggled in disbelief. 'Are you sure?'

'It's what they're saying in the corridors of the House of Lords.'

'You've been talking to your uncle?'

Edward nodded. 'He's up in town for a few days.'

'Well, I'm blessed!' Mr Amery said. 'As you know, they're arranging a peace conference in Paris. One would have thought that the Prime Minister would have been better employed in preparing for that, not playing the fool on the hustings.'

'If he wins – which he will – won't he carry more clout at the conference table?' Edward suggested. 'At the moment, a lot of people regard him as nothing more than the man who ousted Asquith. If he wins an election off his own bat, his prestige will be increased.'

Mr Amery smiled appreciatively. 'It seems that I'm so busy working out what Hindenburg and Ludendorff are up to that I can't see what's going on at home! Yes, you're quite right. Now, let me give *you* a snippet. Assuming that Lloyd George goes to Paris himself, he will be supported by a staff of hundreds.' Edward was not in the least surprised. With an obvious need to redraw the map of Europe and much of the Middle East, those doing the negotiating would need briefing on every topic under the sun. 'A little bird tells me that you and I are likely to be part of the delegation.'

Edward found the prospect exciting, immediately realising that his prospects of promotion were likely to be enhanced. 'How long will the conference last?' he inquired.

'How long is a piece of string?' Mr Amery retorted. 'I don't know – a year? It could take that long.'

The longer the better, Edward decided.

At Cadogan Square that evening, Franklin was in his usual place near the front door with the customary greeting.

'I trust you had a pleasant day, Mr Edward?'

'Yes, thank you, Franklin.' Edward paused to allow the butler to take his hat and coat. 'Got some interesting news . . . I may be going to Paris for the peace conference. Part of the support delegation.'

'Is the task to your liking, sir?'

'Very much so, Franklin. Between you and I, it could stand me in good stead for promotion. It certainly won't do any harm.'

'*Excellent*, sir.'

'Now, Franklin, I'm starving! I take it that my sister's in and we can start dinner?'

'Miss Beatrice telephoned two hours ago, sir. She will not be in this evening. I gather she is visiting friends at St Albans and may stay with them until tomorrow morning.'

Edward frowned. 'Friends at St Albans? That's a new one on me. Do you know anything about them?'

'I regret not, sir. If I understood Miss Beatrice correctly, they are connected with the business – Boothby's, you know.'

'Oh.' At once, Edward's interest evaporated. 'Look, will you bring my meal up to the study? I have some papers I must read – background for the conference, you know.'

Franklin, as ever, was only too glad to oblige.

Half a mile away, in Upper Belgrave Street, Charles Templeton was unaware that Beatrice had already taken the most momentous decision of her life so far. In the sitting-room at Martha's Vineyard, a number of conversations were in progress. Beatrice was talking to a woman who was considering selling a valuable painting; Charles was giving advice on investments to an architect. A larger group were discussing the Armistice. Seven-thirty came round; the architect thanked Charles, caught the eye of the titled lady with Beatrice, and slipped away. In the course of the next few minutes, five more couples did the same, leaving Beatrice and Charles alone. It was what always happened. With no reason to think that this evening was to differ from the others, Charles made himself comfortable in an armchair. To his surprise, Beatrice knelt at his side, gazing at him with a mixture of earnestness and trepidation.

'What is it, my dear?' he asked.

'Charles, I've been thinking very carefully,' Beatrice said. To be sure, she added, 'Very carefully indeed.'

'Yes.' He smiled. 'About what?'

'Us.' For a moment or two, Beatrice wondered whether that was enough, whether he would be able to catch her meaning. It was, of course, an unreasonable expectation. 'Do you think we could be lovers?'

With a great effort, Charles retained the composure the situation demanded. 'I have to say that it has crossed my mind,' he said.

'You like the idea?'

'Frankly, yes.'

Beatrice rose to her feet, reaching for his hand. 'So do I. Come along.'

It was Nancy herself, thrilled by the turn of events, who took the place of the hand-picked maid who normally looked after couples once they were beyond the double doors at the end of the first-floor landing. Beatrice and Charles were shown into a bedroom of sumptuous, blatantly erotic luxury.

Whereas Charles could easily have fallen prey to nervousness, Beatrice generated more than enough calm determination to see them through the preliminary difficulties. Their reward was an experience so overwhelmingly beautiful and satisfying that they promised to cherish its memory forever. So total was their enchantment at what they had done to each other, that it was not until they were ready to make love for a second time that Beatrice became aware of the scars on Charles's broad back.

'Is that why you were discharged from the Army?' she asked, passing her fingertips over the slight ridge and indentations.

'Yes.'

'It seems to have healed up nicely. What about inside?'

'Lost a kidney. Everything seems all right, though. What do you think?' Charles spoke with complete lack of self-pity, or any attempt at bogus jocularity. Beatrice respected and adored him for it.

'I'm not exactly expert,' she said, turning her head towards the towel draped over the linen-basket, a reminder of her virginity. 'But you *do* seem to be in marvellous fettle, Charles.'

To her relief, his face cracked into a broad smile. Ten minutes ago, when she had returned to his embrace after a visit to the *en suite* bathroom, he had seemed ill at ease. Heaven knows why it should trouble him, but had he been assuming that he wouldn't be the first? Thankfully, whatever strange, tortured ideas had been troubling him no longer mattered.

'May I tell you something?' he asked.

'Please do.'

'Until very recently, I had absolutely no idea that a lady could enjoy sex so much.'

'How recently?' Beatrice teased.

'Oh, something like half an hour, I'd say.'

'You've only ever done it with your wife?'

'I'm afraid so,' Charles said.

'I don't think you need to be ashamed of that,' Beatrice laughed. 'Now, let me tell you something. During the last two weeks, I've been reading a book . . . it's called *Married Love* by Marie Stopes.'

'You've got a copy of that?' Charles choked. 'I thought it had been banned out of existence.'

'Nancy lent it to me,' Beatrice explained. 'I suppose it *is* rather sensational . . . but so is our ignorance of our own bodies and feelings. Anyway, Marie Stopes says that women are *meant* to enjoy it – and you'd curl up if you heard what Nancy has to say. It has a lot to do with the man, of course, so there you are.'

'You were somewhat inspiring, my darling.'

'Was I? Really?' Beatrice snuggled closer to him, relishing the excitement of his renewed hardness. 'Let's spend all our spare time turning each other into experts!'

'I'd like that very much,' Charles replied. Curiously, he sounded rather sad, but Beatrice understood. One of the thoughts churning through his mind on this, an exceptionally happy day, was pity for Archie Shackleton. The poor chap would never know how damnably unlucky he had been to be deprived of life with Beatrice.

'We're going to be very, very good for one another,' she sighed. 'Will you let me worry about Archie, please, Charles?'

They went to Paris on 25 November, rather earlier than Edward thought necessary. Leaving London with no idea where they would be living for the duration of the conference, Mr Amery predicted chaos and discomfort.

It had seemed ominously probable. With hundreds of diplomats and thousands of assistants streaming into Paris from every part of the world, even mediocre accommodation was expected to be at a premium. The absence of any information in London encouraged the cynical view that, although Britain might be capable of waging and helping to win the greatest conflict in history, finding lodgings for those who had to tie up the loose ends would prove impossible. In all honesty, the doubters had every justification for their gloomy outlook – but they had reckoned without the British Ambassador in the French capital.

There were those who said that someone on high had made a terrible blunder over the appointment of Lewis Peters. His previous appointments in South America and Spain had revealed a tendency to take risks. To make matters worse, his plans always succeeded. It was generally accepted that Lewis Peters was extremely brave and talented. On top of all this, he was popular throughout the Diplomatic Service. Mention of his name almost anywhere was enough to produce a smile and a kind word. 'Ah, yes, Lewis . . . Do you remember that time he threatened to lock that Bolivian general up if he didn't start learning some manners? What a chap!' Finally – and this was the factor that had shaken the Foreign Office to its foundations – Lewis Peters was young. When given the Embassy in Paris in June 1918, he was a mere stripling of forty-two, nowhere near old enough for the knighthood that should have accompanied the appointment.

Two days after the Armistice, when it became known that Paris was to host the peace conference, Lewis Peters commandeered a pair of hotels. Situated in a peaceful side street of the Quai d'Orsay and only a minute's walk from the Embassy, the neighbouring establishments were named after the brothers who owned them. In total, L'Hotel Jean-Jacques and L'Hotel Jean-Pierre were capable of providing solid, three-star comfort for three hundred people. Some facilities had to be sacrificed to allow a few of the public rooms to be turned into offices, but it was a small price to pay for a home from home. Edward and Mr Amery found themselves billeted in adjoining suites on the second floor of the Jean-Jacques: it was the smaller of the two hotels, but had the best food.

'I stand corrected,' Mr Amery said, after they had unpacked and settled in. 'And I take my hat off to Lewis Peters. I hope such initiative doesn't ruin his career.'

'He's pretty impregnable by all accounts,' Edward replied.

'You don't know him?' Mr Amery asked.

'No, I'm afraid I've never had that pleasure.'

'That's what special duties does for you,' Mr Amery said. 'While you've been stuck in Vienna and lying low between trips to Berlin, you've missed the star performer. I expect you'll get a chance before we're finished with this job.'

'I doubt it,' Edward said. 'A chap in his position can't bother with small fry.'

Mr Amery's reply was an enigmatic grunt.

Their first working day began with a trip next door to have breakfast at the Jean-Pierre with Sir Maurice Hankey, the head of the British delegation. The ex-Royal Marine, who was to be Lloyd George's right-hand man during the conference, wasted no time in demonstrating his no-nonsense approach to the task ahead.

'You two chaps will report directly to me . . . I'll give you a chit to wave at anyone who tries to pinch you for his department. Clear?'

'Yes, sir,' Edward and Mr Amery said.

'The PM will need briefing on *everything*. I've got a list of topics as long as my arm and the luminaries of the FO tell me that I haven't even scratched the surface yet.' Sir Maurice directed a disdainful look at a less than perfectly fried egg. 'One of my most important requirements is an appreciation of the German Army. Obviously, the War Office are working on it, but I want an independent view. I'm told you're the chaps to do it.'

The only possible response to the shrewd stare was an eager nod.

'Here's what worries me,' Sir Maurice went on. 'The Germans have marched home – and in damned fine order by all accounts. Nothing has been abandoned in the War Zone. They've got all their kit and equipment – including artillery – and are beyond our reach. What – if anything – should we be doing about it?'

'Do you want them disarmed, sir?' Edward asked.

'*I* do, Mr Boothby-Graffoe,' Sir Maurice replied tetchily. 'It's common sense, isn't it? However, we have to consider the subtleties of the negotiating-table. In essence, that means being prepared for anything the French might pull out of the hat.' His mistrust of an ally was pointed up by a thin, grim smile.

'And the German attitude?' Edward suggested, only to receive a baleful glare for his trouble.

'What the Germans think about *anything* is totally immaterial,' Sir Maurice snapped. 'They will not be attending the conference.'

'I see. Very well, sir.' Edward was chastened and dismayed.

'I want you fellows to work up an analysis of the problems,' Sir Maurice went on, more friendly now that Edward had been brought to heel. 'I'm sure you know the sort of thing I'm looking for . . . Can we afford to disarm the German Army? How long would it take? What are the risks involved? What sort of risks are we running if we *don't*?'

'I understand, Sir Maurice,' Mr Amery said.

'Good. Report to me here at this time every Monday morning.'

With that, Sir Maurice Hankey abandoned the remnants of his breakfast and strode away.

Mr Amery smiled, first at a nearby group of acquaintances, then at Edward. 'I know what you're thinking,' he said quietly. 'It really would be best if you kept your thoughts to yourself. For the moment, at any rate.'

Until they were back in their own hotel, Edward did. Then, he gave vent to his views. 'It's unprecedented folly to exclude the defeated side from a peace conference. Have the people responsible no idea of the harm they could be doing?'

'Obviously not,' Mr Amery said.

'Why is it being done? Who wants it this way?'

'Let us see if we can find out,' Mr Amery mused. 'Consider the five nations who claim to have beaten Germany and her allies. Shall we start with Japan? Could it be our friends in Tokyo who want Germany excluded?'

'Ridiculous,' Edward scoffed. 'Even if they'd come up with such a damned silly idea, no one would listen.' In fact, most people in Britain were unaware that Japan, without obvious justification, had declared war on Germany in August 1914. The purpose had been to gain possession of German ports and property in the Shantung province of China.

'How about Italy?' Mr Amery suggested.

'Not enough weight. They're petty opportunists.'

'Harsh, but accurate,' Mr Amery conceded. 'Now to the Big Three as they will doubtless wish to call themselves. We can rule out America, can we not? A man like Woodrow Wilson is hardly likely to insist on such an unreasonable pre-condition.' Edward nodded agreement. 'We can also eliminate ourselves. Despite his immoderate utterances, I have it on the best authority that Lloyd George is as displeased as you and me at Germany's exclusion from the conference.' The look on Edward's face was sceptical. 'All that talk about squeezing Germany till the pips squeak and hanging the Kaiser in London is simply hot air – electioneering poppycock. It's what the British public *wants* to hear. Privately, David Lloyd George is disgusted at the way things are being organised.'

'So it's the French,' Edward said.

'Georges Clemenceau, to be precise – the "Tiger" as the pompous old fool likes to be known. Believe me, Edward, that man's intransigence is a serious obstacle. If he has his way, Germany will be blamed and made to pay for every last thing that's been wrong with France since the year dot.'

'Perhaps he and Woodrow Wilson deserve each other,' Edward suggested.

Mr Amery sighed. 'Dear boy, you really should try to hide your cynicism for the next thirty years. It will be invaluable when you *are* running the Foreign Office, in the meantime, we have more mundane work to do and a little altruism wouldn't come amiss. What about this job Hankey's dumped on us . . . Can we cope? Do we have the necessary information?'

Edward's smile had a suggestion of smugness. 'I brought all my notebooks with me.' Mr Amery relaxed. Edward's meticulous records of all that he had learned in Berlin during the War were legendary. 'If we're short of anything, I know a couple of chaps in the military delegation who'll help out.'

'If the worst came to the worst, you could go to Germany,' Mr Amery said.

'Yes, I suppose so,' Edward replied, though without noticeable enthusiasm.

They set to work, attempting to keep their spirits up through day after day of stygian gloom and steady rain. In the evenings, while Mr Amery was content to huddle over a fire with Sir Walter Scott's Waverley novels, Edward was out and about, making himself known in the hotels occupied by other delegations. The Americans were the most hospitable and knew all the juiciest gossip, but it was the Italians who had the best bridge players. Not only did they welcome Edward with open arms, they knew what was happening in Austria.

It seemed incredible that such events were not common knowledge. On reflection, Edward decided that newspaper editors were sick of the War's ramifications and doubted the capacity of their readers to assimilate anything not connected with stringing Kaiser Wilhelm up or bankrupting the German Treasury.

The Emperor, Karl, had abdicated, apparently leaving Vienna in considerable confusion and haste. Some reports said that he and his immediate family were in Budapest, drumming up support for an attempt at restitution. However, since a Transylvanian journalist by the name of Bela Kun was well on the way to turning Hungary into a Communist dictatorship, this seemed improbable. In Vienna, a provisional Government of questionable legitimacy was furiously enacting a mass of anti-Habsburg legislation, confiscating all lands and titles. There was talk of a law that forbade any member of the Family – however obscure and lowly – to set foot inside Austria. Elsewhere, the Empire was in turmoil, seething with the age-old multitude of hatreds and disparate aspirations that had, paradoxically, been given new life by Woodrow Wilson's lofty idealism. In particular, relations between Serbia and Bosnia were dangerous enough to raise fears of war.

'There will be disaster,' Edward was told by a man close to Sonnino, the Italian Foreign Minister. 'Not next week, or next year, perhaps, but it will come. For all their faults, the Habsburgs held the rabble together and kept them quiet. The men with fancy notions are going to set them at each other's throats.'

'Someone else will take the blame, of course,' Edward said. 'Tell me, is anything known about the lesser members of the Imperial Family? Where are they?'

'All gone. Switzerland, mainly. Maybe some are in Spain. There's a rumour that the Emperor is going to Madeira.'

'The Archduke Joseph . . . the one married to the Bavarian princess?' Edward asked hopefully.

A shake of the head. 'We have no knowledge of individuals. Officially, we're like the Austrian people, pretending to be glad that the "accursed" Habsburgs have gone. *Unofficially* . . .' The man smiled and shrugged eloquently.

Returning to L'Hotel Jean-Jacques, Edward wrote a letter to his parents, telling them how miserably dull Paris was. There were frequent interruptions to his work on the catalogue of boredom as he paused to speculate on Annaliese's whereabouts.

On 14 December, the gloom was dispelled by an event that brought the whole of Paris on to the streets.

The American liner *George Washington* had steamed into Brest the previous day, bringing Woodrow Wilson and his aides to a grievously battered Europe. At Paris, after a journey in the luxurious private train belonging to the President of the French Republic, Wilson walked into what was soon being described as the greatest display of mass delirium in the history of the world. Even in victory, millions of Parisians were disillusioned by their own political leaders and institutions; they scrambled and fought for a glimpse of the saviour from an untainted New World. Placards proclaiming, *Wilson le juste*, were on every lamp-post and building. Weeping hysterically, the huge crowd kept up an hypnotic chant of, 'Veelson! Veelson!' for over three hours.

A surge of the constantly shifting crowd, regrouping for a second or third sighting of the redeemer, trapped Edward on the steps of the British Embassy. As luck would have it, the carriage procession swept up the Quai d'Orsay some moments later, and Edward found himself only yards away from Woodrow Wilson. The President of the United States was an austere, aesthetic-looking man, somehow radiating the moral rectitude that was his stock-in-trade. Yet it was something else in his demeanour that struck Edward most forcibly. Wilson had been elected to his high office in November 1912 after a lifetime in the remote, jealously protected peace of Princeton University. Surely, therefore, he should have been overwhelmed, even downright uneasy, at the unnerving tumult taking place within feet of him, a tumult that the soldiers lining the route were finding it difficult to contain. Such an ethereal being would be perfectly entitled to be afraid of the frenzied uproar. But not a bit of it! Although most of his demented admirers were incapable of noticing it, there was a self-satisfied twist at one corner of Woodrow Wilson's mouth: for him, this astounding reception was no more than his due.

What made the whole business completely incomprehensible was that there was no earthly reason for Wilson to be in Paris on this murky December day. He had neither been invited, nor given any intimation that the serious work of the conference was about to begin. Lloyd George was tearing round Britain on the election hustings; Clemenceau had condescended to ride in Wilson's carriage, but had no intention of talking until he was good and ready – another five weeks was the word among those close to the men who were in the Tiger's confidence. Woodrow Wilson's arrogance had lured him into a ludicrous position: having appointed himself guest of honour, the President of the United States of America had arrived at the party long before it was ready to start. The attempt to resolve mankind's greatest problem was beginning with a farce.

Filled with foreboding, Edward attempted to extricate himself from the crush, only to find himself jostled into contact with a woman.

'I say, I'm terribly sorry,' he said. Perhaps because she was not wearing a street coat, he assumed that she was a member of the Embassy staff and addressed her in English.

'You couldn't help it,' she replied, confirming the assumption of her nationality. 'Have you ever seen the like?' She was peering at him closely. 'I say, aren't you young Boothby-Graffoe?'

Not a day over forty herself, her beautiful face was wreathed in mischief as she parodied male chumminess.

'Yes, I am.' Edward was at a loss. 'I'm afraid you have the advantage of me, madam.'

'Of course I do,' she laughed. 'I'm Frances Peters – Mrs Ambassador. Look, *do* come inside. It's pointless you trying to go anywhere until this lot clear off. Besides, I love talking to bright young men.'

She guided him into a small private room. Here, a maid brought coffee and Frances Peters shocked Edward to the core. 'You're the chap who was always popping in and out of Berlin during the War, aren't you?' she said. 'Oh dear, have I put my foot in it?'

Edward shuffled uncomfortably. 'Well . . . no . . . not really. It is frightfully hush-hush, though.'

'I know,' Frances Peters hooted. 'But what's the point of being married to a big-wig if one can't winkle out exciting stuff like that. Rest assured, my lips are sealed.' Her unconventional approach to her role was refreshing and engaging, and Edward capitulated to her charm. Nearly an hour later, he was sent on his way with an invitation to dinner the following evening.

Frances and Lewis Peters were, Edward soon realised, the most united and happy couple, surpassing even the harmony achieved by his parents before Alexander's death had laid Lord Douglas so low. The one sadness for the Ambassador and his fascinating wife, their failure to produce children, had been partially sublimated into their collection of brilliant young men. Edward was far too old to be their son, but he was conscious of being regarded as a favoured younger brother. One of the three other men who sat down to dinner in the Ambassador's private quarters on the evening of 15 December, a brilliant economist in his mid-thirties, was treated as a much-respected equal by Lewis Peters.

John Maynard Keynes, a Cambridge don and one-time member of the Royal Commission on Indian Finance, was an advisor to the Treasury. He needed little prompting from his host to explain why he considered the idea that Germany should be forced to pay colossal reparations to be potentially disastrous – not merely for Germany, but for Europe as a whole. It would, he insisted, ruin national economies. Among the many evils that would stem from this, Keynes saw the threat to jobs as the greatest. Without full employment, Keynes insisted, there was scant hope for the twentieth century.

The intense discussion that ensued went on until nearly two o'clock in the morning. After playing a constructive, if somewhat combative part in it, Edward was left in doubt that he had been accepted into what Mr Amery had called the 'golden band' – the select group that Frances and Lewis Peters believed were destined for great things. As Edward was leaving for his hotel, Frances extended an open invitation to dinner on any evening when she and Lewis were free of official duties.

'Which should keep us going well into January,' she added with undisguised glee. 'Lewis won't tolerate bores until the conference starts and we can't wriggle out of entertaining them.'

Although there was a bit of a fuss about it, Beatrice was pleased by the news that Edward would not be returning to England for Christmas. While Lady Alice was angling for an invitation to Compton Allardyce in Wiltshire, Beatrice arranged to stay with Nancy at Martha's Vineyard for five days. Charles Templeton promised to spend at least two afternoons and one night with her.

Christmas in Paris was very pleasant. Frances created an atmosphere of traditional festivity to offset the deadly seriousness of the golden band's debates. By now, Edward was convinced that the French desire for retribution and recompense would, if unchecked, plunge civilisation into something resembling a new dark age.

The Ambassador's wife suspected that there was more to her new protégé's pessimism than met the eye. 'Do you know, Edward, I'm beginning to wonder if you've ever subscribed to the *Entente Cordiale*,' she said. 'Deep, deep down, you're a reactionary. You think that the French are nothing but a bunch of ghastly foreigners and outsiders.'

'They've always caused trouble,' Edward said. 'Seven hundred years of confounded nuisance.'

'More, if you count William the Conqueror,' Frances replied. 'And what about that bounder Napoleon?'

'He made a terrible mess of things,' Edward pointed out, suffering from the delusion that he was taking part in a serious conversation.

'What do you expect? They eat frogs' legs.'

It was her eyes, wide with mock horror that gave the game away. To Edward's surprise, he was able to laugh at himself. He also allowed Frances to steer him to a spot beneath a bunch of mistletoe and was far from embarrassed during the subsequent kiss.

On 29 December, as the Embassy was being prepared to celebrate a New Year for which mankind had impossibly high hopes, news of the general election result arrived from London. Voting had taken place on 14 December, but the count and declaration of results had been delayed to allow the soldiers who remained in France to vote by post. Of the 707 seats in the House of Commons, Lloyd George's Liberals, together with his Conservative supporters, had won 526, a victory of unprecedented scale. The British Prime Minister would be a figure of commanding authority at the peace conference.

He duly arrived in Paris on 2 January 1919, but nothing happened – at least, nothing that could be reported. Behind locked doors, it was probable that Lloyd George was acting as referee in an argument between Clemenceau and Woodrow Wilson. It was a struggle between the old-style statesman who believed in secret, often venal deals, and the idealist demanding that everything should be open and above board. This was also the time to seek a preliminary settlement of the issue that Wilson had placed above his Fourteen Points in importance. There must, he insisted, be a League of Nations to prevent a repetition of the disaster that had swept across Europe in August 1914. So far, Clemenceau had ridiculed the idea at every opportunity.

Unnoticed, keeping themselves to themselves, Mr Amery and Edward worked away at the briefing papers for Sir Maurice Hankey. At six-thirty each evening they parted: Mr Amery made himself comfortable with Sir Walter Scott, Edward went to the British Embassy. However, on Saturday 11 January, this agreeable diversion was not available: much to Frances Peters's disgust, she had to organise a reception for members of the American delegation.

Edward dined with Mr Amery at L'Hotel Jean-Jacques.

Leaving the restaurant, they found the foyer – which now served as the resident's lounge – abuzz with excitement. A bundle of up-to-date German newspapers had turned up. Grabbing what they could from the pandemonium, Edward and Mr Amery huddled in the quietest corner and began to read. For nearly ten minutes, they were astounded into silence by the reports of civil war.

'This seems to be worse than you predicted,' Mr Amery said at last.

'Yes.' Edward paused to think. 'This is all very confused and contradictory, though.' He brandished the bunch of papers he had obtained from the free-for-all. 'I have three completely different accounts of what purports to be the same event.'

'Which merely emphasises what a mess they're in!' Mr Amery replied. The need to make a point he considered glaringly obvious gave his voice an irritable edge. Edward grunted and they lapsed back into silent study of the newspapers.

Two factors eroded Edward's concentration. His amazement at the press reports was replaced by a sixth-sense insistence that the most extraordinary event of his life was imminent. Then, he began to experience an inner tension that impeded his breathing. Intending to step outside for a breath of fresh air, Edward lowered the newspaper.

At that same moment, the man who had been making fruitless inquiries at the reception desk finally gave up and turned away. He and Edward were looking straight at each other.

Disbelief turned them into statues. They spent an interminable fifteen seconds over recognition and denial, doubting the evidence of their eyes. At last, it was Edward who got to his feet and began to cross the thirty-foot gap between them. Leopold von Habsburg remained rooted to the spot, unsure of whether to go or face it out.

'Hello, Boothby-Graffoe,' he said. 'This is a surprise.'

'Isn't it!' Edward had no idea how to address him and decided not to bother. They shook hands.

'You came through the War,' Leopold said. 'I'm glad.'

'You, too,' Edward replied. 'What brings you to Paris?'

'I'm with the Austrian delegation.'

'Oh.' Edward was on his guard, wondering whether he and Mr Amery had missed something. 'I didn't realise there was one.'

'Officially, no, there isn't. In practice, no one can keep us out of a free city, can they? We thought it would be to our advantage to be here and keep our ears to the ground.'

'*We?*' Edward asked.

'I'm with half a dozen social democrat friends.' Recovering from the shock of encountering Edward, Leopold was starting to exhibit his turkeycock tendency. 'I have become a private citizen – as demanded by the laws of the Republic. I retain my status, of course. One signs a paper, but it doesn't mean a thing. My new colleagues find me quite an asset.'

Edward made no attempt to respond. He was busy congratulating himself on having marked the Archduke down as a man who would go wherever the wind of expediency took him.

'And you?' Leopold asked. 'Why are you here?'

'I'm with the British delegation.'

'Ah, yes!' Leopold was looking over Edward's shoulder. 'Your friend is wondering who I am.'

Turning, Edward saw that Mr Amery was staring at them with unashamed curiosity. 'Come and meet him,' Edward said. 'He may be inclined to give you some advice.'

Although Mr Amery must have been surprised to find himself being introduced to a member of the Austrian Imperial Family, his courteous interest betrayed nothing.

'I'm afraid you're wasting your time,' he told Leopold after learning the reason for his presence in Paris. 'Your country isn't going to be discussed here. They're saying that there will be a separate conference when this one is finished.'

'No matter,' Leopold said airily. 'I'm sure there are snippets and nuances that will never find their way into the newspapers. It will be helpful when it comes to our turn.'

'I trust your parents are well?' Edward said, doing his best to sound no more than polite.

'Thank you, yes. They went to Switzerland last February. For some reason, they didn't like it, so they moved on to Portugal. I believe it's very pleasant.'

'You didn't go with them?' Edward asked.

'No. I expect you find that ironic, eh? I was all for getting out in 'fourteen, if you remember.'

'No doubt you had your reasons,' Edward said. 'What does your sister think of it?'

It was so casual that Leopold had no idea what Edward meant. 'Think of what?' he asked.

'Portugal.' Edward's impatience was near the surface.

'Oh, Liese isn't in Portugal.' Leopold was scanning the foyer, making sure that there was nothing to be learned in L'Hotel Jean-Jacques before he left to sniff round another delegation. 'She's far too altruistic for that sort of thing.'

'Where is she?' Edward's voice rose anxiously, drawing a quiver of interest from Mr Amery.

'She's in Berlin,' Leopold said.

'*Berlin!*' Edward's shout caused heads to turn all over the foyer. 'She's in Berlin?'

'Yes. She went there in November nineteen-seventeen. Is it not rather amusing? If you recall, I was the one who was always accused of being too pro-German.'

'Berlin must be the most dangerous place in the world,' Edward said, fighting to regain composure. 'According to these newspapers, it's as bad as the Western Front used to be.'

Leopold shrugged. 'I suspect that Russia is far worse,' he said. 'But, yes, Berlin isn't good. Mother and Father *are* upset. They've pleaded with her to come out. She won't budge. Apparently her letters are full of rubbish about her duty to a brave people. Mother has been trying to persuade me to go and fetch her. Ridiculous!'

'Have you been in contact with Annaliese?' Edward asked.

'Er . . . no.' For the first time, Leopold was uneasy. 'Too busy, you understand.'

'I . . .' Half out of his chair, Edward stopped himself. In the grip of an insane inspiration, he forced himself to appear outwardly calm. 'What is Annaliese doing?' he asked. '*Why* is she in Berlin?'

'She's a nurse.'

'Where?' Edward demanded.

'The Kaiser Frederick *Krankenhaus*.'

'On Prinz Albrecht Strasse – just off Leipziger Platz?'

Suddenly, Leopold was staring hard at Edward. 'Yes, that's the address. You seem to have an excellent knowledge of Berlin, Boothby-Graffoe.'

'Which hotel are you at?' Edward asked, brushing aside the implied question.

'The Matignon on Rue de Varenne.'

'I will send word to you if I have any worthwhile information,' Edward said.

In his eagerness to trawl for possible openings elsewhere, Leopold von Habsburg attached the wrong meaning to the ambiguous statement. With a stiff bow, and a farewell that verged on the sincere, he was away through the revolving doors into the darkness of another wet night.

'What amazing people you met in Vienna,' Mr Amery said, mildly critical.

'They weren't all like him, thank God!' Edward replied, then slumped back into his chair and stared up at the ceiling. He recalled the details of his last two visits to Berlin, retracing every step, every tram ride round the city. He must have passed the Kaiser Frederick Infirmary at least a dozen times. On each occasion, he had, in all probability, been within a hundred yards of Annaliese!

When Mr Amery abandoned his air of benign abstraction, he was circumspect. 'This nurse . . . in Berlin. I presume that she is the Archduchess who was your friend in Vienna?'

'Only for a few weeks,' Edward countered.

'Granted – although I understand that the attachment was none the weaker for its brevity. Quite the contrary, perhaps?'

Edward's suspicions were aroused. 'How do you know that?'

'Do you remember Edith Rathbone – Sir Lionel's daughter?'

'I do indeed.' Edward said with a distinct lack of warmth.

'She's married now,' Mr Amery said. 'Very happily settled in Washington with a gentleman called Warren. However, there was a time when you were a great disappointment to her. Miss Rathbone had quite a lot to say for herself.' Studying Edward's face, Mr Amery saw that assurances were necessary. 'Don't worry, she didn't blab it all over the place. Only a very few knew about it and they were the souls of discretion. I was put in the picture so that I could make a decision. With hindsight, we know that being in love with a lady on the enemy side did *not* affect your performance and judgement – but I couldn't assume that at the time, could I?'

'I take your point,' Edward muttered.

Mr Amery gazed at him, waiting for a denial that he had been in love with Annaliese. It was not forthcoming.

'Far be it from me to put ideas into your head,' Mr Amery said after observing Edward's mental turmoil. 'Do you have any inclination to go to see the lady?'

The reply was weighed with such agonising care that it seemed it would never come. 'Yes,' Edward said at last.

'You think it might be beneficial?'

'I don't know. One can but try.'

'One can,' Mr Amery agreed. 'On the other hand, one must be careful not to put one's head in a noose.'

Edward smiled. 'One must also be conscious that there is a risk of stirring up a major diplomatic embarrassment.'

'Not necessarily,' Mr Amery replied. 'From what we were reading when your Habsburg chum turned up, I'd say the situation in Berlin mitigates against that. Make a mess of it and you'd end up as just another body. Someone *might* have the time and inclination to try identifying you, but I doubt it.'

They stared at each other. This was the point of no return, the stage at which they either forgot the idea, or committed themselves to it.

'I'd like to have a go,' Edward said.

Mr Amery decided that it was time to carry out a thorough inspection of his finger-nails. 'Those identification papers we made such a good job of forging . . . Did you, by any chance, bring them with you?'

Edward nodded. 'Yes. And my pistol.'

'Do you know, I'd forgotten about that,' Mr Amery said. 'I must relieve you of it one of these days!' He was thoughtful. 'Perhaps it *is* time we found out what the Germans are up to.'

'Could you justify sending me on that basis?' Edward asked.

'Only if I have to – after the event, as it were.'

Edward understood. 'I'll make sure nothing goes wrong.'

'How long do you think you'd need?' Mr Amery asked.

Edward pulled a face. 'Does anyone know what travelling conditions are like between here and Belgium?'

'It's reasonable along the coast. I imagine that the direct route is out of the question.' Everything from Amiens to Lille had, of course, been smashed to smithereens by the War.

They talked round it for an hour, digging up one difficulty after another, assembling a host of good reasons for trying to forget that

Leopold von Habsburg had ever appeared with news of Annaliese. But not for an instant did they give up the assumption that Edward was going to Berlin.

'I'd like you to do two things for me,' Mr Amery said. 'First, sleep on it. Then, if you're still of the same mind, I must insist that you tell your friend Lewis Peters all about it *and* listen to what he says. If he forbids you to do it, that's the end of it. Right?'

Edward agreed.

Soon after ten o'clock the following morning, he was in the Ambassador's private apartments. There had, of course, been no question of sleep, but the interminable night with its elation and despair, hope and fear had left Edward so drained that he appeared calm and lucid. As he told of Annaliese and himself, Lewis listened impassively, Frances with barely suppressed excitement.

'It's the most thrilling and romantic story ever!' she cried when it was over.

'Well, yes, that's one way of looking at it,' Lewis replied. 'I could equally describe it as fantastic beyond belief, ludicrous, dangerous, and totally impossible.'

'Spoil-sport,' Frances hissed and stuck her tongue out at him.

Lewis laughed. 'I said *could*, darling. A mere hypothesis.'

'Does that mean you'll give it your blessing?'

'Yes, I will – if . . .' Lewis curtailed Frances's glee with a stern look. 'Edward must understand what's happening in Berlin. I have up-to-date and accurate information. If he still feels like going after I've put him in the picture, I'll help him.'

To escape from Frances's unruly effervescence, Lewis took Edward into his study. They were hidden away for a very long time and both looked grim when they emerged.

'It isn't possible?' Frances said dolefully.

'Yes, it is,' Lewis replied. 'It's just that I've left him with no illusions about what he'll be facing. Now, look, Frances, will you look after Edward for a few hours? Feed him and *please* try to keep him on an even keel. I want to fix him up with a set of papers.'

That afternoon, as the January dusk was closing in, Frances and Lewis Peters, accompanied by Mr Amery, took Edward to the Gard du Nord for a train to Calais. The documents that Lewis had given Edward, added to those he had used during the War, covered every imaginable eventuality. They were all acutely aware of the *unimaginable*.

In the last minute before the train pulled out, Frances asked the question that exposed the perilous venture's lack of clear purpose.

'What are you proposing to do with this Archduchess?'

Momentarily, Edward was at a loss. 'Well . . . assuming that I can find her, I shall talk to her.'

'With a view to what?' Lewis asked.

'Er . . . perhaps I can persuade her to go to Portugal . . . to be with her parents, you know.'

It was more conjecture than answer.

Lewis and Frances Peters waited until the tail lamps of the train were disappearing into the gloom before betraying their misgivings in an exchange of troubled looks.

'Good luck, my boy,' Mr Amery said quietly.

8

January 1919
'I knew you would come'

Two months after the Armistice, Western Europe seemed to be in worse chaos than at the height of the War. It was, Edward soon discovered, the consequence of a bad-tempered apathy. Without the harsh military discipline that had kept things moving, every minor official was free to do as he pleased: many turned themselves into dictators.

Forced to spend Sunday night in Calais after arriving three hours late, Edward found a *pension* close to the railway station. Disturbed by the noise from the marshalling yards, he slept badly. At five o'clock, he abandoned the uncomfortable bed and decided on an early start. Despite an incessant stream of promises, the first train to the east did not appear until half past eleven. It eventually reached Liege at midnight.

As luck would have it, there was a connection to Hannover within an hour. But, for reasons that were shrouded in sullen secrecy, the 225-mile journey took seventeen hours. After two days with little sleep and food, Edward was close to collapse and dismayed by the prospect of searching for more overnight accommodation.

It was, however, time for a miracle. There was a vacant first-class sleeping-berth on the express that was due to leave for Berlin at 7 p.m. Better still, the train – which had come from Amsterdam – arrived on time. Over a splendid meal in the opulent dining-saloon, the German head waiter moved discreetly down the centre aisle, informing passengers that they were being diverted via Brunswick and

Magdeburg. To Edward, the man made a point of confiding that this route was expected to be 'safer'. With his exhaustion now multiplied by good food and half a bottle of decent wine, Edward scarcely minded where the train went as long as he slept.

He did, for ten hours, not waking until eight o'clock on the morning of the fourth day of his journey, Wednesday 15 January.

The train was stationary. Bleary-eyed, Edward drew the blinds to find himself confronted by a view that was instantly recognisable. The vast expanse of water was the Grosser Wannsee against the sombre backdrop of the Grunewald. The centre of Berlin lay ten miles ahead; not far behind the train was Potsdam. Astonishingly, entry into Germany during the small hours had been achieved without anyone bothering to check papers.

The attendant who answered Edward's call for hot water said that they had been standing here for an hour. In answer to the inevitable question, the man beckoned Edward into the corridor to look out of a window on the other side of the carriage. Away to the north-east, three separate palls of smoke hung over the city, one of them billowing two thousand feet into the crystal-clear morning air. Shrugging, the attendant went on his way.

Edward began to shave. As he lathered his face, the mirror shuddered to the sound of gunfire. That, too, was in the centre of Berlin and had the distinctively percussive thud of heavy artillery.

It was time to focus his mind on what Lewis Peters had told him.

As Sir Maurice Hankey had said, the German Army marched home from the Western Front. Once across the Rhine, the bands played and every soldier held his head high. It must, Edward reflected, have been an astonishing, very moving sight. Each regiment returned to the city or town in which it had been raised. Almost without exception, they found an organisational shambles. The Kaiser had gone, his Government collapsed, and the people who said that they were running the country had no idea what they were about. Gradually, over a period of two weeks, the conscripted men had demobilised themselves, sneaking away in twos and threes to find their families. The regulars went to their garrisons, took a long, hard look at the country for which they had fought, and were disgusted.

The Social Democrats, struggling in a political vacuum, were discredited and reviled from all sides. Those on the right were branding them as the traitors who had stabbed the Army in the back; the left called them incompetent milksops, polluted by half-hearted co-operation with Kaiser Wilhelm, and incapable of facing, let alone solving, the country's problems. What was so difficult to grasp was the sheer, breath-taking speed at which the ensuing disaster had unfolded.

The left, incited by Rosa Luxemburg and Karl Liebknecht, had engineered anarchy on a scale to cause a nervous breakdown of the German psyche. Communists and Spartacists invaded the Reichstag to disrupt debates; their incessant processions and demonstrations turned Berlin into a bedlam; workers were persuaded or intimidated into joining lightning strikes. To hammer the last nail into the coffin of law and order, the hard left armed itself and launched a campaign of violence.

After looking on in outraged disbelief, the Army acted. While the Government sank deeper into paralysis, officers formed new, independent regiments. They were called *Freikorps*. These groups of up to 2,000 battle-hardened men, welded together by a fearsome *esprit de corps*, based themselves in Army barracks, thus acquiring a secure base and full logistic support, including field artillery.

To the best of Lewis Peters's knowledge, *Freikorps* troops began to impose a particularly brutal type of order in Hamburg and Bremen on 18 December. A few days later, there were reports of serious trouble in the south, round Munich. Berlin seemed to be avoiding the worst of the trouble, then, on 8 January, a Spartacist revolt erupted. Fearful that it was losing control of the city, the Government asked the officer commanding the Potsdam *Freikorps* to act.

'You see what this means,' Lewis had said. 'The Government is trying to save its miserable neck by making use of a gang of thugs. And don't run away with the idea that this is a one-sided contest. Our information is that the left is as well-armed as the *Freikorps*. Berlin is an arsenal and they've been helping themselves to weapons. You're probably going into the middle of a pitched battle.'

There never had been a reason to doubt Lewis's assessment. The sound of the big guns echoing across the Grunewald was proof that Berlin was in the throes of something frightful.

The firing stopped at nine-thirty. Fifteen minutes later, the train jolted into timid motion. After covering a mile at a slow walking pace, the brakes were slammed on. Lowering the window and sticking his head out, Edward saw a group of men at the trackside in conversation with the driver: they carried rifles and wore red arm-bands. After five minutes of acrimonious argument, the men gave up and faded into a plantation of fir trees.

There was another hour of stopping and starting before the driver was able to cover the last five miles into the Friedrichstrasse Station without further check. Warily, taking care not to be in too much of a hurry, Edward made his way through the dense crowd in the booking-hall. Hundreds of people, white-faced with fear and stifled panic, were trying to leave Berlin, many with nothing more than the clothes on their backs.

Edward paused outside the station, absorbing the atmosphere. The sense of danger was heightened by the realisation that he was, for the first time in his life, completely alone. Dieter Hoffmann would be up to his neck in the Spartacist cause – assuming that he was still alive – and, to shield her from the risk attached to the venture, dear old Frau Schmidt must not be involved. Crossing Wilhelmplatz, Edward turned towards the Hotel Viktoria on Taubenstrasse, an expensive but unobtrusive establishment that was a favourite with visiting businessmen. Ascending the steps to the entrance, he assumed the well-rehearsed persona of a Swiss journalist.

The clerk on the reception desk laughed at the suggestion that there might not be a room vacant. For the past three weeks, there had been a choice of eighty: for some strange reason, people had stopped coming to Berlin. Pretending to share the man's black humour, Edward signed the register. Taking a suite with a private bath, he scrubbed away the grime of the journey and changed into a fresh shirt and underwear. Before leaving the hotel, he gave instructions that the discarded garments must be laundered that afternoon.

As Edward turned into Wilhelmstrasse, a clock struck two, drawing attention to the silence. There was no traffic and few pedestrians. On the corner of Prinz Albrechtstrasse, a group of communists had set up a machine-gun behind a sandbag barricade. One of the men called a greeting to Edward and brandished a copy of *Die rote Fahne*, the newspaper edited by Rosa Luxemburg. Edward waved and strolled on casually, more grateful than ever for his *Lodenmantel*. He had bought the overcoat during his first winter in Vienna. It made him *look* right in Germany, and its voluminous pockets were an effective hiding-place for all manner of things. Reassured by the concealed pressure of the pistol against his hip, Edward maintained his easy pace, secretly counting each step away from the machine-gun.

The Kaiser Frederick Infirmary was a five-acre sprawl of buildings near to Leipziger Platz, Berlin's most important traffic intersection. Spotting what was obviously the main entrance, Edward strode inside with the air of someone who knew exactly what he was doing and had every right to be doing it.

His confidence was sorely tested by the din of the distraught crowd in the cavernous lobby. Also, there was the smell.

Although they were extremely strong, disinfectant and other medical odours were unable to mask the stench of mutilation and violent death. The people were besieging two orderlies, inquiring after relatives. Mixed up in the jostling mob were badly wounded men in search of treatment.

Edward saw what was happening. The morning's shelling and fires had resulted in a great many casualties and the hospital's administration system was in tatters. In any case, what would he have said if everything had been under control. 'Excuse me, I want to talk to one of your nurses. Her real name is Annaliese von Habsburg, but she's bound to be calling herself something else. Could you tell me where to find her, please?'

Taking advantage of the confusion, Edward headed for the entrance to the wards.

No one challenged him – not even when he went into the larger wards to check that he had seen all the nurses. They and the doctors, harried from pillar to post, many with the blank expressions of people who had forgotten when they had last slept, stared straight through him.

There were more patients than beds. Men and women, injured by shrapnel, broken glass, and falling masonry, were lying on stretchers in the corridors. Some were quiet, too dazed, or near to death; others raved with pain. Their eyes followed Edward, pleading for help. Clenching his fists, he made himself ignore them.

After visiting each of the twenty wards without success, he retraced his steps and repeated the search. Was she working in an operating-theatre? Perhaps it was her turn to rest? How easy would it be to make a night tour of the hospital? Preoccupied, Edward took a wrong turning, walking some way along the corridor before realising his mistake. There appeared to be only one door. It was all of fifty yards away, set in the wall that sealed the passage. Lacking the nerve to explore what was obviously a private area of the Infirmary, Edward was on the point of wheeling round when a nurse emerged from a door that he had missed because it was almost obscured by two massive steel cupboards.

She was escaping from a conversation that had become tedious and came sidling out, her back to Edward. At the same time, she was drawing a heavy cloak over her shoulders. For a fraction of a second, she might have been anyone and he nearly walked away. Then he saw the golden hair beneath the constraint of the starched cap. There was the set of the head, too: as a farewell to the bore who had detained her, she was tilting her chin in that unique imperious way.

Edward's attempt to utter her name degenerated into what sounded like the gasp of a dying man. She was, at the very most, three paces from the door at the end of the corridor. At any instant, she would be through it in a flash.

Instead, she forgot her desire to flee and began to talk, arguing with someone. Just as suddenly, without apparent reason, Annaliese broke off in mid-sentence and turned to face Edward.

His overwhelming impression was that she was totally unsurprised to see him: it was astounding. Very slowly, they were walking towards each other. Edward saw that Annaliese was drawn and haggard, with grey patches under her eyes. The beauty was still there, but she was too weary to understand what was going on: *that* was why she was so calm. None of it was registering in her mind.

Her first words destroyed that idea.

'I knew you would come. I've been expecting it.'

'Why did you think that?'

'Are you here just to ask silly questions?' Annaliese smiled.

It was she who initiated their embrace. There was a brief kiss of greeting, then, with a sigh, she placed her cheek against him. Behind the cloying amalgam of hospital smells, Edward detected the fragrance of that golden summer, four and a half years and an entire civilisation ago.

Somehow, the dream acquired a hallucinatory kind of reality when he took a step back to study her. Instead of the exhausted woman in the unflatteringly shapeless nurse's uniform, Edward saw the staggeringly beautiful Archduchess on the dimly lit terrace of the Hofburg on a hot July night in 1914. Remembering their kiss and his hands on the pale-pink silk dress, he found himself light-headed with desire. As if to compensate for the lack of obvious excitement in their undemonstrative reunion, Edward was lusting after an illusion.

'How did you find me?' she asked, unwittingly bringing him down to earth.

'Oh . . . yes . . . I bumped into Leopold in Paris.' Edward put a great deal of effort into sounding composed and rational.

'Ah!' Her eyes flickered with that sardonic, Viennese amusement. 'He's done something useful . . . at last!' No questions, no attempt to comment on a miraculous coincidence: it was accepted as well-deserved, benign fate. She took his hand. 'Come!'

She led him to the door at the end of the corridor and they were outside, crossing a courtyard towards an imposing building that was set slightly apart from the rest of the hospital. 'This is the Officers' Wing,' Annaliese explained, steering him into a deserted lounge. 'Most of them have gone and no one seems to know what to do with it. Wait.' Edward was comforted by her brisk, no-nonsense attitude. It was a gust of fresh air that dispelled the ludicrous notions that had found their way into his mind. Tiredness and strain were making him vulnerable to flights of fancy. It must stop. There was a job to be done.

While Annaliese was away, two men looked into the room. One was on crutches, the other had lost an arm. Both were prime examples of the stiff-necked, arrogant Prussian officer class – one wore an eyeglass, through which he regarded Edward with distaste before they went away. As Annaliese returned with a tray, the clink of billiard balls came from a nearby room. Edward's mind was in total disarray: instead of jumping up to help Annaliese, he was wondering how one managed to play billiards with only one arm.

'This is the best coffee in Berlin,' Annaliese said. 'Actually, it may be the *only* coffee in Berlin! Someone brought it here from the Unter den Linden Palace after the Kaiser left.' She filled two cups from the jug and sat down. 'Now, what have we been doing with ourselves, eh? Shall I start?'

'Yes, please,' Edward said.

'Well, as soon as the War got into its stride, things were very bad in Vienna. We didn't beat Serbia and it was only a matter of time before Italy attacked us. The Government was discredited. The Emperor died. Father never stopped talking about leaving and it was obvious that Mama would have to give in or be ill. Eva – my maid, remember – was always saying that we should do something useful. I agreed with her, but no one was interested – not in me, at any rate. Any Habsburg was regarded as a liability!' Annaliese paused for a sip of coffee. 'Eventually, Eva and I decided that Germany was worth helping, so we went. That was in November nineteen-seventeen.'

'Without telling anyone?' Edward asked.

'We left notes. It was on an evening when Father and Mama were at the Hofburg. Eva persuaded one of the chauffeurs to take us to the station and we got on a train. We crossed into Germany at Rosenheim and I changed my name to Gruber.' She smiled at the look on Edward's face. 'It was too easy! If you hadn't got proper identification papers, they gave you some.'

'And you became nurses?' Edward prompted.

'Yes – with the Army! Did Leopold tell you that?'

'No.'

'I expect he'd forgotten – or perhaps he wasn't very interested.' Annaliese saw that she was right. 'Well, they gave us two weeks training . . . imagine, a whole two weeks! We were sent to a field hospital in Belgium. It was near a place called Ieper. Have you heard of it?'

'Ypres,' Edward replied. 'British soldiers pronounced it as "Wipers".'

'I won't tell you what the Germans called it,' Annaliese said. 'We were evacuated two months before the end . . . *Waffenstillstand* . . . what's that in English?'

'Armistice,' Edward said. 'This was when Hindenburg and Ludendorff were running the country?'

Annaliese pulled a gruesome face. 'We never realised what a mess things were getting into. As a matter of fact, Eva was talking about this yesterday. We came to the conclusion that we aren't sure why we're still here.'

'You don't think Germany's worth it now?' Edward asked gently.

'Pah!' Annaliese waved a hand disdainfully. 'But where do we go? Eva can return to Austria, but I can't. What about you? What have you been doing?'

'I had special duties during the War,' Edward said. His manner made it clear that he had no intention of elaborating. 'I'm one of the cogs in the British delegation at the peace conference in Paris.'

'And Leopold?' Annaliese asked. 'What's he doing there?'

'He claims to be part of an unofficial delegation representing Austria. But the fact of the matter is that no one's interested in your country at the moment. There's talk of a separate conference later – much later, I expect.'

Annaliese shrugged. 'There's nothing to talk about. What's Austria without its Empire? Six million people with nothing to look forward to – except being part of Germany. And Vienna? What will become of that? It will be the biggest museum in the world.' She lifted her chin defiantly, determined to keep control of her feelings. 'When did you arrive?'

'A few hours ago. It took me nearly four days from Paris. I'm at the Viktoria.'

'And you think I should go to my parents in Lisbon?'

Disarmed by her candour, Edward laughed. 'Naturally.' This was better, he told himself. She intended making his task easy.

Annaliese considered it and shook her head. 'No, Edward, I couldn't do that. I won't forgive Father for the way he betrayed the Family.'

'Annaliese, I'm sure he did no such thing. Self-interest isn't a crime. And what about your mother? She must be worried sick about you.' While the sound of his annoyance reverberated in the high-ceilinged room, their eyes locked and they both asked themselves the same question: had he ever used her Christian name before? Yes, once, on the terrace of the Hofburg when he had declared his love. 'You can't stay here,' Edward said quietly. 'Terrible things are going to happen.'

'They have been for over a week,' Annaliese replied. 'It's been worse in the north. All the sane people believe that Germany will destroy itself.'

'Well?' Edward demanded. 'It's obvious, you *can't* stay.'

'So, what do you suggest?' To his amazement, there was mischief in her eyes: despite everything, that mercurial temperament was unbowed.

'You'd better come back to Paris with me,' Edward said.

'I don't like Paris. It was awful before the War and I expect it's worse now!'

Inexplicably, and at the worst possible time, she was behaving like a spoilt child who rejects a treat because it isn't *quite* right. Edward saw red.

'For God's sake, you don't have to *stay* there. Once I've got you out of this damned place, you can go wherever you please!'

In the ensuing silence, Annaliese was torn between enjoying Edward's contrite misery for having shouted at her, and recognising that he was right.

'I shall have to talk to Eva,' she said at last.

'Where is she?' Edward asked irritably.

'Asleep. She was on duty for over thirty-six hours.' Annaliese frowned thoughtfully. 'It's not only her opinion I want . . . She must come with me.'

Edward said the first thing that came into his head, 'That's impossible.'

'Why?' The spoilt child had been replaced by an angry woman. 'Will I be more than enough trouble?'

'Frankly, yes.' Edward was surly. 'I can't begin to imagine all the things that can go wrong between here and the French border. Can Eva speak French, or English – even a little?'

'No.'

'Then she's a liability. I'm sorry to use such a word, but these are desperate times.'

Annaliese nodded. 'I know that, Edward, believe me. But I won't leave without her.'

They talked and argued until their heads reeled, not noticing that dusk was falling.

'I have to go back on duty,' Annaliese said. 'And you must be in your hotel before it's dark. We've heard that the Spartacists are planning something big for tonight.'

'What have we decided?' Edward asked wearily.

'We shall see tomorrow,' Annaliese replied calmly. 'I will talk to Eva, and you will think – hard. I shall come to your hotel for lunch.'

'But . . .'

She cut him short with a kiss. 'Please be patient. Can another night make any difference after what we've endured? Come, I will show you a quick way out.'

Before they parted, she initiated another kiss, smiling with satisfaction when it was over. 'Go quickly,' she murmured. 'And remember Eva. I will *not* go without her.'

And, knowing that he would want to stand there arguing, she faded away.

At about eight o'clock that evening, what sounded like a full-scale battle was unleashed less than half a mile from Hotel Viktoria. In the dining-room, Edward and the handful of other residents carried on eating with self-conscious concentration.

The din was short-lived, stopping as abruptly as it had begun after barely fifteen minutes. Everyone pretended that the silence was not more unnerving than the frightful din that had preceded it. Without going so far as to admit to being nervous, most of the staff joined the residents in the main saloon. Edward found himself engaged in an earnest discussion of postage stamps with a Dutch engineer who was in Berlin on Government business.

At nine-thirty, a waiter from a neighbouring hotel arrived with news. A group of Spartacists had battered their way into the *Freikorps* barracks in a captured armoured car. Seizing a fortified sentry-post in a corner of the quadrangle, the Spartacists used the *Freikorps*' own machine-guns to carry out a massacre. Over fifty men of the Potsdam Regiment were killed, then, to cap it all, the Sparticists had escaped.

No one wanted to believe it. But nor, as time passed, did anyone show the slightest inclination to go to bed. The Dutch engineer began strumming at the piano; a waiter who had worked in Manila told outrageous stories about Filipino women; Edward found three men who could play bridge – albeit badly; there was a constant supply of coffee from the kitchen. Midnight came and went. People were nodding off, yet no one was prepared to brave the loneliness of a bedroom.

The first artillery salvo shattered the nervous calm at four minutes past one. The roar of the guns was followed by the shell-bursts, close enough to give the impression of an earthquake. While everyone in the saloon tried to think of a joke, a convoy of vehicles, some with caterpillar tracks, clattered down the street. The guns fired again. This time, one of the shells hit the roof of a building opposite.

With a superb show of sang-froid, the manager sighed and rose to his feet. A fine dust drifted down from the ceiling as he spoke. 'Gentlemen, Hotel Viktoria has always been famous for its wine cellars. Since the *Freikorps* appear to be holding an exercise, may I suggest that we go down to ensure that no harm comes to my choice vintages?'

The idea was greeted with the exaggerated joviality of relief. Edward, who was near the end of the disciplined procession, noticed that no one bothered to lock the hotel's front doors.

Because of the wide ventilation slits at pavement level, the cellar gave no reduction in the noise of the artillery. The thudding of guns and shells was deafening and painful. There were several crescendos in the devilish hubbub as nearby buildings were struck and the lights flickered, sometimes going out altogether for as long as ten seconds. Unlike his companions, Edward was entertained by the alarming phenomenon; in the days when he had posed as an expert on electricity generation and distribution, people would have looked to him for an explanation.

The big guns stopped at a few minutes to two, but there was no peace. Several savage street battles broke out, one of them immediately outside the hotel. For a while, part of the fight spilled *inside*: Edward countered the worried looks of those near to him with an airy confidence. It only *sounded* that way, he told himself, it was a freak acoustic effect. His partners in fear read his thoughts and tried to believe him.

Gradually, the conflict – together with its cacophony of shouts and screams – shifted. By four o'clock, it seemed to be concentrated on the warren of narrow streets off Mittelstrasse, slightly to the north of Unter den Linden and five hundred yards from Hotel Viktoria. Twenty minutes more and the crackle of rifles was still further away and becoming sporadic. The manager and Edward exchanged questioning looks, nodded, and led the way upstairs.

The lobby was a shambles. Both inner and outer front doors were wrecked and all the furniture within a five-yard radius was upended. Edward thought that it was a desperate attempt to build a makeshift barricade. Then, between what was left of the entrance doors, he discovered an infinitely more gruesome remnant of the night's mayhem. There was a pool of blood on the mosaic floor, streaked by the victim's heels when he had been dragged away by his comrades. The manager sent for hot water and scrubbing-brushes.

Edward declined the brandy and schnapps that were circulating: far too many cigarettes had made him befuddled enough. He was contemplating going outside for a breath of air when a friend of the manager's arrived, breathless after a frenzied bicycle ride from the *Freikorps* barracks. He was a volunteer civilian cook for the Potsdam Regiment and brought a report of the night's events. Edward listened and was appalled.

Rosa Luxemburg and Karl Liebknecht were dead, the woman clubbed to a pulp by rifle butts, the man shot. To advertise the deliberate act of savagery, their bodies had been slung into the Spandau Canal. Edward lit yet another cigarette.

It mattered not a row of beans whether the story was true or false: the mere suggestion that the icons of the Left had been murdered would be sufficient to rouse what remained of their followers to the final fury. If Berlin had been unsafe hitherto, the next twenty-four hours would see it turn into a veritable death-trap. It was pointless waiting to see if Annaliese were able to keep her promise to come to the hotel for lunch, something had to be done long before then.

Edward considered going to the hospital at once. Hard reason prevailed, however. The calm in the city was deceptive. There would be snipers in every alley, prepared to shoot at anything that moved. Stealing himself to wait for dawn – not due for another two hours – Edward finally went upstairs to his room. After a wry glance at the freshly laundered linen that a maid had placed neatly on his undisturbed bed, he began to bathe and shave, half-convinced that it might be a week before another opportunity to do so arose.

With the coming of an unwilling January sunrise, the artillery began again. Listening to the noise, Edward was sure that the guns had been shifted. Earlier, they were firing from the Alexanderplatz; now they were probably in the Tiergarten, nearly two miles west of their original position. The fall of shot reinforced the impression of a change in tactics: at least three separate areas were being shelled.

Half an hour later, after a terrifying journey through streets littered with rubble and corpses, Edward discovered that one of the targets was the Kaiser Frederick Infirmary.

The scene was horrendous. One end of the main block, badly damaged by two direct hits, was burning from top to bottom. The fire was raging through all four storeys while attempts to control it were hampered by a lack of equipment and blind panic. Plunging into the crowd, Edward heard the opinion that the *Freikorps* intended to destroy the hospital because it was sheltering and treating large numbers of Spartacists.

After wasting precious minutes in an attempt to bring order to a distraught mob who were making things worse for the patients they were rescuing, Edward was overcome by an urge to find the building in which he and Annaliese had spent the previous afternoon. Dodging the shower of debris from a further collapse of the roof, he dashed blindly into the smoke and confusion. Rounding a corner into a courtyard, he collided with a nurse, knocking her flat.

It was Annaliese. Her cap was gone, her apron was spattered with blood, and she was clasping a document case to her bosom.

'Take me away,' she said as Edward helped her up. Her voice, deathly calm, was at odds with her wild appearance.

'What about your maid?' Edward asked.

Annaliese's composure burst into fragments. 'There she is, look. Over there. Third from the left!' She was screaming and pointing.

Peering through the smoke, Edward saw the row of sheet-covered bodies in the shelter of a high wall.

'They've killed her!' Annaliese went on. 'The pigs have killed Eva. We were fools to believe that this country deserved us. Take me away!'

'What about your belongings?' Edward asked.

'They don't matter. This is all I need.' Annaliese hugged the document case tighter still.

'Your maid . . .' Edward groped for words. 'Her funeral . . . don't you want to . . .?'

'What do I care?' Annaliese was on the brink of hysteria. 'It will be attended to. They're good at burying people. They've done nothing else since Cousin Franz was murdered. Don't just stand there . . . I want to go.'

'Where?'

'Anywhere!' It came out as a piercing shriek that brought Edward to his senses. Taking her hand, he started to run.

On the way down Prinz Albrecht Strasse, a gun battle erupted less than a hundred yards in front of them. Edward dragged Annaliese into a side street, but not before they had seen two men collapse in their death throes. Cutting through the Leipzig Strasse, they found *Freikorps* infantry preparing to storm a building in which Spartacists were hiding. Having thrown gas grenades in, the soldiers were fixing bayonets. Edward and Annaliese scuttled past with averted eyes.

They received an extraordinary welcome at Hotel Viktoria. Without a single question being asked, everyone understood and sympathised with Annaliese and Edward.

'You're taking her to Switzerland?' the manager asked, basing the deduction on Edward's bogus nationality.

'Yes. Will you look after her while I go to the station to inquire about trains?'

'Save your time, my friend. There aren't any.'

'Why not?' Edward was dismayed.

'The *Freikorps* guns have destroyed bridges and signal-boxes. There will be no trains for days.'

'This is Bahnhof Friedrichstrasse?' Edward asked.

'Yes.'

'What about Anhalter Bahnhof? Could we get to Dresden – or Leipzig, perhaps?'

The manager shrugged hopelessly. 'Maybe. It depends on how many thousand people have the same idea.'

Edward understood. Looking at Annaliese, who was slumped in one of the few unbroken armchairs, he saw that she had lapsed into shock. Her eyes were dull and unseeing, every line of her body indicated exhaustion and defeat. She had nothing left and he was responsible for her. He had to think of something – *anything* – to get them out of this doomed city.

The Dutch engineer had an idea. 'Why not motor to Dresden? It's no more than a hundred and fifty kilometres. You could do it in three hours with a good machine.'

The suggestion seemed so ludicrously impractical that Edward very nearly laughed. 'I don't have a vehicle,' he said. A thought came to him. 'I suppose it wouldn't be too difficult to "acquire" one in all this mayhem.'

'But there is no need,' the Dutchman said grandly. 'I have a beauty . . . in the garage at the back of the hotel. It's a Benz coupé . . . forty horsepower . . . a wonder. And the petrol tank is full.'

'That's very kind,' Edward said. 'But how do I get it back to you?'

'My friend, there is no need to bother about that,' the Dutchman chuckled. 'It isn't *my* motor. The German Government has lent it to me. If this lunatic asylum ever gets back to normal, I shall tell them that one of their beloved *Freikorps* officers requisitioned it at the point of a gun.'

'Are you sure?' Edward asked eagerly.

'There is nothing easier.'

There was a burst of frantic activity. Edward dashed upstairs for his belongings, created great amusement by insisting on paying for the room that he had been unable to use, then had the hotel turned upside-down for a Baedeker motoring-map. Finally, Annaliese was guided through the kitchens to the garage. She gave no sign of either understanding or caring about what was happening. The Benz's engine fired at the first attempt and everyone shouted their good wishes as Edward drove out of the yard.

It was straightforward at first. Despite the mounting evidence of crisis and total disorder in the city, Edward began to think that they were going to get away without trouble. In Friedenau, a howitzer shell screamed low over the Benz, fired from a battery of guns that the *Freikorps* had set up in the Grunewald. The projectile exploded on a road junction half a mile to the east of the speeding car. Watching the explosion, Edward mentally complimented the gunners on an excellent piece of ranging.

Ten minutes later, in Lichterfelde, an almost-complacent Edward was horrified to see a column of men and armoured cars ahead of him. Swerving into a side street, he began to improvise an alternative route towards the main road for the south. Suddenly, after what he hoped would be the last turn, he was slamming on the brakes to avoid running into a road block. There was a brazier, a red flag, and a tarpaulin hut from which a huge man lumbered. The way his rifle was slung over his shoulder identified him as a Spartacist. With insolent, suspicious slowness, he sauntered to Edward's side of the Benz's cab.

'Papers,' he ordered.

'What authority do you have?' Edward demanded.

The man sneered and tapped the barrel of his rifle. 'This, comrade.'

'Go to hell!' Edward snapped.

'Good.' The Spartacist laughed, exhaling the sickly smell of cheap spirits. 'Very good.' From the corner of his eyes, Edward saw faces at the windows of a house behind the tarpaulin hut: this was probably one of their last hiding places. Instead of lying low or disappearing, the idiots were drawing attention to themselves in this ludicrous, mock-heroic way. The big man's eyes narrowed. He was studying Annaliese, huddled in her cloak. 'That woman's a nurse,' he said.

'No, she isn't,' Edward retorted.

'You're a liar, comrade. We need a nurse. Here, let me see.'

The man climbed on to the running-board and lunged across Edward to tug at Annaliese's cloak. Edward made no attempt to stop him, devoting his energy to extracting the pistol from his overcoat pocket. When he pulled the trigger, the muzzle of the weapon was pressing against the man's chest. The Spartacist spun backwards, crashing to the ground like a felled tree.

For some reason, the men inside the house were slow on the uptake. The Benz was moving – with Edward mounting the pavement to go round the blockage – before any of them made a move. What few retaliatory shots were eventually fired at the accelerating motor were wildly inaccurate.

With Annaliese appearing to be unmoved by the dreadful incident, Edward drove for ten miles at top speed. He was in the grip of a deep satisfaction: a job that was next-to-impossible had been carried out with an efficiency that had proved ruthless when the final crisis threatened to ruin everything. There was not so much as a flicker of regret at killing the self-appointed commissar. The wretched man's comrades-in-arms would be lucky if the *Freikorps* were as mercifully swift. It came as a surprise when Annaliese's voice, now enhanced by a little of its old timbre and musicality, punctured his thoughts.

'I have the oddest feeling.'

'Oh? What's that?' With his eyes fixed firmly on the road, Edward's interest was slight.

'Has this been your first visit to Berlin?' Annaliese asked.

'What makes you think it wasn't?' Edward knew that he sounded evasive.

'You seem to know it very well.'

'Not really,' Edward replied. 'I just followed my nose and hoped for the best.'

For a few moments, Annaliese gave the impression that she was satisfied with this. 'One day, perhaps you'll tell me the truth,' she said softly.

Looking at her, Edward saw that she was smiling in a way that dispelled some of her careworn exhaustion. 'Yes,' he agreed. 'I might.'

After a journey through a countryside that seemed a million miles away from the agony of Berlin and other northern cities, they reached Dresden at twelve-thirty. The trusty Benz coupé was abandoned in a side street near the main railway station. Edward left a note to say that the vehicle was the property of the German Government. Then, while he gave the bonnet a fond pat, Annaliese planted a kiss on one of the front mudguards.

Neither of them had ever visited the old capital of Saxony. Under the clear blue sky of a fine but bitterly cold January day, Dresden was beautiful and untroubled, wistfully reminiscent of the cultured well-being that had been pre-war Europe. Annaliese and Edward exchanged a glance that said they would be happy to stay for a few days, enjoying the urbane serenity. It was, of course, impossible: there was no guarantee that the lunacy of the north would not spread. Even as they shared their unspoken wishes, Edward was itching to go to the railway station for reservations on a train heading west.

But, as they stood on the corner, a most curious thing happened. As if the sleeplessness and strain of the last few days had suddenly descended on him in a great, overpowering mass, Edward was listless, incapable of movement or decision. By sharp contrast, although she was every bit as exhausted, Annaliese was imbued with fresh energy and spirit. She took control.

'We shan't be catching a train until this evening,' she said. 'In the meantime we have to eat and rest. Over there, look!'

She was pointing at the Schweizerhof, Dresden's finest hotel. They crossed the road and Edward took the establishment's best suite. He insisted on paying the daily rate in advance, but explained that he and his friend would actually be leaving after dinner. The attitude of the man behind the reception counter was puzzling.

'Why do you think he looked at me like that?' Edward whispered to Annaliese as they were shown to their rooms.

'Do you *really* not know?' she asked.

'Perhaps he suspects that I'm British,' Edward muttered.

'Let me tell you,' Annaliese said, very earnest and confidential. 'The only thing worrying that man was that you are *desperate* to enjoy an afternoon of passion with a bedraggled nurse that you've picked up off the streets.'

Edward was horrified. Fleetingly, it occurred to Annaliese that his reaction was strange: surely, most men would have treated it as a joke – especially after the experiences of the last twelve hours. Weariness, and her Viennese inclination to shrug problems away, took command.

But Edward's stuffiness re-emerged once they were inside the suite. Excited by the most luxurious accommodation she had seen in eighteen months, Annaliese bounced on the bed, testing its springy comfort. 'This is lovely,' she said. 'Can't we stay here tonight?' Fearing that Edward was about to explode into anger, she quickly added, 'That was *not* meant to be taken seriously.' Seeing that he seemed almost resentful, she distracted him by turning to the immediate future. 'I expect you want to see about a train and I must buy a few clothes. Shall we meet in the foyer in an hour?'

'Yes, that sounds sensible.' Edward reached for his pocket-book. 'You'll need money.'

'My dear Edward, I may have been working as a self-sacrificing menial, but that doesn't mean I'm without funds.' Annaliese's smile was teasingly reproachful as she held up the document case. 'Beneath this disguise, I'm still a Habsburg.'

Edward gave this statement careful thought as he walked to the railway station. It was true. Their short-lived adventure was nearly over. In a few days, it would all be forgotten and Annaliese would have gone her own way. But what on earth was that to be? What *was* going to happen when they reached Paris?

The answer came while he was in the queue at the booking-office window. Frances Peters! *She* would think of something.

The more he reflected on it, the happier Edward became with the idea. Finding a solution to the problem of a stateless Archduchess was something Frances would relish. Banishing himself to the lounge to allow Annaliese to take what she predicted was bound to be an hour-long bath, Edward ordered a large brandy to celebrate the rebirth of the confidence in the future that was so essential to his peace of mind.

The train left Dresden at eleven o'clock that night and arrived in Karlsruhe at seven-thirty the following morning. Annaliese and Edward knew nothing of the journey: they fell fast asleep the moment they climbed into bed in adjacent compartments of a first-class sleeping-car.

There were no connections to Paris. Instead, after a wait of just over an hour which enabled them to enjoy a good breakfast, they boarded a train to Metz. After crossing the Rhine the pace was leisurely for half an hour until, much as Edward had been expecting, they stopped in what appeared to be the middle of nowhere.

'What's happening?' Annaliese asked.

'The French border,' Edward said, getting up to open the window. 'This is the new European order at work.' He looked out.

'Well?' Annaliese asked. It had never occurred to Edward that she could sound so nervous.

'There's nothing to worry about,' he assured her. 'A few formalities, that's all.'

He did not mention the scale of the check that was being made, or that it was in the hands of the military authorities. At this border-post, the wartime allies seemed to be working together. Three French and two British officers boarded the train, the twenty-odd soldiers who lined the track, rifles at the ready, were evenly split between the two armies.

'Are you sure that this is going to be all right?' Annaliese asked, her face lapsing into the tense pallor of Berlin.

'Don't worry!' Edward was using a pocket-knife to unpick the hem of the lining of his overcoat. Annaliese watched in amazement as he withdrew a bulging envelope. 'This will do the trick.'

Fortunately for Annaliese's presence of mind, it was not long before the officer assigned to the coach in which they were travelling reached their compartment. A major in the Royal Military Police, he was taken aback to find himself dealing with a fellow Englishman. Then, the papers provided by Lewis Peters caused him to whistle in astonishment.

'Is this the genuine article?' the major asked.

'See for yourself,' Edward said easily. 'The last two sheets have all the authentication.'

'I believe you.' There was a pause as the officer studied Annaliese. 'What about your friend?'

'She's a German who supplied us with information during the War, 'Edward said. 'She needs protection now, of course, so I'm taking her to Paris.'

Without the faintest idea of how she did it, Annaliese remained silent and kept her face straight under the keen scrutiny that followed.

Satisfied, the major nodded. 'Very good. Have you been anywhere near Berlin?'

'We left it yesterday morning,' Edward replied.

'I understand things are pretty bad there.'

'Very bad indeed,' Edward said quietly. 'We were damned lucky to get out in one piece.'

'You won't have any problems now,' the major said. 'I've heard whispers about chaps like you. Good show! It's a pleasure to be of service.' Before leaving, the major shook Edward's hand.

Sensing Annaliese's need for a period of quiet thought, Edward put the papers away and sat down. Until the train began to move, some ten minutes later, she stared fixedly out of the window. When she finally turned her face towards him, she appeared to be austere.

'Shortly after the War started, Vienna was riddled with scandal,' she said. 'Everyone panicked and started hunting for scapegoats, you see. Dozens of people were arrested, mostly on trumped-up charges that were never pursued. One of them was a man called Anton Leitner. You remember him?'

Edward nodded.

'It emerged that Leitner was a most unsavoury individual,' annaliese went on. 'One of those implicated was a pianist by the name of Beckmann. You know the name?'

'I do,' Edward sighed. 'I presume that he had a great deal to say for himself.'

'He did – it didn't save him, though. He was shot. So was Leitner, by the way.'

'My name cropped up, of course,' Edward said.

Yes.' Annaliese was smiling. 'None of this was common knowledge. Father got it from Willauer – that ghastly man in charge of the Secret Police.'

'So you must think badly of me,' Edward said.

'Is that how it seemed when we met yesterday, in that hospital?'

'Well . . . no.' Edward said it, but he was far from convinced.

'Mama's view was that you were simply doing a job,' Annaliese said. 'She was impressed.'

And your father?' Edward asked guardedly.

'The same. He thought it was a pity Austria didn't have men like you – it might have saved us.'

'Yes . . . er . . .' Edward was uncomfortable. 'I'm sorry, Annaliese.'

'What for?' She made a grand gesture at the passing view. '*That's* all that matters – France and freedom!'

'That's right.' Edward's response was unenthusiastic. Feeling that Annaliese now had him at a substantial disadvantage, he wanted to get the whole thing over and done with.

'How long will we have to wait at Metz?' she asked brightly.

'I've no idea,' Edward replied churlishly, rebuffing her attempt to cheer him up. 'It's in the lap of the gods.'

In the event, the gods were smiling. Fifteen minutes after they reached Metz, a Luxembourg to Paris express steamed in. Diverted from the old route because of the dreadful damage round Verdun, the train was calling only at Bar-le-Duc and Châlons-sur-Marne and was scheduled to reach the capital at five-thirty. The journey that had taken Edward nearly four days on the way out was shrinking to less than thirty-six hours for the return leg. He began to look forward to the end of the mad adventure.

The restaurant-car staff took immense pride and pleasure in providing a lunch of pre-war magnificence. When they had eaten their fill and found secluded seats in the next carriage, Edward tackled the problem that could wait no longer.

'Annaliese, can I ask you to reconsider your refusal to join your parents?'

'You can ask, but it won't do you any good,' she replied, perfectly good-naturedly. 'I know that I shall *have* to make my peace with them eventually, but I'm nowhere near ready yet.'

'What about Leopold? Couldn't you set up some sort of home with him?'

'Where?' Annaliese's exasperation was visible. 'Do *you* know where he will decide to settle? In any case, my brother is playing dangerous games and I don't want to be anywhere near him.'

'Presumably, you have relatives everywhere?' It was a half-hearted suggestion that received the reply it deserved.

'What of it? I don't like many of them and they'll have problems enough without me.'

'That brings us back to Portugal.'

'No, Edward. For God's sake, how many times do I have to tell you? No, no, no!'

They were both angry and took refuge in an uneasy silence until Edward, at his wits' end to find a solution, resorted to pleading. 'Can't *you* think of something, Annaliese? I hate the idea of you sitting around in Paris with nowhere to go and no plans.'

The concentration that sharpened her face suggested that she was, for the first time, giving the matter serious thought.

'What's England like?' she asked abruptly.

'The finest country on earth,' Edward replied. 'I'm prejudiced, of course.'

'Hmm.' Annaliese looked for inspiration outside the window. 'I've heard all sorts of people speak well of it. The two best doctors at the hospital did their training in London . . . They both wished they'd stayed there.'

Edward saw it as a duty to curtail her wishful thinking before it ran out of hand. 'I'm sorry, Annaliese, that *isn't* something you could do. You saw what it was like at the French border: the frontiers are closed.'

'You couldn't tell the same story?' Annaliese asked.

'Not with any serious hope of being believed. That officer wasn't protecting his own country and there wasn't a civil servant in sight. I'm not sure what the position is with Britain, but I do know they're being very sticky about letting anyone in unless they're from the Empire or Dominions. I daren't think what the official line is with respect to the enemy.'

'The War's over,' Annaliese said.

'That's as maybe, but the strength of feeling is very great.' Edward clutched at a straw. 'Look, I'm on very good terms with our Ambassador in Paris . . . he'll be able to tell us if there are any loopholes.'

Annaliese wasn't listening: she was abstracted, struggling with a thought that was too big and exciting for her head. 'Would it make any difference if I were married to an Englishman?' she asked.

'Oh, yes. Definitely.' Edward's outlook and mental processes caused him to take an objective view of the suggestion: he saw it as nothing more than a theoretical possibility. 'That would make you a British citizen.'

Annaliese said nothing. She simply gazed at him, her face devoid of all expression. At least, that was how it began. Very gradually, her manner was changing. As the encouragement came into the blue eyes, making them as startling as in that long-ago summer, she was leaning forward, willing him towards the conclusion that struck her as both logical and desirable.

Thunderstruck, Edward gaped at her, refusing to accept what her mind was telling him.

'Berlin was bad,' Annaliese said. 'It distracted us from what we *should* have been thinking and saying to each other after all this time.' She reached for his hand. 'I've never stopped loving you, Edward.'

'Yes . . and I love you!' he said, close to shouting.

'Good.' Annaliese's smile was radiant. 'That solves *everything*, doesn't it?'

To show that his inhibitions and caution were intact. Edward raised an objection. 'What about your parents?'

'We'll let them know after we've done it,' Annaliese replied. 'They liked you.'

'Shouldn't you be finding a husband from one of the "approved" families?' Edward asked.

'They're all in hiding,' Annaliese said gaily. 'In any case, my reputation is sullied with them – it wasn't very good before the War. Now that I've been a nurse in *Germany* . . . well!' She rolled her eyes in comic horror. 'Will you ask your mother and father to come to Paris?'

'What?' Having failed to realise that the wedding would have to be in France, Edward was momentarily baffled. 'Oh, yes, I'm with you. Let's see how things work out first, shall we?' There were much more important issues at stake than his parents. 'Look, Annaliese, are you sure about this? It isn't one of your jokes?'

'When did I ever make jokes?' she protested. 'I've always been the most serious-minded person in the world.' She was losing the fight against laughter. 'Well, I'd *never* joke about a thing like this.'

'We're to be married?'

'Yes – except for one thing.'

'What's that?' Edward was alarmed. 'Is it because I'm a spy?'

Annaliese frowned. 'Have you stopped now?'

'Yes. When the peace conference is over, I shall go back to being an ordinary member of staff at the Foreign Office.'

'That's one less thing to worry about,' Annaliese said with mock gravity. 'That still leaves the original problem, though.'

'What is it?' Edward gibbered.

'I can't marry you until you've *asked* me,' Annaliese said. 'I think it's the least you can do.'

Flinging all his inherent constraint to the winds, Edward shot out of his seat and knelt before her. 'Your Imperial Highness, unworthy as I am, may I request the great honour of your hand in marriage?'

Joining in the pantomime, Annaliese assumed an imperious demeanour. 'You aren't *totally* unworthy, Mr Boothby-Graffoe, and you seem a steady sort of fellow with prospects. It could be said that you saved my life and that weighs heavily in your favour.' The air of grand condescension dissolved into a glowing smile. 'And I love you dearly. Yes, Edward, I will marry you.'

'I say, this calls for a celebration.' Edward scrambled to his feet. 'I wonder if they've got any bubbly in the diner?'

'They seemed to have everything else,' Annaliese said. 'Before you go dashing off, would you like to kiss me?'

When they reached Paris, Edward took Annaliese straight to the British Embassy. Frances was depressed because there was no official function that evening: despite her dislike of entertaining pompous dignitaries, she would have welcomed the opportunity to be doing something, rather than worrying about Edward. The unheralded arrival of her protégé *and* his lovely Archduchess transformed uneasy boredom into euphoria.

It was a joyous, unruly scene. While Frances indulged in uncontrollable delight over Annaliese, Lewis congratulated Edward on pulling off a remarkable exploit. Curiously, it was the discovery of the marriage that had been agreed during the closing stage of the journey that brought Frances back to earth.

'Annaliese must stay in the Embassy while we make the necessary arrangements!' she said. 'It's the only way.'

Lewis cleared his throat. 'You don't think I should enjoy having a go at pulling strings to get Annaliese into England so that the wedding can be held over there?' The wink he gave Edward showed that he did not expect to be taken seriously.

'How do you rate your chances of success?' Frances demanded.

Lewis shrugged. 'I have no way of telling, my dear.'

'To put none too fine a point on it, you don't have the faintest idea what the official position is, do you?'

'Er . . . no, I'm afraid I don't.'

'So we could be twiddling our thumbs for weeks?' Frances was nicely into her stride now.

'Months, actually,' Lewis admitted.

'Whereas Annaliese will definitely be a British subject if she and Edward marry here?'

'Indubitably.' Accepting defeat, Lewis became facetious. 'So, instead of trying to do things properly, we're going to harbour one of His Majesty's enemies?'

'Don't be ridiculous, darling! The poor girl is a refugee. If you can't handle a simple thing like that, you're not the man everyone says you are.'

Realising that the die was cast, Annaliese and Edward looked at each other. Annaliese was happy enough, but Lewis wondered about Edward: was all this happening too quickly for him? Frances swept the moment aside as she began to organise her adopted daughter.

'Let me show you to your room, my dear. You can have a bath before dinner, if you like. What are we going to do about clothes?'

'I bought these in Dresden,' Annaliese replied, indicating the dress and coat in which she had travelled. 'That's all I have.'

'Don't worry, I'm bound to have something that will do until we can get you to the shops.' Frances was enjoying herself hugely. 'Come along, I expect these men want to talk.'

In the vacuum that followed the departure of Frances and Annaliese, Lewis went to the sideboard to pour two tumblers of whisky. 'How *was* Berlin?' he asked quietly.

'Bloody!' Edward said.

'Reuters are reporting that Rosa Luxemburg and Karl Liebknecht were murdered on Wednesday night.'

'That was the rumour,' Edward replied. 'Because of it, all hell was being unleashed when we left.'

'Perhaps you could write me a report on what you saw,' Lewis said. 'It would be useful for a variety of reasons.'

'Of course.'

Lewis was slightly bashful as he turned to an infinitely more pleasant topic. 'If I may say so, Edward, your Annaliese is *quite* magnificent. My word, those eyes! You're a lucky chap. Frances has taken to her.'

'I noticed that,' Edward laughed.

'And she's very smitten with the romance of it all,' Lewis went on. 'It really is an amazing story.'

'Yes, I suppose it is.' Edward proved that he was slightly ill-at-ease by asking, 'What's been happening at the conference while I've been away?'

'Nothing!' Lewis pulled a face. 'Nothing that can go in the newspapers, at any rate. Lloyd George, Clemenceau, and Wilson are behind locked doors, arguing like cats and dogs. The rumour is that they're further than ever from an agreement on how and when to start the talks.'

Nearly four hours later, Edward heard the same – with cynical embellishments – from Mr Amery, who was still reading in a corner of the foyer at L'Hotel Jean-Jacques.

'Do you think that the conference won't ever start?' Edward said at last.

'On the contrary, I'm very much afraid that it will,' Mr Amery replied. 'But don't expect to see me cheering the outcome.'

There was a gloomy silence in which Edward skimmed through a letter from Beatrice which had arrived during his absence. After taking him to task for his failure to write since Christmas, she made much of the fact that Lady Alice was suffering from a severe chill.

'And this young lady of yours is safe and sound in the Embassy?' Mr Amery said, wanting to know more than the bare details that Edward had provided.

'She is,' Edward replied, smiling at the memory of the kisses he and Annaliese had exchanged before Frances had thrown him out.

'That's all very well, but she can't stay there indefinitely.' Mr Amery spoke as though revealing a great truth known only to himself. 'What are you going to do?'

'Marry her,' Edward said proudly. 'As soon as possible.'

Mr Amery had to overlook the cardinal rule that forbade him to exhibit surprise. 'Good God! Er . . . forgive me for saying so . . . isn't that somewhat *drastic*?'

'Slightly unusual, perhaps. It's what we both want, though.'

'Well, jolly good luck to you,' Mr Amery said warmly. 'Dare I hope for a chance of meeting this extraordinary lady?'

'I shall want you at the wedding,' Edward replied. 'Frances Peters is seeing to all the arrangements, but I shall need a best man.'

'Aren't I too old for that sort of caper?' Touched by the idea, Mr Amery hoped to be overruled.

'Certainly not.' Edward grinned. 'In any case, you'll *have* to do . . . there isn't anyone else I can ask!'

'What about Lewis Peters?'

'From what I gathered over dinner, he sees himself as giving the bride away,' Edward said.

'Hmm . . . in that case, you'll have to make do with me.' Mr Amery rubbed his chin reflectively, thinking that Archie should have been with them. 'You're taking her home after the wedding?'

'Yes.'

'Things don't sound too clever over there, by the way,' Mr Amery said. 'The influenza is bad – much worse than here.'

'My sister says so,' Edward replied, glancing again at Beatrice's letter. 'She reckons it's turning into an epidemic.'

'People are dying.'

'We shan't catch it,' Edward declared with brash confidence. 'Annaliese and I haven't been through the last four years to fall foul of some germ. It wouldn't dare attack us.' He stretched and yawned. 'Bed calls. I may sleep all weekend.'

9

19–28 January 1919
'I've wanted to do that since the day we met'

Not only was Frances Peters a born organiser, she knew people who could get things done at remarkable speed. After reaching Paris late on Friday, Edward imagined that nothing very much could be tackled until Monday. In fact, the jeweller who made a special journey to the Embassy on Sunday afternoon was the last major piece in the grand plan that Frances had drawn up and executed in little more than thirty-six hours. Although exhausted, she remained alert to the possibility that there were still ways in which she could help. An opportunity arose after Annaliese had chosen her rings – a sapphire cluster to mark their brief engagement and a platinum wedding-band – and the jeweller had returned to his shop near Sacre Coeur.

'I've tracked Leopold down and told him you're in Paris,' Edward said to Annaliese. 'He suggested that we went to his hotel for dinner this evening.'

'Which hotel is this?' Frances asked quickly.

'The Matignon on Rue de Varenne.'

'No, I don't think so!' Determination to protect Annaliese made Frances formidable. 'I'm told that your future brother-in-law is mixing with a very funny crowd.'

'I wouldn't put it that strongly,' Edward said.

'Why not?' Frances glared at him. 'He's tagged on to a rum bunch who shouldn't *be* here by rights . . . and it isn't a particle of good you looking like that, my lad. I've had a nice, long chat with Annaliese about *dear* Leopold. I won't have her running the risk of being goggled at by socialists – *especially* in a flea-pit like the Matignon!'

'What am I to tell him, then?' Edward asked, straight-faced in spite of Annaliese's expression.

'That he's to come *here*, of course. Honestly, Edward, Lewis says that you have a brilliant career ahead of you, but you can be such a nincompoop sometimes.'

At Annaliese's request, Edward had told Leopold nothing apart from the fact that his sister was in Paris and in good health. Leopold, in a hurry to keep an appointment and impatient of the merest delay, had not bothered to ask questions. He suggested dinner and dashed off to a waiting taxi. That evening, however, when Edward turned up at L'Hotel Matignon early and alone, it was a different matter. Leopold was suspicious and inquisitive.

'Liese at the British Embassy? Why? Is she some sort of prisoner?'

'Not at all.' Edward was intrigued by Leopold's attitude: he was plainly a man with a great deal to hide. 'She's simply enjoying privacy and protection as a private guest of the Ambassador.' Acting on a hunch, Edward added, 'If the press got hold of her, they might make a fuss – you wouldn't want that.'

'She can't stay there for long,' Leopold said, ignoring the allusion to his activities. 'Does she have plans?'

'Yes. If you come with me, she'll tell you all about them.'

Curiosity got the better of Leopold's wariness. After putting up a token show of distrust, he agreed to accompany Edward.

Frances, who had no wish to see Leopold until their meeting was unavoidable, had made wonderfully cloak-and-dagger arrangements. They entered the Embassy through a side entrance that was rarely used, except for fuel deliveries. A flight of dungeon-like stone steps took them to a remote first-floor landing where the carpet was patched and the ceiling cornices not entirely free of cobwebs. The room in which Annaliese was waiting was pleasant enough, however, with a welcoming fire, easy chairs, and a table set for a meal.

It was a convincing enough reunion – or so the casual observer would have believed. Sister and brother smiled, clasped hands, exchanged greetings, and embraced. But with his growing knowledge of Annaliese and her moods, Edward saw that she was doing no more than enacting a formality. And Leopold was behaving like a man attempting to calculate how embarrassing this rediscovered sister was likely to prove.

When the men had removed their overcoats and were sitting in front of the fire, Annaliese showed that she was not prepared to deal in platitudes. After telling Leopold that he was putting on too much weight, she tackled him about his presence in Paris. 'Edward tells me that you're part of an unofficial delegation. I suppose Neisser is in charge?'

'Yes, as it happens, he is.' Leopold was annoyed. 'You always were good at guessing-games, Liese.'

'And Dohnal will be mixed up in it, too.'

Unable to employ mockery a second time, Leopold became pompous. 'These are serious matters. *Someone* has to look after our country's interests.'

'That's what the family did,' Annaliese said. '*Without* ending up in the pockets of twisters like Neisser and Dohnal.'

'You're talking about the so-called good old days. Things are *very* different now, Liese.' Leopold paused, taking the decision to confront the problem head-on. 'I hope you aren't intending to be a nuisance?'

Annaliese regarded him with pity rather than anger. 'No, Leopold, I am not. Apart from having no desire to be anywhere near whatever games you're playing, I shall be leaving Paris on Thursday morning.' Waiting for his reaction, she added, 'I don't expect to be coming back.'

'Oh?' Leopold was guarded. 'You're going to Lisbon after all?'

'No.' Annaliese gazed at him in silence for a few moments. 'I'm marrying Edward on Thursday. We shall have a short honeymoon at St Malo, then we're going to England. Edward will have to come back to attend to his duties at the peace conference, but it will be a very long time before I return to Europe.'

Leopold's face was blank. Giving Annaliese up as a bad job, he turned to Edward. 'Do you know why she's spouting such nonsense?' he asked.

'It's the truth,' Edward said equably.

Leopold looked again at Annaliese. She smiled and held up her left hand, drawing attention to the sapphire ring. In pre-war Vienna, she had enjoyed access to a huge collection of jewellery: now, she was reduced to a single piece and she was immensely proud of it.

'You really mean this?' Leopold gasped.

'Most assuredly,' Annaliese said.

'Well . . .' Leopold needed another look at Edward to be fully sure. 'Congratulations are called for.' He stood up to shake Edward's hand. 'You're a good fellow, Boothby-Graffoe. I know you'll look after her.'

Edward, working hard to ignore Leopold's insufferably patronising attitude, was given the chance to convert his anger into laughter. Annaliese said, 'What he *will* do, is to keep me away from you, Leopold. You won't have to worry about what I think of your plans for Austria.'

'I'm pleased to hear it, sister dear.' It was an attempt at a joke. 'Am I invited to the wedding?'

'A car will pick you up on Thursday morning,' Edward replied. 'We're going to Fontainebleau to be married by the Mayor.'

'A *civil* ceremony?' Leopold stared at Annaliese with haughty disapproval. 'I don't think our parents would approve of that – particularly Mother.'

'Mama and Father wouldn't approve of lots of things,' Annaliese said sharply. Seeing that her point had been taken to heart, she continued in a more amicable tone. 'I know that Mama would prefer full Catholic rites, but we haven't the time to worry about religion . . . and please don't pretend that you do, Leopold. After the sheer awfulness of what we've been through, it hardly seems to matter.'

'How did you get everything arranged so quickly?' Leopold asked.

'Frances Peters – the Ambassador's wife – has done it all,' Annaliese replied. 'She's amazing. She knows everyone and they all owe her favours.'

'Very good.' Leopold turned to Edward. 'Are your parents pleased about this match?'

'I'm sure they will be,' Edward said. 'There's so much to do in such a hurry that I decided not to tell them. It will be a surprise.'

'Yes.' Leopold put enough meaning into the monosyllable to give Edward pause for thought. *Was* this terribly unconventional way of getting married the right thing to do? There was no alternative. Lord Douglas and Lady Alice – who would adore Annaliese – were bound to see the funny side of it. When people described him as 'solid' and 'dependable', Edward had always suspected that they meant 'dull'. This was going to show them.

'How long will you be staying in England?' Leopold asked.

'Three weeks, I hope,' Edward said. 'I have masses of leave owing to me.'

'And you think the conference can carry on without you?'

Edward decided to give Leopold part of what his facetious question was fishing for. 'It isn't a question of carrying on at the moment – the wretched business hasn't started yet. Nor will it until Woodrow Wilson comes down to earth.'

'Those of us who were defeated and fear exploitation have the highest hopes of President Wilson,' Leopold pointed out.

Edward nodded. 'I understand that and I hope you aren't *too* disappointed. Be careful of Wilson, though.'

'You think that Clemenceau and Lloyd George will wear him down?'

'There's every danger of that,' Edward agreed. 'But let me give you a piece of advice that should be regarded as confidential. Even if Wilson does get away with it at the conference, his own people may disown him and whatever he's negotiated.'

'Surely not?' Leopold was dismayed.

'Yes.' Edward insisted. 'Wilson is politically weak at home and the American Congress detests his scheme for a League of Nations. Be warned.'

Leopold barely had time to mutter his thanks before Annaliese's patience expired. 'That's enough statesmanship,' she said. 'I'd like us to settle down now and act as if we're part of a family. Do you think we can manage that?'

'Why not?' Leopold assumed an air of jollity and moved to his sister's side. Edward went to the dumb waiter that was enabling them to have dinner without interruption. Pressing the bell to alert the kitchen staff down below, he was suddenly disinclined to believe the events in which he was caught up.

Thursday 23 January was a fine, crisp day. Allowing themselves plenty of time for the fifty-mile drive to Fontainebleau, Edward and Mr Amery set out from L'Hotel Jean-Jacques at eight-thirty. In morning suits and silk cravats, they made a brave sight as Edward steered one of the Embassy's Rolls-Royces towards the Porte D'Orleans and the main road to Dijon.

Mr Amery was in a mood that could fairly be described as flippant. Edward refrained from seeking an explanation for the phenomenon, knowing that it would not be forthcoming unless and until his friend was good and ready. It proved to be a long wait. After driving for two hours, they reached Barbizon, a charming town within easy reach of their objective, and decided to kill time in a café rather than in some soul-destroying anteroom, praying that Annaliese would not be too late.

Mr Amery sidled into the revelation in an oblique way. 'I had a word with Sir Maurice Hankey yesterday afternoon.'

Edward stirred his coffee and waited.

'There's no prospect of a start to the conference,' Mr Amery went on. 'Hankey expects that the preliminary haggling could go on until the end of February.'

'Bad show,' Edward said gravely.

'Quite. Well, the upshot is that I thought I might as well grab a spot of leave myself. I'm going home tonight.'

'Cambridge?' Edward asked out of politeness.

'Quite near.' In a froth of exuberance, Mr Amery became tired of his own beating about the bush. 'The fact is, Edward, a lady of my acquaintance has written to say that she would like to see me.'

Edward blinked. 'You mean . . .?'

'I believe I do.' Mr Amery beamed.

There was no stopping him after that. He and the lady – who sounded as though she was something in the literary world – had been friends for ten years. An hour later as they parked in the main square of Fontainebleau, Edward was still trying to piece together the baffling course of the relationship. Sadly, the puzzle had to be abandoned just as it promised to surrender its secrets: Leopold, who was standing on the steps of the Town Hall, began waving his arms excitedly. Looking over his shoulder, Edward saw another Rolls-Royce entering the square. It was Lewis Peters's own vehicle, a brand-new machine that had been delivered only two weeks after the Armistice. Alongside the ethereal vision in white in the back of the Rolls, Frances, dressed up to the nines, was gesticulating furiously.

'What the devil are we supposed to do?' Edward muttered.

'Lord only knows,' Mr Amery replied. 'I've a vague idea what the drill is for church, but this is beyond me.'

Leopold came to the rescue. 'Get inside,' he ordered. 'We ought to be outside the Mayor's office.'

Edward led an undignified scramble up the steps, Mr Amery adding to the comic mayhem by clutching at the tails of his coat. Inasmuch as he was capable of thinking of anything else, Edward imagined Frances being vastly entertained.

Inside the grandeur of the Town Hall, help was waiting. The Mayor of Fontainebleau was proud of his town's historic past; he was also an unashamed royalist. To be granted the opportunity of marrying a Habsburg Archduchess to a man related to an English *seigneur* was an honour that André Duparc intended to execute to the very best of his abilities. Accordingly, the most elaborate and comprehensive preparations had been made. Two officials converged on Edward with respectful determination.

'Monsieur Boothby-Graffoe?'

'Yes, that's me.'

'Be so kind as to follow us. Monsieur le Maire is waiting to welcome you.'

André Duparc was a rotund man of boundless affability. Wearing his very best 'official' clothes, and sporting the sash of a *Chevalier* in the *Legion d'honneur*, he cut an imposing figure. Yet, so completely had his office been converted into a florist's shop, he seemed almost inconspicuous. The discovery that the ceremony was to be witnessed by *another* Habsburg drove him into raptures.

'Gentlemen, I am gratified to be of service to you,' he gushed.

'Today, I am the proudest man in all France. Milady Peters will have my eternal gratitude for allowing me to officiate.' While Edward and Mr Amery were exchanging wry glances at Frances's elevation to the nobility, Monsieur Duparc spotted that they were not wearing flowers in their buttonholes. In the great flurry that accompanied the selection of two blooms from the horticultural riot surrounding them, an attendant produced a clothes-brush and set about ensuring that the groom and his supporter were immaculate enough for the privilege that lay in store.

Calm descended in the nick of time. Escorted by two ushers in splendidly grandiose uniforms, Annaliese came in on Lewis's arm and Edward caught his breath in wonder. The white silk dress, with its tight-fitting bodice and flared skirt, was an evocation of a ball at Schönbrunn and Edward guessed that Annaliese had chosen both the material and design herself. But the amazing veil suggested Frances in full flight. It was a billowing confection of lace and gauze beneath which Annaliese's hair shimmered like a golden halo.

On being introduced, Mr Amery found himself inspired to a rare eloquence. 'If I may be permitted to say so, Your Imperial Highness, you are quite ravishing, my dear. I have to confess that I questioned Edward's wisdom in going to Berlin, but for *you*, no risk is too great.'

Annaliese appeared quite overcome and was able to murmur only a word or two of bashful thanks. As Mr Amery showed signs of wanting to say much more, Frances bore down on him with the air of a woman determined to put a stop to it. At the same instant, Monsieur le Maire launched into a grandiloquent speech that combined welcome with an explanation of how the ceremony would be conducted.

In fact, explanation and actuality merged. Edward found himself guided to Annaliese's side by one of the uniformed escorts: moments later, he was dimly aware that he and the delectably beautiful woman who had always seemed unattainable were exchanging the vows that would make them one. Under Frances's eagle eye, Mr Amery was much more his normal self and produced the ring when required to do so. In no time at all, a beaming André Duparc was urging Edward to kiss his wife. The removal of the veil required Frances's expert help, after which Edward set about his duty with great gusto, aided and abetted by a responsively eager Annaliese.

It was time to sign the register and for the certificate to be issued. Not involved with the mass of paperwork required for a French civil wedding, Frances wandered round the large, flower-strewn office, turning the handles of the five doors that led to other rooms. Four were locked. The last swung open, exposing a spectacle that made her cry out with delight.

'Bless me!' Lewis said to Edward. 'Look at that. A civic lunch, if you please!'

Edward craned his neck to see into the room, glimpsing a superbly prepared table surrounded by more waiters than he could count. 'Did you know about this?' he whispered to Lewis.

'Not allowed to, old chap. Top secret. Frances said she'd fixed something, but there were no details. At least it explains what she was up to on Tuesday!'

After walking into the dining-room and studying what had been done in her honour, Annaliese turned to the organiser and dazzled him with one of her best smiles. 'I must be the first member of my family who hasn't married in a great cathedral or palace in front of hundreds of people – most of them complete strangers, of course. But there can't ever have been a *nicer* occasion than this. Thank you very much, Monsieur Duparc.'

'Highness, the pleasure was entirely mine,' the Mayor boomed. 'And I have been fortunate with the help and encouragement of Milady Peters.' His wink was a most eloquent way of conveying what a mixed blessing that had been.

'*Highness*,' Lewis said quietly, more to himself than anyone else. 'Yes, she still is.' Realising that everyone was looking at him, he gave a self-conscious little grin. 'Just because Austria's turned itself into a republic doesn't mean that Annaliese has lost her title. The thing is, though, what's she called *now*?'

'Mrs Boothby-Graffoe,' Annaliese said firmly.

'Oh, I think you can do better than that, my dear,' Frances interjected. 'You can't go chucking top-class titles away on account of marrying an upstart from the back streets of Belgravia. I think you should be known as "Mrs Boothby-Graffoe, the Archduchess Annaliese von Habsburg".'

'Can't I be Mrs Boothby-Graffoe for everyday purposes?' Annaliese asked, a trifle anxious.

'I suppose so,' Frances conceded grumpily, making everyone laugh.

Throughout a meal that was a banquet of sumptuous quality and quantity, Mr Amery proved to be the life and soul of the party. Exhilarated by Annaliese's beauty and charm, he produced a stream of wit that astonished Edward. In attempting to act as the representative of the Habsburgs at the small gathering, Leopold behaved reasonably well, drawing only two filthy looks from Frances before he gave up the role at about half past two. That was when he started looking at his watch every minute or so.

'What's troubling you?' Annaliese asked after pretending not to have seen her brother's fretting for nearly a quarter of an hour.

'I'm afraid I shall have to be leaving,' Leopold said. 'I promised to meet someone in Paris at six o'clock. It's very important – I mustn't be late.'

'I suppose *we* should be thinking of making a move,' Lewis said.

No one agreed with him. Leopold had to make his farewells with everyone remaining seated at the table. He wished Annaliese and Edward well, but made no mention of when and where they might meet again. It was left to an attendant to escort the Archduke who had renounced his title and birthright for political expediency, showing him the way out and ensuring that he was provided with transport back to Paris. André Duparc turned a diplomatic blind eye to the looks that flashed between Annaliese, Edward and Frances as Leopold left the room.

By four o'clock, with darkness falling, Lewis decided that they really must be on their way. As well as the farewells and thanks to Monsieur le Maire, Edward and Mr Amery had to face a momentous parting. Edward was travelling back in Lewis's car: after a night at the Embassy, he and Annaliese were leaving for St Malo in the morning.

The man who had been his guide and mentor through more than four years of nerve-racking adventure and heartache was pausing at L'Hotel Jean-Jacques only to change. He was booked on a train to Calais and the night boat to Dover. Although they would be reunited in a few weeks, they both sensed that nothing would ever be the same.

Deeply affected by the occasion, Mr Amery shook Edward's hand with great warmth. 'I hope you and your lovely wife are as happy as you both deserve to be,' he said, his voice nowhere near as steady as he would have liked. 'And the best of luck when you get to London.'

'Thank you, sir. We owe a great deal to you.' Edward, too, was feeling the strain of emotion. 'I'm sure things will pan out well with the lady from Cambridge.'

'We shall see.' Mr Amery made an abrupt dash for the motor in which he and Edward had travelled that morning.

Throughout the journey back to Paris, Annaliese was aware of Edward's growing tension. Huddled together in the back of the Rolls, they were wrapped in rugs and holding hands like children. Chatting to Frances and laughing at her observations on Lewis's difficulties with the icy roads, they appeared totally carefree. Yet Annaliese knew that her husband was becoming apprehensive. Squeezing his hand, she gave him a smile that was meant to convey understanding: unhappily, it baffled Edward and sent him further into his shell.

When they reached the Embassy, he was far more interested in discussing the latest rumours surrounding the conference than in accompanying Annaliese to the rooms that had been prepared for them.

'Don't you want to change out of that morning suit?' Frances asked pointedly.

'No, I'm perfectly comfortable, thank you,' Edward replied, looking quite the reverse.

Utterly po-faced, Frances went with Annaliese to help her out of the wedding dress and to carry out a final check on the packing of the going-away wardrobe that had been purchased in a single day's orgy of shopping. They returned over half an hour later to find Edward and

Lewis earnestly raking over Clemenceau's latest objections to Woodrow Wilson's Fourteen Points.

Frances decided that there was no need for dinner after the huge lunch. Accordingly, a light supper was brought in at eight o'clock. Its arrival made not the blindest difference to the flow of political speculation. Thinking it hugely funny, Frances took Annaliese into an alcove where they ate smoked-salmon sandwiches and gossiped about Mr Amery and Leopold.

Two hours later, when Edward was showing signs of wanting to talk indefinitely, Frances decided that enough was enough.

'I'm tired even if you aren't,' she said to Edward. 'And you have an early start tomorrow. Shut up and go to bed.'

'Yes, of course. I'm sorry. Good-night – and thank you for all your help.' Edward's face as he and Annaliese set off for the rooms normally reserved for the Embassy's most distinguished visitors was a picture.

'Do you know, my dear, I think Edward's got the wind up,' Lewis said as he and Frances made for their own apartments.

'I *know* he has,' was the forceful reply. 'It looks like a terrible case of cold feet.' She smiled knowingly. 'Her Highness will cope. You can bet on it.'

To Edward's intense relief, there were separate dressing-rooms. Shooting into his like a startled rabbit making for its burrow, he undressed and washed with a time-consuming attention to detail. After that, he laid out his shaving-tackle for the following morning, checked that he had left nothing in the pockets of the morning suit, and repacked his suitcase. Finally, when there was nothing else to do, he went hesitantly into the bedroom.

Already in bed, Annaliese face was framed by the golden cascade of her loose hair. Struck by the fact that she looked ten times lovelier than ever, Edward stopped dead.

'Thank you,' she said.

'What for?'

'The way you're looking at me. It's a great compliment.'

'Well . . .' Edward shuffled. 'You're very beautiful, Annaliese. I should have told you earlier.'

'I never said how handsome you are.'

'Surely not.' Edward laughed nervously. 'I've always thought I had a face like a horse.' He rubbed his jaw self-consciously.

'A good-looking horse, though.' Annaliese held out a hand, inadvertently drawing attention to the allure of her naked arms. 'Get into bed, *Liebste*. And don't look so worried.'

Edward did as he was told and Annaliese fitted herself into a companionable embrace. 'May I ask you for a big favour?' she murmured.

'Of course.' Edward put both arms round her protectively.

'It's been a very exciting and tiring day, don't you think? Would you mind terribly if we waited until I've had time to recover before we make love?'

'Oh . . . good gracious, not at all, my dear.' Edward realised that he must not allow Annaliese to shoulder all the blame. 'To tell you the truth, I've been wondering whether I was up to it. I don't think we've got over that business in Berlin, you know?'

'You're sure you don't mind?' Annaliese asked.

'Not a bit. We have the rest of our lives, don't we?'

The tenderness of the long kiss that followed was sweetened when Annaliese took her husband's hand and guided it to her breast.

'I want you to tell me the truth about something,' she said.

'Yes?'

'Did you *never* give up hope of us when the War was going on and on? *Never?*'

Edward grimaced as he recalled a host of painful memories. 'Yes, eventually I did,' he admitted. 'What about you?'

Smiling sadly, she nodded. 'I'm afraid so. It was when I was in Belgium with the Army. I thought the whole world was going to end.'

'But look at what you said when I found you in the hospital – "I knew you would come".'

'Yes.' Annaliese nestled deeper into his arms. 'It all changed a few days after the War finished.'

'Amazing,' Edward mused. 'If Leopold hadn't come into Jean-Jacques that evening . . .' His voice tailed off as he closed his mind to frightening possibilities.

'I shall probably never see Leopold again,' Annaliese said.

'I'm sure you will.'

'No.' She considered it afresh and shook her head. 'Leopold will live in Austria, and I shan't go back.'

'You won't?'

'I couldn't bear to watch what will happen to it. I'm going to live in the future, not the past.'

'What do you think will become of Leopold?' Edward asked idly.

'Who knows?' Annaliese was dispassionate. 'He may do something useful, but he's in with dangerous men. He wants *Anschluss* – union with Germany.'

'The peace conference will specifically forbid that,' Edward said.

'That would be sensible. Not that Leopold's associates will take any notice of what the conference says. Anyway . . .' She smiled. 'I'm *British* and nothing else matters. And I'm very tired.'

They fell asleep in each other's arms.

Cheerful pandemonium reigned next morning. As well as ensuring that the newly-weds caught the nine-thirty train to St Malo, Frances had to cope with a breakfast reception for selected members of the peace conference's Japanese delegation. Apparently, none of the visitors spoke a word of English and the only interpreter in Paris was busy elsewhere. It was, Frances declared with a good helping of grim relish, going to be a gruesome business.

So that he could dash downstairs to the reception, Lewis had to say goodbye to Annaliese and Edward much sooner than either he or they liked. As he did so, he gave Edward an envelope containing the documents proving that Annaliese was now a citizen of Great Britain. The lady herself was so engrossed in the papers that she had to be reminded to give Lewis a final kiss.

During the frantic rush to load the motor that was to take them across the Seine and along the Rue Royale to the Gare St Lazare, Edward became aware of the amount of luggage Annaliese had acquired in a single, breathless week. His mild complaint – really no more than a comment – drew an explosion of indignation from Frances.

'You ungrateful toad! Have you no idea how hard we had to work to limit it to *this*? It isn't as though poor Annaliese has anything resembling a *proper* wardrobe yet!'

Grinning an apology, Edward helped to load the boxes into the boot. Having got herself into a state, Frances was virulently critical of the traffic-jam on the approach to the Pont Solferino, becoming ten times worse when the chauffeur suggested that the hold-up was probably caused by Woodrow Wilson's daily procession from his hotel to the Foreign Ministry. For some reason, he travelled in what the Americans called a motorcade: very impressive and very inconvenient for everyone else.

However, when they reached the station, found the train, and the time for departure was drawing near, Frances calmed down.

'My dears, I'm *so* glad I was able to help you,' she said. 'It was an absolute joy. Now, have a simply lovely time and *do* write . . . I want to know what you think of England and your new home, Annaliese.' Frances paused to favour Edward with a look of mock disgust. 'You'll be back in a few weeks and I expect I shall have to put up with your nuisance. But what about you, my precious?' Turning to Annaliese, Frances was suddenly close to tears. 'I couldn't bear the thought of not seeing you again.'

Appreciating how upset Annaliese was at the idea, Edward was quick to provide comfort. 'Our paths are bound to cross before too long.'

'What if Lewis is posted to Outer Mongolia?' Frances said.

'We shall come and spend a holiday with you,' Edward replied.

'Promise?'

'We promise,' Annaliese and Edward said in perfect unison.

When the train began to move, Frances did shed a few tears.

'I will see her again, won't I?' Annaliese asked anxiously.

'Don't worry,' Edward reassured her. 'Lewis won't get an outlandish posting after this. I'll stake a year's salary on him coming back to London.'

Satisfied, Annaliese leaned out to wave and blow kisses at Frances, continuing to do so long after they had lost sight of each other.

*

The journey to St Malo took three hours.

For most of that time, Edward talked about himself. It was an activity he had always hated. When Annaliese said, 'I want to know all about you – tell me *everything*!' his initial reaction had been the resentment that invariably confronted attempts to break down the barriers of his privacy. Then, with something close to shock, he realised that the request had come from his *wife*: if they were to achieve the desirable goal of a unity as close as that enjoyed by Lewis and Frances Peters, Edward recognised that he must unbend. Gradually, with painful slowness at first, he responded to Annaliese's mixture of determination and humour. Before long, he was yielding up his secrets without prompting, going so far as to confess that he had disliked most of his schooldays at Winchester.

Annaliese said very little. Nevertheless, the couple who arrived at St Malo were subtly closer than the two people who had left Paris. They were beginning to form a bond based on the vows exchanged in Fontainebleau Town Hall.

The weather was a nasty surprise. Completely absorbed in each other as the train sped towards the coast, Annaliese and Edward had failed to notice the gathering storm clouds. Leaving the comfort of their carriage, they stumbled into the teeth of a south-westerly gale. Fortunately, they were still within their guardian angel's sphere of influence: Frances had made all the arrangements, spending an age on the telephone to the owner of St Malo's best hotel. One result was the limousine waiting at the wind-battered railway station. The way in which they were conducted to what must have been the establishment's grandest, most luxurious suite of rooms was another. Amidst all the bowing and scraping, there was a fleeting mention of Milady Peters: by avoiding looking at each other, Annaliese and Edward just about managed to keep the solemnly straight faces that were expected of them. Declining the offer to have lunch served in their rooms, they went down to the dining-room and were given a table in a bow-window overlooking the bay.

Despite the continuing deterioration in the weather, they decided to walk along the promenade after finishing the meal. At first, the difficulty of remaining upright against the wind was a joke. It was less funny when Annaliese's hat was torn from her head and sent cart-wheeling along the pavement. Edward, running like a man possessed, almost reached it, only to see it sent on a high curve into the sea by a vicious, swirling gust. Still laughing, Annaliese rushed to Edward, trying to tell him not to worry. No sooner were they together than the rain came, sheets of it, nearly horizontal and stinging cold.

A small army of servants greeted them in the foyer of the hotel, relieving them of their shoes and coats with the promise that they would be dried and cleaned.

'What now?' Edward asked, eyeing the residents's lounge with mixed feelings. In addition to the central heating of which the owner was so proud, there was a fire big enough to roast an ox and the soft chairs *did* look inviting. On the other hand, the threat of boredom was tangible.

'Goodness knows,' Annaliese said cheerfully. 'I tell you what – we ought to have hot baths. That might stop us catching our deaths of cold.'

'I suppose so.'

'We have to look out for influenza,' Annaliese replied, chiding him for his lack of enthusiasm. 'You said so!'

Once inside their suite, Edward made himself comfortable in the sitting-room, poring over a copy of *Le Figaro* in search of fresh information on the peace conference. He was dimly aware of the background activity – wardrobe doors and drawers were opened and closed, the bath was filling. Shutting the distractions out, Edward read a leading article that accused Clemenceau of surrendering to Woodrow Wilson's demands that Germany should be treated leniently. It was a rabble-rousing diatribe that was bound to have the direst consequences. Deeply preoccupied, Edward was only dimly aware that Annaliese was calling out to him.

'Sorry, I didn't hear,' he shouted back.

'I said, have you seen the size of the bath?'

'No.' Edward was disinterested.

'It's *immense*!' Annaliese's voice was closer. He turned and found her standing behind his chair. 'Come and look.'

Edward's exasperation faded when he saw that she was wearing only a flimsy robe that was gathered close to her body. Following

Annaliese through the bedroom, he was looking at a new person. The way she walked, on bare feet, somehow gave a new excitement to the movement of her hips.

'There.' Annaliese laughed, pointing at the vast, square bath. 'It's big enough for an elephant.'

Amused by the huge tub, Edward said the first thing that came into his head. 'We could both get in that.'

'What a good idea.'

The moment the words were out of her mouth, Annaliese saw that Edward was no longer smiling. Far from it, in fact: the silly man seemed to be teetering on the brink of panic. Allowing instinct to dictate her actions, Annaliese unfastened the waist-belt of the robe, shrugged the garment away from her shoulders and let it fall to the floor.

Like most men of his class and background, Edward was a surreptitious admirer of the female form in art and sculpture. In 1910, while he was at Oxford, a holiday in Paris had been made memorable by a Rodin exhibition at the Louvre. But not even that was a preparation for the stunning beauty of Annaliese's nakedness. Plunged into a state of shock, he recoiled as though from a physical blow.

That much, at least, Annaliese understood. But Edward's inexplicable and precipitate dash back to the bedroom posed the threat of things too awful to contemplate. Several long moments passed before she found the courage to edge towards the door. Painfully aware that she might be facing total humiliation, Annaliese prayed for a way of averting disaster.

A few paces short of her objective, she saw a sight that made her heart leap. Edward, sitting down in a corner of the bedroom, was not directly visible. But his reflection in the dressing-table mirror was. The ever-so-proper English gentleman was in a fearful state, undressing as fast as he could, with no time for finesse. A stud flew through the air as he wrenched impatiently at the starched collar of his shirt. Annaliese clapped a hand to her mouth to stifle a giggle at the thought of the time they would have to spend crawling round in search of the tiny piece of gold and mother-of-pearl. Tearing herself away from the half-open door, Annaliese tip-toed back to the bath and slid silently into the warm water.

Edward appeared almost at once. He was calm and self-assured now, untroubled by Annaliese's scrutiny. She was well-pleased by what she saw. Surprised, too. Edward's shoulders were a good deal broader than she had imagined; his arms and chest were strong, his legs sturdy.

'Very nice.' Annaliese smiled.

'I'll do, will I?'

'I think so. Get in.'

Edward grimaced at the perfume that wafted round him as he immersed himself. 'What have you put in this water?' he asked.

'Salts and oil,' Annaliese replied. 'Are your male sensibilities offended?'

'I think they've ceased to exist,' Edward said, reaching for the soap. 'Is this an old Habsburg custom, by any chance?'

'I'd be surprised if it weren't,' Annaliese laughed. 'They never stinted themselves where luxury and pleasure were concerned. All very discreet, of course.'

'Of course.'

The conversation remained flippant while they washed, an activity that ended with Annaliese attacking her husband's back with a loofah. When his unashamed enjoyment of it was over, Edward pulled Annaliese into his arms and kissed her with a forcefulness that both surprised and delighted her. Their hands began to explore, tentative at first, then bolder, caressing and arousing. It was Annaliese's need that got the better of them.

'Now,' she gasped, writhing against the delight of Edward's fingers between her thighs. 'Take me!'

For a few insane moments, Edward imagined that it might be possible. But he had to draw back. 'We shall either drown ourselves, or cause a flood,' he said, his voice sharp with longing. 'We shall have to get out.'

It was a scramble in which they were both desperate to consummate the love that had, even against the odds of their own fears, survived the cataclysm of the Great War. Edward made towards the bedroom, Annaliese had other ideas. She pulled him to the floor where a pile of towels provided what little comfort was necessary for such impetuosity. There was an element of savagery in the union that blazed out of their need for each other. Brief though it was, the frenzy on the bathroom floor seemed to satisfy everything that had been held in check for so long: Annaliese's climax occurred a fraction before Edward was reduced to lunging oblivion.

In the midst of her gasping, wild-eyed wonder, Annaliese revealed her innermost thoughts. 'I've wanted to do that since the day we met!'

'On the train from Budapest?'

'Yes.' Annaliese's eyes glittered with madcap passion. 'What do you think of that, my darling?'

There was no answer. The knowledge that this glorious creature had always thought of him as a lover reduced Edward to dumbfounded amazement.

After the second, infinitely more leisurely and careful spell of love-making, Annaliese and Edward drifted into a half-sleep. It was refreshing, yet left enough of their senses alert to savour the pleasure and comfort of physical proximity. The worsening storm finally dispelled the sensuous idyll at about seven o'clock.

'I'm ravenous,' Annaliese announced.

'So am I,' Edward agreed. 'It must be all that hard work.'

'Believe me, there's a lot more of that ahead of you,' Annaliese said quietly, supplementing the deadly serious words with a luminously voluptuous smile. 'Let's have dinner brought up here . . . Getting dressed seems such a waste of time.'

It was the first step towards a night in which their passion kept pace with the storm that was raging outside, both reaching a tumultuous zenith at four o'clock in the morning. After that, while utter exhaustion drew Annaliese and Edward into a deep, dreamless sleep, the gale gradually moderated.

The following day, after a very late breakfast, they took a long walk. The onset of more rain squalls in the early afternoon caused the exchange of grateful smiles: it was the perfect excuse to return to their suite. As the January dusk fell, they recommenced the voyage of sexual discovery.

On Sunday, when the weather was mild and dry, Edward accepted the offer of a car from the *patron* so that they could spend the day exploring the coast. Following lunch in Dinard they visited Mont St Michel and were pleasantly lethargic when they returned to St Malo. Even so, the seemingly unquenchable desire they had for each other impelled them to make love before dinner.

Afterwards, Edward was in a strange, wistful mood. 'We're leaving for London tomorrow evening,' he said, almost as if he had accidentally unearthed a fact that was worrying him.

'I'm looking forward to it,' Annaliese replied.

'You wouldn't like to stay here for a few more days?' Edward asked.

'No, I want to start my new life.' Annaliese studied Edward closely. 'What's the matter, *Liebste*? Are you afraid we shan't be like this in England?'

'Good Lord, no! I'm sure we shall be very happy. But it is nice here, isn't it? Our own little world.'

'We shall soon find another,' Annaliese said. 'One that's permanent.'

Edward seemed convinced. Throughout the final day of the short honeymoon, he was loving and attentive. They visited the shops in the main part of the town to buy presents for Edward's parents and Beatrice, and he insisted on Annaliese having a diamond pin as a memento of the best three days in their lives.

'So far,' Annaliese insisted. 'The best three days in our lives *so far*. We shall do much better than this, you'll see!'

That evening, they caught a train to Cherbourg and the overnight boat to Southampton. The cabin was comfortable enough, but being at sea made Edward, in particular, realise that the great adventure was nearly over. Annaliese caught his mood and they experienced a strange sense of restless expectancy. Although it was a state that inhibited the composure necessary for sleep, the nervous energy they both felt was highly conducive to love-making.

It evolved into an astonishing night in which their desire for each other became an insatiable delirium. Far from causing fatigue, the increasingly strenuous sexual play spawned a primitive exultation that generated limitless, burning energy. Annaliese and Edward were convinced that they had created a hedonism that was known to few – if any – others. Their mutual pride was close to arrogance as they disembarked at Southampton. Annaliese had no idea that the memory of that night was to haunt her during the years that lay ahead.

The immigration formalities were a disappointment. A solitary, overworked official showed complete disinterest in the well-to-do couple whose papers were obviously in order. After slamming a rubber stamp on the appropriate pages, he climbed on to a chair to scan the people who were pouring out of the steamer's steerage-class accommodation.

'So, this is England.' Annaliese's effort to make a joke of it lacked conviction.

'Never mind, things will improve.' Edward had a protective arm round her waist: he was also keeping an eye on the porter who had their luggage on a barrow and was attempting to stay close to them in the crush to reach the railway platform.

'*Another* train,' Annaliese sighed when she was able to collapse into the deep-cushioned luxury of a Pullman dining-car. 'We seem to spend half our lives in trains.'

'Don't we.' Edward shook his head ruefully. 'This is positively the last one, though.'

'Not for you,' Annaliese replied. 'You'll be going back to Paris.'

'Yes, but you won't have to worry about that, my dear. You'll be nicely settled.'

'Where?' Annaliese asked.

Edward was surprised by the question. Everything beyond the horizon of his immediate happiness could be taken for granted. 'There's plenty of room at both our places,' he said. 'The house in Cadogan Square is very grand, I've an idea you might prefer Upper Overs, actually. That's in Sussex – it's a lovely spot.'

'These are your parents' houses?'

'Yes.'

'Shall we be getting a home of our own?' Annaliese asked.

Edward looked up from the breakfast menu that an immaculate attendant had given him. 'You'd prefer that?'

'I think so.'

It occurred to Edward that Annaliese's wishes on the matter were probably a good deal stronger than she was implying. This gave rise to an unsettling thought: should not this – and several other important matters – have been settled *before* they married? Seeing that she was looking at him in expectation of a reply, he said, 'Yes. Right.'

They both knew that he was evading the issue, but this was not the time to pursue it.

It turned into a bright, crisp morning. Under a cloudless, azure sky, the countryside looked beautiful, despite the time of year. Although it was the end of January and the weeks ahead had endless capacity for harsh weather, the belief that spring would arrive within days was overwhelming. What Annaliese saw of the New Forest and the ancient city of Winchester as they tucked into a huge breakfast convinced her that she was going to like her new country. To cap it all, the arrival in London inspired an outburst of amused admiration.

'Fancy having a terminal called Waterloo,' she spluttered. 'However did the *Entente Cordiale* survive?'

'Do you know, I don't think anyone's ever thought of it like that,' Edward grinned. 'It serves the French right for the Gare D'Austerlitz!'

Annaliese pretended to be furious at the mention of Napoleon's crushing defeat of Austria, but the pantomime was short-lived. Sitting eagerly forward in the cab, determined not to miss a thing, she was rewarded by the sight of Big Ben and the Houses of Parliament from Westminster Bridge. Then, after the driver had taken them down Birdcage Walk, there was a glimpse of Buckingham Palace.

'Is that where King George lives?' Annaliese asked, disappointment mingling with curiosity.

'It's only one of his residences,' Edward replied. Reading her thoughts, he added, 'It *isn't* a very attractive building – especially after the places you grew up with.'

Annaliese shrugged. 'King George is still there,' she said. 'The Habsburgs have gone.'

She turned her attention to the shops and passers-by in King's Road and Sloane Street. She ignored Edward's expression of surprise after the cab had slowed down and turned into Cadogan Square.

'What is it, my darling?' she asked as he continued to mutter under his breath.

'The house appears to be closed up. That's it, look.' He pointed. 'All the curtains are drawn. How odd. Someone must be there . . . they can't *all* be in the country . . . in any case . . .' The confidence drained from his voice and he was silent.

The instant the cab stopped, Edward jumped out and was rushing up the steps to the house, leaving Annaliese to fend for herself. Unconcerned, she smiled at the driver and asked him to begin unloading the luggage.

Something happened to Edward while he was ringing the bell. For no apparent reason, a presentiment of disaster came over him, inciting panic. Although the bell was perfectly audible, he belaboured the heavy knocker.

The way the door was opened indicated that the maid who performed the task was deeply upset. She looked dreadful, deathly pale and with her eyes red from recent tears. At the sight of Edward, she clapped a hand to her mouth, turned tail, and fled.

'Emily!' Edward crossed the threshold, as if he intended pursuing the distraught girl. 'Emily, come back here. What on earth is wrong with you?'

It was no good. Heedless of the consequences, the maid wanted to escape from Edward. Blundering through the door into the servants' quarters, she collided with Franklin, who had been cleaning silver. In that first instant, he was angry with Emily: then he saw Edward.

'Oh, sir, thank God you've come!' Franklin abandoned his customary dignity to hurry forward, wiping his hands on a duster as he did so.

Edward either failed to see the man's agitation or ignored it. 'What the devil's going on, Franklin?' he demanded. 'Why is that wretched girl in such a state and where *is* everyone?'

Franklin made an effort to regain some of his composure and was on the point of speaking. Then he froze, his eyes appearing to start from their sockets. Turning, Edward saw Annaliese framed by the wide-open front door. Not in the least put out, she was surveying her surroundings with calm interest. There was not a vestige of unease. On the contrary, she was completely poised, an exemplar for centuries of breeding. Overcome by remorse, Edward hurried to her side.

'Forgive me, my dear,' he said, taking her arm. 'I can't imagine what came over me. May I present Franklin, my father's butler. He's the best fellow you could wish to meet.' Edward took a deep breath, stuck his chest out, and beamed at Franklin, his fears of a few moments ago forgotten. 'Bit of a surprise for you, I'm afraid. I was married last Thursday.'

'*Married*, sir?'

Annaliese saw that Franklin was horrified.

'Yes. This is my wife.' Edward was unaware of the butler's reaction. 'She's Austrian – but I'll horsewhip any man who holds that against her. As a matter of fact, she's an Archduchess – a member of the Habsburg family.'

Annaliese and Franklin surveyed each other.

'How do you do, madam?' Franklin said, bowing with stiff, over-elaborate formality.

'How do you do?' Annaliese replied, concealing her instant dislike of the man. She saw a lot that Edward was too full of self-congratulation to notice. Franklin resented her. Nor was that all: something was badly wrong. 'Thank God you've come,' had been the man's opening remark. What did that signify?

'My darling, the cab-driver,' Annaliese said. 'The poor man has been struggling with our luggage.'

'Permit me, sir,' Franklin said. He went to the door where the cabbie was waiting patiently by the stack of boxes and trunks.

'Give him a good tip, Franklin,' Edward called. Taking Annaliese's hand, he said, 'Let me show you a few things.'

'Wait,' she replied, disengaging herself from his grip. 'We must find out what's going on.'

'Eh?' Momentarily, Edward appeared to have no idea what she was talking about. 'Oh, yes, quite right,' he said, remembering his concern at the state of the house. Seeing that Franklin had seen to the driver and was now alone, he called out, 'Where are my parents?'

'In Sussex, sir. So is Miss Beatrice.'

'Why?'

Reluctantly it seemed, Franklin moved away from the luggage. 'It's the influenza. Her Ladyship, your mother, contracted the illness. Doctor Murdoch thought that she would make a quicker recovery if she were taken to the country.'

'Quite right.' Edward nodded approvingly.

'Unfortunately, sir, her Ladyship became very poorly.' Franklin added, 'Very poorly indeed.'

Edward's anger was rapid and frightening. 'Why the hell wasn't I told? This is a damned bad show.'

Franklin was uneasy, surprising Annaliese. Her shrewd examination had told her that his overweening confidence could normally be relied upon to cover all eventualities.

'Well?' Edward snapped. 'What's been going on?'

'A telegram was dispatched to you last Thursday, sir,' Franklin said. 'During the morning. Miss Beatrice attended to it personally.'

'I never received any telegram. Are you sure . . .' Edward's bluster evaporated even faster than it had flared up. 'Er . . . this telegram went to my hotel in Paris?'

'It did, sir.'

Edward was puzzled, unable to understand why Mr Amery had failed to act. Then the details of last Thursday began to come back to him. On his return from Fontainebleau, Mr Amery would have been in and out of L'Hotel Jean-Jacques as fast as possible in order to catch the night boat to Dover. After that, the telegram was destined to be ignored, possibly buried in a pigeon-hole under the flood of delegation memoranda that required a dozen messengers to carry it round Paris.

'Yes . . . well . . . I expect that was my fault.' Edward's discomfort was showing up as peevishness. 'Anyway, I'm here, so we'd better get down to Upper Overs.'

Franklin cleared his throat. 'Miss Beatrice sent a second telegram on Saturday, sir. On Sunday, she attempted to contact you by telephone. That proved impossible because of the weather in France –

apparently gales had brought the wires down in many places.'

Annaliese, the forgotten spectator, watched Edward's struggle for words. He eventually gave up, leaving Franklin to answer the unspoken question.

'Mr Edward, sir, I very much regret to inform you that your mother passed away in the early hours of Sunday morning.'

It seemed as if the appalling news had failed to register. Edward remained motionless, apparently unmoved. When he did jerk into life, his behaviour was astounding. Grabbing Franklin by an elbow, he propelled him towards a door. The process of entering the room and shutting Annaliese out was accomplished without so much as a glance in her direction.

She listened to the house's pained silence, felt its chill. Time passed, etched out by the ticking of a long-case clock. Annaliese lifted her chin. It was the only change she made to her stance. Three minutes passed before Edward and Franklin reappeared, the latter talking earnestly – rather like a doting parent, Annaliese thought.

'. . . and His Lordship finally gave in and had the telephone put in at Upper Overs just before Christmas, sir. It would be best if you spoke to Miss Beatrice before setting out . . . Under the circumstances, I recommend it most strongly, Mr Edward.'

'You're right, Franklin. We'll use the instrument in my father's study.' It was a split-second decision, accompanied by a dash towards the stairs.

'Edward.' He was on the first step when Annaliese's voice rang out. The expression on his face confirmed that he had forgotten all about her.

'I'll come with you,' she said, moving swiftly to place herself between Edward and the butler. In response to Franklin's unconcealed animosity, Annaliese's face assumed a mask of chilling authority. 'That will be all,' she said. '*I* will help my husband.'

Since Edward was in no mood to object, Annaliese won the skirmish. As she climbed the stairs, however, she knew that she had made her first enemy in England.

Striding along the landing, Edward spoke to Annaliese for the first time in what seemed like an eternity. 'This is terrible – absolutely terrible.' He flung the remark over his shoulder as he opened a door.

'I know, my darling. I'm very sorry.'

Giving no sign that he had heard her, Edward made for the telephone on the desk. Snatching at the earpiece, he pushed the rest up and down furiously to attract the attention of the operator. While he was saying, 'Hello . . . hello, I want a call to Ashdown four-seven . . . and hurry, please. It's very urgent,' Annaliese seated herself in the leather armchair set to one side of the desk. Slowly and with great deliberation, turning the simple task into an exercise in nerve-soothing, she peeled off her gloves.

The connection was made.

'Hello . . . Bee, is that you? It's Edward. I'm at Cadogan Square.'

Annaliese heard the tirade that was unleashed at the other end of the line. It was simply noise. There was no hope of deciphering individual words, but it conveyed the angry and near-hysterical state of Beatrice with graphic effectiveness.

'I've only just got here,' Edward said when he was able to get a word in. 'No, I didn't get your telegrams or I would have come at once. I wasn't at my hotel, you see. I left on Thursday morning.'

More agitated babble from the remoteness of Sussex. There were questions, a lot of them.

'Something quite amazing happened, Bee. You remember what I told you about Annaliese – you know, the Archduchess. Well, I found her. She was in Berlin, working as a nurse.'

He waited, stopped by a flood of criticism. Trying to speak against the torrent, he was stuttering. At last, it came out.

'Bee, I married her. That was Thursday. We went away for a short honeymoon in St Malo. We came over from Cherbourg last night.'

Annaliese was sure the connection had been lost. All too soon, she knew otherwise. The silence was, of course, the consequence of stupefaction, not a technical fault. When it was shattered, the strident racket seemed unbearable. Rising to her feet, Annaliese moved unsteadily to the window. Keeping her back to Edward, she gazed down into the Square, barely seeing the comings and goings.

'Bee, I *told* you it was serious about Annaliese,' Edward was saying. By a cruel twist, his attempts to assert himself and bring some rationality into the one-sided conversation made him sound ineffectual. 'We *had* to do it like that . . . I'll explain it all later. How could I possibly know that Mother was going to die? What we did seemed perfectly right and logical.'

Instead of participating in mutual condolence on the death of their mother, Edward was attempting to convince his sister that he had married sensibly. Annaliese felt sick.

'Yes, she's with me now,' Edward said. After another pause, he was blustering again. 'I don't know . . . it might be best, I suppose. What would you do, Bee? Do you think she ought to stay here?'

This time, what came from the other end was more moderate – inaudible, at any rate. Edward was grunting agreement at frequent intervals. Finally, he said, 'All right, Bee, I shall be there as quickly as I can.'

He replaced the receiver on its rest. Annaliese remained facing the window, struggling to come to terms with the mounting nightmare. An hour ago, she and Edward had been closer than any other two people on earth: now, they had walked into a tragedy that was changing them into strangers. Turning, she saw it on his face – dawning shock at his mother's death, the beginnings of the realisation that he had not been at her side because of their impulsive, hastily arranged marriage.

'This is awful for you,' Edward said, his voice wooden.

'Oh, no, my darling.' She was at his side in an instant, an arm round his shoulders. 'You mustn't worry about me.'

For some strange reason, he nodded: it was nothing more than a pretence at activity while he thought of a way to approach the disagreeable problem that was vexing him.

'Look here, my dear, this is a frightful pickle for you to find yourself in.' He sounded absolutely sincere, yet avoided meeting her eyes. 'To be frank, I have to question the wisdom of taking you down to Sussex at the moment. Poor Father has enough on his plate without having a surprise daughter-in-law sprung on him. Don't you think it would be best if you stayed here for a few days – until the worst is over?'

Annaliese was shocked by the feelings that welled up inside her.

This dithering individual, who didn't even have the courage to look at her, was supposedly the same man who had risked his life to get her out of Berlin. Briefly, she came close to despising him. It was horrifying.

'What would become of me here?' she asked tonelessly.

'You'd be perfectly all right. Franklin will look after you.'

'I doubt that very much indeed.' There was an edge to Annaliese's voice that forced Edward to stop staring at the blotting-pad and raise his eyes to hers. 'The man took an instant dislike to me. I don't think I've ever seen anything quite like it – particularly in a servant.'

Edward's face was a kaleidoscope of disagreement and denial. But he made no attempt to put his repudiation of Franklin's demeanour into words. Instead, he said, 'Perhaps you could go to an hotel. The Dorchester is very good.'

'Or Lisbon?'

'What?' Edward was mystified. His mental state rendered him incapable of understanding the bitter suggestion.

'Perhaps you'd prefer it if I went to Lisbon,' Annaliese said. 'It's what you wanted before I had the *brilliant* idea that we should marry. Now that I've become a liability . . . that's what you called Eva . . . perhaps I belong somewhere else. Portugal should be far enough away for you.'

Edward was appalled. 'My dear, that isn't what I meant at all,' he said. 'You must forgive me . . . please . . . I'm not thinking straight.'

'I understand.' She was stroking the nape of his neck. 'I want to help you, *Liebste*. I can't do that if you leave me behind. What is it you have in your British wedding ceremony – "For better and worse" – something like that?' He nodded. 'That applies to us, too, Edward, even though we married in France.'

'Yes.' Edward was making an effort to collect himself. 'Yes, you're quite right.' He looked at her beseechingly. 'Are you sure you can face it?'

Annaliese's smile was as brave as she could make it. 'No, I'm not,' she said. 'I can try, though, can't I?'

'Of course you can.' Edward reached for her hand.

'How shall we get there?' Annaliese asked.

'There's bound to be a motor in the garage. It won't take more than two hours.'

'The sooner we start, the sooner we get there,' Annaliese said resolutely.

Franklin, making himself busy in the hall, glanced up expectantly as Edward and Annaliese descended the stairs. They were holding hands and the new Mrs Boothby-Graffoe looked uncompromisingly strong and dignified.

It was a plucky display that concealed Annaliese's assessment of her predicament. She had never imagined that joining her new family would be without its problems, but the reality had proved to be totally awful.

Behind the valiant façade, a dreadful thought was taking root in Annaliese's mind: her five-day-old marriage was on a knife-edge.

10

28 January–18 February 1919
'Use your brain, there's a good girl'

Once they were on the road, Edward abandoned Annaliese. He did so by means of silence. After his effusive farewell to Franklin, not another word passed his lips for nearly two hours.

Annaliese made no attempt to start a conversation. She studied the towns they passed through and wondered if they would ever mean anything to her. The stark, winter beauty of the Ashdown Forest was pleasing, but she sensed they were nearing the end of the journey and was apprehensive. When they finally turned into the drive, Annaliese would have liked to say that Upper Overs and its surroundings were very beautiful, but the words refused to form.

Long before Edward had brought the motor car to a halt, Beatrice was outside. She had made good use of the interval since the distressing telephone conversation and was resolved to do her best. The black of mourning emphasised the pallor of her grief and loss of sleep: her chestnut hair seemed lacklustre. As soon as Edward climbed out of the car, she embraced him. They stayed folded together for a long time, unmoving, not speaking. When they parted, Beatrice walked towards Annaliese.

'Hello,' she said and they shook hands. 'I'm Edward's sister, Beatrice. I know you were meant to be a surprise, but I expect you understand that we shall have extra difficulty in these circumstances.'

Annaliese inclined her head in acceptance of the point. Surely, the fact that she had been told next to nothing of this attractive, brave woman was a ludicrous state of affairs: how many more shortcomings of the whirlwind marriage to Edward were waiting to be exposed? Aloud, Annaliese said, 'Please accept my deepest sympathy, Beatrice. It must have been a terrible shock for you and I'm sorry to begin by being such a nuisance. I hope you will forgive me.'

Very briefly, a flicker of animation lit up Beatrice's colourless face as she responded to the beauty of Annaliese's voice. Flustered, she turned to Edward. 'Let's go inside, it's turning colder.'

The house exuded its customary welcome, warm and fragrant. Edward paused in the long entrance-hall to remove his overcoat and hang it on an oak peg.

'Father?' he asked.

'He's in the library,' Beatrice replied. 'He's hardly left it since . . .' Beatrice cleared her throat. 'Uncle William is with him and they asked to see you as soon as you arrived.' Beatrice shot a nervous, apologetic look at Annaliese. 'On your own.'

Edward nodded and made a start down the corridor, but Beatrice caught his arm. 'Wait,' she said urgently. 'Mother's death has affected him badly, Edward. *Very* badly. Do you understand?'

'I think so.' Edward shifted uneasily. 'Have you spoken to him since our . . . er . . . chat on the telephone?'

'Yes.' Beatrice breathed deeply. 'He was baffled. To be honest, I don't think it registered. I expect Uncle William has tried to explain.'

Edward set off, only to stop after a few paces. 'The luggage . . . I must bring it in.'

'Old Ben and Matthew will see to it. They've been here every day since Mother was taken ill. Go on, it will all be taken up to your rooms.'

Edward went and Beatrice guided Annaliese into the sitting-room, taking her coat and hat, pointing to an armchair beside a log fire.

'Are you hungry?' Beatrice asked. 'I can arrange for tea and sandwiches.'

'That would be nice,' Annaliese replied.

Wearily, as though every bone in her body ached, Beatrice sank into a chair facing Annaliese. 'Father was devoted to Mother,' she said. 'Much more than I realised.' She grimaced. 'Does that sound dreadful of me?'

'One's parents are often a surprise,' Annaliese murmured.

'The *big* trouble is that Father hasn't really recovered from Alexander,' Beatrice went on.

'Alexander?' It was a natural reaction that took place before Annaliese could even think of preventing it.

'Our brother,' Beatrice said. 'He died in the War. Hasn't Edward mentioned him?'

'No.' Annaliese felt herself flush with embarrassment. So much for Edward's supposedly frank account of himself on the train from Paris to St Malo.

'Do you know, I'm not surprised,' Beatrice said. 'Edward thought the world of Alexander, but it isn't the done thing to show too many emotions – at least, that's what Edward believes.' To Annaliese's relief, Beatrice pushed the topic aside. 'This is not much of a homecoming for you. We must do better after the funeral – that's the day after tomorrow, by the way.'

'It's a good thing my coat is black,' Annaliese replied. 'I don't have a suitable dress, though.'

'One of mine should do. You're a couple of inches taller, so we may have to let the hem down.'

'Thank you.' There was an awkward little pause. Annaliese decided to be bold. 'I was with Edward while he was talking to you on the telephone,' she said. 'I gathered that he must have mentioned me to you some time ago.'

Beatrice nodded. 'It was last April. We'd been entertaining some Americans at Cadogan Square and got pretty miserable after they'd gone . . . we were both upset about Archie.'

'Archie? Is that the man who worked with Edward in Vienna before the War?'

'That's right.' Assuming that Annaliese knew nothing about Edward's activities in Berlin, Beatrice decided to tread carefully. 'Archie was my fiancé, but he was killed just before Christmas, nineteen-seventeen. This is his ring.' She held out her left hand. 'The night the Americans came, we were thinking about Archie – and Alexander – and it all got on top of us.'

Annaliese nodded understandingly.

'I climbed on to one of my hobby-horses,' Beatrice continued. 'I told Edward that he ought to be looking for a wife – someone to take care of him and help with his career. He hates being lectured. He probably started talking about you to shut me up. He said he'd fallen in love with you in Vienna and that he thought about you every day. I'm afraid I told him that it was hopeless. Even if he ever did meet you again – and I couldn't see that happening in a million years – his status and yours were incompatible.'

'A reasonable point of view,' Annaliese smiled. 'Fortunately for Edward and me, the War has changed most things.'

'How *did* you and Edward come to find each other?' Beatrice asked.

Glad of an opportunity to talk, Annaliese sketched out the salient facts. Beatrice was an appreciative audience, wide-eyed, gasping with disbelief, and asking questions in order to clarify the more fantastic parts of the story. When it was over, she shook her head and said, 'Incredible.'

There was nothing more. Bemused, Beatrice stared into space while Annaliese became aware of the house's clocks, chuntering away to themselves: otherwise, there was an intimidating silence.

It was broken by a fresh-faced girl in a maid's cap and spotlessly white pinafore. 'Begging your pardon, ma'am,' she said in the distinctive tones of the Weald. 'Mrs Grove was wondering if you'm ready for a snack.' She bobbed a dutiful curtsy towards Beatrice, but avoided looking at Annaliese.

Beatrice came to with a start. 'Yes, please, Polly, I'm sure we are,' she said. 'I expect you'd like to see your rooms, Annaliese? Let me show you – then I can make sure you have everything you need while we eat our sandwiches.'

'That would be nice,' Annaliese said dutifully.

'When you get used to it, you'll find that it isn't so far as it seems,' Beatrice chattered as she led the way up the stairs. 'Much as I adore this place, I have to admit that it's a maze. Sometimes, if I don't have my wits about me, I can still get lost.'

From the landing, their course turned repeatedly, and, at every corner, there were shallow steps up or down. 'It's the way the house was built,' Beatrice explained as part of her polite, over-bright babble. 'I don't think there was ever any question of design, it just sort of *evolved*, if you know what I mean.'

At last, when Annaliese was starting to wonder how much longer she could maintain the display of interest, they turned yet another corner to find that the passage ended about thirty feet away. There was a window with a view of the Forest skyline and the luggage that Annaliese and Edward had brought with them was piled between the two doors on the left-hand side of the corridor.

'Oh, well done,' Beatrice gasped thankfully. 'To be honest, I was worried about Ben and Matthew. They're part-time as a rule, you see, and strictly outside – Mrs Grove won't allow them in the house. Anyway, they've done splendidly. Now this is what you might call the south wing. To be *strictly* accurate, I think it's more south-west. That's the bathroom.' She pointed to the solitary door on the right. 'And *this* is your own, private sitting-room.'

Everything was spotless, a fire cast its warm glow, and two vases were full of fresh flowers from the greenhouse. Annaliese was aware of what must have been a fearful panic of preparation while she and Edward were travelling from London. Looking quickly into the adjoining bedroom, she found the same atmosphere of welcome and warmth. 'Thank you,' she said to Beatrice. 'You worked wonders.'

'We all pitched in and did our bit,' Beatrice replied. 'Polly was the mainstay – she's a demon when she gets going. Ah . . . here she is with our sustenance!'

They sat down to take their pick from the marvellous selection on the huge tray and Beatrice pressed on remorselessly with her efforts to make Annaliese feel at home.

'Another of our maids – a girl called Gwen – will look after you. As soon as you're ready, she'll see to the unpacking. You don't seem to have all that much luggage.'

'That's all my worldly possessions,' Annaliese smiled. 'I left Berlin in a nurse's uniform!'

'Er . . . what about your parents?' Beatrice ventured.

'In Lisbon,' Annaliese said. 'They're exiles.'

'Do they know about you and Edward?'

'No. I must write.' Annaliese decided that an addition to her rather curt response was justified. 'Father and Mama knew Edward quite well before the War and liked him. They will be pleased . . . I hope.'

'Your father is an Archduke?' Beatrice asked, trying to make a start on exploring the delicate question of Annaliese's status.

'Yes. The new Austrian Government have introduced laws that strip us of all titles and possessions, but he's . . .'

The knock at the door stopped her short. In their shared nervousness, the two women exchanged worried looks before Beatrice called, 'Come in.'

In the instant that preceded Beatrice's sigh of relief, Annaliese knew who the distinguished-looking man must be. The resemblance to Edward was startling. She also spotted that, although he looked grave, there was no sign of debilitating, directly personal sorrow, therefore, this was not Edward's father. Annaliese rose to her feet, smiling bashfully.

'Uncle William!' Beatrice, too, sprang to her feet. 'This is Edward's wife, Annaliese.'

'I'm honoured, Your Grace,' Annaliese said.

His eyes twinkled with amused appreciation of her courtesy. 'The honour is entirely mine, Your Imperial Highness,' he replied, bowing.

Coolly, taking their time, Annaliese and the Duke of Lincolnshire weighed each other up. When they were good and ready, they shook hands. Beatrice could have sworn that they exchanged the knowing looks of kindred spirits.

'Welcome to the family, my dear,' the Duke said. 'You're a devil of a surprise – and a damned beautiful one. May I kiss you?'

Annaliese presented her cheek, the deed was done, they laughed, and sat down.

'I can understand my nephew's point of view,' the Duke said. 'I didn't know he had such taste – or charm.' When the weak laughter had subsided, he was serious. 'Sadly, this isn't the best time to be springing a surprise.'

'I know,' Annaliese said. 'I feel awful.'

'Don't.' It was an order. 'It's the most filthy bad luck, but we shall have to lift ourselves over it. Alice's death is a tragedy. She was a delightful woman – one of the very best. You'd have loved her, Annaliese.'

'I'm sure I would.'

'My brother Douglas – that's your father-in-law – is pretty low.' The Duke paused to reconsider his opinion. 'To tell you the truth, m'dear, he's in a terrible state. Alice was as fit as a fiddle, but she went so suddenly – and just as we were rid of that *bloody* war.'

'I do understand,' Annaliese murmured.

The Duke gazed at her intently. 'What I'm saying is that I suspect you're going to find it dashed difficult to strike up any sort of friendship with my brother. The poor fellow's quite off his head with grief. Inasmuch as he knows what's going on, he thinks all the talk of an Austrian princess is some kind of joke.'

'I'm not a princess,' Annaliese said.

'You're the next best thing.'

'Not at all. There used to be so many Archdukes that they were practically worthless. Archduchesses were even worse.'

'Be that as it may, you've come as a fair old shock,' the Duke said. 'Like it or not, you're a member of Europe's oldest Imperial Family and that husband of yours is having the devil's own job explaining you to his father. I'd say that it's going to be some time before Douglas takes any notice of you.'

'Thank you for the warning, Uncle William,' Annaliese said. 'I shall do my best to be patient.'

'Good girl.' Obviously delighted by the way she had addressed him, the Duke eyed the tray longingly. 'Any chance of some tea?' he asked Beatrice.

'You'll have to use my cup,' she told him. 'I'm not dragging Polly all the way up here with a clean one just for you.'

'Anything you say, dear niece.' The Duke gave Annaliese a conspiratorial wink.

Beatrice had dinner with Lord Douglas that evening. Their whereabouts remained a mystery, a fact that Annaliese found unsettling as she ate her meal with Edward and her new friend, Uncle William.

Three hours in his father's company had done nothing to improve Edward's frame of mind. On the contrary, he was morosely uncommunicative when he emerged from the library. Annaliese soon gave up the struggle to talk to him, acutely aware of his mounting self-disgust and guilt at the death of his beloved mother while he, for the first time in his life, was yielding to impulse.

Left to his own devices, Edward would probably have said next to nothing over dinner. But he had Uncle William to contend with.

'What's the plan?' the Duke asked as they made a start on the meal. 'What are you two going to do and where will you do it?'

'I have to go back to Paris for the peace conference,' Edward said. 'Annaliese will stay here, of course.'

The Duke stroked the back of his head, a gesture that Annaliese guessed denoted perplexity. 'Are you sure that's the right way to go about things?' The question sounded vague enough, but his eyes were shrewd. Rather than allow Edward to be dismissive, Annaliese jumped in.

'We think so. I don't like Paris and Edward will be awfully busy – mostly during the evening and night from what I can gather.'

'Picking over what the Big Three have been saying to each other during the day?' the Duke asked.

'That's about it,' Edward agreed. 'We expect to be up half the night and twiddling our thumbs for the rest of the time. No fun for a lady – even if we could find decent accommodation.'

'Paris is full, I take it?'

'Packed.'

'And after the conference?' the Duke asked.

'Back to the Foreign Office and some richly deserved promotion, I hope.'

'You'll live in London?'

'Yes. I expect we shall be at Cadogan Square for most of the time. Ultimately, Annaliese would like us to have a place of our own. I expect it will be in the country somewhere and I'll go down for weekends.'

Annaliese, keeping her face steady, told herself that Edward was upset and was speaking without thinking. Excellent though her efforts at concealment were, she saw that Uncle William had spotted that she was deeply unhappy.

She was also exhausted. This extraordinary, upsetting day had followed the hectic, sleepless night on the cross-channel steamer. Helped by the Duke, who made a tactfully kind comment about her tiredness, Annaliese excused herself at the first opportunity and went upstairs. She took a bath, then, as she liked to do every night, spent five minutes brushing her hair. Seated at the dressing-table, she studied herself in the mirror. It was like looking at a stranger, attempting to work out what she was thinking.

But the image in the glass remained inscrutable, yielding nothing. When she was settled in the comfort of the feather bed, Annaliese found that she was able to put the events of the day behind her. Terrible though it had been, love and patience would restore the rapturous happiness that she and Edward had known at St Malo.

The room was full of sunlight when she woke the following morning. Edward was finishing dressing, his face sleek and glowing from the razor. He smiled as she struggled to sit up, squinting against the brilliance of the light.

'Good-morning, sleepyhead.' He perched on the edge of the bed to kiss her, full on the lips with great tenderness.

'Good-morning. What time is it?'

'Nearly half past eight.'

'The sun!' Annaliese shielded her eyes.

'Not bad for January, eh?' Edward's boyish pride in England was touching.

'Nearly February,' she corrected, rubbing her cheek against the early morning smoothness of his chin. 'What time did you come to bed?'

'It was past midnight! Uncle William can talk the hind legs off a donkey when he gets going.'

'Why are you up so early?'

'This isn't really *early*,' Edward said. 'Wait until you see what the Foreign Office expects.' There was no change in his mood as he went on to what lay ahead of him. 'I have to make sure that everything's fixed for tomorrow. Bee has done wonderfully well, but there are some loose ends.'

Annaliese clasped his hand in a gesture of commiseration, understanding his need to make sure that his mother's funeral was well-organised. 'Is there much to do?' she asked.

'I'm afraid so. Do you think you can manage without me until this evening?'

'Of course.' She squeezed his hand reassuringly. 'I think that Beatrice and I are going to be great friends.'

'That would be splendid,' Edward said. 'Bee's the very tops – you won't find one better – and she's taken to you.' He frowned. 'I must be off.' He kissed her again. The way in which he stroked her neck and breasts showed his regret at leaving. Annaliese stayed in bed after he had gone, savouring the afterglow of his touch, promising herself sensual treats in the not-too-distant future. Not until she heard an engine barking into unwilling life on what was, despite the sun, a cold morning, did she get up. Soon afterwards, Gwen appeared with a breakfast-tray.

The seventeen-year-old girl and the Archduchess had yet to make up their minds about one another. Gwen, pretty but with a stubborn look about her, had been taken from an orphanage four years ago by Lady Alice. Saddened by the death of her revered mistress, Gwen felt that Mr Edward turning up out of the blue with a wife was a scandal. Even so, it had to be admitted that the Austrian lady was very beautiful and had nice manners. That counted for a lot with Gwen. So did the quality of clothes. The Princess – or whatever she was supposed to be – hadn't brought all that many with her but they were the finest that money could buy. Nothing was said while Annaliese ate her breakfast and Gwen made a start on the cleaning. However, in a way that was curiously companionable, they were heading towards an affinity.

When Beatrice came in with a black dress that proved to be far too long, Gwen showed her how to pin the hem up while Annaliese, trying not to laugh at the garment's pre-war length, stood on a stool. Later, after muttering something to Beatrice, Gwen took the dress away.

'What did she say?' Annaliese asked.

'She's going to sew it and press it.' Not entirely sure of herself, Beatrice went on with obvious trepidation. 'Look, Annaliese, you don't want to be stuck indoors on such a lovely day – would you like me to show you some of the country round here? It's well worth looking at.'

'That's kind of you, Beatrice,' Annaliese said. 'I'd love it.'

'We can take a motor.'

'You drive?' Annaliese was astounded and impressed.

'Well . . . sort of. Edward says I'm not fit to be let out.'

'I think I'm going to enjoy this,' Annaliese laughed.

Ready to grab at any opportunity to escape from the cruelty of tragedy, Beatrice became gleeful. 'You'll need to wrap up well – the Sunbeam is somewhat draughty!'

It was indeed, but immense fun. When they were in danger of getting too cold and Beatrice's arms were dropping off from the struggle with the steering-wheel, they stopped and walked along a ridge that gave breath-taking views across the Vale of Sussex towards the coast.

'Isn't that the sea?' Annaliese asked, indicating the distant shimmer.

'I'm never sure whether you can see quite that far from here,' Beatrice replied. 'It's about twenty-five miles to Eastbourne – a bit less to Brighton.'

'Miles.' Annaliese wrinkled her nose. 'That's something I have to get used to.'

It took Beatrice a few moments to see the point. 'Do you know, your English is so absolutely brilliant that I've forgotten you're a foreigner.' She laughed. 'What do they have in Austria?'

'Kilometres.' Annaliese was amused by the way the question had come out.

'Oh Lord!' Beatrice frowned furiously. 'I should know the answer to this – let me see if I can remember. Yes, I know – you multiply by eight and divide by five – so twenty-five miles is forty kilometres.'

Annaliese made facetious use of her native tongue. '*Ach so! Vierzig kilometres. Danke, Liebe Schwester*! Now I understand. That's the distance from Vienna to Ebenfurth.' She gazed at the distant horizon again. 'No, perhaps that isn't the sea.'

'I'd love to know all about you,' Beatrice said as they walked on. 'It would help us to become friends, don't you think?'

'Mmm.' Lost in thought, Annaliese sounded aloofly discouraging.

'Tell me to mind my own business if you think I'm being nosy,' Beatrice said nervously.

'No, you're quite right,' Annaliese said, taking her sister-in-law's arm. 'Where would you like me to begin?'

'At the beginning!' Beatrice urged. 'Were you born in a very grand palace?'

'I don't know about "grand",' Annaliese replied. 'But it's very, very beautiful – better than Versailles according to some of the "experts".'

'Schönbrunn?' Beatrice cried excitedly.

Annaliese was delighted. 'You see, you know everything. My father was the son of one of the Emperor Franz Joseph's younger brothers. Mama was a princess of the House of Wittelsbach in Bavaria.'

It took nearly an hour for the story to unfold, mostly because of Beatrice's frequent questions. Returning to the Sunbeam, they drove into the charming village of Uckfield for a lunchtime snack at a tea-shop-cum-grocers. There, with people milling around the table in the jolly, gossip-swapping commotion of market-day, Annaliese was given an indication of what the locals thought of her new family. At least half the crowd in the shop knew Beatrice and wished to express their deep sympathy at Lady Alice's death.

When they were finally alone at the end of the meal, Beatrice asked, 'Would you like to see where Mother is being buried?'

'Yes, I would,' Annaliese replied after a moment's consideration. 'It would help me get used to things.'

'That's what I thought,' Beatrice said. 'It's a little place called Hatchetts Green, sort of halfway between Upper Overs and Crowborough.' She became dreadfully serious. 'The road's reasonably good for most of the way, so you won't get shaken about like we did this morning.'

Beatrice had tremendous difficulty with the Sunbeam's gears on the steep hill out of the village. When the crashing and grinding had subsided, she regained her breath and asked, 'What did you think of the house at Cadogan Square?'

'I didn't see enough of it to form a proper opinion,' Annaliese said. 'It seemed very elegant.'

The politely evasive reply made Beatrice pull a face. 'To tell the truth, Annaliese, I've never been able to make my mind up about it. It *can* be pleasant enough, but it's very cold and formal sometimes.'

'Do you spend much time there?'

'I have to. I run Boothby's. Has Edward told you about *that*?'

Annaliese ignored the emphasis on the last word. 'Yes. He mentioned it when we were in Vienna.'

'We've closed it down for a few days because of Mother,' Beatrice said. 'It will have to open again after the weekend, though. I suppose you met Franklin?'

The rushed question was made to sound too casual.

'Yes, I did,' Annaliese replied, bestowing a wealth of meaning on the simple phrase.

'What did you think?' Beatrice asked edgily.

'I disliked him intensely.'

'Oh.' Beatrice was shaken by the outspoken response. 'Why?'

'Because he took against me *and* showed it.'

'He didn't!' Beatrice wailed.

'He did.'

Beatrice's agony of indecision was betrayed by the way she gnawed at her lower lip. 'That man is a menace,' she said.

'Why is he tolerated?'

'It's a long story,' Beatrice said wretchedly.

'Tell me.'

Beatrice sighed, as if the task were irksome. 'Years ago, when I was small, we used to go to Cornwall for a whole month every summer.' She saw that an explanation was needed. 'Cornwall is the bit at the bottom left-hand corner of England that sticks out into the Atlantic.' Annaliese nodded. 'We rented the same house every year. It was virtually on a beach that we nearly always had to ourselves. One year . . .' She screwed up her eyes in thought. '. . . Edward was four, so it must have been eighteen ninety-four, he nearly drowned. At least, that's the story.'

'There is some doubt?'

'Oh, I don't know.' Beatrice was cross, both with herself and the twenty-five-year-old story. 'The sea *is* very dangerous down there. Even on the nicest, quietest day, you often get huge waves rolling up the beach. It's very deceptive and treacherous.'

'What happened?' Annaliese prompted.

'It was afternoon. Mother and our nanny decided to go to the village for cream ices. They took me with them – I was only one. Father stayed on the sands to keep an eye on Alexander and Edward who were larking about – building a sand-castle and paddling. Father had eaten too much lunch and dozed off. He admitted that. What's *supposed* to have happened is that Edward was caught by an extra-big wave, knocked over, and dragged into deep water. A young man walking along the beach dashed in and rescued him.'

'The young man being Franklin?' Annaliese said.

'Yes. He was about twenty-three at the time and working in the household of an earl. While Father was thanking him, it came out that he wasn't happy and was looking for a change. You can work the rest out for yourself.'

'*Was* Edward in danger?' Annaliese asked.

'There were arguments about that,' Beatrice replied. 'Alexander said not. He was only six, but Mother always insisted that he was very grown-up and sensible for his age. There was a fisherman who agreed with Alexander, but two other holiday-makers swore that Edward was in serious trouble. He was very frightened and backed up Franklin's version.'

'At the time?' Annaliese asked shrewdly. 'There and then, on the spot?'

'No, I think it was the following day,' Beatrice said. 'I'm afraid that it's one of those stories that changes every time it's told.'

Annaliese nodded slowly. 'And neither Edward nor your father has ever allowed a word against Franklin since?'

'Absolutely not,' Beatrice agreed. 'Mother was very unhappy with him, by the way. I think she and Father occasionally fell out over

Franklin. They never quarrelled about anything else.'

'What do you think he's up to?' Annaliese asked.

'I've often wondered that,' Beatrice said reflectively. 'I don't think he's *up to* anything in particular. He's carved himself a very comfortable niche and Edward is under his influence.'

'I noticed.' Annaliese's tone was caustic.

'I doubt you'll be able to do anything about Franklin,' Beatrice warned.

'*That* remains to be seen.'

They were entering the hamlet of Hatchetts Green. As a diversion from Annaliese's uncomfortable attitude towards Franklin, Beatrice made much of the church which had been built between 1390 and 1410 during the full flowering of the Perpendicular style of architecture. Annaliese, who had never seen anything remotely like it before, was enchanted.

'It's exquisite. But why is it so big? Hardly anyone seems to live here.'

'They did when this was built,' Beatrice said, bemused by her first encounter with one of Annaliese's mercurial swings of mood. 'There used to be several hundred people in Hatchetts Green.'

'What became of them?'

'They drifted off to towns and cities.'

Annaliese shook her head, unable to comprehend such apparent lunacy. 'Exquisite,' she said again after another look at the graceful fifteenth-century building. When she turned her attention to the churchyard, surrounded by centuries-old oak trees with an inner boundary of yews, she was equally impressed. Far sooner than she had dared to hope, she was experiencing the birth of an affinity with England.

The freshly dug grave was easy enough to spot. It was in a corner, sheltered from everything but a southerly wind.

'I'll have a closer look if you don't mind waiting,' Beatrice said.

'Please do.'

Left alone, Annaliese walked round the church, inspecting and admiring it from every possible angle. She also looked at the headstones of the graves nearest the path. They were old and weathered, with the inscriptions indecipherable. A group of half a dozen were for members of the same family whose deaths had occurred between 1800 and 1840. Now, they were either extinct or had moved away: Annaliese felt for them.

Then her attention was caught by a simple stone that looked almost new. Although it involved crossing a patch of long grass, Annaliese was drawn to it, half knowing what she would find. Sure enough, the dedication confirmed her instincts.

In Memoriam

Archibald Sturrock Shackleton

(1890–1917)

Sadly missed by his fiancée

Beatrice Boothby-Graffoe

Raising her eyes, Annaliese saw Beatrice watching her from the path. For a long time, they stood motionless in the slanting glow of the January sun which was etching out the skeletal silhouettes of ten thousand trees as it sank towards the Forest skyline. The pull that Annaliese felt towards Beatrice was the beginning of true friendship. They came together and left the churchyard hand-in-hand, without a word or backward glance.

They arrived at Upper Overs only a couple of minutes after Edward. He was standing in the doorway of the sitting-room, telling his father what he had achieved during the day.

Thrown off-guard by the unexpected encounter, Lord Douglas and Annaliese stared at each other in utter dismay. Although seeing her father-in-law for the first time, Annaliese realised that grief was having a terrible effect on him. He was, she sensed, a man who was normally bright-eyed and with the fresh complexion of robust health. Now, his careworn face was the colour of dirty chalk and his eyes had the blank dullness of complete despair.

The seconds stretched into a mortifying eternity. Lord Douglas's mental state appeared to deteriorate, as if he was alarmed by the beautiful, golden-haired woman. When Beatrice finally appreciated that Edward was incapable of action, she made a valiant – if rather strained – effort.

'Father, this is Annaliese. I told you about her yesterday.' Lord Douglas's obvious bewilderment flustered Beatrice into adding, 'You do remember, don't you?'

Lord Douglas came out of his trance-like state with frightening abruptness. 'How do you do?' he snapped at Annaliese. Before she had time to attempt a response, he turned on his heel and scuttled away. The lamps had not yet been lit and the gloom of the long entrance-hall swallowed him.

While Edward tried to pretend that nothing had happened, Annaliese and Beatrice exchanged tense looks.

'Please don't worry,' Annaliese rushed to say. 'I quite understand. This must be terrible for him.' She was, Beatrice saw, dangerously close to tears. 'If you'll excuse me, I shall go up and rest for half an hour.'

'Do you want some tea?' Beatrice asked. 'Or coffee? Would you prefer coffee?'

'Nothing, thank you.'

Beatrice frowned at Edward as the sound of Annaliese's hurrying footsteps receded along the landing at the top of the stairs.

'No,' Edward said. 'There isn't any point in following her.'

'Why not?' Beatrice demanded.

'She'll get over it on her own. She said she understood. I might make things worse.'

'In your present mood, that's probably true,' Beatrice stormed. 'Where are you going?' He was edging away from her.

'To find Father. I was in the middle of telling him how things stood for tomorrow.'

'I'm sorry we interrupted you,' Beatrice retorted bitterly. 'I know that the arrangements for the funeral are important, Edward, but you ought to have another go at explaining Annaliese to him.'

Two hours later, Edward was apologising to Annaliese as they prepared for dinner.

'Do try to forgive Father, my dear. This is most unlike him.'

'I know that,' she replied. 'He must have loved your mother very much.'

'Oh, he did – still does, of course. They were a wonderful couple. Just like us.'

Annaliese was sitting at the dressing-table, Edward stood close behind her. Their eyes met in the mirror and they smiled. Edward, who had just returned from the bathroom, placed his hands on Annaliese's back. Initially, his caresses were intended to be nothing more than soothing reassurance. But everything was different after the stroking movements dislodged the peignoir from her shoulders. The loose-fitting garment fell to her waist. Beneath the wrap, Annaliese was naked.

She sighed when his hands fluttered over her susceptible breasts. For a few moments, she enjoyed a contentment that was tinged with sensual promise: after dinner, they would plead tiredness and slip away. Making love would help them face up to the funeral. But the feeling of delicious anticipation faded when she looked at his reflection in front of her. Edward's face was burning with desire.

'Annaliese, I must have you,' he muttered.

She was confronted by a stranger, a man she had never seen before. He was mauling her, watching the fluid movement of her breasts in the mirror with hard, sharp eyes. She could feel his arousal pressing hard against her spine.

'My darling, there isn't time,' she protested. 'We must get ready to go down.'

'Don't be silly, there's plenty of time.' His recklessness seemed dangerous. Would he create a scene if she denied him? There was no question of risking that, not on top of all the other problems. Annaliese extricated herself from his clumsy pawing and stood up, intending to untie the knot that held the peignoir at her waist.

Elated, Edward cast aside his bathrobe and snatched her up in his arms. 'Don't bother about that,' he said. 'Let's try to be natural . . . spontaneous . . .'

What in God's name do you think we were doing in St Malo and on that steamer? Annaliese wanted to shriek at him.

They were on the bed, and Edward, making no attempt at delicacy, was forcing himself into her, oblivious to Annaliese's pain and humiliation. All that mattered was his omnipotence and need.

Although it lasted a mercifully short time, Annaliese saw it all in a dreadful sort of slow motion from which she was somehow detached. For about thirty seconds, Edward wallowed in pleasure and believed that he was magnificent. But spurred on by whatever demon had taken possession of his mind, he lost control. Even as he groaned out the brutish ecstasy of his climax, he seemed conscious of Annaliese's frozen lack of participation and the way she was staring at him. Already in the grip of self-disgust, Edward was quick to roll away from her, ducking to the floor for his robe and making an undignified dash to the bathroom.

When he returned, it was to play a part in a charade that had similarities with a medieval courtly dance. He and Annaliese dressed for dinner without once looking at each other or speaking, moving round the bedroom in a pavane-like display of chagrin and confusion.

At dinner, Beatrice was quick to spot that something was badly wrong, but attributed it to Lord Douglas's unfortunate reaction upon being confronted by Annaliese. It was Beatrice's anxiety to pour oil on that particular patch of troubled water that had led her to join the party in the dining-room, leaving her father to fend for himself.

'I hope tomorrow will see the turning-point,' Beatrice said to Annaliese. 'Things are bound to improve after we've buried Mother.'

'I expect so,' Annaliese replied, wondering how on earth she was supposed to face food.

'There might be something I can do to help,' the Duke chipped in. While Edward ignored him, Annaliese looked politely curious, only to be disappointed. 'Can't say anything at the moment,' Uncle William added. 'I haven't broached it with Douglas.'

No one pressed the point and the conversation became laboriously brittle. Giving up the unsuccessful struggle with the meal's main course, Annaliese invented a headache. She met Gwen on her way upstairs and made up her mind to begin a task that was becoming daunting as it nagged away at the back of her mind.

'I want to write a letter,' Annaliese said. 'Where can I find paper and ink?'

'I'll bring it,' Gwen replied, bustling on her way as though resenting the interruption. But she was as good as her word and showed an inclination to linger when she returned after carrying out the errand, fussing over the fires and making sure that the curtains were closed properly.

'My parents,' Annaliese said, explaining why she needed stationery. 'I must get in touch with them.'

'Don't they know, neither?' Gwen asked with a perception and blunt directness that somehow – but only just – avoided insolence.

'No.' Annaliese laughed nervously. 'They're in Portugal. Actually, I haven't seen them for some time.'

Gwen shrugged. 'Everything'll be all right, I expect.' Without the slightest pause, she said, 'Looks like Mrs Grove and us girls is going to be up all night.'

'Why?'

'Getting ready for tomorrow. You should see the baking. Two hundred guests don't half need some feeding.'

'Two hundred!' Annaliese was appalled.

'That's what Miss Beatrice reckoned.'

'How am I supposed to face that lot?' Annaliese whispered, her self-control in tatters.

'You don't need to worry about them.' Touched by Annaliese's distress, Gwen hid her true feelings behind scorn. 'Most of them won't be worth a light. I mean, they're not like Lord Douglas and his brother – they're *real* toffs and nice gentlemen with it. Most of what you'll get tomorrow are the folks who *think* they're something . . . nothing to make a lady of your quality fret.'

'My quality?' Annaliese said weakly.

'You're royalty. Been going on for hundreds of years.' As if expecting that all would be made clear, Gwen added, 'Matthew says so.'

'Matthew?'

'Me and him are walking out,' Gwen said. 'He's got a book about all the kings and queens in Europe and your lot are in it. Habsburgs, ain't it?'

'That's right.' Annaliese wanted to laugh. Goodness only knew how, but Gwen had produced a complete reversal of her mood.

'So, you've got nothing to worry about.' In dramatic contrast to her habitual seriousness, Gwen smiled broadly. It was as if the sun had emerged from cloud. 'If they get uppity, give 'em a look! Here, I'd best get on or Mrs Grove will be after my guts for garters. Good luck!'

For some time after Gwen's departure, Annaliese remained staring into the fire. Over and over again, she told herself that everything would come right. Soon!

Or would it? Lord Douglas was not a serious problem. The poor man's perfectly understandable distress would heal. But what about Edward? What *had* possessed him before dinner? Resolutely, Annaliese went to the writing-table.

It was a good thing that Gwen had brought so much paper. Nine sheets – three of them almost covered by Annaliese's flowing writing – went on to the fire. At long last, she found a way of starting that would enable the letter to develop as she wanted and worked steadily until the clock on the mantel said half past ten. Placing the incomplete letter in one of her linen-drawers, Annaliese undressed and climbed into bed, believing that she would fall asleep at once.

Although furiously pretending otherwise, she was still awake when Edward came up at midnight. He crept round like a thief, taking elaborate care not to make a sound. It was interminable, almost driving Annaliese into telling him to hurry up. When he did finally slide into bed to arrange himself gingerly beside her, she caught the smell of brandy. Wanting to think the best of him, she decided that he had been drinking only to keep his father or uncle company.

Despite the awfulness that hung over them, it was a comfort to feel Edward's back against hers. He was, Annaliese realised, all she had in the world.

On a day that threatened but never brought snow, Lady Alice Boothby-Graffoe was laid to rest at twelve noon after a church service of sad, dignified beauty. At least two hundred people came, some from as far afield as Scotland. The true size and rambling complexity of Upper Overs was revealed when they all went back for the buffet that had indeed kept Mrs Grove and the maids up all night. Certainly the house was full, yet it never gave the impression that it was crowded.

Nervous of the weather, the guests began to leave at two o'clock. An hour later, with only about thirty people left, Annaliese felt able to relax: she was no longer an object of curiosity and speculation.

Beatrice, Uncle William, and – somewhat less effectively – Edward, had protected her. Annaliese was introduced to a small, carefully selected fraction of those who had come to pay their last respects to Lady Alice. The people she met were politely cordial – though Annaliese suspected that it would be a different matter once they were out of earshot.

The majority, those who had to be satisfied with furtive inspections from a distance, registered every emotion from raffish disapproval to disgust. Generally, the men were in favour, the women against. There were exceptions. It was a man who advanced the theory that Annaliese was probably pregnant by a high-ranking German officer and had been disowned by her family. Why else would she marry a comparative nonentity like Boothby-Graffoe?

Not all the women took an instant and powerful dislike to Annaliese's striking looks. Nancy Shenstone – welcomed as a supporter of Boothby's, but staying in the background to avoid Edward's disapproval – was the centre of a small group who thought that the young Archduchess was splendid. As she was leaving, Nancy startled Annaliese by giving her a smile of such warmth that it seemed they were old friends.

When the worst was over and Annaliese had retreated to what had been Lady Alice's drawing-room with Beatrice and the Duke, she raised an issue that had been intriguing and nagging at her for over an hour. Franklin had been notable by his absence, so had the man who had given rise to almost as much gossip as Annaliese. 'Who is Ralph?' she asked.

'My son and heir,' the Duke replied.

'Our cousin,' Beatrice added.

Annaliese waited for more. It was not forthcoming. 'Everyone seemed to be talking about him,' she said. 'And not in a pleasant way.'

Uncle William nodded. 'On this particular issue, my sympathies tend to be with the common herd. Ralph has several faults – big ones, I might say. The one exercising minds today is that he was absent from his aunt's funeral.'

'Where is he?' Beatrice asked.

'Nassau, in the Bahamas. We exchanged telegrams about this sad business, naturally. It *was* out of the question for him to get back in time – which begs the question of him being there in the first place.'

'Who's he with?' Beatrice asked.

Uncle William shook his head. 'One doesn't bandy names. I'll say this, though – the husband isn't pleased. There's every chance that Ralph will get himself cited as a co-respondent again.'

'*Again!*' Beatrice wailed.

'Hmm . . . I must learn to be more careful.' Annaliese saw that Uncle William wasn't nearly so upset as he pretended. 'Yes, I fear so, Beatrice. He was dragged into a divorce last summer. Needless to say, he wasted no time in dumping the wretched woman.'

'Why didn't I know about it?' Beatrice asked.

'It was rushed through a court in the wilds of Norfolk,' Uncle William replied. 'Not a single gentleman of the press bothered turning up. By all accounts, that's the way the wronged husband wanted it . . . He was anxious to plight his troth with another lady.'

'Really!' Beatrice's exasperation was threatening to get the better of her. 'You know that I blame you for most of this, Uncle William: you've been too lenient with him.'

Deciding that it was time Annaliese was given an explanation, the Duke turned to her, his eyes twinkling waggishly. 'My son is over-fond of the ladies, m'dear.'

'It isn't a crime,' Annaliese said flippantly. 'Lots of men are like that. It wasn't unknown in Vienna, I can assure you.'

'Oh, I know that, but Ralph makes such a *thing* of it, d'you see? And he does have a mania for other men's wives. I wouldn't be a bit surprised if he isn't the country's most notorious womaniser.'

'He is,' Beatrice snapped, not caring for the touch of pride that she suspected was creeping into the Duke's tone. 'No woman is safe from him.'

Uncle William guffawed. 'I'm sorry, Beatrice,' he gasped. 'You sound awfully like the maiden aunt in a Victorian melodrama when you get going about Ralph.' Subdued by Beatrice's glare, he became ruefully pensive. 'But, yes, you're quite right, it *is* a bad show.' He turned to Annaliese again. 'I worry about it. In this country, the aristocracy mustn't draw too much attention to themselves if they want to survive – that's something else I think the War's changed. The prospect of Ralph inheriting the title is not one I relish.' His face lit up with mordant relief. 'I, of course, won't be around to see it.'

'Doesn't he have a title already?' Annaliese asked, trying to remember what Edward had told her when they first met.

'Yes, he's Marquess of Axholme. Wait until he's a duke, though . . . then you'll see the sparks fly!'

'He sounds rather interesting.'

In reality, Annaliese was simply introducing a touch of mischief: for Beatrice, however, it was the last straw. Insisting that she and Uncle William ought to be seeing the more persistent of the guests off the premises, she dragged him away. Left alone, and unable to spot Edward, Annaliese went upstairs to continue writing the letter to her mother.

Gwen appeared at six o'clock, ostensibly to check on the fires. The bulky envelope on the writing-table was an opportunity to demonstrate a desire to be helpful.

'Do you want that taking to the post?'

'Could you?' Annaliese was glad of the offer.

'Matthew's going to Crowborough. He'll see to it.' Before pushing the envelope into the bosom of her apron, Gwen, who was secretly very proud of being able to read, scrutinised what was written on it. 'Hasn't your mother got a title?' she asked in her direct way.

'Yes – for what it's worth. I never use it because I don't know how things are in Portugal. People in exile usually want as much anonymity as possible.'

Gwen's look was a masterpiece, combining understanding with disgust at the necessity for such tactics. 'How did you get on with the crowd?' she asked.

'I survived,' Annaliese said. 'By the skin of my teeth.'

'You should have heard some of 'em chattering about you.' Gwen sniffed contemptuously. 'I don't know why they always think servants are deaf.'

'What were they saying?' Annaliese asked, by no means certain that she wanted an answer.

'Oh, all sorts of rubbish. Only to be expected.' Having dismissed the subject – if only to her own satisfaction – Gwen turned to something she considered far more important. 'His Lordship is asking if you'll be coming down to dinner.'

Annaliese was uncertain what Gwen meant. 'Do you mean the Duke of Lincolnshire?'

'No, Mr Edward's father, Lord Douglas.' Although there was absolutely no need for it, Gwen lowered her voice and edged closer. 'Miss Beatrice and His Grace have had a right old go at him on account of his being rude to you.'

'Oh dear! That wasn't necessary.' Annaliese was horrified.

'Yes it was,' Gwen declared stoutly. 'Anyway, how about it? Will you come down?'

'When?'

'Now. It ain't going to be much of a meal . . . Mrs Grove's done enough cooking to last her a lifetime and the leftovers have got to be finished.'

'Don't I need time to change?' Annaliese asked, desperate for an excuse to escape.

'No, it's still mourning.' Gwen surveyed the black dress disapprovingly. 'I wish I'd had more time to make a proper job of altering that. Can't be helped!'

Annaliese dithered, then committed herself. 'Very well, I'll go . . . on one condition.'

'What's that?'

'You must come with me.'

There never had been such a girl for eloquent looks. Gwen's latest effort said that of course she would; it was what she had intended all along – anything else was out of the question.

They were in the smaller of the house's two dining-rooms, a cosily cheerful place with an ingle-nook in which a pile of apple logs were burning. A cluster of armchairs was set apart from the table. Lord Douglas turned at the sound of footsteps and was on his feet with surprising agility, hurrying to meet Annaliese.

'Heaven knows what you must think of me,' he said. 'I've been a total bore.'

He was a different man, suavely urbane and with a flush of colour in his cheeks. His eyes were a fraction too bright, possibly as a result of drink. It was a very minor point that did nothing to diminish Annaliese's heartfelt relief.

'Please don't think about it,' she told him. 'I chose a difficult time to appear.'

'If only these things *were* a matter of choice,' Lord Douglas smiled and kissed Annaliese on the cheek, she clasping his hands as he did so.

'May I call you "Father"?' she asked.

'My dear, that would be wonderful.'

While they smiled shyly at each other, Beatrice said, 'Thank you, Gwen, that will be all.'

Annaliese had assumed that the girl had faded away when they reached the door. Glancing over her shoulder, she saw that Gwen was standing her ground. Her eyes, fixed on Annaliese, were asking what *she* thought.

'Yes, you may go, Gwen,' Annaliese said, and she did, as meek as a lamb.

The Duke chuckled. 'You've made a conquest there, m'dear. I've never seen her like that with anyone else.'

'She's very obliging,' Annaliese replied.

'Let's go to table,' Lord Douglas said. 'Annaliese, will you sit next to me so that you can tell me all about yourself?'

It soon became a pleasant occasion, the sort of evening that Annaliese had imagined and hoped for. There were two difficulties.

Lady Alice's absence, although steadfastly ignored, exerted a palpable sadness, and Edward was in a detached frame of mind. He had enough to say for himself, but never managed to sound convincingly involved. Indeed, when it was eventually time to start making tracks for bed and Lord Douglas told Annaliese of his immediate plans, Edward seemed to be radiating disapproval.

'William is travelling back to his place in Wiltshire tomorrow and he's taking me with him,' Lord Douglas said.

'This is Compton Allardyce?' Annaliese asked.

'My word, you have been learning.' Lord Douglas smiled. 'It's a lovely spot. I lived there until I was twenty-three. With me out of the way, you'll have the peace and quiet to get to know Edward.'

'You mustn't think of going on my account,' Annaliese protested.

'There's no need to look at it that way,' Lord Douglas replied. 'I like Compton Allardyce. It will do me good. And William is excellent company.' The two brothers exchanged affectionate smiles and that was the end of it.

But there was something wrong and Annaliese tackled Edward about it when they reached their rooms.

'You don't approve of Father going with Uncle William, do you?'

'No, as a matter of fact, I don't.' He was guarded, resenting the question.

'Why?'

'I happen to believe that he'd be better staying here. There's nothing for him in Wiltshire.'

'It's his childhood home,' Annaliese replied. 'That means a lot to him.'

'Be that as it may, I worry about him being subjected to bad influences.' Edward was trapped and starting to sound pompous.

'Your cousin, Ralph, is out of the country,' Annaliese said, fighting the urge to laugh. 'And even if he weren't, I can hardly see a man like Father falling under his spell.'

'If you must know, I suspect that Uncle William isn't as innocent as he appears,' Edward blustered. 'There are stories about him.'

Long afterwards, Annaliese saw that her reaction was wrong, compounding the error of having started the ridiculous conversation.

That, however, was the invaluable gift of hindsight: at the time, she yielded to the instinct to burst into scornful laughter. 'Really, Edward, how can you be such a prude? As to bad influences, your performance yesterday evening suggests that if anyone's been exposed to them – you have!'

As she slammed off, Edward was dismayed by the fire in her eyes. Following her some minutes later, he found that Annaliese was already in bed and had turned the light out.

The Duke was in a hurry to be away the following morning – but not before he had taken Annaliese on one side for a quiet word.

'Goodbye, m'dear. I hope it won't be long before I see you again.'

'I hope so, too.'

They were standing outside the house and Annaliese was troubled by Lord Douglas, already in the Duke's Rolls-Royce. Last night's cheerfulness had given way to the bleak-faced melancholy of previous days.

'Don't worry about him,' the Duke whispered. 'The poor chap is going to be up and down for a long time.' He sighed. 'Not a thing you can do about it. I mean to say, how the devil do you tell a chap not to miss a woman like Alice? Now, promise me that you'll look after yourself.'

'I will, Uncle William.'

'And take care of that husband of yours, eh? Edward's a good chap – very sound and steady – but he can be an ass when he puts his mind to it. Use your brain, there's a good girl!'

They kissed warmly and the Duke climbed into the Rolls to sit by Lord Douglas. There was a brief flurry of last-minute shouting and waving and they were gone, leaving Annaliese and Edward staring at each other across an expanse of gravel. They decided that they were going to ignore the last two days and start again. After he had made the first move, she jumped at the chance to close the gap between them.

'Poor Father,' Edward said.

'Yes.' Annaliese slipped her arm through his.

'Perhaps going away *is* the best thing for him,' Edward said. 'God alone knows, this place must make him think of Mother incessantly.'

Annaliese's heart went out to him. 'Let's see,' she replied quietly. 'Perhaps I shall be able to help him – especially when you have to go back to Paris.'

The idea appeared to surprise Edward. 'I say, would you?'

'Of course.' Annaliese planted a kiss on his nose. 'I'm your wife, *Liebste*. What do you expect me to do?'

'Yes . . . well . . .' Edward did not know quite how to express his gratitude. 'That's marvellous.' He looked up at the sky. 'It's a decent sort of day, shall we take the Sunbeam for a jaunt? I think Beatrice would rather we were out of the way.'

'Really?' Annaliese's eyes widened with alarm.

'She wants the whole place cleaned from top to bottom,' Edward explained. 'If she gets rid of all trace of those people who were here yesterday, she can put the funeral behind her – at least, that's my opinion.'

'You are amazing,' Annaliese said.

'In what way?'

'You understand *some* things about women.'

Instead of rising to the bait of the implied criticism, Edward laughed. 'Come on, let's get ready. We shall need to wrap up well.'

Letting him pull her indoors, Annaliese heaved a secret sigh of relief at their rediscovered happiness. She must do better in future. *Use your brain*, Uncle William had said.

The outing took them in a forty-mile circle, with lunch at Horsted Keynes, the halfway point. Returning with the dusk at half past four, they found the house in repose and smelling of polish. Heading for the stairs without bothering to turn on the lights, Edward almost collided with Beatrice. She was crouched over the telephone and raised a hand, leaving it unclear whether the gesture was greeting or dismissal. As they crept away, Annaliese accidentally caught a snatch of what Beatrice was murmuring into the instrument.

'. . . Yes, so have I . . . very much indeed. *Could* you? Yes, I'm sure I can . . . There's nothing more I can do here . . .'

Later, when it was evening and they had eaten a simple meal, Annaliese watched Beatrice becoming more and more restive. She fussed around, fiddling with curtains and cushions, moving ornaments a fraction of an inch, never happy in whichever chair she had chosen only minutes ago. The point at which she tried to relax and build up an air of indifference was, to Annaliese – but not Edward – glaringly obvious.

'I think I might go to London tomorrow,' Beatrice said. 'I ought to.'

'Boothby's?' Edward asked, not taking his nose out of *The Times*.

'Naturally.' Beatrice was cross at the suggestion that it could be anything else.

'You'll stay in Town?'

'Yes – for a few days. There's a lot to do.'

'It's Saturday tomorrow,' Annaliese pointed out.

'A normal working day,' Beatrice responded and looked defiant, daring Annaliese to mention Sunday.

She did not. But turning a blind eye to Beatrice's demeanour when Matthew turned up to drive her to Crowborough railway station after Saturday's early breakfast was another matter. Fizzing with barely concealed excitement, Beatrice was carefree and radiant. Boothby's *was* an important factor in her decision to go to London, but Annaliese was convinced that another force was at work. There was the man at the other end of the previous afternoon's telephone conversation. A curious fellow, Annaliese thought. Beatrice and he had missed each other very much during the past few days – they had said so. Yet he had no objection to her continuing to wear Archie Shackleton's engagement ring.

Left alone at Upper Overs, Annaliese and Edward adopted a routine that was very pleasant. When the weather was reasonable, they explored a huge swathe of country encompassing the coast from Eastbourne to Worthing. On days when rain or snow flurries allowed nothing more than a hurried dash round the garden, they sat before a blazing fire and studied maps. Once Annaliese had made herself an expert on Sussex, she wanted to know everything about the British Isles: where was Carlisle? what happened at Swindon? – and so on. In the evenings, after Gwen had served dinner, they talked about the future. The Foreign Office was never far away.

'How important *do* you intend being?' Annaliese asked once. It was an idle question as they sat close together on a sofa, her head on his shoulder.

There was nothing idle about the response. 'Very important indeed,' Edward said firmly. 'I would like to run it.'

'I shall do my best to help you.'

'I know you will, my dear.' Drawing her closer, he kissed her forehead.

It was all very cosy and companionable. But, to Annaliese's mounting dismay, that was as far as it went. When they reached their bedroom, Edward turned into a bashful apology for a man who categorically refused to lay a finger on the wife he professed to love so much. Not that achieving the privacy of their suite was easy. Annaliese came to dread the tactics Edward employed to avoid going upstairs until she was nearly falling asleep with exhaustion. There was always a rattling window to be investigated, or a strange noise from an outbuilding. Once, he decided to wind every clock in the house at midnight.

Behind her mask of contentment, Annaliese racked her brains incessantly, sifting through all that she knew of Edward's character and mental processes. Her conclusions were extremely discouraging.

Essentially, Edward was a creature of habit and conformity. Although he claimed to have disliked his public school, he was an unwitting prisoner of the conventions it had championed. The only true, deep-seated passion that Annaliese had been able to unearth was for bridge, the card game of which she knew nothing. Several times since their wedding Edward had complained – albeit mildly – of not being able to play.

For Edward, nothing was ever done out of impulse. At least, that had been the golden rule until two weeks ago. What else was their marriage but an impulse? Annaliese wondered if it could have happened without Frances Peters: it was a profoundly disturbing thought. And what had that impulse done for Edward? It had kept him from his dying mother.

Perhaps the confused ripples from his distress at that fact had helped to instigate the second impetuous act. Annaliese suspected that Edward's disgust at the way he had taken her the evening before Lady Alice's funeral was growing, not abating. Guilt and self-loathing: what a mixture. His only answer was to hide behind defences that were higher and stronger than in the days when shyness had made him a tongue-tied cripple with women.

The days passed. Edward received a letter instructing him to be back in Paris on 20 February: apparently the peace conference was starting to move. Visibly cheered by the prospect, Edward said that he would travel on the previous day, a week before Lord Douglas was intending to return from Compton Allardyce. As the days passed, the conviction that Edward intended to leave without making any further attempt at restoring the physical aspect of their marriage took root and grew stronger in Annaliese's mind.

What was he hoping for? That a few months of separation would wipe the slate clean so that they could make a completely new beginning? The notion was not unattractive, but the pitfalls were even more obvious. Annaliese's greatest concern was for the duration of the enforced parting: no one had breathed a word about when the conference might end. Indeed, Edward had said that the process of peace-making might take as long as the War itself.

The prospect was intolerable. That afternoon, when driving rain kept them indoors, Annaliese acted.

'My darling, there's something I would like,' she said. They were sitting by the fire, Edward with a sheaf of newspapers, she with a book.

'Yes?' he said, eager to help.

'Will you take me to bed, please? Now.'

His face remained expressionless in the ensuing silence. The absence of shock or disapproval was a good sign, surely? Slowly, with studious care, Edward folded the newspapers into a neat pile. 'Yes,' he said at last, standing up and holding out a hand to her. 'I think that's a very good idea.'

Annaliese had every reason to believe that she had done the right thing. Edward was loving and tenderly attentive, helping her to undress, stroking her body as he did so. When they came together in a sweet, naked embrace, they both said the same thing.

'Mmm . . . you feel lovely!'

Annaliese encouraged Edward to caress her breasts. 'You like them, don't you?' she whispered.

'Yes . . . very much. Do you like me doing that?'

'I do. It's lovely. Why don't you kiss me there?'

Tentatively, he did. Seeing how much Annaliese enjoyed it, Edward became more adventurously expert, making her moan with pleasure. Paradoxically, the sweet euphoria proved to be the prelude to disaster. Despite all Annaliese's efforts at stimulation, Edward was unable to gain the arousal necessary to enter her. Eventually, the protracted teasing was exposed as a futile struggle. Annaliese carried on only because she had no idea what to do if she stopped. As a consequence, Edward endured the mortification of an ejaculation that came without warning, providing neither enjoyment nor release from tension.

Annaliese lay very still, making her breathing as shallow as possible. Perhaps if she kept quiet for a few minutes, she would be inspired to say something helpful.

It was not to be. 'This is terrible.' Edward muttered. 'Terrible. I'm impotent.'

'I'm sure you aren't,' Annaliese said. She spoke with the absolute confidence of someone who knew nothing whatsoever about the disorder.

'So what's wrong with me?' Edward asked angrily. 'I was perfectly all right in St Malo.'

'Ssh!' Annaliese whispered, stroking his face. 'You've had a dreadful time since we arrived. Perhaps it's affecting you. I'm sure it won't last long.'

'It wasn't like this the last time,' Edward said. His face clouded at the memory. 'Look, I've been meaning to speak to you about that . . . I think I made a mistake there . . .' His voice tailed off, leaving Annaliese with the feeling that an opportunity to repair the wreck of their marriage had been lost.

They spent the remainder of that day being uncomfortably over-polite to each other.

*

Annaliese missed Beatrice, who stayed away from Upper Overs until it was very nearly time for Edward to go back to Paris.

'I've been awfully busy,' Beatrice explained when they had hidden themselves away in her bedroom. 'And I thought you and Edward would welcome a chance to be alone. You seem to be getting along nicely.'

'Yes, we are.' Annaliese was dismayed by the ease and conviction with which she lied.

'Will you be staying here while Edward is at the conference?'

'Oh yes. I wouldn't like to be at Cadogan Square without him.'

Beatrice nodded. 'This place is perfect in spring . . . you'll love it. And I'm sure you're going to be great friends with Father.'

'Yes.' Annaliese moved restlessly to stare out of a window. 'I've been wondering if I might find something to do,' she said. 'Something *useful*, you know.'

'There's a Women's Institute branch in Crowborough,' Beatrice replied. In response to Annaliese's blank look, she explained. 'They do good works around the parish – making jam, raising money for the needy, *organising* everybody. They did a splendid job during the War.'

'That wasn't quite what I had in mind,' Annaliese said, attempting to steer a difficult course between firmness and courtesy. 'I was wondering if you could find something for me to do at Boothby's.'

'Oh . . . I see!' Beatrice was surprised and embarrassed. 'Yes . . . well . . .' Her mind was working furiously. 'I suppose it might be an idea to bear in mind for the future. But not yet, I'm afraid.'

Annaliese was torn between meek acceptance and risking conflict. She chose the latter, asking, 'Why not?'

'It isn't appropriate at the moment.' Beatrice was clearly irritated. 'It's best if you stay here until Edward comes back from the conference. It will give people a chance to get used to you.'

'Get used to me?' Annaliese pretended to be puzzled. 'Why can't I just be accepted?' She allowed Beatrice to struggle for a few moments before providing her own answer. 'Is an Archduchess *and* an enemy alien too much for your friends and clients?'

'Well, to be brutally honest, yes,' Beatrice said wretchedly. 'I don't like it, but it's what people will think.'

In a way, it was a relief that the inevitable had happened and that Beatrice, rather than a stranger, was responsible for breaking the unpalatable news. With the problem more or less out in the open, Annaliese was in a much better position to deal with a show of hostility from a man who really should have known better.

On the day before his return to Paris, Edward suddenly realised that he had made no provision for Annaliese to receive money in his absence.

'This won't take long,' he said. 'Probert will arrange it.'

Mr Probert managed the Crowborough branch of one of England's biggest banks. Aged about fifty, his behaviour towards his unfortunate staff was that of a vile-tempered martinet. With customers, however, he was unctuously charming. Since he never listened to gossip and no one had given him official notice of Edward's marriage, the appearance of the new Mrs Boothby-Graffoe was a splendid opportunity to display the affable side of his nature – in tandem, of course, with ladling out the condolences on the sad demise of Lady Alice.

Edward explained what was necessary and Mr Probert, after due consideration said, yes, that would be in order. Was twenty pounds a month sufficient? After opening his mouth to agree, Edward decided to consult Annaliese. The moment she spoke, Probert detected the faint accent and his face narrowed with suspicious antagonism.

'Your wife is *German*, Mr Boothby-Graffoe?' The wretch actually addressed himself to Edward as though they were alone in the oak-panelled room.

'Good Lord, no.' Edward treated it as a joke. 'She's Austrian. Different thing altogether.'

It was obvious that Mr Probert failed to agree. As he stared frostily at Annaliese, she drew several sheets of paper from her handbag. They had come from Berlin in the document case that was her sole possession.

'I have money of my own at a bank in Liechtenstein,' she said. 'Are you able to arrange for the transfer of some of it?'

Probert reached across his desk to take the papers, doing so with a boredom that was designed to be insolent. However, one glance at the documents made his jaw drop.

'This is a very substantial sum . . . er . . . Mrs Boothby-Graffoe,' he said, visibly shaken.

'Isn't it?' Annaliese smiled. 'I'd like part of it moved to this country, please.'

'Certainly.' Reaching for a pen, Probert prepared to copy down the details of the Liechtenstein deposit. 'I think I can promise that the funds will be in your husband's account within two weeks. Now, how much am I to request?'

'Can't I have my own account?' Annaliese asked.

Mr Probert leaned back in his leather chair, made a steeple with his fingers, and smiled sagaciously. 'This bank doesn't encourage that sort of thing, Mrs Boothby-Graffoe.'

Annaliese simply stood up, removed her papers from the desk, and popped them back in the handbag. 'In that case, I shall look for one that does,' she told the open-mouthed Probert.

In spirit, Edward was already halfway to France and counting the hours until his departure. Not much interested in any little nest-egg that Annaliese had hidden away in a toy bank in the Grand Duchy, he was glad that the interview was at an end. 'You'll manage perfectly well with the allowance I've made you, my dear,' he said. 'There's no need to use whatever you managed to scrape together in Berlin.'

Watching them go, Probert was astounded. Did Boothby-Graffoe know that his devilishly attractive wife had well over £100,000 to her name in Liechtenstein?

Two days later, Probert telephoned Upper Overs, only to discover from Gwen that Edward had gone to Paris.

11

May 1919
'Annaliese needs something to do'

London was at its best on a Sunday in late May. During the morning, Beatrice and Charles Templeton had taken a rowing boat on the lake, then cooked themselves a simple lunch. Now, at nearly six o'clock, they were pleasantly weary following an afternoon of love-making. A soft breeze stirred the curtains of the open bedroom window, bringing the scent of blossom and the sound of bells from at least half a dozen churches. They were alone in a house overlooking Regent's Park.

Charles had taken it on a long lease soon after the Armistice. The beautifully appointed property – which was inside the Park – belonged to a man who had been Charles's friend since their shared schooldays. 'It will give you a chance to enjoy yourself away from that freak you're married to,' the man had said. 'And I shall find the rent useful.'

It had been a great success. Far from objecting to being abandoned, Charles's wife used the new freedom to move deeper still into the bizarre world of her religion. Their son, Nigel, was in the day-to-day care of Charles's mother, a charming woman who had found an entirely new, much-improved life as a widow. After an illness that made him ten times more foul-tempered than usual, Charles's tyrannical father had died during the last summer of the War. Beatrice had deflected Charles's hint that, with the old man out of the way, there was nothing to stop him seeking a divorce.

'Aren't you happy enough as we are?' she asked.

'Well . . .' Charles hesitated, feeling slightly guilty. 'To be honest, yes. Very much so.'

'Good. Let's just enjoy what we have. Why draw attention to ourselves with a divorce?'

'Fair enough – but if you ever change your mind about marriage, you'll let me know?' Charles asked anxiously.

'Don't worry,' Beatrice laughed. 'You shall have first refusal.'

Within the secure privacy of the house in the Park, they enjoyed each other at every possible opportunity. Not that they gave up visiting Lady Shenstone. Nancy was constantly seeking ways to heighten the wickedly erotic ambience of Martha's Vineyard, a fact much appreciated by Beatrice and Charles who were now dedicated, unshamed hedonists. Every two weeks or so, when they felt the need for an extra fillip of sexual excitement, they spent an evening at the extraordinary house in Upper Belgrave Street.

'You've worn me out, you beast!' Charles complained as they lay in a weary tangle on that lovely May evening.

Beatrice shook with silent laughter. 'Call a cab and we'll dash round to Nancy's,' she gurgled. 'That *always* perks you up.'

'We can't, not tonight,' Charles replied. 'The lady is throwing a terribly posh dinner-party. Your sister-in-law is the guest of honour.'

'I'd forgotten all about that,' Beatrice gasped. 'I wonder if she'll be all right.'

'I defy anyone to make her otherwise,' Charles said.

'She's staying the night at Nancy's,' Beatrice pointed out, making it sound like a terrible warning.

'What of it? Are you afraid that Nancy will reveal all her secrets – not to mention ours?' Charles found the idea absurd and Beatrice had to agree with him. 'Don't worry, my love,' Charles went on. 'Everyone's talking about your Archduchess and my spies tell me that it's good for Boothby's.'

'It is,' Beatrice admitted. 'We've never been so busy.'

Charles gave her a look of mock censure. 'And you didn't want her anywhere near the place.'

'True.' Beatrice pulled a rueful face.

'May one ask why?' Charles asked facetiously.

'Well, I don't know now.' Beatrice tried to tie her fingers in knots. 'I was afraid some of our clients wouldn't take to an ex-enemy –

especially a woman who'd actually helped the Germans.'

'Nursing is hardly fraternising with the enemy,' Charles pointed out. 'It's an honourable, neutral profession. In any case, she's *royalty*, Beatrice. That takes precedence over everything in London.'

'I know that – *now.*' Beatrice grabbed at another straw. 'And I was worried what Edward would think about her doing a job.'

'Hmm.' Charles was thoughtful, intent on treading carefully. 'It was bad luck he had to leave her so soon after their marriage. I suppose he keeps in touch?'

Beatrice winced. 'Yes, he does. Often.'

'Hello, do I detect a problem?' Charles asked.

'Well . . . sort of, yes. The fact is, sweetheart, Edward writes the most tedious letters you could *ever* have the misfortune to come across. I've seen some of them.'

It had begun the very day that Edward returned to Paris and L'Hotel Jean-Jacques. Not surprisingly, he had conducted an investigation into the whereabouts of the telegrams sent by Beatrice in connection with Lady Alice's illness. The convoluted account of what had happened to the buff envelopes occupied six sides of quarto notepaper. To make matters worse, this was followed by a three-page account of the failure of Mr Amery and an unnamed lady near Cambridge to reach an understanding. It was Edward's old weakness running riot: he had to get to the bottom of things which, although important once, were now irrelevant.

Subsequent letters had contained a few lines that were vaguely personal, but were mostly interminable rigmaroles about the conference, full of names that meant nothing to Annaliese. Who, for example, was John Maynard Keynes? He had, apparently, resigned from the British delegation in protest at the punitive financial penalties that were to be imposed on Germany. According to Keynes, this would ruin the whole of Europe.

'He churns out the most boring twaddle,' Beatrice told Charles. 'Annaliese gave up trying to read them after three weeks – she just skims through to make sure that he hasn't said something important by accident.'

'Oh dear.' Charles shook his head. 'Edward seems a decent fellow, but he takes his work so seriously.'

'There was Father, too,' Beatrice pointed out. 'As well as putting up with those *terrible* letters, Annaliese looked after Father. Heaven knows how, but she worked wonders with him.'

'No wonder she broke out, though.' Charles laughed.

'Thank goodness she did,' Beatrice said.

In fact, it had been Lord Douglas's idea.

As they did at every possible opportunity, he and Annaliese were sitting in the garden. On a beautiful morning towards the end of April, they were sipping the Viennese-style coffee that Gwen took such a pride in making. Old Ben was busy in the herbaceous border, Matthew was mowing the lawn.

'Annaliese, my dear, you've been an angel,' Lord Douglas said, breaking into her thoughts much more abruptly than he had intended. 'What would I have done without you?' Although he was still eating and sleeping erratically, there was a new animation in his face as he patted her hand.

She had realised early on she must not, under any circumstances whatsoever, leave Lord Douglas to his own devices. Grief, loneliness, and the brandy bottle were wicked companions. So, for ten weeks, she had barely let him out of her sight. It had been a gruelling time, both physically and emotionally.

'You need a break,' Lord Douglas went on. 'Why don't you pop up to London for a few days?'

'Could I take Gwen with me?' Annaliese asked, having taken time to think about it.

'Of course. I imagine that she'd play merry hell if you *didn't*. You'll stay at Cadogan Square?'

'Do I *have* to?' Annaliese asked.

They stared at each other shrewdly. 'I understand,' Lord Douglas said softly. 'I shall speak to Franklin on the telephone.' He nodded. 'I *am* aware of the man's shortcomings, my dear. It's Edward who believes he can do no wrong.'

'I'd be grateful for that,' Annaliese said in a way that made her opinion of Franklin plain.

Later that same day, while preparations were in progress, Lord

Douglas asked, 'What will you do in London?'

'Oh, all sorts of things,' Annaliese replied airily. 'Shop, I expect.' Suddenly, she was looking at Lord Douglas with an especially beguiling expression in her eyes, like a child bent on winning a treat. 'Actually, Father, what I *would* most like is to see Boothby's.'

'Then go there,' Lord Douglas said.

'I did ask Beatrice,' Annaliese confessed. 'It was some time ago – in February. She thought I shouldn't.'

'Stuff and nonsense!' Lord Douglas retorted. 'She's worse than a mother hen with that place. I can't begin to imagine what she thinks will go wrong if she lets you look round.'

'Actually, I was hoping it might be possible for me to help out,' Annaliese said. 'I mean work there occasionally.'

The idea interested Lord Douglas. 'That could be useful,' he mused. 'Perhaps we could do with some new blood. Hmm . . . No, you go and give it the once-over.' His manner became conspiratorial. 'I won't tell Beatrice you're coming, if you keep the secret I shall have to let you into.'

'What?' Annaliese asked excitedly.

'Since you're going to pop up without warning, you may catch Beatrice at an embarrassing disadvantage,' Lord Douglas confided. 'You see, she's having an affair. It's all meant to be totally hush-hush because the man is married. He's a frightfully good chap called Charles Templeton – he's saddled with an appalling wife whom he can't divorce. It seems that Beatrice found consolation with him after Archie Shackleton was killed and it's gone on.' A terrible thought occurred to Lord Douglas. 'Please don't imagine that I've been snooping around – this is from my brother. It's *amazing* what he knows!'

'Men like Uncle William are *always* well-informed,' Annaliese said.

'He is, by Jove! Goodness knows how he does it. Anyway, it's entirely possible that you'll find Beatrice isn't quite at Cadogan Square, if you catch my meaning.'

'I do. She's already told me that she sometimes stays with "friends" – at a place called St Albans.'

Lord Douglas chuckled. 'It's a damned sight nearer to Marble Arch than that, I don't mind telling you. Be prepared to turn a blind eye, my dear, and be discreet.' Another thought struck him. 'And *whatever* you do, not a word to Edward. He can be very difficult about such matters.'

'You can trust me,' Annaliese promised. Leaning across the gap between their two chairs, she kissed his cheek. 'Thank you for telling me. It helps to understand these things. Now, are you sure you're going to be all right while I'm away?'

'Don't be silly. You won't be gone for a *very* long time, will you?'

'Two or three days.'

'There you are, then,' Lord Douglas said. 'Mrs Grove and Polly will make sure I keep on the straight and narrow – and I tell you what, I owe your mother a letter, so that will take care of at least one day . . . You know what a terror she is for asking questions.'

It was the strangest, yet most sincere and touching of friendships. When the Archduchess Elsa had replied to Annaliese's first letter, she had enclosed a short note for Lord Douglas, expressing her sympathy for Lady Alice's death. After ignoring it for nearly four weeks, he had written a reply. Now the letters were exchanged almost as fast as the Union Castle mail ships could carry them between Southampton and Lisbon.

'I heard from Mama yesterday,' Annaliese said. 'She mentioned that you're late.'

'That's what I mean,' Lord Douglas said. 'She's a slave-driver. Tell me, does she still think you made a sensible move in marrying Edward?'

'Most definitely,' Annaliese assured him. 'And the answer to your next question is that I am continuing to think about going to visit Mama and Father.'

'All right, all right.' Lord Douglas held his arms up in a gesture of mock surrender. 'But try not to leave it too long, my dear.'

Annaliese gave one of her Viennese shrugs. 'Not until I'm ready,' she said firmly. Straight away, her mood swung and she was smiling again. 'So, I shall go to London to learn all about everything.'

'Don't be too hard on them,' Lord Douglas said.

'I shall be as good as gold, Father dear,' Annaliese replied, her face truly alight for the first time in months.

Matthew drove them and their luggage to Crowborough for the eight-thirty train. After getting them organised on the platform, he hung around, fiddling with the chauffeur's cap he had donned for the occasion, and looking like a fish out of water.

'Go on,' Annaliese laughed. 'Kiss her and have done with it.'

Despite Gwen's attempts to convey the impression that she loathed every second of it, there was a lustre in her eyes when Matthew finally broke away.

'His Lordship will let you know when we're expected back,' Annaliese told Matthew. 'I hope you'll be able to meet us.'

'I'll be here on the dot, Your Highness,' Matthew said. He bowed gravely, gave Gwen a last smile and was gone, leaving Annaliese staring after him in amazement.

'It's what we've decided to call you,' Gwen explained as they settled down and the train drew away from the station. 'Matthew reckons it's right. Anyway, I don't like "ma'am" – it's what we have to use for *all sorts*!'

'But, Gwen, I don't want to be bothered with all that business,' Annaliese protested. 'My Imperial status is over and done with.'

'How can you be an Imperial Highness one day and nothing the next?' Gwen asked.

'It's the way of the world,' Annaliese replied. Suddenly, she was saddened by the way Austria had changed, not for herself or her parents, but for the idealistic young Emperor, Karl.

'Not round here, it ain't,' Gwen retorted. 'Me and Matthew's going to give you your proper due and I'll make sure that snotty so-and-so *Mr* Franklin knows all about it.'

'Gwen, you mustn't speak about Franklin like that,' Annaliese chided, stifling the urge to laugh.

'Yes . . . Well . . .' Gwen folded her arms, looked very stern, and made it clear that there would be no more chatter until they reached London.

Annaliese was deeply moved. Gwen's difficulty in finding an appropriate form of address had been impossible to ignore. In nearly three months, she had never called Annaliese *anything*, a practice that had often brought her to the very brink of insolence even as they were drawing closer together. Now, thanks to Matthew, it was to be 'Highness'.

For the first fifteen minutes of the journey towards London, Annaliese's close interest in the passing view hid her struggle against tears.

She was composed and in command when the train reached Victoria Station. 'We'll go to Cadogan Square, Gwen. You stay there to get things arranged while I carry on to Boothby's.'

'Right you are,' Gwen said, showing that 'Highness' was to be rationed out carefully.

Someone must have been keeping a watch from the house. The cab had barely stopped in Cadogan Square before the front door was open and a footman was dashing out to help Gwen with the luggage. Two maids hovered in the background, apparently eager to help if required. Lord Douglas's words of encouragement to Franklin – who was nowhere to be seen – had obviously worked wonders. Smiling to herself, Annaliese asked the driver to take her to Boothby's in Bond Street.

It was, she discovered, in *Old* Bond Street, facing Burlington Gardens. Her first impression was disappointment at the narrow frontage, squashed between a vintner's and a furniture depository. As if to make up for the lack of width, the premises were very high – four storeys and what looked like the sort of attic that no one had visited for fifty years. It struck Annaliese that no attempt had been made to use the street-level façade to anything like its best advantage. There was a door, a display-window only eight feet wide, and far too much brick wall. The window contained one item, an oil painting on an easel that had seen better days. Yet the painting – which looked as if it might have been put in the window as a hurried afterthought – was a Canaletto, an outstandingly fine one at that. Annaliese smiled at the casual, almost apologetic way the masterpiece was being shown and realised that she had already learned all she needed to know about Boothby's. She went in.

There was a porch behind the door. Negotiating its awkward confines, Annaliese was transported to a world of breath-taking elegance and space. The building was immensely deep: the chamber in which she found herself was at least eighty feet long and had other rooms beyond it. There were pictures on the walls and a few pieces of good furniture, but it was mostly space, thickly carpeted, softly lit, serene space.

At the centre of it all there was a glass showcase and table. A group of five women was gathered there, three sitting in straight-backed chairs, two standing. Those sitting were the bemused spectators of a conversation between the other two, one of whom was Beatrice.

The look on her face when she turned to see who had come in was proof that Lord Douglas had not said a word. Watching Beatrice convert her initial reaction into something resembling pleasure was entertaining.

'Annaliese . . . what a surprise . . . how wonderful!' Beatrice gasped after putting several big strides between herself and the gathering at the showcase.

'Father said that I should come,' Annaliese said quietly.

'Yes . . . of course . . .' Beatrice turned to her friends. 'Ladies, this is my sister-in-law, Annaliese. I expect you all heard about how Edward swept her off her feet.' Three of the women obviously knew no such thing: the fourth gave Annaliese that same smile of warm understanding that had characterised her departure from Upper Overs after Lady Alice's funeral.

'Hello there,' Nancy said, raising a hand in a whimsical salute.

'That's Lady Shenstone,' Beatrice explained and Annaliese returned the smile. 'Mrs Barbridge and Lady Milford.'

They surveyed Annaliese. Mrs Barbridge, fiftyish, rather plain, and fat, was jealous of Annaliese's beauty; Lady Milford, proudly svelte, possibly as young as forty and with a blatantly sensual confidence that had a great deal to say for itself, nodded and smiled.

'And this is Eugenia Benbow,' Beatrice said, presenting the woman with whom she had been talking. 'Miss Benbow has come to me with a problem, but I can't help.'

'Oh?' Annaliese thought that it was nothing more than a piece of polite small-talk.

'She's a singer,' Beatrice went on. '*Rather* a famous one, actually.' It was easy to imagine the handsome Miss Benbow dominating a stage or concert platform. 'A man is offering her the original manuscripts of two songs and she came in to ask if they were likely to be genuine. I'm afraid I've no idea.'

'They're pieces by Schubert,' Miss Benbow said.

'Which ones?' Annaliese's manner changed dramatically. She was, Nancy thought, as sharp as a razor.

'*Auflösung* and *Thekla*,' Miss Benbow replied.

'*Auflösung* was composed in March eighteen twenty-four,' Annaliese said. 'The manuscript is in the library of the Gesellschaft der Musikfreunde in Vienna – at least, it was two months before the War began and I can't imagine *them* parting with it.'

'Are you sure?' Although obviously impressed, Miss Benbow remained sceptical.

'Absolutely. I saw the manuscript with my own eyes.'

'Annaliese is Austrian, you see,' Beatrice said. 'Actually, she's . . .'

But she was cut off. 'Which version of *Thekla*?' Annaliese asked Miss Benbow.

'The second, apparently.'

'Eighteen-seventeen,' Annaliese said. 'The Curtis Institute in Philadelphia has that. It was bought as part of the Apponyi collection.'

Beatrice's face was a picture: so, in a different way and for a different reason, was Nancy's.

'You're really sure about this?' Miss Benbow asked, perversely determined not to be convinced.

Annaliese ignored her disbelief. 'What about the man who's offering them? Is his name Johann Muller?'

'No.'

'Frederich Stoll?'

'No.' Miss Benbow was becoming bored.

'Wilhelm Jenger?'

Miss Benbow paled. 'Yes . . . er . . . that *is* the name he gave me, as a matter of fact.'

'Do you know, this is very bad.' Annaliese's flashing anger opened her eyes wide. 'What on earth are the immigration people doing? He should never have been allowed into England.' Calmer, she faced Miss Benbow. 'He's a short, bald-headed man with a waxed moustache. Inclined to sweat easily.' Miss Benbow was speechless. 'Jenger, Stoll, and Muller are the same man,' Annaliese continued. 'He used to be one of Austria's most notorious forgers – his work is quite accomplished, by the way. Things are obviously bad for him in Vienna, so he's decided to try his luck here.'

'The rogue.' Miss Benbow's theatrically ruffled feathers subsided and she turned to Beatrice with a grateful smile. 'I knew that coming to Boothby's was the right thing to do. Lord Hammerwich advised it, you know.'

Behind her back, Nancy and Lady Milford exchanged looks that were pregnant with meaning, most of it derisory. Annaliese guessed that the gentleman whose name Miss Benbow flaunted with such conceit was her lover.

Mrs Barbridge, deciding that the morning's excitement was over, was hoisting herself upright when Annaliese had an idea.

'I don't think he should be allowed to get away with this,' she said to Miss Benbow. 'There must be dozens of others who might be taken in by him.'

'They must look after themselves . . . as I did,' Miss Benbow declared loftily. 'I have no intention of becoming involved with the *police* . . . my reputation, you know.'

'I wouldn't *dream* of suggesting anything so crude,' Annaliese purred. 'Do you have an appointment for lunch?'

'No, not today.' Miss Benbow made the admission with the greatest reluctance.

'If you will guide me to a suitable restaurant, I'll explain how we could put a stop to Wilhelm Jenger with the *utmost* discretion. I would consider it an honour if you would be my guest.'

'Oh, how kind!' Miss Benbow came close to preening. 'There is rather a nice little place nearby . . . it's just round the corner in Cork Street.'

'I know it.' Nancy was already on her feet. 'Is it all right if I join in the fun?'

'I don't see why not,' Annaliese smiled.

Miss Benbow was given no choice in the matter, nor could a bemused Beatrice do more than watch as the singer was swept off.

Nearly two hours later, Annaliese and Nancy stood on the steps of Whitaker's restaurant as Miss Benbow persuaded her Junoesque bulk into the back of a cab.

'Lord Hammerwich must be a glutton for punishment,' Nancy murmured.

'That's exactly what I was thinking,' Annaliese whispered.

The looks they exchanged set the seal on the rapport that had sprung up between them over the meal. They waved as Miss Benbow was borne away.

'I like the plan,' Nancy said. 'It's real smart.'

'I think it will be effective.'

'Bound to be.' Nancy studied Annaliese admiringly. 'You're what we'd call a honey over in the States. Clever, too.'

'Thank you,' Annaliese said. 'Why am I clever?'

'Because La Benbow has no idea who you are – or used to be. Beatrice was gonna tell her, but you chipped in very nicely.'

'I didn't want to give her the vapours,' Annaliese said, deadly serious in the instant before they both erupted into laughter. 'I'd better go back to Beatrice – I expect she feels like wringing my neck.'

Nothing was further from Beatrice's mind. Before leaving for her own, terribly mysterious luncheon appointment, Lady Milford had given her a piece of advice.

'If your sister-in-law has nothing else to do, you should persuade her to lend a hand here.'

'I hardly think that's necessary,' Beatrice replied, determined to stick to her guns.

'Think again, darling. We're heading for difficult times – all my financial friends say so.'

Beatrice and Cordelia Milford had become close through their association with Martha's Vineyard. Although Cordelia did not number the Governor of the Bank of England among her lovers, she was certainly close to him.

'Hasn't Charles Templeton warned you?' Cordelia went on.

'Yes,' Beatrice admitted.

'An attraction like Annaliese could give Boothby's quite an advantage,' Cordelia said. 'Think about it.'

The telephone call that Beatrice made to her father a few minutes later reinforced Cordelia Milford's view.

'Your Uncle William isn't at all happy with the country's economic prospects,' Lord Douglas said. 'And remember, he's in touch with the people who know. You've got to look at anything that might improve business. There's something else I'd like you to consider.'

'Yes?'

'Annaliese needs something to do. She's been cooped up down here for too long.'

'I must admit that she made a big impression,' Beatrice said.

'Well, see what you can arrange,' Lord Douglas advised. 'Edward will probably disapprove, but he'll get over it . . . He might even thank you in the long run.'

So, when she returned to Boothby's, Annaliese received a welcome that came as a surprise. After introducing an extremely good-looking man called Paul Marks, Beatrice left him in charge of the front showroom while she took Annaliese on a conducted tour.

Behind the spacious reception area was the first of two sale-rooms. This one, as big as the anteroom, had rows of utilitarian chairs facing a platform and auctioneer's rostrum. Its smaller neighbour jutted out beyond the line of what Annaliese had assumed to be Boothby's premises, occupying the rear of the neighbouring wine-shop. With no floors above it, this room had the benefit of skylights. There were no chairs, but hundreds of pictures, some hanging, most wrapped in sheets and leaning against the walls.

'Most of this lot will be going next week,' Beatrice said, encompassing the pictures with a wave of her arm. 'Tuesday and Wednesday are public sale days.'

Annaliese made a rapid inspection of what was visible and gave her verdict. 'Everything from five pounds to five thousand.'

'Five pounds may be optimistic for some of them,' Beatrice replied. Nevertheless, she was pleased by the accuracy of the assessment. 'Shall we go upstairs?'

Apart from a group of offices at the front of the building, the first floor was a single, vast space, full of furniture. There was everything from the English simplicity of Chippendale to the baroque extravagance of central Europe, together with some unusual pieces from the

Orient. Annaliese's attention was immediately caught by a piano. It was in a shockingly bad state, looking as though it had spent ten years in the open air.

'That's a Pleyel,' Annaliese said. 'One of his earlier instruments.' She used both hands to strike a chord, producing a sound of astonishingly good quality. 'It could be worth more than a Broadwood.'

'I don't think we realised that,' Beatrice admitted. 'We only took it in as part of a debt settlement.'

'If this is restored, it will take care of a very big debt,' Annaliese said, and Beatrice did not question the judgement.

Soon afterwards, Annaliese found a sideboard by Andreas Ruckert, a German contemporary of Thomas Sheraton. The hunt was on, lasting until well after four o'clock when a girl appeared with a tea-tray.

'The second floor will have to wait,' Beatrice said, as they retreated to her office. 'It's pretty much the same as this.'

'And above that?'

'Workshops and the attic. What did you and Eugenia Benbow decide to do about the man who's trying to rob her?'

Annaliese explained. 'We hope this will happen tomorrow evening,' she concluded.

'Will you be staying in London tonight?' Beatrice was uneasy.

'Yes. I left Gwen at Cadogan Square to pave the way.'

Beatrice was uncomfortable. 'I'm afraid I have things planned for this evening . . . If I'd known you were coming . . .'

'Don't worry, it doesn't matter,' Annaliese said. 'Will you be staying with your friends at St Albans afterwards?'

'Yes . . . yes, I'm afraid I promised, you see,' Beatrice grasped the ready-made excuse gratefully. 'But will you manage? What about Franklin?'

'Tell me, Beatrice, has Franklin ever come across Gwen?' Annaliese asked the question with mischief dancing in her eyes.

Beatrice searched her memory. 'I don't think he has,' she said at last. 'No, he can't have done. He never goes to Upper Overs and this must be Gwen's first trip to London.'

'In that case, our friend Franklin has a treat in store for him,' Annaliese said. 'I can hardly wait to see if he enjoys it.'

She then persuaded Beatrice to begin revealing some of Boothby's business secrets. Another two hours were to pass before Annaliese got back to Cadogan Square – but her return was well-worth waiting for. Once again, the front door was opened as the cab drew up: this time, it was Franklin himself and he hurried out to pay the driver.

'Good-evening, Your Highness,' he said respectfully. 'I trust you had a pleasant day?'

'Very good indeed, thank you, Franklin,' Annaliese replied in her grandest manner. 'Where's my maid?'

'Awaiting you, madam.' Franklin's magisterial sweep of the arm drew the eye to Gwen, poised on the stairs.

'Excellent.' Annaliese dazzled Franklin with her broadest smile. 'I think I shall have dinner in my room.'

'Gwen has already indicated as much, Your Highness. The matter is in hand.'

'*Thank* you, Franklin,' Annaliese said and set sail towards Gwen, somehow keeping her face poker-straight. Until they were safely away from flapping ears, a tight-lipped silence was maintained.

'What have you done to him?' Annaliese laughed when they were safe.

'Put him right on certain matters.' Gwen was more truculent than ever.

'You weren't *too* rude, I hope,' Annaliese said, patently not meaning it.

'Not specially. He made it easy.'

'In what way?'

'He started chucking his weight around.' Gwen's grin hovered between the angelic and the diabolical. 'So I had to stick up for myself. While I was at it, I told him a few things about you. Is this all right for you?'

Annaliese glanced round the sitting-room, then made a quick inspection of the bedroom and bathroom. '*Very* nice,' she said. 'How much argument was there over this?'

'A fair bit,' Gwen conceded. 'Franklin wanted to shove you in Mr

Edward's room. I thought this was better.'

'Where are we?' Annaliese asked.

'The main guest suite. This is the one His Grace, the Duke, has when he comes to stay.'

'I'll bet that's raised a few eyebrows,' Annaliese replied. 'When you go down for my dinner, bring your own meal up. We shall dine together.'

'That'll make it worse,' Gwen pointed out gleefully.

'Good.'

While they ate, Annaliese told Gwen about the attempt to rob Eugenia Benbow and the action she proposed taking.

Gwen enjoyed the story. 'This caper could make you quite famous with the nobs,' she said.

'Perish the thought!' Annaliese pretended to be horrified.

The telephone call came during the following afternoon, while Annaliese was rooting round the second floor of Boothby's. Miss Benbow reported that she had made contact with Wilhelm Jenger, who had agreed to call on her at nine that evening. In anticipation of concluding the sale, he was bringing what he claimed were the original manuscripts of the two songs with him.

'By the way, how much is he asking for them?' Annaliese asked.

'Five hundred guineas.'

'That wouldn't be a bad price for two genuine Schubert songs,' Annaliese said. 'Especially *that* pair.'

'He wants that for *each* of them,' was the aggrieved response.

Annaliese felt a grudging respect for the scoundrel. Jenger, who couldn't hurt a fly if his life depended on it, was a likeable individual with the cheek of the devil, a quintessential Viennese. There was a strong temptation to yield to the lure of homesickness, but Annaliese resisted it, telling herself that Vienna was no longer a place for rose-tinted dreams.

She arrived at the imposing block of flats in Kensington at the agreed time of eight o'clock to find the singer not knowing what to do about an excited Nancy Shenstone who had beaten Annaliese by ten minutes.

'You don't mind, do you?' Nancy asked. 'I *had* to see this guy get stitched up.' Ignoring the owner of the ostentatiously furnished set of apartments, Annaliese agreed.

They chatted until ten minutes to nine, then went into Miss Benbow's music-room, where Annaliese and Nancy took up their positions. On the stroke of the hour, the doorbell rang.

Several minutes passed before Jenger allowed himself to be manoeuvred into the music-room. Although Annaliese could not make out what was being said, she assumed that he was attempting to complete the transaction on the doorstep. Miss Benbow was having none of it. Her voice, always somewhat mannered, became positively theatrical once she had achieved her objective and they were in the music-room.

'So, these are they? You have no objection to my inspecting them?'

'Please to be careful, *Gnadige Fräulein*,' Jenger pleaded. 'Do not hurt or crease the beautiful paper.'

'I do *not* need lessons on handling great music, thank you,' Miss Benbow said crushingly.

There was silence but for the slow rustle of pages. Miss Benbow played a few bars on the piano.

'Is good, *Ja*?' Jenger said.

'You give me your absolute assurance that these manuscripts are genuine?' Miss Benbow asked.

'Of course. Look, I have a letter from . . .'

Annaliese had heard enough. Parting the heavy, full-length curtains that covered the spacious bow-window, she stepped into the room. She did so quietly and slowly, at pains to avoid creating undue shock. Nevertheless, the effect on Jenger was sensational: he was appalled by the discovery that he and his intended victim were not alone. But Nancy, unable to resist joining the exit from their hiding-place, saw that there was much more to it than that. Jenger had recognised Annaliese.

'Well, well . . . I never thought our paths would cross again, Otto,' she said, speaking in German.

Pulling himself together, he responded in the same language. 'Your Imperial and Royal Highness! This is a great pleasure.'

'Unexpected, though.' Annaliese smiled. She extended her right hand and Jenger bowed to brush it lightly with his lips. 'What brings you to England?'

'Things are not what they were in Vienna, Highness. Germany is a madhouse and the French are Philistines. Where else could I go?'

'Wasn't it difficult getting in?' Annaliese asked.

'False papers,' Jenger replied. His smile veered from guilt to professional pride.

'Ah, your stock-in-trade,' Annaliese laughed. 'I'm a British subject now, by the way. I'm married to an Englishman.'

'I hope that Your Highness is happy?'

'Very much so, thank you, Otto.'

Nancy was having a wonderful time. She had no idea what was being said, although the friendly courtesy of the exchanges was apparent. The look on Miss Benbow's face was priceless. It seemed that the singer had some knowledge of the German language, nowhere near enough to follow the conversation, but sufficient to understand that Annaliese's pre-marriage status had been exalted. Jenger, ignoring both Miss Benbow and Nancy, had eyes only for his Archduchess and fellow-Viennese.

She turned to the piano where the manuscripts were spread on the lid. 'Well, Otto, you rogue, what have you been up to this time?' she asked.

'Nothing to trouble Your Highness,' Jenger said. 'A little game, that's all.' He made an attempt to gather the songs up: Annaliese froze him with a look.

'Let's see,' she said. Selecting one of the sheets, she held it up to the light provided by a cluster of electric bulbs. 'Very good,' she muttered. 'Very good indeed. Is this paper part of the batch you stole from Schratt's in nineteen-eleven?'

'It was nineteen-twelve, Highness.'

'Mmm. Good, isn't it?' Annaliese made what was to be her sole concession to Miss Benbow. 'The watermarks and sheet-numbering are right,' she said in English. 'This is genuine paper of a type frequently used by Schubert.' There was mockery in her voice as she turned back to Jenger and reverted to German. 'The ink and script aren't too bad. However, you're no musician, Otto. *Everyone* knows that Schubert's original version of *Auflösung* cast the first six bars in F major – he didn't decide to change it to E minor until he was correcting the printed proofs.'

'I'm deeply sorry, Highness. A stupid error. If you will permit me to go?'

'That would be best.' Annaliese frowned at his second attempt to gather up the sheets of manuscript paper. 'Otto, you really are incorrigible. You cannot seriously imagine that I intend letting you walk away with these travesties?' His mobile face crumpled into wry resignation. 'I will not have you wandering around London in search of other gullible fools! It would be best if you went back to Vienna. You must certainly leave England.'

'Yes, Highness. Tomorrow.'

'Good. If you ever give me grounds for suspicion again, I shall be very cross.' Smiling sweetly, Annaliese took Jenger's elbow and escorted him from the room.

Miss Benbow appeared to be in danger of exploding. Cocking her head to listen to the earnest conversation that was taking place in the entrance-lobby, she sidled towards Nancy.

'Do you speak German?' she whispered.

'No.'

'Well, I have what you might call a working knowledge. That wretched man called Mrs Boothby-Graffoe "Highness". He did it repeatedly.'

'That doesn't surprise me,' Nancy said nonchalantly.

'Why?'

'Her maiden name was Habsburg. She was a member of the ruling clan – I guess they must be the crowd who used to be Holy Roman Emperors. It's a hell of a shame they got shoved out by the War.'

A door closed, footsteps clicked on a parquet floor and Annaliese was back. 'There,' she said. 'Simple, wasn't it?'

Of all the questions that a spluttering Miss Benbow wanted to ask, the one that escaped was the least important. 'Why did you call him Otto?'

'Because it's his real name,' Annaliese replied, looking as though she were burdened with a complete idiot. 'Otto Fischer. Quite a nice fellow with a good family background – he could have amounted to something if his wife hadn't run off with a Bulgarian.' Crossing to the piano, she picked up the forgeries and tore them into pieces which she threw into the empty grate. '*Such* a shame to have to destroy such lovely paper. Matches, anyone?'

'Sure.' Grinning at Miss Benbow's thunderstruck inability to speak, Nancy rummaged in her handbag.

It was Lord Hammerwich who began to spread the story, taking great care that his beloved Miss Benbow did not look *too* foolish. As her detractors were quick to point out, not everyone was prepared to believe that original manuscripts were to be had from an individual who sounded like a door-to-door salesman. The criticism was countered by bestowing powers of fiendish cunning on Otto Fischer, alias Muller, Stoll, and Jenger. Miss Benbow was further helped by London Society's eagerness to relish and embroider the story of the beautiful young Archduchess who had outwitted the hellhound. It was a perfect antidote to the despondency that was affecting so many people – an inexplicable phenomenon at a time when post-war elation should have been firmly in the ascendant.

Gaining in strength and colour by the hour, the story circulated with tremendous speed. Beatrice received the first telephone call about it while Annaliese and Gwen were on a train back to Sussex, less than twenty-four hours after Otto Fischer had faded away from Eugenia Benbow's flat. The following evening, Charles mentioned it over their evening meal at the house in Regent's Park.

'How do you know about this?' Beatrice wailed.

'My darling, half of London is talking about it.'

'What are they saying?'

Charles smiled. 'Quite a number are disappointed that Eugenia *didn't* get robbed. The rest are carrying on blind about your sister-in-law. She's being hailed as the finest thing that Boothby's have ever acquired.'

'I haven't acquired her,' Beatrice insisted.

'I'd keep quiet about that if I were you,' Charles said.

Two days later, Nancy became outspoken after Beatrice had shown signs of wanting to resist the inevitable.

'What makes you think you have a choice? Are you telling me that Boothby's is doing so well that you can afford to ignore all this?'

'We're clearing a colossal amount of stock,' Beatrice retorted hotly. 'Over five hundred lots went at last Tuesday's open sale.'

'Great. How much ended up in the till?'

'Well . . . just under four thousand pounds,' Beatrice admitted. 'But that was an exceptionally bad day.'

'No, it wasn't,' Nancy snapped back. 'You've been grumbling about the decline in item values for eighteen months, to my certain knowledge. All right, I know you tend to do the big stuff in private, but there isn't enough of it. Get Annaliese in here and Sotheby's will be wondering what the hell they're doing wrong.'

Beatrice travelled to Upper Overs that evening. Lord Douglas, who was a willing party to the discussion, was all in favour of Annaliese putting in at least two days a week at Boothby's. He also saved her the trouble of voicing a serious doubt.

'I'm right, am I not, in thinking that you and Miss Benbow were very lucky with this forger?'

'Yes,' Annaliese said with great feeling.

'I'm sorry, I don't understand,' Beatrice said.

'Annaliese knows a great deal about Schubert and his music,' Lord Douglas said patiently. 'She was ideal for the circumstances. But how much does she know about, say, furniture?'

'Very little,' Annaliese was quick to point out. 'I'm all right on pianos and the sort of furniture in Schönbrunn and the Belvedere, but I know nothing about English and French types.'

'The answer is quite simple,' Lord Douglas said before Beatrice could start worrying. 'I shall teach her.'

'How?' Beatrice asked as though it were the most improbable idea that she had ever heard.

'Dear child, this house is full of books on the subject and I'd be surprised if we didn't have every worthwhile type of furniture – added to which, my own experience is reasonably extensive.'

Beatrice looked at Annaliese. 'What do you think? *Could* we get away with it?'

'I don't see why not. I'll work tremendously hard.'

She was as good as her word. Somehow – and there were times when she herself was at a loss to know how she did it – Annaliese kept one step ahead of the clients. To supplement Lord Douglas's tuition, she always had her nose in a book. She studied while she ate, when she went to bed, and during the increasingly frequent train journeys between Crowborough and London. Gwen was a constant and perfect travelling companion, watchful but unobtrusive, and never wasting time with chatter.

Sure enough, exactly as Charles Templeton and Nancy had predicted, new clients began to appear at Boothby's. It scarcely mattered that their initial motive was curiosity; a significant number decided to do business. One, a near-penniless dowager who was struggling to survive in circumstances made infinitely worse by the deaths of her two sons in the War, became a far greater and more popular talisman than Eugenia Benbow. Two dining-suites, each with twelve chairs and a pair of sideboards that had been dismissed as junk by various experts, proved to be the work of David Reisner, Marie Antionette's favourite craftsman. Having spotted the possibilities of the pieces, Annaliese persuaded Lord Douglas to leave Upper Overs in order to confirm her intuition.

The exertions of a day in London exposed the fragility of his constitution and he made no secret of his desire to get back to his beloved Sussex as soon as possible. Nevertheless, he spent nearly two hours examining the furniture and was happy to agree with Annaliese: it *was* by David Reisner.

The two suites were sold within ten minutes. A French nobleman who was prowling round Boothby's simply to catch a glimpse of Annaliese, looked on while the authentication was in progress, decided that the furniture was ideal for the ancestral château he was renovating, and made an offer. Although it was a private sale, none of the parties involved objected to details of the transaction becoming common knowledge: the 'pile of junk' had realised £12,000. At a stroke, Annaliese had confounded the 'experts', solved the much-loved Lady Leintwardine's financial problems, and shown that Boothby's was an establishment where supply and demand could blend into a felicitous partnership.

*

Despite the hectic pace of that eventful May, Annaliese and Nancy created the time and opportunities to convert their rapport into deep friendship. A week after the Eugenia Benbow episode, Annaliese paid her first visit to Martha's Vineyard.

It was late afternoon and the big house was deserted save for the servants, who put on their well-drilled act of remaining discreetly out of sight and hearing, unless summoned. Over tea and cakes, Annaliese discovered one important aspect of Nancy's life and sensed another.

'You have a husband,' Annaliese said, once the brief formalities were out of the way and they were at ease in the conservatory in which Nancy talked to her special confidantes.

'Indeed I do. He's a dear, sweet man. I gave him a quarter of a million as a marriage gift and he visits me twice a month. We have a very satisfactory life.' Correctly interpreting Annaliese's inquisitive expression, Nancy chuckled throatily. 'No, we don't do it – not any more. Poor Harold has lost the yen. Let me be the first to tell you that I have lovers. Plural. Are you shocked?'

'Not in the least.' Annaliese was perfectly at ease. 'I was brought up in Vienna – in privileged surroundings, and with some very promiscuous relatives.'

Nancy smiled at the revealing statement and they drifted into a discussion of London's more prominent socialites.

That first call lasted for no more than an hour and Annaliese saw little of the house. Even so, she detected the first traces of its distinctively sybaritic atmosphere. Subsequent visits reinforced the impression that Nancy and her lovers were by no means the only source of excitement at Martha's Vineyard.

From the outset, Nancy was pressed to give a dinner at which Annaliese would combine the roles of novelty and guest of honour. Arranged for the last Sunday in May, with Annaliese agreeing to sleep at Martha's Vineyard afterwards, it was the occasion that caused Beatrice to express concern to Charles.

In addition to Nancy and Annaliese, twelve others sat down to dinner at eight o'clock. Annaliese thought it very unlikely that every one of the eight men and four women were unmarried – indeed, all the women wore rings – yet none of them had partners in the accepted sense of the word. They were, however, a close-knit clique, with their own language and sophisticated undercurrents. Cordelia Milford was present, exhibiting a lazy sexuality that the other women copied. The men had an easy lack of pretension that Annaliese was sure concealed their power. None of them seemed particularly famous or pre-eminent, but the influence they exerted in their various professional fields was great and far-reaching, Annaliese felt.

As the evening drew to its close, Cordelia Milford, making no bones about it, chose a man to escort her home. The other women selected their partners more subtly. When she was alone with Nancy in the conservatory after all the guests had gone, Annaliese mentioned the way the party had dispersed.

'Cordelia doesn't mess about,' Nancy said. 'She sees something she likes and she takes it. But all my group are like that.'

'You seem to be a very adventurous crowd,' Annaliese said.

'We are,' Nancy agreed. 'Do you think we're pretty bad?'

Annaliese shrugged. 'Why? Where's the harm in it?'

'The way we do it, there isn't any,' Nancy said. 'It needs control – not much, though, they're a decent bunch who know when they're on to a good thing. That keeps them steady. They took to you. That will count for something.'

'At Boothby's?' Annaliese asked.

'They'll spread the word,' Nancy said. 'There could be other benefits, too.'

'Being able to work is making a huge difference,' Annaliese said, deciding to ignore Nancy's hint. 'It's settling me down.'

'Which is no mean achievement after the start you had – hell, what a thing that was!' Nancy cast her eyes up to the glass roof and the heavens beyond. 'Beatrice tells me that your father-in-law is holding his own these days.'

'Just about,' Annaliese said. 'He's very brave and cheerful, but I'm sure there isn't much underneath. To be honest, I *do* worry about him. I hope he'll go to stay with his brother again in the summer.'

'I hear you got on well with the Duke,' Nancy said.

'Yes, he's a lovely man. What about his son, Ralph, though? People say the most awful things about him.'

Nancy's face clouded. 'He's a bastard!' she said vehemently.

'Oh. I was starting to think that he sounded rather intriguing.'

'You aren't the first to get that idea,' Nancy retorted bitterly. 'Just forget it. Take it from me that the Marquess of Axholme is a piece of dog dirt.'

'I'll remember,' Annaliese said dutifully. Secretly, she thought that her friend's condemnation made Ralph sound even more fascinating.

'Make sure you do.' After driving home the point, Nancy's mood changed. 'Have you told Edward about your work at Boothby's?'

'Yes.' Annaliese's reply was wary.

'And?' Nancy said. 'What does he think?'

'I suppose you'd call it over-polite tolerance,' Annaliese replied. 'My impression is that I'm expected to stop doing it when he comes home.'

'Mmm . . . I see.' Nancy was pensive, seeking a way to approach a very difficult subject. 'It's a brute him having to be in Paris so soon after you were married.'

'It is,' Annaliese agreed.

Nancy waited, watching and biding her time. Eventually, she decided that she had to barge straight in. 'You and Edward have problems, don't you?' she said.

12

May–September 1919
How did you learn to do that?

There were two possible responses. The first was emphatic denial. To be effective, it needed to be immediate. Annaliese said nothing, thereby committing herself to the truth.

First, however, she was curious. 'What makes you think that?' she asked.

'Lady Alice's funeral,' Nancy replied. 'I watched you and Edward for a couple of hours.'

Annaliese's nod was an admission that, for someone of Nancy's perception, the scrutiny could have been revealing. 'I want to be *absolutely* clear about one thing,' she said. 'I love Edward – very much indeed – and there is no reason to believe that he doesn't feel the same way about me.'

'Right,' Nancy said. 'I've got that.'

'Although we're different in so many ways, we seem to complement each other,' Annaliese added.

'Fine.' Nancy smiled and waited.

'But there appear to be problems . . . at least, I think so.' Annaliese was in trouble. 'You see, I simply don't know.'

'Most people are the same at the start,' Nancy said soothingly. 'They have no idea what to expect from marriage.'

'The first few days we spent in France immediately after the wedding were marvellous . . . and crossing the Channel was even better.' Annaliese laughed nervously. 'But it was dreadful when we got here . . . and I'm not convinced that Lady Alice's death can be blamed for all of it . . .' Annaliese stopped, staring at Nancy's quizzical expression with mounting desperation. At last, she gave in. 'It's the sex thing,' she said wretchedly.

'Do you want to tell me?' Nancy asked gently.

Annaliese was hunched-up, studying the intricate patterns of the conservatory's mosaic floor. 'Yes,' she said. 'I have a feeling that you might be able to help.'

'I just might,' Nancy murmured.

It was difficult to get started. Annaliese repeatedly hesitated and stumbled over the account of how she had saved Edward from his inability to consummate the union on their first night. Then, it became much easier. Reassured by Nancy's quiet sympathy, Annaliese found that she enjoyed describing the passion of St Malo and the splendid night on the ferry. Her baffled bitterness at the subsequent fiascos was brief but lucid.

'Yes,' Nancy said when it was over. 'That sounds typical.' She refilled their coffee-cups and reached for a gold cigarette-case. 'I suppose you've heard of that guy, Sigmund Freud?'

'Of course. He's Viennese. Most people thought he was mad.'

'That doesn't surprise me.' It was clear that Nancy considered the people, not Freud, to be at fault. 'I've read quite a bit of his stuff,' she went on. 'I won't say that he's got it all absolutely right, but he's headed in the right direction. Hell, sex *is* important, and it's time somebody said so instead of all the sniggering and winking. You couldn't count the number of times a day I think about it.'

'That's a relief,' Annaliese said. 'I was wondering if there was something wrong with me.'

Nancy shook her head. 'Forget *that*. You're telling me that you want to let yourself go and have fun but Edward doesn't . . . is that right?'

'More or less. The time he virtually raped me – which was the day before the funeral – I think he was trying to get rid of his inhibitions. He said something about being natural and spontaneous, but it turned into such a disaster . . . Especially when we tried again, after a few days.'

'I don't like the sound of that,' Nancy was forced to admit. 'But look on the bright side . . . there's nothing wrong with an incompetent dumbo that a woman can't put right. Most men have to be shown what they're missing.'

'I've wondered whether it was beginner's luck in St Malo,' Annaliese said. 'We were both virgins and neither of us had the faintest idea what we were doing. Does that matter?'

'Very much,' Nancy replied. 'It took me two years to get the hang of the basics and another three to work on the goodies . . . and that was with guys who were experts.'

Annaliese threw up her hands in a gesture of despair. 'What chance do *I* stand?' She looked hard at Nancy. 'I expect you could introduce me to a man who would "educate" me?'

'No trouble at all. At least two of that lot at dinner tonight would jump at the chance. But that's no good to you, is it?'

'Definitely not,' Annaliese said firmly. 'I have no intention of being unfaithful to Edward.'

'Sure.' It was what Nancy expected. Not entirely seriously, she suggested, 'Would it help to see what other folks get up to? I've got hundreds of pictures.'

'The ones I came across weren't any good,' Annaliese replied. She saw that Nancy was surprised. 'When I lived there, Vienna must have been the pornography capital of Europe . . . my brother had a huge collection.'

'He showed you?' Nancy asked incredulously.

'Don't be silly.' Annaliese laughed. 'I stumbled across his hiding-place one day. Some of the pictures *were* interesting – that's how I learned what little I know. But most of them were dreadfully self-conscious and *lifeless* – they made you want to laugh.'

Nancy drew deeply on the cigarette, then tilted her head back to blow smoke towards the glass roof. 'How about watching a couple actually doing it?' she asked.

'I'd probably die of embarrassment,' Annaliese replied.

'Because they could see you watching them?'

'Yes.'

'And if that problem could be solved?' Nancy murmured.

'That might be different,' Annaliese said in a small, tense voice.

Nancy stood up, stubbing out her cigarette. 'Come with me,' she ordered.

They moved stealthily, not disturbing the house's expressive silence. At the end of the second-floor landing, Nancy unlocked a door, turning on the lights as she shepherded Annaliese inside. The room was windowless, about twenty feet square, and fitted with a crimson carpet. Its furnishings were an armchair, a *chaise-longue*, and what appeared to be two mattresses, lying on the floor and covered by white silk sheets. The walls were hung with rich tapestries with gaps for the two doors and a huge mirror. Nancy allowed Annaliese time to inspect the room thoroughly before beckoning her into the corridor. There was another door to unlock and they were in a much smaller room, lit by a glow that was coming through what appeared to be a sheet of plain glass. It was the other side of the mirror.

'That's amazing,' Annaliese gasped.

'Clever, huh?' Nancy said proudly. 'I'm told it's the only one in London.'

'And we can't be seen from the other side?' Annaliese asked.

'Go take a look. I'll stay here.'

Annaliese did so. She peered into the mirror from every possible angle, but there was nothing apart from her own reflection. To be absolutely certain, she tapped on the glass: Nancy's answering knock was eerily invisible.

'Well?' Nancy asked, returning to the extraordinary room.

Looking round yet again, Annaliese became conscious of the second door. 'What's that?' she asked.

'Dressing-room.' Laughing, Nancy corrected herself. '*Un*dressing-room.'

'And people really don't mind doing things in here while others watch through that?' Annaliese pointed to the mirror.

'*Mind*?' Nancy hooted. 'Look, honey, let me tell you straight, so you know what's what round here. I have friends who *complain* if they aren't allowed to show how good they are.'

'And do they know who is behind the mirror?' Annaliese asked.

'That depends,' Nancy said. She relocked the room as they left it. 'They always ask, of course. Sometimes I tell lies – not just to protect people. If a man thinks he's being watched by a woman who's expressed an interest in him it increases the fun.'

They strolled to the head of the stairs in contemplative silence. 'I'd want you to lie for me,' Annaliese said.

'That's easy enough.' Nancy took her arm. 'Does that mean you're gonna give it a go?'

Annaliese exploded into recklessness. 'Yes.'

They were on the first-floor landing, moving towards the bedroom in which Annaliese was to spend the night. 'I'll fix a special show for you as soon as possible,' Nancy said. 'What's your schedule for this week? How long are you planning to be in London?'

'I was thinking of going back to Upper Overs on Wednesday evening,' Annaliese replied. Anticipating what Nancy was about to suggest, she added, 'Gwen didn't come with me this time.'

'That's fine. Don't go to Cadogan Square. Stay here.'

'Very well.'

After an extremely full day at Boothby's, it was nearly seven o'clock when Annaliese arrived at Martha's Vineyard on Monday evening. Nancy was bursting with news.

'I've managed to fix something for tomorrow,' she said, offering Annaliese a Martini cocktail. 'Can you make it for six?'

'Yes . . . it should be a quieter day.'

'Be as prompt as you like,' Nancy said. 'This one was tricky because of other engagements.' She smiled. 'One of the players has a dinner-date at St James's Palace afterwards.'

Annaliese was astounded by the speed at which Nancy had made the arrangements: it was a powerful demonstration of the influence she exerted over her amazing coterie. The two women spent a pleasant, gossipy evening together, Annaliese fighting a constant battle against her nerves and the urge to tell Nancy that she had changed her mind, that she no longer wished to hide behind the mirror. Outwardly, however, she remained calm, went to bed soon after ten, studied a book on Jacobean furniture for an hour, and fell asleep.

After keeping an eye on the clock all afternoon, Annaliese was at Nancy's house soon after five-thirty on Tuesday. She was met in the entrance-hall by Christina, one of Nancy's maids, who was looking after her.

'Lady Shenstone will be pleased you're in good time,' Christina said. 'Would you like to freshen up?'

'Er . . . yes . . . all right,' Annaliese agreed, sensing that it was expected of her. Left alone, she dabbed toilet water on her face, fiddled with her hair, and was on the point of starting to pace the bedroom when Christina re-appeared.

'We can go up, Your Highness,' she said, a sweetly reassuring smile emphasising her beauty.

'Where is Lady Shenstone?' Annaliese asked as they climbed to the second floor.

'She isn't far away,' Christina replied. 'She said you're not to worry.'

Oddly enough, Annaliese found that she was disinclined to worry. On the contrary, she was looking forward to whatever lay in store.

They reached the two doors, halting at the second where Christina pressed a bell-push that Annaliese had not noticed on Sunday night. Almost at once, there was a muted buzz in response.

'They're ready,' Christina said. 'Would Your Highness like me to come in with you?'

'Yes, I think I would,' Annaliese said on the spur of the moment.

It was as well that she did so. One of the mattresses had been positioned virtually against the mirror. It was so close that Annaliese felt that she could have reached out to touch the woman and two men lying on it. All stark naked, they were an attractive, shockingly magnetic spectacle. Instinctively reaching for the hand that Christina offered, Annaliese sank into a chair.

One of the men was Jack Nesbitt. On Sunday evening at dinner, he had appeared almost dull. The other, a fair-haired, superbly muscled individual, was much younger than Jack – no more than twenty-three, Annaliese thought. The woman, on whom they were lavishing sensuous attention, was Cordelia Milford. Jack Nesbitt was stroking her breasts, teasing at the proud nipples with the tip of his tongue; the young man had a hand busy between Cordelia's legs. Annaliese saw that the trio were deeply involved in conversation as well as intimate fondling.

'Can they hear us?' Annaliese whispered to Christina.

'No. The glass is quite sound-proof.'

'Who is the young man?'

'That's Tommy Weston. He works in the Baltic Exchange.' Christina sounded affectionate. 'He plays cricket for Middlesex sometimes. Isn't he magnificent?'

'Yes, I suppose he is,' Annaliese said, bemused by young Weston's lithe muscularity and the almost terrifying scale of his fiercely aroused manhood.

'Lady Milford will choose Tommy,' Christina said. 'She hates him . . . She says he's stupid and bumptious. But she can never resist him.'

She was soon proved right. Cordelia Milford coaxed Tommy on to his back, swung astride his hips, and impaled herself, wincing at the pleasure of it. Jack Nesbitt left them, going to the *chaise-longue* to watch.

Cordelia began to ride Tommy Weston savagely, spurred on by the way he was rubbing her breasts. She was, Annaliese thought, an astonishingly attractive woman with a firm, shapely body in excellent condition.

'Tommy's trouble is that he never seems to last long enough,' Christina said. 'Especially with her like *that*! I did nice things to him about an hour ago, but it won't help him!'

'How old is Lady Milford?' Annaliese asked.

'Forty-four, I think,' Christina said. 'And Tommy's only twenty-two.' She smiled. 'Terrible, isn't it?'

Annaliese hardly knew what she thought. She was transfixed by the sight of a sex act in which the woman was ruthlessly dominant. Selfishly, using both strength and skill to extract the utmost from the instrument of her pleasure, Cordelia Milford was driving herself towards climax. It was a relentless struggle that she was determined to win. A few moments after she achieved her carnal triumph, falling on to Tommy Weston's chest in writhing ecstasy, his body arched and he was clutching at his head. Watching the way his lips curled back in a snarl of excruciating pleasure, Annaliese made a resolution: one day, at an appropriate time, she would do that to Edward.

Despite what appeared to be complete exhaustion, Cordelia Milford recovered quickly. If her manner was any sort of guide, what she said to Tommy Weston was viciously uncomplimentary. He laughed it off and enjoyed the view of her backside as she stalked towards the door of the dressing-room. It opened as she approached it and a second woman emerged. Annaliese clapped a hand to her mouth, stifling a shriek of surprise.

The new arrival had a black mask covering the top half of her face, yet it hardly prevented identification: the angular cheek-bones and mane of copper-coloured hair were quite unmistakable.

'Why is Lady Shenstone wearing that thing?' Annaliese asked.

'She always does in there,' Christina replied, very matter-of-fact. 'I think it's just because she enjoys it – everyone always knows who she is.'

Apart from the mask, Nancy was naked. With her full breasts, narrow waist, and exceptionally long legs, she looked ravishing. Jack Nesbitt, who was still sprawled on the *chaise-longue*, eyed her appreciatively. They exchanged a few pleasantries, then Nancy knelt down beside him. Slowly, with calculating deliberation, she raked her finger-nails along his erection. Jack Nesbitt shuddered. Unhurried, obviously enjoying his helpless craving, Nancy repeated the torture. And again. In all, she did it sixteen times. Annaliese counted.

'What a state that wretched man's in,' she whispered to Christina.

'Lady Shenstone can keep them like that for *ages*,' Christina said. 'She loves making them squirm and beg.'

'He certainly seems to be doing that,' Annaliese said.

'I think she may make it even worse for him,' Christina replied. 'Yes, here we are, look.'

Leaning forward, Nancy took the tip of Nesbitt's penis into her mouth. After registering bliss, his face became distraught.

'Good God!' Annaliese breathed.

'Poor Tommy,' Christina murmured. 'Look how excited he is – *again*.' It was true enough. At first, Annaliese was surprised that he should be ready so soon after Cordelia Milford: then she understood that watching Nancy at work on Nesbitt was bound to have an effect on a man. 'Would you excuse me, please, Your

Highness?' Christina asked. 'He needs help.'

Annaliese muttered her agreement and Christina slipped away. In no time at all, she was hurrying through the door opposite the transparent mirror. She must, Annaliese realised, have been wearing few, if any, clothes beneath her nondescript grey dress: it was the only explanation for the speed at which she stripped. Young Weston responded joyously to her loveliness and, before she had time to adjust to the rapid progress of events, Annaliese was witnessing another bout of love-making.

At eight o'clock, Annaliese and Nancy had dinner. Christina waited on them. It was the sheer normality of the meal that finally threatened to destroy Annaliese's composure. Eventually, she accepted the fact that the two women who had given themselves up to sexual abandon in the mirror-room were, without the slightest difficulty, going to behave as though butter would not dare melt in their mouths.

Driving the point home, Nancy initiated a discussion that involved Boothby's. She knew of two aristocrats who were hard-up. Their dilapidated mansions were packed with treasures that meant nothing to them, but they had a horror of the publicity that a sale might attract. Nancy's inquiries suggested that they would be amenable to a discreet approach from Annaliese. Using pencil and paper brought to the table by a respectfully straight-faced Christina, Annaliese noted the details.

Only at the end of the meal, after they had moved into the conservatory, a place of secrets and intimate conspiracy, did Nancy come to the topic that had kept Annaliese on tenterhooks.

'Well, did you learn anything behind that mirror?'

'Heavens, yes. I can't begin to thank you,' Annaliese enthused, glad of a chance to unleash some of her repressed excitement.

'Before you get carried away, let me tell you something.' Nancy raised a long, steely forefinger in admonition. 'Hear this and hear it good, right? Do not – I repeat, *not* – jump on Edward the minute he gets back and start showing him what you've picked up.'

'I wasn't intending to,' Annaliese replied. 'What makes you say that?'

'Firstly, we don't want to give him the idea that you've been playing whoopee while he was away.'

'Exactly.'

'Second, he's bound to find out that you and I are friends.' Nancy looked grave. 'That is bad news. Edward does not approve of me. He believes I indulge in every vice known to man and beast *plus* a few new ones that I've invented myself.'

'The very idea.' Annaliese laughed.

'Give him an excuse to start using that brain of his and you're in trouble.'

'There's another thing I have to look out for,' Annaliese said.

'What's that?'

'I suspect that Edward has a puritanical streak in him,' Annaliese replied. 'It isn't beyond the bounds of possibility that he might enjoy something, *then* decide to be angry about it.'

Nancy whistled. 'If that happens, honey, you and me will have to have a real serious talk.'

Later, when Christina was helping Annaliese prepare for bed, she was eager for an opinion on the view through the mirror.

'What do you expect me to say?' Annaliese laughed. 'It was astounding. I thought that you and Mr Weston made a very good show . . . You *did* enjoy yourselves.'

'I like Tommy,' Christina said. 'He's got to marry soon. By all accounts, she's perfectly horrible, but his parents think it's a good match. He'll still come here for his *real* entertainment, though.'

'I presume it was Cordelia Milford who was dashing off to St James's Palace?' Annaliese asked.

'Yes. She's well in with the Prince of Wales.'

'They aren't lovers, surely?'

'I wouldn't think so,' Christina replied. 'I've heard it suggested that she advises the Prince on his lady friends.'

'Of whom there are many, I understand,' Annaliese said.

'Far too many.' Christina was disapproving. 'So, you enjoyed the performance,' she said, reverting to her customary cheerfulness.

'Yes, Christina, I did.' Annaliese was suddenly tense. 'I wish my husband were here,' she said plaintively.

*

Seven weeks and a few days later, Edward came home, slightly before the official conclusion of the peace conference.

Someone with an eye for theatre and history had decided that the German delegation would be marched into the Hall of Mirrors at Versailles on 28 June, the fifth anniversary of Franz Ferdinand's assassination at Sarajevo. In the chamber where Bismarck had proclaimed the German Empire after the defeat of France in 1871, the representatives of the vanquished nation were made to sign a treaty they had scarcely had time to read. Seeing no point in staying for this final, grotesque charade, Edward left Paris on the evening of 24 June, reaching Dover the following morning. He found Annaliese and his father waiting for him with the Rolls.

At an hotel on the outskirts of the town where they stopped for breakfast, Lord Douglas surveyed Edward with mock-resignation and said, 'I suppose you think that the treaty is the most flawed instrument ever concocted and that it will lead to all manner of problems?'

'Yes, I do,' Edward replied.

Lord Douglas sighed and rolled his eyes at Annaliese. 'We must brace ourselves,' he said. 'There will be endless lectures, during which every last point will be explained in remorseless detail.'

'There will not,' Edward said firmly. 'It's very likely that the problems created by that treaty will keep me busy for the rest of my working life. But I've made a vow that I shall not be boring about it. I'm very glad to be home. I'm thrilled that you've come to meet me, and delighted to see you both looking so well.' Taking Annaliese's hand, he drew her closer and kissed her.

'Is this completely official?' Lord Douglas asked.

'Yes, Father, on my honour.' Edward laughed.

'Didn't Mr Amery travel with you?' Annaliese asked. After rereading Edward's letters as a preparation for the reunion, her husband's mentor seemed almost like an old friend.

'He's taking an extended holiday to explore France,' Edward replied. 'The Foreign Office has finished with him.'

'Isn't that rather short-sighted of it?' Annaliese asked.

'He was on secondment,' Edward said. 'I know it's gone on for ages, but his heart is in Cambridge and he wants to get back. In any case, I refuse to be drawn into arguments about the Foreign Office.'

They all laughed and Annaliese saw that Edward meant what he said. For the time being, he was sick to death of diplomacy's devious byways. The happy mood continued once they were on the road, Lord Douglas driving, Annaliese and Edward sitting very close together in the back of the Rolls. The conversation flitted around like a butterfly, never staying in one place long enough to have a chance of becoming serious. Annaliese was expecting that Edward would defer the inevitable question about Boothby's until they were alone, but it came out as part of the animated banter.

Annaliese phrased her reply with great care. 'I go there two or three days a week. I seem to be useful and I enjoy it.'

'You're a damned sight more than that, my dear.' Lord Douglas had lowered the glass partition so that he could listen to what was being said in the back and join in when necessary. 'I'd say you'd got a fight on your hands, Edward.'

'I'm sorry, I don't understand.' Edward was so puzzled that he tore himself away from Annaliese to lean forward.

'I suppose you'll want to put your foot down,' Lord Douglas said. 'Dash it all, we can't have your wife working in a junk-shop, eh?'

Edward laughed. 'Boothby's is hardly a *junk-shop*, Father.'

'Next best thing, though.'

'Who wants to stop Annaliese working there?' Edward asked.

'You will,' Lord Douglas said. 'It's the sort of dog-in-a-manger caper that's right up your street.'

'This is outrageous!' Edward shouted, still in a good humour. 'Have I said or implied that I want Annaliese to give up Boothby's?'

'If you want my advice, you won't,' Lord Douglas said earnestly. 'Otherwise, Beatrice will skin you alive. The fact is, my boy, what with the War and a few other things, Boothby's was starting to slide downhill. Not any more, by Jove! Turnover has gone up in leaps and bounds since Annaliese got cracking.'

'That's very good news,' Edward said.

'It is – and Beatrice won't thank you for trying to upset the applecart.'

'How many more crimes am I to be accused of?' Edward asked. Leaning back into the comfort of the seat, he clasped Annaliese's hand. 'I must say, this is a funny way of welcoming a chap home.'

Annaliese offered silent thanks to her adopted father. Under the guise of being an amiable, interfering old buffer, Lord Douglas had exercised considerable skill. Without a word passing between them, Edward had given his blessing to Annaliese's continued presence at Boothby's. The remainder of the day was to prove that his sunny mood was durable.

Reaching Upper Overs, Edward declared his need for what he called 'a damned good scrub'. Snatching at their first moment alone, he told Annaliese that he would like her to sit by the bath and talk to him.

'You're looking wonderfully well, my dear,' was his first comment when they were settled. 'I'd nearly forgotten how beautiful you are. I hope that doesn't sound awful?'

'It sounds *lovely*,' Annaliese assured him. 'Forgive me for saying so, *Liebste*, but you're slightly pale and tired.'

'No fresh air and ridiculous amounts of work,' Edward grumbled. 'It was worse than I'd imagined . . . never mind, I shall soon get over it. Father's in good form.'

'He's getting better,' Annaliese agreed. 'But don't expect too much. He's very pleased because you're back – he still has bad days, though.'

Edward nodded. 'Beatrice hinted at that in her last letter. She also said you'd worked miracles with him.'

'Teaching me enough to stop me looking a fool at Boothby's was the best thing for him,' Annaliese said.

'Yes, I can imagine that. You don't know how relieved and grateful I am. A couple of days after I went back to Paris, I started to feel terribly guilty about leaving you with him.'

'*Dummkopf!*' Annaliese reached for a huge sponge, made sure that it was saturated, and pushed it into Edward's face.

Not only did the laughter continue, Edward was eager to confront *the* problem. The long, late-June day had thirty minutes of dusky light left when he suggested that an early night was in order. Annaliese agreed at once.

Their love-making was gentle, with satisfaction flowing from tenderness. While Edward was being almost *too* considerate, Annaliese found her mind wandering to the scenes she had watched through the mirror at Martha's Vineyard nearly two months ago. Far from feeling ashamed, she used the images to augment her husband's carefully loving efforts. It proved to be good, an exquisite start to the new beginning for which she had prayed.

Lord Douglas particularly wanted to join Annaliese and Edward for breakfast the following morning.

'It's high time we did something about a wedding present,' he said, very businesslike.

'Oh.' Edward was at a loss.

'I'll bet you never had any,' Lord Douglas said. Annaliese wanted to laugh at the way he turned it into an accusation.

'We didn't make it easy for people to give us presents,' Edward said, rising to the bait.

'Well, of course you didn't,' Lord Douglas growled. 'Anyway, let's rectify the situation.' He beamed across the table. 'I want you to have the house in Cadogan Square.'

Annaliese and Edward gasped but said nothing.

'It will be yours, in any case, once I'm dead and gone,' Lord Douglas added.

'Father!' Edward shifted uneasily.

'I thought it would be useful for you to have it now. You need a decent house where you can cut a bit of a dash. And before you start wasting time, let me tell you that I'm more than happy with this dear old place. I daresay you'll give me a room and a crust when I have to be in London?'

'Don't be silly, Father.' Edward turned to Annaliese. 'What do you think about this, my dear?' he asked solicitously. 'You were talking of us finding our own place, weren't you?'

'I say, am I speaking out of turn?' Lord Douglas was worried. 'Look here, I don't want to spoil any plans you two might be making.'

'It's quite all right, Father,' Annaliese said. 'I see things differently now.' She turned to Edward. 'You'd like to live at Cadogan Square, wouldn't you?'

'Very much so, my dear. But your opinion matters, too.'

That, and their love-making of the previous night, was more than enough for Annaliese. She stood up, walked round the table and hugged Lord Douglas. 'Thank you,' she said. 'We'd love it – and we're very grateful.'

'I suppose you want it all decorating to suit you?' Lord Douglas said, pretending to be grumpy.

'Yes, please,' Annaliese said, planting a kiss on his cheek. 'And a few alterations.'

'Consider it all taken care of,' Lord Douglas said. 'I expect I'm going to lose Gwen and Matthew?'

'I'm afraid so,' Annaliese said gaily. 'Always assuming that they want to come with me.'

'Oh, they will. You can depend on it.' Lord Douglas's gaze became shrewd. 'What other changes do you imagine you might want? Should I do something about Franklin?'

Annaliese was acutely conscious of Edward, looking at her with an anxiety that was tangible. It was tempting, very tempting indeed. For a few moments, she teetered on the brink of accepting the offer, but Edward was distressed and she decided to make a concession.

'No,' she said to Lord Douglas. 'I think we'll keep Franklin. Edward would be lost without him.'

The look on her husband's face persuaded Annaliese that she had done the right thing. She did not notice that Lord Douglas failed to share her optimism.

Buoyed up by five idyllic days at Upper Overs, Annaliese and Edward travelled to London by the early train on Monday 30 June, a busy and exciting day ahead of them. She was going to Cadogan Square to talk to an interior designer; he was bound for the Foreign Office where he hoped to learn of his future.

Annaliese had a good day, Edward a bad one. That evening, she was sympathetic and patient, eventually dispelling his ill-humour. It seemed that the men who mattered had been unavailable, so Edward had mooched around in search of old friends. It was, he said, a worse shambles than when he and Archie were hunting for a job at the start of the War.

Over a sandwich lunch at Boothby's the following day, Annaliese was discussing her ideas for the transformation of Cadogan Square with Beatrice and her beautifully good-looking assistant, Paul Marks. To their utter astonishment, Edward came bounding up the stairs from the ground floor.

'Goodness!' Beatrice exclaimed. 'This *is* an honour – and doesn't he look pleased with himself?'

Two seconds later, Edward burst into the office. 'Sorry to interrupt,' he said breathlessly. 'I thought you'd like to know the news as soon as possible. I'm going to be working for Lewis Peters.'

Annaliese's heart sank. 'You're going back to Paris?' she wailed.

'No, no! Lewis is posted home, promoted, and put in charge of the Commonwealth Administration Department. I'm to be his deputy.'

'How splendid!' Annaliese knocked a wastepaper basket flying in her haste to reach Edward and kiss him. 'You're *so* clever, my darling.'

Beatrice tapped Paul Marks on the shoulder, saying, 'I think we should leave this pair alone for a few minutes . . . Let them get it out of their systems.' Annaliese and Edward smiled sheepishly at Beatrice as she abandoned her office.

'What about promotion?' Annaliese asked. 'Are you getting it?'

'My word, yes.' Edward felt a sudden need to sit down. 'I can't believe this, yet. Guess what?'

'If you can't believe it, how can I be expected to guess it?' Annaliese laughed.

'I've been bumped up three grades,' Edward said. '*Three*! It's unheard of – I think.'

'Well-deserved, though.'

'Of course.' Edward's conceit was short-lived. 'They seem to have more vacancies than they know what to do with. It looks as if they've been pensioning off some of the dead wood.'

'What of it?' Annaliese perched on Edward's lap. 'You're going to be someone important, that's all that matters. When does all this come into force?'

'Lewis is due back in three weeks. I'm to have everything ready for him.'

'You're going to be busy.'

Edward pulled a face. 'That's the one snag – I'd been hoping that we could have a really first-class holiday together.'

'Oh!' Annaliese was pleasantly surprised. 'It can wait.'

'I'm afraid it will have to, my dear. But not for long.' Edward was exuberant again. 'September will be fine – I've already asked.'

'Won't that depend on Lewis?'

'Strictly speaking, yes. Can you see him objecting? He, of *all* people, knows how much we deserve a proper honeymoon.'

Reluctant to let Edward go while he was in such a rare mood, Annaliese found ways of keeping him talking for nearly half an hour. Finally, however, he said that he must return to Whitehall. As he stood up and caught sight of Beatrice and Paul Marks, inspecting a set of dining-chairs while they kept out of the way, Edward's face clouded.

'Be careful of Marks,' he said, right out of the blue.

'What on earth do you mean?' Annaliese asked, taken aback by the change in his attitude.

'He's an extremely unsavoury character.'

Annaliese gaped. 'He's nothing of the sort, Edward. He's a knowledgeable, very charming man. I owe him a great deal.'

'He's a pervert,' Edward whispered angrily.

'I'm sorry, you must be mistaken,' Annaliese replied. She was determined to remain calm. 'Beatrice thinks very highly of him.'

'Beatrice *protects* him,' Edward hissed.

'From what?'

'He's a homosexual, Annaliese. I know. I had to deal with that creature Beckmann in Vienna.'

'What am I supposed to do?' Annaliese asked.

'Stay away from him.'

'How can I? We work together.'

'Be careful. A man in my position can't afford scandal.'

'How can there be a scandal?' Annaliese's hands were clenched tight.

'What do you think people are likely to say if they find out that my wife is associating with a homosexual?'

The awful thing about it was that Edward was becoming annoyed with her. It was as if their beautiful few days at Upper Overs had never happened. Annaliese's patience snapped.

'I can't see what there is to worry about,' she said, her face twisted by a sardonic smile. '*If* Paul is a homosexual, then *I* am perfectly safe, am I not?' She watched Edward attempting to absorb the idea. 'And he doesn't seem to have corrupted Beatrice.'

'Just be very careful,' Edward retorted and left in a bad-tempered hurry.

There was so much to do that Annaliese was soon able to put the unpleasant scene behind her. Even so, she studied Paul Marks with a new, curious interest, an interest that she failed to conceal completely.

'Has my dear brother been having a go at Paul?' Beatrice asked when they were alone together.

'I'm afraid so.'

'Honestly, he is the limit!' Beatrice was annoyed. 'One of these days, I'll sit on his head.' She sighed. 'It's his favourite phobia and there are far too many like him. Paul would be in prison if they had their rotten way.'

'So he does prefer men?' Annaliese asked.

'Yes. You don't object to that, do you?'

'Of course not,' Annaliese replied.

'Edward's so naive in some things!' Beatrice fumed. 'I don't suppose he knows that there are women who incline towards their own sex.'

'As well as liking men,' Annaliese pointed out.

'Really? That's interesting.' Briefly, Beatrice was fascinated. Then, flushing with embarrassment, she became very busy again.

At Cadogan Square that evening, Annaliese and Edward began to establish the routine foundations of a marriage that promised to be busy. Now that her mind was made up, Annaliese wanted Edward's approval of her scheme for redecorating the house. He wanted to tell her what further surprises had emerged during his afternoon at the Foreign Office. Totally preoccupied with his professional future, Edward gave a somewhat absent-minded blessing to the renovation plans, leaving Annaliese with the impression that he had not listened to a word of her explanation. However, when they went to bed, he set all else aside and loved her with a devotion that was all the more affecting for being bashful.

Especially since the days that followed never had quite enough hours in them, Edward's harsh comments on Paul Marks were forgotten. Annaliese was in constant turmoil and argument with painters and people who swore they could make the curtains she wanted, yet subsequently displayed every sign of indifference. Meanwhile, Edward was engaged in what sounded like a life-or-death struggle to find offices for Lewis Peters, himself, and the thirty-odd staff who were to work for them.

At some point in the chaos, Edward became a member of a Club. It most definitely had a capital C; Annaliese was never in any doubt about that. And there was no question of it being a simple question of 'joining'. One was recommended, proposed, seconded, and, after due deliberation, invited to submit oneself for interview. The Club was called Fisk's and occupied imposing premises in Ashley Street at the very heart of St James's. Founded in 1791, Fisk's was, in effect, a top-class hotel, hidey-hole, and gossip-factory for men, drawing its membership from the upper echelons of the civil service, the legal profession, and banking. Membership was clearly advantageous to Edward's career, and – wonder of wonders – it was a tremendous place for bridge. Having Edward out of the way for at least two evenings a week while the house reeked of paint, and the curtain crisis worsened by the hour, seemed like manna from heaven. Moreover, in the fullness of time, when the chaos at Cadogan Square was over, Edward's Club nights would provide opportunities to visit Nancy.

During the second week of Annaliese's full-time residence, the chaos found itself confronted by two implacable enemies: Gwen and Matthew arrived. They were taking the place of three servants who had decided to leave as a consequence of the house's changed ownership. The instant Gwen had Annaliese to herself, she asked the most important question.

'How're you getting on with that muck-stirrer, Franklin?'

'He's behaving himself very well,' Annaliese said.

'No he isn't,' Gwen retorted. 'Why do you think three people have left?' Annaliese looked blank. 'It's because he's *staying*,' Gwen went on. 'There was a chance he'd be got rid of when you took over. Now, it's obvious he's going to be here for another twenty years, so them with the sense are getting out.'

Annaliese was dismayed. 'Are you sure of this Gwen?'

'Certain.' Gwen grinned. 'Look on the bright side – they weren't all that good, and you'd have had to get rid of them yourself to make room for me and Matthew if Franklin hadn't done the job for you.' Pausing for breath, Gwen gave the assurance that Annaliese had been about to request. 'Don't worry. If Franklin's nice to us, we'll be nice to him.' She sniffed disdainfully at the odours of decorating. 'Things are in a fair old state. I'll have a word with Matthew to find out what we can do about it.'

Annaliese never doubted that Gwen and Matthew would be worth their weight in gold. But when, two days later, Frances Peters turned up out of the blue, Gwen assumed the role of saviour.

'Oh Lord! Have I come at a bad time?' Frances asked.

'Yesterday was even worse,' Annaliese responded.

'I've been sent on ahead to find somewhere to live,' Frances explained. 'Perhaps I should go to an hotel.'

'I won't hear of such a thing,' Annaliese said. 'Things are getting better all the time, so there *must* be a habitable bedroom somewhere.'

There was, Gwen tracked it down and settled Frances in. Until Edward came home, there was an enormous amount of news and gossip to be exchanged. Then, at half past six, the greetings and laughter started all over again.

At dinner, Edward wondered about a house for Frances and Lewis. 'What sort of place are you looking for?' he asked.

'Oh, you know . . . big, imposing. Plenty of room to swing cats and keep a *huge* staff. Well, two or three, perhaps. And a big garden.

Lewis is talking of *cultivating* things.' Frances waved her arms a great deal.

'I think I know of a place that might fit the bill,' Edward said. 'A chap was talking about it at the Club the other evening. His aunt wants to let it and find a cottage in the country.'

'Where is it?' Frances asked.

'St John's Wood,' Edward replied. 'A bit out of the way, I'm afraid.'

'Never mind that.' Frances was excited. 'Is this house anywhere near Lord's Cricket Ground?'

'Two minutes away.'

Frances let out a shriek of delight and clapped her hands. 'Lewis will forgive all my sins and love me forever if I get him fixed up that close to the blasted thing,' she cried.

By some means or other – and no one knew how – everything fell into place by the end of July. Free of noise, dust, and smells, Cadogan Square looked a picture: even Edward was impressed and said so. In Whitehall, the Commonwealth Administration Department was all present and correct. To cap it all, Annaliese had been away for three days, valuing the entire contents of a country house in Shropshire in preparation for what Lord Douglas thought would be the biggest sale that Boothby's had ever undertaken.

A firm pattern had emerged. Annaliese and Edward dined with Frances and Lewis Peters twice a week, alternating between Cadogan Square and St John's Wood. On another two evenings, Edward went to his Club after work, staying until half past ten. Now that the house reflected her own tastes, Annaliese was perfectly content to be alone at Cadogan Square, spending many a happy hour at Lord Douglas's old roll-top desk in the study, poring over books on fine art. She also liked to visit Nancy, and often slipped round to Martha's Vineyard on foot.

On such an evening in August, Annaliese had a piece of news that she knew would interest her friend.

'We're going away for two weeks in September. It's to be our honeymoon.'

'Where?' Nancy asked.

'St Malo,' Annaliese replied. 'To the hotel where we spent those three days.'

'Ah!' Nancy's green eyes shone in the glow of the conservatory's soft lights. Her hair was flowing loose and her lush body was half-covered by a flimsy silk robe. She had been in bed with her current lover until little more than half an hour ago. Now, her languid distraction was replaced by keen interest. 'This sounds like *the* opportunity.'

'Yes. I'm looking forward to it.'

'So am I.' Nancy laughed. 'I can't wait to hear how you make out.'

'I'll be round as soon as we get back,' Annaliese promised. '*However*, before we go, I've got to organise a dinner-party for thirty people.'

'Honey, it's August,' Nancy said. 'There aren't thirty people in London. I'm only here because my man can't get away.'

'The Foreign Office hasn't gone on holiday,' Annaliese wailed. 'I'm supposed to fascinate the beasts.'

'No problem,' Nancy said carelessly, more concerned with admiring her legs. 'You'll kill them.'

To Annaliese's surprise, she did. Frances and Lewis came, of course, providing the moral support to help her through the tricky preliminaries. Once everyone was seated and the meal was being served, Annaliese realised that she had no cause to worry. The men whom Edward was seeking to impress were all nearing the end of their careers. They and their wives ranged from jaded cynicism to affably resigned acceptance of what life had done for them. There was an undercurrent of waspishness and a desire to be clever, usually at the expense of absent colleagues or politicians. Above all, there was respect for Annaliese, extending to awe in some cases.

The irony of it was not wasted on her. From her mother's letters, Annaliese knew that the Habsburgs were reviled in Austria, bearing the blame for practically everything. But in England, the name seemed to carry immense prestige. Once she had grasped what lay behind the treatment she was receiving, Annaliese played up to it shamelessly.

Because she enjoyed herself, she proved to be a great success.

Edward was delighted. 'You did wonderfully well, my dear,' he enthused when they were able to collapse after the last guests had gone. 'I was proud of you.'

'Oh, thank you, *Liebste*. Did I create the right sort of impression?'

Edward laughed and hugged her. 'They'll be talking about you for weeks. You have definitely been marked down as a Permanent Under Secretary's wife.'

Having heard it mentioned countless times during the past few weeks, Annaliese knew that the curious-sounding title belonged to the Foreign Office's most senior civil servant, a man of virtually unlimited power and influence. Apparently, a knighthood went with the post.

'Sir Edward Boothby-Graffoe,' Annaliese murmured, trying it out for the first time.

'It has a ring to it, don't you think?' he said. 'It's about the only way you can make my name sound half-decent.'

With three days to go before their holiday, the omens were propitious.

They had the same suite, the staff at the hotel made it plain that they were dedicated to ensuring perfection, and the weather was as fair as January had been foul.

After a first day in Rennes, where they spent hours marvelling at the great cathedral, there were walks, steamer trips, and bathing in the sea. The discovery that they were both strong swimmers gave Annaliese and Edward increased faith in the power of their affinity. On the hotel's tennis courts, they developed their own highly idiosyncratic version of the game. The fact that neither of them had held a racquet before was not lost on the appreciative, much-amused audiences they invariably attracted.

They made love every night before falling asleep and again on waking in the morning. Edward still lacked the confidence to create a resurgence of January's unrestrained passion, yet the very placidity of it all showed their dependence on each other in a way that raw excitement had failed to do. And every time, Annaliese's instincts told her that they had moved a step closer to the moment she longed for.

It came at the start of the second week, on a day that was less fine than its predecessors. Over lunch, Edward said that he thought it would rain. He repeated the observation five times in as many minutes. Annaliese, who considered the clouds harmless and likely to disappear with the freshening breeze, waited patiently.

At last, when he was forced to declare his intentions, Edward cleared his throat, took a last look at the sky, and said, 'I think we should stay in this afternoon. No point in getting wet. What do you think, my love?'

'I agree.' Keeping a straight face, Annaliese leaned closer to him. 'Why don't we go to bed?' she whispered. 'It's even more fun than tennis. Besides, I want you.'

Edward escorted her from the dining-room with slow, careful dignity. Eyebrows rose. Was Monsieur Boothby-Graffoe quite well? Why did Madame seem so full of excitement? *Les Anglais!* Who could understand them?

Annaliese encouraged Edward to prolong his unhurried, rather meditative approach into half an hour of embrace and caress. Then, coaxing him on to his back, Annaliese straddled his hips, exactly as Cordelia Milford had done with Tommy Weston.

It was clear what Edward thought: as she guided him into her, his face was vividly eloquent. Even so, Annaliese thought that an explanation might be helpful. 'I thought you'd like it if I did all the work for a change,' she said. He groaned his approval, his eyes fixed on her breasts.

Unlike Cordelia Milford, Annaliese was slow and careful. She was soon revelling in her new-found capacity to give them both unparalleled pleasure. Her own sensations were particularly acute. When she succeeded in focusing her gaze on him, Annaliese saw that he was watching her avidly.

'I seem to be able to get more of you this way,' she gasped. 'It's good. *Very* good.'

'God, it is,' he muttered.

She was agreeably surprised at how long they made it last. They savoured the voluptuous novelty for what seemed like a joyous eternity before Edward was forced to surrender, adding his own thrusts to her gyrations. The intensity of her climax took Annaliese by storm: nevertheless, she retained enough of her faculties to appreciate that Edward experienced an orgasm of paralysing ferocity.

The afterglow was sublime, with delicious satisfaction seeping through them like a healing balm. But very gradually, Edward's face took on a troubled, questioning expression. Annaliese watched it grow, her heart sinking with every moment that passed. The words that were on the tip of his tongue had an awful, tangible certainty.

How did you learn to do that?

Propping herself up on an elbow, Annaliese stared at him challengingly.

'I thought that might be good,' she said.

'Oh.' Edward was wary.

'I wanted to show you that a mere Viennese can be as clever as the best brains in the Foreign Office.'

'You invented that? All on your own?' Edward was starting to smile.

'What do you think I did?' Annaliese shrieked. 'Took lessons? Asked the porter on Crowborough station to show me?'

'Don't be silly!' He was laughing. 'I wouldn't suggest anything so ludicrous.'

'Good.'

'You *are* clever.' Edward drew her back into his arms. 'I'm a lucky man.'

'So long as you appreciate that, we shall get on famously,' Annaliese told him with mock severity. 'By the way, have you noticed what a nice afternoon it is outside? All your blethering about rain was nothing but a ploy.'

'I admit it,' Edward said. 'In all seriousness, my dear, I *do* think your idea is better than tennis – quite a lot better, I'd say.'

'Yes, I suppose I agree.' It was meant to sound grudging. 'But we need other exercise and fresh air, you know.'

After dinner, they took a turn along the causeway, with Annaliese attempting to stride out as though on a route-march and Edward resenting every step.

'Could we go back now, my dear,' he pleaded when they were almost in the harbour quarter of the newest part of the town.

'Why? Aren't you enjoying this?'

'Not much.' He grinned. 'If I'm to be absolutely honest, I'd far rather be having another go at your new invention.'

It was even better than their first attempt, with Edward's seed bursting into her with an eruptive force she had never before felt. When subsequent diagnosis confirmed her pregnancy, Annaliese knew exactly when the child had been conceived.

13

June–August 1920
'I trust the matter will be rectified'

Annaliese was pleased to have brought a happy event to the church at Hatchetts Green. It has been her idea, intended to wipe out the memory of that dire February day when Lady Alice had been buried. Now, with the June sun streaming through the lofty windows, it was a different world, all light and space. Gazing up into the intricate delicacy of the fan-vaulted roof, she decided afresh that she truly loved the church. How strange that an exile from Austria should feel so much at home in this most *English* of buildings.

Her choice of location was much appreciated. So was the name she had insisted on for her son. Born three weeks ago, on 1 June, a fortnight before her own twenty-fourth birthday, Annaliese's little boy was being christened Douglas. There were no other names: it was plain, simple Douglas Boothby-Graffoe. He was an outstandingly bonny child, guaranteed to be devastatingly good-looking in the fullness of time and breaking female hearts by the dozen. As Nancy Shenstone had been the first to point out, with Annaliese and Edward for parents, Douglas was bound to be attractive. Nancy had invited herself to Sussex for the ceremony, and Edward was such a proudly happy father that he was actually civil to her.

In addition to Beatrice, Frances and Lewis Peters stood as godparents. Frances, who played her part in the ceremony with great solemnity, seemed unusually subdued. The occasion was, Annaliese realised, a poignant reminder of Frances's inability to have children of her own. She cast off the cloud the moment the service was over and set about being the life and soul of the party.

Beyond the unstinting adoration of his family circle, young Douglas had already made a considerable conquest. At Annaliese's request, Gwen had been present during what had turned out to be a remarkably easy birth. Annaliese's abiding memory of it all was the way Gwen's face had lit up when she got her first look at the child.

'He's beautiful,' Gwen whispered. 'Real beautiful.'

Before too long, the baby was demonstrating that he was endowed with a sturdy personality.

'Like my father,' Annaliese lamented. 'Everyone always said what a brute he was as a child.'

'It's no more than high spirits,' Gwen said, taking the infant into her arms. Douglas, having studied her long and hard with his amazingly blue eyes, stopped howling and began to gurgle contentedly. Annaliese knew that she need look no further for a nanny.

In a way that was both remarkable and typical, Gwen insisted that her new role need not interfere with her other duties. After three weeks, it was clear that she was making a great success out of what most girls would have found impossibly hard work. When the motor cars returned from church. Gwen was waiting in the porch at Upper Overs, eager to take charge of the bundle of lace christening robe that contained her precious charge.

Briefly, in the happy confusion of twenty-odd people alighting from Rolls-Royces and Daimlers, Edward was the focus of attention. Refreshments were being served in the garden and everyone looked to him for a lead. He was in his element, organising and pointing the way. Slightly apart from the main group, Annaliese was lost in her own proud thoughts for some time before realising that another isolated member of the gathering was watching her, a mischievous half-smile playing with his mouth and eyes.

'Uncle William!' Annaliese laughed. 'What are you plotting?'

'Nothing at all, m'dear. Just enjoying myself – same as you.' She took his arm and they began to walk away from the crowd, heading towards the more remote part of the gardens where the natural woodland held sway over attempts at horticulture.

'I'm not much of a one for babies,' the Duke said. 'Couldn't stand my own. But I must say, Annaliese, that little fellow of yours is a charmer.'

'Thank you. Even Edward approves.'

'*Even* Edward,' the Duke chuckled. 'My word, you *are* getting the hang of things. He's a good boy, though.'

'He is indeed,' Annaliese said happily. 'How are you keeping, Uncle William?'

'Busy,' he growled. 'I've been seeing far too much of the House of Lords.' He shook his head in a sad, bewildered sort of way. 'You wouldn't believe the mess the Government is making of things.'

'I'd gathered there were problems,' Annaliese said.

'Ah . . . has Edward been going on about it?'

'No, he's very good.' There was just a hint that Annaliese was working hard to be kind. 'I hear him and Lewis Peters talking. They aren't pleased.'

The Duke made a rumbling noise and dismissed the subject with an irascible wave of his hand. 'You're going from strength to strength, m'dear. What's all this I hear about you getting five thousand guineas for some grubby old daub you found in the lumber-room at Woodseaves?'

Annaliese's musical laugh rippled through the trees. 'That's another story that went wrong in the telling,' she said.

'Oh. It wasn't five thousand, then?' The Duke was disappointed.

'The correct figure was *six* thousand,' Annaliese said. 'It isn't true that *I* discovered it. Lord Drayton's grandfather suspected that he had a Rubens – he made a note about it in his journal. I simply took the trouble to look for the wretched thing after sixty years of neglect.'

'It's still a deuced good story,' the Duke said. 'Another feather in your cap.' Seeing the way her mind was working, he squashed Annaliese's protest before she uttered it. 'Spare me the modesty. You're doing a splendid job. The old firm has never been in such fine fettle.'

'Father *does* seem pleased,' Annaliese said.

'Douglas is over the moon about you. Mind you, I've got a complaint.'

Annaliese was dismayed. 'What have I done?'

'It's what you haven't done, m'dear. There's no sign of you visiting me in Wiltshire.'

'I know.' Annaliese hung her head penitently. 'There's always so much to do.'

'I appreciate that,' the Duke said. 'And if you are going to make the time to dash off somewhere, I couldn't expect to be first in the queue.'

'I don't understand.' Annaliese stopped walking to gaze at him intently.

'*Your* parents. You must want to see them?'

'Mmm.' It was a very ambiguous sort of sound. Annaliese frowned, looked into the far distance, then started walking again. 'I'm not ready yet,' she said. 'Actually, I'm beginning to wonder if I ever will be. Does that sound terrible?'

'I shouldn't think so. You might be worried about what you'd find in Lisbon – or wherever they are.'

'That's part of it,' Annaliese admitted.

'And there's never any point in going back, is there?' the Duke said. 'There never was. These days, with everything upside-down, I'd say it was impossible.'

'Will you keep a secret?' Annaliese asked diffidently.

'Naturally.'

'As far as Austria is concerned, my head is firmly in the sand. There are dreadful things going on and I can't bear to hear about them. But my father *will* be keeping in touch – he couldn't do anything else.'

'And you're afraid of what it will be doing to him?'

'Yes.' Annaliese paused. 'There's something else, too. My parents left Vienna several months before the end. I'm certain that Mama would have hated it, but Father put his foot down. He wanted to run away in nineteen-fourteen before it all started.'

'*Run away*,' the Duke repeated thoughtfully. 'Do you know, it strikes me that you're judging him a shade harshly.' He was mild, thinking aloud, but it took them into nearly twenty minutes of profoundly serious discussion. Annaliese was so absorbed that she was unaware they had walked round in a wide circle and were back at the front of the house. Then the Duke broke off in the middle of a sentence to say, 'There's Lady Shenstone . . . I think she's looking for you.'

Nancy came towards them. 'Hello, William. You're looking pretty damned fit and chipper.' She favoured him with her broadest smile.

'My dear Nancy, the sight of you always puts life into my poor old bones,' the Duke replied.

'You are a silly old fool.' The expression on Nancy's face gave a substantial coating of affection to what sounded like severity.

'That's what they all say,' the Duke laughed. He patted Annaliese's arm. 'I'll go and mingle, m'dear.'

Nancy watched him until he had disappeared round the side of the house.

'What is it?' Annaliese asked, thinking that her friend seemed perplexed.

'Him, of course,' Nancy said. 'I can never make up my mind.'

'About what?'

'Whether to accept his invitation to bed.'

'*Nancy!*' Annaliese's explosion was a mixture of outrage and amused disbelief. 'You're mad. Uncle William is a sweet, harmless old man.'

'Your Uncle William is certainly sweet,' Nancy agreed. 'I like him a lot. But being over sixty does not make a man "harmless", honey. One of the best lovers I've ever had was your uncle's age.'

'Yes . . . but . . . I mean . . .' Annaliese was incoherent. 'He isn't like that.'

'You didn't see the look he gave me when you came round that corner,' Nancy said. 'I was *naked*.'

'Oh, Nancy, you're being fanciful.' Annaliese was struggling to convince herself.

'No, I'm not. Take it from me, that gentleman has a way with him and an eye for a woman. I've never heard a breath of scandal about him, but you can bet your socks that there's a lady tucked away somewhere who could tell you amazing things about His Grace, the Duke of Lincolnshire.'

Annaliese's respect for Nancy's instincts in such matters got the better of her scepticism. 'I'm very surprised,' she said weakly.

'Don't be. The old boy deserves his fun. I'm afraid I must dash away, honey. I'm having dinner with a gorgeous new man.' Nancy rolled her eyes. 'Be in touch soon, won't you?'

'I will,' Annaliese laughed. 'Good luck!'

It was the Friday evening of the week following the christening. Boothby's was closed and deserted save for Annaliese and Beatrice. They were in the office on the first floor, ostensibly catching up on paperwork. Beatrice had become distracted ten minutes ago and was restless, fiddling with a pencil, looking out of the window.

'London's beastly in this weather,' she said.

'I don't think it's been so warm today,' Annaliese replied, not looking up.

'No. Perhaps not.' It seemed that the brief, trifling conversation had ended. Annaliese worked on. But Beatrice wanted to say more. 'I think I shall go away for a holiday. I need it.'

What she said was ordinary enough: it was the quiet desperation in her voice that arrested Annaliese. Setting aside the sale catalogue she was drafting, she gave Beatrice her full attention. They stared at each other across the table for a long time, Annaliese doing her best to convey encouragement and sympathy.

'My friend wants us to go to Skye,' Beatrice said abruptly. 'That's an island off the west coast of Scotland. It's very beautiful.' As an afterthought, she added, 'And very romantic.'

'That sounds pleasant,' Annaliese said.

Once more, Beatrice fell silent. She reached for the pencil, but changed her mind, irritated with herself. 'Annaliese, there's something I want you to know,' she said.

'Yes?'

Never had Beatrice's nervous habit of trying to tie her hands in knots been so hectic. 'My friend is a married man. We sort of . . . well . . . the fact is, we more or less live together.'

'I presume he's a very nice man,' Annaliese murmured.

'Yes, he is!' The burst of animation froze as Beatrice appreciated what lay behind Annaliese's remark. 'You don't disapprove?'

'Disapprove?' Annaliese was puzzled. 'No. Why on earth should I?'

Beatrice had great difficulty coming to terms with such broad-minded generosity – even though she ought to have expected it from her sister-in-law. 'People do,' she muttered. 'At least, they would if they knew. It's a secret.'

'Of course.' Briefly, very briefly, Annaliese toyed with the idea of explaining that Lord Douglas had been aware of the relationship almost from the start. The tacit endorsement of his silence might reassure Beatrice. But the chances of her seeing it in that light were slender; she was much more likely to treat it as an acute embarrassment. Annaliese remained still and quiet, waiting.

'We don't want to marry,' Beatrice went on. 'I don't suppose we ever will. We're happy as we are. He would like to divorce his wife, though.'

'There are difficulties?'

'For someone in his predicament, the law makes it virtually impossible,' Beatrice declared bitterly. 'He's determined not to drag me into it, you see. It *is* awful being named as "the other woman" – the disgrace might affect Boothby's.'

'He has no grounds for divorcing her?' Annaliese inquired gently.

'Tons of them. But her co-operation is needed and she's making unreasonable demands. She wants custody of their son and a *huge* sum of money. The money isn't *too* much of a problem – although it would hurt him by putting his business at risk.'

'I take it that he loves his son very much?'

'Yes. In any case, the poor boy couldn't be left with his mother. She's wrong in the head.' Attempting to clarify the matter, Beatrice added, 'It's a weird religion. She's involved with a bunch of fanatics and bigots . . . That's why she wants lot of money . . . They've got some scheme for creating their own exclusive community.'

'Does your friend still live with his wife?' Annaliese asked.

'No, he left her eighteen months ago.' Beatrice smiled bashfully. 'We share a house . . . if you see what I mean.'

'And your friend's wife leaves you alone? She doesn't turn up creating scenes – or have you followed?'

'No, she ignores us. But I'm sure it preys on Charles's mind. He's been on edge for some time now.'

'A week or two on that island you mentioned will do him the world of good,' Annaliese said.

'You think we should go?' Beatrice asked, pathetically eager for moral support.

'Why not? You're an independent human being, so make up your own mind – you're more than capable of it, Beatrice. The thing to remember is that you have one life, one chance at happiness. Worrying about what other people may or may not think is not the best way to go about it.'

Beatrice was pensive, as if she were trying to put a name to a vaguely familiar face. 'That sounds like Nancy Shenstone,' she said.

'That wouldn't surprise me.' Annaliese laughed. 'By the way,' she was serious again, 'I shall not mention a *syllable* of this to Edward. Rely on it.'

'Oh, that is good of you.' A tidal wave of relief brought Beatrice to the brink of tears. 'I was suffering agonies wondering how to ask you about it.'

'Well, there you are, there's no need to worry.' Significantly, Annaliese went on to say, 'It's a poor wife who doesn't know her husband.'

'Edward is a good man,' Beatrice said.

'He is,' Annaliese replied staunchly. 'However, his moral judgements are slightly inflexible. This can make things decidedly awkward for us mere mortals.'

'What a lovely way of putting it.' Beatrice was giggly, a sign that she continued to be plagued by nerves. 'There's something you could do for me, Annaliese,' she said hesitantly.

'Of course.'

'Charles – that's his name, Charles Templeton – wants to meet you. I told him that I wanted to let you in on the secret and he was sure you'd be on our side.'

'I'm flattered.'

'Charles believes that we must have some contact with my family and friends,' Beatrice said. 'You fit the bill perfectly.'

'Beatrice, I'm delighted that you asked me.'

'Oh, he *will* be pleased!' Beatrice cried. 'Perhaps you would like to come to our house one evening?'

'With pleasure. I shall choose a time when Edward is at his Club.'

'Will he want to know where you've been?' Beatrice asked anxiously.

'Probably.' Annaliese shrugged. 'I shall tell him part of the truth – that I'm with you. He will assume that we're talking business and that always sends him to sleep.'

'He's never shown the slightest interest in what goes on here,' Beatrice said.

'All the better for us in this instance,' Annaliese replied. 'What *is* your Charles Templeton? How does he earn his living?'

'He's a merchant banker.'

'Ah.' Annaliese nodded. 'I see what you mean about his wife and money. Look, do you think your friend, Charles, would do something for me?'

'I'm sure he would.'

'I have money in Liechtenstein. My mother put it there after I'd left Vienna. I asked Mr Probert in Crowborough . . .' She stopped, bemused by the gruesome look on Beatrice's face. 'What's wrong?'

'Probert's a *toad*. He thinks the only place for a woman is at home, warming her husband's slippers.'

Annaliese laughed. 'That's the conclusion I came to. Naturally, I didn't bother.'

'I should think not. Between you and me, Annaliese, I'm trying to get our business away from Probert's bank. Yes, Charles will be pleased to help you.'

By unspoken consent, they decided it was time to finish for the day and began to collect the papers on which they had been working.

'How did you meet Charles?' Annaliese asked. 'Did our friend Nancy have anything to do with it, by any chance?'

Any hope that Beatrice might have entertained of denying it was ruined by her uncontrollable reaction: she blushed vividly. 'Yes, she did, I'm afraid.'

'Why be afraid?' Annaliese asked. 'I can't imagine a better way of finding a good man.'

Bereft of speech, Beatrice lost control of an armful of ledgers. After a rueful survey of the chaos on the floor, she joined in Annaliese's laughter.

*

Nancy's admirers and close friends called February and March the 'contractor's months'. It was the time of year when changes were made to the structure of the house. The disruption was a signal for animated speculation as well as tolerance: alterations were designed to give new opportunities for epicurean excitement. In 1920, an indoor swimming-pool was constructed. It was part extension and partly the conversion of a large room at the back of the house that had never served any useful purpose. The water could be heated when necessary and the four changing-rooms were miniature temples of sensual luxury.

It soon became an unwritten rule that the pool was not available between the hours of two and four on Monday afternoons. That was when Nancy and Annaliese swam. They did so without the constraint of bathing-suits, which they both detested.

On 19 July, they were not particularly interested in exercise. After five minutes, they paddled to the steps, where Christina waited with robes. Nancy, who left the water first, turned to study Annaliese as she climbed out.

'Having that child hasn't made any difference to you,' she said. 'You're *marvellous*!'

'So are you.'

For a few moments, they admired each other, openly and unashamedly displayed a mutual attraction.

'C'mon, Chrissie, cover us up before we get carried away,' Nancy said, trying to turn it into a joke.

Shapeless in the voluminous robes, and with towels wound turban-like round their hair, they soon had a genuine reason for laughter. 'What a pair of frumps,' Nancy spluttered. 'Let's go and talk.'

Leaving by a side door, they padded across the lawn to the conservatory. Nancy flung herself into a chair, reached for cigarettes and said, 'I guess you know what's eating me up with curiosity?'

Annaliese decided against teasing. 'Charles Templeton,' she said.

'Right. You met the guy on Friday. What did you think?'

'I was very taken by him,' Annaliese replied. 'Handsome, impeccable manners, and a good sense of humour.'

'He's as straight as a die, too,' Nancy added. 'That isn't too common these days.'

'Beatrice and he are happy together,' Annaliese went on. 'That was *very* obvious.' She looked at her companion quizzically. 'What's he like as a lover?'

'I have no personal experience, you understand,' Nancy said.

'That doesn't stop you knowing,' Annaliese smiled.

'He's definitely on the good side of adequate,' Nancy replied. 'How's Edward?'

There was a pause, during which Annaliese accepted that the change of subject was nowhere near as extreme as it appeared.

'He's very well,' she said. 'Spending far too much time at the Foreign Office.'

'There seems to be a crisis on every time I look at a newspaper,' Nancy complained. 'I was amazed to see that they're still arguing about peace treaties. I thought that had been sorted out in Paris.'

'Oh, no. There are separate arrangements with Hungary, Bulgaria, and Austria.' Annaliese smiled mordantly at the last-named country. 'They're still working on the one with Turkey. I believe Edward is involved with that because Australia and New Zealand have a lot of points.'

The words were straightforward enough and made sense, yet the way they were uttered clouded them in a strange ambiguity. Nancy puzzled over it, then gave up. 'Go on,' she urged. 'Give me the *real* facts.'

'Edward is surprising me,' Annaliese said.

'In what way?'

'Although he's told me about it often enough, I'd quite underestimated the extent and strength of his ambition. He truly *does* intend to be running the Foreign Office by the time he's fifty-five – earlier, given a chance.'

'There's nothing wrong with wanting to get to the top,' Nancy pointed out. 'We Americans think of nothing else.'

'Yes.' Annaliese was distant. 'He considers it vital that he should know as much as possible about what goes on. He's there until eight o'clock most evenings, prowling round, sticking his nose into things that aren't his immediate concern.'

'You mean he searches other folks' files – things like that?' Nancy asked. She sounded slightly shocked.

'There's no need for anything so crude,' Annaliese retorted. 'His Majesty's Foreign Office is populated by men who have no homes to go to. It seems that many of them are only too willing to tell Edward whatever he wants to know.'

'I can figure that,' Nancy said. 'I've heard talk that he's going places, so everybody wants to be his friend. That way, they reckon they'll be looked after when he gets there. He's already big enough to be worth creeping to, isn't he?'

'Probably,' Annaliese said.

'And how much does the job pay?' Nancy grinned. 'That's something a Yank always wants to know.'

'I've no idea.' Considering the question to be absurd, Annaliese was faintly amused. 'Ladies don't poke their noses into things like that, Nancy. My impression is that we live on money from Edward's family.'

'Fine. That's taken care of the material side of things. How about the rest?'

'Edward's a good man.' Even as she made the statement, Annaliese knew that it was starting to sound tired and forced. 'We manage very well. We appreciate each other.'

'*Appreciate*?' Nancy fastened on to the word, repeating it several times. 'That's an interesting angle.'

'It's very important.' Annaliese was defensive.

'Sure. A hell of a lot of folks don't. Come to think of it, I suppose Harold and me appreciate each other.' Annaliese stirred uncomfortably at the mention of Nancy's outlandish marriage: she had a fair idea what was coming next. 'We don't do much else, though,' Nancy went on. 'Not that I *mind*. Hell, look what I have instead . . .'

Annaliese decided to tell the truth and have done with it. 'Edward and I are both very busy people. It was lovely when we conceived Douglas and I hope that we shall be able to repeat it one day. In the meantime, I think I envy Beatrice.' Mistaking the look on Nancy's face, Annaliese believed that she had failed to make herself clear. 'We hardly ever make love, these days. Even when we do, it isn't worth the trouble and effort . . .'

Nancy was spared the necessity of replying. Flustered and tight-lipped, Annaliese dashed out of the conservatory, hurrying back to the swimming-pool to dress. Nancy decided that it was best to leave her alone.

Matthew was driving Annaliese and Edward back to London on a Sunday evening in August. The weekend at Upper Overs had been at the request of Lord Douglas. He was entertaining an old, valued friend who was proposing to refurbish a neglected country house that he had acquired. Money appeared to be no object and Annaliese's task was to persuade him to buy from Boothby's.

Fully aware that he was present merely for the sake of appearances, Edward had hated every minute of it. Having spent most of Saturday on the telephone, talking to colleagues at work, he was pompous and boring over dinner. On Sunday morning he had taken himself off for a drive round the forest. Now, as they neared London, his mood was undoubtedly worsening. Annaliese expected trouble.

He tried to start a row as soon as they reached Cadogan Square, while Matthew was parking and unloading the Rolls.

'I realise that you make a valuable contribution to Boothby's, my dear, and I understand that there is little chance of you giving it up. But I do wish that I didn't have to be a spectator. I felt quite foolish.'

Annaliese was tense and in no mood to waste energy on placating him. 'I'm very sorry about that,' she said. 'The answer is quite simple – I shan't bother you in future. If Father needs my help again, I shall attend to it alone.' Taken aback, Edward opened his mouth, only to be cut down before he could get the words out. 'If you'll excuse me, I'm going to the nursery.'

Young Douglas and Gwen had not been to Sussex and were overjoyed to see Annaliese. As sharp-eyed and sensitive as ever, Gwen asked, 'What's wrong?'

'Nothing,' Annaliese said, taking Douglas into her arms. 'A slight difference of opinion, that's all.'

'Hmm . . .' Gwen sniffed. 'That's the first time I've heard you say so. Things are changing.'

'You're a terror,' Annaliese chided. 'Aren't you anxious to see Matthew? Go on, I'll put Douglas to bed.' She winked. 'It's a good excuse for keeping out of the way.'

Gwen made a pretence of unwillingness: she would die rather than show how she was longing to dash down to Matthew.

Annaliese stayed with her son long after he had fallen asleep. When she did eventually creep away, it was in the expectation that she would be able to bathe and prepare for bed in solitary peace. She had to curb the surge of exasperation she felt at finding Edward pottering round their bedroom.

'Is the boy all right?' he asked.

'He's very well. Fast asleep.'

'Good.'

They busied themselves with minor tasks, Annaliese knowing that the ensuing silence was temporary: Edward was looking for an opportunity to get something off his chest.

'I've been wondering about Gwen,' he said, ridiculously over casual.

'Oh? Why?'

'I suppose she *is* the right sort of person to be looking after Douglas?'

'I'm sure she is,' Annaliese replied. Trying to stop him going any further, she added, '*Absolutely* sure.'

'Yes. Hmm.' Edward made great play of peering into his wardrobe, as though seeing it for the first time. 'I suppose it's inevitable that you and she seem rather close, but I wonder if you aren't a shade too familiar with her. The girl gets away with blue murder, you know.'

This time, Annaliese saw the need to keep calm. 'I'm not aware of this,' she said evenly. 'Are you saying that there are problems?'

'Not *problems* as such – but she is resented for her impertinence and intimacy with you.'

'Edward, Gwen is my personal maid and nanny. We're bound to be close – how else could it work?'

'Well, I wish you'd think about it, my dear,' he said, making no attempt to answer her question. 'As I say, it's causing ill feeling.'

'How do you know?' Annaliese asked.

'Eh?' Edward looked positively shifty.

'How do you know? You never go near the servants, so how do you know they resent Gwen?'

'Franklin has had a word with me,' Edward said stiffly.

Franklin!

It was the ultimate test of Annaliese's resolve to control her temper. She passed it by the simple expedient of saying nothing. If Edward saw the danger in her glacial attitude, he promptly proceeded to ignore it.

'There is another point we ought to resolve,' he said doggedly. There was no help for him this time, no question to give him a lead into the disagreeable issue: Annaliese remained silent. Steeling himself, Edward plunged in.

'It seems that you're seeing far too much of Nancy Shenstone,' he said, the effort of conquering his nerves making him aggressive. 'I'm surprised that you aren't aware of her terrible reputation and how easily we could be tainted by it.'

Aghast at his effrontery, Annaliese appeared meek. 'I'm sorry, I don't understand. What reputation?'

'Really, my dear, you can hardly be unaware of her highly irregular life style. That husband of hers must be a complete buffoon.' Edward was starting to enjoy himself. 'Actually, I'm at a loss to know how she makes the time to see you. Her army of men friends must keep her pretty busy – and I shall say nothing about the other stories one hears.'

'Surely, you don't get this tittle-tattle at the Foreign Office?' Annaliese said with brittle sweetness. 'Where *do* you hear such scandal? At the Club? Or is it your faithful Franklin?'

'Both, as it happens,' Edward retorted. 'Not that it makes a jot of difference to the point I'm making. I've already told you that a man in my position can't afford *any* suggestion of scandal. I'm disappointed that you should need so obvious a problem pointing out to you. I trust the matter will be rectified.'

Numb with shock and anger, Annaliese realised that, as far as Edward was concerned, this was the end of it. In just the same way that he ordered her to avoid Paul Marks, he was now warning her off Nancy.

'Yes, the matter will be rectified,' she said, very, very softly.

At breakfast the following morning, it was difficult to decide whether Edward's cheerfulness or insincerity was the most galling feature of his performance. The prospect of a day in Whitehall had obliterated all memory of his annoying weekend and the unpleasant episode of the previous evening – which had culminated in them ignoring each other even after they were in bed. This morning's schoolboyish humour, hard on the heels of heavy-handed arrogance, was intolerable. Staring at *The Times*, behind which Edward disappeared when he decided to stop being cheerful, Annaliese reminded herself that this was the man who had come to Berlin with his heart full of courage and hope.

While Matthew was driving Edward to the Foreign Office, Annaliese went to the kitchen to discuss the week's menus and special arrangements with Mrs Powell, the cook. The six servants were clearing up after their own breakfasts: as usual, Gwen was upstairs in the nursery.

'I'm told that there have been complaints about Gwen,' Annaliese said in a strong, assertive voice that surprised her listeners and seized their attention. 'Apparently, she's regarded as a disruptive influence.'

The silence was electric. Mrs Powell was perplexed, acutely conscious that the others were looking to her to do the talking. All except Franklin: originally standing near the cooking-range, he was edging towards the still-room.

'Well?' Annaliese demanded. She noticed that poor Matthew was petrified.

Mrs Powell stuttered into life. 'I . . . I can't think where you heard this, ma'am. I think it's a wicked lie. Gwen's very popular – and *such* a worker. She does her turn with the pans even though there's no need . . . I mean, skivvying isn't her job, is it?' There was a chorus of assent.

'You're telling me the truth?' Annaliese asked.

'Yes, ma'am, on my life.' Mrs Powell was flushed with emotion. 'I can't imagine who's been trying to get Gwen into trouble, but there's no cause for it, none at all.' Actually, the righteously indignant Mrs Powell was more than capable of deducing the identity of the culprit: she shot a sidelong glance at him as he continued his attempt to go into hiding.

'Is there anyone who disagrees with Mrs Powell?' Annaliese asked. 'In any respect, no matter how small?'

Heads shook.

'Very well, that's the end of it,' Annaliese said. 'I shall go through the week's work with you shortly, Mrs Powell.' She swung round to stare at the butler. 'A few moments of your valuable time, *Mr* Franklin,' she said, her tone pure acid.

He followed her to his pantry at the end of the corridor, trying to ignore the feverish whispering that broke out when they left the kitchen. When she turned to face him, Annaliese's face was pale with anger.

'At the time Lord Douglas Boothby-Graffoe gave this house to my husband, he asked for my views on the servants.' She paused to gain control of her breathing. 'I insisted on bringing Gwen and Matthew from Upper Overs. After we'd settled that, Lord Douglas asked what I thought about *you*.' She savoured the man's look of astonished alarm. 'You will doubtless be surprised to learn that his Lordship is not so convinced of your virtues as you suppose. He was of a mind to get rid of you. Out of deference to my husband's preferences, I said that you should stay.'

Another pause, this one to allow him time to digest what she had said. He did, wisely making no attempt to speak.

'You have a strange way of repaying my consideration, Franklin,' Annaliese continued. 'I object strongly to your remarks about my maid. Very strongly. Spreading stories about Lady Shenstone is far worse. It is utterly reprehensible. At the moment, I can't be bothered to have *another* quarrel with my husband, so I will not demand your dismissal. But you will bear in mind that there will be no second chance. When I lived in Vienna, I was used to the very highest standards and you will keep to them. If you fail, one of us will be leaving this house. Do you understand me, Franklin?'

'Yes, Your Highness.'

He gave the impression that he was crushed. However, Annaliese turned unexpectedly as she reached the door, catching him off-guard. His hatred was implacable.

Later, when Mrs Powell was telling Gwen all about it, she was bursting with admiration. 'You can see what she's made of. She give that Franklin a right going-over, then she comes straight in here to do the menus, cool as a cucumber, bless her. If that ain't class, I'm blowed if I know what is.'

Especially since Mrs Powell had said such nice things about her, Gwen pretended to be agog. The reality was that she knew what lay behind her mistress's apparent composure. After deciding on the week's menus, Annaliese went up to the nursery and told Gwen the truth.

'It wouldn't worry me if I never saw this place again,' she concluded. 'I've a good mind to take Douglas to Lisbon and stay there – forever.'

'You don't mean that,' Gwen said.

'No, I don't expect I do,' Annaliese sighed. 'But I could spit, Gwen, I really could. Why does my husband listen to a wretch like Franklin?'

'No idea.' Gwen was resolutely determined not to be drawn anywhere near the dangers of criticising Edward. 'I tell you what, though – I'm going to give that bugger Franklin an even worse time.'

'Good,' Annaliese said savagely, abandoning the idea that she had a responsibility to urge restraint on Gwen. 'If you're foul enough to him, he might leave. From what I saw this morning, the others would buy you a present. A big one.'

As she spoke, Annaliese was aware that she was spouting childish bravado. A premonition whispered that Franklin's ability to make trouble was far from exhausted.

'Cheer up,' Gwen urged. 'It's Monday. You're going swimming with Lady Shenstone. That always makes you feel better.'

But, as Gwen told Matthew during the five minutes they usually managed to have to themselves after lunch, it seemed that Annaliese's despondency would take some shifting.

'I reckon Mr Edward's gone too far,' Gwen said.

'That doesn't surprise me,' Matthew muttered. 'I've always thought he was a funny devil. Cold, as well, very cold when he wants to be.'

Once in a while, when he was not *too* preoccupied with his adoration of Gwen, Matthew fancied that he was ever so slightly in love with Annaliese.

After exchanging troubled, questioning glances, Nancy and Christina silently agreed to ignore Annaliese's mood. Arriving late enough to create the belief that something had gone wrong, Annaliese hovered between suppressed fury and melancholy. As usual, she shared a changing-room with Nancy, Christina flitting around to ensure that their clothes were put away neatly in the wardrobes. When she was completely naked, Annaliese studied herself in the full-length mirror fixed to the back of the door. She was keenly narcissistic, looking for self-assurance. Apparently satisfied, she spoke to Nancy over her shoulder.

'I've rather neglected God since I was a child. Do you think he'd listen to me if I asked for his protection from pompous, arrogant, interfering prudes?'

She opened the door and was gone, not waiting for an answer. Nancy and Christina heard the splash as she dived into the pool.

The furious energy that Annaliese put into her swimming suggested that she was seeking to dissipate a deep-seated anger. Deciding that it was best to let her get on with it, Nancy stayed at the shallow end of the pool, making only a token gesture at exercise. After ten minutes, Annaliese seemed calmer and swam towards her friend.

'What's wrong?' Nancy asked gently. 'Want to tell me about it?'

Annaliese was unutterably dispirited. 'It's Edward,' she said. 'And Franklin!'

'Franklin?' Nancy's eyes narrowed. 'What's he done?'

'Oh, to hell with it,' Annaliese muttered. She was shaking her head. 'No, I don't want to talk about it.'

Touched by Annaliese's distress, Nancy drew her into an embrace. It was nothing more than an impromptu act of friendship.

Christina, who was returning from the house with fresh towels, had a good view of Annaliese's reaction to the gesture of compassion. The way she pressed herself against Nancy was a sign of much more than friendship. Nancy detected the deep, physical hunger at once. She was stroking Annaliese and talking to her. The responses seemed eager. Although she was unable to hear what was passing between them, Christina saw that they were moving towards the steps and hurried to help. They came out together, with Annaliese's head on Nancy's shoulder.

Reading Nancy's signals, Christina accompanied them to the changing-room. Grabbing one of the towels, Nancy began to rub Annaliese dry. Unbidden, Christina did the same to Nancy: when the time was right, she helped lift the submissive Annaliese on to the divan.

'Okay, Chrissie,' Nancy whispered. 'Make *real* sure we're not disturbed, huh?'

Nodding, Christina slipped away. Before closing the door, she turned for a last look and saw Annaliese's wide-eyed joy at what Nancy was already doing to her.

Christina went back to the main part of the house, holding her breath to listen for sounds of any unexpected guests. All was quiet – or very nearly. Cordelia Milford was spending the afternoon in a first-floor bedroom with two men: the expansive luxury of Martha's Vineyard was muffling most of their turbulence. Glad that Tommy Weston was expected at five o'clock, Christina returned to the pool.

Noiselessly, she busied herself in the three empty changing-rooms, making sure that they were in immaculate condition for the evening. Eventually, however, she gave in to temptation and pressed an ear against the door of the fourth room.

Christina smiled at what she heard. With hindsight, it was slightly surprising that Nancy had never previously ventured into this secret labyrinth of physical love. She certainly seemed to be making up for lost time. And Mrs Boothby-Graffoe had found a way to what sounded like desperately needed fulfilment that did not, strictly speaking, betray her stupid husband.

14

May 1921
'I think I could cope with it'

Annaliese knew that she would never forget her first sight of Allardyce Castle, the Duke of Lincolnshire's Wiltshire seat. The experience was gloriously memorable, lifting her in an instant from the persistent gloom of the difficult months that had preceded it.

Change, unexpected and disruptive, had been at the root of it all. In October 1920, quite without any warning or hint of dissatisfaction, Mrs Powell had give notice. Annaliese's repeated attempts to get to the bottom of it failed. Mrs Powell would say nothing apart from the fact that she had been offered a position at a splendid house in Belgravia, the London home of an earl. It was, the cook insisted, a chance that was far too good to miss. More than that she refused to divulge her reasons and rejected all offers of increased wages. Her intransigence was revealing and, although neither she nor Gwen could unearth a shred of evidence, Annaliese was certain that Franklin was responsible.

After three days of interviewing applicants, Annaliese congratulated herself on finding a gem: a young woman of thirty who was one of a new breed of cooks, very bright, well-educated and only available because her previous employer was bankrupt. Her first task was to prepare a dinner for ten of Edward's colleagues and their wives. It was a masterpiece that fully deserved the praise heaped on it by the guests.

Five days later, the gem walked out.

Annaliese was still reeling from the shock and nerving herself to begin another search when Edward announced that he had found and appointed a suitable candidate. In all honesty, her principal emotion was relief – although she did make a token display of annoyance at the way she had been excluded from the decision. Mrs Darbishire was not the most agreeable of women, but what came out of her kitchen was at least as good as Mrs Powell's offerings.

In the strained, secretive atmosphere that was now all-pervasive below stairs at Cadogan Square, even Gwen took a week to unearth the truth. The new cook was a war widow. Her maiden name had been Franklin: she was the wretched man's cousin. Observing the extent of Annaliese's dismay, Gwen refrained from talking about it again. Not too long afterwards, Annaliese yielded to her Viennese nature: with a metaphorical shrug of the shoulders, she turned her back on the problem. Deep down, she knew that it still existed, but she was determined to pretend that it didn't.

Immediately after the celebrations for the New Year of 1921, there was upheaval at the Foreign Office. The sudden death of a man in the second level of the hierarchy led to a host of changes that struck Annaliese as excessively out of proportion with the need to fill one vacancy. Edward explained that what looked like musical chairs was a very necessary reorganisation to shift men out of posts in which they were proving less than useful. The upshot of it all was that Lewis Peters was moved, given more responsibility and lined up for the knighthood that was, in any case, overdue. Edward was promoted into Lewis's erstwhile job. He was immensely pleased.

There were more people to impress at more dinner-parties and Edward spent longer than ever in and around Whitehall. Annaliese did her best to be proud of him and put in extra hours at Boothby's.

But the harmony was fragile. Annaliese's insistence on taking up the Duke's invitation to visit Allardyce Castle had given rise to what was virtually a month-long battle, with Edward claiming that he could not spare the time. Irritated, then rattled by the way Annaliese stuck to her guns, he finally gave in. The concession was made with poor grace and the insistence that the visit should be an extended weekend of no more than five days' duration. Annaliese's acquiescence was conditional upon their son accompanying them. To her surprise,

Edward agreed at once, telling her to make whatever arrangements were necessary.

As it happened, that last stage in the negotiations took place while Edward was dressing on a Monday morning, a time when he often found himself wary of Annaliese's jaunty, somehow *invincible* mood. Why, he sometimes wondered, was she like that on Mondays? Inasmuch as he ever gave it any thought, he came to the conclusion that she was probably glad to be seeing the back of him after the weekend. It was a measure of the extent to which the relationship had deteriorated that he accepted this state of affairs as normal.

The truth would have stupefied him.

After their first sexual exploit together, Annaliese and Nancy had taken stock. Calmly, without a trace of embarrassment or shame, they agreed that they had enjoyed it immensely. They wanted to know why it had happened. Annaliese had, of course, been profoundly distressed and frustrated, but enthusiastic indulgence in activities widely regarded as 'unnatural' required more justification than that. The admission that they found each other powerfully alluring paved the way for regular repetitions of that first excitement.

They regarded themselves as partners in adventure, rather than lovers. Annaliese was always willing to encourage the few half-hearted advances which Edward made to her, and Nancy found that their exquisite Monday afternoons gave her a new perspective on her more conventional partners.

They travelled to Wiltshire on the last Thursday in May, using two motor cars. Edward drove a Rolls that was loaded with luggage. Annaliese was at his side. Accompanying them in a brand-new Morris that Edward had bought on his father's recommendation, were Matthew, Gwen, and the eleven-month-old Douglas. Delighted at the prospect of a few days in the country with his beloved Gwen, Matthew had only one reservation.

'The master doesn't seem to be putting too cheerful a face on this,' he said as they approached the centre of Reading, keeping what Matthew considered a respectful distance behind the Rolls.

Gwen's reply was delayed by an expressive sniff. 'He's in a worse mood than ever,' she said.

'Not very nice, is it?' Matthew ventured. 'You'd think he'd make an effort for a job like this.'

'He's got two choices,' Gwen retorted. 'Between you, me, and young Douglas here, I reckon Her Highness has got to the point where she don't give a damn which one he takes.'

The great shout that Douglas let out at that moment was not agreement, but delight at two magnificent shire horses easing a load of biscuits out of Huntley and Palmer's bakery.

Twenty-five miles later, Matthew overtook the Rolls, Annaliese and Douglas laughing and waving to each other as he did so. The pre-arranged move was to allow Matthew to lead the way through an area of which Edward knew next to nothing. Following Matthew, who had often been to Compton Allardyce with Lord Douglas, was preferable to looking a fool by becoming hopelessly lost in a maze of lanes that were mostly little better than farm tracks.

Beyond the first of several villages that had the word Bedwyn in their names, they were following the River Kennet along a valley of water-meadows and lush woods. With each quarter-mile that passed, Annaliese was conscious that they were moving deeper into an enchanted, *private* landscape. Beautiful though Sussex was, this place was much more impressive. It was rare and flawless. The trees were greener, the scent of the hedgerows, on a peerless morning following a damp dawn, almost overpowering.

After skirting the southern edge of the great and ancient Forest of Savernake, they passed the village of Bedwyn End, where Annaliese saw thatched roofs for the first time. They crossed the main road from Marlborough to Salisbury and another half a mile took them into the Vale of Pewsey, hemmed in to the north by the chalk ridge of The Wansdyke.

'This is incredible,' Annaliese said. 'I had no idea that England was *this* lovely.'

Edward's grunt was the response of a man anxious to perpetuate the silence that had lasted since Hungerford. Unconcerned, Annaliese concentrated on her surroundings and was soon rewarded by the village of Compton Allardyce, an almost ludicrously picturesque straggle of cottages, all with walls of the same mellow stone and roofs covered with pantiles. The only thatched roof was the inn, whose sign, complete with heraldic devices, proclaimed it to be The Lincolnshire Arms. Busy craning her neck to take in Uncle William's armorial bearings, Annaliese very nearly missed the village's most striking feature. After a bend, the road approached a pair of massive, wrought-iron gates and ceased to be a public highway.

Ahead of them, the Morris was at a standstill while Matthew spoke to the man in the gatehouse, a small, single-storey structure. The delay was short and they were soon on their way, the gatekeeper waving from his window as the Rolls passed. Annaliese saw that he was using a telephone: the estate was efficient.

For several hundred yards, the road twisted through woods that were thick enough to form an impenetrable screen even in winter. Now, at summer's burgeoning, it was like driving through a tunnel. Annaliese guessed, correctly, that this was a deliberate device to conceal what lay beyond.

Emerging from the eerie, green twilight of the screen, Annaliese found that her eyes needed a few moments to adjust to bright sunlight. When they did, she gasped at what she saw.

The manorial demesne of Compton Allardyce had been well-established at the time of the Norman Conquest and was recorded in Domesday Book. It was a rectangular piece of land measuring four miles by three, set four-square on the face of Wiltshire by someone with an eye to symmetry. The long boundary lay on an east-west line, the shorter sides were north-south. Nearly nine centuries had made no difference to the size and disposition of the estate: Allardyce Park covered twelve square miles, getting on for 8,000 acres. It was ten times bigger than Schönbrunn, and, although there were no fountains, much more interesting. For one thing, it was not hemmed in by a city: the journey had shown Annaliese that the open, unspoilt countryside extended for miles beyond the boundary.

Much of the Park, especially the eastern side, was thickly wooded. In the south-western corner, cows were grazing in an enclosure that was clearly a farm. The landscape was full of interest, but it would all have to wait: Annaliese had eyes for one thing only.

It was, of course, precisely what the builders had intended. The highest point of the gently indulating land lay at the centre of the Park. Here, between 1425 and 1450, they had constructed Allardyce Castle.

'Why is it called a castle?' Annaliese was to ask Uncle William. 'It isn't in the least bit like a fortress.'

'I expect affectation entered into it,' he replied. 'The original owners – a family called De Willoughby – were a pretty bombastic bunch. In all fairness, though, there'd been two previous buildings on this site and they were definitely proper castles – moat, drawbridge, all the trimmings.'

The two cars were approaching from the south, giving their occupants a breathtaking view of one of England's greatest architectural glories. By means that had baffled his contemporaries, Godfrey De Willoughby secured the services of John Craxton, master mason to the City of London and designer of the Guildhall. Despite the prestige he must have enjoyed, John Craxton was a disheartened man, building for commerce rather than God. It was always said that, during his apprenticeship with the incomparable Henry Yevely, John Craxton had designed a magnificent church, but, to his everlasting vexation, was never given an opportunity to convert the dream into reality.

Seen in that light, there was no mystery surrounding his acceptance of De Willoughby's commission. Naturally, the grand design had to be changed. The massive central tower, together with smaller twins intended for the west end, had to go. Nor were transepts appropriate. In the event, this lead to a cheaper, more stable building. A little ingenuity was required with the windows, breaking them up to meet the requirements of a three-storey domestic structure while conveying the impression that the tracery was continuous for an eye-catching sixty feet. Finally, the design was extended. John Craxton's original concept of ten bays was not grand enough for De Willoughby, who begged, borrowed, and stole the money for an extra six.

The result, measuring 850 feet from end to end, was the most elegantly lovely building that Annaliese had ever seen, a celebration of the Perpendicular style that had so impressed her in the church at Hatchetts Green. Faced in the same mellow limestone that was such a striking feature of the village, and with a crenellated parapet, it was aesthetically perfect.

Three hours later, after lunch, Annaliese discovered that there was much more to Allardyce Castle than was obvious from the south. Behind the original building, three wings had been added during the 18th century. At right angles to John Craxton's nave-like structure, there was one at each end, with a slightly shorter one in the centre. A bird's-eye view of the Castle showed it to be a huge E-shaped structure.

The Duke's conducted tour brought them to the end of the Central Wing and a view of the stables, coach-houses, and workshops. Annaliese shook her head wonderingly.

'I can't take all this in,' she said wonderingly.

'It takes about twenty years,' the Duke replied. 'And it helps if you were born here.'

'What I want to know,' Annaliese said cheekily, 'is how your family came to own all this. I don't for one moment suppose that the De Willoughbys sold it to you?'

'You suppose correctly,' Uncle William chuckled. 'I expect you've heard of our Civil War?'

'Yes. The English beheaded their king long before the French thought of it.'

'It caused a fair upheaval – especially after we decided to restore the monarchy in sixteen-sixty. There were some dramatic changes of fortune. The De Willoughbys backed the Roundhead cause – that was Oliver Cromwell and his lot. There was nothing wrong with that – quite a few people did the same thing and came out of it all right. But the De Willoughbys were a nasty, vicious bunch. King Charles the Second wasn't at all keen on them. He booted them out of the country and confiscated this place.'

'And gave it to you?' Annaliese suggested.

'Not straight away, no. Charles thought he'd keep it for his own use, but he never came here. Too far from London, I suppose. In sixteen-seventy, he made my ancestor, Henry Boothby-Graffoe, Duke of Lincolnshire and gave him Compton Allardyce.'

'Your man, Henry – had been a Royalist in the Civil War?' Annaliese asked.

'Very much so. By all accounts, he was a fierce sort of chap . . . He wanted to hang Cromwell and his cronies. So, there you have it, m'dear.'

'And very beautiful it is.' Annaliese's face clouded. 'But I could easily be cross with Edward for keeping it such a secret.'

'Hey, hold on. In fairness to Edward, he hardly knows this place.'

'That's his fault,' Annaliese said brusquely.

'Where is he, by the way?' There was unease in the Duke's question.

'In our rooms with his nose struck in Foreign Office junk.' Annaliese made a belated, unconvincing attempt to make a joke of it. 'When Matthew and Gwen were unloading our luggage, I found that he'd brought half a ton of papers with him.'

'Affairs of state, I expect.' Uncle William glanced at his watch. 'Look, will you be all right on your own, m'dear? There are people I have to see . . . estate business, you know. It's never-ending, I'm afraid.'

'I shall manage,' Annaliese smiled. 'I'm going to have another look at everything.'

'Try not to get lost.' The Duke had taken the first steps away from her when he stopped suddenly. 'You'll be meeting my son, Ralph. I expect he'll turn up at dinner. He arrived yesterday with a friend.'

Annaliese was not allowing herself to be intimidated by something that sounded ominously like a warning. 'I shall look forward to it,' she said and they parted.

There was no risk of getting lost: Annaliese knew exactly where she was. In next to no time she had become perfectly familiar with the vast house. Nor was that all: comprehension had been accompanied by an equally rapid sense of compatibility. Upper Overs was cosy and quaint; Cadogan Square was grand and just about bearable after the changes; but Annaliese felt that she could be happy at

Allardyce Castle in any circumstances that the world chose to throw at her. She had fallen head-over-heels in love with the place and it loved her. Mocking her own fancifulness with a wry smile, Annaliese went back to John Craxton's sublime contribution to the beauty of Wiltshire.

She was on the first floor of the Central Wing, the main corridor of which led into the Long Gallery. The Duke had whisked them through it in less than a minute. Now, Annaliese wanted to study it and absorb its special atmosphere.

It was a stupendous room, directly above the main door of the Castle. Two hundred feet long, it occupied the full eighty-foot width of the original building. The south-facing wall seemed to be nothing but window, the others were oak panelling from floor to ceiling. On the inner walls, there were paintings, over a hundred of them, mostly portraits of men with those distinctive Boothby-Graffoe features and colouring. There was not a stick of furniture and the floor-boards were uncarpeted, proudly showing the patina acquired from nearly five centuries of polish. The noise of her footsteps as she walked to the windows was music to Annaliese's ears. Kneeling on a low sill that was all of three feet deep, she looked out.

The commanding view across the southern half of the Park brought a surprise. Barely two hundred yards from the front of the Castle, there was a lake, slightly larger than the one in St James's Park. It lay in a hollow and was easy enough to miss from ground level – particularly when the eyes were being bombarded with delights. There was a tiny island at the centre of the lake with two swans cruising round it, grandly indifferent to a horde of ducks and other water-fowl.

Gazing towards the eastern woodland that was well over a mile away, Annaliese eventually noticed breaks in the trees. In two of the clearings, chimney-pots were visible. They were, she concluded, the homes of estate workers. Did they realise how lucky they were to live in such idyllic surroundings? Yes, they probably did. No matter what the backstreet firebrands of the Communist and Socialist parties had to say about class and privilege, the system's employees generally had other ideas. Scanning the trees again, she spotted what must be a solitary house, at some distance from the others: in such a prime spot, it must be for someone special.

She was turning her attention to the farm when a heavy, confident footfall disturbed her. There was a triumphant cry of, 'Aha! At last.'

The sound continued to reverberate round the Long Gallery as she turned to look at the man. He had come from the Central Wing, taking a few steps across the bare boards before stopping. He regarded her with a mixture of challenge and curiosity.

'Are you my elusive cousin-in-law?' His voice was strong and bold: he could, she thought, be a good singer if ever he put his mind to it.

'I'm Annaliese.' She eased off the window-sill.

'And I'm Ralph.'

They began to walk, studying each other as they closed the vast gap between them. Amazement put Annaliese at a disadvantage. Ralph was totally unlike what she had come to expect. His long, sleek hair was almost jet-black, his deep brown eyes could easily appear to be the same colour. And he was noticeably taller than his male relatives. Unnerved, Annaliese glanced up at the portraits on the walls, reminding herself what Boothby-Graffoe men *always* looked like. He saw what was passing through her mind and laughed.

'My maternal grandam was Spanish,' he said. 'It all came out in me. The poor old guv'nor is alleged to have thrown a dozen fits when I was born.'

'Oh. I see.'

His physical presence was becoming overwhelming as they drew near to each other. Annaliese had never seen such lithe, animal grace in a man and his complexion was astounding. Instead of the sunny duskiness that would have complemented his hair and eyes, Ralph, Marquess of Axholme, had skin that was the colour and texture of alabaster. In a moment of insanity, Annaliese wanted to touch his face to discover if it felt as perfect as it looked.

She knew exactly what his kiss would be like. This gorgeous, dangerous creature had no truck with chaste pecks on the cheek. And while his lips were planted on hers and his arms held Annaliese tightly, his tongue inveigled its way into her mouth. It went on for much longer than the occasion demanded, with Annaliese powerless to stop it and far from certain that she wanted to. Indeed, for a few insane moments, her tongue was responding to his. At last, he was holding her away from him, studying her.

'It's been my experience that *they* hardly ever know what they're talking about,' Ralph said. 'You prove it, by God!'

'I don't understand.' Annaliese scarcely recognised her voice and there was something wrong with her knees.

'The gossiping classes never came within ten thousand miles of doing you justice.' Ralph laughed.

'Thank you.'

'You are *magnificent*!' There was a passionate authority in the way he said it. Finally letting go of her, Ralph stood back to conduct a thorough, top-to-toe inspection. 'So. You're Edward's wife. However did he do it?'

'Do what?'

'Persuade *you* to marry him.'

'Oh, it was quite easy – bravery and love soon did the trick.'

That was better. Annaliese's presence of mind was returning, nonplussing Ralph. 'Edward, *brave*?' he said.

'Very,' she replied firmly.

He laughed without either humour or sincerity, yet there was a strange charm about it. Annaliese sensed that this was the way he dealt with all tricky situations, big or small. Mostly, because of who he was and his devastating looks, he would get away with it.

'What do you think of the old place?' Ralph asked.

'It's lovely.'

'Would you care for a tour?'

'Your father has seen to that,' Annaliese said.

'Damn!' Ralph's pretence at disappointment was most engaging. 'You've seen all of it . . . the Chapel, the Great Hall, the Library?'

'Yes.'

'I'll bet he never gave you time to draw breath.'

'It was rather brisk,' Annaliese admitted.

'Why don't you let me do the job properly?'

'Very well,' Annaliese agreed.

They went down the main stairs to the Great Hall, where Ralph proved to be unexpectedly knowledgeable, able to provide a wealth of interesting historical detail. But he soon spoiled it by sliding a hand round Annaliese's waist while they were staring up at the hammer-beam roof. Resolutely, making sure that he understood what she was doing, she disengaged herself and put a safe distance between them.

'Your father mentioned that you were here with a friend,' Annaliese said, driving the point home. 'Tell me about her.'

'This is the Habsburg way of putting a chap in his place, is it?' Ralph wavered between admiration and annoyance. 'She's called Sybil Turner – *the* Sybil Turner.'

'Should I know her?'

'She's an actress. Quite famous.'

Annaliese was apologetic. 'I'm afraid I know nothing about the theatre.'

'I'm not exactly the world's leading authority,' Ralph replied. 'At the moment, Sybil is in a thing by a new chap called Noël Coward – the critics seem to think that he's going to be important. What else can I tell you about her? She's unmarried – which is quite unusual for a lady-friend of mine, and she's very keen on being a marchioness, with a view to becoming a duchess in the fullness of time. She's prepared to do anything for that.'

Annaliese gave Ralph the most Viennese of her smiles. 'Does Miss Turner realise what a cynical swine you are?' she asked.

'Good Lord, I don't think she's anywhere near clever enough for that,' he replied coolly.

He was deluding himself, of course. Annaliese knew as much within minutes of meeting Sybil Turner shortly before they went in to dinner. The actress, whose beauty stemmed from an inner strength and fire, was showing signs of irritability. A less arrogant man than Ralph Boothby-Graffoe would surely have seen that something was badly wrong.

The issue was complicated by the two guests whom the Duke had invited to share the meal. Sir Andrew Younger, the local Member of Parliament and a self-styled expert on foreign affairs, was there to provide Edward with interesting conversation. Lady Younger, a woman who struck Annaliese as having a lot in common with Cordelia Milford, made no secret of her interest in their host. She manipulated the seating arrangements to put herself next to the Duke, with Edward and Sir Andrew opposite each other. Annaliese, Ralph, and Sybil Turner were left to fend for themselves. Ralph retaliated by dragging Annaliese to the other end of the long table; reluctantly, because she had no alternative, Sybil joined them.

Feeling duty-bound to do so, Annaliese did her best to strike up a worthwhile conversation with the actress. It was hard work. Sybil Turner had been at Allardyce Castle for little more than twenty-four hours, but was already regretting her decision to come. To her, Annaliese was simply another high-born ignoramus bent on patronising her with fatuous remarks about the theatre. Worse, Ralph acted as if he had the exclusive rights on speech, making it brutally plain that his pearls of wisdom were intended solely for Annaliese.

Edward and Sir Andrew Younger hit it off famously, tearing into Lloyd George. Indifferent though she was to politics, Annaliese knew that the Prime Minister's reputation was in tatters. According to Younger, the man once known as the 'Welsh Wizard' was hanging on to power only by a thread. Next year, the coalition would fall apart. Before Younger and Edward lowered their voices and became positively anti-social, Annaliese heard the words, 'Bonar Law' and 'merely a stop-gap'.

Resignedly, she allowed her attention to drift to the Duke and Lady Younger, only to be shocked into watchfulness. There was no mistake about it, Uncle William *was* responding to the woman's provocative behaviour. As the evening wore on, they began to look more and more like prospective lovers. Nancy had been right!

A bigger surprise lay in store. At the end of the meal, the Duke and Lady Younger disappeared. No one saw them go. One moment they were there: when Annaliese next looked, it was as if they had melted into the vastness of the Castle. Complaining of a headache, Sybil Turner announced that she was going to her room. Soon afterwards, Edward mumbled about the need for total confidentiality and withdrew to the smoking-room with Sir Andrew Younger.

Annaliese and Ralph eyed each other across the table.

'Everyone is very obliging,' he said.

'What do you mean?'

'Leaving us alone like this. It gives me an opportunity to coax you into my bed.'

'I don't really believe that's what they had in mind,' Annaliese said, injecting a note of levity into a situation that she feared was about to become deadly serious.

'No, you're probably right,' Ralph smiled. 'Even so, I'd be a fool not to try.'

'What of Miss Turner?'

'She's a bore,' Ralph said. 'And not unduly rewarding. She should have stayed a virgin for all the good she does a man.'

'Oh dear.' Annaliese stood up. 'Actually, Ralph, I think you're a liar.'

'Why?' he was offended.

'If the lady is as inadequate as you suggest, *you* wouldn't have given her the time of day, let alone brought her down here. I'd say she was *very* good in bed . . . certainly exciting enough for you to run the risk of offending Josephine Underwood. Isn't she rather jealous and possessive?'

Not even such a consummate dissembler as Ralph could avoid a brief betrayal of surprise before his face broke into a broad grin. 'You *are* in the know,' he said. 'That's meant to be frightfully hush-hush. Who told you?'

'Don't be silly, Ralph,' Annaliese laughed. 'My sources are no concern of yours. Good-night.'

She was halfway to the door before he managed to shout, 'Where are you going?'

'To see my son,' Annaliese replied over her shoulder. 'I shall then go to my husband's bed.'

'He won't be there,' Ralph retorted. 'Not for hours. That dreadful man Younger talks all night if he's given half a chance.'

'I'm a patient woman,' Annaliese said and went.

It was a long trek to the guest-rooms on the first floor of the West Wing, with dozens of dark nooks and crannies to be negotiated. Annaliese found herself wondering where Uncle William and Lady Younger were. And was Ralph stealing after her, or attempting to make some sort of peace with Sybil Turner? After one wrong turning that alarmed her more than she cared to admit, Annaliese reached the nursery.

In the room allocated to Gwen, she and Matthew were sitting on a battered old sofa, solemnly holding hands. Matthew leaped up like a startled rabbit, intending to go back to his cubby-hole in the servants' quarters, but Annaliese shook her head.

'Stay where you are,' she ordered. 'It's nice to see you so happy together.' She glanced at the open door of Douglas's bedroom. 'Is everything all right, Gwen?'

'He's been asleep since eight.'

'Lovely.' Annaliese perched on the foot of Gwen's bed. 'Well, what do we think of this place?'

'Matthew's tried to tell me about it several times,' Gwen said. 'I never believed him, though.'

'Does that mean you approve?' Annaliese asked.

'Not half! It's smashing.' It was the highest praise Gwen had ever given. 'Be all right living here all the time, wouldn't it?'

'I think I could cope with it,' Annaliese smiled.

'Have you come across that Ralph?' Gwen asked, her brow furrowing in disapproval. Matthew shifted uneasily: he hated Gwen to tear into people they were paid to respect.

'Yes, I have.' Annaliese's smile was mocking. 'He's quite extraordinary.'

They chatted for a while, then Annaliese tip-toed into the next room to peer into her son's cot. Satisfied, she left Gwen and Matthew to make eyes at each other and went across the corridor to the suite she and Edward had been given.

A maid had opened the bedroom windows, attracting the scents of the night. Enchanted, Annaliese turned off the lights and sat on a window-sill. Gradually, as her senses accustomed themselves to the darkness, she was certain that she could see and hear some of the Park's secrets.

Content and pleasantly tired, she prepared for bed, unconcerned by Edward's continuing absence. She was asleep the moment her head touched the pillow.

*

In London, Annaliese was invariably up and about by seven, but it was well past eight when she woke the following morning, disturbed by Edward's fumbling with the tea-tray. Fully dressed, he was in a good mood – the first for weeks.

'You look as if you could stay there all day,' he said, pouring her tea.

'Why are you up so bright and early?' Annaliese asked.

'I didn't sleep too well . . . had a lot on my mind. Don't worry, I feel chirpy enough.'

'I can see that,' Annaliese replied. Not expecting to hear anything of importance, she asked, 'What's been happening in the world?'

'Oh, there's tremendous excitement,' Edward said. 'It seems that Sybil Turner has cleared off during the night. She's gone back to London.'

'How?' was the first thing that sprang into Annaliese's mind.

'She has her own car.'

'Does she?' The idea seemed to appeal to Annaliese. 'Do you know, I think I should take up driving . . . Beatrice could teach me, couldn't she?'

'So that you could escape from me in the middle of the night?'

'It's an idea, isn't it?' Annaliese said and they both laughed. 'What does Ralph think about Sybil going like that?'

'Officially, he's claiming to be glad. Behind all the bluster, I'm sure he's livid – and rather embarrassed.'

Annaliese studied her husband. '*Schadenfreude!*' she said. It was an accusation of sorts. 'Is that why you're so cheerful this morning?'

'No, that's to do with an idea Andrew Younger came up with while we were talking last night.' Edward smiled. 'Mind you, I'm not sorry to see Ralph put down. What did you think of him?'

Annaliese's reply was slow and careful. 'He's appalling. Totally and utterly appalling.'

'There you are . . . I told you so.' Edward's smugness was at its worst. 'What are your plans for today?'

Although she had no idea why, Annaliese wanted to scream at him: it was the most peculiar sensation.

'Is there something wrong, my dear?' Edward asked as she closed her eyes in search of composure.

'No, it's nothing.' She was smiling. 'Today? I was wondering if I could take Douglas round the Park.'

'What a good idea!' Edward said warmly.

Annaliese cocked her head to one side. 'Am I right in assuming that you have other things in mind?' she asked.

'Yes, I do, as a matter of fact. Younger suggested that I might join him for lunch.'

'To carry on talking about this idea?'

'Yes.' Edward decided that it was safe to say more. 'There are some papers he'd like me to look at.'

'Very secret and damaging to some poor soul?' Annaliese suggested mischievously.

'You can rest assured that the individual concerned is no "poor soul",' Edward said huffily. 'He'll do incalculable damage if he isn't stopped soon.'

Annaliese gave him a shrewd, searching stare. 'You aren't going too deeply into things that don't concern you?' she asked gently.

'I don't think so.'

'You're a civil servant, Edward, not a politician.'

'Don't worry. I know what I'm doing.' He patted her hand.

Even though it was a rather patronising gesture, Annaliese smiled. 'In that case, enjoy yourself. Where is this lunch taking place?'

'At Younger's house in Marlborough. I should be back by five at the latest.'

After he had gone, Annaliese bathed and dressed, paid a quick visit to the nursery, and took a late breakfast with the Duke.

'Nocturnal alarums and excursions,' he whispered, winking wickedly.

'So Edward tells me,' Annaliese replied. 'I'm not in the least surprised. Sybil Turner was at the end of her tether at dinner.'

'What a shame! I didn't notice anything amiss.'

'No, you wouldn't,' Annaliese replied.

'And what's that supposed to mean, eh?' the Duke asked, all injured innocence.

'Lady Younger,' Annaliese said, putting a wealth of meaning into the name.

'Ah.' There was a long pause while the Duke calculated what, if anything, he could get away with. In the end, he decided not to bother with evasion. 'She and I enjoy ourselves occasionally.'

'Oh. So last night wasn't the first time?'

'Did you think it was?' The Duke chuckled. 'No, we always have a pretty good idea when that husband of hers is going to spend half the night gassing. We knew we were on to a good thing once Edward got going.'

Annaliese wanted to laugh. 'I presume that Lady Younger simply reappeared when you and she had finished "enjoying yourselves" and Sir Andrew assumed you'd been showing her some paintings?'

'That's about it, yes.'

'Really, Uncle William, you're no better than your son.'

'I jolly well am,' he said earnestly. 'For a start, I'm not nearly so prolific.' They enjoyed the joke. 'And I don't make a nuisance of myself or wreck decent marriages. It doesn't happen very often – honestly. As a rule, I make proper commercial arrangements for my disgraceful needs.'

In her anxiety to explore something that was nagging at her, Annaliese disregarded the curious phrase. 'What sort of man is Sir Andrew Younger?' she asked. 'Politically, I mean.'

'He's an extreme Conservative. Says the most frightful things, but most people think he's a joke.'

'You don't,' Annaliese was quick to spot.

'A joke is usually regarded as being harmless,' the Duke replied. 'Younger *isn't*. Lately, he seems to be attracting a group of like-minded fanatics. Why do you ask?'

'Edward is having lunch with him,' Annaliese replied. 'Today. At his house in Marlborough.'

The Duke was thoughtful for a few moments. 'Do you know, m'dear, I'm not altogether sure that I like the sound of that,' he said. 'Someone ought to have a word with him.'

'I tried to sound a note of caution.'

'How did he take it?'

Annaliese smiled wryly. 'I was brushed aside – very politely.'

'He might listen to me,' the Duke offered.

'I'd be very grateful, Uncle William.'

Those intriguing words, *I make proper commercial arrangements for my disgraceful needs*, returned to Annaliese's mind in the course of a fascinating morning. What *had* Uncle William meant? Reminded of her brother, Leopold, she jumped to the conclusion that the Duke made use of prostitutes. At once, the very idea seemed ridiculous. A man of his status and influence wouldn't have to sink to such depths: she must have misheard.

In any case, it was impossible to devote too much attention to it. A dog-cart, drawn by a beautiful grey mare with the most docile temperament, had been provided for a ride round the Park – or that part of it that could be covered in two hours, which turned out to be not very much. Matthew drove, Gwen carried Douglas, and Annaliese relaxed against the cushions, admiring the constantly changing surroundings and trying to work out what Uncle William had meant. Very soon, the scenery won: there was far too much to admire.

Annaliese found that the park, with its ever-present view of the magnificent building at its heart, began to unsettle her. Gradually, but with insidious persistence, Compton Allardyce was taking her back to pre-war Vienna, acting as a reminder of what she, along with the rest of the Imperial Family, had lost. Ashamed of what was passing through her mind, Annaliese was feeling envious.

The sensation grew worse, making her edgy and bad-tempered. After lunch with Douglas and Gwen in the nursery, Annaliese decided that she would go for a walk. Without any clear plan, she followed the road towards the north-western corner of the Park, eventually finding another gate. By that time, she had covered nearly three miles and was painfully aware that her shoes were not suitable for such distances. She was contemplating walking back in stockinged feet to escape the threat of blistered heels when a motor roared in through the gate. It was a huge, green sports car that radiated reckless power and the way it screeched to a stop was alarming.

'Do you want a lift back?' Ralph demanded. There was no charm this afternoon.

'Yes . . . thank you.' Annaliese was shaking. This was far worse than yesterday's first encounter.

He gave no help. She had to scramble up to the running-board and deal with the door on her own, and the brutish machine was lunging forward before she could sit down. But, after half a mile that brought Annaliese's heart into her mouth, they were slowing. Relief was short-lived, however. Ralph had braked in order to turn off the road leading back to the Castle. They were on a rough track, heading into a wood. When he pulled up, they were completely hidden and alone.

With the engine turned off, the silence was unbearable. To break it, Annaliese said the first thing that came into her head. 'I believe your friend Sybil has left. I'm sorry.'

'Don't be,' Ralph snapped, staring straight ahead. 'She was of no consequence.'

After that, Annaliese endured the silence. When Ralph finally spoke, his tone was more reasonable, although he remained staring ahead at an imaginary point in the wood. 'You like this place, don't you?'

'The Castle and estate?' Annaliese said, seeking to establish that he did not mean this particular, isolated spot. 'Yes, it's very charming.'

Slowly, Ralph turned and she saw that his dark eyes were thunderous. Was it hatred or passion? 'It's very charming,' he echoed mockingly. 'I think there's more to it than that, *Your Highness*. Much more. *Charming* . . . Ha!' He sat back, striking a flamboyantly nonchalant pose. 'I watched you this morning.'

'When?'

'While you were parading round in that dog-cart. Do you know what I saw?'

'I can't begin to imagine,' Annaliese said, her voice nowhere near as firm as she would have liked.

'You let your true feelings show,' Ralph said. 'I believe you'd give anything to be mistress of Allardyce. Compared to you, Sybil Turner was nothing.'

'How ridiculous!' Annaliese's laugh was a fraction too high-pitched. 'By the way, I didn't see *you*.'

'I was in my study. For your information, that's on the second floor of the East Wing.'

'Well, even if I were thinking what you suggest – and I wasn't, of course – you couldn't possibly have seen it from there.'

'There is a very powerful telescope in my study,' Ralph said, his voice velvet with menace. 'On a tripod that always stays rock-steady. I inherited it from my brother Gerald. You can be assured that I saw you clearly enough *and* what was going through that Habsburg mind of yours.'

'This is absurd,' Annaliese said.

'It is not,' Ralph replied softly.

Aware of danger, she sat very still and quiet.

'I know of a way for you to get what you want,' Ralph said when he was good and ready.

In the full knowledge that she was behaving like a mesmerised fool, Annaliese asked, 'What is it?'

'Divorce Edward and marry me. It's that simple.' Ralph was tracing a finger along the line of her chin. 'You *must* know that you made a mistake with him . . . British citizenship is all very well, but Edward's too high a price to pay for it. You and he are incompatible.'

'We aren't,' Annaliese insisted through clenched teeth.

Ralph laughed. 'Are you suggesting that I can't spot a deeply frustrated woman when she's thrust under my nose? Edward's no good, is he? He doesn't satisfy you. Just look at your mouth. Can Edward keep up with *that* appetite? He doesn't even try, does he? Whereas you and I, Annaliese . . .' His smile was unadulterated, stomach-churning lust. 'You and I are worthy of each other. I can give you all the pleasures you dream about. It appeals, doesn't it? Which do you want most, me, or this place?'

There was no point in wasting time and energy in telling him that he was a deluded lunatic; Annaliese tried to get out of the car. The speed and force with which Ralph grabbed her suggested that he had been half expecting it. Annaliese found herself fast in a savage embrace and kiss. Obeying her instincts, she offered no resistance, believing that struggle would inflame him.

Ralph mistook inertia for submission. With grunting jubilation, he pushed a hand beneath the hem of Annaliese's dress. The advantage of surprise took the tips of his fingers to the tops of her stockings.

Contact with the soft, inner-thigh flesh produced a gloating noise in his throat. Then, all hell was let loose.

Annaliese bit Ralph's lower lip. Hard.

He drew back, roaring with pain. For a moment or two, he seemed bewildered, apparently incapable of comprehending that Annaliese was standing up. The sight of the blood on the hand he had rubbed across his mouth unleashed his anger.

'You bitch,' he snarled. 'You vicious, Austrian bitch. I'll make you pay for this.'

Constrained by the steering-wheel, he was attempting to get to his feet. As he did so, Annaliese struck him across the face, using every ounce of a desperate strength. It hurt him. The arrogant, beautiful face was as fragile as the porcelain it resembled. While he was off-balance and cursing the pain, Annaliese got out of the car. Rather than waste time with the fiddling mechanism of the catch, she climbed on to the seat and took a flying jump over the door.

Landing safely on soft grass, Annaliese began to run, taking several strides before realising that her shoes had gone. So much the better. How far was it to the road? Four hundred metres? Not more, surely to God!

To her horror, she heard the engine of the motor car roar into life. Willing herself not to diminish her effort by looking back, Annaliese went on. There was a wild revving, followed by a tremendous, thudding crash. The engine died. This time, she not only looked back, she stopped in order to do so. In his crazed haste to turn his vehicle, Ralph had reversed it into the trunk of a three-hundred-year-old oak tree. The engine was refusing to restart. For as long as Ralph persisted in his attempts to coax it back into life, Annaliese felt safe walking. When he started to run, so did she, leaving the cover of the trees and coming within sight of the road.

There was a car rolling gently down the hill from the Castle, and, before she could see who was in it, Annaliese was flailing both arms to attract attention. Veering off the road, the motor bumped across the turf towards her and she realised that Edward was the driver. Ralph charged out of the trees, saw what was happening, and slowed to a walk.

Quick though Ralph had been to size the situation up, Edward was quicker. Out of the car in a flash, he looked at Annaliese's feet, saw that one stocking had fallen round her ankle, that her dress was torn at the shoulder and set off towards Ralph. He was in no great hurry, yet Annaliese was reminded of the day he took her away from the Kaiser Frederick Infirmary in January 1919.

Ralph kept walking because there was nothing else he could do. In an ostentatious pantomime of martyrdom, he was dabbing at his mouth with a handkerchief. Behind the pained façade, he was marshalling his thoughts. Annaliese had flown into an uncontrollable rage, assaulted him, accused him of attempted rape, and been responsible for wrecking his brand-new car, the first Bentley Tourer to come out of the factory.

But the Marquess of Axholme was deprived of a chance to utter so much as a syllable. Not pausing in his unhurried gait, Edward hit Ralph. It was a stylish, almost lazy sort of punch, straight to the point of the jaw, and it sent Ralph flying backwards to measure his length on the ground.

As soon as he was able, Ralph made the mistake of trying to get up. Edward promptly knocked him flat again.

'You're very lucky,' Annaliese told the dazed, badly shaken man on the ground. 'You should have seen him in Berlin. He killed a man who was trying to get his hands on me.'

Nothing else was said. Gently, but very firmly, Edward was guiding Annaliese towards the car in which he had arrived. She was shaking, strangely elated by the events of the last few minutes. Above all else, she now knew why she had wanted to scream at Edward that morning: he had not bothered to ask *why* she thought Ralph was appalling. After she had laid such heavy emphasis on the scathing opinion, he should have wanted to know what lay behind it, thus providing the chance for her to say that Ralph had invited her to his bed the previous evening. But no sooner did Annaliese understand, that it ceased to matter. The most handsome amends had been made for what could, in any case, have been nothing more than carelessness. Nor was that all: as they drove back to the Castle, it was apparent that Edward was in the most thrillingly masterful mood. Would he put it to good use, matching her excitement?

*

Four days later, when Annaliese was telling the story to Nancy in the conservatory, she paused to sip coffee.

'Go on, go on,' Nancy laughed. 'What happened next? No. Hold on.' She waved a hand in exasperation. 'Why was Edward cruising round the estate?'

'Looking for me,' Annaliese said. 'He'd got back sooner than he expected from Younger's and asked where I was. Gwen told him that I'd gone for a walk and was probably suffering from sore feet – the cheek of the girl.'

'Right. Proceed.'

But something was worrying Annaliese. 'Younger,' she muttered. 'Oh, hell!'

'What's wrong?' Nancy asked.

'Uncle William promised to have a word with Edward about associating with Andrew Younger. All that got forgotten, of course.'

'It isn't important,' Nancy said dismissively.

'It is,' Annaliese retorted grimly before bowing to Nancy's impatience. 'We got back to the Castle and went up to our rooms. Edward wanted to know what Ralph had done. I told him. He said I should take a bath and stormed off. He was away for about fifteen minutes . . . afterwards, I found out that he'd given poor Uncle William a terrible time, then ordered Gwen to make sure that we weren't disturbed until she brought us dinner at eight o'clock. He came back and got into the bath with me.'

'Jumping Jesus!' Nancy hooted.

'It wasn't the first time he's done it.' Annaliese was earnest, at pains to make it clear that her husband was not completely dull.

'I do hope that this didn't lead to sexual intercourse,' Nancy said, terribly prim and proper.

'It most definitely did.'

'Do I detect satisfaction?'

'You do indeed!' Annaliese laughed. 'We were like mad things – and I'm sure it was all because of Ralph. We had to have a rest while we ate, of course, but it was even worse afterwards.'

'Better, you mean,' Nancy suggested.

'Yes. Absolutely. I'd be very surprised if I'm not pregnant again.' Annaliese liked the idea that she had conceived at Allardyce Castle: it would make the child very special.

'And you came back to London the following morning?' Nancy asked.

'Yes.' Annaliese pulled a rueful face. 'I hated it, but what else could we do? Edward was threatening to knock Ralph's head off and Uncle William didn't know where to put himself.'

'Well, well, well.' Nancy shook her head wonderingly. 'Your husband, eh?'

'Believe it or not, he's already back to normal,' Annaliese said. 'To see him at breakfast this morning, you couldn't imagine what he did to Ralph last Friday.'

'Or to you,' Nancy pointed out.

'Yes.' Annaliese looked unhappy. 'It's a terrible shame it turned out like that. Goodness only knows what we do now – about Ralph and Uncle William, I mean.' She remembered something. 'By the way, you were right about Josephine Underwood. He did his best to hide it, but Ralph was quite shocked when I trotted her name out.'

Nancy nodded. 'Ralph Axholme's a fool to get mixed up with *her*,' she said.

'Ralph *Axholme*?' Annaliese was puzzled. 'Why call him that?'

'Hasn't anyone explained this?' Nancy asked. 'No? Okay, welcome to another quaint British custom. Aristocrats tend to use their title as a surname – so, your uncle is William Lincolnshire.'

'Good gracious!' Annaliese thought about it for a few moments, then asked, 'Why is Ralph a fool to be involved with Josephine Underwood? Isn't she worth it?'

'Oh yes – very much so. She came here for a spell . . . but with her husband. They were a popular pair.' Nancy's look was full of suggestive meaning. 'But Underwood doesn't like Josephine arranging her own entertainment without him. He's a very nasty piece of work. Charles Templeton can give you the details on what Underwood's capable of.'

'Charles?' Annaliese was surprised.

'It was Charles who told me what Josephine was up to,' Nancy said. 'He may be the perfect gentleman, but that bank of his sometimes gets him close to things that you and I would rather not know. Strange things happen to men who fool around with Josephine.'

'Oh dear.' Despite the way he had behaved, Annaliese was concerned for Ralph; it was something to do with family ties and the well-being of Compton Allardyce.

'Forget it,' Nancy advised. 'Ralph doesn't listen to women – least of all *you* – not after the way you treated him.'

While she was nodding glumly, Annaliese thought that she might drop Ralph a line to warn him.

Nancy lit a cigarette. 'So, you liked Compton Allardyce?' she asked casually.

'It's *wonderful*! The tragedy is that I may never see it again.'

'And what about Ralph?' Nancy asked. 'Don't give me any crap – tell me what you *really* thought about him.'

'I thought he was gorgeous,' Annaliese said in a very small voice. 'If I weren't married . . .' She stopped herself, but added, 'I expect he's a marvellous lover.'

'Yes, he is,' Nancy said. 'Or so my friend, Mary-Ann Wexler, tells me. She came over for a holiday last year – she's from New Hampshire, married to a guy who runs a big insurance outfit. Mary-Ann and Ralph took one look at each other and hightailed it for the nearest bed. I didn't see her for over a week and she looked a wreck when she did show up. But was she happy. She said Ralph was the greatest – and Mary-Ann's a bigger tramp than me, so she knows. She's hoping to see him again in the fall.'

Annaliese said nothing.

'How right was Ralph about you and Compton Allardyce?' Nancy asked. '*Would* you marry him to get it?'

'Don't be silly, Nancy. Have you ever heard a more ridiculous notion?'

'No, to be honest, I don't think I have,' Nancy said. 'And I'll tell you why, huh? You just couldn't trust the bastard. Apart from that one little defect, it's not a bad idea at all.'

'That's rubbish,' Annaliese said angrily.

It was a good response, Nancy thought. The only thing that spoiled it was the delay: Annaliese spent several moments thinking about it before she shouted.

15

November 1921
'I think she's dangerous'

On a dank, foggy afternoon, Boothby's was lifeless.

'You can't expect people to venture out in filthy weather like this,' Beatrice grumbled. 'It hasn't looked like clearing all day.'

'I think I'll go home,' Annaliese replied. She was tired, looking slightly unwell, what Gwen called 'peaky'. Her second pregnancy, now in its sixth month, was turning out to be far more troublesome than carrying Douglas.

'Yes, why don't you,' Beatrice agreed. 'There won't be any . . .'

The telephone rang.

There was no tangible reason for apprehension, but they felt it surely enough. Before reaching for the instrument, Beatrice looked as if she were expecting it to bite her. At once, she was placing a hand over the receiver to whisper, 'It's Father. He's awfully upset about something.'

Incoherent, too, Annaliese guessed: Beatrice's face mirrored her difficulty in making sense of what she was being told.

'When did this happen?' she asked eventually. The attempt at an answer was clearly incomprehensible. Beatrice closed her eyes in an attempt to concentrate. 'What about the funeral?' she asked, cutting into a flood of babble. 'Next Monday . . . We're going, presumably? Yes, as a matter of fact, Annaliese is with me now, so she can tell Edward. I expect that he'll be in touch with you this evening.'

There was more as Beatrice struggled to bring the conversation to an end. At last, after repeated assurances, she achieved it. With shock draining her face of colour, she gave Annaliese the bare facts.

'Uncle William has died. A heart attack. It was very sudden. The funeral is next Monday . . . at Compton Allardyce, of course.'

'When?' Annaliese asked, her eyes filling with tears.

'That could be something of a mystery,' Beatrice said heavily.

'It can't be,' Annaliese protested. 'Surely.'

'Let me try to explain.' Beatrice made the effort to recall what Lord Douglas had said and make sense of it. 'Father got the news ten minutes ago from a man called Montagu Ponsonby. He's *the* senior partner in the firm of solicitors who've looked after the family's affairs since the year dot. As a rule, Ponsonby is very long-winded and old-fashioned – he never says a word out of place. But this time, he seems to have been worked-up and let something slip.'

'What?' Annaliese asked.

'That's the beast of it,' Beatrice wailed. 'Father doesn't know. He's awfully upset and confused, poor darling, but he's *almost* certain that Ponsonby implied Uncle William might have died several days ago.'

'No,' Annaliese gasped. 'That can't be true.'

'No, it can't,' Beatrice said firmly, trying to convince herself.

At that moment, the telephone rang again. It was Charles Templeton.

'I'm told that your uncle has passed away,' he said at once.

'Yes.' Beatrice was surprised and suspicious. 'How did you know?'

'I've just come back from lunch with a couple of chaps who mentioned it.'

'Darling, *we* didn't get to know until about fifteen minutes ago,' Beatrice said. She was starting to tremble.

'Look, I'm not saying that these fellows actually *knew*,' Charles said uneasily. 'Now I come to think of what they said, it was more of a rumour. They'd heard that he died in London on Sunday evening – possibly Monday.'

'In *London*!' Beatrice shrieked. 'He can't have been. He always looks in at Cadogan Square when he's in Town and we didn't see him.' Annaliese made a series of gestures signifying agreement.

Several interminable minutes passed before the call ended and

Annaliese was able to hear all the bizarre story. Her reaction was cautiously sceptical. 'This doesn't sound right to me,' she said. 'It isn't *likely*, is it? But what about Ralph? Don't you think it's strange that he didn't get in touch with Father, rather than leaving it to a lawyer?'

'No, I don't,' Beatrice snapped. 'It's exactly the way you'd expect him to behave.'

'Are you *sure*?' Annaliese asked. 'I could see him crowing – discreetly, of course, behind crocodile tears. He is now the Duke of Lincolnshire.'

'He's still Marquess of Axholme, too, until he marries and produces a legitimate heir.' Beatrice tangled her fingers into knots. 'What *is* going on?'

'Nothing, probably,' Annaliese said. 'I'm sure it's all perfectly simple. You know what people are like once they start gossiping . . . everything gets distorted and blown-up out of all proportion.'

They carried on chatting while Annaliese prepared to go home, neither of them believing the reassuring platitudes they were exchanging. The charade lasted until the telephone rang for a third time.

'It's Nancy Shenstone,' Beatrice announced. 'She wants to speak to you.'

Annaliese drew the instrument across the table. 'Nancy, I'm on my way home,' she said. 'I want to hide from this awful weather and we've just had some very bad news.'

'About the Duke?'

'Yes. Isn't it sad?'

'Very.' For once, Nancy sounded curtly insincere. 'It could also be peculiar.'

'Oh?' Annaliese was despairing.

'I think you ought to call in here on your way home,' Nancy said. 'You ought to hear the story that Cordelia Milford picked up last night.'

Beatrice made up her mind in a flash. Leaving Paul Marks in charge for what was left of the miserable day, she accompanied Annaliese to Martha's Vineyard.

*

Edward was in a bad mood when he reached Cadogan Square at a few minutes to seven. A day fraught with problems at the Foreign Office had been made infinitely worse by the cancellation of a bridge game due to the illness of one of the players.

At first, it seemed that Annaliese's statement of Uncle William's death had simply failed to register: Edward did not respond until Beatrice mentioned the funeral.

'I suppose we shall have to go,' he grumbled.

'Oh, Edward, you are the limit,' Beatrice said. 'Of *course* we must go. Apart from anything else, we shall be looking after Father – he's expecting you to telephone him, by the way.'

'It isn't all that convenient,' Edward muttered. 'Especially if this fog keeps up. I refuse to spend a night down there, so we shall have to go there and back in the day.'

Although unable to face an argument, Annaliese felt bound to question Edward's churlish attitude. 'What's the matter with you?' she asked. 'You surely aren't worried about facing Ralph, are you?'

'What, after the last time we met!' Edward was scornful.

Left to her own devices, Annaliese would have gone upstairs and prepared for a very early night. Already worn out before the strain of the last few hours, she felt she might have slept the clock round given half a chance. But Beatrice, driven on by worry, was determined to have her say.

'We think that there's something peculiar about Uncle William's death,' she said to Edward.

'Such as?' he asked.

'When Montagu Ponsonby was telling Father, he seems to have implied that it happened several days ago.'

Edward frowned. Whatever else he was thinking, there was impatience to get to the study where he would read Foreign Office documents while Franklin brought his dinner. 'Some mistake, I imagine,' he said dismissively.

'No,' Beatrice insisted. 'Uncle William's death was being discussed in clubs and bars *before* Ponsonby spoke to Father.'

'How do you know?' Edward asked sharply.

'My . . .' Beatrice stopped herself in the nick of time. 'One of our clients called into Boothby's this afternoon to say that he'd heard things.' Seeing that Edward was unmoved, Beatrice pressed on. 'Cordelia Milford claims that someone told her last night.'

Edward frowned, searching his memory. 'Cordelia Milford? Isn't she one of Nancy Shenstone's set?'

'Yes – Nancy telephoned and we went to her house to see Cordelia.'

'*We?*' Edward's tone was threatening.

'Yes . . . Annaliese and me.' Beatrice's reply was made in all innocence, leaving her appalled by the consequences.

Edward's anger as he turned to Annaliese was sudden and dreadful. 'I told you to stay away from that damned woman!' he shouted. 'Are you incapable of obeying simple instructions?'

'I wasn't aware that I was supposed to *obey*,' Annaliese said. 'You have the servants for that.' There was an indignant flush on her cheeks.

'Nancy Shenstone is an out-and-out trollop!' Edward roared. 'How the devil am I supposed to preserve dignity and integrity while you persist in associating with a creature like her?'

'Edward, you're . . .'

'This is nothing to do with you,' Edward snapped at Beatrice. Initially, his purpose had been to crush her interruption, but he pursued a thought that occurred to him. 'I suppose you still see this woman regularly?'

'Yes,' Beatrice retorted. 'You know perfectly well that she's always been a great help to Boothby's.'

'I know no such thing,' Edward said. 'What I *do* know is that you're running a devil of a risk in letting her anywhere near the place. Has it crossed your mind that she might have invented this story about Uncle William? Look at the facts, for God's sake . . . Have you ever known him come to London without at least calling on us?'

'A few hours ago, I would have said, "no",' Annaliese replied. 'But Beatrice and I were told that he's been doing it twice a month for several years.'

'Poppycock!' Edward was amused, but the respite from his anger was transitory. 'The whole country has gone mad since the War. People never used to spread filthy scandal the way they do nowadays. I may not be able to stop what's happening in the gutter, but I'm damned if I'll tolerate it in this house. Annaliese, I forbid you to go near that Shenstone woman ever again! Is that understood?'

'I *understand*,' she replied icily. 'I have no intention of *obeying*, though. If you'll excuse me, I'm going upstairs to lie down.'

In the mortified vacuum that followed Annaliese's departure, Edward and Beatrice did their best not to look at each other. Although shocked by the discovery that her brother had a side to his character that made him a stranger, Beatrice knew that it was up to her to repair the damage.

'Look here, Edward, this won't do at all,' she said in the most reasonable tone she could muster. 'It's no way to treat Annaliese – especially in her condition. This pregnancy is turning out to be very trying for her.'

Edward made a strange, throat-clearing noise and looked uncomfortable.

'Father would hate it if he knew how you were behaving,' Beatrice went on.

'It has nothing to do with Father,' Edward replied. 'Or you, Beatrice. Are you intending to stay here tonight, or are your friends expecting you?'

'All right, I'll go,' Beatrice said dispiritedly. 'Remember to telephone Father . . . I promised you would.'

She paused at the front door to ask, 'By the way, are you sorry that Uncle William has died?'

'Of course I am,' Edward said irritably.

'Oh, I see.' Beatrice's eyes were furious. 'It's very odd that you didn't say so instead of flying off the handle at your wife.'

When Annaliese woke the following morning, she found that Edward had not slept in their bed. Gwen said that he had used a spare room prepared by Franklin. Initially, Annaliese was deeply offended; Edward's action was obviously meant to show his displeasure and she felt it like a slap in the face. Then, when calmer counsels prevailed, she decided that she had no feelings one way or the other. She was, however, certain of one thing: there was no longer any point in pretending that her marriage was satisfactory.

The next few days were hideous.

Annaliese and Edward spoke only to discuss the arrangements for travelling to the funeral – and those bad-tempered snatches of conversation would have been briefer still had it not been for the difficulty of getting Lord Douglas to Compton Allardyce. Beatrice spent a day at Upper Overs, returning with the not unexpected news that their father was laid very low by his brother's death.

'He can't drive himself to Wiltshire,' Beatrice told Edward. 'He simply isn't up to it.'

'If he comes here for Sunday night, he can travel with us,' Edward replied.

'No, he won't do that,' Beatrice said. 'It's best if Matthew drives Father . . . He can go down to Sussex on Sunday afternoon.'

'That won't do at all. I want Matthew to drive us.'

'Oh, Edward, for goodness' sake be reasonable.' Beatrice exploded. 'You're perfectly capable of doing that trip yourself.'

'I have a very busy and important day on Tuesday,' Edward replied, his voice growing louder. 'I don't intend to wear myself out by driving to Compton Allardyce and back.'

While Beatrice washed her hands of him and stormed off to make alternative plans, Annaliese felt compelled to take Edward to task for his boorishness. His response was to stay at his Club for the three nights preceding the funeral. Annaliese was incensed. Using another bedroom within the privacy of Cadogan Square was one thing, making a public display of their difficulties was something else entirely.

'Keep your hair on,' Gwen insisted. 'Think of that baby before you start getting het up. And don't give that sod Franklin the satisfaction of seeing you in a state.'

On Sunday evening, Beatrice telephoned to say that she was at Upper Overs and would drive Lord Douglas to the funeral herself.

The fog that had plagued most of southern England for two weeks cleared during the night, leaving a clear blue sky. It was cold but bright, a champagne-like day more suited to beginnings than the finality of funerals.

Obeying instructions, Matthew drove carefully, keeping a sharp look-out for ice, and never exceeding thirty miles an hour. As a result, the 80-mile journey took over three hours, and, for every single minute of it, Matthew was painfully conscious of the stony silence behind the glass partition that separated him from Her Highness and Mr Edward. Gwen had warned him that things were bad, but the grim faces in the back of the Rolls went far beyond her gloomiest predictions.

The sight of the Castle and Park brought Annaliese to life. Everything looked very different. May's fertile profusion had been replaced by the spare, windswept gauntness of winter, yet the intrinsic beauty was still there. It was like seeing a truly attractive woman without make-up or finery: although the effect was not so immediately striking, the underlying perfection was visible. Glad that at least one of them seemed to have cheered up, Matthew devoted himself to the task of finding where to park the Rolls.

There was excellent organisation to ease his way, with Salisbury's most respected firm of funeral directors determined to ensure that everything about the occasion was a dignified success. Expecting hundreds of motor cars, they had posted men to direct new arrivals to the yards at the rear of the Castle. There, other marshals arranged for vehicles to be parked in neat lines, making the best use of the space. Annaliese spotted that an old coach-house had been turned into a rest and refreshment room for chauffeurs and told Matthew to get along in. Then, purely for the sake of appearances, she took Edward's arm and they headed for the Great Hall where the mourners were gathering.

Beatrice was hovering anxiously near the main entrance, Lord Douglas at her side. His eyes lit up when he spotted Annaliese and he clutched gratefully at the hand she offered him.

'This is a terrible business, my dear,' he muttered. 'William was no age at all.'

'Sixty-six?' Annaliese asked.

'Not very old, is it?'

Deeply shocked by his appearance, she murmured a sympathetic phrase or two. Emotionally, he was in reasonable control, but his face had that same pasty pallor that had persisted for so long after Lady Alice's death. 'William and I started off with a brother and two sisters,' something compelled him to say.

'What became of them?' Annaliese asked.

'They all died before they were three. It wasn't uncommon in those days – the 1860s, you know. Even so, I've often wondered if our parents and nanny were quite up to the mark. Father never took the blindest bit of notice of us and Mother was wild . . . like Ralph.'

Gazing at him in numbed disbelief, Annaliese saw that Lord Douglas had awful bags under his eyes, a sign of incipient ill health. 'What a lot of people have turned up,' she said, desperate to lighten the atmosphere.

'I imagine most of the top families in *Debrett* have sent someone,' Beatrice added gamely, taking up the lead. She grabbed Annaliese's elbow, lowering her voice. 'Over there, look, by the middle window . . . Do you see that tall man . . . the one with the tremendous opinion of himself? That's Lord Curzon, the Foreign Secretary. They say that he and Lloyd George are at daggers-drawn.'

Annaliese nodded and there was a slightly cynical twist to her mouth. Following the direction of her gaze, Beatrice puffed with exasperation at what she saw. Edward, distributing perfunctory courtesies to those he was easing out of his way, was making a determined attempt to get close to Lord Curzon. 'Isn't he the limit,' Beatrice hissed. Shrugging, Annaliese devoted herself to Lord Douglas.

For the time being, Edward's objective was to be thwarted. Montagu Ponsonby saw that it was turned half past eleven, time to start people moving into the Chapel for the burial service which was due to start at twelve. Using a gavel on a block of wood to gain attention, he made the announcement in the unctuous tones of the professional sympathiser. Behind the mask demanded by the occasion, Annaliese detected a ruthless, stony-faced individual. Montagu Ponsonby was not a man to trifle with.

Members of the family of the late Duke – a very small group by aristocratic standards – were to be seated in the front row of pews. Entering on Lord Douglas's arm, with Edward and Beatrice some way behind them, Annaliese saw the man who had been plaguing her thoughts all the way from Cadogan Square. Ralph Frederick Gainsborough Boothby-Graffoe, the new Duke of Lincolnshire, was standing in the centre of the left-hand row of pews. He stared straight at her, and, for a moment or two, Annaliese felt sure that he was going to ignore her. Then his eyes beckoned. As Lord Douglas nodded curtly to his nephew and turned pointedly to the right, Annaliese was unable to resist approaching Ralph.

'Thank you for your letter about Underwood,' he said, his eyes boring into hers. 'I took your advice.'

'Oh . . .' Annaliese felt herself blushing. 'Good. I was warned that he was a nasty piece of work.'

'You were right,' Ralph replied, as forcefully as he felt able in the funeral brooding of the Chapel. 'And I want to apologise for the way I behaved to you when you were here in May. That was wrong.'

Annaliese nearly fell over. Had he ever said anything remotely like that before? Her confusion was made worse by Edward, glaring at her from the aisle. 'That's quite all right,' she told Ralph and hurried to join Lord Douglas in the right-hand pew. After a gratuitous scowl at Ralph, Edward guided Beatrice to the seat beside Annaliese and positioned himself on the outside.

As the places behind them began to fill, Annaliese was struck by how totally *alone* Ralph seemed. Still standing, he seemed strangely torn between pride and embarrassment in his isolation. According to Nancy's grape-vine, he was without the consolation of female company. After he had dumped Josephine Underwood, all his other women had disappeared and there was no sign of anyone prepared to take him on. *You need to marry, my lad*, Annaliese thought. *Looking so vulnerable doesn't suit you. Perhaps being the Duke of Lincolnshire will attract the right woman*.

Then, the oddest thing happened. With a visible sigh of boredom, Ralph turned for a last look at the growing congregation before he sat down. At once, after catching sight of someone, his whole demeanour changed: confidence surged through him and his eyes became almost tender. Turning quickly, Annaliese was lucky: a narrow gap through the jostling crowd let her see the woman who was returning Ralph's look. She was tall, blonde, and very attractive. A moment later, everyone moved. The woman was lost to sight and Ralph sat down, staring fixedly ahead.

The woman fascinated Annaliese to the extent that her mind was distracted from most of what followed. Only later, for example, did she discover that the service had been conducted by the Bishop of Salisbury. Instead of paying any sort of attention to what was being said or sung, Annaliese manufactured excuses for looking over her shoulder, trying to find the woman, her obsession undeterred by Edward's glowering disapproval. That one brief glimpse of the blonde, and what had passed between her and Ralph, was a tormenting riddle that screamed for an explanation.

At the conclusion of the service, the coffin containing Uncle William's body was carried down to the crypt for interment in the family vault. Edward decided not to accompany it, leaving Annaliese and Beatrice to help Lord Douglas down the worn, twisting steps. It was an eerily memorable experience, with part of the cavern illuminated by oil lamps, and, beyond the orb of light, shadows fading into impenetrable darkness.

The coffin was placed on a deep ledge containing the remains of all seven previous dukes. In the dimness of the recess, Annaliese could make out three small boxes, covered by dust and cobwebs: she assumed that they were the other uncle and two aunts that Edward should have had. As the last prayers were being intoned, Annaliese and Ralph exchanged looks: was it a trick of the strange light, or was his valedictory?

By the time they came out of the crypt and made their way back to the main part of the Castle, the mourners had spread out, some in the Great Hall, others upstairs in the Long Gallery, and another, much smaller group in whichever hiding-place Ralph had chosen. Old friends who rarely met these days, apart from funerals and weddings, were banded together in corridors and on the broad staircase. Beatrice heard someone say that food and drink were available in the Long Gallery; having failed to spot Lord Curzon anywhere else, Edward said they should go up.

Fifty-odd trestle-tables had been set up in the vast chamber. At the centre, refreshments were spread out in a display on four huge refectory tables. People were helping themselves and going off to form groups at the scattered trestles, each of which was covered with an immaculate white cloth and surrounded by chairs. As Edward sat down, he spotted Sir Andrew Younger near the entrance to the Central Wing and was off, not bothering to excuse himself. Annaliese and Beatrice pulled faces at each other.

There was a constant stream of visitors to the table, men and women who were anxious to have a word with Lord Douglas. In the space of twenty minutes, Annaliese was introduced to five dukes and eight earls. She found them courteous and impressive. Without exception, they and their elegant wives were deeply concerned about Ralph succeeding to the title. The Countess of Torksey summed it up in her usual blunt style. 'What about your blasted nephew, Douglas? Everyone's afraid that he's going to get us all a bad name. Five years of him and we could find ourselves abolished – or even worse. You know what a bloody funny mood the country's in these days. What's to be done, eh?'

'Lavinia, my dear, I wish that I knew,' Lord Douglas told her. For a few harrowing moments, he seemed to be close to tears. Seeing his distress, Lady Torksey grabbed his arm and hoisted him on to his feet.

'What you need is ten minutes with my two gals,' she said firmly. 'You know what screams they are and they think you're the cat's whiskers. Let's find them before they run off with a groom apiece. Come along, Douglas, old thing, quick march!'

'I like her,' Annaliese said after Lady Torksey and Lord Douglas had set off towards the main stairs.

'She's one of the best,' Beatrice agreed. 'Actually, her daughters aren't nearly so much fun as she is, but Father's always adored them and they might cheer him up.' She looked round. 'Is it my imagination, or is it starting to thin out already?'

'People *are* going,' Annaliese said. 'Look.' She pointed to the windows with their view of the road to the south-east entrance to the

Park. Three limousines were drifting down towards the gate. 'Just gone two o'clock,' she said, glancing at her watch. 'I wonder if Edward and Sir Andrew Younger have run Lord Curzon to ground?'

Beatrice was saved from thinking of a response to the barbed comment by the approach of a pretty woman in a plain but beautifully cut black dress. She was probably aged about forty, Annaliese thought.

'Miss Beatrice, so nice to see you again,' the woman said. 'A terrible shame about the circumstances, though. I'm very sorry about your uncle – we all thought the world of him.'

'Thank you, Mrs Pritchard,' Beatrice said. 'You know my sister-in-law, don't you? I expect you met her when she was here in May.'

'I'm afraid I never had the honour,' the woman replied. 'As I recall it, the visit ended rather suddenly – in difficult circumstances.'

'Oh . . . well . . . Annaliese, this is Mrs Pritchard, the Castle's housekeeper.'

'How do you do, Your Highness?' the woman executed a neat curtsy.

'Hello, Mrs Pritchard,' Annaliese smiled. 'It looks as though you've done very well today. It can't have been easy.'

'Easier than you'd imagine,' the housekeeper replied. 'There's been no one giving orders, so Mr Baskerville and I have been able to get on and do the necessary.'

'Baskerville is the butler,' Beatrice explained to Annaliese. 'Wonderful man.' To Mrs Pritchard, she said, 'You'll be expecting big changes, I suppose.'

Mrs Pritchard's face darkened. She bent forward slightly and lowered her voice. 'Between ourselves, Miss Beatrice, I'm not at all sure that Mr Baskerville and I will stay to find out what happens. We were both devoted to His late Grace, you see.'

The hidden meaning was plain enough. Annaliese was on the point of telling Mrs Pritchard not to consider a move before talking to her when she caught sight of the blonde woman from the Chapel. She appeared to be looking for someone, prowling round the Gallery like a cat, sensually proud of herself, especially the long, shapely legs.

'Who's that?' Annaliese whispered to Mrs Pritchard when the

woman was in their direct view and there was no need to turn.

'Blanche Hamilton,' Mrs Pritchard answered, a chill in her voice. 'She's the wife of the estate manager.'

'Of course.' Beatrice was remembering. 'Her husband's called Richard . . . Didn't he have a bad time in the War?'

'Wounded twice,' Mrs Pritchard said. 'Shell-shock, as well. The poor devil's never been the same since. Mind you . . .' She stopped abruptly and Annaliese understood the code of behaviour that the housekeeper had felt herself to be in danger of breaking. However, there was something she felt able to say that gave a fleeting glimpse of a clue. 'He's older than her, of course.'

Looking up, Annaliese saw Blanche Hamilton from a revealingly new angle and much was made clear. Everything about the striking blonde – the arrogant eyes, greedy mouth, and the way she *used* her voluptuous body even when standing still – suggested a woman who valued sexual pleasure above all else. Almost certainly, she was the permanent mistress that Ralph kept hidden in the background.

'Where do the Hamiltons live?' Annaliese asked.

'They have a cottage in Keeper's Wood,' Mrs Pritchard said. 'It's rather nice – very secluded.' Annaliese remembered the house on its own that she had been studying from the windows of this very room only moments before her first meeting with Ralph.

Blanche Hamilton was giving up the search and leaving the Long Gallery. Men were watching the alluring swing of her hips – all part of hypnotic sexuality. As she strutted out of sight, Annaliese had a premonition. The feeling was strong enough to make her shiver.

'Are you all right, Annaliese?' Beatrice asked anxiously, aware of Annaliese's pregnancy.

'Don't worry, it was only someone walking over my grave.' Annaliese passed it off as a joke.

Mrs Pritchard was inclined to take it more seriously. 'It's easy enough to get that notion in this place since His Grace passed away,' she said. 'Please excuse me, Your Highness, Miss Beatrice – I must be getting on.'

She went and Beatrice asked, 'Who walked over your grave?'

'That Hamilton woman,' Annaliese replied. 'I think she's dangerous.'

'In what way?' Beatrice was curious rather than alarmed.

'I don't know . . . It was a feeling that came over me.' Frowning in concentration, Annaliese paused to re-examine her feelings. 'Actually, it's not *her*, as such, that's dangerous, it's something she's involved in. She's mixed up in a situation that could easily turn into a disaster.'

'What?' Beatrice demanded.

'I've no idea,' Annaliese said ruefully, conscious that Beatrice thought she was ever so slightly wrong in the head. 'I've never had a feeling like it.' Quickly, she changed the subject. 'People really are going now,' she said.

It was all too easy to slip away: there was no host. Even if Ralph were anywhere to be seen, few would have bothered speaking to him. Someone had placed a condolence book on a table in the Great Hall, and, once an appropriate entry had been made, those who had come to pay their last respects to the old Duke disappeared. Mrs Pritchard became a centre of attraction when she returned to the Long Gallery to inspect the remains of the buffet. Several peers seemed to treat her as though she were the lady of the house; from what she saw, Annaliese deduced that an earl offered Mrs Pritchard a job.

Then, when the great chamber was almost empty, Edward turned up, obviously pleased with himself. Lord Douglas came back, escorted by Lady Torksey. An immaculate, handsome man emerged from the main stairs, caught Mrs Pritchard's eye, and moved swiftly to her side. It was Baskerville, the butler, Annaliese assumed, liking the look of him. The Duke and Duchess of Dorchester, who were already talking to Mrs Pritchard, drew him into their conversation.

'We're the last,' Beatrice whispered. 'Time we made a move.'

Annaliese nodded and looked at Edward.

At that moment, with a crashing of feet on the bare boards, Ralph strode in. He was accompanied by Montagu Ponsonby and four other men. Three of them were so grey and self-effacing that they were obviously junior members of Ponsonby's firm. The fourth was Bertie Christopherson, an inane nuisance who imagined himself to be Ralph's bosom pal.

In a flash of insight, Annaliese saw that Ponsonby and his three subordinates were ill at ease: they did not want to be here, like this, with Ralph. Why were they? Perhaps they had been engaged in the post-funeral ritual of transferring deeds and titles and had simply followed the new Duke like sheep. Annaliese was also aware that Ralph and his crony were the worse for drink. Swaying idiotically, Bertie Christopherson showed it; with Ralph, it was more in his manner, very careful and precise, a favourite ruse with drunks who believe they are stone-cold sober.

When the reverberation of footsteps had faded, the Gallery was filled with silence, tense and expectant. Ralph made the most of it.

'I owe you an apology, Uncle Douglas,' he said in a clear, ringing voice. He was an actor playing a part.

'Do you?' Lord Douglas bristled, willing his nephew to shut up.

'I fear so. It was *I* who should have told you that Father had popped off, not old Ponsonby. I hope I'm forgiven.'

'Yes.' Never had a man meant it less. Lord Douglas lied in the hope that it would put an end to the matter; he was disappointed.

'The fact is, I was frantically busy,' Ralph went on. 'Didn't have time to wipe my nose.' He paused, relishing his command over the dozen or so people who made up his captive audience. Unseen by most of them, there was an extra spectator. Blanche Hamilton was at the end of the corridor that led to the Central Wing. Sensing the atmosphere, she edged back into the deep recess of the doorway. Only Annaliese could see her, was able to study the way she was looking at Ralph. According to Nancy's friend, Mary-Ann Wexler, Ralph was a very accomplished lover: the expression on Blanche Hamilton's face confirmed it.

'Father croaked it a week last Saturday,' Ralph said. 'As far as I know, *none* of the rumour-merchants got it right!'

'That's enough, Ralph,' Lady Torksey said in a voice that would have stopped most men dead in their tracks.

Not Ralph. 'You will all bear in mind that this is *my* house now, won't you?' he said, apparently amiable. 'I feel sure that you would all like to know that the dear old guv'nor went out in style – with a bang, you might say. To put none too find a point on it, he was in bed with a whore when he breathed his last.'

The Gallery pulsated with reaction. In the midst of the outrage and disbelief, Annaliese recalled Uncle William's own words: *I make proper commercial arrangements for my disgraceful needs.*

Ralph was carrying on. 'I need hardly say that she was a very high-class whore . . . the guv'nor always had impeccable taste! This was in London, by the way, so there was a good deal to do, eh, Bertie?'

'Oh, rather.' Christopherson brayed. 'What a performance it was. Wouldn't have missed it, though. Not for anything. Great fun, don't you know?' The idiot was grinning from ear to ear.

'Is that all, Ralph?' Lady Torksey asked.

'It is,' he replied.

'I presume you're satisfied?'

'Very.' Ralph's smile was vindictive.

Lord Douglas erupted into a burst of pathetic anger. 'By God, Ralph, you're more rotten than I thought! You care for nothing, do you?'

Montagu Ponsonby had heard enough. Moving to Ralph's side, he said, 'This is *most* unseemly and uncalled-for, Your Grace. I urge you to respect your father's memory and entitlement to privacy.'

The tone was authoritarian and verging on the contemptuous. It took most of the wind out of Ralph's sails, but the onlookers, hearing him called 'Your Grace' found no comfort in his deflation.

Ralph glared round sulkily. 'You have homes of your own, go to them,' he said nastily.

Turning, he saw Blanche Hamilton and headed toward her with an elated spring in his step. They disappeared together, followed by Ponsonby and his retinue. Bertie Christopherson, abandoned in the sudden burst of movement, began to wander round in search of a drink.

As if hypnotised by what had happened, none of the people in the Long Gallery seemed capable of leaving. The Duke and Duchess of Dorchester were attempting to comfort Lord Douglas; Edward was agreeing with Lady Torksey that Ralph was the world's worst; Beatrice was sympathising with Mrs Pritchard and Baskerville, both of whom were appalled. Only Annaliese was alone, still sitting at the trestle-table and gazing blankly into space, mulling over the image of

Ralph and Blanche Hamilton rushing off together.

It was concern for Annaliese that made Beatrice take action to disperse the gathering. Slowly, bowed down by the unpleasantness to which they had been subjected, they made their way back to the cars where Matthew was waiting, anxious and impatient. Lord Douglas and Annaliese parted sadly, sharing an additional grief.

'We shall never be able to come here again,' Lord Douglas whispered as he embraced Annaliese.

'I know,' she replied. 'I can't bear to think about it.'

Once they were started and on the way to the south-east gate, Matthew's heart sank. It was going to be another grim, silent journey with Her Highness and Mr Edward ignoring each other.

After travelling three miles, Matthew thought he might have been wrong. Passing a stretch of the River Kennet that was bathed in the scarlet glow of the November sunset, Annaliese spoke.

'Can what Ralph said about Uncle William's death be true?'

'Of course not,' Edward retorted angrily. 'It's one of his disgraceful jokes.'

'It would explain why we thought there was a delay in letting us know,' Annaliese said.

'There was no delay.' Edward had an ideal way of preventing further discussion of the subject. 'What was Ralph saying to you in the Chapel?'

'He wanted to apologise for what he did when we were here in May.'

'*Did* he? How interesting.'

Annaliese was surprised. Instead of launching into what should have been a predictable diatribe about his cousin's deviousness, Edward seemed impressed. Eventually, Annaliese gave up watching him out of the corner of her eye and settled into the silence that was to last all the way to Cadogan Square.

When Matthew jumped out to open the door for Annaliese to alight, she shook her head. 'Just a moment, please,' she said and pulled the door shut. The way she turned to Edward caused Matthew to retreat across the pavement.

'Are you intending to return to your Club?' Annaliese asked Edward.

'Yes.'

'I suggest that you do so merely to pick up whatever you have left there,' Annaliese replied. 'If you aren't back within the hour, I shall go to Nancy Shenstone's house and *stay* there. Douglas, Gwen and Matthew will go with me!'

Edward gaped at her. 'Have you taken leave of your senses?' he asked.

'On the contrary, I believe I'm regaining them,' Annaliese snapped. 'We must be one of the most fortunate couples in London, yet look at the way you behave. Because you don't like me seeing Nancy Shenstone, you take yourself off like a bad-tempered child. I must say, Edward, your idea of "for better or worse" strikes me as quite eccentric.'

Six months pregnant or not, Annaliese made quite a show of getting out of the Rolls and stalking up to the front door where a puzzled Gwen was waiting.

Edward was back in under half an hour, sufficiently chastened to make a gesture of goodwill: he installed himself in their bedroom, rather than the one Franklin was keeping ready for him. It remained to be seen whether this was anything more than a gesture. Despite Edward's concession, Annaliese felt bitterly unhappy, two months short of her third wedding anniversary, she had been forced to issue a dire threat in order to preserve the outward show of her marriage.

There was, however, one source of profound thankfulness in the six weeks that passed before Christmas. No scandal blew up to sully Uncle William's reputation as a wise, kind man who had served England to the best of his ability.

Dozens of people must have known of the circumstances in which he had died, yet, after that flurry of rumour four days before the funeral, it was all forgotten. More remarkably, after his outburst in the Long Gallery, Ralph – who seemed to have disappeared from public view – kept his mouth shut. Annaliese's gratitude was mostly on behalf of Lord Douglas, spared the disgrace of an uproar in the more sensational elements of the press.

16

1922

'She must be a harmless nonentity'

The child conceived at Allardyce Castle was born in February, during a spell of outstandingly harsh weather. Afterwards, Annaliese took three days to recover.

'It's another boy,' Gwen said, before either the doctor or nurse could draw breath. 'And this one's very special.'

'Why do you say that?' Annaliese asked wearily.

'I don't know, but he is. That's gospel.' Gwen was convinced.

When Annaliese had recuperated and attempted to take an interest in the baby, she found him an odd little scrap, with great big eyes, and, poor thing, what looked like a Habsburg lower lip. There was a strong suggestion of the long-suffering and bewildered about him: this one had definitely *not* asked to be born and was at a complete loss to know what to do about it. Temperamentally, he was a million miles from the increasingly extrovert Douglas, a factor that counted against him – as did the trouble he had caused for the past nine months. On the whole, Annaliese was inclined not to like him. Edward, who had spoken of a daughter, made no attempt to hide his disappointment.

Matthew bore the brunt of Gwen's indignation. 'That pair want their heads banging together,' she fumed. 'They've no time at all for that *lovely* little chap. Come to think of it, they've no time for anything except glaring at each other.'

'It's been the same ever since His Grace's funeral,' Matthew said. 'They came back from that even worse than they went. God knows what went on while they were inside the Castle.'

'It'll be something to do with that Ralph,' Gwen said. 'You can bank on it. That's no cause to take it out on this poor mite, though, is it?' She was nursing the child as they sat by the fire in the day-nursery.

'Maybe things will get better when Her Highness goes back to work,' Matthew suggested. 'Boothby's always cheers her up and Miss Beatrice is struggling without her. She was going on blind about it when I drove her and Mr Templeton down to Upper Overs last week. What's wrong?' After giving vent to a sniff, Gwen was looking cross.

'I don't like the way Miss Beatrice and Mr Templeton are doing things,' she said.

Matthew was puzzled. 'That's not like you, Gwen,' he said. 'I know they're what you might call living in sin, but . . .' He shut up, attempting to suggest that Miss Beatrice and her lover, both first-class toffs, should not be the subject of moralising by servants.

'Don't be daft,' Gwen chided. 'I ain't bothered about what they get up to behind closed doors.' There was a sparkle of roguishness in her eyes: for some months, Gwen had been thinking that it was high time she and Matthew went a good deal further than kissing. 'No, what worries me is that they're getting too easy-going. They don't seem to care who knows about them.'

'As I heard it, Lord Douglas had specially asked for Mr Templeton to go with Miss Beatrice,' Matthew said. 'Polly reckons he's been in on the secret from the start.'

'I know that,' Gwen replied. 'It's other folk that worries me.'

'Like who?'

'Oh, Matthew, you are dim sometimes. Mr Edward isn't the most broad-minded person, is he?'

'What Miss Beatrice does is her own business.'

'That isn't how Mr Edward sees things,' Gwen said. 'He seems to be getting worse . . . you should hear him when he starts going on about Lady Shenstone. How old would you say he was?'

Matthew foundered. 'I'm hopeless at guessing ages.' He took a stab. 'Forty? A bit more?'

'He's thirty-two,' Gwen said triumphantly, her point proved. 'He's doing ever so well at the Foreign Office, but it's turning him into a proper old fuddy-duddy before his time.'

A fortnight later, Frances Peters thought the same. Because Edward and Lewis no longer worked together, their lives had separated. No one had intended that the break should be so complete: it was one of those unfortunate oversights that build up week by busy week.

'Do you know, it must be well over a year since I've seen Edward,' Frances said to Lewis as they motored down to Sussex for the christening.

The response took a long time. 'I had lunch with him last week,' Lewis replied. 'It's possible that you may see changes in him – quite big ones, actually.'

Frances, who knew better than to ask questions when Lewis was being this cautious, settled down to be patient.

No one had ever thought it remarkable that Douglas should have been given only one Christian name. Conscious of their status, the Boothby-Graffoes had tended to heap names on male children, but the tradition was flexible – as in the case of Edward. There was no conscious effort to make amends for the frugality shown towards Douglas: it was more by accident than design that his brother ended up being called George William Joseph Francis. Joseph and the anglicised Francis were Habsburg names. After they had been chosen, Annaliese added a memento of Uncle William to Edward's lukewarm preference for George. Lord Douglas approved.

'George William Joseph Francis Boothby-Graffoe,' he recited at the conclusion of a christening at Hatchetts Green that had left the infant more bemused than ever. 'That's splendid. I think it's got a nice ring to it.'

'Are you sure?' Annaliese tended to be in strange, uncertain moods these days. Currently, she was always on the brink of finding everything funny – but in a sardonic, twisted sort of way. 'It sounded a terrible mouthful to me.'

'Well, he'll always be known as George, of course,' Lord Douglas said. 'Nothing wrong with that – it's good enough for the King. But, do you know, I have a notion that this little chap will find a use for an impressive handle. He's going to amount to something when his time comes.'

'Whatever makes you say that?' Annaliese asked.

'For heaven's sake, my dear, where's your maternal pride?' Lord Douglas was making light of a defect that he found worrying. 'Unless I'm very much mistaken, this fellow will turn out to have your looks and his father's brains. Doesn't that strike you as a pretty useful combination?'

'Are you sure?' Annaliese made no attempt to conceal her disbelief.

'We shall have to wait to see about the brains,' Lord Douglas admitted. 'But I'm surprised you haven't spotted the looks. Can't you see it . . . forehead, chin, the way his eyes are set? Most striking, I'd say.'

'Ye . . . es.' Annaliese was either unconvinced or loath to admit it. Nevertheless an idea had taken root. After lunch, she drew Lord Douglas aside and re-opened the conversation.

'I'm sure it's not the wishful ramblings of a dotty old man,' he said. 'That boy has a damned good head on his shoulders . . . I can see it in his eyes.'

'You think that's important?' Annaliese's interest was growing.

'Very. The way the world's starting to look, a chap needs all the brain-power he can lay his hands on. Our family has never been *dense* – at least, nowhere near as bad as some of the upper crust. But we haven't been bright. From what I can make out, Jeremy was pretty sharp – he's the one who started Boothby's off. Then there's Edward. The rest of us have been pretty mediocre. Mark my words, George William Joseph Francis will be the best yet.'

The transformation began that afternoon on the way back to London. Taking charge of George herself, Annaliese conducted a non-stop monologue, talking to him as if he were the most knowledgeable adult for miles around. Enthralled, the infant never took his eyes off her. Thereafter, and much to Gwen's satisfaction, Annaliese was to spend at least half an hour a day talking to George.

After becoming godparents for the second time, Frances and Lewis Peters travelled the first few miles back to London in companionable silence, feeling their way round each other's thoughts.

'I wouldn't say that Edward is starting to look *old*,' Frances said at last.

'Definitely not,' Lewis agreed wholeheartedly.

'Even so, he's aged,' Frances added.

'I think so.'

'To what do you attribute this phenomenon?' Frances asked in the facetious way she liked to approach ticklish problems.

'He's taking his work tremendously seriously,' Lewis said, so careful that there had to be a hidden meaning.

'Whereas you, my darling, treat the whole shooting-match as one big joke.'

'Point taken,' Lewis smiled.

'And does this taking things *tremendously seriously* have any undesirable consequences?' Frances asked shrewdly.

'Frankly, yes.' Lewis was a good deal less comfortable now they had reached the crux of the matter. 'Edward's getting a reputation as a back-stairs man – a bit of an intriguer. He seems to be on good terms with Lord Curzon.'

Frances whistled. 'Fraternising with the politicals, eh? Isn't that frowned upon?'

'Officially, yes. In practice, nearly all successful civil servants do it. Actually, it isn't the thing with Curzon that's the main cause of resentment. Edward's involved with a group of Tory MPs led by a chap called Younger.'

'Andrew Younger? Isn't he a trouble-maker?'

'Very much so,' Lewis replied. 'They're a frightening bunch.' An idea occurred to him. 'Do you think you could have a word with Annaliese?'

'Saying what, darling?'

'That Edward is playing a risky game. A gentle warning might save a great deal of trouble.'

Frances considered it. 'No, I don't think that's a runner,' she said at last. 'For one thing, on the basis of that performance at the christening, one would have to question how much notice Annaliese and Edward take of each other these days.'

'You noticed that, too?'

'Stuck out like a sore thumb.'

'Was there another reason?' Lewis asked.

'I'm afraid so, my old fruit. It seems that Annaliese and I have rather grown apart.' Frances sounded sad.

Realising that there was nothing useful to be said, Lewis drove on in silence.

Annaliese returned to Boothby's six weeks after George was born. She was soon in the thick of things, enjoying herself, and displaying much of the old sparkle. But full recovery from a long period of directionless depression had to wait until May.

Although Annaliese and Nancy had maintained their close friendship, they had refrained from erotic adventure throughout Annaliese's pregnancy. The decision was arrived at by unspoken, mutual consent, without a vestige of awkwardness or weakening of the bonds between them. They both missed their exquisite Monday afternoons and longed for them to begin again. But, with Annaliese inhibited by the odd feeling that her body would never recover from George, Nancy was close to giving up hope. Then, on a perfect afternoon near the end of May, Annaliese turned up at Martha's Vineyard with a glint in her eyes.

'Shall we swim?' she asked. Even though the house looked and sounded deserted, excitement made her whisper.

'Do you mean what I hope you mean?' Nancy whispered eagerly.

'Sex!' Annaliese laughed, putting her arms round Nancy. 'I want oceans of our lovely, lovely sex.'

'Let's not waste time and energy, huh? We'll skip the swimming and go to my bedroom.'

'That's fine by me.' Annaliese was proud of her developing American accent.

They dashed upstairs like lunatics and Nancy undressed with whirlwind haste, flinging herself on the bed so that she could watch Annaliese.

'That new baby did you nothing but good, honey,' was Nancy's verdict. 'I'll bet Edward's impressed?'

'Not really,' Annaliese replied distantly.

'I don't think I like the sound of that,' Nancy said.

'Edward's very busy.' As soon as the words were out of her mouth,

Annaliese knew they sounded pathetic. The one thing she never confided to Nancy was the trouble *she* caused at Cadogan Square. There was the danger that Nancy, who could be big-hearted to a fault, might take herself out of Annaliese's life if she thought it would improve things with Edward.

'Are you telling me he isn't laying a finger on you?' Nancy asked.

'Yes, I am.'

'Then come here and let me put things right.'

As soon as Annaliese had fallen on to the bed, Nancy slipped a hand between her thighs and was conjuring up blissful magic. As a rule, they worked on each other in harmonic unison, but for once, Annaliese needed to be selfish.

'Relax,' Nancy said reassuringly. 'Leave it all to me . . . How's that? Good?'

'It's going to be,' Annaliese murmured. 'It's going to be very good indeed.'

It was so good that Annaliese wept with relief. Nancy hugged and stroked her until she was calm, secretly dismayed at her friend's overwrought state.

'We've been over this before,' Nancy said gently when Annaliese was calm. 'But I really would like you to take another look at it.'

'You think I need a *proper* lover – a man?' Annaliese said.

Nancy laughed. 'I don't know whether I'd call it *proper*, honey – I was wondering whether you need a guy to stop you going off your head.'

'I expect you have a list of probables?'

'There are men who never miss a chance of asking after you,' Nancy replied. 'It's all very casual and polite, but I can tell what's underneath.'

'And you'd recommend them?' Annaliese asked. She was starting to treat it as a joke.

Nancy shook her head. 'No . . . at least, not all of them. There is one, though.'

'And you consider him worthy of me?'

'Yes, you could say that.' Nancy was in no hurry. 'Yes, I reckon he might be right for you.'

'Who is this paragon?' Annaliese had to ask.

'John Brandon.'

As Nancy had expected, the effect on Annaliese was dramatic. Eyes wide, she sat bolt upright, struggling for words.

John Brandon was a regular client at Boothby's, appearing every two months to arrange a sale or purchase. Annaliese always looked after him, ensuring that the transactions were cloaked in the total discretion required by a very special client. Since the death of King Edward VII in 1910, Queen Alexandra had lived in almost permanent isolation at Sandringham House in Norfolk where John Brandon was a member of her staff. Apart from her interest in charities, the Queen's main activity was getting rid of 'bits and pieces' that she had never liked. As often as not, a disposal was followed by an acquisition: Her Majesty was especially fond of paintings by Sir John Millais.

Invalided out of the War in 1916, John Brandon had been a major in the Royal Artillery. He returned home to find his life in ruins: his wife had run off to Canada with a man whose main purpose in fleeing Britain was to escape debt. There was a year of misery, then his luck had changed: the mysterious forces that organised such things spirited him off to Sandringham.

He was about forty-five and unmarked by the horrors of the Western Front. Tall, rather distinguished-looking, and a thorough-going gentleman of the old school, John Brandon had shown nothing but impeccable courtesy on his visits to Boothby's. Obviously used to command, he was, in his quaintly circumspect way, quite ruthless in his service to the old Queen. Annaliese had liked him from their very first meeting.

Eventually, words stuttered out. 'I don't believe you, Nancy. No . . . I do not . . . You're making this up.'

'I most definitely am not!'

'Rubbish!'

'Honey, I promise you, John Brandon would give anything to be able to swap places with me at this moment.'

'Are you asking me to believe that you and John Brandon have sat down together and talked about him taking me to bed?' Annaliese shrieked.

'Not in so many words,' Nancy replied. 'People like us aren't so unsubtle, for Christ's sake! But there was *absolutely* no doubt what was going on and you'd better believe it.'

'Look, Nancy, what I don't understand is . . .' Confused, Annaliese shook her head and started again. 'John Brandon *can't* be the sort of man that you would know. He doesn't come here, to this house, does he?'

'Certainly not,' Nancy hooted. 'He wouldn't be seen dead anywhere near a joint like this.'

'So how . . .' Annaliese began, then gave up.

'How did he get to talk to me?' Nancy suggested.

'Well, yes.'

'He knew you and me are friends,' Nancy said. 'You'd mentioned it, right?' Annaliese nodded. 'He made inquiries about me. You know this guy, so you can imagine what that was like . . . He has contacts *everywhere* and they all owe him favours. So, he found out what gives and invited me to have lunch with him.'

'When was this?' Annaliese asked weakly.

'About a year ago – it was the week before Ascot. He took me to the Savoy Grill and we settled two things. First, your marriage was shaky – he pretty much knew that already, by the way.'

'How?' Annaliese asked.

'Folks talk,' Nancy said, irritated by her friend's naivety. 'It's obvious that there's something wrong every time you and Edward are seen out together. That Diplomatic Corps Ball last year was a disaster for you. So was Douglas's christening.'

Annaliese nodded. 'All right – what was the other thing you agreed with him?'

'That you don't have a man. He gave me the third degree about what you got up to when you were here and I convinced him that you were no Cordelia Milford.'

'He knows about her?' Annaliese asked.

'Honey, *everybody* knows about Cordelia,' Nancy said. 'That's why she isn't news. Anyway, it ended up with John Brandon asking me to work something out. While I was mulling it over, you found out that you were pregnant; I dropped him a note.'

'That's the end of it, then?'

'No, ma'am, it certainly is not.' Nancy was studying Annaliese closely, looking for confirmation of what had sounded like disappointment. 'The good major and I met up again last week. He remains *very* interested . . . I'd say that the poor sap was in love with you.'

'He can't be!' Annaliese said.

'Why not? Have they passed a law forbidding it?' Nancy asked facetiously.

Annaliese did not reply. She was naked on Nancy's bed, being propositioned in his absence by a man whose unbending respectability was a by-word, yet she seemed perfectly calm. Watching her closely for a reaction Nancy was agreeably surprised when Annaliese began to stroke her breasts.

'Hey, you want more?' Nancy whispered.

'Yes. Yes!'

Annaliese was recklessly passionate. With a tigerish grace, she shifted her position and was kissing Nancy's taut stomach, gradually inching towards the lush triangle of soft hair. When her tongue began the ultimate sorcery, Nancy was moaning and helpless. No one – not even Michael Richardson – did this as sublimely as Annaliese. Staring up at the mirror suspended above the bed, Nancy amplified her pleasure by watching herself writhe towards orgasm. At the height of the climax, she was struggling to move, desperate to bury her face between Annaliese's thighs. She succeeded and they were locked into the closed loop that gave them incredible, self-perpetuating passion. This one, the most furious yet, went on and on for over half an hour until they finally fell apart, worn out by the sheer effort of giving and enduring almost continuous sexual fulfilment.

'Jesus Christ,' Nancy gasped. 'That was great. Who needs men?'

Annaliese reared up in a way that made her seem panic-stricken. 'You didn't tell John Brandon about us?' she asked.

'Will you do me a favour!' Nancy howled. 'Do you think I'm dumb, or something?' They stared at each other for a few moments, regaining composure. 'What shall I do about him?' Nancy asked.

'Nothing.' Annaliese flopped back to spread-eagle herself into hedonistic indolence. However, despite the languor, her mind was busy. Happy enough to conceal or deprecate the fact for much of the time, she *was* a Habsburg, with no reason or inclination to allow conventional morality to govern what she chose to do in securely discreet privacy. Faithfulness to Edward had been dictated by her views on loyalty, a force infinitely more powerful than bourgeois codes. But his efforts to erode her resolve were acquiring a churlish determination.

'Don't do anything,' Annaliese mused. 'At least, not yet. I want time to think about it.'

It was, Nancy realised, just about the most significant statement she had heard Annaliese make. Edward needed to get a grip on himself: his wife was no longer rejecting the idea of a lover.

Lloyd George was in a frightful mess. Even Annaliese, who resolutely turned her back on political tittle-tattle, knew that the Welsh Wizard's days were numbered.

The Prime Minister's behaviour was increasingly irrational and cavalier, especially in his dealings with the Foreign Office. A long-running argument culminated in Lloyd George attending the Genoa Conference without Lord Curzon, let alone the other diplomats who would normally provide support for such an important event. The ill feeling that boiled up was heightened by the suspicion that Lloyd George was sympathetic towards the new Russian Government. The merest suggestion that the British Prime Minister was soft on a gang of blood-stained Bolsheviks set the seal on his political death-warrant.

For two weeks before 11 June, Annaliese believed that Edward was somehow involved in the plotting to get rid of Lloyd George. What happened that evening turned her worst fears into reality.

It was a humid Sunday night. At eleven-thirty, Annaliese was in the nursery with George, who was restless and running a temperature. Gwen was downstairs in the kitchen, brewing a potion that she promised would make George better. As ever, Edward was in his study, relentlessly poring over documents.

Despite the hour, someone came to call. Annaliese heard the bell, the distant murmur of voices, and, after a few moments, Edward. He was flustered. There was a burst of irritatingly inaudible conversation, then footsteps hurried towards the study, the door closed and silence descended.

Five minutes passed before Gwen appeared, carrying a jug covered by a muslin cloth. 'Did you hear that to-do?' she asked.

'Yes. Do you know what it was?'

'It's Lord Curzon,' Gwen replied. 'In person! The Foreign Sec'tary, if you please.'

'Surely not!' Annaliese gasped.

'That's what Franklin said, and he's the know-all.'

As a distraction from the incredible news, Annaliese devoted herself to persuading George to swallow some of Gwen's elixir. Fifteen minutes later, the child seemed better; another fifteen minutes and he was asleep. Annaliese watched over him until she could barely keep her eyes open. At one o'clock, when she finally obeyed Gwen's orders to go to bed, Edward and Lord Curzon were still in the study. On Monday morning, Gwen reported that the conversation had rumbled on until well past three.

Two days later, Annaliese was given the task of organising a dinner-party from which she was excluded. Sir Andrew Younger and eight other Conservative Members of Parliament had the air of conspirators when Annaliese caught a glimpse of them as she was taking herself off to Nancy's for the evening. At midnight, the mutter of plot and counter-plot from the library had such a distasteful sound to it that Annaliese resolved to tackle Edward. The encounter, over breakfast, followed an all-too-predictable path.

'Edward, I'm worried,' she began, using a deferential tone.

'What about, my dear?' He was pleasant enough.

'Are you sure you know what you're doing?'

'In what respect?'

'Well . . . I don't know much about these things, of course, but shouldn't a man in your position avoid contact with politicians – especially having them here?'

'You're right, you don't know much about such matters.' The mood had changed in an instant to outright hostility. 'I don't interfere with your work at Boothby's, kindly extend the same courtesy to me.'

Soon afterwards, Edward left for his office. Annaliese noticed that only the few words he exchanged with Franklin on the way out lifted his foul mood for a moment or two.

That night, Lord Curzon came to Cadogan Square again.

The weather during the last week of June was more appropriate to November than mid-summer. The 29th was an outstandingly unpleasant day, with gale-force winds, driving rain, and the need to have the lights on in the middle of the morning. Beatrice, suffering from a streaming cold, was conducting an auction, with Paul Marks standing by in case her voice failed. Annaliese was in the office, working her way through a valuation for the entire contents of a house in Eaton Place. It was a tedious job, complicated by the inclusion of half a dozen near-priceless gems in an inventory of over five hundred pieces of junk.

Pausing to clear her mind, Annaliese noticed that it was a quarter to twelve. She closed her eyes, hoping that the columns of swimming figures would have disappeared when she opened them again. For all she knew, they might well have done: the shock of seeing John Brandon framed in the doorway obliterated all else.

'Good morning, Mrs Boothby-Graffoe,' he said. 'I'm sorry I startled you. Please forgive me.'

'Major Brandon!' Annaliese *was* startled, but she recovered quickly. 'I was miles away. This is an unexpected pleasure.'

'I should have telephoned for an appointment,' he said. 'The fact is, I happened to be in London with an hour or so to kill, so I thought I'd look in to see if you had anything that might appeal to Her Majesty.'

Annaliese believed him. He was that sort of man. If he said it was a purely spur-of-the-moment visit, then that's what it was, not an element of some devious scheme. She waved at the chair in front of the table. 'Please, Major Brandon, sit down. I think you've called at a bad time. To the best of my knowledge, we've nothing that might suit Her Majesty – no, I tell a lie . . . I'm sure there's a Whistler buried in this lot from Eaton Place.'

An economical gesture from Major Brandon stopped Annaliese's search through the inventory before it began. 'Oh, no, Mrs Boothby-Graffoe, I fear not. Between ourselves, HM can't *stand* Whistler.'

'I see.' At a loss to know what to say, Annaliese asked, 'How is the Queen?'

It was an inspired question, keeping Major Brandon talking for a good ten minutes. Almost stone-deaf for thirty years, Alexandra had never enjoyed good health. Now seventy-seven, she was a cause of great concern to her loyal servant.

'But I mustn't carry on like this,' he concluded. 'I'm keeping you from your work.'

'Not at all, Major,' Annaliese said. 'To be honest with you, I was thinking of lunch. What are your plans?'

'I have to be at the Palace for two-thirty,' he replied.

'Could we have lunch together?' Annaliese ventured.

'That would be an exceptional honour, Mrs Boothby-Graffoe.' It was a quiet, sincere statement, with no trace of the bombastic gallantry that many men would have felt bound to employ.

They scuttled through the rain to Whitaker's in Cork Street, Annaliese clutching Major Brandon's arm while he held his umbrella over her. A nod at the head waiter while her companion's back was turned was enough to secure Annaliese a table in a booth that gave almost total privacy.

'Major Brandon, you and I have matters to discuss,' Annaliese said as soon as the waiter had taken their order. 'May I get down to brass tacks?'

'Please do, Mrs Boothby-Graffoe.'

'Nancy Shenstone was speaking of you recently.'

'I see.' Major Brandon was unruffled.

'I understand that you wish us to have some sort of liaison?'

'Yes, I'm afraid I did advance that idea to Lady Shenstone.'

'You're not in the least afraid, Major Brandon,' Annaliese teased. 'As a matter of fact, I find it difficult to imagine you being afraid of *anything*.' The compliment left him unmoved. Annaliese decided to verify one aspect of what Nancy had told her. 'One thing puzzles me,' she went on. 'You aren't the sort of man to make a ridiculous suggestion that has no chance of success, so why did you think that

I would even entertain the idea? Surely, I'm perfectly content with my life?'

There was a quick nod, recognising a valid point. 'Before we go any further, Mrs Boothby-Graffoe, I must say that I don't consider myself special. The best I can hope for is exceptionally good luck.' Major Brandon's smile was self-deprecating. 'As to the suggestion that you are content, I must beg to disagree.'

'Oh?' Annaliese's eyebrows rose and she leaned forward. 'Why?'

'Please understand that I move in what one might call rarified circles and hear things that the average person will never encounter. As a result of your skill and kindness in our business dealings, I have mentioned you to a number of people. Some of them have volunteered information about you. I did not ask for it, nor did I take it seriously – at first.'

'I accept that,' Annaliese said.

'People have always been interested in you, Mrs Boothby-Graffoe. Ladies of your quality don't turn up in London every day, and the stories of how you met and married your husband were irresistible.'

'I suppose you're going to tell me that tongues have been wagging about how unhappy I look in unguarded moments?' Annaliese knew that she had allowed bitterness to creep in.

'Exactly so. As I said, I ignored the first few. However, when unconnected people keep saying the same thing, one begins to take notice.'

'Especially when those people are of the quality and discernment of, let us say, Lady Torksey,' Annaliese said, taking an inspired stab in the dark.

Major Brandon inclined his head. It was the nearest he was ever likely to get to dropping a name. 'In the meantime,' he said, 'I had the good fortune to continue meeting you and was forming opinions. To the best of my knowledge, you aren't involved with another man, we've always got on well, so I thought I'd try my luck.'

'Nancy Shenstone implied that you'd gone to some trouble to winkle her out,' Annaliese said.

'Yes, I did,' he admitted frankly.

Two waiters arrived to serve the meal. Leaning back against one of the padded partitions that gave the table its privacy, Annaliese was grateful for the interruption. It was an opportunity to gather her thoughts and make the final decision, a knife-edge choice. When they were alone once more and she began to speak, she was still wavering.

'We must stop all this formal business. "Mrs Boothby-Graffoe" and "Major Brandon" are such mouthfuls. Let's have "Annaliese" and "John". Agreed?'

'With the greatest of pleasure.'

Annaliese smiled. 'I know that I can confide in you, John, so I shall be frank. Although I am doing everything in my power to preserve it, my marriage *is* less than satisfactory in some respects – one in particular. Nancy Shenstone thinks that it would help if I had a lover – and I find it difficult to argue against the idea.' With only the slightest pause, Annaliese resolved the problem. 'However, while there is still hope of keeping my marriage alive, this would be a betrayal of my husband. For the time being, I can't bring myself to do that.'

John returned her steady gaze. 'I understand and respect your sentiments,' he said. It was clear that he was not going to attempt to make anything of that crucial, enigmatic phrase *for the time being*.

'But I do want us to be friends,' Annaliese said. 'Very good friends. Can you bear that?'

'Why shouldn't I?' There was a suggestion of mischief in his smile; it came as a surprise.

'Nancy Shenstone seems to think that your feelings for me are pretty strong,' Annaliese said.

'They are,' John replied, cheerfully providing the assurance that she had been seeking. 'But I'm not a juvenile idiot – at least, I hope I'm not. Your friendship will be highly valued, Mrs . . . er . . . Annaliese.' Charmingly, the first hesitant use of her Christian name brought a flush to his cheeks.

'Lovely.' She gave him a special smile. 'We must make plans. Do you ever have to spend a night in London?'

'Yes, I do.' He was baffled, wondering why Annaliese appeared to be heading in a direction that she had barred.

'And do you like music – proper, serious music. The classics?'

'Well . . . yes . . . actually, I do.' It sounded like a confession. John Brandon had spent most of his life against a background that regarded such tastes as not quite 'manly'.

'Good.' Annaliese was excited. 'Artur Schnabel is coming to London. He's playing all the Beethoven sonatas at the Wigmore Hall in July and I'd love to hear some of them. It's *years* since I went to a decent recital.'

'You have the dates?' John smiled as Annaliese produced a handbill out of thin air. 'May I keep this?' he asked and she nodded eagerly. 'I can contact you at Boothby's, of course?'

'Naturally. No one will suspect a thing.'

Everything was settled and they embarked on forty minutes of relaxed chatter. Annaliese made several attempts to unearth details of life at Sandringham, but got absolutely nowhere. John was never less than polite and sometimes gave the impression that he *was* about to indulge in a revelation, but it never came. Deftly, with subtle wit, what had been so tantalisingly close faded like a mirage. Unless he expressly wanted it, no one would ever gain so much as a glimpse of John Brandon's vast array of confidential knowledge.

As they were preparing to leave the restaurant, there was a fleeting chance for Annaliese to offer encouragement to her new friend. All the waiters were busy, so they had to retrieve their own coats from the cubby-hole of a cloakroom. Realising that they were alone and invisible, Annaliese kissed John on the lips. Brief though it was, the tender gesture affected him deeply.

'Your husband is a very lucky man,' he muttered. 'Does he appreciate that?'

'Probably not,' Annaliese replied. 'Not any more. Another thing that he doesn't appreciate is that my patience is not limitless. Do you understand, John?' She turned her back so that he could help her with her coat.

He nodded. 'I expect you know that your husband is getting himself talked about,' he said. 'For all the wrong reasons, I'm afraid.'

'Too friendly with certain politicians?' Annaliese said, turning to face him.

'Yes.'

'He refuses to be told. I've tried and had my head bitten off.' Leading the way out to Cork Street, Annaliese was grim-faced. After they had parted, however, she returned to Boothby's with a jaunty swagger in her step.

Charles Templeton abhorred gossip. Normally, he walked away from it, pausing only to give the scandal-monger a piece of his mind. But, on an August evening when Annaliese was dining with him and Beatrice at the house in Regent's Park, Charles demonstrated that he did, very occasionally, take notice of a good story.

'What's your friend the Duke of Lincolnshire up to?' he asked out of the blue.

Annaliese and Beatrice exchanged puzzled looks.

'I've no idea,' Beatrice said.

'We've been avoiding each other,' Annaliese added.

'Oh.' Charles stirred his coffee and began to take an elaborate interest in the view from the window.

'Come on, you beast,' Beatrice said. 'Spit it out. What do you know?'

'I doubt if it's earth-shattering,' Charles said.

'Do I have to beat it out of you?' Beatrice laughed, looking round for a suitable weapon.

'No, I suppose I'd better give in gracefully,' Charles sighed. 'By all accounts, Ralph is seeing rather a lot of a young woman.'

Beatrice shook her head dismissively. 'That doesn't sound very exciting, darling,' she said. 'There's a constant procession of them. The lucky ones last three or four weeks.'

'This lady has been in favour for at least six months,' Charles said mildly. 'Consistently, and to the total exclusion of all others. Ralph takes her everywhere. She appears to be unmarried.'

'What's her name?' Beatrice asked.

'Celia Jameson.'

Beatrice repeated it several times. 'That doesn't mean a thing,' she said. 'Who is she?'

'No one knows,' Charles said. 'She's a complete mystery.'

'What's she like?'

'Very nice, I'm told.' Charles's tongue was in his cheek.

'Well, I'm blowed if I know,' Beatrice muttered. 'And does it matter?'

'No,' Annaliese said firmly. 'Definitely not.'

Two days later, she was not so sure.

'What do you know about Ralph's girl-friend?' Nancy demanded.

'I didn't hear about her until Tuesday,' Annaliese replied. 'Charles mentioned her.'

'Her name's Celia Jameson,' Nancy said. 'What else?'

'Nothing,' Annaliese replied. 'Beatrice has never heard of her, so she can't be important.'

'That depends on what you call important, honey,' Nancy said. 'Ralph's never stuck to one woman like this . . . that makes Miss Jameson important.'

After the disgraceful performance at his father's funeral, Ralph's fellow peers tended to ignore him. One of the very few exceptions was the Marquess of Yeovil, whose friendship with Ralph went back to their earliest schooldays. The Marquess, also the proud owner of an extremely dubious reputation, gave a weekend house-party in early September at which Ralph and Celia Jameson were guests. So was Cordelia Milford.

'You can judge for yourselves what sort of party it was,' Cordelia said when she visited Martha's Vineyard to tell Annaliese and Nancy about it. 'They wanted *me* there . . . Yeovil insisted, God bless him!'

Her suggestive smile made sure that the meaning was absolutely plain. Annaliese recalled the sight of Cordelia driving herself mad on Tommy Weston, certain that it was the appropriate image for the weekend.

'You had a good time?' Nancy asked.

'Heavenly, darling, heavenly.' Closing her eyes, Cordelia assumed an ecstatic expression.

'And you met Celia Jameson?' Nancy prompted.

'I did indeed.' Cordelia struck a portentous pose. 'What would you like to know?'

'*Everything!*' Nancy shrieked. 'How old is she?'

'Not very. No more than twenty, I'd say.'

'Why don't we know anything about her?' Annaliese asked.

'Because there's nothing to know,' Cordelia replied. 'She seems to be a nobody. At a pinch, you could say that she was lower-middle class – but that really would be stretching it. Her father died in the War and her mother remarried and went to live in Tasmania – of all places – leaving Celia with a widowed aunt in Esher.'

'What's she like?' Nancy asked.

'Very pleasant. I had quite a long chat with her – no thanks to Ralph, I might say. She's reasonably easy to talk to. Although she keeps it well out of sight, I'd say she has quite a strong character. Doesn't know anyone, of course, and appears to think that the sun shines out of Ralph's backside.'

'She sounds like a harmless nonentity,' Nancy mused. 'How strange.'

'Darling, did I say she was *harmless*?' Cordelia purred. 'I'm sure I didn't.'

'You implied it,' Nancy accused.

'Why don't you ask me how she looks and acts?' Cordelia suggested archly.

'Consider it done.'

'She's quite plain and demure. At least, that's how she *can* seem – and she does it without too much effort.'

'You're saying that it's a cover?' Nancy asked.

Cordelia exploded into shrieking laughter. 'Darling, you should *see* her. She's got a body I'd sell my soul for and she knows how to use it.'

'Was this one of those get-togethers where everyone joins in the fun?' Nancy asked.

'Yes – except that Ralph wouldn't let any of his friends near Miss Jameson.' Smiling at the expression on Annaliese's face, Cordelia explained. 'There were eleven men, but only five women in this party . . . that meant plenty to go round for the ladies. After dinner on Friday evening, Jack Beresford and I set the ball rolling . . .' Cordelia laughed at the memory. 'We did it on the table in the dining-room.'

Annaliese and Nancy exchanged raised-eyebrow smiles. 'With the rest watching?' Nancy asked, just to be sure.

'Of course. Yeovil and his gang are far worse than this place.' By 'worse', Cordelia meant 'better'. 'Then various people did various things. It had been going on for about an hour when Ralph and Miss Jameson gave their first demonstration.'

Cordelia Milford paused, shaking her head in what looked like awe.

'Good, were they?' Nancy asked.

'Stupendous,' Cordelia sighed. 'I've always suspected that Ralph was brilliant – and he is. But, my God, you should have seen *her*. I tell you, she's better than me. The men all thought they were in for the treat of their lives when it was "pass the parcel" time, but Ralph wouldn't allow it. He has the sole rights on Celia Jameson – and very happy she seems with it.'

There was a long silence as they pondered Ralph's unusual behaviour with the unknown girl. It was Annaliese who finally spoke.

'If Celia Jameson *is* what she claims to be, how on earth did Ralph ever come to meet her?'

Cordelia Milford nodded furiously. '*That* is the big question,' she said. 'Ralph's circle simply doesn't include lower-middle class nobodies from Esher.'

'What's the answer?' Nancy asked. 'It must have been mentioned.'

'No, it wasn't. Ralph and Celia are very proud of themselves. Once they started, they didn't stop – not for very long, at any rate. As I said, they were stunning and no one bothered asking questions.'

'Not even *you*?' Nancy protested.

Cordelia gave her a pained look. 'Darling, when the men found that Celia was out-of-bounds, I was the second favourite. What time did I have for carrying out investigations? I was fully occupied – it was almost too much.' Responding to Nancy's crestfallen disappointment, she added, 'I can't see that it matters. Miss Jameson has probably been dumped by now.'

On 19 October, a fateful meeting of MPs took place at the Carlton Club, that bastion of Conservative beliefs that had once counted Uncle William among its members. By special invitation, Edward was in an adjacent room, waiting to give advice on foreign policy, together with the last-minute opinions of Lord Curzon, who had zealously avoided any direct contact with the conspirators. In the event, the men who made up what was destined to become known as the 1922 Committee reached their decision without calling on Edward. When they broke up, however, he was thanked for his assistance during the preceding months and invited to join them for dinner.

The following day, the leader of the Conservative Party, Andrew Bonar Law, was summoned to a private room in the House of Commons by the man who had led the Carlton Club intrigue. Shortly afterwards, he withdrew from the coalition that made up the Government, thus ending Lloyd George's term as Prime Minister. A General Election in November made Bonar Law the leader of a Conservative Government, the first since 1905. Lord Curzon would continue as Foreign Secretary, his position apparently unassailable.

Two weeks later, in good time for it to make him overbearingly smug for Christmas, Edward received another promotion. Certain that it was a reward for services that should never have been rendered, Annaliese was disgusted. She was also convinced that such rapid and tainted progress through his career would be building up a store of ill feeling that might come to haunt Edward. With bizarre irony, only the soothing good sense of John Brandon, the man who wanted to be her lover, held Annaliese back from telling her husband exactly what she thought of him.

17

1923–1924

'His Grace is still up to his old tricks'

On 17 July 1923, the Court and Social page of *The Times* carried an announcement that stunned Society.

Six weeks previously, on 5 June, Ralph Frederick Gainsborough Boothby-Graffoe, ninth Duke of Lincolnshire and Marquess of Axholme, had married Miss Celia Jameson, of Esher, in the County of Surrey. It had been a simple, private ceremony in the Chapel of Allardyce Castle. The bride had been given in marriage by the Marquess of Yeovil, while the Honourable Bertram Christopherson had acted as best man. Four little girls from the Duke's estates in Scotland and Bristol had attended the bride. The children were, the announcement was at pains to point out, supervised by Mrs Blanche Hamilton. What was *not* mentioned was that the service had been conducted by a retired clergyman from St Helier, in the Channel Islands. Immediately afterwards, he and the bridesmaids had been whisked back to their homes with promises of substantial sums of money if they kept their mouths shut for six weeks.

Normally, the wedding of a duke, a member of the aristocracy's first rank, would have been regarded as one of the year's most important social events. In addition to the family of the participants, at least 500 people had a right to expect an invitation, and, bad though Ralph's standing was, few would have failed to turn up. The gathering for such an occasion could be expected to give rise to arrangements for at least half a dozen dynastic marriages, and dislike of Ralph was no excuse for interfering with a time-honoured process. One could, after all, ignore the couple who imagined themselves to be the centre of attraction and get on with the serious work. A place like Allardyce Castle had countless far-flung rooms where negotiations might be conducted without fear of interruption.

But Ralph had snubbed the lot of them, spectacularly and with blatant, scheming malice. The fury in Belgravia, Mayfair, and in country houses the length and breadth of Britain would be uncontrollable.

The announcement in *The Times* concluded by pointing out that the six weeks since the wedding had been devoted to a honeymoon in Monte Carlo and Antigua.

Nowadays, two copies of the newspaper were delivered to Cadogan Square. Annaliese never took all that much notice of the one she had asked for, it was merely for show, something to keep her company at breakfast while Edward was immersed in his copy. She always glanced at Births, Marriages, and Deaths in search of possible business. It was amazing how often arrivals, unions, and departures gave rise to changes that led to the auction-room.

Annaliese saw the wedding details the instant her eyes scanned the page. Folding the paper she read the announcement twice in slow, thoughtful silence. Then she passed it across the table without comment. Initially annoyed by the irritation, Edward's interest was soon aroused.

'Well, that's a turn-up for the book,' he said. 'Noses will be out of joint.' The prospect obviously pleased him. His dislike of Society – with its capital S and affectations – was strong.

'What about the new Duchess?' Annaliese asked. 'Celia Jameson . . . Do you know her?'

'No, of course I don't,' Edward replied. 'Does anyone?'

'Apparently not,' Annaliese murmured.

'I wonder if we should make our peace with Ralph,' Edward said casually.

'Why?' At once, Annaliese was sorry for sounding so hostile; any sort of conversation at breakfast was a rarity to be welcomed, not treated churlishly.

'It doesn't do to be on bad terms, you know. I expect Ralph will calm down now that he's married.' Edward's fierce interest in a piece of toast betrayed his unease; he knew that he sounded unconvincing. Resisting the temptation to point out that neither marriage *nor* Blanche Hamilton would make Ralph 'calm down', Annaliese waited.

'After all, it could be to our mutual advantage,' Edward said airily.

'How?'

'It all depends on whether Ralph wants to take his seat in the House of Lords. I think he should.'

'And make interesting statements on foreign affairs?' Annaliese suggested.

'That's an idea . . . It could be useful all round.'

Edward was so preoccupied with the possibilities that he failed to notice Annaliese's cynicism. She was thinking that there was no point in attempting to make him change his mind, so she might as well ignore the issue. The decision to walk away from the problem was helped by self-interest: reconciliation with Ralph might bring an invitation to Allardyce Castle.

'Yes, perhaps we should try,' Annaliese said. 'I don't suppose it can do any harm.'

'I'll think about it,' Edward said, even though his tone and manner suggested that his mind was already made up. 'A letter is probably the best way to tackle it.'

'As you wish, my dear,' Annaliese replied, pleasing him by her docility. He seemed unaware of the fact the she no longer called him '*Liebste*', or 'my darling'.

Annaliese was far from docile, however, when she told John Brandon about it over lunch at Whitaker's. As he did so often, John defended Edward's viewpoint.

'It's the Foreign Office, Annaliese. This is what it does to all the men who become its creatures.'

'That's ridiculous,' she protested. 'What do they imagine they're playing at?'

John smiled wryly. 'You're nearer the truth than you realise,' he said. 'Diplomacy *is* mostly a game. The chaps who become obsessed with playing it find all manner of things spoiling their fun – reality and democracy are the two worst offenders.' They both laughed. 'It's natural for Foreign Office people to become devious and secretive.'

'Edward's taking it to excess,' Annaliese grumbled.

'What's his position in the hierarchy?' John asked.

'That promotion last December made him a Deputy-Under-Secretary.'

John was impressed. 'That is *very* senior,' he said. 'There are only four or five at his level. There aren't many above him and they're all old men. But it's a very strange, insidious world at those heights. I'm sure they spend more time plotting against each other than they devote to the country's enemies.'

'How idiotic.' Annaliese was exasperated. 'Edward upset a lot of people by being involved with that gang who got rid of Lloyd George. Now he has the insane idea that Ralph may be useful.'

'Don't be surprised if events prove him right,' John warned. 'Politics is a funny business at the best of times, but things are in a most peculiar state at the moment. I wouldn't trust this man Baldwin with anything more important than patting babies on the head.'

'I thought he was supposed to be all right,' Annaliese said. The avuncular, 'steady' Stanley Baldwin had become Prime Minister in May, following the death of Bonar Law.

'He's an incompetent,' John said, uncharacteristically agitated. 'I doubt if he'll be able to hold his own party together, let alone do the job he's there for.' He smiled apologetically. 'Sorry, I mustn't get on my high-horse. Let's talk about something else, shall we? How about your cousin-in-law's wedding? That's put the cat among the pigeons. No one seems to have had the faintest idea it was going to happen.'

'I certainly didn't,' Annaliese replied.

'By chance' – John's eyes were twinkling – 'I overheard Lady Torksey holding forth on the subject an hour ago. We bumped into each other at Kensington Palace.'

'How was she?'

'Incandescent.' John chuckled. 'The idea of a mystery duchess who is almost certainly a complete "outsider" doesn't appeal to her.'

'I've been wondering . . .' Annaliese traced imaginery patterns on the table cloth with a fingertip. 'It's tempting to assume that Ralph did it that way to cock a monumental snook at Society.'

John nodded. 'That was certainly Lady Torksey's attitude.'

'Well, I'm sure that *did* enter into it,' Annaliese said. 'But I wonder if there might be another reason.'

'Such as?'

'I don't know.' Annaliese paused. 'I think Ralph has behaved very strangely over this. It's as though he's *hiding* his wife, not just being secretive to stir people up.'

'Why would he want to do that?' John asked.

'I've no idea,' Annaliese confessed. 'Aren't you able to shed any light on the mystery?'

'Me?' John's attempt at mock innocence was priceless. 'No, I'm sorry to say that I'm as stumped as everyone else.'

'Are you telling me that the invincible Brandon information service has broken down?' Annaliese joked.

'Completely and utterly.'

They laughed and clasped hands across the table. From the corner of her eye, Annaliese caught sight of their reflection in a mirror on the other side of the restaurant. They looked well together: it was easy to picture them as an exceptionally happy husband and wife. In fact, a shrewd observer would have assumed they were lovers.

That their relationship remained platonic baffled and slightly annoyed Nancy.

'How does he put up with it?' she had asked Annaliese. 'Have you hypnotised the poor guy into submission?'

'It's quite simple,' Annaliese insisted. 'We're such good friends that we never worry about it.'

'You expect me to believe that?' Nancy howled.

'Yes.'

'Well, I'm hanged if I know.'

Glancing across the restaurant at their reflection, neither did Annaliese.

Ten days had passed since Edward's letter to Ralph was posted. Studiously avoiding all mention of the topic with Annaliese, Edward assumed that his attempt to institute a reconciliation had failed. Then, late one evening, Ralph telephoned. Edward took the call in the study.

They talked for ages. At the end of it, Edward said only that Ralph had promised to make contact again. Believing that Edward was turning what should have been a perfectly simple matter into one of his convoluted intrigues, Annaliese expected to hear no more and banished the idea from her mind.

She was wrong. After several more telephone calls, Ralph and Celia came to Cadogan Square for Sunday lunch in mid-September. When Annaliese asked whether a dinner, possibly on a Friday or Saturday evening was not more suitable, she was told that Sunday lunch had more of a 'family atmosphere' to it. Later, Edward accidentally revealed that Ralph and Celia were spending a weekend with the Marquess of Yeovil at his house in Hertfordshire, but wanted to avoid someone who had been invited to join the party on Sunday. It sounded very much as though Ralph *was* doing his best to hide Celia.

Their arrival was fraught with tension. Only Franklin, who liked dealing with the aristocracy, was at ease. In the ten minutes that were needed to break the ice, Edward overdid the part of genial, welcoming host, while Annaliese was *too* calm. Her detachment proved to be an advantage, enabling her to see things that might have been overwhelmed by a more friendly attitude.

Ralph, although clearly determined to be on his best behaviour, was like a coiled spring, waiting to explode into disruptive life. Given a large pre-lunch gin and tonic, he became loud and cheerful, complimenting Annaliese on the changes she had made to the house. Since Edward was anxious to monopolise Ralph, Annaliese could ignore him and concentrate on Celia.

The young woman who had surprised everyone by making herself Duchess of Lincolnshire was very much as Cordelia Milford had described her. At first sight, she was no more than pretty, with colouring that matched her profusion of light-brown hair. But her features were supported by an exceptionally good bone structure, and it was not long before her body, strikingly shown off in a yellow dress that was obviously French and fitted like a glove, drew attention to itself. Edward disapproved of the dress. Yards away, in the deep bow window of the drawing-room and in earnest conversation with Ralph, he scowled at Celia as she went to a side table to look at the latest photographs of Douglas and George.

She moved with a lithe grace that was strikingly sensual. It must, Annaliese realised, be a natural, inborn characteristic: no one as nervous as Celia could have feigned such poise. Her insecurity was even more apparent when they sat down to eat. While struggling to cope with Annaliese's small-talk, Celia never took her eyes off Ralph for more than a few seconds.

In all fairness, he was a commanding focus of attention, especially after his opening remark.

'I've decided that I shall take my seat in the House of Lords. It's about time I did something useful. Who knows, people may decide I'm not so bad.'

Despite the patent cynicism, Edward was enthusiastic. Urged on by Ralph, he began to explain the political climate. Annaliese was struck by how different his opinions were to those of John Brandon. According to Edward, it was a long time since things had looked so promising and Baldwin was the man to make the most of it. Bored, Annaliese gave Celia her full attention.

Most of what Edward was spouting should have been way over the young Duchess of Lincolnshire's head, yet her face said otherwise. It was Celia's eyes which alerted Annaliese to a sharp intelligence based on animal cunning. They were pale green and volatile. Perfect windows for weaving spells of sexual enchantment, they were also capable of betraying a hard shrewdness. Politics was about men claiming to be motivated by high principles, whereas their actions were often governed by venality. The longer the meal and Edward's lecture progressed, the more Annaliese adhered to the view that Celia had a deep, calculating knowledge of such weaknesses.

Eager to take his conversation with Ralph into the realms of secrecy, Edward dragged him away to the study slightly sooner than it was polite to leave the table. Ralph's parting look, shared between his wife and Annaliese, was a patronising injunction for them to enjoy a nice chat. Celia's nervous fragility showed in the flicker of panic she darted at Ralph's back.

'Would you like to see my two terrible sons?' Annaliese asked. 'They went to the zoo this morning, but they should be quiet by now.'

Celia jumped at the offer. 'That would be lovely. I was admiring their photographs.'

The easy grace was in evidence again as they climbed the stairs. Celia paused on the landing, wanting to ask a question. Although her mind was perplexed, the gorgeous body retained its slightly flamboyant poise.

'Forgive my asking,' she said diffidently. 'Are you royal?'

'Not in the least,' Annaliese laughed, wondering whether this was the reason for the nervousness. 'My Family used to rule Austria, but they've been abolished. In any case, I wasn't at all important.'

'Oh. I see.' Celia clearly didn't. 'Ralph hasn't said all that much about you – except that you were an Archduchess.'

'Strictly speaking, I suppose I still am. No one bothers, though.' They walked on, with Annaliese wondering if Ralph had told Celia anything about *anything.*

Gwen, half-expecting a visit to the nursery, was in no mood to be fazed by a jumped-up nobody who had become a senior peeress simply by climbing into Ralph Boothby-Graffoe's bed and persuading him that she was sufficiently over-sexed and adept to be allowed to stay there.

'Good-afternoon, Your Highness,' she said to Annaliese, driving the point home with a wicked curtsy.

'Hello, Gwen,' Annaliese replied, keeping her face very straight. 'This is Her Grace, the Duchess of Lincolnshire. She's come to inspect the wretches.'

If anything did pass between Celia and Gwen, it was inundated by Douglas's boisterous arrival from the playroom. Now three and a quarter and precociously advanced, he took an instant liking to Celia and regaled her with his version of the visit to the zoo. By contrast, the eighteen-month-old George was shy. At least, Celia was quick to place that interpretation on his unwillingness to approach her.

Annaliese, who understood George almost as well as she knew herself, made no attempt to deny the facile idea. George was soon happy enough in her arms, leaving Douglas to dump himself on Celia to hold forth about his favourite animal, the 'rhinopotamus'.

Responding to Douglas, Celia changed completely. No matter how roughly he jumped up and down, punching the air and sometimes her in his lather of enthusiasm, she remained captivated. Annaliese almost envied the way Celia was able to talk to him, rather like a big sister egging him on to greater feats of verbal bravado. When, after about half an hour, Gwen intervened to prevent Douglas getting sick with excitement, he took it badly.

'That's enough,' Annaliese said, more sharply than she intended. 'If you're good, Aunt Celia will come again. Otherwise . . .' She left the threat hanging and Douglas, good soul that he was, cheered up.

'Shall we go and hide ourselves away for a nice chat?' Annaliese whispered to Celia, striking a note of feminine conspiracy. 'Edward and Ralph will be *hours*.'

'I'd like that,' Celia said gratefully.

They went to Annaliese's first-floor sitting-room, the same retreat that Lady Alice had favoured in the years before the War.

'Douglas really took to you,' Annaliese said. 'I don't always know how to deal with him.'

'It doesn't seem to matter,' Celia replied. 'They're both devoted to you in their different ways.'

'I can see you care for children. You'll be having some of your own, I expect?'

'God, I hope so. I'd love a son.' Celia paused, rather embarrassed. 'Giving Ralph an heir will make me think I matter,' she went on. 'I'm not much of a duchess at the moment.'

'Whatever makes you say that?' Annaliese cried, taken aback by Celia's frankness.

'I'm hardly the sort of person you'd expect the Duke of Lincolnshire to marry, am I?' Celia said. 'And the way we went about the wedding is turning out to be a disaster. It seemed good fun at the time – and I can't say that I was sorry to avoid a huge wedding. But no one wants to know us. Even Ralph feels it . . . I'm sure that's what this House of Lords business is really all about. He's hoping to sort of reinstate himself.'

'English Society is very hidebound,' Annaliese pointed out. 'I haven't done badly, but that's because I married a man whose mother and father were popular and respected. And lots of people have been curious to find out what a Habsburg looks like . . . that's helped.'

'I don't have those advantages,' Celia said. Her pause indicated that she was plucking up the courage to divulge a tremendous secret. 'I . . . er . . . I believe you know the circumstances in which Ralph's father passed away?'

'I'm afraid I do, Celia. Ralph announced them at the funeral.'

Celia nodded miserably. 'I heard about that. I expect it was awful for you all.'

'It was,' Annaliese said grimly, trying to guess what Celia was leading up to.

'I must have been one of the first people to know about the Duke's death,' Celia said. 'You see, I used to work as a receptionist for a Mr Napier – he's a doctor in Harley Street. It was Mr Napier that Ralph sent for after he'd been told.'

'Oh, I *see*.' Annaliese nodded sagely. This was the answer to the question everybody had been asking: how had Ralph ever come to meet Celia? Now it was being volunteered. 'Who contacted Ralph about this dreadful business?' she asked.

'The woman the Duke was with . . . the prostitute . . . looked in his wallet, found one of his visiting cards and telephoned the number – which was Allardyce Castle. As luck would have it, Ralph was at home.'

'And Ralph knew Mr Napier?' Annaliese asked.

'Yes – although he wasn't a patient. I was never told anything like the full truth, but I imagine Ralph must have been very busy the day after his father died – which was a Sunday. I met him when he came to Mr Napier's consulting-rooms on Monday to pick up the death certificate.'

'Whatever happened to the woman?' Annaliese asked.

'I've no idea.' Celia shuddered. 'After Ralph had insisted on taking me out to dinner and more or less swept me off my feet, he said she wasn't in the least bothered. He'd given her some money and she'd promised to keep quiet.'

'Incredible,' Annaliese murmured.

'Can you imagine it?' Celia whispered, her face ashen. 'To be doing *that* with a man and he dies. It doesn't bear thinking about.'

'Indeed not,' Annaliese said. 'How are you finding the Castle?'

'I don't think I'll ever get used to it,' Celia replied, her saucer-like eyes pleading for sympathy. 'If I'm coping, it's only by the skin of my teeth. At first, I thought things were going to be even worse.'

'Why?'

'The butler and housekeeper gave notice the week before Ralph and I married.'

'Baskerville and Mrs Pritchard?' Annaliese asked, checking that they had not carried out their threat to go sooner.

'Yes. Ralph had fallen out with them.' Celia changed her mind. 'Actually, I think they'd fallen out with him. They seemed such nice people that I decided I *had* to talk them into staying. I practically went down on my hands and knees and it worked.'

'And you're managing?' Annaliese said.

'Yes – except that there's hardly anything for me to do. With everyone ignoring us, there isn't any entertaining.'

For the next hour or so, Annaliese pretended to listen to Celia's complaints about the intimidating size of Allardyce Castle and its loneliness. While Annaliese attempted to reach some sort of conclusion about Celia, she remembered what Cordelia Milford had said about the way she and Ralph had behaved during the Marquess of Yeovil's weekend party – presumably at the same house where they were currently staying.

It was turned half past eight before Ralph and Celia left after what had to be counted a successful day. Edward and Ralph were dragged out of the study at seven, but they still had plans to make and Ralph wanted more to drink. Edward did his best to ignore Celia. On the two occasions when she inadvertently forced herself to his attention by trying to persuade Ralph to leave, he regarded her with unconcealed distaste.

'You weren't very polite to Celia,' Annaliese said when they were finally alone together. 'As a matter of fact, you were downright rude.'

'I don't like her,' Edward snapped. 'She isn't right for Ralph.'

'She used to be a doctor's receptionist,' Annaliese said.

'Oh.' Edward was surprised. 'Is that what she told you?'

'Yes. The poor girl is completely out of her depth at Allardyce Castle. She's terrified of the place.'

'There you are, then!' Edward was satisfied that his point was proved.

'Are you sure that you aren't *slightly* frightened of her?' Annaliese asked, testing the idea that she had seen a brief spark of something other than contempt in the looks that Edward had given Celia.

'Me, frightened of *her*?' he laughed. 'How could I be? What is there to be frightened of? She's an empty-headed girl who's bamboozled Ralph. There's nothing to her.'

'Of course.' Annaliese smiled, indicating that she believed him. 'What have you and Ralph been up to? Am I allowed to know such deep, devious things?'

Gratified by her interest, Edward sat beside her on the sofa and began to explain it all. As if he expected the gesture to clarify matters, he reached for her hand. Smiling attentively all through his account of what had been discussed during the private conversation, Annaliese understood not one word of it.

'Thank you,' she said when he finished, just as the clocks were striking nine. 'I suppose you're going back to your study now?'

'No, I'm not,' Edward replied amiably. 'Nothing was further from my mind. To tell you the truth, I was thinking that we might have an early night.'

'Were you?' Annaliese said teasingly. Much to her own surprise, not only was she in the mood for love-making, a secret voice was telling her that it would be memorable. 'You're quite sure about this?'

'Yes.'

'Very well.' Annaliese stood up. 'Shall we retire?'

There was a strange, unaccountable urgency about Edward, a

determined lustfulness that was reminiscent of the night before Lady Alice's funeral. The difference was that Annaliese was in a mood to play an active part in the near-savagery. Edward's rare willingness to enjoy himself made him something of a stranger and, as she watched him, Annaliese found the oddest thought creeping into her mind. Edward was imagining that she was someone else. How extraordinary and exciting. What on earth had come over him?

Merely as an experiment, Annaliese began to think of John Brandon. The results astounded her: there had been nothing quite as good since St Malo. Wonderfully pleased with himself at the end of their frenzy, Edward tried to persuade her not to make a quick visit to the nursery to check that all was well with the boys.

'They'll be all right,' he said. 'They always are. Stay here. I want you again.'

'Be patient, you monster.' Annaliese laughed, wriggling free and reaching for a wrap. 'A couple of minutes, that's all . . . It should make you even stronger.'

Not content with the exertions of Sunday evening, they played the game again before Edward left for his office on Monday morning – something they had not done since the belated honeymoon in St Malo. This time there was no doubt at all. Annaliese was astride Edward, watching him closely. He was committing mental adultery. It was so fascinating that Annaliese forgot to do the same: instead, she assisted his tortured progress towards orgasm and wondered what had become of her strait-laced, frequently joyless husband.

Afterwards, she was quick to shelve the mystery. Some Viennese recess of her mind was able to accept and be amused by Edward's aberrant behaviour, rather than allow it to become a source of worry. Annaliese was also preoccupied by a task she had set herself.

The moment Edward was out of the house, she went to the study and looked up the telephone number of Mr Napier's consulting-rooms in Harley Street. Her call was answered by a woman who managed to sound both efficient and friendly. Annaliese adopted her prized American accent.

'Hi there. May I speak with Celia Jameson, please?'

'I'm sorry, Madam, Miss Jameson left Mr Napier's service three months ago.'

'Hell! Is this why I'm getting nothing from her flat?'

There was a slight hesitation. 'Er, yes, I expect so. Celia has married, you see. As a matter of fact, she's now the Duchess of Lincolnshire.'

'No kidding,' Annaliese hooted. 'I go back to the States for three months and she turns into a duchess.'

'If it's helpful to you, madam, her home is Allardyce Castle in Wiltshire.'

'Thank you, that's great.' Belatedly, the woman at the other end was thinking of asking to whom she was speaking, but the call was abruptly terminated.

Annaliese paced round the room. 'What does that prove?' she asked herself. 'Anything?'

Taken at it's face value, it confirmed Celia's account of how she had met Ralph. Was there a good reason why it *shouldn't* be accepted? No. Indeed, to do otherwise, one had to believe in the possibility of a conspiracy involving Celia, Napier, and his current receptionist. That was surely too far-fetched for words?

'No, it isn't,' Annaliese said out loud. 'Not with Ralph involved.'

Nevertheless, when she reached Boothby's to find Beatrice clamouring for details, Annaliese was careful to stick to Celia's story, allowing no hint of her misgivings to creep in.

'And she's really quite nice?' Beatrice asked for the umpteenth time.

'I thought so. She's totally out of her depth, largely because Ralph doesn't seem to have told her anything, but she wants to do well. She's very fond of children and desperate to have some of her own.'

'Well, I'm amazed,' Beatrice said. 'Has Ralph done something sensible at long last?'

'We can but hope,' Annaliese said.

Things were very different when the story was repeated at Martha's Vineyard that afternoon.

'It stinks,' Nancy declared without hesitation.

'That's my feeling,' Annaliese agreed.

'It's a good story, though,' Nancy pointed out. 'Clever. They've gotten real close to poor old William's death, so you think, "Hey, that *must* be true. Why else would they bother with anything so *squalid*?"'

'That's what puzzles me,' Annaliese said. 'So what *is* the truth?'

Nancy shook her head. 'It could be that we'll never know, honey. I tell you, I have had London *scoured* over and over for something on that lady and no one's come up with a thing.'

'Maybe you're talking to the wrong people.'

'Sure.' Nancy shrugged. 'Who are the *right* people?'

'Perhaps she really was that doctor's receptionist,' Annaliese suggested.

'Which is what we're *supposed* to believe,' Nancy grumbled, making it plain that she remained to be convinced. 'What did Edward make of her?'

'Oh, he thought she was dreadful.' Annaliese laughed. 'It wouldn't surprise me if he doesn't start feeling sorry for Ralph before too long.'

'Something else for him to get crabby about.' Nancy chuckled. 'Aren't you the lucky one?'

'He wasn't in the least crabby,' Annaliese said gleefully. 'Almost as soon as Ralph and Celia had gone, he wanted sex. We did it twice last night and again this morning before he went to work.'

'Was it good?' Nancy asked, always eager for details.

'Yes. There was something strange, though. I'm certain that Edward was dreaming he was making love to another woman – not me at all. It's ridiculous.'

'Don't you be so sure,' Nancy said. 'Men are always doing it . . . even when they're with *me*!' She laughed at the image of herself as the perfect answer to a man's desires.

'I don't think he *knows* any other women,' Annaliese said. Catching sight of the look on Nancy's face, she laughed. 'Yes, I know what they say – the wife is always the last to know, but I'm not a brainless ninny, am I? Edward's whole life these days is all-male. There isn't a woman anywhere near him.'

Nancy was deep in thought. 'What's Celia like?' she asked quietly. 'Was Cordelia right? *Is* she a sex-bomb?'

'Definitely,' Annaliese replied. 'It's how she trapped Ralph and it's her only hope of hanging on to him. The minute she . . .' She stopped, staring at Nancy in dawning disbelief. 'You don't think that Edward took a fancy to her?'

'I've no idea, honey. I suggest you keep your eyes open.'

During the next four weeks, Annaliese and Edward made love only once, an unsatisfactory encounter, brought about largely through a vague sense of mutual duty. Ralph and Edward met regularly, but Celia was hidden away in Wiltshire, apparently complaining about her isolation in a particularly wet and murky autumn.

Ralph was introduced into the House of Lords and, within a week, made a speech that attracted a great deal of favourable attention. He spoke at erudite length on the potential problems in the Balkans, largely brought about by the 1919 Paris Peace Treaty. According to Ralph, the deliberate breaking up of the old Austro-Hungarian Empire left a vacuum which disparate nationalistic elements were filling with all manner of hatreds and dangers. Reading a transcript of the speech a few days after it was delivered, Annaliese was impressed.

'This is what you think?' she asked the true author of the words that Ralph had uttered.

'Yes,' Edward replied. 'That whole region, from the Hungarian border down to Greece, is a powder-keg.'

'Why did you want Ralph to make *this* speech?' Annaliese asked. 'Why not something on the League of Nations?'

'Hmm.' Edward's shrewd stare was a compliment. 'You understand a thing or two, don't you? Isolationism is taking a grip. People are burying their heads in the sand. I thought it was time to put up an Aunt Sally to gauge opinion. The League is sacrosanct – unjustifiably so, I might say – so I tried the Balkans.'

'And have you discovered anything?' Annaliese asked.

'I'm afraid so.' Edward was grim and bitter. 'Everyone thinks that Ralph made a damned interesting speech and that something should be done – but not by us. Britain can't afford it, in any sense of the word.'

'What's your next move?'

'I don't know. Lord Curzon will contact me in a week or two.'

But it was not to be. Quite unexpectedly, and for reasons that not even Edward was able to explain, Stanley Baldwin requested a dissolution of Parliament and called a general election, an event that should not have been necessary for another three years. In the poll, which was held in December, the Conservatives lost 87 seats. With 258 winning candidates, they were still the largest group in the House of Commons, but were unable to command an overall majority. Baldwin, the man in whom Edward had put his faith, had created the most unholy mess.

The indecision, not resolvable until Parliament assembled in the New Year of 1924, plunged Edward into a deep depression. Annaliese knew that he was apprehensive for his future after the way he had aligned himself with the Conservative cause. Whatever happened in the political arena, there would be a new Foreign Secretary; the sixty-five-year-old Lord Curzon declared that he would not wish to be a member of the Government if Baldwin managed to hang on.

Looking into Cadogan Square for a drink and a moan one evening, Ralph came up with an idea that lifted some of Edward's gloom and delighted Annaliese.

'Why don't you two come down to Allardyce for Christmas? Bring the boys, of course, and a couple of servants. To tell you the truth, you'd be doing us a favour.'

'How?' Edward asked.

'Celia wants a "proper" Christmas – you know, carols and decorations. But she doesn't much care for spending it cooped up with me on our own.' He laughed nervously.

'It would give us a chance to put our heads together,' Edward said, needing to prove to himself that there was a better reason than mere relaxation for making the trip.

'Good idea,' Ralph agreed.

'What do you think, my dear?' Edward asked Annaliese.

'Yes, please,' she replied.

Celia, Mrs Pritchard, and the maids worked tremendously hard to decorate the Castle, concentrating most of their efforts on the West Wing living quarters. Nor had Ralph been idle. In all there were six huge Christmas trees: their selection, felling, and positioning in eye-catching corners was Ralph's work. When Annaliese, Edward, and the boys, together with Gwen and Matthew, arrived on 22 December, everywhere was cosy and spiced with pine needles and a dozen other festive smells. The first thing that Annaliese did was to revel in her surroundings; after fearing that she might never see the Castle again, it was like a home-coming.

Then she watched Edward, waiting to see how he reacted to Celia.

On that first day, he seemed perfectly at ease with her. Tired and cold after the drive from London, and anxious to be rid of his worries about the formation of a government, Edward accepted Ralph's offer of two large whiskies in rapid succession and spent what was left of the day in a mellow haze. Following a supper of steak and kidney pie, it was as much as he could do to keep his eyes open until it was time for bed.

The following morning, 23 December, Edward and Ralph took a short walk after breakfast, then hid themselves away in Ralph's East-Wing study – the room that boasted the powerful telescope, Annaliese remembered.

'What do you think they're up to?' Celia asked as she and Annaliese set off on a drive round the Park with Douglas and George.

'Preparing for doomsday,' Annaliese replied facetiously. 'Edward believes that we're going to have a Labour Government.'

'Is that a bad thing?'

'I've no idea,' Annaliese said. 'Edward thinks so. I expect Ralph will agree, so they should have plenty to moan about – don't worry, it will keep them happy for hours.'

When they all came together for lunch, the two men certainly seemed to be carrying the whole of the world's troubles on their shoulders. But, preoccupied though he was, Edward began to react to Celia. This time, it showed up as punctilious politeness with a succession of strange looks. Once, when he thought no one was watching him, Edward stared at her in a way that Annaliese was at a loss to describe, let alone understand.

Although the afternoon and evening passed pleasantly enough, Annaliese was conscious of the energy and tension building up in Edward. After spending nearly an hour exchanging highly charged looks with Celia, it was Ralph who suggested an early night. To Annaliese's astonishment, Edward's agreement was coloured by a roguish eagerness that almost had him winking. Sure enough, once they were inside their rooms, he had one thing only in mind, achieving it by means of a delightfully persuasive seduction.

Christmas Eve saw the same pattern of unease and tension during the day. That night, Edward's mood and lunging vigour somehow conveyed the impression that he was using Annaliese as a whore. She rather liked the feeling, and began to act the part, behaving with wanton abandon to ensure that she and Edward experienced intense climactic pleasure. Afterwards, she was not unduly surprised when his mood indicated that he was feeling ashamed of himself.

Edward was like a fish out of water when they went to the nursery on Christmas morning to watch the boys open the presents that filled the pillow-cases at the foot of their beds. Douglas, armed with an outlandish explanation of how Father Christmas had found them in the middle of Wiltshire *and* come down the right chimney, took no notice of his father's frame of mind – but then he never did. George, however, seemed wary of it, looking at Edward in a way that seemed to be critical. Not for the first time, Annaliese told herself that she had to be careful with George: he must not be allowed to develop a dislike of Edward.

Ralph, struggling to improve his standing locally, had decided that they must go to Morning Service in the village church. Before they set off, Annaliese put through a telephone call to Upper Overs to wish Lord Douglas a happy Christmas. He sounded in good form, enjoying himself in the company of Beatrice and Charles Templeton. No mention of Charles's presence was made, especially to Edward, who spoke to his father and sister after Annaliese had spent ten minutes saying everything there was to say. While Edward and Lord Douglas were ignoring the spirit of goodwill to tear Stanley Baldwin to shreds, Annaliese thought how ridiculous this enforced secrecy over Charles was: it would have to stop.

They sat in the family pew in church, a boxed-in enclosure which put them on display to the packed congregation. Douglas, who stood on a pile of hassocks so that he could see over the sides of the oak structure, attracted a good deal of friendly interest, but it was painfully obvious that Ralph was wretchedly unpopular. When they left at the end of the service, Annaliese heard the gossiping hubbub that was unleashed the instant they passed through the outer door.

What followed was even worse. Ralph's father had always toured the estate on Christmas Day, visiting every cottage for a convivial chat and a drink. On leaving, he would slip a five-pound note into someone's hand. It was a substantial sum of money, given without fuss and bother, and was much-appreciated. Ralph had decided to raise the gift to ten pounds. The stench of ostentation was exacerbated by the patronising bluster accompanying each presentation. Part of the problem was that Ralph had no idea of who was who; Annaliese saw that he had not taken the trouble to get to know the staff he had inherited. Before acting the grand seigneur, Ralph should have torn himself away from political games in London and devoted time to his birthright.

It was turned two o'clock before the task was done and they headed back to the Castle, ravenously ready for turkey and plum pudding. In the embarrassing progress round the cottages they had not, Annaliese noticed, visited the Hamiltons. Had they left, or was the estate manager important enough to be excused from Ralph's attempt to ingratiate himself with the peasants?

That only four people should sit down to Christmas lunch in a place like Allardyce Castle struck Annaliese as completely wrong. Perhaps conscious of this, Ralph was in a hectic mood, drinking far too much and encouraging Edward to do the same. At five o'clock, after an exchange of knowing stares and nods, Annaliese and Celia left their husbands slumped in armchairs and went up to the nursery.

They found Gwen tidying up after what had clearly been a rip-roaring party.

'Where are they?' Annaliese asked.

'Playing hide-and-seek with Matthew and Mr Baskerville,' Gwen replied. 'You wouldn't believe their energy.'

'This place should slow them down,' Annaliese replied. 'If they're not back in an hour, we'll send out a search-party. Gwen, I'm dying for a decent cup of coffee.'

'Viennese?' Gwen asked.

'Of course. What about you, Celia, coffee or tea?'

'Tea, please.' Celia seemed touched by Annaliese's consideration. When Gwen had gone to get the beverages, she said, 'I'm sorry you're leaving tomorrow.' She sounded wistful.

'I am, too,' Annaliese admitted. 'I'm afraid it's Edward. The fact is, I was lucky to keep him away from London for this long.'

Celia nodded understandingly. 'You and the boys have made a big difference . . . I don't know what it would have been like without you.' She paused. 'Edward doesn't like me very much, does he?'

'Oh, no, you mustn't think that!' Annaliese was rattled, not only by Celia's directness, but by a hint of slyness in her eyes. It disappeared as quickly as it had come, leaving a doubt whether it had ever been there at all. 'No, it's just his way,' Annaliese went on with an effort. 'He's dreadfully *gauche* with women.'

'I thought it must be my fault.'

'Goodness me, no.' Annaliese laughed. 'Give it two or three years and he'll be quite friendly.'

'Was he like that with you?' Celia asked.

'Funnily enough, no, he wasn't. Our circumstances were rather exceptional, though.'

'Like mine.' Suddenly, Celia was both bitter and fragile, somehow exposed. 'I'm beginning to wonder if I haven't landed myself in a mess.'

Annaliese's brain raced, looking for the right thing to say, something that might take advantage of Celia's relaxed guard to get at the truth. 'You need patience,' was all she could think of.

'I realise that,' Celia replied and the moment passed: although she remained sorry for herself, she was no longer vulnerable.

'Things will be much easier for you if Ralph can persuade people to think more kindly of him,' Annaliese said. 'And you need an ally, Celia – Lady Torksey, for example. With someone like her on your side, life would be *very* different.'

Possibly because she only knew of Lady Torksey as a battle-axe, possibly because she wasn't interested, Celia ignored the suggestion. 'The big problem is being stuck here on my own while Ralph's away, trying to make a good impression,' she said. 'And he's asking me to *do* things – He wants me to take charge of the maintenance of everything.'

'There must be an estate manager, or someone like that,' Annaliese said, concealing the sudden upsurge of interest.

'Richard Hamilton.' Celia shuddered.

'What's wrong?' Annaliese asked, all innocence.

'He's a weird man.' Celia screwed her face up. 'He hardly ever says anything and he's always looking at you in a creepy sort of way. They say he had a bad time in the War.'

'There are a lot like that,' Annaliese said quietly, realising that Celia was probably too young to understand the horrors that Europe had endured. 'It's very sad.'

'I know that – but it doesn't help me.'

'Is this poor man married?' Annaliese asked.

An unnatural calm descended on Celia. 'Yes, he is.' After a long pause, she added, 'To Blanche.'

A wealth of meaning was poured into the name. Although they talked for another hour, Annaliese was unable to get any idea of what lay behind it. Gradually, Celia cheered up, chatting brightly about everyday things, a pretence she kept up until Annaliese said goodbye to her after lunch on Boxing Day.

'You're very thoughtful,' Edward said after they had travelled several miles in a silence that he found uncomfortable after their three nights of wild love-making. 'Nothing wrong, I hope?'

'No.' Annaliese returned to earth with a jolt. 'I was wondering about Celia.'

'Hmm . . . Yes.' Edward shook his head. For several long moments, it seemed that he was intending to express an opinion about Celia, but he remained quiet before alighting on a subject that took Annaliese's breath away. 'I don't think we should leave it *all* that much longer before we visit your parents.'

'Heavens above, what makes you say that?'

'I often think about them.'

'So do I,' Annaliese replied. 'You're right, of course. We *should* go.'

Inconclusive though it was, Edward was content to leave it there, certain that the idea would take root.

On 21 January 1924, Stanley Baldwin was defeated in the House of Commons and resigned. The next day, King George V sent for James Ramsay MacDonald and asked him to form an administration. Britain had its first Labour Government – albeit a minority one. A Clydeside radical declared, 'Bishops, financiers, lawyers, and all the polite spongers upon the working classes know that this is the beginning of the end.'

There *was* panic in the upper reaches of Society, some of which was visible at Boothby's. Was it best to buy, sell, or sit tight and do nothing? For a month, the latter view prevailed and business died. Soon, however, people came to see that Ramsay MacDonald's dependence on Liberal support ruled out any possibility of far-reaching Socialist legislation and confidence returned.

Not so for Edward. Of Ramsay McDonald's many problems, perhaps the greatest was his party's total lack of experience in government. Forming a cabinet was a nightmare and, when it came to filling the critical post of Foreign Secretary, Ramsay MacDonald saw no alternative to doing the job himself.

'What a disaster,' Edward fumed. 'Even if the stupid man knew anything about foreign affairs – which he doesn't – how can he possibly share the job with the premiership?'

By spring, British foreign policy was in the hands of a few civil servants. Annaliese's impression was that Edward, in common with many of his colleagues, did little except plan for a future beyond Ramsay MacDonald. There was some work coaching Ralph for House of Lords debates, but time hung heavily on Edward's hands. He spent more and more of it at his Club, playing bridge or gossiping.

After much agonising, Annaliese raised the question of the visit to her parents. 'Would you like to go to Lisbon this summer?' she asked Edward at an appropriate time, a Sunday morning in May when they were on their way down to Upper Overs for lunch with Lord Douglas.

'Are *you* ready to make the trip?' he asked, sensing her lingering ambivalence.

'Yes and no,' Annaliese said. 'We must take the boys, so I'd rather leave it until next year. George should be all right with the journey when he's three.'

'Why suggest this year, then?' Edward asked good-naturedly.

'With so little going on, I thought you might be happy to be away from the Foreign Office for three weeks – we need that length of time, you know.'

'Yes, I understand. The fact is, my dear, this is *not* the time to be away. I've never known things so tricky.'

'Abroad, or inside the Foreign Office?' Annaliese asked with a hint of mischief.

'Inside,' he laughed.

She felt duty-bound to admit that, with Boothby's enjoying levels of business that were tantamount to an epidemic, and with Beatrice talking of going to Cornwall with Lord Douglas for anything up to four weeks, a holiday might be difficult to arrange.

'That's settled,' Edward said. 'We shall go to Portugal next year. Definitely. Consider it arranged.'

Annaliese was surprised to experience feelings of relief. Without her being consciously aware of it, repeated failure to face up to the problem posed by her parents had been preying on her mind. The longer it had been put off, the easier it had been to find excuses for more delay. Once it had been decided, she was much happier, despite Edward's black moods caused by Ramsay MacDonald and the Foreign Office.

During August and September, when Nancy spent two weeks in Nice and was strenuously preoccupied with a new lover, Annaliese saw John Brandon with increasing frequency. They went to concerts, the theatre, art galleries, and had lunch together at least once a week. On 27 September, John insisted that they try the restaurant at Claridge's.

'My treat,' he said. 'I've had a bit of luck on a horse.'

'You're a gambler?' Annaliese shrieked, pretending to be horrified.

'Only very, very occasionally,' John replied. 'And only when I have information from impeccable sources.'

'Just like everything else you do,' Annaliese joked.

They did themselves proud, ordering the most expensive meal on the menu. After a first course made up of smoked salmon with a delicious concoction of prawns and poached egg, Annaliese was gazing contentedly into space, pretending to listen to John's latest concerns about Queen Alexandra's health. The plate-glass doors of the restaurant were in her direct line of vision. Beyond them, a newly constructed mezzanine floor served as a promenade-cum-lounge. It was all very art deco and so fascinating that it was a long time before she saw the man leaning against a pillar.

'What's the matter?' John asked when recognition drained her face of colour.

'That man,' she whispered. 'Outside.'

John turned his head, slowly and unobtrusively. 'Ah. The Duke of Lincolnshire,' he murmured.

'Please don't let him see us,' Annaliese said to a nameless deity.

'Those palms are pretty good cover,' John pointed out. 'Added to which, His Grace is far too taken up with himself to worry about his surroundings.'

'He's waiting for someone?' Annaliese asked.

'I'd say so. That languid boredom is really impatience. Could it be . . . yes, here she is now.'

A woman emerged from the powder-room. Elated, Ralph strode towards her.

'I presume that isn't the Duchess?' John said mildly as the couple on the landing merged in a gluttonous kiss.

'No,' Annaliese said in an icy, distant voice. 'That's Blanche Hamilton.'

'You know her?'

'I know of her,' Annaliese said quietly.

Ralph and Blanche were entering a lift. Not caring whether he could be seen, Ralph was running a hand down her back. It came to rest well below Blanche's waist.

'His Grace is still up to his old tricks, I see,' John observed drily.

'I think this is more serious than that,' Annaliese said slowly. '*Much* more serious.'

Ramsay MacDonald's flirtation with power and a brave new world ended on 4 November. The second general election campaign in a year began rather tediously, then flared into hysterical life over allegations about links between the tiny Communist Party of Great Britain and the Bolsheviks in Russia. Labour was believed to be well-disposed towards Communism in its British form and the stage was set for scare-mongering. It came in the form of the Zinoviev Telegram, an incitement to insurrection and class war.

The telegram fell into the hands of a national newspaper, was published four days before the poll, and made the voting and counting a mere formality. The Conservatives were returned with a massive overall majority. Prime Minister again, Stanley Baldwin put Austen Chamberlain in charge of the Foreign Office, a choice that pleased Edward enormously.

On an evening when Edward had cancelled a game of bridge in order to dine quietly at home with Annaliese, she asked a question that had nagged at her for over a week.

'Why do I think you had something to do with getting that telegram into the newspaper?'

He smiled in a way that put the clock back a long time: for a few precious moments, Edward had the sheepish look of a schoolboy in need of a cast-iron alibi. 'I could insist that your imagination was running away with you,' he said.

'You could – but I'd have to ask about the strange goings-on just before Comrade Zinoviev's message to the struggling proletariat got itself splashed on the front page.'

Edward nodded and appeared to make his mind up about something. 'I'm going to mend my ways,' he said. 'Politics is a dirty game and I'm steering clear of it in future.'

Was this voluntary, or had a warning been given? Annaliese simply said, 'Yes, that may be for the best.'

'By the way, there's something I should have mentioned earlier,'

Edward went on. 'Ralph's been asking if we'll go to Allardyce again for Christmas.'

On the verge of unthinking, automatic agreement, Annaliese stopped herself. 'What about Father?' she asked. 'What will he be doing?'

'I don't know,' Edward admitted. 'I suppose Bee will be with him for some of the time.'

'I think we should go to Upper Overs,' Annaliese said.

'But you like Compton Allardyce.'

'So I do . . . I also love your father. In any case, I can't expect you to put up with Celia for a second Christmas!'

'Amen,' Edward said. Then, his mood changed suddenly. 'Oh my God!' He was sitting bolt-upright, looking foolish. 'I forgot to tell you . . . Ralph mentioned it a couple of weeks ago and it slipped my mind.'

'What?'

'He's going to be a father.'

'How lovely! When's the baby due?'

Edward searched his memory. 'End of June, I think.'

'I expect Celia's pleased,' Annaliese said. It was disconcerting that the news had come this way: following the previous Christmas visit, Celia had kept in touch for a while, but had been silent since the summer and – just as with Frances Peters – Annaliese had done nothing to rectify the situation. 'She'll like being the mother of a son and heir.'

'It would consolidate her position,' Edward conceded.

'Careful you don't strain yourself,' Annaliese scolded. 'To change the subject, a horrible thought is occurring to me.'

'What's that?'

'If things are going to be so perfect at the Foreign Office now that Austen Chamberlain is in charge, what are the chances of us going to see Mama and Father next year?'

'Aha! I can tell you,' Edward was triumphant. 'My application for three weeks' leave was approved yesterday. This lunchtime, I went to the Union Castle offices and confirmed my provisional booking. We sail for Lisbon on the thirty-first of May.'

18

28 May–7 June 1925
. . . Not this time, my friend!

Thursday 28 May was Annaliese's last day at Boothby's before the great adventure. Friday and the weekend were for packing – even though Gwen swore that it was all under control.

The weather that Thursday matched Annaliese's mood, breezy and sparkling. Even so, over lunch with Beatrice and Charles Templeton, she confessed to nervousness about what lay ahead.

'I've reached the stage where I feel guilty at leaving it so long,' she said. 'I can't for the life of me imagine how it happened. What if we don't recognise each other?'

'That doesn't seem likely,' Charles suggested. 'Not as far as you're concerned, anyway.'

'You are rather eye-catching, Annaliese,' Beatrice said, explaining Charles's half-baked gallantry. 'And you haven't changed at all.'

'I was thinking about up here,' Annaliese replied, tapping her forehead. 'Thoughts and attitudes – they're strange things. It's over seven years.'

'And your parents are living in exile,' Charles said sympathetically. 'Yes, I see your point, Annaliese – it might be sticky for a while.'

'Don't listen to him!' Beatrice shrieked, frightening the living daylights out of people at nearby tables. 'There won't be a single thing to worry about – everything will be *lovely*.'

'Yes, I agree,' Charles laughed. 'Let me be helpful for a change. Do you have all the money you need for this trip, Annaliese?'

'Yes, thank you, Charles, there's no need to go to the piggy bank.'

That was how she referred to her account in Liechtenstein. Helped by Charles, she had used some of the interest, mostly to supplement the generous dress-allowance she received from Edward, but the original capital sum was still intact and appreciating.

By the time they had polished off an extra bottle of wine and Charles was muttering about the need to get back to his office, Annaliese was convinced that she was going to have the time of her life in Portugal. Outside Whitaker's, Charles kissed both women, wishing Annaliese *bon voyage*, and begging Beatrice not to be *too* late that evening: she was having dinner at Cadogan Square before joining him at their house in Regent's Park. When leaving Charles, both women were standing with their backs to the roadway, so they did not see Franklin as he passed from Cork Street into Clifford's Passage. Charles *did* notice the man who took a quick, furtive interest in them, but didn't know him from Adam and thought nothing of it.

At five o'clock, Annaliese and Beatrice left Boothby's and went to Cadogan Square, going straight up to the nursery.

Douglas was beside himself. 'Auntie Bee, Auntie Bee. Hurrah!' He was roaring his head off and jumping round like a dervish. 'We're going to Por-chew-girl on Monday to see Grannie and Grandpapa Habsburg.'

'I know you are, darling. Isn't it exciting?'

'Are you coming to wave goodbye when we go on the big ship?'

While Beatrice was giving Douglas ten good reasons why she would not be at Southampton, George was scrambling into her arms, his expressive eyes full of love.

Gwen brought tea, Douglas calmed down, and a sensible conversation developed. Douglas, who liked to keep an eye on the comings and goings in the Square from his bedroom window, dashed into the sitting-room to announce that Edward was on his way.

'Good, he's nice and early,' Annaliese said brightly. Then, straight away, without rhyme or reason, she felt the chill of an unease so great that it approached menace.

'Papa looks cross,' Douglas said after a second peek from the window.

Annaliese went to the door, put her head into the corridor and listened. Edward was downstairs in the hall, angrily calling for Franklin. From the sound of his footsteps, he was impatient and heading towards the butler's pantry.

'What's going on?' Beatrice asked.

Annaliese shook her head.

'Why is Papa so cross?' Douglas asked. 'Is it that horrid Pry Minster?'

'I expect that's what it is, darling,' Annaliese said. 'Aunt Bee and I will see what we can do to help him. Be good, and Gwen will let you have extra jelly for supper.' Jelly was a sure-fire way of guaranteeing Douglas's best behaviour.

Annaliese and Beatrice walked to the head of the stairs, sharing a feeling of apprehension.

'I thought he was usually in a pretty good mood these days?' Beatrice whispered.

'He *has* been,' Annaliese replied. 'Come on.'

They were halfway down the stairs when Edward emerged from the servants' quarters. It seemed that the sight of his wife and sister gave him a kind of grim satisfaction.

'Very handy,' he snapped. 'Come with me, you two.' Not pausing in his stride, he made for the drawing-room. Mystified, exchanging looks that swung between amusement and fearful disbelief, Annaliese and Beatrice followed. They found Edward standing in front of the fireplace, feet apart, hands behind his back, shoulders braced resolutely: it was a pose that could easily have given rise to mirth.

'Close the door,' he ordered.

Dumbfounded by his tone and manner, Annaliese and Beatrice did so together. When they faced him, he was in no hurry to speak. Edward was a man in the grip of an all-consuming rage.

Annaliese's patience snapped. 'For heaven's sake, Edward, what is it? You look like something out of a third-rate melodrama.'

'I had lunch at the Club,' he said slowly. Briefly, his voice was quiet, but the thunder came as he went on. 'To my complete and *utter* embarrassment, I found myself sharing a table with two fellows who took it for granted that I knew my sister was virtually living with a married man.'

Beatrice tried to speak: 'Edward, this has . . .' She stopped when Annaliese gripped her arm.

'No,' Annaliese said softly. 'Let him say his piece.'

'*Thank* you,' Edward responded, bitingly sarcastic. 'It appears that this disgraceful state of affairs has been going on for years. Not only that, what do I find when I get home?'

'I have no idea,' Annaliese said coolly. 'I suppose you're going to tell us.'

'Knowing that Franklin keeps his ear to the ground, I talked to him.' Beatrice gasped; Annaliese's grip tightened and she stayed silent. 'As if I hadn't been subjected to enough for one day, Franklin informs me that you, Annaliese, have known about this unsavoury business for a long time. It so happens that he saw you with Beatrice and this man outside Whitaker's this afternoon.'

'Fascinating,' Annaliese said, astonishing both Edward and Beatrice by the mildness of her tone. 'Does Franklin *know* Charles Templeton? I mean, how did he recognise him?'

'He studies the illustrated papers,' Edward retorted, obviously uneasy with the point. 'Mrs Darbishire confirmed the man's identity.'

'Ah, I see.' Annaliese nodded to herself. The cook had been very careful: until now, there had been no definite link between her and the frequent unpleasantness below stairs. 'I wonder how Franklin happened to see us?' Annaliese mused. '*Was* it a coincidence?'

Edward's anger exploded. 'Don't bandy words with me. This is not the time for nit-picking over irrelevant detail, Annaliese. Good God, half of London must be laughing up its sleeve at me. As for you, Beatrice, I'm appalled, absolutely appalled!'

'I love Charles,' Beatrice screamed.

'Do you know, I'd expected you'd come out with that sort of clap-trap,' Edward sneered. 'It won't wash, do you hear? Have you no idea of what this will do to the family name? I doubt I can wipe it out, but I can show people what I think about it. You are no longer welcome in my house, Beatrice. I won't have it thought that I condone your disgusting—'

The sheer unexpectedness of the slap across the face was more damaging than the physical pain. Edward was left with the impression that Annaliese had covered the three yards separating them in a single, lightning stride. After reeling back against the fender, he found her eyes boring into him, ablaze with a terrible fury.

'You are a pompous hypocrite!' Annaliese hissed. 'Not content with trying to impose your puritanical tyranny on those you claim to love, you encourage that *despicable* creature Franklin to tell tales about them!'

Leaving Edward speechless and rather frightened, Annaliese turned to Beatrice and saw that she was sobbing. It was all very quiet and gentle, but she was heart-broken. Placing an arm round her shoulders, Annaliese led her from the room.

'I want to go home . . . to Charles,' Beatrice whispered.

'Are you sure? Wouldn't you like to sit down for a while. Don't go back to Charles like this.'

'No, no. I must go . . . I can't bear to stay here. If I can find a cab . . .'

There was one cruising round the Square after dropping a passenger. It swooped in response to Annaliese's raised arm and Beatrice was into it like a frightened rabbit. Annaliese called out that she would see Beatrice before Monday, but it went unheard.

Back in the house, Edward had left the drawing-room and was hovering in the hall.

'Look here, my dear, this won't do,' he said, torn between bluster and conciliation.

'You're right, it won't,' she responded, the fury burning back into her eyes. 'Your behaviour is contemptible.' She stepped back, hardening her stare. 'I'm curious about something.'

'Yes?' he asked uncertainly.

'When we're in bed, making love, you sometimes think of another woman. Her image is fixed so firmly in your head that it's as if you were having intercourse with her. It's Celia, isn't it – the woman you claim to despise? I'd like to know how *that* squares up with these morals you ram down my throat whenever it takes your fancy.'

Annaliese waited long enough to watch his initial flush of guilt drain away to ashen pallor, then went upstairs.

'I'm having my meal here,' she told Gwen.

'But I thought that Miss Beatrice—' Gwen shut up as she understood the force of her mistress's mood.

'There has been a disagreement,' Annaliese said, struggling to be calm. 'The boys didn't hear anything, I hope?'

'Not a sausage,' Gwen replied. 'This place has *some* good points.'

Annaliese looked at Gwen sharply. 'I never realised you didn't like it.'

Gwen shrugged. 'It's all right, I suppose, but it's still stuck-up and heartless – even after what you had done.'

'Hmm. You're right. Perhaps we should think of going somewhere else?' Gwen was so struck by what seemed to be both a threat and a promise that she decided not to ask questions.

Annaliese spent half an hour humouring Douglas's latest theories and telling the ever-solemn George how much he was going to enjoy sailing to Portugal. Behind the placid exterior, her mind was inching towards a decision that she knew would be a watershed. When she reached it, Annaliese went in search of Edward.

He was nowhere to be seen, not in the study, nor any of the downstairs rooms. A nervous maid was pretending to be busy in the dining-room; the girl obviously knew that something was awfully wrong.

'Have you seen my husband?' Annaliese asked.

'I think he's talking to Mr Franklin, madam . . . er . . . Your Highness. In the pantry.'

'Thank you.'

It beggared belief that Edward should be skulking with Franklin instead of trying to redeem the situation. They both looked alarmed when she arrived: Franklin, frozen by her eyes, thought that she was ready to kill.

She addressed Edward softly, in a voice that had the cold precision of a scalpel. 'What is now *my* bedroom will be locked in thirty minutes' time.' She glanced at her watch. 'If you wish to remove any of your possessions, please do so before then.'

Later, when they shared a meal, Gwen marvelled at Annaliese's composure. This, of course, was 'class': it was what six hundred years of breeding did for you. During the visit to the kitchen for their food, Gwen had discovered that the row between Mr Edward and Her Highness had been a bad one. And Miss Beatrice was in tears when she shot off into a cab.

'This holiday?' Gwen asked nervously. 'What are we doing about it?'

'We are going to Portugal on Monday, exactly as arranged,' Annaliese replied. 'At least, you, me, and the boys are. Whether Edward comes with us remains to be seen.'

'Oh,' Gwen said in a very small voice.

'Precisely. There is no more to be said at the moment.'

When she put out the light and settled down in the locked bedroom, all that exercised Annaliese's mind was the question of Franklin's dismissal. The timing of her ultimatum was important. It was probably best left for at least a day: in that time, Edward might have summoned the sense and courage to act on his own initiative. What if he did: would it make any difference to what looked for all the world like an irreversible catastrophe?

Annaliese fell asleep before a solution suggested itself.

Next morning, Gwen provided the unaccustomed luxury of breakfast in bed, together with the news that HE had gone to work. By all accounts, he was in a *mood*.

'Well, that's neither here nor there,' Annaliese said blithely. 'We shall have a nice, quiet day, Gwen. I *must* make sure that we packed everything for the boys. Have you persuaded Douglas *not* to take the kitchen sink?'

'I don't know about a nice quiet day,' Gwen said. 'I think summat's up.'

'What?'

'Lord Douglas has been on the blower – that special one in the kitchen for tradesmen. He asked to speak to Matthew most particular.'

'Good gracious!' Annaliese's interest in ham and eggs was suspended. 'What was it about?'

'Well, Matthew wasn't supposed to say,' Gwen replied. 'His

Lordship swore him to secrecy.' After a pause, she added, 'But he told me before he went.'

'Went where?' Annaliese asked.

'To Upper Overs, of course. He's under orders to bring Lord Douglas here.'

'What for?'

'Now that, I do not know,' Gwen admitted.

'How extraordinary.' Annaliese frowned. 'What time are they due to arrive?'

'I suppose you could work it out. Matthew left here just before eight. He took the Rolls and he said he'd been told not to hang about.'

Annaliese decided that twelve o'clock was the sort of time at which Lord Douglas might be expected and planned the morning accordingly, wondering what had prompted him to take such unusual action. It was something serious and Boothby's seemed the only possibility. But what was it about?

Midday came and went without sign of Lord Douglas. At half past, Edward turned up, flustered and ready to be cantankerous.

'What are you doing here at this time of day?' Annaliese demanded, letting him see that he was unwelcome.

'I had a telephone call from Father. He said he wanted to see me – here. He insisted. As it happens, I was thinking of taking the afternoon off.'

'He hasn't arrived yet,' Annaliese replied curtly. Swinging round abruptly, she left him and went upstairs, only to be met by Gwen trotting excitedly along the landing.

'They're here,' Gwen whispered, bouncing up and down. 'The car should be outside *now.*'

Franklin seemed perfectly at ease as he went to the door. Watching him from the top of the stairs, Annaliese seethed at the man's effrontery. How *could* he be so calm? Even Lord Douglas's greeting left him unruffled.

'Why the devil are you still here?'

'I beg your pardon, My Lord, I don't understand,' Franklin replied, giving one of his self-righteous little bows. 'If I may say so,

Your Lordship is looking somewhat tired.'

'Damn it, you may not say so,' Lord Douglas thundered. He was in a stupendous, quite unbelievable rage. Gwen edged closer to Annaliese. 'How dare you speak to me like that?'

Franklin was no longer at ease: on the contrary, he looked scared stiff.

'Father. What's going on?' Edward dashed out of the drawing-room.

'That's what I've come to ask *you*,' Lord Douglas replied. 'I had reason to contact Beatrice last evening.'

'Oh,' Edward said.

'Gawd blimey,' Gwen whispered to Annaliese.

'The poor girl was very upset,' Lord Douglas said. 'She was distraught!'

'Yes . . . well . . .' Edward was inept and wretched, incapable of defending himself.

'I see you haven't even had the decency to get rid of *this* individual,' Lord Douglas said. Turning to Franklin, he let rip. 'You are dismissed, damn you! I should have done it years ago. If you're out of the house within the hour, I'll consider giving you a reference, otherwise you can go without.'

Franklin made an attempt to fight. 'If I'm pushed out like this, Mrs Darbishire will give notice.'

'Who's Mrs Darbishire?' Lord Douglas asked.

'She's the cook,' Edward said. 'A very good woman.'

Lord Douglas was suspicious. 'Is she the woman you set on without having the decency to consult Annaliese?'

'Er . . . yes . . . she is.'

'This man's cousin, if I remember rightly?'

'I believe so,' Edward admitted.

'She's dismissed as well,' Lord Douglas roared. 'Now I come to think, I remember Beatrice mentioning her in connection with this odious business of spying on Charles. Is this all perfectly clear and simple? Is there anything else you'd like to threaten me with, Franklin?'

'No,' was the sullen answer.

'Just a minute, Father,' Edward said. 'I can't allow you to dismiss my servants like this.'

'You will if you know what's good for you,' Lord Douglas retorted. 'Go on, Franklin, get out of my sight.' As the ex-butler headed for the servants' quarters, painfully aware that a barrage of jeering awaited him, Lord Douglas glared at Edward. 'I want to talk to you,' he said ominously.

'The study,' Edward suggested. 'Perhaps we shan't be overheard *too* much up there.' Ignoring the petulant jibe, Lord Douglas was taking the first strides towards the stairs.

Anticipating the movement by a fraction of a second, Annaliese had grabbed Gwen's hand and was dragging her out of sight.

'Well, blow me!' Gwen gasped when they reached the safety of the nursery. 'I never would have thought that dear old Lord Douglas had it in him.'

'Nor I,' Annaliese said.

Lord Douglas's five-year-old namesake emerged from the play-room. 'Had what in him?' he asked. 'Who's got what in him?'

'Not now, darling, *please*,' Annaliese said.

Gwen was more brisk. 'Curiosity killed the cat *and* bedtime stories.'

Douglas shut up and went away. Although he was *far* too old for stories, George adored them and Douglas was turning into a doughty guardian of his younger brother's interests.

While the boys played with their train set, Annaliese and Gwen pretended to talk about the arrangements for Monday, when they had to be at Southampton no later than ten o'clock. After a few minutes, Annaliese's patience expired.

'This is no good,' she said, rising impulsively from the chair. 'I want to know what they're talking about.'

'Be careful,' Gwen warned. 'Don't get caught.'

Automatically, Annaliese nodded. Then she changed her mind. 'What if anyone *does* see me? What can they do about it? Damn it, I'm an Archduchess.'

'That's the ticket.' Gwen's huge, cheeky grin declared that the boldness was overdue. Watching from the door of the nursery suite, she saw Annaliese march down the corridor towards the study with no pretence at stealth. That was reserved for the last few paces and the careful positioning of an ear against the door.

Lord Douglas was speaking. Although the peak of his rage was past, his voice remained uncharacteristically harsh.

'. . . a perfectly splendid chap. I tell you, there is nothing wrong with Charles Templeton.'

'How do you know?' Edward asked. 'You surely can't believe what Beatrice says . . . she's obviously besotted.'

'In the first place, that's a very insulting attitude to adopt,' Lord Douglas said. 'Your sister is a remarkable woman, Edward, and you should be proud of her, not standing ready to belittle her at the drop of a hat. I really can't imagine what's come over you. Secondly, I must tell you that Charles and I are good friends . . . We get together quite often. You remember that holiday Beatrice and I had in Cornwall last year? Charles was with us and a jolly good time was had by all.'

Outside the door, Annaliese enjoyed the silence and tried to imagine Edward's face.

'Why wasn't I told?' he said at last.

'That's a very good question.' Lord Douglas let out a short, mirthless laugh. 'We were all afraid of how you'd react, so we put our heads down and prayed for a quiet life. Isn't it ridiculous, eh? We've made a rod for our own backs.'

'Am I that bad?' Edward asked petulantly.

'Yes, you are. You're a total pain in the neck and I feel an absolute fool for putting up with it all these years. And I dread to think what Annaliese feels. I made Beatrice tell me that yesterday wasn't the first time you've caused a row like this – *and* you were using information provided by that blackguard, Franklin.'

Annaliese went back to the nursery.

'What's happening?' Gwen was bursting to know.

'Father is laying down the law.'

Gwen was restive. 'What shall we do?'

'Sit here and wait patiently,' Annaliese said.

It took longer than she expected: nearly an hour elapsed before someone tapped on the door. Annaliese jumped up to let him in. At the sound of their beloved grandfather's voice, the boys racketed into the sitting-room. Lord Douglas was the only person on earth who could inspire George to a boisterous enthusiasm that put his extrovert brother in the shade. When Grandpa had inspected the model railway and made several suggestions for improving the track layout, the boys were content to be diverted by Gwen, leaving Annaliese and Lord Douglas free to go into a huddle.

'First things first,' he said. 'You won't be losing any sleep over Franklin and the cook?'

'None whatsoever,' Annaliese assured him.

Lord Douglas's eyes twinkled, momentarily drawing attention away from the fact that he did not look at all well. 'I saw you and Gwen skedaddling away from the stairs,' he said. They smiled, and he plunged into seriousness. 'Well, my dear, this is a bad business and no mistake. I've read the riot act to Edward – I hope it does some good.'

'I'm sure it will,' Annaliese replied. 'He respects you very much.'

'Hmm, we'll see,' Lord Douglas said gruffly. 'Mind you, I haven't left it at that. Beatrice and Charles are coming down to Upper Overs this evening – they'll be staying for the weekend. I've told Edward to come to lunch tomorrow. He can grovel to Beatrice and be decent to Charles. I take it that you've no objection to having him out of the way?'

'No, but shouldn't I . . .'

'No, you shouldn't,' Lord Douglas said firmly. 'I want him to do this on his own. Having you there would be an extra embarrassment for him. I suppose you might even go soft and help him to wriggle out of the worst?'

'No, Father, I wouldn't,' Annaliese said. 'But, yes, I'll stay away.'

'He's pretty chastened,' Lord Douglas replied. 'Actually, he's afraid that you and the boys will go to Portugal without him.'

Annaliese followed her instinct to be brutally frank. 'I have yet to make up my mind about that,' she said.

'Oh. Oh dear.' Lord Douglas gazed at her sombrely. 'Are things that bad?'

'Yes, Father, I'm afraid they are. This isn't the first time Edward has been so unreasonable and unpleasant.'

'I gathered as much from Beatrice.'

'Edward's outbursts are bad enough in themselves,' Annaliese added. 'The big trouble is that they make me even more aware of the other things that are wrong.'

'Do you know, poor old Beatrice was wondering about this,' Lord Douglas replied. 'She mentioned that "marry in haste, repent at leisure" thing.'

'We shall have to see.' Annaliese's concern for something else made her brisk. 'At the risk of sounding like that creature Franklin, I have to say that you *do* look tired.'

'Yes.' He was quiet for a moment or two, accepting that 'tired' was a euphemism. 'All this hasn't done me much good. I was dashed upset after I'd spoken to Beatrice . . . didn't sleep too well, and flying off the handle at Edward has taken it out of me.'

'Would a spot of brandy help?' Annaliese asked.

'That's a good idea.'

When Gwen returned with the decanter and a glass, Lord Douglas asked her if she was looking forward to Monday.

'I am, sir. It's very exciting.'

'You'll be away from Matthew for nearly three weeks,' Lord Douglas pointed out.

'Can't be helped,' Gwen said bravely. 'At least he won't have to put up with that Franklin while I'm away.'

Lord Douglas chuckled and winked at her. 'Be a good girl and tell Matthew that I shall be ready to leave in about half an hour.' When she had gone, he asked Annaliese, 'I expect you can manage without a butler and cook until you get back from Lisbon?'

'Oh yes. There are at least two kitchen maids who can do as well as Mrs Darbishire.' Annaliese smiled mischievously. 'I don't care whether we have a butler or not. Now, if I could have Baskerville from Allardyce Castle – that would be different.'

'He's a first-class man,' Lord Douglas agreed. 'That reminds me, isn't Celia's baby due soon?'

Annaliese screwed up her face as she ransacked her memory. 'While we're away, I think. I have an idea it's the middle of June.'

'You obviously don't keep in close touch?' Lord Douglas said.

'Not with Celia, no. She doesn't seem to want it. Edward and Ralph still meet occasionally, but they aren't close – not like when Edward was writing speeches for Ralph.'

'Good thing, if you ask me,' Lord Douglas said. He sniffed at the brandy and gave Annaliese a searching look. 'You must be suffering mixed feelings about next week,' he said.

'Yes.' Annaliese sighed. 'The main worry is that I've left it far too long. I'm almost afraid of what I shall find.'

After a moment's hesitation, Lord Douglas said, 'I'll let you into a secret if you promise not to breathe a word.'

'I promise.'

'Your mother feels the same. Her last letter was full of it – she's as nervous as a kitten.'

'Do you know, I'd forgotten that you two wrote to each other,' Annaliese laughed.

'Oh, we're demons. If anything, we've got worse over the last year. Not a week goes by without six or seven pages travelling one way or the other.' He became serious again. 'Your mother is quite worried about it all. I've done my best to set her mind at ease, but the ultimate answer lies with you, my dear. Once the first ten minutes is out of the way, I'm sure you'll both feel that you've never been apart.'

'I shall remember that,' Annaliese said. 'And thank you for today. At least it's stopped me killing someone.'

'Good.' Lord Douglas drained the last drops of his drink and held the glass out expectantly. 'One for the road, eh?' Correctly interpreting Annaliese's expression, he laughed. 'Don't worry. I shall have Beatrice fussing over me all weekend. It's odds-on that she'll want me to see a doctor.'

'And you will?' Annaliese asked.

'There won't be any option, believe me. Come on, my dear, a spot more please. It's the least you can do after I dismissed Franklin for you.'

While Edward was away at Upper Overs on Saturday, Annaliese spent several hours at Martha's Vineyard. She told Nancy all about the row over Charles Templeton and what Lord Douglas had done. They swam and enjoyed each other in one of the changing-rooms. Afterwards, Nancy persuaded Annaliese that, even though her marriage was in a state that made recovery look improbable, Edward should accompany her to Portugal.

'You've got to consider your folks,' Nancy said. 'What are they gonna think if you turn up without a husband?'

'I hadn't seen it that way,' Annaliese said. 'You're right, Nancy.'

The liner *Caerphilly Castle* was calling at Lisbon *en route* to Cape Town. Her 35,000 tons of gleaming-white splendour towered over the quayside. Douglas was vastly impressed, George not so sure. Later, he confessed to Annaliese that he was worried about how the great thing could possibly move, and, as so often, Douglas's grandiose theories had been the reverse of reassuring.

The bustle and excitement that had persisted since the six o'clock departure from Cadogan Square reached its height outside the terminal building. As well as Matthew with the Rolls, Edward had hired a second car and driver to be sure that five people and their luggage for three weeks would be safe and comfortable. Annaliese revelled in the chaos of boxes and trunks, and porters who seemed hell-bent on packing them off on the wrong ship. She unashamedly admitted to herself that a great deal of the pleasure came from seeing how much Edward hated it.

When they sailed, promptly at eleven o'clock, he was still embroiled in the purser's office. There was no good reason for Edward to be worrying: the first-class cabins were superb and all the luggage was accounted for. He really should have been on deck, watching the hawsers being hauled in as the tugs set about inching the *Caerphilly Castle* away from her berth, and waving to Matthew, who looked diminutive and forlorn from a height equivalent to a six-storey building.

Eventually, however, Edward ran out of excuses not to be alone with Annaliese. As the ship headed into Southampton Water, and Gwen took the boys exploring, husband and wife were together in the lounge of their luxurious accommodation.

'This is extremely nice,' Annaliese said, waving a hand at their surroundings. 'You did us proud.'

It was the first time she had displayed friendship for nearly four days and she was nervous. Sensing that her mood could go either way, Edward knew that he must be careful. 'It is rather posh, isn't it? Seems a pity we're only on board for one night.'

'Yes.' Annaliese made a gesture towards the doors that gave access to their own private sun-deck. 'And we have a lovely day for it. I'm sure I heard someone say that it was going to be like this all the way to Lisbon.'

'It is. A chap in the purser's office reckoned we were sure of a good passage – flat calm throughout Biscay even.'

'Good.' Annaliese was bright and cheerful. 'How about lunch? I'm starving.'

'Bound to be. What time did you get up?'

'Half past four,' Annaliese replied.

'Beat me by ten minutes,' Edward said with a weak, jittery smile. 'Yes, by all means, let's go to lunch. Yes.' He was wandering, taking an interest in the furniture and fabrics, working his way to the door of the night-cabin. 'Er . . . what about this?' He cleared his throat. 'They have spare cabins . . . I asked. Do you want me to take one?'

Purely to give herself time to think, Annaliese joined him in the doorway, discovering that the room was equipped with two single beds. 'For my parents' sake, we have to appear to be happy on this holiday,' she said. 'I think you'd better sleep here. Now, may I have some food, please?'

'What about the boys and Gwen?' Edward asked as he locked the outer door of the suite.

'What about them?' Annaliese asked. 'They're perfectly capable of looking after themselves. Gwen will see that they get something to eat . . . *when* Douglas has finished with the engine-room, of course.'

'Are you sure?'

'Perfectly sure, Edward. Believe me, I *do* know our children and have complete faith in Gwen.' Without further ado, she took his hand and dragged him towards the dining-saloon.

Towards the end of a delicious meal, Annaliese tired of their nervously banal small-talk. 'I deliberately haven't asked you what happened at Upper Overs on Saturday,' she said. 'There's no point in raking over old ground.'

'Actually, I'd rather like to tell you about it.' Edward leaned forward eagerly.

'Very well.'

'It was a pretty humiliating experience.'

'You put things right with Beatrice?' Annaliese asked.

'I hope so. If I didn't, it wasn't for want of trying – and Beatrice is a very forgiving person.'

'Good.' Annaliese nodded. 'And Father?'

'Yes, I think we patched it up.' Edward's face clouded. 'It occurred to me that he didn't look all that well.'

'He's very tired,' Annaliese replied. 'He's been thinking about your mother a great deal and not sleeping.'

'You spoke to him?' Edward seemed surprised.

Annaliese went out of her way to be gentle. 'He came to see me and the boys after he'd finished with you in the study.'

'Yes, of course. He would. Perfectly natural. When I left Upper Overs, Beatrice was talking of sending for the doctor to give Father the once-over.'

'In that case, I'm sure it happened,' Annaliese said. 'You met Charles Templeton?'

'Yes.' Edward would have liked to crawl into a hole and hide.

'What did you think of him?'

'He seems a splendid fellow. I felt a complete and utter fool. Does that please you?'

'Not in the least,' Annaliese said.

'I wish you'd told me about him.'

'I didn't dare,' Annaliese replied. 'And you might have had the sense and decency to realise that Beatrice wouldn't involve herself with any Tom, Dick, or Harry.'

'That's exactly what Father told me.'

'I hope this is a lesson to you,' Annaliese said.

'If only for the sake of your parents,' Edward murmured.

'*Especially* for my parents,' Annaliese corrected. She stood up.

'Let's find the boys and enjoy ourselves.' She was extremely businesslike. Edward suspected that there was little or no real feeling behind the act. But then, as they began the search, he remembered that he had apologised to everyone except Annaliese for last Friday's outburst: he lacked the courage.

Douglas and George were on the boat-deck, in earnest conversation with one of the ship's officers. At least, Douglas was. George was taking it all in, wide-eyed and sagacious. Gwen looked on from the comfort of a chair.

'What's going on?' Annaliese whispered.

'That gent is explaining all about knots – and things,' Gwen replied. 'We're doing twenty-eight knots,' she added.

Edward, looking round, pointed to the chalk stacks at the tip of the headland about two miles away. 'The Needles,' he said. 'Isle of Wight. And look at that.' He turned to the stern, facing the boiling wake that seemed to stretch for miles. 'We're going at a bit of a lick.'

'Don't we need to?' Annaliese said. 'We're due in Lisbon at one o'clock tomorrow.'

'There's no time to waste,' Edward agreed. 'I'd better let that poor chap get on with his work.'

He detached Douglas from the officer, collected George, and they set off on what promised to be a complete tour of the ship, leaving Annaliese to put up a chair beside Gwen. They exchanged platitudes about the blueness of the sea and sky, with Gwen bursting to ask a question.

'There's a truce in operation,' Annaliese said, forestalling it.

'Is that *all*?' Gwen sounded disappointed.

'We must be grateful for small mercies,' Annaliese replied.

'Anyway, it's nice to see him spend some time with the boys,' Gwen said, determined to look on the bright side.

'Isn't it, though,' Annaliese agreed. As a father, Edward was probably no worse than other men of his class and outlook. Nevertheless, it always seemed that he spent very little time with his sons.

He made handsome amends that afternoon. It was nearly seven o'clock when they finally turned up, the boys worn out by traipsing *and* an awesomely good tea. Gwen took one look at them and whisked them off for a bath and bed.

'You won't laugh at me?' Edward said as Annaliese helped him with his white tie in preparation for dinner.

'Probably,' she threatened. 'What is it?'

'Douglas and George.' Edward looked at himself in the mirror, patted his hair and was satisfied. 'I had no idea they were so bright. I don't mean intelligent – though they are – it's how much they *know*. From what I picked up, I understand that Douglas is reading books like *Treasure Island*. How did that come about?'

'I've done a bit, but it's mostly Gwen,' Annaliese said. 'She's always trying to improve herself and she passes it on to the boys.'

'Very good,' Edward said.

'She is. While we're on the subject, Douglas ought to go to school in September.'

'I was thinking that only the other day,' Edward said. 'Would you like to find a place that might suit him?'

'Yes, I will.'

Much to his surprise, Edward found his generous concession rewarded with an exceptionally hard stare. *My word, aren't you on your best behaviour?* Annaliese was thinking. *But don't run away with the idea that you can keep it up for a few days, then slip back into your old ways – not this time, my friend!*

Despite that unspoken yet clear warning, the evening was enjoyable. After dinner, the tables were whisked away and a dance band materialised. Annaliese and Edward shuffled round the floor for a while before agreeing to a stroll on deck. It was a perfect night, clear and still,with only the throbbing of the engines to remind them that they were at sea.

'Where are we, do you think?' Annaliese asked.

'At a very rough guess, I'd say that Ushant is somewhere over there.' Edward made a grand gesture into the darkness.

'Is that starboard?' Annaliese asked.

'No, it's port – the left-hand side when you're facing forward.'

'I give up.' Annaliese was suddenly painfully aware that on a beautiful night such as this, on the high sea, with a great adventure ahead of them, she should be snuggling into Edward's arms. And what about their special, shipboard love-making? 'Come along,' she said brusquely. 'We have a very busy day tomorrow.'

Annaliese was up and about at six the following morning, leaving Edward fast asleep. Douglas was dead to the world after yesterday's non-stop excitement and novelty, but George, who had tremendous reserves of strength, was ready for anything. Clutching the map that she had acquired for the journey, Annaliese took her younger son up on deck. It was a superb morning, with the rising sun playing dazzling games on the sea. Annaliese was so entranced by the fresh morning air that it was quite some time before she realised that there was no sign of land.

'We'll give it another hour, darling,' she said. 'Let's go for breakfast.'

Although there was a thin smudge of something on the horizon at seven o'clock, another hour passed before Douglas identified Cape Carvoeiro – and for once, he was right. Yesterday afternoon's officer was passing as the pronouncement was made and confirmed it.

'So we have another hundred miles to go?' Annaliese asked.

'A fraction over, madam. We're expecting to be about half an hour early – we did very well during the night.'

Particularly after the ship had entered the estuary of the River Tagus and reduced speed, Annaliese found the morning interminable.

'You'll be ill if you don't calm down,' Gwen scolded.

'I can't help it,' Annaliese wailed. 'What if—'

'What if be blowed,' Gwen retorted fiercely. 'If you're going to behave like a jack-in-the-box, go somewhere else and do it. Even Douglas is getting nervous.'

'I'm sorry,' Annaliese said wretchedly. 'Perhaps I'll be better off on deck.'

At last, the long wait was nearly over. *Caerphilly Castle* seemed to be in the centre of the city and Edward was pointing to a quay no more than half a mile away. 'We shall be docking there,' he said.

There was no grand terminal building as at Southampton, just a collection of sheds that were hidey-holes for the dockers who emerged at the vessel's approach. On the broad, open space of the quay, an impromptu market had been set up, taxis were jostling for position, and hundreds of people were milling around in what could easily have been a riot. Surveying it all through a pair of binoculars, Edward spoke so quietly that Annaliese barely heard him.

'I can see your parents.'

'Where? Show me.' Annaliese was tugging at the glasses while the strap was still round Edward's neck.

'You can't miss them,' he replied, escaping from the threat of strangulation. 'They've got two enormous Mercedes motor cars.'

There was a delay as Annaliese fiddled with the focus, then she let out a squeal of delight. 'Father has binoculars, too!' she said and waved furiously. 'Yes, they've seen us. My God, I do believe they haven't changed at all.'

'I didn't think so,' Edward murmured. 'A few grey hairs, perhaps.'

'Those two cars . . . I don't believe it . . . I'm *certain* the drivers were at Schönbrunn with us. They were. Kurt and Ludwig . . . well!' Annaliese's eyes were bright with tears. 'Edward, bring the boys up. They *must* be here.'

The next twenty minutes were pandemonium. As soon as the mooring-lines were out and the ship was winching itself up to the quay, Annaliese and Elsa began to shout at each other, not in the least deterred by being able to hear only one word in five, or by Douglas's deafening contribution. Slightly apart from the group on the rail, Gwen held George in her arms. They exchanged eloquent looks as the two Archduchesses carried on their unintelligible but obviously joyous conversation.

'It's a devil of a long time since your mama's used her mother tongue,' Gwen told George.

Once the gangways were in place, chaos ensued. Elsa and Joseph, followed by the two chauffeurs, came on board. Dashing to the entry-port, Annaliese jumped into her mother's arms, apparently intending to stay there forever. In thirty seconds of tears, laughter, and endearments, all the anxieties were dispelled. Beside them, Edward and Joseph shook hands with great gravity, then, deciding that this was not enough, embraced.

'I am very glad to see you again,' Joseph said. 'Very glad indeed.'

'The pleasure is mutual, sir.' Edward studied his father-in-law and was struck by his wariness: even surrounded by loved ones and two trusted servants, he was watchful. Later, it came as no surprise to learn that this was the first time in over two years that the Archduke had been into Lisbon.

For once, Douglas and George reacted in the same way: both were mightily impressed and slightly overawed by their Habsburg grandfather, both found Elsa totally adorable. It was a natural product of her radiant warmth: when Edward was clasped in her embrace, he found that the mysterious sensuality of Vienna remained potent.

'Edward, my dear boy, I can't tell you how thrilled I am,' she said. 'It's a miracle. Your marriage was the only good thing to come out of the War . . . I'm sure of it. Now, who's this charming young woman?'

'This is Gwen,' Edward replied. 'She looks after the boys.' As he spoke, Joseph was also taking an interest.

'It's a very great honour to meet Your Imperial and Royal Highnesses,' Gwen said and curtsied.

'How lovely,' Elsa cried, clapping her hands. She kissed Gwen, thereby destroying the poor girl's carefully nurtured aplomb. Joseph took her hand and bowed.

Annaliese became involved in an emotional reunion with Karl and Ludwig, servants from the old, sweet days at Schönbrunn. The two men combined friendship with devotion and respect: for a few affecting moments, it was as though *Ihre Hoheit Die Erzherzogin* Annaliese was being welcomed back to Imperial Vienna. George, normally the most reserved of children, was competing with Douglas for Elsa's attention; Gwen was chatting to Joseph as though they were old friends and had softened the wariness in his eyes.

Letting them get on with it, Edward organised porters and stewards. Within ten minutes, all the luggage was ashore and distributed between the two Mercedes cars. Douglas and George refused to be parted from Elsa, So Gwen joined them in one vehicle, leaving Annaliese, Joseph, and Edward to spread out in the other.

'We have to go thirty kilometres,' Joseph said as, with much hooting and fist-shaking, the cars eased out of the madhouse on the quay.

'Is it nice, this place, Cascais?' Annaliese asked.

'One gets used to it,' Joseph grumbled. Immediately, he was ashamed of his churlishness. 'Yes, I must be fair . . . it *is* agreeable. But Vienna . . .' His voice tailed off.

Before reaching the road to the west, they saw enough of Lisbon to appreciate that it was an elegant, well-planned city, with wide streets and handsome buildings.

'All rebuilt after the earthquake in seventeen fifty-five, I suppose?' Edward said.

'So I believe,' Joseph replied, disinterested. There was, Edward saw, an air of spiritual exhaustion about him.

They left the city behind and entered a rural world that had not changed in centuries. It was fertile country, with lime and lemon groves and a riot of colourful flowers and shrubs. The hills to the right were thickly wooded, to the left, there was a lush, verdant plain extending to the River Tagus. Only the road was dry – and very dusty, getting worse as they ascended a gentle but never-ending hill. The leading car, with Elsa, Gwen, and the boys, was fifty yards ahead, yet almost invisible in its cloud of dust. The speed – a steady sixty miles an hour – made it worse. Edward felt sure that the headlong dash was part of the Archduke Joseph's all-consuming suspicion and fear.

There was no slackening of speed through the pretty village of Estoril. Chickens scattered and half-naked children, brown as berries, paused in their games to wave and shout at the growling monsters. Another five minutes and they were in Cascais. This time the speed was reduced to make a sharp turn at the end of the main street. Then, they were climbing a steep hill.

After a mile or so, the narrow road came to an end. At first sight, there was nothing but high stone walls and hedges; close inspection revealed three concealed gateways. A man was standing in one of the entrances. He was bareheaded, he wore no tie, and his shirt sleeves were rolled up, but his trousers and highly polished boots were part of the old Imperial Guard uniform. And he was carrying a rifle. He snapped to attention, swinging the rifle into a ceremonial salute to which Joseph raised a hand in acknowledgement. Not believing his eyes, Edward turned to study the guard and so missed their entrance into the grounds of the villa.

The buildings nestled in a miniature, semi-tropical forest. The main residence was a bungalow, immense and L-shaped, with pink colour-washed walls and windows set beneath semi-circular arches. To Annaliese's delight, the roof was covered with pantiles, very similar to those in the village of Compton Allardyce.

When the powerful engines of the motor cars were turned off, the only sound was that of the breeze stirring the trees. While she was enjoying the almost silent whispering, Annaliese picked up the scents.

'Where are we?' she laughed. 'In the middle of a perfumery?'

'It's the flowers,' Elsa said. 'You can probably smell the orchids and bougainvillea . . . and the gardenias, they're delicious – but there are dozens of others.'

'Beautiful.' Annaliese made several turns in a full circle, drinking in her surroundings. 'And so peaceful. No one for miles.'

'We're not *quite* that isolated,' Elsa said. 'We have two neighbours – though you can hardly see them for all these trees. Your Uncle Max lives over there' – she pointed – 'and there's a Russian gentleman beyond him. It's very cosy.'

Edward was surprised. The proximity of another Habsburg had obviously never been mentioned in the hundreds of letters that Elsa had written. But Annaliese, bent on seeing the interior of the bungalow, shrugged it off.

Indoors, it felt almost chilly. To supplement the insulating effect of the thick walls, many of the shutters were closed.

'You probably think we're mad to block out the sun,' Elsa said as she led the way along a broad passage. 'But it's vital, believe me.'

Glancing at the pictures on the walls, Edward marvelled. Whatever the circumstances of their flight from Vienna, Elsa and Joseph had contrived to bring a great deal with them. This applied to the footman and two maids who were waiting in the background, ready to provide assistance.

They turned a corner into the other half of the bungalow's L-plan and Elsa was opening doors, showing off rooms. 'These are for Gwen and the boys.'

Douglas and George raced in and voiced their approval. Annaliese joined in the praise. 'This is *lovely*,' she said. 'It's nicer than the rooms we had at Schönbrunn – or is that heresy?'

Elsa shook her head. 'My darling, we're better off than ever,' she replied. 'Your father won't admit it, but we *are*. Now, I thought these rooms would be nice for you . . . the bathroom has one of those shower-bath things. I like them.'

'I'm going to try it at once,' Annaliese said.

'Be as quick as you can,' Elsa ordered. 'Douglas told me that you didn't have lunch on your ship, so I'm arranging for a buffet on the terrace.'

She slipped away and Annaliese, assisted by a maid originally from the household of the Archduke whose assassination at Sarajevo had turned the world on its head, plunged into a whirlwind of activity.

Edward prowled, exploring, sniffing things out. He studied the enormous double bed, came to the conclusion that it was big enough to provide both isolation and comfort, and wandered into what he presumed was his dressing-room. Drawing back the blinds, he had a view of the garage, beyond which were several cottages, presumably for the servants. The big Mercedes motor cars were outside the garage and two men were already washing off the dust that had smothered them during the dash from Lisbon. Like the man on duty at the gate, they wore Imperial Guard trousers and boots. Standing on a chair so that he could peer into the shadowy interior of the garage, Edward spotted two rifles leaning against a work-bench.

Annaliese, fresh from the shower and wearing not much more than a simple cotton dress, found him still on the chair, craning to see what lay beyond the cottages.

'What *are* you doing?' she asked.

'Er . . . looking round, you know . . . getting my bearings.' Edward felt rather foolish.

'You'll do that much better outside,' Annaliese replied. 'I'm off to the terrace. I hope you're going to wear something more comfortable than that suit and starched collar?'

'Yes . . . I thought flannels and a sports shirt.'

With a curt nod, Annaliese left him.

Elsa and Joseph virtually lived on the terrace during the summer and autumn. Beneath a huge canvas awning that could be raised and lowered like a shop sun-blind, there was furniture enough to duplicate the facilities of the dining-room and lounge.

Most of the ten-acre garden was invisible from the terrace. In addition to the screen of trees and shrubs, the land fell away in a series of terraced steps, the work of a landscape artist of long ago. Annaliese was delighted to learn that there was a swimming-pool in the garden, and, even better, a secret path down to the beach.

'Tomorrow, darlings,' she promised Douglas and George, who wanted to set off for the sea at once. 'Today, we rest and catch up with all the news.'

When he joined them, Edward pointed out what everyone had been too absorbed to notice: the *Caerphilly Castle*, looking no bigger than a tiny toy at a distance of five miles, was heading out to sea and the long, fifteen-day voyage to Cape Town. After that, he was content to contribute nothing more than the occasional smile or nod to confirm what Annaliese was telling Elsa.

It was all about London, the way people behaved, what they thought of Germany, King George, and, of course, Boothby's. When those subjects had been exhausted – for the time being, at least – Elsa wanted to know about Upper Overs. 'Lord Douglas has tried to describe it, but I'm sure he hasn't done it justice,' Elsa said to Annaliese.

At about six o'clock, the boys decided that they must see something of the garden and went off with Gwen. Soon afterwards, Edward agreed with Joseph that they, too, should take a stroll.

'Foreign affairs,' Elsa sighed after they had gone. 'That's what it will be. Your father never stops worrying about Europe.'

'*You* seem happy enough,' Annaliese said.

'Yes, I am. To be perfectly honest, I don't miss Vienna – but I was always an outsider, anyway.'

'I'm sure Edward will stoke up Father's worst fears.' Annaliese said.

'Don't be unkind,' Elsa said with a smile. 'They were right about nineteen fourteen and that's what counts with Joseph. If Edward can put the fear of God into him, he'll be as happy as my lovely grandchildren. Now, you must tell me about Beatrice . . . she sounds a wonderful person.'

Sure enough, when Edward and Joseph returned as the shadows were lengthening, they both looked grim.

'Is the world in ruins, Joseph?' Elsa called as the men trudged across the lawn.

'Definitely.' The Archduke's face lit up with sardonic glee. 'We've finished it off – left it in ruins. Time for a drink, Edward. I've taken to terribly dry Martinis.' As he spoke, a manservant appeared with a tray.

'Oughtn't we to be changing for dinner?' Edward asked, slightly miffed at hearing serious international problems turned into a joke.

'Bless you, we don't bother with that rubbish,' Elsa said. 'Sit down, my dear. Enjoy yourself.'

If the look on Edward's face made Annaliese want to giggle, there was greater fun in store. The meal arrived in bits and pieces, with Elsa helping to ferry it from the kitchen. It was a single course, albeit one that went on forever. Moreover, Elsa insisted on it being taken *en famille*. For the first time in their lives, Douglas and George ate with both their parents. Gwen also sat at the table. To crown Edward's discomfort and simmering disapproval, Elsa's maid drew up a chair and joined in. Having spent the afternoon in Estoril, she had collected a vast amount of gossip for which Elsa was agog.

Eventually, Edward began to relax, drawn into the strong feeling of family. Without being aware of it, he was drinking much more than usual: following two large Martinis, he was refilling his wine-glass at ten-minute intervals. It was very easy: there were always two nearly full bottles on the table, white Bordeaux and unlabelled, the same as at Schönbrunn before the War.

Dusk came suddenly. Lamps were lit and hung from the metal stays supporting the sun-blind. George fell fast asleep in Elsa's arms and Douglas, slumped across Edward's lap, was going the same way.

Quietly, Gwen took them to their room. At a suggestion from Elsa, Joseph stepped indoors, through the wide French window and sat down at the piano. When he began to play, it was music of such wistful intensity that even Edward was moved by it.

'Schubert,' Annaliese said. 'The soul of Vienna.'

It had to be reunion with her parents that was causing this, Edward thought. As far as he knew, Annaliese hadn't mentioned Vienna in over five years. Now, she was acting as though she were its guardian. Resentful, he was dimly aware that mother and daughter were turning to more serious matters than the exchange of news that had occupied them so far.

'What do you know of the family?' Annaliese asked.

'Very little. Max is next door, of course. I told you that Karl had died, didn't I?'

Annaliese nodded. The deposed Emperor had succumbed to pneumonia at the age of only thirty-five. 'Are Zita and the children still in Madeira?' she asked.

'Yes, but they loathe it. Zita put a note into her last Christmas card to say that she wants to go to Spain, but they can't get permission.'

'Does everyone hate us *that* much?' Annaliese asked.

'Darling, it isn't a question of hate,' Elsa replied. 'The Austrian Government is *terrified* of us. They believe that allowing one Habsburg back into Vienna would restore the monarchy. They're in league with nearly everyone to keep us out.'

Edward knew nothing more until Annaliese shook him awake the following morning.

'Drink this,' she said, wafting a cup of strong, black coffee under his nose.

After screwing up his eyes against the light and taking a few moments to gauge the awfulness of his headache, Edward began struggling upright.

'How did I get to bed?' he asked.

'Father and me,' Annaliese replied. 'It wasn't difficult. You weren't unpleasant, just unconscious.'

'I'm sorry . . . I had no idea I'd drunk so much. That wine is very nice.'

Annaliese shrugged. 'There's no harm done. You've missed breakfast. Do you want me to get you some toast?'

'No, thank you.'

'We're going to the beach,' Annaliese announced. 'You'll be having lunch with Father, Uncle Max, and Vassily.'

'Who's Vassily?' Edward asked plaintively.

'Vassily Kondrashin. It's what our Russian neighbour calls himself.' And with that, she went, leaving Edward to his coffee and a thundering headache.

It was eleven-thirty before he made an appearance in the bungalow's main lounge, where Joseph was immersed in a book. He rose to his feet when he saw Edward, smiling sympathetically. 'How do you feel now?' he asked.

'Not much better,' Edward confessed.

'Will you risk my cure-all?'

'I'll try anything.'

'Did Annaliese tell you about lunch?' Joseph asked, busy at a sideboard with a fearsome collection of bottles.

'Yes.'

'Max and Vassily are looking forward to meeting you. They want to pick your brains – if we can get them working again.' Joseph held up the tumbler, inspecting the mixture he had prepared. 'Yes, that looks about right. This tastes utterly vile, so it's best to get it down at one go.'

Edward did so, closing his eyes as the room began to rotate. 'Sit down,' Joseph advised. 'Keep still and pray.'

Five minutes later, Edward stopped clutching his head and smiled. 'Miraculous,' he said. 'I . . .' He stopped, distracted by Douglas's shouts from the garden. 'I thought they were going to the beach.'

'They're waiting for Aurora,' Joseph replied.

'Who's Aurora?' Edward asked, wondering if there was any end to the villa's novelty and mystery.

'You'll soon find out,' Joseph said and winked.

She arrived with Maximilian von Habsburg and Vassily Kondrashin on the stroke of midday. A devastatingly beautiful woman with a smile that made Edward fear he was drunk again, Aurora dos Santos de

Sequieria was at least thirty years younger than Max, who took colossal pride in presenting her as his mistress. She was, Edward discovered later, the only Portuguese who had ever been allowed into this remote enclave.

Elsa came in from the garden, greeted Aurora, and took her outside to join Annaliese, Gwen, and the boys. Equipped with hampers and beach-bags, they set off, followed at a respectful distance by a man with a rifle. As Edward joined Joseph and his guests at the table on the terrace, he saw another of the ex-soldiers concealing himself in a shrubbery.

Joseph introduced Edward to Max and Vassily, suggesting that they converse in German, their most effective common language. Edward nodded abstractedly: he was fascinated by Vassily Kondrashin.

'What is it, my friend?' Vassily asked, smiling at Edward's bemusement. 'Are you, perhaps, imagining that you detect some sort of likeness to a certain family?'

'Not at all,' Edward replied in his best diplomatic style. 'Please forgive my rudeness – I'm not entirely myself this morning.'

'The poor man has a hangover,' Joseph interjected. 'He is digesting one of my cures.'

Max and Vassily laughed, entertained by Edward's discomfort. As the Russian's face subsided into repose and he turned to grab a bottle of vodka from a tray presented to him by the manservant, the new perspective on his features put his pedigree beyond doubt. Vassily Kondrashin was a Romanov, most probably the Grand Duke Peter, a man whose whereabouts were exercising evil minds from Moscow to Rio de Janeiro.

The meal was served. Aided by the charcoal-grilled steak and fresh orange juice, Edward began to feel much better, able to put up a reasonable show of enjoying Max's hair-raising account of Aurora's sexual appetites. Not to be outdone, Vassily described the proclivities of a woman in Estoril to whom he paid frequent visits. Coffee was served, Vassily clung to the vodka bottle and the conversation turned to international politics.

Two men, Joseph Stalin and Benito Mussolini, dominated the conversation until five o'clock. Although he made many useful contributions to the debate, Edward began to dread the inevitable question.

'What does the British Government think of this pair?' Joseph asked.

Edward had decided that forthright honesty was his only course. 'Nothing,' he replied. 'They hope that Russia under Stalin will be in too much of a mess to cause trouble to the rest of the world. As for Mussolini' – he smiled wryly – 'they simply don't take him seriously.'

'Incredible.' Max shook his head and scowled.

'So, Great Britain *is* pursuing a policy of isolationism?' Joseph asked.

'I wouldn't call it a *policy*,' Edward said. 'That implies that it's been thought out and agreed. As things stand, it's happening by default. Britain has no time for anything but its own domestic problems; France is the same; and look at America, for God's sake.'

'An understandable reaction to the War, I think,' Vassily said. 'Necessary, too, I imagine.'

'Of course,' Edward agreed. 'Dangerous, though. It's creating a vacuum. Mussolini sees himself filling it, but I doubt he can.'

'Can this new rabble-rouser in Germany do it?' Joseph asked.

'You mean Adolf Hitler?' Edward said. 'I don't think the British Government has heard of him.'

'Not heard of him,' Vassily spluttered. 'What about that fiasco in Munich – you know, the beer-hall business with Ludendorff? That damned nearly worked.'

Edward shook his head. 'It isn't regarded as significant.'

After that, as Max and Vassily conjured up a picture of a Europe at the mercy of madmen and tyrants, Edward wished that the conversation would end. This was not possible until the beach-party returned shortly after six o'clock. In the midst of all the shouting and laughing, Annaliese saw that Edward was in a bad mood, cut off from what was happening around him. With a flamboyant display of flashing eyes and innuendo, Aurora insisted that Max should take her home at once and Vassily left with them. George was determined that his version of an exciting afternoon on the beach should prevail over Douglas's bawling.

In the midst of the happy uproar, the evening meal was appearing. Elsa thrust a plate at Edward, telling him to help himself. Deciding to cheer him up, Annaliese slipped into the seat beside him.

'Not such a good afternoon?' she asked sympathetically.

'Oh, it's not been so bad,' Edward replied, making an effort to shake of his disgruntled boredom. 'Your father and his friends weren't too pleased with what I had to tell them.'

'They never will be,' Annaliese said. 'Mama believes that there's *nothing* that will please them. But they're ever so happy being miserable.'

'It must be easy enough to get into that state after what they've been through – especially Vassily.'

'Sssh,' Annaliese whispered, squeezing his hand. 'I knew you'd recognise him . . . I told Mama as much.'

'He did come as rather a surprise,' Edward admitted.

'It will be different tomorrow,' Annaliese promised. 'You can come to the beach with us. Max and Vassily aren't here *every* day.'

'*Nearly* every day?' Edward asked, picking up the hint.

'I'm afraid so.'

Annaliese saw that Edward was considering a protest, but Douglas decided it was time for the story of how he had caught a shark with his bare hands. George – who contested each detail of the yarn with a comical scepticism – reduced Elsa and Joseph to helpless laughter. At the end of a hectic day, the bravura story-telling performance soon wore the boys out and they were whisked away to bed.

'Do you think you could ever get used to this way of living?' Elsa asked Edward.

'Don't be silly, Mama,' Annaliese laughed. 'If we carry on like this, he'll be out of his mind in two days.'

But Edward was thinking. 'I wouldn't be too sure about that,' he said eventually. 'I admit that this is going to take a bit of getting used to, but I can't help wondering if hiding away in a beautiful place like this isn't the best way of dealing with the twentieth century.'

'Good God!' Annaliese gasped and slumped against the back of her chair in a mock faint.

Elsa wanted to know what was at the back of Edward's mind. 'You think there will be more trouble?' she asked. 'Another war?'

'It's very likely.'

'Why?'

'The terms imposed on Germany at Paris are a prescription for disaster,' Edward replied. 'Marshal Foch called it a twenty-year armistice, and influential people – who know a thing or two – are starting to agree with him. As Annaliese knows, *my* pet hate is the break-up of the Austrian Empire. It's thrown a very volatile region into a dangerously unstable condition.'

'There, Joseph,' Elsa declared, 'the Habsburgs *were* useful.'

'What did Aunt Elisabeth always say?' Joseph teased. 'According to her, the world would still be in the dark ages if it weren't for us.'

When the subsequent bout of joking died down, Elsa began to reminisce and the balmy evening drifted into a nostalgic haze that went on until Annaliese and Joseph were almost falling asleep.

'It's been a lovely day,' Annaliese said when she and Edward were alone in their room and ready for bed. 'You will come to the beach with us tomorrow?'

'Yes, I will.'

'We can swim. And tennis. Do you remember St Malo?' Briefly, Annaliese was wide-awake, her eyes dancing at the memory. Just as quickly, however, the dream was gone. 'I'm sure we could organise something on the beach.'

'Leave it to Douglas,' Edward laughed, doing his best to gloss over Annaliese's disheartening change of mood.

'Was there any mention of Leopold when you were talking to Father and the others?' she asked.

'No. What about your mother? Does she talk about him?'

Annaliese shook her head vigorously and they climbed into bed, carefully keeping themselves apart. Uneasy at the prospect of silence, Edward asked, 'Why is your father so frightened?'

'What do you mean?'

'Is it *really* necessary to have armed men round the place? This afternoon, there was one skulking in the bushes and another patrolling the grounds.'

'And I have no doubt that one of them is out there now, at this minute,' Annaliese said. 'Yes, Edward, it is necessary. Father, Max, and Vassily have many enemies.'

'I appreciate that the Bolsheviks want Vassily, but aren't your father and Max laying it on a bit thick? Surely, they aren't important enough to trouble extremists?' Too late, Edward realised that he sounded patronising.

'All Habsburgs are important,' Annaliese retorted. 'That's why we're banned from setting foot inside Austria. The gangsters in the Government are terrified of us because they know the public is on our side. If they couldn't get anyone else, most of Vienna would be happy to have a joke like Max as Emperor. I'm going to sleep.'

And, in less than a minute, she did. That, and her acidic calm, was a more crushing display of contempt than the blazing anger she had shown in the row over Charles Templeton.

During the next six days, they rubbed along in an alliance that was, by turns, comfortable and uneasy. Attempting to work his passage back to favour, Edward did his best to comply with the way life was conducted at the villa. He joined in several of the expeditions to the beach, felt relaxed enough to make a fool of himself, and allowed Aurora to flirt with him. On Thursday and Saturday, he sat through two more lunches and afternoons with Joseph, Max, and Vassily.

He came to accept the informality of the evenings, even starting to enjoy the free-for-all that replaced his idea of what dinner should be. Yet there was an extraordinary irony in the long, casual summer days that baffled Edward and made him prey to feelings of resentment. Lounging on the beach, chasing Douglas and George into the waves, eating sea-food salad with her fingers, Annaliese became more remote with each day that passed. In pre-war Vienna, she had been careless of her status. Most of her friends and contacts in England needed reminding of her background – and Annaliese was never the one to do it. Here, on an isolated spit of land jutting into the Atlantic, where she had given up wearing cosmetics and stockings, Annaliese somehow acquired an aura that was undeniably *royal*.

Having failed to get close to her by all other means, Edward tried to initiate love-making when they went to bed on Sunday evening. The rebuff was crushing and, he suspected, final.

19

8–10 June 1925

'The disgusting spectacle has been covered'

The following day began badly. Waking at seven, Edward found himself alone. When she returned, nearly an hour later, Annaliese said that she had wanted a walk before breakfast. Her tone implied that she disliked being asked to account for her movements.

Douglas and George set off for the beach earlier than usual, accompanied only by Gwen and Aurora. There was vague talk of a trip in a boat belonging to a fisherman who was a friend of Aurora's. Annaliese, who intended spending the day with Elsa, annoyed Edward by failing to issue a warning about the possible dangers of going to sea with a strange man.

'Don't worry,' Annaliese said, understanding Edward's look only too well. 'You don't imagine that Gwen would let them come to any harm, do you? Why waste breath?'

Sullenly, Edward went off to lose himself in the garden. After allowing a tactful interval to pass, his father-in-law tracked him down.

'God bless the ladies, eh?' Joseph said. 'One really can't live without them, but it's often impossible to live *with* them.'

'True, very true.' Edward forced a laugh and looked expectantly at Joseph, certain that he wished to say something important. The Archduke guided him to a bench beside a lily-pond.

'Annaliese is having a difficult time,' he said.

'Why?' Edward asked.

Joseph shrugged. 'I think it's the old story, the *Viennese* thing.

We're a peculiar bunch – as a "foreigner", Elsa can tell you all about it.'

'Isn't it strange that this place should bring it out?' Edward ventured. 'You can't imagine anywhere *less* like Vienna.'

'Not at all. My dear boy, where *is* your common sense?'

'You and her mother?' Edward asked.

'It has to be. Annaliese has had no contact with Vienna for eight years, yes? She's in England, fully adapted to your ways and making a good job of it.' Edward nodded. 'Everyone – including Annaliese herself – thinks she's cured. Then, at long last, she comes to see us and poof, bang! The old disease takes hold.'

'You think so?'

'I'm sure of it. Be patient with her.' Joseph became very earnest. 'Do you know what we Viennese often do with things we don't like?'

'You turn your backs.'

'Good boy.' Joseph smiled, considering the problem solved. 'Not only do we turn our backs, we tip-toe away if we get half a chance.'

'Is that what she's doing to me?' Edward laughed.

'Yes – but it's more complicated, you see. There are some problems we only *pretend* to ignore. Deep down, Annaliese knows that she will never go far from you. You've always been happy enough together, haven't you?'

'Of course.'

'All that she needs is room,' Joseph said. '*Spiritual* room. Give her that and she'll come back soon enough.'

They stayed on the bench, chatting of this and that until the manservant came to announce that Max and Vassily had arrived.

'I'd forgotten that we were lunching today,' Edward said as they went towards the terrace.

'Be brave.' Joseph smiled. 'We have so little entertainment here . . . we rely on you for amusement and information. Is that asking too much?'

'No, it isn't,' Edward said happily.

Reality was a different matter, however. Max was worked up about Hitler. A friend had sent him a copy of a four-week-old Munich newspaper that was determined to sensationalise the National

Socialist Party and its leader. Max, goaded by Vassily, constructed a scenario in which the streets would be running with blood inside two years. Annoyed that his powerful arguments against such an eventuality were disregarded, Edward became restive.

His impatience with Max's lurid theories was heightened by a growing unease about Annaliese and Elsa. Were they talking about him? If so, the conversation could hardly be as comfortable as the one between him and Joseph on the bench by the pond, a sham that had taken no account of the rumbling after-effects of the terrible row at Cadogan Square ten days ago. It was ridiculous wasting time with the mischievously apocalyptic visions of old men when his marriage was in such a parlous state. He must find Annaliese and talk to her – *properly.*

The chance came when one of the maids was clearing the table after lunch. 'If you'll excuse me, I'll go and look for Annaliese,' Edward said. 'There's something I want to ask her.'

Max and Vassily exchanged looks of mock horror and disbelief. What on earth did a man want with his wife when there was the intellectual thrill of solving the world's problems?

Joseph understood. 'At the swimming-pool, I think,' he told Edward.

Nodding his thanks, Edward hurried off and promptly lost his way. The pool was situated in the garden's fourth tier, an especially pleasant and secluded area. Anxious and not bothering to count the levels, Edward found himself at the end of the garden. Flustered, he retraced his steps, nearly ending up back at the house before spotting the right path. Last-minute uncertainty made Edward hesitant, fearful of losing his way again. Without meaning it to be so, his approach to the pool was quiet and unobtrusive.

Certainly, Elsa was unaware of him. She was lying on a sunbed in front of the pavilion that served as a changing-room and store. Until ten minutes ago, she and Annaliese had been talking about Ralph, Celia, and Allardyce Castle: now, Elsa was miles away, mulling over what she had learned. Her swimming-costume was in the very latest fashion. Its wanton daring astounded Edward: it also confirmed that the fifty-five-year-old Archduchess had a body to make many much younger women jealous. Beside Elsa, another sunbed had a towelling robe draped across it.

Lazily, hardly disturbing the surface of the pool, Annaliese was swimming. Not moving or calling out for fear of startling Elsa, Edward watched as his wife paddled towards a ladder and started to climb out of the water. She had her back to him.

At first, what he saw simply failed to register. Annaliese was standing upright on the stone edge of the pool before Edward's mind finally accepted that she was naked.

His first reaction was unashamed admiration of her supple, clean-limbed beauty. That was soured by memory of the way she had refused him the previous evening. Then he thought of the guards, the men who were everywhere, unseen, hiding in bushes. A blind, unreasoning anger took him by storm.

'Annaliese! What the *hell* do you think you're playing at?'

The enraged roar had very different effects on the two women. Pulling her sun-glasses off, Elsa sat bolt-upright, bewildered and slightly frightened. In sharp contrast, Annaliese turned with deliberate composure to face Edward. The width of the pool did nothing to dim the flare in her eyes.

'What is it *this* time?' she demanded.

'*What is it?* Are you mad?' This was an argument that Edward, boiling with indignation, had no intention of losing. 'Why aren't you wearing your costume?'

'Because I prefer to swim without it!' Annaliese shouted. 'Mama doesn't mind.'

'What about those blasted guards?' Edward bellowed. 'Don't you care if they see you like *that*? I do. I care very much!'

'The guards aren't here,' Annaliese retorted. 'They know they have to keep away when we're using the pool. *They* respect us.'

'So much for your safety,' Edward sneered.

'They're still protecting us. Avoiding this place doesn't mean that they have to neglect the boundaries, you idiot.'

'Don't argue with me!' Edward bawled, stung by the insult. 'Cover yourself up.'

She thought of defying him. He sensed it and a battle of wills developed across the still water of the pool. Annaliese's final decision stemmed only from the need to put an end to her mother's excruciating embarrassment. Running to the sunbed, she snatched up the robe, put it on, and tied the waist-cord with a savage flourish.

'Is that better?' she called to Edward, introducing a note of mockery. 'The disgusting spectacle has been covered.'

'Don't be childish.' Edward was riled by her derision. 'It's beyond me why I should have to tell you these simple things. I really—'

Catching sight of Elsa, Edward felt light-headed, at a loss to know how he could possibly have forgotten her presence. She was gaping at him, utter dismay on her face. Drawing breath to begin an apology, Edward found that his mind had stopped working. Conscious only of crushing mortification, he turned tail and fled.

Tripping up a flight of steps gave him a jolt that edged him towards reality. He could see the terrace and decided to go back to it; if he rejoined the conversation, there would be a chance to think of a way of putting things right. But, as he neared them, the three men at the table were staring at him with intense curiosity. At least, Max and Vassily were; Joseph was concerned. They must, of course, have heard the screaming and shouting from the pool. Averting his eyes, Edward veered off at a new angle, making for the front of the villa. Perhaps if he went for a walk, everything would have changed when he came back.

The guard patrolling the area between the three entrances heard Edward's footsteps and turned to give him a respectful wave. But there was something else competing for the man's attention: so faint that it was barely audible, a motor was labouring up the hill from Cascais. To Edward, the very unusual event was a potentially face-saving diversion; he joined the one-time member of the Imperial Army to wait for the outcome. As the noise grew louder, it was apparent that the engine, a fairly small one, was in a bad way, misfiring and howling repeated protests. Growing louder and louder, the noise was enough to wake the dead in the thirty seconds before the thing appeared.

Edward was tense. He had seen the guard cock his rifle and release the safety catch. After the suspense, what finally came round the bend was laughable: a boy of no more than fourteen, astride the most amazing motor cycle. Built from parts of at least three different machines, it was, in its bizarre way, an engineering miracle.

The boy and the guard knew each other and were chatting in Portuguese. But Edward did not remain baffled for long; the boy pulled a buff-coloured envelope from inside his ragged shirt and made a stab at saying, 'Boothby-Graffoe'.

'Sir, are you ill?' Edward, who had felt himself go as white as a sheet, was so surprised to hear the guard speak English that he dropped the envelope.

There were other distractions. Disturbed by the fearful noise of the motor cycle, Joseph was hurrying to the gate. Behind him, Max and Vassily were wondering whether to be brave or cautious. Still further back, Annaliese and Elsa were emerging from the garden. Elsa was now muffled in a long robe, identical to Annaliese's.

Edward smiled stupidly at the guard, who had picked the envelope up and was holding it out to him.

'Is it a cablegram?' Vassily asked.

'Looks like it,' Max replied.

From far off, Annaliese's voice said, 'I know what that is – it *can* only be one thing.'

Slowly, unwillingly, using time-wasting care, Edward tore the envelope open. He read the words pasted on to the slip of paper three times before looking up. Because his eyes happened to meet Elsa's, he spoke directly to her and no one else. 'He's still alive,' he said.

Elsa took the cablegram from Edward's inert hand. Annaliese looked over her shoulder. Then Joseph had it, sharing it with Max and Vassily, muttering a translation for Vassily's benefit. Annaliese was staring at her feet, knowing nothing except the desire to be a hundred miles away. The paper was back with Edward and he read it again.

FATHER HAD A HEART ATTACK ON THURSDAY. QUITE A BAD ONE, THEY SAY. HE IS MAKING PROGRESS.
BEATRICE

The boy on the motor cycle was talking. Elsa moved swiftly to Edward's side. 'He's asking if you want to send a reply,' she said.

'Yes. I think so. Er . . . yes.' Edward looked helplessly at the envelope. Grinning proudly at his skill in keeping it there during the ascent of the hill, the boy took a pencil from behind his ear and offered his back as a makeshift desk. Using impeccably clear capital letters, Edward wrote Beatrice's name and address – she was bound to be at Upper Overs. Elsa became concerned as he stared up at the sky to consider the point. Satisfied, he wrote: COMING AT ONCE. EDWARD, and handed the pencil and envelope to the boy.

'Joseph, we need money,' Elsa said.

There was a moment or two of confused searching. In the end, it was Vassily who produced a banknote. Thrilled by the scale of the tip, the boy shouted thanks and farewells to everyone, coaxed his incredible machine back into howling life, and pointed it at Cascais.

Elsa shepherded Edward towards the villa. After a muttered consultation with Joseph, Max and Vassily decided to make themselves scarce. Annaliese and Joseph were left outside the gate, staring at each other.

'This is what happened with his mother,' she said.

Joseph was mystified. 'I'm sorry . . . I thought that was influenza.'

'No, no.' Before reverting to a toneless voice that was devoid of all emotion, Annaliese was irritated by his failure to grasp the point. 'She was taken ill and died while Edward was out of the country with *me*!'

'My dear child, that's no more than an unhappy coincidence.' Joseph tried to put a comforting arm round Annaliese but she stepped away from him.

'I sometimes think that Edward has never forgiven me for keeping him away from his mother. Now *this*.'

Joseph recognised the need to be firm. 'Come inside, my dear. We must see what we can do to help.'

Reluctantly, Annaliese agreed.

They found Edward slumped in a chair, dazed and incapable of action. Elsa, crouching at his side, was worried.

'You're going back to see your father, of course,' Joseph said.

'Yes, I must,' Edward paused. 'I mean, there's no question of me *not* going.'

'I understand that,' Elsa said gently. 'How?'

Edward looked blank. 'I beg your pardon?'

'How are you going to get there?'

'By boat. There must be a fairly frequent service from Lisbon.'

'I don't know, my dear. It isn't a thing that's ever interested us.' Elsa turned to Joseph. 'Do you know anything about sailings to England?'

'I'm afraid not.' Joseph's face lit up with an idea. 'How about the train?'

It was while Edward was considering this that a dramatic change swept over him. One moment he was numbed, apparently useless, the next he was alert and incisive.

'No, that's out of the question,' he said. 'Going through Spain and getting over the Pyrenees would take longer than a boat to Southampton. I need the telephone, please.'

Elsa sprang into action, bringing in the guard who spoke Portuguese to deal with the exchange in Estoril. Edward dashed to the bedroom, collected the travel documents, and discovered that both Union Castle and P & O had offices in Lisbon.

Ignored in the sudden outburst of activity, Joseph went out to the terrace where Annaliese was standing like a statue, hands thrust deep into the pockets of her robe.

'What about the boys and Gwen?' Joseph asked.

'They'll be back when they're ready,' Annaliese replied, not bothering to find out precisely what her father had meant. 'I'm going back to the pool.' Seeing Joseph's amazement, she added, 'To dress. My clothes are in the pavilion.'

It was no sort of response to the situation and Joseph's face was troubled as he watched her stride across the lawn. Before disappearing into the trees, Annaliese tossed her head; it may have been involuntary, but it was awfully like the gestures of defiance she used to make as a child. Defiance against what? Joseph wondered.

When Annaliese returned after a deliberately drawn-out thirty minutes, Elsa was being very, very calm. It was her way of counteracting panic, a disgraceful condition that she always refused to tolerate.

'Darling, where *have* you been?' she asked.

'Dressing,' Annaliese replied curtly. 'Essential, I would have thought.'

Elsa winced at the unsubtle reminder of the scene at the pool. 'There's a ship at midnight,' she said. 'Edward has a berth on it.' She hesitated. 'He seems to be under the impression that he will be travelling alone.'

'Where is he?' Annaliese asked.

'In your rooms, I think.'

'I'll see,' Annaliese said and went.

Busy packing a small case, Edward stared at her distractedly. Momentarily, he gave the impression that he had no idea who she was. 'Did your mother tell you?' he said.

'There's a sailing tonight?'

'Yes. It's a cargo ship that carries a few passengers – plenty good enough.' Edward cleared his throat. 'I assumed that . . . er . . . I thought you would want to stay here – with the boys, of course. I mean to say, you've waited so long to see your parents, you can't leave now.' He tried to smile. 'Besides, George wouldn't take too kindly to being snatched away from Grandmama at such short notice.'

'Yes, I would prefer to stay here,' Annaliese said. 'There isn't anything I could do if I came with you.'

'Well . . . Father's devoted to you,' Edward said. 'He'll understand, though.' Conscious of the conversation's painful awkwardness, Edward pointed to a pile of papers on the dressing-table. 'That's everything you need for getting back – tickets and whatnot.'

'Thank you.'

'I'm going to leave most of my stuff here,' Edward said. 'I need to travel light. That won't make things difficult for you, will it?'

'Gwen and I will cope.'

'Splendid.' Edward rubbed his hands together in a show of bogus good humour, pretending that everything was as it should be. 'I was wondering about Father's heart attack.'

'Yes?' Annaliese asked.

But Edward thought better of it. 'Nothing,' he said. 'It was nothing.'

Do you think that row over Charles Templeton had anything to do with him being ill? That was what he had wanted to ask and Annaliese came close to telling him what she thought. 'He looked unwell,' she said. 'You'll give him all my love and very best wishes, won't you? Tell him that I shall be down to see him as soon as I get back.'

'Of course.' Edward looked as if he were bracing himself to have a tooth dragged out. 'Look, Annaliese, my dear, that nonsense at the pool . . . I'm sorry if . . .'

'I don't think we should attempt to discuss that at the moment,' Annaliese snapped. 'Your main concern must be your father.'

'Yes, I see that,' Edward mumbled.

'I'll go and keep a look-out for the boys,' Annaliese said.

They both knew that it was an excuse to get her out of that room and away from him.

Annaliese approached Douglas and George with the skill and concern that had been so glaringly absent from her conversation with Edward.

It was gone six o'clock when they returned, bursting with enthusiasm for their boat trip. While Aurora, after a quick word with Elsa, slipped away to Max's villa and Gwen made threatening noises about two young gentlemen who needed a good scrub, Annaliese listened to the story of the great voyage. Then, when the boys had been dumped in the bath, Annaliese joined Gwen, ostensibly to help with the washing.

'While you were away on the high seas, we've had some news from home,' Annaliese said. 'Aunt Bee sent us a cablegram.'

Douglas was excited: Gwen and George knew better.

'Grandpa Douglas isn't very well,' Annaliese went on. 'Papa is a little bit worried about it.'

'I expect I would be if Papa was poorly,' Douglas said.

'Yes, I'm sure you would, darling. Papa feels that he should go home to look after Grandpa.'

'To help Auntie Bee?' George suggested.

'That's *just* what Papa said,' Annaliese replied. 'Now, the big thing is, what do *we* do? Papa didn't think it was right for us to spoil our holiday, so he says we should stay here.'

In the middle of a silence that she found nerve-racking, Annaliese noticed that Douglas was watching George closely, looking to him for guidance on how to react.

'Papa's right,' George said at last. 'Grandpa Douglas isn't going to die, is he?'

'Good gracious me, no!' Annaliese laughed. 'Not for ages and ages and ages.'

George was satisfied. 'When's Papa going?' Douglas wanted to know.

'Tonight,' Annaliese told him. 'Luckily, there's a ship that can take him.'

'In that case, we shall have to be good,' Douglas said.

'Yes.' George gave his all-important agreement.

Seeing that the boys would be content to play with their model boats for a few minutes, Annaliese beckoned Gwen out of the bathroom. They went to the room that Elsa had set aside as a day-nursery: because of the superb weather, it had yet to be used as such.

'What's the trouble?' Gwen asked.

'Heart attack. Last Thursday.'

'Poor man.' Gwen was upset. 'How is he?'

'Beatrice said that he was recovering.' Annaliese sighed. 'I really don't know what that means.'

'He's at Upper Overs?' Gwen asked.

'Either that or the hospital in Crowborough,' Annaliese surmised.

'I hope Miss Beatrice has sent for Matthew,' Gwen said. 'There are all sorts of things he can do and he loves Lord Douglas.' She gave Annaliese a shrewd stare. 'Whose idea was it for us to stay here?'

'Call it mutual consent,' Annaliese said wearily.

Gwen's eyes sharpened. 'Has something happened while we were away?'

'Yes.' With a quiet, simmering anger, Annaliese told the story of the row at the swimming-pool.

'One of them guards *might* have been getting a crafty eyeful,' Gwen said. 'Be fair, see it from his side.'

'But he was so insufferably *dictatorial*, Gwen. Mama was dreadfully upset by it. And right on top of that shocking business over Mr

Templeton – wouldn't you have thought he might have learned *something*?' Annaliese paused. She was quivering with anger. 'I tell you straight, I cannot begin to imagine what might have been said or done if that cablegram hadn't turned up and changed everything – for the time being, at least.'

'So . . .' Gwen was thinking hard '. . . you've got two weeks to think about it.'

'That's what it boils down to,' Annaliese said.

By eight o'clock, the boys were in bed, enjoying the very rare treat of being told a story by Edward. Next door, Gwen was clattering round in her bedroom; under the pretext of tidying up, she was attempting to blot out the argument that Annaliese and Elsa were having on the terrace. Their voices weren't all that loud, but with the windows and shutters open to obtain the benefit of the breeze that always sprang up at this time in the evening, you never knew.

'. . . I do, I really do,' Elsa was saying crossly. 'I find your attitude incomprehensible, darling.'

'It isn't really necessary,' Annaliese retorted. 'And I'm in no mood to put myself out after that business at the pool.'

'Annaliese, the poor man's father is very ill. You should forget a quarrel.'

'Not this time, Mama. And that was much more than a *quarrel*.'

'*This time?*' Elsa repeated. 'Are you saying that this has happened before?'

'That doesn't matter,' Annaliese snapped, wanting to retreat from having said too much. 'I do not want to go to Lisbon to wave at Edward.'

'Someone must,' Elsa said.

'You do it then,' Annaliese flared.

'Very well, I will.'

An hour later, Edward was ready to leave. After deluging him in platitudes, Annaliese tried to inject warmth into their kiss. The look on Edward's face told her that she had failed. She was untroubled; he was stern, more sure of himself, probably glad to be going. When he went to the waiting motor, Annaliese stayed at the door of the villa.

After making sure that Elsa was comfortable, Joseph turned to Edward and said, 'I hope everything will be good,' with a wealth of meaning.

'Thank you.' Edward returned the Archduke's heartfelt embrace. 'I'm sure you'll look after Annaliese.'

'Of course. Worry about your father, not that.' On impulse, Joseph attempted a joke. 'Send the word, and we'll pack her off to you by the next boat.'

'That isn't a job I'd envy,' Edward said grimly and climbed in to take his place alongside Elsa.

As the Mercedes moved forward, Annaliese and Edward waved to each other. They both stopped too soon, Annaliese because she couldn't be bothered to prolong the display, Edward because he was distracted. The passenger compartment was flooded with light from the powerful headlamps of the other big Mercedes which was following them.

'Joseph insisted on it,' Elsa said, not waiting to be asked. 'Safety in numbers, you see. There are two men behind us, I expect.'

'Do you believe in all this?' Edward asked.

'Yes. That doesn't mean I like it.' Briefly, Elsa's handsome face was infinitely sad. 'When we first came here, one of Joseph's cousins was in the house that Vassily has now. He was shot and killed while he was gardening.'

Nothing more was said until, after another high-speed dash that was all the more worrying in darkness, they reached the docks in Lisbon. Edward's ship was easy to find, well-illuminated and still loading cargo, and an officer was waiting at the foot of the passenger gangway.

'Is it Mr Boothby-Graffoe, sir?' the man called.

'That's right.' Edward turned to Elsa. 'Look, don't bother to hang around. I shall be all right now.'

He saw that she toyed with the idea of arguing, then thought better of it. 'Goodbye, Edward,' she said. 'Please give my love and *very* best wishes to your father.'

'I will.'

'And remind him that he owes me a letter. I shall expect to hear from him within days.'

'I'll let him know,' Edward laughed.

The driver was holding the door open, the foot of the gangway was five yards away. As Edward gathered himself to make the move, Elsa laid a hand on his arm. 'A kiss for your mother-in-law,' she smiled.

Mechanically, he pecked at her cheek, only to find that she was shaking her head. 'No, that won't do,' she murmured. 'Like this.'

It was a full, sensual kiss that left him uncertain of his surroundings. 'Think of Annaliese,' Elsa whispered. 'And learn to relax, for God's sake. There are far better things to do with a beautiful body than shout at it. Go on, be off with you.'

The two powerful motors burst into life and Edward found that he was on the gangway, watching as the cars roared away, back to the lonely hill above Cascais.

Conscious that it was pointless, he waved.

It was five-fifteen on the morning of 10 June when Edward left the Customs' shed at Southampton. Even before he discovered that there was an hour to wait for the first train to London, he had been hoping to find a way of avoiding the capital. A journey across country would be much quicker.

The taxi-driver kicking his heels outside the Cunard offices needed little persuading to undertake the journey.

'It'll cost a bit, mind,' he warned after Edward had pointed out their destination on a map.

'Will ten pounds cover it?'

The man, who had been hoping for half that, promised to be at Upper Overs by nine o'clock.

It was a few minutes to when Beatrice heard the crunch of wheels on the gravel. Not bothering to look through a window, she dashed outside. Edward was out of the cab in time to cushion her wild leap into his arms.

'Oh, thank God,' Beatrice gasped. 'You did wonderfully well to get here so quickly.'

'I wasn't making any mistakes with this one,' Edward said quietly. Turning, he waved his thanks to the departing taxi-driver, then steered Beatrice into the house.

'You've come on your own?' she asked,

'Yes. It was quicker.' For the moment, that was all Edward wanted to say about it. 'How's Father?'

'He's had a very good night,' Beatrice replied. 'The best yet. And he insisted on a cooked breakfast . . . That's the first time.'

'Good.' They were in the sitting-room and Edward was studying his sister with concern. 'You look done-in,' he said gently.

'I am,' she admitted. 'Things will get easier now – the worst is over.' She crossed her fingers and touched wood. 'It's Polly's turn to sit with him tonight. Ah . . . here she is.'

Hearing the arrival, Polly had come to see if anything was needed from the kitchen. Edward decided on tea and toast.

'Tell me what happened,' he said when he and Beatrice were settled.

'Last Thursday . . . yes. I was in London, of course.' Beatrice collected her thoughts. 'It was about a quarter to twelve, coming up to lunchtime. Father was in the garden talking to old Ben. Apparently, Father thought he was suffering from indigestion. He told Ben that it was getting worse. Then he sort of fainted. Polly telephoned Doctor Thomas who said to make Father comfortable, but not to move him.'

'Good job it's summer,' Edward said, releasing some of his tension with a wry smile.

'It started to rain,' Beatrice went on. 'Quite heavily. Ben covered him up with a tarpaulin . . . You should have heard Mrs Grove. Anyway, Doctor Thomas got here. Father was conscious and it wasn't very difficult to diagnose what had happened. Oh, I forgot . . . by this time, Polly had telephoned Boothby's and I was on my way down.'

'I suppose Doctor Thomas wanted Father to go to hospital?' Edward said.

Beatrice pulled a face. 'I had to agree to him staying here. I didn't like it, but we'd reached the stage where Father was so upset that Doctor Thomas thought he might have another attack.'

'In his shoes, I don't think I'd want to go to hospital,' Edward said.

'Why?'

'You know how much he loves this house, Bee. It's where he'd want to die.' He took her hand. 'I know its awful to say such things, but it *is* what Father would be thinking.'

Beatrice nodded. 'Yes, I understand.'

'You've told him that I'm expected?' Edward asked.

'Yes. In any case, he saw the telegram arrive. He's allowed to potter round his room . . . Doctor Thomas says it's good for him.'

'I believe that's the current thinking,' Edward said. 'Lying around too much can bring on another attack.'

'Don't.' Beatrice shuddered.

Doctor Thomas was due to make a visit at ten-thirty and Edward decided to wait for that before going upstairs. To fill in the time, they rambled through a series of mundane issues.

'What about Ralph?' Edward asked suddenly. 'Should we let him know that Father isn't too well?'

'I tried,' Beatrice said. 'He's in America . . . not due back until the seventeenth.'

'Oh, yes.' Edward clapped a hand to his forehead. 'I helped to arrange that visit.'

'What's it in aid of?'

Edward had to search his mind. 'Basically, he wants to find out what the Americans think on various issues. He's hoping to see the Secretary of State. A couple of Congressmen have definitely promised to speak to him.'

'Why?' Beatrice asked, bluntly sceptical.

'It will be the people who are against isolationism,' Edward said. 'The idea is that Ralph can make a speech or two and change opinion at Westminster.'

'Could he?'

'I doubt it very much. Stanley Baldwin is determined to ignore everything beyond Dover. Everyone knows that, but it won't stop Ralph enjoying himself. A lot of Americans will talk to him because of what he is – a real live duke.'

'Celia isn't happy at him being away,' Beatrice said.

'Hasn't she gone with him?'

'Hardly.' Beatrice was amused by Edward's forgetfulness. 'She's expecting the baby in two weeks . . . You can't expect her to go gallivanting across the Atlantic in that condition.'

'I wonder if she was ever given a choice?'

'You still don't care for him, do you?' Beatrice asked.

'No, I don't,' Edward sighed. 'To be honest, I'm beginning to regret this alliance with him. I'm looking for a way to finish it.'

'You don't think he's useful?' Beatrice asked, then regretted her cynicism.

'No, it isn't that,' Edward replied. 'It isn't a good idea for me to be involved in politics – in any form.'

Beatrice gave her brother a concerned look. 'Have you been told that?' she asked. 'Officially?'

Shuffling, Edward stared at his feet. 'Yes,' he said at last. 'As a matter of fact, I was given quite a ticking off.'

'When?'

'A few days before I started my holiday.'

Beatrice remained silent, wondering what part this might have played in Edward's foul mood on that Thursday evening when the row over Charles had erupted.

Doctor Thomas arrived and went up to Lord Douglas. The examination lasted nearly half an hour and the doctor, an old family friend, professed himself satisfied at the end of it.

'I'd say the immediate worries are over,' he said. 'No wild optimism, or stupid behaviour, though. Am I making myself clear?' Beatrice and Edward nodded. 'It won't be too long before your father imagines that he's as fit as a flea. He can get outside for the sun and fresh air – that will do him a power of good – but you'll have to watch him like a hawk to make sure there are no mock heroics.' Again, Beatrice and Edward nodded and Doctor Thomas's severity faded. 'He knows you're here, Edward, so you'd better go up – otherwise he's in danger of boiling over.'

Edward hesitated in the doorway, turning to look at Beatrice in a way that showed he was nervous. She gave him a quick smile. Squaring his shoulders, he set off.

Lord Douglas, propped up against a great mound of pillows, was reading *The Times*. When Edward poked his head round the door after a tentative knock, the old man's face was illuminated by a smile of sheer delight. Crossing to the bed, Edward realised that all the windows were open. Instead of the awful frowstiness one expected from the sick-room, the air was full of the scent of late blossom from the garden. Lord Douglas extended a hand, Edward grasped it, bent to kiss his father's cheek, and sat down on the chair that had obviously been used for many hours of anxious vigil.

'I'm damned glad to see you, my boy,' Lord Douglas said. 'It's an awful shame about your holiday, but I feel much better now you're here.'

'I came as quickly as I could,' Edward replied.

'You certainly did, by Jove!'

They studied each other, Edward coming to the conclusion that his father looked ill. More disturbingly, he seemed to have aged badly. He was sixty-five, not a great age, yet he suddenly looked much more.

'Yes, it knocked me about a good deal, I'm afraid,' Lord Douglas said, reading his son's thoughts. 'You came on your own?'

'Yes. There didn't seem much point in uprooting Annaliese and the boys.'

'Quite right. I expect they were having a good time?'

'Very nice. It's a marvellous spot – lovely gardens, the sea, and the weather, of course.' Edward did his best to be enthusiastic.

'What about my friend, Elsa?' Lord Douglas asked. 'Is she in good form?'

'Very much so. She sends her love and asked me to remind you that you owe her a letter.'

Lord Douglas chuckled admiringly. 'She's a remarkable woman.' He savoured the thought for a long time, then his eyes became serious. 'There are two things I want you to do for me, Edward.'

'Yes, Father?'

'I shall be doing my best to get better, but if things don't work out like that, you are *not* to let them take me into hospital. Agreed?'

'Agreed,' Edward promised.

'Your dear mother died in this house and I'm going to do the same when my time comes. Now, my will.'

'Father!' Pretending to be shocked was the best defence Edward could muster.

'Don't start having the vapours,' Lord Douglas said gruffly. 'You're old enough to know better. Ponsonby has all the necessary documents, but I'll tell you what's got to be done. Beatrice is to have this place. It's to be hers and she can please herself who she invites here. Do you understand me?'

'There'll be no more trouble over Charles Templeton,' Edward said.

'Make sure of that. Beatrice is to carry on the business at Boothby's. If you'll take my advice, you ought to think of George as a successor. That boy has brains and talent. Will you bear him in mind?'

'Yes, Father.'

'Don't go packing him off to Winchester and Oxford and trying to turn him into a damned civil servant. You're my executor and I shall want you to look after the money. See to the death duties and make sure that Beatrice gets *at least* half of what's left. You might feel the need to be more generous than that.'

Edward nodded. 'None of this is going to take place for a very long time,' he said.

'Those are my sentiments,' Lord Douglas said. 'The Almighty may have different ideas and I want to make sure that we're ready for him.'

'Consider it done,' Edward assured him. 'Can we *please* talk about something else?'

'Most certainly. I want to know how my grandsons are getting on in foreign parts. What did Elsa think of them?'

They chatted until Polly brought up Lord Douglas's frugal lunch and a message. 'Miss Beatrice says you're not to tire His Lordship, Mr Edward.'

'I'm not. Look at him. He's improved since I've been here.'

Secretly, Polly agreed, but orders were orders and Edward was sent packing.

'It's time you had a proper meal, anyway,' Beatrice said when he was downstairs. 'Your journey can't have been very comfortable.'

Edward, already tucking into a plate of cold beef and Mrs Grove's famous fried potatoes, agreed. 'The timing was the main problem –

midnight on Monday to five o'clock this morning. I tell you, Bee, if I last that long, I shall sleep tonight.'

'Will you be spending the rest of your holiday here?' Beatrice asked.

'Yes. I'll get in touch with the Foreign Office tomorrow to let them know where I am – it's purely a matter of form.'

'And Annaliese?'

'She'll stay with her people until the date we planned to come back.'

It struck Beatrice as a little bit offhand. Something was being swept under the carpet. It was best not to ask any more questions, not for the time being, at any rate.

20

12–17 June 1925

'I was an afterthought'

During the three days following Edward's return to England, Annaliese behaved like a carefree holiday-maker. She spent up to eight hours a day on the beach with the boys and Gwen. On Thursday Aurora joined them while Joseph, Max, and Vassily talked on the terrace. In the evenings, Annaliese wrote two long letters, one to Nancy, the other to John Brandon. In both, she described the peaceful beauty of her surroundings and told of Edward's departure. Nancy was given exact details of the scene at the swimming-pool; John's letter contained a number of hints that something had gone wrong just before news of Lord Douglas's heart attack reached the villa. In one passage – over which she took great care, trying it out several times on separate sheets of paper – Annaliese implied that the problem was serious. In a postscript, added after the subconscious thoughts of a night's sleep, she stated categorically that it was very serious indeed.

Throughout this period, Elsa never mentioned Edward, not even to wonder if he had arrived safely. On Friday, however, she decided that the time had come to tackle what she believed was a dangerous problem. While Gwen looked after the boys on the beach, Annaliese and Elsa were sunning themselves after a swim.

'Do you have a lover?' Elsa asked. The impact of the bolt from the blue was heightened by the quiet, detached way in which the question was posed.

Annaliese responded in the same manner. 'No, I don't.' Somehow, she left a cloud of ambiguity hovering over the answer.

'I wonder if that's wise.' Elsa remained detached, staring into the nearby trees as though looking for something in particular.

'Might it be *unwise*?' Annaliese asked.

'It isn't often that a husband can provide everything that a woman wants.' Elsa still sounded as if she were theorising. Perhaps this was an idea she had picked up from a book?

Annaliese thought not. 'Would you like to explain?' she asked.

'There are men who make very good *providers*,' Elsa said. 'They confer status, children, and security – and they are loyal. Unfortunately, their interest in the sexual side of love is erratic and frankly inadequate. Don't ask me why, but it *is* a fact of life.'

'Perhaps it's because they're busy with another woman?' Annaliese suggested.

'In some cases, yes. But I'm talking about the men who lose interest completely. Strange, isn't it? They're supposed to think of nothing else.'

'Are you implying that Edward is like that?' Annaliese asked.

Laughing gently, Elsa eased herself into a sitting position. For the first time, she looked directly at Annaliese. 'My dear girl, *you* must be the judge of *that*. However . . .' Her eyes flashed with mischief: 'If I were *forced* to give an opinion, I'd say, yes, he is.'

'What's wrong with him?'

'He has ridiculously rigid codes of conduct, my dear. It's a great shame, because his father's letters indicate that *he's* very free and easy. Men sometimes suffer from the most awful confusion and inhibitions and God knows where they get them.'

'You sound very sure about this,' Annaliese pointed out.

She was fishing and Elsa knew it. Mother and daughter stared at each other in quizzical amusement.

'Is Father like that?' Annaliese asked.

'Yes, he is.' There was no bitterness or anger. On the contrary, the admission brought great relief to Elsa. 'Your father is a very dear man and I've never regretted marrying him, but he has never been able to satisfy me.' With a wry smile, she added, 'Not even when he was interested in trying.'

'So . . .' Annaliese hesitated. 'You took a lover?'

'What possible alternative was there?' In the mildest of ways, Elsa conveyed the impression that any censure of her action would be regarded as an outrage. 'There were enough frustrated, cantankerous women in the family. They caused a great deal of trouble and I had no wish to add to their number. Besides, it wouldn't have been fair to Joseph if I'd turned out like the others – he gave me a good life, so why should he be saddled with a vile-tempered harridan?'

Annaliese laughed at the logic, then fell to attempting to recreate the subtle nuances of a vanished world. 'I suppose it must have been easy to arrange in Vienna?' she said.

'Of course it was. Organising and protecting liaisons was virtually a full-time profession. Your friend Katerina Leinsdorf was one of the main brokers.'

Viennese insouciance had brought Annaliese this far in complete impassivity. Now, she was astounded. 'Katerina Leinsdorf? That old crow?'

'Hush.' Elsa was vastly entertained by the eruption of disbelief. 'Katerina had a heart of gold underneath that forbidding exterior – which was mostly sham. She was very good to me. Why else do you imagine she gave you a little job in the gallery?'

'I always thought it was because of my *tremendous* talents,' Annaliese laughed.

'Well, as a matter of fact, she *was* very pleased with the way you turned out,' Elsa replied. 'But the original idea was no more than a favour.'

'*Another* one?' Annaliese teased.

'Yes. Dear Katerina made life so easy with her introductions,' Elsa sighed. 'It was much more difficult here.'

Annaliese was silent, evaluating what she thought she was being told. 'You have a lover *now*?' she asked, not quite succeeding in the attempt to keep incredulity and disapproval at bay.

'Why on earth not?' Elsa demanded. 'My age?'

'Well . . . yes.'

'I have some bad news for you, my darling child,' Elsa said sternly. 'Desire does not disappear when one reaches forty-eight – or any other age you care to dream up. In my case, it actually got worse. Imagine that happening to you. How many empty years is that? At least thirty.'

Annaliese side-stepped the issue. 'How do you manage here?'

'It's perfectly simple. About three years ago, the hotel in Estoril was bought by an Italian gentleman – he was alarmed by developments in his own country and decided to get out. We met one day while I was shopping. We became friends.' Elsa smiled luminously. 'I visit him regularly.'

'How?'

'Such prying,' Elsa said. 'If you *must* know, Karl drives me down. He sees his lady-friend from the flower shop while I spend the siesta with Gian-Carlo. Mondays and Thursdays are our favourites.'

'You haven't done that since I arrived,' Annaliese said.

'I've been playing the dutiful hostess,' Elsa replied. 'Both Gian-Carlo and I are thoroughly fed-up with that and we shall make amends tomorrow.'

'That's Saturday,' Annaliese said.

'What does that matter?' Elsa cried. 'I've made tremendous sacrifices and I don't intend waiting until Monday.'

'How old is your friend, Gian-Carlo?'

'Rather younger than me,' Elsa replied. 'He values my experience and we have *great* fun. Now, that's enough of that. What about *you*?'

There was to be no more dodging: Annaliese knew that she had to face the truth. 'Yes, Edward is as you suggest,' she admitted. 'There have been good times, but not all that many and certainly not recently.'

'Some women don't mind,' Elsa said. 'Are you one of them?'

'No,' Annaliese said firmly. 'I am not.'

'So, what do you do?' Elsa was challenging. 'Will you leave him?'

'I don't think so,' Annaliese said slowly. 'The fact is, Mama, I don't know.'

'It's that bad?'

'You saw how things are,' Annaliese said with a funny, lop-sided grin that, for some strange reason, was meant to be apologetic. 'The truth is, we had a terrible argument only a few days before we started our holiday – I very nearly came without him.'

'Oh,' Elsa said.

'Exactly. While we're still wondering how to patch it all up, he produced that performance by the pool. Have you tried to imagine what would have happened if Edward hadn't been called back home? How *would* we have got over it – especially cooped up here together with no means of avoiding each other?'

Elsa nodded unhappily. 'Yes, that had occurred to me.'

'So, you see, I don't know what I shall do,' Annaliese said. 'Separation is an awful thing. It would upset the boys terribly.'

'And Edward's father,' Elsa murmured. 'He's very fond and proud of you.'

Annaliese shuddered. 'With this illness, it doesn't bear thinking about. On the other hand, I don't think I can go on like this – in fact, I know I can't.'

'There have been other arguments and rows, I gather?' Elsa asked.

'Yes.'

'All of which brings us back to the original point,' Elsa said. 'You should have a lover. If you could find the right man it would make a tremendous difference to your life.'

'I can see that.' Annaliese was pensive. 'What about Father? Does he know what you get up to?'

'I imagine so. He can't really believe that I spend all that time in Estoril admiring the harbour, or looking at shops.'

'He obviously doesn't mind.'

'No. We're such very good friends, you see. His attitude has always been that if my little transgressions are necessary to keep me sane and us together, then so be it.'

'Edward isn't like that,' Annaliese grumbled. 'He's utterly intolerant. I work with a lovely man called Paul Marks. Boothby's would be lost without him – he's brilliant. Edward has *ordered* me to have as little as possible to do with him because he's a homosexual.'

'Why on earth does that upset him?' Elsa asked.

'I think men like that make his flesh creep,' Annaliese replied. 'But his main objection is a phobia about anything that might have the tiniest effect on his reputation at the Foreign Office.'

'So we needn't expect him to turn a blind eye to you being another man's mistress?' Elsa said.

'Hardly. He's as bad over "loose" women as he is over poor Paul. That terrible row just before we came was caused by him finding out that Beatrice has been having an affair with a married man for the last seven years.'

Annaliese went on to tell the full story. Elsa was quick to spot the possibility that had proved to be a forbidden topic between Annaliese and Edward.

'Did this have anything to do with Lord Douglas's heart attack?'

Annaliese shrugged expressively. 'That's bound to prey on Edward's mind for a long time,' she said. 'I don't see how it can have failed to have at least *some* effect.'

'Isn't that rather a harsh judgement?' Elsa asked.

'Probably.' Annaliese was contemplative for a moment or two before exploding into fresh life. 'According to Edward, I shouldn't even be seen within half a mile of Nancy Shenstone.'

The new name stirred Elsa's curiosity. 'Who's she?'

Glad of the diversion from a problem that seemed to be worsening by the minute, Annaliese embarked upon an enthusiastic and comprehensive description of Nancy, her obsessions, and remarkable house.

Elsa responded with a sensual chuckle. 'I think your friend and I would get on well together. What a shame that Katerina Leinsdorf didn't have an establishment like Martha's Vineyard.' She stopped, struck by a thought. 'Isn't it an ideal meeting-place for lovers?'

'Perfect,' Annaliese said.

'There you are.' For Elsa, the problem was solved. 'I expect you're going to tell me that you don't know a man who is even remotely suitable for your purpose?'

'No,' Annaliese said softly. 'I'm not going to tell you that at all. As a matter of fact, there is someone who could be splendid.'

Elsa smiled knowingly. 'Am I right in assuming that you have known this man for some time?'

'Yes.'

'And he *is* interested?'

'Very much so,' Annaliese said.

'Look at it this way,' Elsa said. 'You are likely to find life quite uncongenial when you return to London. Unless you provide yourself with a pleasant distraction you may start screaming and throwing vases.'

'Actually, Nancy thinks I'm a fool for not starting an affair with him some time ago,' Annaliese said.

Elsa's look was eloquent. 'And you say her house is perfect *and* secret? What more do you want?'

'Mmm . . . yes.' For a whole range of reasons, Annaliese decided on confession. 'There is a reason why I didn't start screaming and throwing vases ages ago. You see, Mama, Nancy and I are what you might call lovers.'

'*Really?*' Elsa's face was a picture of wide-eyed astonishment that was childlike. To Annaliese's relief, there was no hint of disapproval. 'How fascinating.'

'It hardly counts as adultery, does it?' Annaliese said. 'I used to believe that I mustn't be unfaithful to Edward – however bad things were.'

'Quite so,' Elsa said, noticing that Annaliese had put her conviction in the past tense. 'Do you know, my darling, I've often wondered what it would be like with another woman.'

'It's quite lovely,' Annaliese said. A moment or two passed before she realised that Elsa was eager for details. Laughing, she began to let her mother – the sophisticated woman who visited a young Italian twice a week – into the secrets of another kind of love.

That same afternoon, in equally fine weather, Lord Douglas went out of doors for the first time since the heart attack eight days ago. Deriding the wheelchair that some well-meaning soul had delivered, he walked round the garden for twenty minutes. He was cautious and sensible, using a stick in one hand and holding Edward's arm with the other. When they were back indoors, Polly brought tea and scones, and Lord Douglas told Edward they were expecting a weekend guest. Much as she disliked the idea, Beatrice had gone to London that morning, forced to conduct an auction for a client who was both important and troublesome. At the merest suggestion that anyone other than the head of the firm would be in charge of finding the best price for his precious possessions, the wretched man had threatened to take his business to Sotheby's. When Beatrice returned, she was bringing Charles Templeton with her.

'I want you on your best behaviour,' Lord Douglas said to Edward.

'Father, I've told you, I'm sorry for being such a dog in the manger. And I *like* Templeton.'

'Make sure it stays that way,' Lord Douglas growled.

'Please don't upset yourself,' Edward pleaded. 'If you do and Bee finds out, I shall be hauled over the coals – again.'

'Serve you right,' Lord Douglas retorted.

In fact, Edward treated Beatrice's friend and lover with a courtesy that was, if anything, slightly exaggerated. The only awkward moment in a pleasant evening came when Charles, not to be outdone in the civilities, asked after Annaliese and the boys.

'They're very well,' Edward replied effusively. 'Very well indeed. Having a marvellous time with their grandparents, of course. And this villa they have is *perfect* – you should see it.'

'I presume they're coming back on the date you originally arranged?' Charles said.

'Oh, absolutely. Yes. I didn't see the point of disrupting *their* holiday. And that trip was very overdue, you know. It's been a ridiculously long time since Annaliese has seen her parents, so she had to stay with them. Mind you, there's an amazing thing – they hadn't changed at all. Not a bit. I'd say that was miraculous after what they must have been through.'

Beatrice was puzzled and worried by Edward's forced jollity. Later, when she tried voicing her concern to Charles as they were preparing for bed, he went out of his way to defend Edward.

'He was pretty on edge and unnatural all evening – and what can you expect after what he's been through over the last ten days? Look at that lunch we had before he went to Lisbon.' Charles shook his head sympathetically. 'That must have been awful for him. Then your father being ill. I doubt whether the poor chap knows where he is at the moment.'

Beatrice admitted that, as ever, Charles was probably right.

Saturday 13 June dawned fine and promised to be a scorcher. After an exceptionally good night's sleep, Lord Douglas decided to make the most of the feeling of well-being that enveloped him by staying in bed until lunchtime. When Beatrice went to his room to check that he had taken his medicine, he suggested that she, Charles, and Edward should go out for lunch.

'They do a good meal in The Plough at Hatchetts Green,' Lord Douglas said. 'One of these days, I'm going to take my friend Elsa there.'

'Do you think she'll ever come to England?' Beatrice asked.

'One never knows,' Lord Douglas replied owlishly. 'The Archduke won't. He never goes anywhere for fear of his life. But Elsa . . . well . . . as I say, one never knows. I'm certainly going to suggest it.'

More to humour her father than from any conviction that it was the right thing to do, Beatrice dragged Charles and Edward off to Hatchetts Green. Against all the odds, it was an enjoyable and interesting two hours. Edward seemed to be without a care in the world and, as a result of his exceptionally relaxed frame of mind, he began to criticise the Foreign Office, inferring that it was a shambles.

Beatrice leaned across the table to place a hand on his brow. 'Are you feeling all right?' she asked with mock concern. 'You're not going down with a fever, are you? What did you have for breakfast?'

'There's nothing wrong with me,' Edward laughed. 'I just think it's time I let a few cats out of the bag.'

'Weren't things supposed to improve when you got rid of Ramsay MacDonald?' Beatrice asked.

'Hah!' Edward made a noise that combined a mirthless laugh with a snort of exasperation. 'Yes, that's what I thought. I believed Austen Chamberlain would be good.'

'But he isn't?' Beatrice said.

'Between ourselves, he's a menace.'

Charles chipped in with a banker's viewpoint. 'The Chancellor of the Exchequer worries me to death. He's a gambler, I'm sure of it. This nonsense of going back on the gold standard is sheer bravado. The exchange rate is causing untold problems.'

Not only did Edward agree, he launched into a denunciation of Winston Churchill's decision that impressed Charles by the grasp of economics that it displayed. Then, while Beatrice was open-mouthed at her brother's knowledge of a difficult subject that was nothing to do with his normal work, he returned to his dissatisfaction with the Foreign Office.

When Edward finally shut up, Charles flew a kite. 'You sound like a man who could cheerfully pack it all in – or am I misunderstanding you?'

'No, you could be right,' Edward agreed. 'It's not only the politicians.' He gave a quick, sheepish smile. 'I'm not exactly in tune with the top men at the Foreign Office.'

'Nor they with you?' Charles suggested.

'No. That's a fact, I'm afraid.' Edward was rueful. 'But the thing is, what can a thirty-five-year-old civil servant hope to do in the real world outside Whitehall?'

'We could talk about banking,' Charles said.

'Really?' To Beatrice's amazement, Edward seemed eager.

So was Charles. 'Very much so. If that doesn't appeal to you, I'm always coming into contact with men who need a chap with a brain like yours. I have two industrialists at the moment who actually admit that they haven't got the know-how to organise the big schemes they want *me* to finance.'

'That's very interesting.' Edward was looking at Charles keenly. 'Let me mull it over. You must come to dinner at Cadogan Square when Annaliese is home – and perhaps you'd care to be my guest at the Club?'

'I shall look forward to it,' Charles smiled.

Beatrice made a mental note to tell him not to waste his time finding a position for Edward. She was certain that this disenchantment with the Foreign Office was nothing more than a temporary aberration caused by the reprimand for dabbling in politics. And Edward's strange moods since his return from Portugal had a lot to answer for. No, this talk of a change of career was rubbish: the root of the unhappiness was in that villa at Cascais, not the Foreign Office.

Beatrice did not allow her misgivings to mar a convivial meal, and they returned to Upper Overs in high spirits. Lord Douglas, in the best of form after his long rest, was ready for a turn round the garden. Charles wanted to change into more comfortable clothes and Beatrice went upstairs with him, anxious to warn against involvement in Edward's willingness to flirt with a new career.

'Let's get going,' Lord Douglas said to Edward. 'I want to see what Ben's done to the roses. Beatrice and Charles will have to catch up.'

He was far more sprightly today, stepping out confidently, without much reliance on the stick. By keeping a firm hold on his arm, Edward made sure that there were none of the mock heroics that Doctor Thomas had forbidden. They went to the end of the garden in silence, then, after commenting on how beautiful the surrounding forest was looking, Lord Douglas said, 'I take it you had a good lunch?'

'Very good,' Edward replied. 'Charles said that he can help me find a new job.'

'New job?' Lord Douglas found the idea fanciful. 'Going through a bad patch at the Foreign Office?'

'Yes.'

'You'll get over it.'

'Don't be too sure of that,' Edward replied. 'The last six months have been miserable. Charles mentioned banking.'

'It's fine for some,' Lord Douglas said. 'But I'd have to question whether you'd be happy – it's a matter of utilising *all* your faculties.'

'What do you mean?'

'What do I *mean*?' Lord Douglas chuckled. 'My dear boy, you are one of nature's plotters and schemers. You're never happy unless you've got an intrigue on the boil. Is there much scope for that sort of thing in a bank?'

'Father, I'm not like that at all,' Edward protested good-naturedly.

'Don't be silly. Of course you are. Let me tell you something. Your mother was the first person to spot your talents in that direction.'

'Oh.' Edward was taken aback.

'Bit of a shaker, eh?'

'Yes.'

'Alice was a clever woman – as well as the nicest person I ever met in all my life,' Lord Douglas said. 'If I were you, I'd think very carefully before you come to any conclusions. You might be sick of the Foreign Office *now*, but in a year's time, everything could have turned full circle.'

'Yes . . . yes . . . there's something in that.'

They talked it over until they were distracted by Beatrice's cry of, 'Cooee!' as she and Charles emerged from the house.

Turning to wave, Lord Douglas's attention settled on two huge clusters of flowers. 'The lupins are exceptional this year,' he said. 'I don't remember—'

He stopped, his face registering bewilderment. He said, 'Oh . . . dear me,' very quietly and looked offended. There was also pain, terrible pain. 'Alice,' he said. Despite the pain, he smiled. Edward steadied him as he swayed, but was not prepared for the shock of having to support the whole of his father's weight.

As the two men fell, Beatrice lost sight of them behind the lupins. She screamed and started to run. Charles followed her.

They found Edward wrapped in an unearthly serenity. There would be time enough for affliction and grief; for the moment, Edward was thanking God for allowing him to be with his father at that last terrible moment.

It was late on Sunday afternoon before Beatrice suggested that a cablegram should be sent to Annaliese. Edward did it by telephone, via a helpful man in London. The message was transmitted to Lisbon within the hour, but, for a variety of reasons – including sheer incompetence – was not delivered to the villa until Monday evening. The delay was glaringly apparent to Elsa; to make matters worse, she found Annaliese's reaction distressingly close to indifference.

'Calm down, Mama. I don't think it would have made a jot of difference if the people in Cascais – or wherever – had been more efficient. I couldn't possibly have got there in time.'

'You might have tried,' Elsa retorted. 'Surely you still can?'

'Don't be silly,' Annaliese scolded. 'They're going to bury the poor man on *Wednesday*. In forty-eight hours it will be all over.'

Elsa was determined. 'Shall I see about a sailing?'

'No, Mama.' Annaliese was on the verge of losing her temper. 'What if there is a ship today? It would get me to Southampton at some unearthly hour on Wednesday morning.'

'That's what must have happened to Edward,' Elsa said, far from sure that the point was significant.

'To the best of his knowledge, he wasn't rushing to get to a funeral,' Annaliese snapped. 'Nor did he have two children and a ton of luggage. No, there's nothing I can do about this.'

'It's a terrible shame about Lord Douglas, though,' Elsa said, giving up the argument.

'Yes, it is,' Annaliese said, calming down. 'He was a lovely man . . . I shall miss him.' She was studying the cablegram again, frowning thoughtfully. 'This must have been one of the last things they did,' she said. 'I was an afterthought.'

'That's ridiculous,' Elsa said.

'Is it?' Annaliese's blue eyes had acquired a tinge of grey that was hard and steely. 'The funeral was arranged before anyone thought of me. That would have taken time, Mama. All sorts of important people were contacted to make sure that Wednesday suited them.'

'Well . . . it may have been like that,' Elsa conceded.

'I think it *was*,' Annaliese insisted. 'No one bothered to think about me and whether I could get there.'

'So what will you do?' Elsa asked.

'I shall go back as arranged,' Annaliese said. 'On the *Caerphilly Castle* at ten o'clock on the twenty-first.'

'Shouldn't you go sooner?' Elsa suggested. 'Even if you can't get to the funeral, isn't your place with Edward?'

'No,' Annaliese replied curtly.

Elsa sighed. 'You must let him know,' she said.

'Yes, I suppose so. Can I send a cable over the telephone?'

'I don't know, darling. I'm sure your father or Max will be able to tell you. Otherwise, we can go to Estoril – there's a proper post office in the square.'

'I'll decide when I come back.' Annaliese stood up, dreading what lay ahead of her.

'Where are you going?'

'To the beach. I must talk to the boys. They'll be very upset.'

After Annaliese had gone, Elsa wept for Lord Douglas, the dear friend whom she had never met.

As it had been for Lady Alice, the church was packed for Lord Douglas's funeral service. Afterwards, on a lovely, still afternoon in which larks sang a requiem, he was laid to rest beside the wife whose loss had marred the last six years of his life.

When the ceremony was over, many of the mourners went to Upper Overs. Among them was the indefatigable Lady Torksey.

'Damned good turn-out,' she said to Beatrice as they collapsed in the sitting-room, away from the crowd.

'It's nice, isn't it?' Beatrice replied. 'It makes you realise how popular Father was.'

'Delightful man.' Unexpectedly, Lady Torksey's eyes were bright with unshed tears. 'He always was, you know – even forty years ago. Quite amazing when you consider what odious specimens most young men are. Your dear mother beat me to him.'

'Good gracious!' Beatrice blinked in astonishment. 'Were you and Father sort of fond of each other?'

'I *think* we were. There were at least two others after him but none of us stood a snowball in hell's chance once Alice turned up. He fell for her like a cart-load of bricks and that was the end of my hopes.' Lady Torksey, dry-eyed now, smiled and patted Beatrice's hand. 'You've given him a good send-off, my dear and I can't tell you how glad I am to see you and Charles Templeton out in the open at long last.'

'It's a *huge* relief,' Beatrice said.

'Does this mean that your brother is acting like a human being instead of an overbearing prig?'

'Yes.' Beatrice pulled a gruesome face. 'It wasn't easy, though.'

'I've often thought that there's nothing wrong with Edward that drowning at birth wouldn't have cured,' Lady Torksey said, dreadfully straight-faced in the instant before she and Beatrice giggled wickedly. 'Anyway, make sure that you and Charles enjoy yourselves. There's no second chance in this life, my dear.'

'So Nancy Shenstone always says.'

'I see Edward's new broadmindedness hasn't extended as far as inviting her,' Lady Torksey said drily. 'She'll be sad about that. Now, my dear, to other absent friends. Why isn't your *delightful* Austrian sister-in-law here?'

'Oh, Lady Torksey, we made a complete hash of it,' Beatrice wailed. 'I suppose you know what happened on Saturday? Father had another heart attack and died. He was in the garden with Edward.' Lady Torksey nodded. 'It was appalling. To take our minds off it, Edward suggested that we made ourselves busy – and we did. By Sunday lunchtime we'd arranged everything – Charles was a great help, of course. We couldn't have done it so quickly without him. On Sunday evening, when we stopped to draw breath, I remembered Annaliese. We'd organised everything and hadn't let her know. Naturally, we sent a cablegram off straight away, but she didn't get it until late on Monday afternoon and that was that. To tell you the truth, we originally thought that the funeral should be tomorrow, but the Duke of Dorchester had an appointment that he couldn't break – and Father would have wanted him here, so we made it today. Tomorrow might have given Annaliese a better chance.'

'I hope she doesn't take it badly,' Lady Torksey said.

'Oh, I'm sure she'll understand.' In all honesty, Beatrice was far from sure of anything since Edward had told her about the row with Annaliese and his growing fear that she might not come back to England at all.

'And what of our errant peer, His Grace of Lincolnshire?' Lady Torksey asked, naming the other notable absentee.

'Ralph's in America,' Beatrice said. 'He probably doesn't know that Father had the first heart attack.'

'Or care.' Lady Torksey snorted. 'What the devil is he over there for? It must be a tart.'

'*Officially* . . .' Beatrice was very careful with the word '. . . he's talking to politicians about isolationism.'

'I've heard it called some things in my time,' Lady Torksey said. 'Mark my words, Beatrice, there's strumpet involved.'

'I think he's back today,' Beatrice went on. 'About eleven o'clock,

Celia thought. So he would never have been able to get here in time.'

'Tchah!' The explosive noise expressed Lady Torksey's profound doubt that Ralph would have wanted to be present at the funeral, opportunity or not. 'Isn't *she* due to give birth soon?'

'Any day now,' Beatrice replied. 'I think she'll be glad when the time comes. I haven't seen her for ages, but I gather it hasn't been the happiest of pregnancies.'

'Serve her right,' Lady Torksey said vehemently. 'I mustn't monopolise you any longer . . . there must be dozens of people waiting to give you their condolences.'

'I can't bear it,' Beatrice said, lowering her voice to a whisper in case anyone was in the long entrance-hall. 'It's marvellous talking to you, but I know I shall burst into tears once the sympathy starts flowing.'

Nevertheless, she set off bravely.

Ralph arrived at Allardyce Castle at about the same time – three o'clock.

It was an unflatteringly late home-coming. One of the chauffeurs had left at six o'clock that morning, driving the big Bentley to Southampton to meet Ralph from New York. A telephone call had told Celia that the *Mauretania* had docked, as scheduled, at eight o'clock. The journey should have taken two hours, not six or seven. The delay made no sense: setting herself aside, Celia knew that there was a powerful reason why Ralph *should* have wanted to be home as quickly as possible. Not bothering to ask questions that would inevitably lead to a quarrel in which she would come off worst, Celia broke the news of Lord Douglas's death, providing what detail she knew.

It was a thankless chore. Ralph made no pretence at interest. Instead, while Celia was talking, he examined the mail that had piled up during his absence. There were one or two patently insincere tokens such as: 'What a shame. Uncle Douglas was a good sort', and 'The funeral was today? Hell!' but for the most part, he was immersed in letters.

'What was America like?' Celia asked when there was nothing more to say about Lord Douglas.

'Oh, you know – mostly tedious. I met one or two useful people, though. Picked up some good ideas, too.' Ralph looked squarely at Celia for the first time. 'How are you?'

'So-so. I shall be better when I've got rid of this.' Celia patted her stomach.

Ralph studied her. Being pregnant suited some women, but Celia was not one of them. He made no attempt to hide his distaste as he asked, 'You will get your figure back afterwards?'

'What if I don't?' It was a taunt rather than a simple question. 'Will I be replaced by the sort of upper-class bitch you *should* have married?'

'We shall have to see.' Ralph was sneering at her anger. 'Do remember, darling, that I'm not one for convention.'

Celia nodded. 'And you don't mind scandal.'

'I miss it,' Ralph responded. 'I was thinking the other day how dreadfully *dull* things have been since I was fool enough to make you a duchess.'

'I must have been mad,' Celia muttered bitterly.

'Possibly we both were. I think you're plotting something, my sweet – have been for months. If it amuses you, fine. But don't build your hopes too high, will you? You have no leverage here.'

'Is that an American expression?' Celia asked.

'Yes. You know what it means?'

'I can guess!'

'Excellent.' Ralph collected up his correspondence. 'I must go to the library to make some calls. There are people anxious to know what I discovered in the States.'

Left alone, Celia rang for a servant. The butler, Baskerville, answered the summons himself.

'I shall be dining alone this evening,' Celia told him. 'Seven o'clock, please.'

'Very good, Your Grace.' Baskerville's look included a hint of sympathy, which she hated.

Celia not only knew that Ralph would be going out, she knew his destination. Whatever cock-and-bull story he decided to tell her, he was on his way to the house in Keeper's Wood. Richard Hamilton, the estate manager, was away in Devon.

Sure enough, Ralph came back from the library spouting a list of names, men who were frantic for news of his American trip. A special dinner was being laid on at a house near Marlborough.

'It won't be worth waiting up for me,' Ralph said. 'God alone knows what time it will be before I can get away.'

'I shall be in bed by nine,' Celia replied. 'I'm worn out carting this thing round.'

'Not for very much longer, eh?' Ralph was cheerfully affectionate. 'Look after yourself.'

Although she couldn't predict the steps of the charade with total accuracy, Celia left their private quarters in the West Wing to watch the opening gambit from the vantage point of the Long Gallery. Alone in the most nondescript of his cars, Ralph trundled down to the Park's south-eastern entrance. That *was* the way to Marlborough, but he wouldn't be taking it. Instead, after an eight-mile drive along lonely, rarely used lanes, he would reappear at the north-western gate, taking a track that hugged the boundary wall and was concealed from all eyes except anyone who happened to be working in the immediate vicinity. In that event, there would be a great deal of forelock tugging and a grandiose wave from His Grace as he went on his way.

At the end of it all, Blanche Hamilton was waiting.

Celia had known about Blanche from the start. Until pregnancy had made Ralph regard her as untouchable, Celia had reigned supreme, keeping her husband away from Keeper's Wood by the simple process of satisfying his every demand. Complying with her side of the bargain they had struck over their marriage, Celia made sure that Ralph was incapable of thinking of another woman, let alone matching thought with action. It was no mundane or unpleasant duty; Celia had enjoyed it, invariably going out of her way to instigate Ralph's desires.

For Celia, pregnancy had proved to be a disgusting experience. She hated the sickness and lassitude, and the mental changes were alarming. Why she had ever imagined that she wanted a child was beyond her. But above all else, she loathed being robbed of her hold over Ralph because of what the baby had done to her superb body.

'Don't worry, dear Ralph,' she murmured to herself as she waddled back to the West Wing. 'I shall soon look wonderful again . . . But you won't be enjoying it. As for leverage . . . well, we shall see!'

Keeper's Wood was the only part of his estate that evoked deep feelings in Ralph. Its 300 acres, densely packed with elm and beech trees, had been his secret kingdom as a child. In those days, the solitary house in the hollow had been unoccupied and semi-derelict, a pirate's castle that was the envy of the children who were brought in to play with Ralph and his brother, Gerald. Renovated for the Hamiltons in 1913, it still provided delights, albeit of a very different kind.

Coasting down the last, steepest part of the hill, Ralph parked his car so that it was almost out of sight in a thick copse of lilac. Walking across to the house, he saw Blanche watching him from a bedroom window. Only her head and shoulders were visible above the sill. She was smiling wickedly. Ralph waved and went in through the front door.

By the time he reached the foot of the stairs, Blanche was at the top. She was stark naked in a confidently provocative pose, feet apart, hands on hips. 'Hello, stranger,' she said.

'Hello, yourself.' Ralph removed his jacket, hanging it on a row of pegs. 'Where's the idiot gone?' Their very brief telephone conversation had revealed only that Richard Hamilton had left the previous morning, saying that he would be back on Thursday evening – tomorrow.

'Your farms at Crediton,' Blanche replied.

'Have I got farms at Crediton?' Ralph was surprised.

'Apparently so.'

'Why's he gone there?' Ralph was undressing.

'From what I was able to pick up, he thinks the tenants are defrauding you. He intends putting the fear of God into them.'

'That's bloody noble of him,' Ralph laughed. 'All in all, I'd say your husband was a splendid chap.'

'Isn't he, though.'

'Far be it from me to quibble, but why is it taking him so long?' Ralph asked.

Blanche shrugged, exaggerating the gesture so that her breasts moved provocatively. 'He intends going through the ledgers, line by line.'

'What a splendid fellow.' Ralph threw the last of his clothes on to the heap that had been growing during their exchanges.

Blanche feasted her eyes on the lithe body that was as translucently pale as his face. 'You're a beautiful bastard,' she said.

Slowly, Ralph began to climb the stairs, his dark eyes glowing as they devoured her. 'And you, my precious, are the best thing I've seen for nearly two weeks.'

'Is that how long it is since you were with Mary-Ann Wexler?' Blanche demanded.

Laughing, Ralph reached the top step and grabbed her into a rough embrace. Blanche sighed as he kissed her and flung her arms round his neck. Ralph's hands were all over her, one skimming down her back, plunging through the cleft to discover her viscous arousal.

'God, you're screaming for it,' he gasped.

'What about you?' Blanche demanded, rubbing furiously at his erection. 'Have you been saving yourself for me?'

'Since last Saturday.'

There was an oak blanket-box on the landing that suddenly struck Ralph as perfect for the needs of the moment. Guiding Blanche to it, he pushed her into a kneeling posture against the box. She rested the top half of her body on the lid, shuddering as Ralph went down behind her.

'I suppose you enjoyed that bitch Mary-Ann Wexler?' Blanche said, her voice distorted by lust.

'Of course.'

'And who was it last Saturday?'

'A woman on the boat. Sadly, she was never able to elude her husband again.'

'Was she good?' Blanche asked, squirming against the relentless probing of his fingers.

'Not bad.'

'Not as good as me,' Blanche retorted.

'Let's see, shall we?' Ralph rammed himself into her, making sure that the penetration was ruthlessly deep and searching.

'Well?' Blanche groaned.

'Not bad,' Ralph sighed. 'Not bad at all.'

'By the way, how's her hideously pregnant Ladyship?'

'Terrible! Feeling sorrier than ever for herself.'

'She soon won't be and you'll forget me again.'

'No. It was wrong of me to neglect you,' Ralph conceded. Starting to sweat with exertion and excitement, he was inclined to be generous. 'It isn't sensible to let her have all of me . . . it gives her too much power. Be good to me tonight, Blanche, and I'll see that you get looked after. It will be like the old days . . . before she turned up . . . remember . . . when we couldn't get enough of each other . . . it was always like this, wasn't it?'

Drowning in waves of passion, Blanche Hamilton was incapable of a coherent reply, but Ralph, losing himself in her voracity, took her staccato gasps to indicate agreement.

21

18 June 1925
'This is going to suit her'

It was a few minutes past midnight when the car turned into the north-western gate of the Park, which, like its south-eastern counterpart five miles away, was always left open and unattended after dusk.

Richard Hamilton had been to the Duke of Lincolnshire's two farms near Crediton purely to escape from Compton Allardyce, to give himself a breathing-space. The Walker brothers, Josh and Walter, were honest to a fault and would never dream of doing any man down, not even a landlord like Ralph. It was good to see them twice a year. There was Mary, too. She was Josh's daughter, thirty-two, widowed by the War and serenely beautiful. Mary had a dignity that reached out to and comforted Richard Hamilton's ravaged soul.

Sometimes, when she slipped into his bedroom after the old farm had fallen asleep, they made love with an ethereal tenderness that let them both believe in the future. But the threat of Richard's impotence was an ever-present menace, an unpredictable nemesis lying in wait for their brief periods of happiness. It had struck last night.

'The War,' Richard had sobbed into Mary's shoulder. 'The bloody War . . . Is there anything – any damned thing on earth – it didn't ruin?'

'It has a lot to answer for,' Mary murmured. God knows, it had taken another Richard from her, less than two months after they were married. 'But so does your wife. Why don't you divorce her? Come and live here with us.'

It was the best idea that Richard had heard for many a long year and it was enough to give him a peaceful night without dreams of gas attacks and artillery bombardment. Morning was a different matter.

'What about that devil, Lincolnshire?' Richard asked Mary. 'I'd have to cite him as a co-respondent.'

'He won't mind,' Mary replied. 'He lives on scandal.'

'Not if it's stirred up by one of his hirelings.'

'It'll be a new experience for him,' Mary smiled.

'All right, let's imagine I did come here,' Richard said. 'Do you honestly think that your father and Uncle Walter would still have farms to work?'

'I don't see why not.'

'I do,' Richard retorted savagely. 'He's a vindictive swine. We'd be served notice to quit – at once, never mind the next quarter.'

Mary refused to accept this and the day that had promised so much degenerated into grumbling argument. At six o'clock, Richard decided to take himself off. Making no attempt to stop him, Mary repeated her advice. 'You need to be free of Blanche, Richard. The War might have made you ill, but any woman worth her salt would have put things right by now. She's no good to you.'

He drove slowly, his mind swinging between blind rage and blankness. Conscious of hunger, he stopped at a wayside inn between Sherborne and Shaftesbury. The place was quiet – most of the regulars had travelled to a pub three miles away for a games night. No one took any notice of Richard Hamilton as he sat in a dim corner of the bar. He ate a pork pie and two cheese sandwiches, sipped at a pint of beer, and reviewed the past.

The old Duke had taken him on in 1912 when he was thirty-two and beginning to worry that the best of life was destined to elude him. Then, after less than a month, Blanche turned up. She was the daughter of some people who were staying at the Castle for a weekend. In those days, before she acquired that sleek, carnal gloss, her beauty had a stunning simplicity and clarity. She was like the most perfect of May mornings, fresh and unspoilt. Richard closed his eyes and jumped. Miraculously, she fell for the Duke of Lincolnshire's handsome estate manager.

They married the following year and moved into the renovated house. Blanche was twenty-two and a virgin, but she had an instinctive sexuality that transformed their lives into paradise.

It lasted until the autumn of 1914 when he volunteered for Kitchener's Army. Blanche told him not to be such a fool; there were stories of women giving white feathers as a badge of cowardice to men who refused to go, but not Blanche. She wanted him at home. The Army – especially after he was promised a commission – won the argument.

When they carried him away from the outskirts of a village near Bapaume in July 1916, there was talk of a Military Cross. A few days later, they discovered that his mind had gone and the hero became an embarrassment. The convalescent home at Aylesbury was comfortable and safe, staffed by nurses and doctors who wanted to understand the blank faces and inexplicable ravings of the poor devils they were hiding from the world. But Compton Allardyce was a nightmare, far worse than the Somme.

For most people, sympathy meant forced jollity – but only as a last resort, when their attempts to avoid coming face-to-face with Richard had failed. For Blanche, even that was too much trouble. 'I told you not to go,' was her response, backed up by the dreadful logic of, 'If you'd waited for conscription, you wouldn't have *been* there.'

In one respect, his condition was a blessing. It had taken him the best part of two years to realise that Blanche was Ralph's mistress. The memory of his shell-shocked naivety caused a jeering, self-mocking smile; the grimace was observed by a barmaid, as was the head shaking that followed it.

After the painful years of clawing his way back to what passed for normality, there was one thing above all else that stuck in Richard's gullet: Blanche and Ralph were not in love, nor did they seem particularly fond of each other. When it suited him, Ralph ignored her for months on end. The arrival of Celia seemed to have put a stop to it altogether: she would be more than a match for Blanche. She was – until she got pregnant. Then, as though there had been no interruption to their games, Ralph and Blanche were together again – *using* each other.

The landlord called for last orders. There was something deeply disturbing in the way the tense, pale man in the corner gathered himself together and made for the door.

Landlord and barmaid exchanged looks. 'It takes all sorts,' he said.

'That's what they reckon,' she replied. 'Us can do without his sort, though.'

After the north-west gate, Richard followed the boundary track used by Ralph seven hours previously.

Winter or summer, hail or shine, he always drove with at least one window open. He liked to smell the countryside, especially the last few miles to Compton Allardyce. The scents told him how much further he had to go. Tonight was exceptionally beautiful: entering Keeper's Wood, the land and its fruits made the air sensual.

Stopping the car, Richard listened, breathed deeply, and got out. Not bothering to close the door, he set off down the hill, softly on the grass verge, respecting the stillness of the night. An owl watched him, following his movements to the last bend before the house.

There was a light in a bedroom. It was the electric lamp she kept on a table to give a cosy, intimate glow. Richard studied the square of dull radiance for a long time, recalling the days when he shared that room.

Attracted by the heavy smell of lilac blossom, Richard wandered into the copse and found Ralph's car. He was back from America, then; not wasting time, either. Idly, as if he were considering an arcane, totally impersonal conundrum, Richard wondered if this had ever happened before. No, they normally made sure he was out of the way. He was supposed to be, of course: wasn't expected back until tomorrow. What to do? Find a place to kip down in the wood? There were plenty of good spots – along the stream, for instance. A man could lose himself there.

There was no conscious decision. Richard climbed a low fence and walked across the lawn to the back door that was never locked. The catch and hinges made no noise. Richard was obsessed about keeping things well-oiled: it was one of the multitude of habits and foibles that were the object of Blanche's ceaseless derision.

Motionless in the darkness, he listened. The silence was shattered by a burst of laughter, both of them, crude and raucous. Richard reached for the light switch. Adjusting quickly to the glare, he saw that the kitchen was a shambles. The remnants of a makeshift meal for two were everywhere; they had eaten eggs on toast and cold apple pie; one of the half-finished cups of coffee was upset, staining the pine table.

They had left the door into the entrance-hall open. After gliding to the foot of the stairs, Richard surveyed the discarded clothes on the floor, looked at the jacket on the peg, and, without altering his blank expression, noticed the silk knickers draped over the newel post at the top of the banister.

Laughter again – more gentle this time, apparently very near. Almost certainly, the bedroom door was ajar. Blanche spoke, a low intimate murmur followed by a throaty chuckle. The bed creaked. Blanche sighed.

Richard moved at lightning speed. Remote from himself, a casual onlooker, he was surprised. Outside the house now, he was at the door of the wood-store, reaching up to the cavity of a missing brick for the key. Darkness was no obstacle: in fact, for some strange reason, he made himself do it with his eyes closed. At the first attempt, his hand found the distinctive smoothness of the twin barrels, nestling side-by-side in cool harmony. He broke the gun and reached for the box on the shelf, removing three cartridges. Two went into the breeches, the other into a pocket. Locking the door, Richard returned the key to its hiding-place. He cocked the gun and walked slowly towards the garish brilliance of the kitchen.

Long ago, in a previous existence, they had joked about the noise the bed made. There was a slight fault in one of the joints that he had never bothered to repair. As well as creaking, it could cause the headboard to bang against the wall. It was doing so now, beating time to Ralph Lincolnshire's prowess. Whenever Richard had been stupid enough to challenge her, Blanche had taunted him with it. There was nothing, she declared, absolutely nothing in the whole bloody world as good as sex with Ralph: *he* knew how to do it, by God! The noise grew louder. It was in his head, the remorseless pounding of another ten thousand pieces of gun-fodder tramping along a road in Flanders, on their way to hell.

Slowly, Richard began to climb the stairs, the shotgun in the regulation two-handed grip, making an angle of forty-five degrees with his body – just like the infantry on the Somme. One of the treads creaked, but the couple on the bed were deaf to everything except their own mounting pleasure.

The door *was* open, letting out their ruttish panting. At first, they were unaware of his presence, even though he almost fell over the tangle of blankets on the floor. There was nothing on the bed but two meshed, writhing bodies; it had never occurred to Richard that he would find the sight shockingly beautiful. Blanche, underneath Ralph, had her eyes shut in tortured ecstasy and was pouring out a stream of obscene encouragement.

Something – there was no reason for it – made her open her eyes. The muzzle of the gun was less than a foot from the back of Ralph's head.

The last five seconds of Blanche Hamilton's life were unutterably hideous. The first, ear-splitting roar of the gun left her choking on her lover's brains. Then she felt the soft kiss of gun-metal on her throat. In the fraction of an instant before he pulled the second trigger, she saw the blankness in Richard's eyes turn to wild triumph.

Richard broke the gun, ejecting the spent cartridge case. Satisfied that the ghastly mess on the pillows retained no spark of life, he backed towards the door. Despite death, the voluptuous legs remained wrapped round the Duke of Lincolnshire's headless corpse. Accepting the irony, Richard went downstairs.

With fastidious care, he took a damp dishcloth and wiped the end of the gun's barrels. Reloading the weapon with the single cartridge from his pocket, Richard went through to the sitting-room. He took a bottle of brandy from the sideboard, filled a tumbler, and moved to the armchair beside the telephone.

It was an eternity before the operator came through. The man, who had been dozing, was annoyed by Richard's repeated jiggling of the receiver bracket.

'All right, all right! Keep your shirt on. I've only got one pair of hands.'

'They shouldn't be too busy at this time of night,' Richard replied. He sounded amused.

'There's no need for sarcasm. What do you want?'

'The police, please.'

'Hold the line.'

Richard snuggled deeper into the armchair and drank brandy.

'Wiltshire Constabulary. Marlborough station. Duty Officer speaking.'

Richard recognised the voice. 'That's Sergeant Vernon, isn't it? Richard Hamilton here.'

'Hello, Mr Hamilton, sir. What can we do for you at this time of the morning?'

Richard looked at the clock. It was a few minutes to one. 'I'm in my house,' he said. 'I've just killed my wife and the Duke of Lincolnshire. I used a shotgun.'

During the long, incredulous pause, Richard took more brandy. 'Are you *quite* sure about this, sir?' the Sergeant asked. He was wary, prepared to believe in a mental collapse that had dragged Richard back to the dark days of early 1917.

'Absolutely serious, Sergeant,' was the level reply.

'You're sure you're feeling all right?'

'Yes.' Richard was unable to remember the last time he had felt so content.

'Well . . . er . . . you're going to stay there, are you, Mr Hamilton – in your house?'

'Yes, Sergeant, I am.'

'I'll get someone to pop over and have a word with you, then. You're *sure* you'll be there?'

'Don't worry, I'm not going anywhere,' Richard said in a voice that convinced Vernon that he *was* off his rocker.

Richard replaced the receiver, threw back the last of the brandy and shuddered as the spirit hit his guts. He went to the front door, unlocked it and flung it wide: it would make things easier for the police. Back in the kitchen, he sat in an upright chair with the shotgun, muzzle up, between his knees. As he had suspected, with the barrel in his mouth, the trigger was just beyond his reach. Looking round, he saw the very thing – a long-handled wooden spoon. He tried it on the trigger of the empty barrel: yes, it was ideal. Richard took the gun and spoon into the sitting-room. Looking round – rather as if he were a stranger – he decided that none of the chairs was right. Intent on perfection, he returned to the kitchen for the upright chair.

A minute later, the owl, returning from a foray for mice at Home Farm, flew inquisitively close to the open front door, only to veer away sharply as the gun went off for the third and last time.

Following Richard's call, Sergeant Vernon made contact with the police house in Compton Allardyce. The constable was told to get dressed and cycle into the Park. His instructions were to humour the estate manager and report back. PC Johnson knew the area and was able to locate the house in Keeper's Wood without getting lost. Even so, because he had been led to understand that the incident was nothing more than Richard Hamilton having one of his funny turns, he did not rush. It was two-fifteen before he peered through the open front door, calling, 'Hello, Mr Hamilton. Where are you?'

Soon afterwards, the constable was remonstrating with the telephone operator. 'I don't care if this is the second time tonight, put me through to the police.' As an afterthought, he added, 'Anyroad, I *am* the police.'

Sergeant Vernon had known Johnson for over twenty years. He was a steady, reliable chap. When his voice quavered, it was time to pay attention.

'It's a slaughter-house, Sarge . . . We've never had anything like it and that's for sure.'

'What about Mr Hamilton?'

PC Johnson turned to look at the body on the floor. 'There's a chap here done himself in. The gun again.'

'Is it him?'

'Bloody hell, Sarge, how do I know? His head's spread all over the wall. And as for that pair upstairs . . . God Almighty! Look, you'd better get cracking.'

Another hour passed before the first car arrived, most of the delay due to the driver having no idea of the Park's layout. A second vehicle was close behind, bringing a Chief Inspector from Salisbury. He said that a doctor and an ambulance were on their way. The first light of a dawn close to the summer solstice was touching the sky, bringing Keeper's Wood to life with a dawn chorus of prodigal variety. Listening to it as he regained consciousness, the young constable who had driven the Chief Inspector thought he had gone to heaven.

'Are you going to be all right?' Johnson asked, crouching at his side.

'I don't know,' the lad whispered.

'You wouldn't be told, would you?' Johnson said with gruff kindness. 'You had to go up to that bedroom. My fault, I suppose . . . it was daft of me to mention her legs.'

The youngster blenched at other memories.

'We think the man upstairs is the Duke of Lincolnshire?' the Chief Inspector was asking.

Sergeant Vernon, a passenger in the first car to reach the scene, said, 'That's what I was given to understand by Mr Hamilton, sir.'

'But the woman isn't the Duchess?'

'Apparently not.'

'Where is Her Grace?'

The discussion went round in circles for half an hour. A doctor was examining the bodies, a fresh bunch of policemen – plain-clothes detectives – were studying the gun and taking measurements. Someone found Richard's car where he had left it, the offside door still open. Meanwhile, the story was going the rounds of the County Constabulary grape-vine: shortly before five o'clock, more cars arrived, one with a Superintendent. Sensing the helpless inertia, he demanded action.

'It's no good standing around like this,' he said. 'We must rouse the Castle. They need to be told and asked to help.'

Sergeant Vernon, the man who knew most about Allardyce Castle and its workings, was detailed for the thankless task. To add official weight to his mission, the Chief Inspector accompanied him.

They drove to the sleeping Castle, approaching it from the rear, through the maze of garages, stables, and workshops. To Vernon's relief, some servants were already up and about. They were, of course, alarmed by his presence at that hour.

'I must see Mr Baskerville,' Vernon told a maid. 'We'll come in and wait.'

The message was relayed and the girl guided the policemen to the kitchen where cups of tea were provided. Vernon, the Chief Inspector, and two scullery maids stood around awkwardly, trying to ignore each other.

Baskerville did not keep them waiting long. Already shaved and dressed for the day, he concealed his surprise and consternation. 'Good-morning, Mr Vernon,' he said. 'You're bright and early.'

'Well . . . yes . . . that's how things are, Mr Baskerville.' The Sergeant eyed the maids apprehensively. 'Do you think we could have a word somewhere more private?'

'Certainly. Please follow me, gentlemen.'

A walk down a corridor took them into the main part of the Central Wing, where Baskerville ushered his companions into a billiard-room. 'We shan't be disturbed here,' he said. 'Now, Mr Vernon, what's wrong?'

'A devil of a lot, Mr Baskerville. It looks as though we've got a disaster on our hands.'

'I see.' Baskerville took a seat, indicating that his companions should do likewise. 'Go on, please.'

Sergeant Vernon did the only thing possible – he recited the facts at his disposal. Uninvolved, the Chief Inspector watched Baskerville's face as the horror unfolded. The butler was dismayed, but not surprised, very definitely not surprised. When Vernon had finished, there was a long silence as Baskerville worked out the priorities.

'Her Grace is expecting a baby,' he said. 'The child is due in four or five days.'

'Blimey!' Vernon muttered. He rubbed his chin and stared at the floor.

'We shall have to be extremely careful how we break the news to her,' Baskerville went on. The Chief Inspector nodded sagely, then looked baffled; how could you be *careful* about news like this? 'Mrs Pritchard will do it,' Baskerville went on. 'She's reasonably close to Her Grace. I'll go and wake her.'

'Are there any other children?' the Chief Inspector asked.

'No. This is Their Graces' first.'

'So there's no heir to the title?'

Baskerville ignored the question and stood up, inhibiting further discussion of the matter. 'I will fetch Mrs Pritchard,' he said.

It was over half an hour before he returned with the housekeeper. Still recovering from the shock of what she had been told, Mrs Pritchard was fighting to regain her composure.

'I won't have the Duchess woken before seven-thirty,' she said. 'That's her usual time. I want the doctor here when she's told . . . I shall speak to him.'

'Yes, that seems fair and sensible,' the Chief Inspector said. 'Look, can I ask you two a question?' Baskerville and Mrs Pritchard nodded. 'We have three bodies in Hamilton's house. According to a telephone conversation that Sergeant Vernon had with Mr Hamilton, the two upstairs are the Duke and Mrs Blanche Hamilton. Without going into the gruesome details, it isn't going to be easy to identify them – not for Coroner's purposes, anyway. What we need to know is this.' He cleared his throat. 'Is it likely that His Grace and Mrs Hamilton would have been together . . . er . . . like that?'

'Like what?' Mrs Pritchard asked.

'It looks as though they were engaging in a sexual act when they were killed,' the Chief Inspector said in a rush of bravado.

'Yes.' Mrs Pritchard, though pale, was her normal self again. 'They had been having an affair on and off for seven years.'

'Did Mr Hamilton know about this?'

'*Everyone* knew,' Mrs Pritchard replied.

'Including Her Grace?'

'Yes,' Mrs Pritchard said.

'And is it true to say that Mr Hamilton wasn't exactly right in the head?'

As Mrs Pritchard was stating the facts about Richard Hamilton, a man for whom she had considerable sympathy, Baskerville left; while he had been away from the billiard-room to fetch Mrs Pritchard, he and she had agreed that there was important work to be done.

On his way to the West Wing, Baskerville broke into a trot. A maid who goggled at the sight was still more amazed when she escaped without a telling-off. Baskerville knew that rumour was inevitable; damn it, with police on the premises at five-thirty in the morning, the servants must already be in uproar. Darting into the Library, he locked himself in.

The old Duke had kept a special notebook for important family information. Baskerville was confident of finding it in the drawer it had occupied for years. In fact, it was lying on the desk, yet another display of Ralph's high-handed carelessness. Baskerville soon found what he wanted – Montagu Ponsonby's private telephone number.

The manservant in Wimbledon was not inclined to be helpful. 'Have you no idea of the time? It's ten minutes to seven. To the best of my knowledge, the master is shaving.'

'I'm Baskerville, the butler at Allardyce Castle. I can assure you that I wouldn't dream of troubling Mr Ponsonby at *any* hour of the day without the most compelling reason. A dreadful situation has arisen that Mr Ponsonby will wish to know about. We could all be in trouble if he isn't informed immediately.'

There was a last show of resistance and Baskerville was told to wait. As he did so, he pictured the operator in the telephone exchange at Marlborough. By now, speculation would be rife in the town and it was a near certainty that every word he was about to say would travel like wildfire. There was no way out of it: Mr Ponsonby *had* to be told at once.

He came to the telephone with his face covered in shaving-soap, but there was no annoyance. Mr Ponsonby had a high regard for Baskerville. The story was told economically, without extraneous comment or emotion. When it was over, Mr Ponsonby permitted himself the very rare luxury of a spontaneous, revealing comment. 'Dear me, trust *that* man to get himself murdered!' The tone was one of profound exasperation, without a trace of pity or regret. Once it was out of the way, Mr Ponsonby was businesslike. 'Given the circumstances, Baskerville, you have done extremely well to let me know of this deplorable occurrence. Now, do I take it that Her Grace has not yet given birth?'

'That is correct, sir.'

'Difficult, Baskerville, very difficult. As soon as I have finished shaving and dressing, I shall be on my way down to you.'

'I'm relieved to hear it, sir.'

But no sooner had Mr Ponsonby spoken, than his mind was jumping ahead. 'No, on second thoughts, I must stay here, in London. There are matters that need *my* attention. I shall send Mr Fowler. He is an excellent man and you can place your full confidence in him.'

'Thank you, sir.' Baskerville smiled ironically. Briefly, he was being treated like a lord.

'Mr Fowler will be instructed not to waste a *minute* over his journey,' Ponsonby concluded. 'In the meantime, hold the fort, Baskerville.'

After interrupting Ernest Fowler's breakfast, Montagu Ponsonby put through a second telephone call, to London's leading authority on the peerage.

In her room at Allardyce Castle, Celia awoke to find Mrs Pritchard sitting by her bed.

Mr Fowler drove like a madman and was accepting coffee from Baskerville at ten o'clock. An hour and a quarter later, he was alone in the Library, connected by telephone to Montagu Ponsonby.

'What is the position?' Ponsonby asked.

'As you'd expect, quite dreadful. The press are here, by the way.'

'They'll make something of this.'

'Won't they just! Oh, yes, one piece of good news – the police have decided to identify the deceased by their fingerprints. They've already done this with the Hamiltons – his prints were all over the gun, of course, and they got hers from a cosmetic jar.'

'Was there any doubt as to who they were?' Ponsonby inquired superciliously.

'*Legally*, yes. A coroner can't accept hearsay or circumstantial evidence.'

'What about the late Duke?' Ponsonby asked, a note of anxiety creeping in as he evaluated the legal complexities of failing to make proper identification of *him*.

'They're taking samples from his belongings. There's a Chief Superintendent in charge and he tells me that they'll be moving the bodies to the mortuary no later than one o'clock.'

'I'm gratified to hear it. What of the Duchess? I presume that you have spoken to her?'

'Yes. In her condition, one has to be very careful – although her doctor and Mrs Pritchard seem to be working miracles.'

'At the risk of sounding fatuous, how did she receive the news?'

'Quite well.' Fowler paused. 'Actually, it isn't strictly true to say that I've spoken to her.'

'Come along, man, get a grip on yourself. What's going on?'

'I've been talked *at*,' Fowler explained unhappily. 'After I'd been introduced to her, she spent half an hour telling me what was going to happen.'

'In what way?' Ponsonby was deeply suspicious.

'She believes that her son will inherit the title – and everything that goes with it – and that she will have the controlling interest until he attains his majority.'

'In the first place, one has to consider the possibility that she will give birth to a girl.' Ponsonby's reply was casual. He was stating the obvious almost as though it was irrelevant.

'I didn't mention that,' Fowler said.

'Quite. The poor woman has enough to worry about.'

'And in the second place?' Fowler prompted.

'I'm still looking into it. The facts are straightforward enough, are they not? His Grace, the ninth Duke died without issue. The feeling seems to be that a posthumous heir is invalid in this case.'

'Even if he's born today?' Fowler suggested.

'I said *in this case*,' Ponsonby replied, tetchily emphatic.

'Really?'

'Frankly, I have no idea,' Ponsonby admitted. 'Not yet. You will say nothing, of course. Provide what comfort you can, but make no commitment to *anything*. I may know more after lunch.'

'Shall I wait here?' Fowler was puzzled.

'No, I think not. When you've run out of sympathy, come back to London.'

*

Montagu Ponsonby lunched at The Athanaeum. His companions in the private room were the Earl Marshal, two other dukes, the Lord Chancellor, and the editors of *Debrett's* and *Burke's Peerage*, acknowledged authorities on the esoteric secrets of the aristocracy.

By the time they convened, the first editions of the London evening papers had splashed the Allardyce Castle blood-bath on their front pages. A keen and not particularly scrupulous journalist had contacted several of Ralph's ex-mistresses. Most of them were 'not at home', but two had perceived a chance to settle old scores. Their comments on the murdered duke's treatment of women – with particular reference to Blanche Hamilton – had been watered down to make them printable. The convention of not speaking ill of the dead was conspicuously absent. It was obvious that both the Castle and the village of Compton Allardyce had proved hostile and uninformative to the press. Because of this, and since next to nothing was known of Celia, the sensationalism included inferences that the Dukedom of Lincolnshire was now without an heir.

The Earl Marshal reported that he had received a telephone call from King George. 'His Majesty believes that there should be no delay or dispute in fixing the succession. I'm sure that I do not need to remind you that this title is of great importance.' The Earl Marshal's attentive listeners nodded; Lincolnshire was reckoned to be third in the ducal rankings, and dukes were the most senior members of the peerage. 'Any unseemliness could have an adverse effect on public opinion. We all know that certain elements of the press are rabidly opposed to the present structure of Society. We must not give them an excuse to preach dissent.'

'How long do we have, My Lord?' Ponsonby asked.

The Earl Marshal made a cynical assessment. 'Gory multiple murder, heavily spiced with adultery, gives us a breathing-space.' He paused to stare at Ponsonby with a curiosity that was blatantly prurient. 'Tell me, is it true that Lincolnshire was actually *having* this Hamilton woman when he got his head blown off?'

'That would seem to be the case, My Lord,' was the reply, delivered in a measured tone.

'Good God!' The Earl Marshal gazed round the table, exchanging eloquent looks with all present. 'However!' His mood shifted back to shrewd calculation. 'The press and its public will be happy with lurid titillation for three or four days. After that, we must have the answer. Frankly, I would prefer it to be done sooner.'

In any of the records that could be relied upon, there was no precedent for the situation confronting the Dukedom of Lincolnshire. Opinion round the table was divided. Two of the men advising Montague Ponsonby thought that Ralph's unborn child, if a son, could lay legitimate claim to the title. Two others were convinced that this was not the case. The Earl Marshal and the Lord Chancellor had nothing to say, but gave Ponsonby the impression that they were biding their time.

It was suggested that, for an ordinary family, without titles, a son born after his father's death could inherit property and money through his mother. This was ordinary, common law. The contrary argument, that the aristocracy did not permit women to inherit a single penny, was compelling. History had produced a tiny number of exceptions to this harsh rule, but the Boothby-Graffoes were not one of the families who had ever seen the need for such an accommodation.

A long and often almost incomprehensibly erudite discussion finally produced stalemate. Fearing that there was nothing more to be said, Ponsonby was uneasy; it seemed that he was to receive no guidance on how to deal with a dilemma that now looked impossible.

The Earl Marshal cleared his throat.

'We are assuming that the child is legitimate,' he said.

'Naturally, My Lord,' Ponsonby replied.

'What evidence do we have to sustain that assumption?'

'I . . . er . . .' Ponsonby squirmed, imagining a legal minefield. 'If I may say so, My Lord, by what right would we assume that the child may *not* be legitimate?'

The ensuing silence was heavy with tense conjecture. Finally, the Earl Marshal asked, 'What is known of the widow? *Who* is she?'

'Your Lordship may recall the circumstances of the wedding,' Ponsonby said. 'The Duchess was – and remains – something of a mystery.'

'Do you think it likely that she was a complaisant spectator to Lincolnshire's repeated infidelities? Could she not have gone in search of her own entertainment?'

'Well . . . yes . . . *anything* is possible, My Lord, anything at all. We are, however, faced with the burden of proof.' Struggling, Ponsonby was inspired to say. 'You stated that a speedy solution was required. That is not consistent with what Your Lordship is intimating.'

'Quite.' The Earl Marshal was thoughtful, gathering his resources. 'I have it in mind that Lincolnshire's widow is not a fit person to exercise any authority in this matter. She does not deserve her status and her child must not inherit.'

'I concur,' the Lord Chancellor said. 'Completely.'

No one said a word. Ponsonby noticed that the Earl Marshal and Lord Chancellor, firmly agreed though they were, did not wish to look at each other or amplify their comments. Suddenly, from nowhere, a brick wall had appeared and the twenty-two-year-old Dowager Duchess was on the wrong side of it.

The Lord Chancellor smiled hopefully at Montagu Ponsonby. 'I understand that you have a perfectly satisfactory heir standing by?'

'Not exactly standing by, My Lord. As yet, I doubt very much whether he knows anything of this wretched business. And he will be distracted by the fact that he buried his father yesterday.'

'Hmm. Yes. Douglas was a good man. His son seems to have the right ideas. He was very useful to Curzon when Lloyd George had to go.' A quick glance at the Earl Marshal brought a nod of approval. 'Well, gentlemen?' The Lord Chancellor studied the members of the gathering, his aquiline features posing the question. One by one, they signalled their assent.

'There you are, Ponsonby,' the Lord Chancellor said. 'You have an heir. I suggest you talk to him.' He took a last look round the table before adding, 'You may rely on our unequivocal support for all eventualities. I can guarantee that the House of Lords will share my sentiments.'

The full weight of the Establishment was against Celia and her unborn child.

*

During the morning, Beatrice and Edward drove to Hatchetts Green to ensure that the wreaths on their father's grave were neatly displayed. Charles accompanied them: at Edward's suggestion, he was staying on at Upper Overs until Sunday evening. After lunch, Beatrice and Charles went for a walk in the Forest and Edward settled down to prepare himself for the task of acting as Lord Douglas's executor.

Montagu Ponsonby's telephone call soon after three o'clock seemed to be no more than a happy and welcome coincidence.

'I was just thinking that I might have to get in touch with you,' Edward said.

'*Really?* Why might that be?'

Ignoring the fact that the lawyer sounded more wary than ever, Edward replied, 'I'm looking at Father's papers and one or two queries have cropped up. I'm sure there's nothing wrong – I feel rather dense today.'

'My word, we can't have that,' Ponsonby was positively jocular. 'If you will allow it, Mr Boothby-Graffoe, I shall come to see you. I'm sure that we shall find that there is a ready explanation for your little . . . ah . . . misunderstandings.'

'That's extremely good of you,' Edward said. 'When had you in mind?'

'I can be on my way in ten minutes.'

'Oh.' Edward was stunned. 'It isn't *that* important, Mr Ponsonby.'

'I'm sure it is,' Ponsonby enthused. 'Nothing is too much trouble for a client like yourself, Mr Boothby-Graffoe. As it happens there *were* one or two matters I wanted to chat over with you, so this will be an excellent opportunity to kill several birds with one stone, won't it?'

'If you're sure I'm not putting you out,' Edward said. He was becoming mystified.

'Not in the least,' Ponsonby replied. 'I shall have my man drive me down, so shall we say five o'clock?'

Beatrice and Charles returned from their walk half an hour before the appointed time to find Edward bemused.

'I don't know,' Beatrice said after hearing about it. 'You're head of the family now. I think Mr Ponsonby always looked after Father pretty well and he's going to do the same for you.' She turned to Charles. 'Don't you think so, darling?'

He was dubious. 'Edward's right, it *does* sound rum. Montagu Ponsonby's a big wheel. He must have plenty to keep him busy without making a longish journey to answer minor questions.'

'Perhaps he's sick of London,' Beatrice said. 'It's beastly in weather like this. He was glad of an excuse to escape for a few hours.'

'Hmm . . . we'll see,' Edward muttered.

Mr Ponsonby was a few minutes early. Beatrice took his driver to the kitchen to be looked after by Mrs Grove and arranged for tea and cakes to be brought to the sitting-room. While they waited for the tray, Ponsonby and Charles, who were acquainted, chatted with forced affability about precisely nothing. As soon as Polly had delivered the tray, Ponsonby's manner changed.

'I am here on the most momentous business,' he announced. He was so awe-inspiring that Edward looked downright scared. 'Is it in order to speak in Mr Templeton's presence?'

'Oh . . . yes.' Edward pulled himself together. 'Charles is a good friend.'

'Excellent.' Montagu Ponsonby struck a magisterial pose. 'I take it that you have not seen this afternoon's London newspapers, or had any contact with Allardyce Castle?'

'No, we haven't.' Edward, perched on the edge of his chair, glanced uneasily at Beatrice.

'As I thought.' Ponsonby reached for his capacious Gladstone bag. 'Last night – or in the early hours of this morning – *the* most appalling and regrettable chain of events took place at Compton Allardyce.' He pulled several copies of the *Evening News* from the bag. 'The account given by these people is probably the least sensational of those on offer and may be the nearest we are ever likely to get to the truth.' Edward and Beatrice were each given a copy of the paper; Charles looked over Beatrice's shoulder.

Apart from a whispered, 'Dear God!' from Beatrice, the impact and contents of the front page produced horrified silence. Montagu Ponsonby waited while they read what was, had they but known it, a surprisingly accurate reconstruction of what had happened at the lonely house in Keeper's Wood. The only question remaining unanswered was where Richard Hamilton had been during the two days preceding the slaughter. With that exception, the reporters had ferreted out or deduced all that was relevant.

Edward was the first to lower the newspaper and have a stab at rationality. 'There's an inevitability about this,' he said. 'One's inclined to think that this was almost *bound* to happen.'

'I fear so.' Ponsonby was at his most statesmanlike. 'The liaison between your cousin and Mrs Hamilton was long-standing.'

'Annaliese thought she was dangerous,' Beatrice said suddenly.

'Who?' Edward asked.

'Blanche Hamilton. Annaliese took one look at her and said she was dangerous.'

'When was this?'

'At Uncle William's funeral,' Beatrice replied. '*Before* Ralph's disgraceful performance.' Ponsonby winced at the memory.

'Tomorrow morning's papers will go to town on this,' Charles said grimly.

'What about Celia?' Beatrice asked.

'Her Grace is as well as can be expected under such shocking circumstances,' Ponsonby replied. 'I sent my best man to the Castle this morning.'

For the moment, there was nothing to say. Edward and Charles were lost in shocked thought, Beatrice scanned the front page of the newspaper again. Looking up abruptly, she saw that the lawyer was keeping a hawk-like watch on Edward.

'Who will succeed to the title?' Beatrice asked. 'If Celia's child is a girl . . .' She turned to gaze at Edward.

His face was blank, 'Yes? What of it?' he asked.

Montagu Ponsonby sat very still and quiet. Instinct told him that it would be best if it came from Beatrice.

'A daughter can't inherit.' Beatrice glanced at Charles for verification: he nodded. 'That would make you the heir, Edward. If Celia gives birth to a daughter, *you* become Duke of Lincolnshire.'

He gaped, broke into a nervous laugh, then stopped. Ralph's

brother, Gerald, had been killed in the War. Alexander, his own elder brother, had gone the same way. Yesterday, they had buried Lord Douglas. There *was* no one else.

Edward shook his head, like a man in a trance. 'No, that can't be right,' he said.

'It is.' The voice was Ponsonby's, quiet but firm.

'I don't want to be a duke. I couldn't cope with it.'

'There isn't much to it, is there?' Beatrice looked to Ponsonby for guidance.

'I don't know that I can *quite* agree with you, Miss Boothby-Graffoe.' He was transforming himself into the urbane man of affairs. 'The Lincolnshire estates are extensive and imply substantial responsibility.'

'There you are,' Edward said. 'I'm no good at that sort of thing.'

'How do you know?' Beatrice was quick to ask.

Anxious to stop this singularly pointless avenue of conversation, Ponsonby cleared his throat brusquely. It failed.

'You can't *make* me a duke against my will,' Edward said. To Beatrice's dismay, he was starting to sound like a fractious child. That impression was strengthened by his gleeful reaction to a sudden thought. 'What if Celia produces a son? Yes, that's it. Why are we assuming that it will be a girl?'

Beatrice frowned. 'This is all dreadfully sad, you know,' she said. 'And the most rotten bad luck.'

'What do you mean?' Having seen a way out of his predicament, Edward resented the diversion.

'This dreadful affair at Compton Allardyce involves *our* family,' Beatrice said. 'You can't turn your back on that, Edward. What are a very young, inexperienced woman and a baby supposed to do? If ever we needed Father, it's *now*. He'd have known how to handle it.'

Ponsonby murmured sympathetically, then made his play. 'Mr Boothby-Graffoe, I have to advise you that there is considerable doubt as to whether your cousin's child – even if a boy – should inherit the Lincolnshire estates and titles.'

While Edward glowered, Beatrice said, 'Because he wasn't born at the time of his father's death?'

'That is the starting point of the argument,' Ponsonby agreed.

'That's rubbish,' Edward snapped. 'I will not be dragged into any scheme to disinherit an unborn child. If we wait a few days, this will look very different.'

Ponsonby was prepared. 'Without wishing to offend your sister or Templeton, Mr Boothby-Graffoe, there is an aspect of this *dire* business that you and I should discuss in private.'

Nervously eager to oblige, Beatrice sprang to her feet. 'Charles and I will leave you to it.'

'No, I won't hear of putting you out.' Ponsonby's affability belied his resolve as he, too, stood up. 'Aren't I to be allowed some of your refreshing Sussex air? Your brother and I will take a turn round the garden.'

Reluctantly, Edward, looking as though he might attempt to run away and hide once he had access to the garden, led Ponsonby outside.

'Well!' Beatrice exclaimed.

'A hell of a shaker,' Charles agreed.

Beyond that, they were at a loss for words and Beatrice was soon wandering from room to room in search of a window that gave her the best view of Edward and Ponsonby. One of the upstairs landings provided what she wanted and Beatrice watched for three-quarters of an hour as both men went through a range of emotions and attitudes. At one point, Ponsonby appeared to be telling Edward something that seemed to be more shocking than anything in the newspapers. Edward's reaction was strange: it certainly surprised the lawyer. Was he discounting the information – or was he, perhaps, telling Ponsonby that he already knew? In the end, Beatrice decided that she was probably imagining it all. One thing was certain: on several occasions, Edward and Ponsonby were angry, not at each other, but with the state of affairs they were discussing. When they finally made their way back towards the house, they had reached some sort of agreement. Edward was unhappy, but determined.

Montagu Ponsonby declined Beatrice's invitation to dinner. He was anxious to be away, thus avoiding further debate, which might jeopardise whatever he had achieved. Edward was in a strange, tense mood, forbidding Beatrice to ask questions.

'I'm sorry, Bee, but I've no intention of telling you what we were talking about, so don't be a nuisance.'

'Steady on, old chap,' Charles said. 'I know this is all beyond belief, but there's no need for that.'

'You're right,' Edward replied miserably. 'Forgive me.' He ran a distraught hand through his hair. 'As if the mess you know about isn't enough, there are complications that make it *far* worse.'

'In that case, I'll keep quiet,' Beatrice promised.

She was as good as her word. That did not prevent discussion of Ralph's terrible death and the more obvious problems it raised. That went on until nearly midnight, when, with the best of intensions, Beatrice blundered into another difficulty.

'We're forgetting Annaliese,' she cried. 'You must get in touch with her.'

'What for?' Edward was frosty.

'To let her know what's happened – what might happen.'

'There's no point,' was the curt reply. 'By the time she gets back, there shouldn't be any need for speculation. I think I'll go to bed.'

After his abrupt, churlish departure, Beatrice asked, 'What do you make of that?'

'I think he's hoping to find a way out of being Duke of Lincolnshire,' Charles said.

'I'm certain that isn't what Mr Ponsonby thought when he left,' Beatrice said.

Charles agreed with her.

But, capable though Montagu Ponsonby was, the matter had not been entrusted to him alone.

A visit to the offices of *The Times* in Printing House Square by the Earl Marshal was not an unduly rare event. More often than not, His Grace simply felt the need for an informal chat and a glass or two of sherry. There was never any doubt, however, that his unheralded arrival at four o'clock that afternoon had a very specific purpose.

'Damned bad show about Lincolnshire,' he said, savouring the first taste of a new Amontillado. 'The bloody man's been asking for it, of course.'

'He won't be remembered as an adornment to the peerage,' the editor said.

'I take it you aren't thinking of printing anything about the widow?'

'Certainly not.' The very idea was repugnant. 'I believe that other papers will be observing the same silence.'

'Good.' The Earl Marshal helped himself to a cigar from the silver box on the desk. 'There's something of a difficulty with the succession.'

'Indeed?' The editor was indolently calm, unmoved by the fact that he was about to be given an exclusive story.

'The child isn't due for a day or two. Some people think that bars it from the title.'

'These people are authoritative?' the editor asked.

'Totally. Others don't like the mother.'

'Hardly surprising, is it?' There was the ghost of a cynical smile on the editor's face.

'The upshot is, we're thinking of the cousin,' the Earl Marshal said.

'Ah . . . yes. We did his father's obituary the other day.'

The Earl Marshal shook his head sadly. 'Poor Douglas.' The regret and affection were genuine. 'We could have done with him now. He'd have been first-class for Lincolnshire.'

'The son is sound, I hear,' the editor said.

'Seems to be. He's blotted his copy-book at the Foreign Office by dabbling in politics – but he's on the right side, so we mustn't hold that against him, eh?' Smiles were exchanged. 'His wife will keep him up to the mark.'

'Yes, indeed. The lovely *Arch*duchess!'

'Rather appropriate, what? I think she'll be a great success.' The Earl Marshal held out his empty glass for a refill.

It was nearly three weeks since Nancy had seen Annaliese, and, for a variety of unconnected reasons, it had been a fairly miserable time. Many of the regulars at Martha's Vineyard were out of London; others were exceptionally busy; the remainder seemed to have fallen out with each other. But, on that Thursday, 18 June, two of Nancy's favourite men turned up only a few minutes apart, both wanting to take her to lunch before spending the afternoon in her bed. Not wanting to disappoint either of them, or deny herself much-needed pleasure, Nancy suggested that they shared her meal before accompanying her upstairs.

It was six o'clock before two weary but satisfied men dragged themselves away and Christina, who had been boiling over with impatience since the delivery of the *Evening News* at four-thirty, was able to get at her mistress.

'The Duke of Lincolnshire's been *murdered*!' she screamed, throwing the paper at the naked, half-comatose Nancy. Instantly, she was wide awake, devouring the lurid front page.

'Holy Moses!' she whispered.

'You know what this could mean?' Christina said.

'Don't I just! Wowee!' Nancy collapsed again, kicking her legs high in exuberance. 'This is *something*! I wonder if Annaliese will get to know about this?'

'Probably.'

'Perhaps I ought to write?'

'When's she due back?' Christina asked.

'Monday . . . which means she'll be sailing from Lisbon on Sunday.'

'And you won't catch tonight's post,' Christina pointed out.

'Hell! Okay, I guess I'd better forget it.' Nancy whistled. 'What sort of state will Edward be in, for Christ's sake? He buried his father yesterday.'

'I know. I was sorry about that.'

Nancy was looking at the paper again. 'This is *sensational*,' she said. 'I thought things like this only happened in the States. Good old England!' Seriousness returned as she thought of Annaliese. 'This is going to suit her,' she said. 'This will suit her real good, Chrissie.'

22

19–20 June 1925

'I think it's going to pour down!'

By seven o'clock on Friday morning, Mrs Pritchard and Baskerville had read all the newspapers. The coverage of the three violent deaths was comprehensive and, in many cases, sensationalised. It was, however, *The Times* that contained the biggest shock.

'Oh, dear, we mustn't let her see this,' Mrs Pritchard muttered.

'What's wrong?'

'They say that Lord Douglas's son will probably inherit – whether Her Grace has a boy or not.'

Baskerville thought about it. 'That would be good,' he said.

Mrs Pritchard nodded. 'Yes, I can see what you mean. We'd get a proper family, ready-made. And Mrs Boothby-Graffoe wouldn't half smarten things up.'

'She's what this place needs. She's royalty, you know – as good as. We've forgotten what a *real* duchess is like.'

'I know you've never liked that poor soul upstairs, Ted, but we must take care of her.' Mrs Pritchard was desperately earnest. 'She's got nobody now.'

'All right.' Much as he loathed the young Dowager Duchess, a word from Doreen Pritchard was always enough to instil kind-heartedness into Baskerville. 'Which paper don't you want her to see?'

'*The Times*.'

He pulled it away from the pile. Methodically, as was his unvarying habit, Baskerville folded it neatly, as the old Duke had liked it by his breakfast place, before setting it to one side. Later, after doing his morning rounds, he would get rid of it.

Celia woke with an inexplicable sensation of physical well-being. For the first time in months, she was not aware that she was pregnant. Making herself comfortable against a pile of pillows, she began to assess her circumstances.

Now that the initial shock of Richard Hamilton's ghastly farewell gesture had subsided, Celia's emotional state was not at all what the majority of people would have expected. Indeed, her most difficult task over the next few days would be to play the part of the grieving widow. At long last, pregnancy was an advantage: in her state, no one expected anything but a pathetic lump, avoiding excitement and emotional extremes. She could also shut herself away, seeing no one but Mrs Pritchard and the doctor. If those who had so cordially detested Ralph descended to the hypocrisy of calling to express their condolences, they could be sent packing because the baby was imminent. After its birth, she would be too tired.

Both she and Ralph had ridiculed the idea of love. Their marriage had been founded on sexuality, Ralph's rather cruel sense of the bizarre, and Celia's belief that she would enjoy being the Duchess of Lincolnshire. That vain hope had proved to be the Achilles' heel of a flawed relationship. Far from enjoying her status, Celia had found that she was the prisoner of a system that treated her with contempt. During Ralph's absence in America, when no one but Mrs Pritchard had shown the slightest interest in her, Celia realised that divorce was unavoidable – desirable, even. Moreover, despite what Ralph thought, she had the power to dictate timing and terms. Given a week in which to make observations, any private investigator worth his salt could transform Blanche Hamilton into an asset worth at least £250,000.

As well as wiping out that dream, the shotgun had destroyed another valuable resource. *Society*, those arrogant, mostly shadowy people who wielded so much influence, either regarded Ralph as utterly beyond the pale, or were fearful of him. As a consequence, he had provided an apparently invincible degree of protection. That had died with him and the nagging doubts about David Blake came back to the surface.

Despite his cool-headed assistance in a terrible crisis and his need for secrecy, Arabella had always worried about David. She had mentioned him, albeit in passing, in her last letter a month ago.

Arabella Fenton! The memory of the woman who had been her best friend and mentor curved Celia's lips into a warm smile.

They had met in the cocktail-lounge of a London hotel when Celia was seventeen. She went there most evenings, easily passing for twenty and turning heads with her looks. Men were also fascinated by her poise and lithe movement: was she *really* as natural and unaware of herself as she looked, or was she proclaiming her expertise and availability? She knew exactly where to draw the line between finding what she wanted and being a nuisance. The staff accepted her as a decoration who was good for business, and she never put a foot wrong. When she did finally make a mistake, it rapidly turned into a miracle.

The man, fiftyish, distinguished, and radiating wealth was waiting. Celia's error was to assume that he was looking for a commodity, rather than waiting for a specific person to provide it. When she went to his table and sat down, his welcome was warm, his subsequent enchantment total. Celia imagined that they were on the point of agreeing terms for the night when a cool voice behind her said, 'Hello, what have we here?'

Standing to greet the woman, the man was easily in complete control of the situation. 'Bella, my angel, you were nearly too late. This delightful creature was about to poach me from you.'

'*Was* she?'

The woman walked round the table to study Celia, who stared back unflinchingly. Bella was around thirty, with a beauty she had been at pains to understate in her preparations for the evening. She was the most sensually self-possessed woman Celia had ever encountered.

'I'm Arabella Fenton,' she said, calmly sitting down. 'And you are?'

'Celia Jameson.'

'Ah!' Arabella's interest became keener still. 'Yes. I've been hearing about you. Where do you live?'

'Two rooms near Paddington. It isn't very nice.' Determined not to be fazed, Celia grinned. 'I have to rely on gentlemen who are staying here for a few days.'

Arabella turned to the man. 'What do you think of her, Hugo?'

'She's wonderful! I have to confess that I was tempted.'

'What about your promise to take me to Covent Garden?' Arabella asked, pretending to be cross. While the man was laughing it off, Arabella turned back to Celia. 'Do you want to carry on as you are?' she asked. 'Two rooms in Paddington and risking arrest practically every evening?'

'It isn't much of a risk,' Celia claimed.

'Don't delude yourself,' Arabella retorted. 'Remember what I said – I've heard of you. So have others.' Her smile was mocking. 'But you don't know about me, do you?'

'No,' Celia admitted.

'So, answer my question – are you satisfied with your lot?'

'Good God, no,' Celia replied. 'It's only temporary.'

'Until what? Something turns up?'

'Well . . . yes.' Celia was a good deal less confident now that her weakness was exposed.

Arabella turned to the man. 'What do you think, Hugo?' she asked. 'I've heard that Miss Jameson is exceptionally promising. Shall we forget the ballet and find out how good she is?'

'What a splendid idea,' Hugo said, smiling broadly.

Celia found herself bundled in a cab and taken to Arabella Fenton's flat, deep in the entrenched respectability of St James's. It was a big, luxurious place in which, Celia soon realised, two women could conduct a lucrative business. Inspired by the possibilities, Celia gave Hugo the full benefit of her skills. Unlike many of her previous clients, he was a competent, considerate lover. In addition, he was surprisingly virile and flamboyantly extrovert. He enjoyed Celia twice, then produced a *tour de force* with Arabella which finally exhausted him. And he was generous. Before leaving, he gave Celia £25, a princely sum that dwarfed her expectations.

After Hugo's departure, Celia and Arabella talked until midnight.

Twelve hours later, Celia left Paddington and became a resident of St James's, taking the place of Arabella's previous partner, who was now married to the owner of a South African diamond mine.

On her first day, Celia learned that there was one principle that transcended all else. Arabella's patrons were men of great wealth and discernment. Many of them were not especially unhappy with their wives and some kept mistresses. The only possible reason for their willingness to part with substantial sums of money was the assurance that they would be granted access to epicurean pleasures that were not obtainable elsewhere. Celia's innate talents were considerable: Arabella's tuition and advice soon transformed her into a carnal virtuoso.

The most appreciative of Celia's clients was William Boothby-Graffoe, eighth Duke of Lincolnshire. She enjoyed making love to him and was charmed by his old-world courtesy. For over a year, Celia looked forward to his visits. Then, on a night in November 1921, the excitement and exertion proved too much for him and he died in her arms.

Before recalling the help provided by David Blake, Celia was distracted by her sudden realisation of a grisly coincidence. Both father and son had expired while in the throes of sexual intercourse. What an achievement!

It had been a terrifying, traumatic experience, momentarily destroying Celia's resilient mettle. Plunged into blind panic, she began to scream. Fortunately, not only was Arabella in the adjoining bedroom, she was entertaining David Blake, a barrister who had recently become a King's Counsel.

Later, when all the difficulties were resolved or swept decently under the carpet, Ralph took the credit for the smooth handling of the matter. In fact, he did very little except drive up to London from Wiltshire, bringing an undertaker with him. The rest, including the all-important death certificate, was arranged by David Blake, and he it was who organised the deception that Celia had worked as a receptionist for Mr Napier in Harley Street.

As the days passed, it became clear that the Duke's death had unnerved Arabella, precipitating the 'retirement' she had been considering for some time. Although life carried on much as normal for three months, there were disruptive elements at work. Arabella was trying to decide whether she would be happiest in Monte Carlo, Nice, or Antibes, and Celia had begun an affair with Ralph.

In order to satisfy his warped sense of humour, he paid her £50 for their first night together. Ten crisp, crackling five-pound notes were waved under her nose then tossed on to the bed.

'Go on,' he urged. 'How can you miss a chance to make history? The first whore to do it with *two* Dukes of Lincolnshire in less than a month.'

Celia had matched his brutal cynicism. 'As the son of a much-valued regular, I'm surprised you don't expect a reduction.'

That was the only occasion on which they ever attempted to make a mockery of what they were about to do. In the maelstrom of thrilling lust that followed, Ralph and Celia were dragged into the delusion that they had been created for each other. She was overwhelmed by his savage, insatiable potency, he was convinced that he had, at long last, found a woman who was worthy of him.

The devouring passion grew by the day, inducing Ralph to suggest marriage. It was while Celia was attempting to make sense of her feelings that Arabella issued the warning.

'If you do marry him, you'll be turning yourself into a target.'

'That doesn't worry me,' Celia retorted. 'Have you any idea how rich and powerful Ralph is?'

'He's supposed to be one of the wealthiest men in the country,' Arabella said dismissively. 'And I know that his performance as a lover is out of this world. That doesn't mean you have to marry him, though.'

'I quite fancy the idea of being a duchess,' Celia said coquettishly. 'Imagine the bowing and scraping, and everyone calling me "Your Grace".'

'Let me tell you something.' Arabella was quiet and purposeful. 'Not all our clients use their real names when they visit us.'

'Of course they don't.' Celia was impatient, wondering what Allardyce Castle was like.

'My man, Mr Dickens, for instance,' Arabella went on. 'You like him, don't you?'

'Yes, he's nice.' Celia often spent time chatting to the man in question when he was relaxing with a glass of whisky after Arabella had taken care of his needs.

'Dickens isn't his name,' Arabella said. 'He calls himself that because he's very fond of *David Copperfield*. He's actually the Lord Chancellor. And "Mr Smith" is the Earl Marshal. How do you think you'd manage as a duchess with people like *that* knowing who you are – or were?'

'What difference does it make?' Celia's eyes were crafty. 'They can hardly shout their mouths off, can they?'

'They don't need to shout, Celia. They whisper – that's all it takes.'

'Let them.' Celia was defiant. 'Come to think of it, I hope they do. Just think of those fearful snobs looking at me and saying to themselves, "She must be wonderful in bed." All the women would be as jealous as hell and the men wouldn't know what to do with their erections.' She laughed wickedly.

'All right, what about David Blake?' Arabella said.

'He can be trusted. You said so.'

'I did,' Arabella agreed. 'David can't afford anyone to know about his visits here. His wife has the money and she's an utter bitch. She'd cut his balls off before she threw him out.'

'There you are, then,' Celia said. 'He won't breathe a word.'

'Not unless the one-in-a-million chance crops up when there's a blue moon and an R in the month,' Arabella murmured.

Suddenly, Celia's reckless confidence faded. 'You sound as though you know how that *could* happen,' she said uneasily.

'David is a member of a Club called Fisk's,' Arabella said. 'Apparently, they take bridge very seriously there and David's an addict. Ralph's cousin, Edward Boothby-Graffoe is also a member of Fisk's *and* another bridge maniac. He's something at the Foreign Office, he can't stand Ralph, and he's a puritanical pain in the rectum!'

'How do you know all this?' Celia asked.

Arabella was vastly amused. 'Sweetheart, I've spent seven years working some of London's most influential men into every sort of lather. When they aren't chewing the sheets, they *talk*.'

Arabella went to Monte Carlo and Celia became Ralph's duchess. Eyebrows were raised and tongues wagged, but it was all well away from the lonely safety of Compton Allardyce and the scandal-mongers eventually turned to other topics. The regular letters from Arabella – who had found a demand for her services in the South of France – were entertainingly packed with details of a life that made Celia restive. From time to time, there was a mention of David Blake, but it was easy to forget that he was a potential danger and meeting Edward reassured Celia.

Some men, those who were permanently preoccupied with great intellectual or spiritual issues, were a closed book to Celia. They were, however, very few in number and Edward – though he did his best to pretend otherwise – was not one of them. From the very beginning, his hostility had stuck out like a sore thumb. Behind her mask of bashful innocence, Celia was quick to spot the hungry discomfort that caused it. Far from being a threat to her, Edward was a rag-bag of repressed desires, a confused idiot who neglected his very attractive and passionate wife, then hated himself for lusting after another woman.

Although Ralph's death appeared to leave Celia alone and exposed, it would not be for long. In a matter of days, her son would be born, bringing with him power of a kind that Celia had never imagined: she, and she alone, would control the tenth Duke of Lincolnshire and one of the country's biggest fortunes. Well pleased, Celia reached for the bell-push to signal that she was ready for her morning tea.

The kitchens were in the grip of bad-tempered hysteria. Even before the frying-pan caught fire, everyone had been out of sorts: with the flames threatening to spread, the air was thick with abuse and recrimination. Hearing the bell, Celia's maid added to the chaos in her scramble for boiling water and milk. As she was leaving, Baskerville rushed in and set about restoring order. He was far too busy to notice that the maid had picked up the inviting, immaculately folded copy of *The Times* and placed it on the tray.

*

It was mid-morning before Edward bothered to sit down to read what *The Times* had to say about Richard Hamilton's handiwork. Not interested in even a tastefully edited version of the squalid details, he skimmed quickly through the columns of text, arriving at a paragraph that had been tacked on at the end.

Our Special Correspondent GD writes:
It is understood that the succession to the Dukedom of Lincolnshire presents the relevant authorities with some difficulty. The ninth Duke was without live issue at the time of his murder, but his young widow is expected to give birth to a child within the next few days. If the baby is a girl, the dukedom will pass to Mr Edward Boothby-Graffoe, cousin of the late Duke, and son of Lord Douglas Boothby-Graffoe, whose death we reported last week. If, on the other hand, the bereaved Dowager Duchess gives birth to a boy, it is tempting to assume that the child would become the tenth Duke. However, official sources have expressed doubt as to the validity of this. It appears that Mr Edward Boothby-Graffoe's claim to the title may be incontestable.

Edward spent several minutes coming to terms with it. What the devil was going on? The initials 'GD' were almost certainly meant to imply Geoffrey Dawson, editor of *The Times*, a man of great power who invariably clung to the shadows of anonymity. Why was he lending his weight to the story? Edward went to the telephone.

Holding the receiver away from his ear, Montagu Ponsonby waited for the first wave of anger to subside before attempting to speak.

'I'm afraid that *The Times* has a lot to answer for,' Ponsonby said. 'Her Grace, the Dowager Duchess was on the line a short while ago.'

'I can't say that I blame her,' Edward retorted. 'It's insufferable. What does Geoffrey Dawson think he's playing at? And who's been talking to him, eh?'

Ponsonby lied with polished sophistication. 'Mr Boothby-Graffoe, I have no idea, no idea at all. One could say that it was an unfortunate piece of speculation.'

'What, from Geoffrey Dawson? That's rubbish, Ponsonby, and I suspect you know it.' Edward was seething. 'After fourteen years at the Foreign Office, I can smell a conspiracy at ten miles. Kindly do not insult my intelligence!'

Smarting from the use of his unadorned surname by a man who was not *yet* a duke – and never would be if he carried on acting like a fool – Montagu Ponsonby allowed some of his anger to show. 'It seems that you have failed to grasp the significance of the conversation we had in the garden yesterday afternoon. Allow me to make it clear to you. In view of your late cousin's deplorable life style and his wife's history, we have to ask ourselves who the father of this child might be. When you face up to *that*, Mr Boothby-Graffoe, you will realise that the baby's sex is irrelevant.'

'That's a monstrous suggestion,' Edward replied. 'There's no such thing as illegitimacy for a child born to a married couple.'

'That may be the *legal* position,' Ponsonby replied. 'But are you prepared to stand by while your family's lands and money fall into the hands of an unscrupulous woman and a child of dubious parentage?'

'I don't care whose hands they fall into as long as they're not mine,' Edward said firmly. The heat of his temper was being replaced by ice. 'Am I not right in saying that the estate would be under the control of trustees until the boy came of age?'

'Er . . . yes . . . that is one of the conditions of the entailment deed given to the first Duke by Charles the Second and Parliament.' The admission cost Ponsonby dear.

Edward could not resist a morsel of family folklore. 'The first Duke was illegitimate. His mother had no idea who the father was.'

'You wished to say something about trustees?' Ponsonby asked, knowing that Edward's statement about his distant ancestor was correct.

'I presume that I would be expected to serve on this body?'

'That is not unreasonable,' Ponsonby conceded.

'In that case, you can rest assured that nothing untoward would be allowed to take place.' Edward grasped at what had to be the final escape. 'I have no intention of becoming the Duke of Lincolnshire. To ensure that, I shall support the boy's claim to the title – publicly, if need be. Perhaps you would be kind enough to make that clear to your meddlesome friends in high places.'

'There remains the question of a girl,' was the acid response.

'We will cross that bridge if and when it happens!' Edward roared. 'Good day to you.'

Terminating the call with a flourish, he turned to find Beatrice and Charles framed in the front door. Back from a walk, they were studying him with a mixture of curiosity and awe.

'That sounded pretty hair-raising,' Charles said.

'So I should think. Here.' Edward was still clutching *The Times*. 'Look at this.' Thrusting the newspaper at Charles, he stabbed a finger at the offending passage. 'What do you make of that?'

Charles's eyebrows shot up as he read the piece. 'My word, someone *has* been busy,' he said.

'Haven't they just.' Edward was working himself up again. 'Did you hear what I told Ponsonby?'

'That you would back Celia's child – assuming it's a boy?'

'Yes.'

'That's a shame.' Charles was whimsical. 'If you became a big-wig, Beatrice would move up in the world – *Lady* Beatrice Boothby-Graffoe. We've decided that we rather like the idea.'

Edward was not in the mood for joking. Treating Beatrice to a baleful look, he strode off, heading for the garden.

'You've been and gorn and done it now, my old darling,' Beatrice giggled.

'Oh, he'll soon come round,' Charles said.

'I don't know . . . I have the horrible feeling that it's going to be one of *those* days.'

Beatrice was right. Edward kept out of their way until dinner, at which he was very bad company.

After her outburst over the telephone to Montagu Ponsonby, Celia was perfectly calm. When her doctor paid a routine call during the afternoon, he was pleased with her.

'But you're not quite ready to get rid of the little chap yet,' he said.

'Believe me, Doctor, I'm doing the best I can,' Celia assured him. 'This baby is *very* important.'

He had read *The Times*. 'I *do* understand, Your Grace,' he said and looked thoughtful. 'If he hasn't made his presence felt by, say, Monday, I think it might be a good idea if you went into hospital – purely as a precautionary measure, you understand. How do you feel about that?'

'It seems very sensible,' Celia agreed.

'Good.' It was an opportunity for beaming and hand-rubbing, generating a furious cheerfulness designed to ward off any mention of Ralph and what the newspapers were saying. 'Mrs Pritchard will be relieved to hear that.' The voice dropped towards simpering confidentiality. 'She's *very* worried about you.'

Celia sighed. 'She's been good to me.' For a moment or two, she looked dreadfully sad, then the bravado and its concealed underpinning of shrewdness returned. 'With any luck, I shall be in that hospital of yours before Monday.'

'Everything is ready and waiting for Your Grace. You can be confident that we shall be doing our very best.'

On Saturday morning, Beatrice and Charles set off for London at seven o'clock. They were spending the morning at Boothby's, preparing for Monday's resumption of normal business following the closure caused by Lord Douglas's death and funeral. After lunch with Nancy, who was overjoyed by the prospect of hearing the very latest development in the Compton Allardyce furore, they were going to the house in Regent's Park. Edward had been warned not to expect them back at Upper Overs until lunchtime on Sunday: Beatrice and Charles wanted some time alone so that they could begin to put sadness and tragedy behind them.

Edward was plagued by an idea. It had taken root the previous afternoon and gnawed away at his mind throughout a restless night. At one point he had been on the verge of action, but more mental turmoil led to the feeling that it was an impulse that must be resisted. That remained Edward's view until the postman arrived with a surprise, a letter from Sir Arthur Hawkins, the Foreign Office's Permanent Under Secretary and Head of the Diplomatic Service.

My Dear Boothby-Graffoe,

Allow me to offer my belated condolences upon the death of your father. The tributes paid to Lord Douglas bore testimony to the very high regard in which he was held. I hope that you and your sister were able to draw comfort from this in your bereavement.

I and many of your colleagues are shocked and saddened by subsequent events. It seems that, no sooner had you completed the duties associated with your father's burial than you were afflicted by the appalling circumstances of your cousin, the Duke of Lincolnshire's, death. I extend my sympathies for this, also.

I understand that there is every possibility that you will succeed to your cousin's title. Under the dreadful circumstances, congratulations do not seem appropriate, however. Instead, I would ask you to consider a point which I am sure has already occurred to you.

The status of a most senior member of the peerage is, as you will have concluded, not compatible with your duties at the Foreign Office. Most especially is this true in respect of your eligibility to sit in the House of Lords. The political aspects of this would, I need hardly point out to you, present difficulties which would be quite insurmountable.

At such time as your future is determined, I know that I may rely upon your judgement of what is right and proper.

Yours faithfully,
Arthur Hawkins

Edward was stupefied. Contrary to what Sir Arthur's letter stated, it had *not* occurred to him that becoming the Duke of Lincolnshire would mean giving up the Foreign Office.

It was the last straw. The dissatisfaction he had expressed to Beatrice and Charles in the pub at Hatchetts Green meant nothing now. A future without his carefully nurtured career in Whitehall was unthinkable. The idea that had troubled him all night was now a pressing necessity.

Mrs Grove and Polly were alarmed by Edward's precipitate arrival in the kitchen. Afterwards, they wondered if he was losing his mind.

'I'm going out,' he announced. 'It will take some time . . . er . . . I could be away overnight.'

'Shall I pack you a bag?' Polly asked.

'No, there isn't time for that. I must leave at once.'

'Where are you going?' Mrs Grove shouted after him. 'In case anyone asks.'

By the time Polly decided to go outside to repeat the question, Edward was driving into the lane.

The 100-mile journey to Compton Allardyce took three and a half hours. At ten minutes past twelve, Mrs Pritchard and Baskerville were wondering what on earth to do about Edward.

'I'm not at all sure that Her Grace will want to see you,' Mrs Pritchard said. Although she was not exactly hostile, her manner embarrassed Baskerville. 'And after what she's been through, I don't know that I can allow it.'

'I've come to help her,' Edward replied. 'Will you *please* tell her that I had no part in what *The Times* said yesterday. The very last thing I want to do is deprive her child of his inheritance.'

Mrs Pritchard was unmoved. Before she could speak, however, Baskerville intervened.

'May we offer you refreshment, sir? You must need something after your long drive.'

'Yes . . . that would be very nice.'

Baskerville and Mrs Pritchard withdrew, leaving Edward alone in a sort of general purpose room, a place where Uncle William had often entertained his political and business cronies. A maid brought sandwiches and tea, performing the task without a look or a word from Edward. He was at a window, gazing across the Park and being surprised by his distaste at what he saw. The vast majority of people would sell their souls to gain possession of an estate like this and the money that accompanied it, yet he wanted to go away and never come back.

He went to the table, picked up a sandwich, and nibbled at it as he prowled round the room. Eventually deciding that food had no appeal, he stopped wandering and poured a cup of tea. He was adding sugar when the door opened and Celia was there.

For several long, awkward moments, her intentions were

ambiguous: was she going to enter the room or not?

'Hello, Edward,' she said at last. 'Why are you here?' Making up her mind, she came in and closed the door.

'To offer you my sympathy – of course – and support.' He sounded a good deal less assured than he would have liked. Celia's most potent weapons were neutralised by pregnancy and the shapeless maternity dress, but her eyes retained their power to disturb. Edward struggled on. 'I'm very sorry about Ralph – I hope that doesn't sound too woefully inadequate.'

There was not the slightest sign that Celia had heard him. She was looking round with a studied curiosity: this was one of the many rooms in the Castle that she had never seen. When she spoke, it was to ask, 'Did you pass through the village on your way?'

'Yes, I did.' Edward was mystified.

'Baskerville says it's crawling with newspapermen. Was there any sign of them?'

'There were a lot of people who didn't seem to belong,' Edward replied. 'Most of them were outside The Lincolnshire Arms – waiting for opening time, I suppose.'

'It's me they want,' Celia said. 'I don't know whether to be flattered or frightened. How long do you think they'll stay?'

'There's no knowing,' Edward said. 'Until they get tired, or their editors decide to send them somewhere else.'

'I wondered about inviting them up for a chat. They'd probably go away then.'

'Oh no, I wouldn't do that,' Edward replied.

'That's what Baskerville said. I thought he was going to have a fit.' Celia's eyes continued to roam. They settled on a glass-fronted drinks-cabinet. Crossing to it, she took out a bottle of whisky and a cut-glass tumbler.

'Do you want one?' she asked.

'No, thank you. Rather early for me.'

She picked up the hint. 'Mmmm . . . perhaps I shouldn't, but what the hell.'

'I'm sorry,' Edward said hurriedly. 'I didn't mean to . . .'

She waved his apology aside, poured herself a modest measure and looked for soda. Accepting the fact that there was none, she sipped the whisky, grimacing at its fiery, undiluted strength. 'It's bad about Ralph,' she said tonelessly.

'Dreadful.' Edward spread his hands in a gesture of hopelessness. 'I don't know what else I can say.'

Celia nodded, finished her drink and poured another. Dragging a heavy Carver chair clear of the table, she sat down, perching in an upright position that looked uncomfortable. 'Ralph was a fool,' she said quietly. 'Everyone knew Hamilton was unbalanced.'

'Ralph and Blanche Hamilton must have thought they were safe,' Edward said, sitting down to drink the cup of tea. 'The newspapers suggest that Hamilton was in Devon.'

'He came back early.' Celia shrugged. 'Sooner or later it was bound to happen. Ralph could hardly wait to get to her when he arrived from America.' She sipped her whisky. 'Why else did you come?'

'To assure you that I don't want the title,' Edward said.

'Really?'

'I'd hate being a member of the aristocracy. *And* it would mean giving up the Foreign Office. I had a letter about it this morning. To be honest, that's what finally made up my mind to see you . . . I wanted you to know that I'm not interested in being a duke.'

'The Foreign Office is that important to you?'

'Yes, it is. I couldn't bear to give it up.'

'Not even for fifteen million?'

'I beg your pardon?' Edward had no idea what Celia was talking about.

'Fifteen million pounds. That's what the title's supposed to be worth. I heard Ralph telling someone just before we were married. At least half of that is in hard cash. In banks. Gathering interest.'

'I had no idea,' Edward gasped.

'Couldn't you force yourself to feel quite happy about leaving the Foreign Office on those terms?'

'Absolutely not.' Edward was annoyed at the suggestion that he could be bought. 'I have all I want.'

'I expect your father left you a penny or two – and you own the house in Cadogan Square, I believe.'

'That's right.'

'I'm sorry about your father, by the way,' Celia said. 'Everyone says he was a nice man. It's a shame I was never able to get to know him.'

Unable to contain himself any longer, Edward boiled over. 'Look here, Celia, I want you to know that I intend backing your son's claim to the title.'

She was surprised: it was her first show of real feeling since she had come into the room. 'You had nothing to do with that thing in *The Times* yesterday?'

'Most definitely not. I was disgusted when I saw it.'

She stared at him over the rim of the glass. Her silence emphasised the one-sided nature of the conversation: whereas Edward was a bag of nerves and emotions, Celia remained detached.

'Have you any idea what *The Times* was up to?' she asked. 'What was behind it?'

'I have my suspicions.' Edward's clipped tone indicated his unwillingness to be frank.

'Go on,' Celia urged. 'Don't I have a right to know?'

Edward thought he detected a flicker of mockery in her eyes. 'I wondered if you had enemies in high places,' he said.

'Me?' She found the idea laughable, but there was unease behind the façade. Her glass was nearly empty and she was staring at the bottle.

'Allow me,' Edward said and went to the cabinet. After helping herself to more whisky, Celia shook her head when he tried to take the bottle away: she wanted it within easy reach.

'So, you think I have enemies in *high places*.' There was a jeer in the last two words. 'Why should that be?'

'Something Ponsonby told me might have a bearing on it.' Edward knew that there was no need to embellish the simple statement, yet her eyes made him want to say more. 'As a matter of fact, Ponsonby's disclosure wasn't necessary. I've known all along – well, since quite soon after you married Ralph.'

'Known what, Edward? *What* have you known all along?' Celia's voice was as beguiling as her eyes. Semi-mesmerised, he felt strangely relaxed.

'That you were the woman with Ralph's father when he died.'

Celia nodded, slowly and repeatedly. 'This was David Blake,' she said, a statement, not a question.

'Yes.' Edward peered at her closely. 'You knew that he and I came into contact?'

'I knew.'

'If it matters to you, I'm certain that Blake has never mentioned this to anyone else,' Edward said. 'It came out late one night when we were alone and only because I was Ralph's cousin.'

'Of course.' Celia believed him.

'I'm at a loss to imagine how anyone else could have found out,' Edward said. 'My wife used to be very friendly with Nancy Shenstone – she probably still is. Have you heard of her?'

'Oh, yes! Ralph was livid because she wouldn't have him in her circle.'

'Nancy Shenstone is one of London's prime scandal-mongers, but it's obvious that she never found out – otherwise Annaliese would have brought the story back.'

'And you haven't told her?' Celia asked.

'Certainly not.' The very idea was repugnant to Edward, touching raw nerves in the maze of his inhibitions.

'Don't worry,' Celia said soothingly. 'I always thought that David Blake might be a problem after I heard that he played bridge with you. But I'd disregarded the others. It's more than likely that one or two of these men "in high places" were clients of mine – or my friend. What better proof could they have that I'm a whore?'

Edward squirmed and blushed at the word. 'This is the foulest bad luck for you. If Ralph had lived to a proper age, all this nonsense about your . . . well, past as it were . . . would have been forgotten. In any case, what can they do about it now? They can hardly come out into the open, can they?'

'Very true,' Celia smiled. 'All I have to do is face them down. A war of nerves.' It was a prospect she relished. 'And with your support . . .'

Edward was only too willing to complete it for her. 'There won't be any difficulty. Your son will inherit.'

'With you as a trustee?'

'I hope so.' Edward's enthusiasm was bubbling. 'I forced Ponsonby to admit that it would be a satisfactory arrangement. No one could argue against it.'

'I like the sound of this.' Celia's mind soared to a peak of elation. 'Now, tell me, Edward, what would you expect in return for all this generosity?'

'Nothing at all.' He was bemused and slightly offended.

'Surely not.' Celia eased herself out of the chair and took a pace or two so that Edward was given a full view of her. 'I'm not exactly attractive in this state, am I? But that isn't going to last for much longer. I shall soon be worth drooling over again.'

It was as if Edward had seen a ghost. Every last drop of colour drained from his face and he was clutching at the edge of the table to stop his hands shaking. Celia, euphorically unaware that she was making a terrible mistake, proceeded to build on it.

'It's more than just old-fashioned craving with you, isn't it? You believe that you might actually be able to let yourself go and *enjoy* yourself with me . . . You could forget all about your lovely wife and wallow in sex!'

'That is completely untrue,' Edward whispered. He looked ghastly.

Celia was deaf. 'And, do you know, you might be right. I mean, if any woman *is* capable of working the miracle, it would be me . . . I must know tricks you haven't even *dreamed* about. So, what's it to be? How about every Friday? You could say that you were spending the night at your precious Club and drive down after you'd finished at the Foreign Office. Total privacy and secrecy. This place has dozens of back doors and bedrooms I've never seen. It wouldn't be one-sided. I shall soon need a man again and you could be ideal as a stop-gap – until I can make permanent arrangements. And who knows, the fair Annaliese might find it useful . . . If you were being looked after, she'd be able to find a nice, strong, straightforward man for herself. It's marvellous! Shall we do that? I warn you, though, I have a dreadful appetite.'

Edward exploded. 'You're mad! Stark-raving mad! I came here to *help* you, not listen to this filth.'

Celia was muddled, conscious only that his furious shouting seemed to be making her giddy. It was a pleasant enough feeling, with no sense of danger.

'I loathe and detest the thought of being an aristocrat,' Edward bellowed. 'It's abhorrent to me. I'd do anything to avoid it. That's the only reason I'm here, tolerating your company. As to your *odious* suggestion . . .' The sheer surging force of his anger made him stand up. 'I wouldn't go to bed with you if you were the last woman on earth. Get that into your stupid, depraved head!'

In an involuntary attempt to drive his words home, Edward took two steps towards Celia.

After plunging from exhilaration to bemusement in a few perplexing moments, Celia's mind was vulnerable to delusion. Believing that Edward intended to strike her, she moved away from him. It was a clumsy, badly judged and light-headed action that left her right foot in mid-air when she thought it was on the ground. Falling, Celia clutched at the back of the Carver for support but bungled it. Collapsing to the floor, she dragged the heavy chair down on top of her.

The scream was more from fear and shock than pain. Even so, it was loud, very alarming, and coincided with Mrs Pritchard's panic-stricken dash into the room. Deeply uneasy at the meeting, she had been loitering at the end of the corridor and came running at the sound of Edward's raised voice.

Celia was lying on her side, the chair across a hip. While Mrs Pritchard froze in dismayed indecision, Edward started towards Celia, wanting to help. But she was already freeing herself and her mood had changed again.

'Don't you dare come near me!' she spat. 'You tried to damage my child.'

'I did no such thing,' Edward protested. Then he saw the look on Mrs Pritchard's face and started to sweat. He had no verifiable defence against the damning accusation: it was her word against his.

Mrs Pritchard was helping Celia. At first, she was concerned and soothing, but her face registered repugnance when she caught a whiff of the whisky. 'Come along, My Lady,' she said firmly. 'Let's get you lying down . . . That might make you feel better.'

Suddenly, Celia was doubled-up, white as a sheet and clutching at her distended stomach. 'It's starting!' she gasped. 'It is. Oh, God, what will happen to me? My baby's being born.'

'We'll get you to hospital,' Mrs Pritchard said. 'You'll be all right. Don't worry.'

Edward turned away, retreating to a window where he stood like a statue, staring fixedly ahead, seeing nothing. Behind him there was considerable activity. Two maids were helping Mrs Pritchard, doing their best to reassure Celia, who was whimpering in fear and self-pity.

At last, the door closed and silence descended. Edward left the window and flung himself into an armchair. It was a mess. Much to his surprise, he was able to clear his mind. He sat and waited like a simpleton, without the faintest idea of what he was waiting for.

When Baskerville appeared, ten, twenty, or thirty minutes could have passed for all Edward knew.

'One of the chauffeurs is driving Her Grace to hospital,' Baskerville said. 'Mrs Pritchard has gone with her.'

'Thank you.' Looking at the butler, Edward found his thoughts wandering off in a direction that had nothing to do with the present crisis. 'Did you know that we had to get rid of Franklin from Cadogan Square?'

'No, sir, I did not.'

'I have to find a new butler. My wife will be returning on . . .' Edward gave up trying to work out when Annaliese was due to sail and what day it was now. 'Well, anyway, I have to get something arranged quickly or we shall be at sixes and sevens. Would you be interested?'

'As it happens, sir, I believe that it may be time to make a move.' Baskerville paused. 'However, I would not consider going without Mrs Pritchard.'

'Oh.' Edward looked blank.

'Mrs Pritchard and myself have an *understanding*, sir.'

'Have you? Yes . . . right . . . I shall bear that in mind.' Edward was at a loss to know why he had started the conversation.

'May I make a suggestion, sir?' Baskerville was deeply concerned.

'Please do.' Edward would have agreed to anything.

'During the past three weeks or so, Her Grace has drunk rather more whisky than may be good for her.'

'*Has* she?'

'Indeed she has, sir.' Baskerville removed the bottle from the table and returned it to the cabinet. 'You must not worry. Mrs Pritchard doesn't believe what Her Grace was saying about you – not after she smelled the drink.'

'Thank you, Baskerville,' Edward said. 'I'm relieved to hear it. Look, what do you think I ought to do now . . . clear off back to Sussex? Would that be best?'

'I would advise not, sir, unless you have an engagement.' Edward shook his head. 'My instincts are that you should stay at the Castle tonight.'

'You think so?'

'Most definitely, sir.'

'I brought nothing with me,' Edward said. 'No pyjamas, linen, shaving-tackle – nothing like that.'

'We are able to supply everything for our guests, sir. May I conduct you to your room?'

It was, Edward realised, a scorcher of a day and he was suffering from the heat. He took a bath, then lay down and dozed for a couple of hours. At four o'clock, Baskerville and a footman brought tea and a selection of comfortable clothes. It was known that Celia had arrived safely at the hospital near Marlborough, but there was no other news.

Edward mooched round the Castle, viewing it with the eyes and mind of a sightseer, a privileged outsider allowed in while the owners were away. His ancestors were everywhere. In the Long Gallery, he spent several minutes staring at Sir Joshua Reynold's portraits of the third and fourth Dukes, painted within two years of each other when father and son were seventy-three and thirty respectively. The family likeness was striking: at one point, Edward half believed that he and

Lord Douglas were together again, looking into a mirror. He told himself that it was a trick of the light, that his imagination was playing overwrought games: there was no feeling that he belonged to this place, not a scrap of affinity.

During dinner, which he ate in the lonely privacy of his room, Edward became restive and bored. It was half past eight. Determination and a little effort would get him back to Upper Overs by midnight. Instead, he surrendered to Baskerville's strange, compelling advice, finished his meal and went outside for a stroll.

A breeze was cooling the evening and wafting the perfumes of midsummer across the Park. Walking towards the lake, Edward remained unmoved by the beauty of his surroundings. If anything, he felt apprehensive. Away to the east, Keeper's Wood seemed forbidding as the sun dipped towards the horizon: it was a place of deceit, madness, and murder. Doing his best to avoid looking at it, Edward skirted the lake, watching ducks and moorhens settling down for the night before making his way back to the Castle. At the sound of his footfall in the great entrance-hall, Baskerville materialised from a door in the shadows.

'I beg your pardon, sir, forgive me for startling you,' he said. 'Mrs Pritchard came on the telephone while you were taking the air. It seems that Her Grace has been safely delivered of a son.'

'Really?' Edward wanted to embrace the butler. 'When was this?'

'About an hour ago, I imagine.'

'And the boy is all right?'

'It would appear so, sir.'

'Splendid! Absolutely splendid!' Edward was about to release his jubilation in a dash up the great staircase when he noticed Baskerville's demeanour. 'You don't seem very pleased about this,' he said accusingly.

Baskerville stiffened and took a pace backwards. 'It is not my place to express opinions,' he said. 'I regret giving the impression that I was doing so.'

There was an underlying hauteur at which Edward could easily have taken offence. But it had turned into far too marvellous a day to bother with such distractions. Grinning happily, he launched himself up the stairs.

*

It was Annaliese's last evening at the villa near Cascais. To conceal his sadness, Joseph was visiting Max; presumably, Vassily was with them, stoking up the argument about Hitler.

By nine o'clock, all the packing was complete and Gwen was settling the boys down for the night. Alone in her bedroom, Annaliese was carrying out a last check on tickets and travel documents. She looked up, smiling, as her mother appeared.

Elsa was carrying a flat, rectangular object wrapped in linen. She placed it on the dressing-table and asked, 'All finished?'

'I think so.' Annaliese's laugh was edged with the tension of the parting to come. 'I expect there'll be a thousand and one things in the morning.'

'Remember that we must leave no later than seven-thirty,' Elsa warned. 'Eight at the *very* latest.'

'Don't worry, we shall manage.' Annaliese sighed heavily. 'I don't like leaving you.'

'No harm is going to come to us, if that's what you mean,' Elsa said, bravely cheerful. 'I want you to have a memento.' Delving into a pocket of the pinafore she had donned to help with the packing, she brought out a tiny jewel box and pressed it into Annaliese's hand. 'Go on, open it.'

It was an enamel brooch, an elegant oval with a black silhouette of the Habsburg double-headed eagle on a pure white background edged with gold. 'Oh, that's beautiful,' Annaliese cried.

'The Emperor presented that to me on my wedding day,' Elsa said. 'It was made for Maria Theresa.' She frowned and raised a hand to suppress the protest before it started. 'No, you *shall* have it. What use is it to me? It needs someone young and full of energy to look after it and hope . . . Who knows, you might live long enough to see the Habsburgs back in Vienna.'

'Not if Leopold has any say in the matter,' Annaliese said bitterly.

'Hush.' Elsa was pinning the brooch on to Annaliese's dress. 'Leopold is a poor, misguided man and we must pray for him. There, now.' She gave the heirloom a final pat. 'Lovely.'

Annaliese went to a mirror. 'I shall wear it all the time,' she said.

'Don't wear it out.' Elsa laughed. There was a pause while they admired the brooch, then Elsa's face became serious. 'You're going home,' she said with stark simplicity. 'What do you think you're going to find there?'

'I have no idea.' Annaliese counteracted the catch in her voice by a defiant tilt of the chin. 'Edward hasn't bothered to write.'

'Nor you to him,' Elsa pointed out.

'I had nothing to say,' Annaliese retorted. 'At least, nothing that was any of his business.'

'Very harsh, my darling.'

'I don't think so, Mama. Was I supposed to tell him about your advice to take a lover?'

'Of course you weren't.'

'Well, then, there was nothing.'

Elsa was contemplative. 'It seems that you're returning to uncertainty,' she said at last.

'I'm afraid that's true,' Annaliese replied. 'If the worst happens, Edward and I will break up.'

'What's the worst?' Elsa asked. 'Things carrying on as they are?'

'Yes.' Annaliese reinforced it with a vigorous nod.

'I see.' Elsa moved to the dressing-table to pick up the linen-wrapped package. 'Because of the circumstances of your marriage, your father wasn't able to provide you with a dowry – and we've never put that right. Here it is.' She held up the bundle. 'You're to do whatever you like with these.'

It was heavier than Annaliese had anticipated. Weighing the parcel in both hands, she was puzzled, slightly wary, even.

'See for yourself,' Elsa said.

Laying it on the bed, Annaliese set to work on the tapes that secured the linen cover. Unrolling the contents from what proved to be a very large square of fabric, she found strong, brown paper. Inside that was a thick wad of tissue paper protecting a silk bag. As she emptied its contents on to the linen square, Annaliese's breath caught in her throat at the stream of flashing viridescence.

'The emeralds,' she gasped. 'The Wittelsbach emeralds.'

'Actually, they've always been known as the Falkenberg emeralds,'

Elsa said. 'My grandfather used to tell a story that connected them with Schloss Falkenberg – that's in the Alps, near Grafenau. I was taken there once when I was small – it's a terribly *eerie* place.'

Annaliese gaped at the treasure. On his second visit to Schönbrunn during the intoxicating summer of 1914, Edward had commented on the beauty of the stones which, at that time, Elsa was wearing in a tiara. Annaliese remembered suggesting that he might spirit them back to London for sale at Boothby's. The admiration displayed by Edward on that occasion had been for ten of the stones: now, Annaliese was looking at the full set of sixty.

'Oh, no,' she said. 'No! I can't take these. You and Father need them.'

'What for?' Elsa demanded. 'Our old age? For when Gian-Carlo no longer wants me?'

'Yes,' Annaliese replied. 'I know it's an unpalatable subject, but it has to be faced.'

'It already has been,' Elsa said, determined to be even more resolute than her strong-willed daughter. 'We have plenty of money in Switzerland, and I have a guaranteed source of regular income.'

'I never knew about that,' Annaliese said. 'What is it?'

'Aha, that's a secret.' Elsa smiled mischievously. 'I don't even tell your father where the money comes from – but it's safe.' She pointed at the emeralds. 'They aren't. This country isn't what it appears to be, my darling. No one can be trusted – *especially* if they have a position of authority. If I put those stones in a bank, it would be robbed inside the month. If I tried to sell them, the *best* I could hope for would be a ridiculously poor price. There's actually every chance that a prospective buyer would decide to murder us and simply take them. If that isn't bad enough for you, Portugal is waiting for a revolution.'

'Surely not,' Annaliese said.

'They deposed King Manuel in an armed rising and proclaimed a republic. But since then, things have got far worse, not better, and the people are sick of waiting.'

'Will it be dangerous for you?' Annaliese asked anxiously.

'Not if we keep quiet and don't draw attention to ourselves,' Elsa said. 'Those gems are a liability, not an asset. It's much better for you to have them.'

'I still have that money you sent to Liechtenstein,' Annaliese said, thinking that she had found a way out.

Elsa blinked. 'I'd forgotten about that. How much do you have left?'

'All of it,' Annaliese said. 'It's still in the bank you sent it to, gathering interest. Charles Templeton keeps an eye on it for me.'

Elsa shrugged. 'That wasn't our own personal money, my darling. When it became obvious that things were going horribly wrong, the young Emperor released funds from the Family's secret wealth. It was to enable people to escape and be sure of their future. I merely let you have a portion of what was given to us. It wasn't a *proper* gift – those emeralds are.'

'I don't know what to say,' Annaliese confessed.

'Then don't try,' Elsa advised. 'They are your insurance against *everything*. What's the English phrase – something about being prepared for a rainy day, isn't it?'

Annaliese laughed mirthlessly. 'I think it's going to pour down!' she said.

Elsa relaxed. She could see that the argument still had some way to run, but the main objections were over; the Falkenberg emeralds were destined to travel with Annaliese.

23

21–22 June 1925

'We must obey my rules, or it will fail'

After three days of stress and crisis, Edward was exhausted, both mentally and physically. The birth of Celia's son lifted a crippling load from his mind and he was fast asleep as soon as his head touched the pillow. He did not wake until eight-thirty on Sunday morning. It was 21 June, the summer solstice.

It took some time to recognise and adjust to his surroundings. As Celia had said, Allardyce Castle was a very private place, quiet and secretive. The sheer silence of the building, which was too old and at ease with itself to have so much as a single creaking floor-board, was unnerving. Eager to escape from it, Edward shaved and dressed, not noticing the impeccably precise preparations that had been made for him.

Unwilling to ring for a servant, he made his way from the West Wing to the head of the main stairs. It was a long, demoralising walk. What was he to do when he reached the ground floor? Wander about until he found someone?

In the event, he was saved that embarrassment. Baskerville and Mrs Pritchard were waiting for him. But the way they positioned themselves at the foot of the stairs made relief short-lived. The air of portent was so overwhelming that Edward experienced difficulty with the last two steps of his descent.

There were no greetings. Edward realised that the housekeeper, haggard and tired, was searching for words.

'What is it, Mrs Pritchard?' Edward asked. Watching closely,

Baskerville saw the change come over him: Edward was dreading the news, but was preparing to accept it. A stoic calm was beginning to encircle him.

'The little boy died during the night,' Mrs Pritchard said. 'About three o'clock, it was.'

'Why? What went wrong?' Edward's voice was quiet and steady.

'He couldn't breathe.' Mrs Pritchard was deeply distressed. 'There was something wrong with his lungs. They don't know why.' She stopped, biting back tears. 'The poor little mite hadn't been baptised . . . well, not by a vicar . . . I did it with ordinary water . . . It's supposed to be all right, isn't it? I'm sorry, sir, you'll have to excuse me.' Shaking her head, she hurried off.

'That's a bad business,' Edward muttered.

'Indeed, sir.'

Edward and Baskerville surveyed each other, recognising the beginnings of a mutual dependence.

'You'd better forget about that job at Cadogan Square,' Edward said. 'It seems that you and Mrs Pritchard can help me best by staying here.'

'I agree entirely, *Your Grace*,' Baskerville said, pleased to be the first to acknowledge that Edward Boothby-Graffoe was now the tenth Duke of Lincolnshire. 'Mrs Pritchard will take the same view when she recovers from a most upsetting night. We shall both do our utmost to support you in whatever difficulties you may encounter.'

'Thank you, Baskerville.'

'If I may speak personally,' Baskerville went on, 'your succession to the title will be regarded with great approval by everyone on the estate and in the village – which you now own. There has been considerable discontent since Your Grace's uncle passed away. He was much loved.'

'Things can only get better, you think?' Edward said.

'That is the way people will see it.' Baskerville's manner changed to indicate an end of the personal remarks. 'May I suggest breakfast?'

'Yes.' Edward was agreeably surprised by the discovery that he was hungry: the die was ineluctably cast and a voice was telling him that he must now do the best with what fate had thrust at him.

'The small morning-room is prepared for Your Grace,' Baskerville said.

As Edward was guided into the corridor that ran the full length of the West Wing, the two maids who were waiting at an open door sprang into action. Smoothly, with nothing more than a nod from his butler to set the process in motion, Edward was given his first taste of pampered privilege.

'Is there anything important I should do?' he asked Baskerville, who was waiting, sentinel-like by the sideboard.

'Perhaps you should contact Mr Ponsonby?'

Edward was doubtful. 'On a Sunday?'

'Under the circumstances, that hardly matters,' Baskerville replied. 'I imagine that there are legal moves which Mr Ponsonby will wish to put in train.'

'You're right. I'll talk to him – but not before this afternoon when I get back home.' Edward frowned, starting the painful and complex process of re-arranging his outlook on life. 'I mean Sussex,' he said. 'I suppose this is home, now. Er . . . what about Celia . . . my cousin's wife?'

'Yes?' Baskerville's right eyebrow rose by a barely perceptible fraction of an inch, yet it was disdainfully eloquent.

'Perhaps I should visit her – in hospital?'

The eyebrow moved again. 'You don't consider that the lady is best avoided?'

'Well . . .' Edward saw that it merited careful thought. 'One has to be civil, you know. And she deserves sympathy.'

'I wouldn't dispute that,' Baskerville said. 'One wonders, however, if the question of dealing with the Dowager Duchess is not one that should be entrusted to Her Grace.'

'Who?' Edward asked, baffled.

'Your wife, My Lord.'

Everything came back to Edward. 'My God, Baskerville, I'd forgotten all about *her*! She's coming home tomorrow and I have to be at Southampton to meet her and the boys.' He looked at his watch: it was nine-fifteen. 'If I remember correctly, her ship is due to leave Lisbon about now.'

*

Annaliese, Gwen and the boys were at the rail of the promenade deck, waving frantically as the *Caerphilly Castle* edged away from the quayside into the strong ebb tide flowing down the River Tagus. Elsa, Joseph and two guards brandished their hats.

It had been an emotional parting, a disjointed mayhem of laughter, weeping, promises and fears. Douglas had destroyed all hope of avoiding distress by dissolving into tears when the time came to leave Elsa. After that, Annaliese was praying for it to end, wishing that her father would stop believing that he would never see her and his grandsons again. She was grateful for the ringing of the engine-room telegraph as the captain asked for more power. The vessel shuddered slightly and began to pick up speed.

'I'm afraid you can't see Grandmama now,' Gwen said to Douglas.

'No, but I expect she's still there.' Since realising that blubbing was setting a bad example to George, his innate toughness had reasserted itself. 'We shall be seeing her next year, shan't we?'

'I hope so,' Annaliese said. 'We certainly mustn't wait a long time before we come again.' She gave a last wave towards the indistinct specks on the quay. 'Come on, it's time to get you two settled in.'

After allowing Baskerville to persuade him to address the servants, reassuring them of their future, Edward left Allardyce Castle at ten-fifteen. He was pleased to see that the village was deserted: either the newspapermen had gone, or, more likely, they were attempting to sleep off their Saturday-night hangovers.

Edward had every intention of going to Upper Overs as quickly as possible. However, when he saw a sign pointing to Marlborough, he followed it. He stopped on the outskirts of the town to buy a huge bunch of flowers and ask the way to the hospital. When he arrived, there was considerable fuss and bother about allowing him to see Celia, but the formidable matron eventually relented and he was shown into an elegant private ward.

Celia was resting, propped up against a pile of pillows. A pair of French windows were open on to a pleasant garden, freeing the room of the antiseptic smell that permeated every corner of the building.

'I . . . er . . . thought you would like some flowers,' Edward said lamely. He held the blooms out for her inspection before a nurse whisked them away to find a suitable vase. Celia was uninterested. With her face bleached of colour and her eyes lifeless, she looked at least ten years older.

'I'm sorry about what happened,' Edward muttered. 'Very sorry indeed. It's the last thing I wanted.'

She made no attempt at a response. After a few moments of excruciating awkwardness, Edward sat down, positioning the chair well away from the bed. 'Mrs Pritchard told me that she did her best to baptise the boy,' he said. 'What name did you give him?'

'I didn't,' Celia said. 'She called him William.'

'Oh. That's nice.' Edward smiled feebly and waited.

'They're going to blame me,' Celia said at last.

'Surely not.'

'They've already started.' She was bitter.

'I was told that the birth was perfectly normal,' Edward replied.

'Drink,' Celia said. 'It's because I'd been guzzling whisky. Even Mrs Pritchard was disgusted with me.'

Edward was silent.

'Ponsonby will have to be told.' Suddenly Celia seemed more alert and lucid.

'I'm putting that off until this afternoon,' Edward admitted.

'He'll be pleased. It will be the best news that he and his friends "in high places" have heard in years.'

'I doubt it.'

'Don't be stupid, Edward. I'm sorry – Your Grace. How does it feel?'

'I don't know,' he replied. 'It will take weeks – months – to get used to the idea.' Inconsequentially, he added, 'I stayed at the Castle last night. Strangely enough, Baskerville recommended it.'

'He's too clever by half,' Celia said angrily. Then she was calm again. 'Very good at his job, though. The place would fall apart without him and Mrs Pritchard.'

'I'll remember that,' Edward said earnestly. 'By the way, I didn't see any sign of the press in Compton Allardyce this morning. Perhaps they've cleared off.'

'I wouldn't think so,' Celia said. 'What about you? Are you staying, or going somewhere?'

'I'm on my way back to Sussex. I have to meet Annaliese and the boys tomorrow morning.'

'Does she know anything about all this?' Celia asked.

'No.' For some unaccountable reason, Edward felt compelled to explain himself. 'A cablegram would have been the only way of reaching her in time.'

Celia saw the point. 'And you couldn't find a way of putting all this into a few words?'

'I didn't even try.'

'It will be a nice surprise for her.'

'I've no idea how she'll react,' Edward said and forced himself to shut up before he betrayed his doubts and fears.

'What are you going to do about me?' Celia asked.

Edward was taken aback by the question. 'Do? What do you mean, *do*?'

'You're the head of the family now – Duke of Lincolnshire and everything that goes with it. Your biggest problem is probably a young dowager duchess who used to be a prostitute. She might also take it into her head to stick to the story that you attacked her at a critical time in her pregnancy.'

'You wouldn't get away with that,' Edward said, close to bluster.

'We can but try,' Celia said with a brittle gaiety that was more frightening than threats. 'It depends on what plans you make for my future. Even that creepy bastard Ponsonby will tell you that I'm your responsibility. It's how the aristocracy works, Edward, *dear.*'

'What have you in mind?' Edward asked warily.

'You could provide me with a home,' Celia said. 'God knows, there's plenty of room at Allardyce. I'd need an allowance, too, of course.'

'That doesn't sound a very good idea,' Edward replied, hoping to get away without explaining why he thought that.

Celia was not interested in pursuing the point. 'Alternatively, you could stump up enough money to get rid of me,' she suggested, her eyes crafty.

'How much?'

'Let's see. What's a troublesome dowager duchess worth?' Playing with him, she decided to double her planned divorce settlement. 'Shall we say half a million?'

'Half a million!' Forgetting himself, Edward shouted. Looking round furtively, afraid that a nurse would come rushing in, he lowered his voice to a theatrical whisper. 'That's a ridiculous figure.'

'It doesn't strike me that way,' Celia said with an amiability that was patently false. 'What was I worth when Ralph was alive? What *would* I have been worth if my son had lived? Think about it, Edward.'

He was already doing so. 'Let's suppose – purely for the sake of argument – that I give you the money. Can I trust you?'

'You'll have to make your own mind up about that, won't you?' Celia teased. 'Which is best – pay me off, or have me where you can keep an eye on me?' She laughed. 'Go away and think about it. I want to rest.'

But Edward stayed put and tried to reason with her. Coldly, Celia rang for a nurse to escort him off the premises.

During the last half-hour of his journey back to Upper Overs, Edward hoped that Beatrice and Charles would have changed their minds and decided to spend the whole day in London. They both had to make an early start at work on Monday morning, so, if they did return to Sussex, they would need to leave no later than seven o'clock. With any luck, they would find it too much trouble and stay put. Edward looked forward to solitude, the opportunity to think, to begin working out what had happened to him. There was also the question of tomorrow: how were he and Annaliese going to react to one another?

Turning into the drive, his hopes were dashed: Charles's motor car was parked near the front door. Disappointment turned into something close to horror when Edward saw the second vehicle, a Daimler which, almost certainly, belonged to Montagu Ponsonby.

Beatrice and Charles had arrived at eleven to be greeted by Mrs Grove and Polly with the news that Edward had dashed off yesterday morning, refusing to say where he was going. They had waited and worried, unsure what to do about lunch; eventually, when the leg of lamb was on the verge of being ruined, they sat down to eat. No sooner had they done so, than Montagu Ponsonby turned up, full of news and dismayed by Edward's continuing absence. So, when Beatrice rushed outside at the sound of her brother's car, her state of mind was agitated and unsettling.

'Edward, what *have* you been playing at?' she shouted. 'We've all been out of our minds with worry! You should have seen the state Mrs Grove and Polly were in when we got here . . . Thank heavens for Mr Ponsonby. He's been able to tell us most of what's been going on.'

Making no attempt to respond to Beatrice's overwrought tirade, Edward saw that the lawyer was standing at the front door. He was all smiles.

'I telephoned Baskerville this morning,' Ponsonby explained. 'Keeping my finger on the pulse, you know.' He congratulated himself with a laugh. 'This was ten minutes after you left the Castle. Naturally, Baskerville apprised me of the latest developments. I do feel bound to say that going to Compton Allardyce as you did was not a prudent course of action.'

'Whatever made you dash off like that?' Beatrice asked.

Again, Edward made no reply. He was going inside, where Charles was waiting expectantly. Further along the corridor, Mrs Grove and Polly dithered between scuttling back to the kitchen and the desire to hear what Edward had to say.

In an attempt to dispel the unease, Ponsonby was cheerful. 'Never mind, I'm sure no harm has been done – and we have a most satisfactory outcome. Yes, *most* satisfactory.'

Edward stopped and turned towards Ponsonby. He was puzzled: something was wrong. His face hardened as he realised what it was: no one – apart from Mrs Pritchard – was grieving for the child, not even his mother.

'I fail to see how the death of a new-born baby constitutes a satisfactory outcome,' Edward snapped. 'In my view, it adds to the terrible tragedy of my cousin's murder. You would do well to see it in that light, Ponsonby.'

The lawyer seemed to shrink. 'Yes, of course,' he stammered. 'I wasn't thinking.' He held up his Gladstone bag. 'As it happens, I brought a number of important documents with me. If Your Grace would care to inspect and sign them, I shall be able to expedite certain matters tomorrow morning.'

Your Grace!

The two words made the atmosphere in the entrance-hall electric. Beatrice, Charles, Mrs Grove, and Polly had been assuming that Edward *was* the Duke of Lincolnshire, but were unable to absorb anything like the full enormity of the idea. With two words, Montagu Ponsonby stupefied the onlookers.

'Very well, we shall go to the study,' Edward said. He was on his way when he caught a lingering whiff of roast lamb. 'If there's anything left, Mrs Grove, I'll eat it,' he called over his shoulder, not pausing in his purposeful stride. Montagu Ponsonby, definitely a few inches shorter, trotted after him.

When they had disappeared, Beatrice broke the silence. 'If you can scrape something together, Mrs Grove, I'll take it in,' she said.

Charles cleared his throat and shuffled. 'I feel the need for a little air, my dear,' he said mildly. 'A turn round the garden, I think.'

Nodding, Beatrice followed Mrs Grove to the kitchen.

It was ten minutes before Beatrice went outside. Charles sauntered across the lawn to meet her, a bemused half-smile on his face. 'How goes it?' he asked.

'Edward's *very* upset,' Beatrice said in an awed whisper.

'I'd managed to work that out for myself,' Charles replied, gently ironic. 'Ponsonby *is* an ass. No one with a grain of sense would deal with Edward that way.'

'He knows that now,' Beatrice replied. 'When I took the tray in, Edward was really putting him through it.'

'Very rude awakenings could be in order,' Charles said. 'You know Edward and his sense of duty. He might not have wanted to be a duke, but he'll make a job of it now there's no choice.'

'We'll see.' Beatrice was enigmatic.

'What's that supposed to mean?'

Beatrice weighed her words carefully. 'Tomorrow is a very important day,' she said at last. 'Very, *very* important. We can't be sure of what Edward will decide to do until he comes back from Southampton. If you can manage it, darling, I'd like to talk about something else.'

Miraculously, for very nearly an hour, they did. Then, Beatrice yielded to the temptation to go back into the house to listen at the door of the study.

'Well?' Charles asked when she returned, pulling a gruesome face.

'From what I can gather, they're having a blazing row over Celia,' Beatrice said. 'Edward seems to want her out of the way.'

'That could be expensive,' Charles mused.

'I think that's what the argument is about. Half a million pounds was mentioned.'

'Hmm!' Charles said and shut up.

After killing time for another hour, he and Beatrice were at the front of the house when Montagu Ponsonby emerged. He was alone and far from happy.

'All settled, Mr Ponsonby?' Beatrice called cheerfully.

'The legalities have been attended to,' Ponsonby replied. 'Though I must say, Lady Beatrice, that your brother's attitude leaves a lot to be desired.'

'Oh, I'm sorry to hear that,' Beatrice said, realising that a title was not something she would learn to live with easily. 'I expect you'll soon find a way of rubbing along together.'

Ponsonby's offended expression turned to one of monumental pain. 'We may do – *if* we are given the chance. There is talk of terminating the long and very fruitful relationship that your family and my firm have enjoyed. It's quite incomprehensible.'

Without waiting for a response, Montagu Ponsonby clambered into his motor car and drove himself away, demonstrating that the state of his nerves was not conducive to changing gear.

'It seems that Edward's chucking his weight around,' Charles said.

Before Beatrice could think of a suitable reply, Edward himself appeared, looking for them. 'Ah, Charles, the very man,' he said. 'Would you be prepared to take on the job of looking after the family finances?'

'Aren't you happy with Martin's?' Charles asked. For someone in his profession, it was common knowledge that Martin's had been the Lincolnshire and Boothby-Graffoe bankers for over 200 years.

'No, I don't think I am,' Edward replied. 'Would you like to come in and talk about it?'

'Of course.' Giving Beatrice a quick, rueful smile, Charles headed indoors.

Beatrice and Charles finally left Upper Overs to head back to London at half past eight. Suddenly, out of the blue, Edward said, 'Don't forget that this is your house now, Bee. As soon as I have probate for Father's will, the deeds will be transferred to your name.'

'Oh, yes.' It was starting to prove too much for Beatrice. Edward had given her a letter to post, explaining that it was his resignation from the Foreign Office. When she had asked if he knew what he was doing, he had showed her the letter from Sir Arthur Hawkins, the one that had caused him to dash off to Compton Allardyce.

'Where will you go tomorrow?' Beatrice asked. 'After you've collected Annaliese and the boys?'

Edward's hesitation showed that he hadn't thought that far ahead. 'Cadogan Square, I suppose,' he said doubtfully.

'You might be better off here,' Beatrice suggested.

'We'll see what Annaliese wants,' Edward replied. It was obvious that his resolve was collapsing and that the uncertainties of the future were starting to bear down on him.

'You will telephone me tomorrow, won't you?' Beatrice said. 'To let me know how you get on and everything. I shall be at Boothby's at least until six.'

'Yes, of course. Well, cheerio, Bee.' In a quick, awkward movement, Edward kissed his sister.

'Cheerio . . . Your Grace!' She smiled, willing him to laugh. Instead, he shook hands solemnly with Charles and would have hurried into the house but for the arrival of the Rolls-Royce.

Matthew, who had gone back to help at Cadogan Square after Lord Douglas's funeral, was needed for the trip to Southampton: he would drive the Rolls while Edward took another car.

'Ah! The very chap,' Edward said, edging away from Charles and

Beatrice. 'I want to talk to him. Bye-bye you two – look after yourselves.'

They were well on the way to London before Charles said, 'Well, my darling, what do we think of things?'

'I only wish I knew,' Beatrice replied unhappily. 'I don't believe I've ever come across a worse mess.'

'That's a pretty extraordinary statement.' Charles laughed. 'Look, I know your cousin's death was frightful – and one hates to think of a baby dying – but everything has turned out for the best, surely? Edward won't be *bad* as a duke and by ten o'clock tomorrow morning, I'll have a dozen people to testify that Annaliese is just what the title and Compton Allardyce need.'

'*If* she comes home,' Beatrice said. 'Edward is very afraid that she won't.'

Charles, who knew nothing of the difficulties in Portugal before Edward's premature return, was amazed. 'Do you want to tell me about it?' he asked.

Beatrice shook her head. 'Let's wait until we hear from Edward after he's been to Southampton,' she said.

At about midnight, Annaliese sat on the private verandah of their suite. It was a beautiful evening, flat calm, with scarcely a breath of wind, and *Caerphilly Castle* was making very fast progress towards England. A soft footfall heralded Gwen's return. She had been to look at Douglas and George, both fast asleep for over three hours.

'All right?' Annaliese asked.

'Lovely.' Gwen sat down in the chair close to Annaliese and stared at her. 'What's going to happen when we get home?' she asked.

Annaliese turned her head to study her maid and friend. The dim glow from the curtained windows behind them accentuated rather than concealed Gwen's truculent determination to have the truth. 'Do you mean what I think you mean?' Annaliese asked.

'Probably.'

'Well. . .' Suddenly, it wasn't so easy. Annaliese collected her thoughts. 'Edward and I aren't the best of friends.'

'Tell me something I don't know,' Gwen said.

'That business by the swimming-pool was bad. The more I think about it, the worse it gets.'

'I know.' Gwen waited before asking, 'Are you going to leave him?'

'I don't know. It depends on how he feels about things, I suppose. If he wants to carry on as though everything is normal, there will be serious trouble. Damn it, after that row over Mr Templeton, wouldn't you have thought that he might have changed?' Gwen said nothing, and, after a moment's hesitation, Annaliese made up her mind. 'Yes, I think I shall leave him.'

Gwen asked the most important question first. 'You'll take me with you, won't you?'

'Of course. I couldn't manage without you – or Matthew.'

With that resolved, the minor details had to be considered. 'Where will you go? Back to your parents?'

'No, I'm staying in England. I'm sure Beatrice will let me carry on at Boothby's and I should want to be near Lady Shenstone.'

'What will you do for money?' Gwen asked, rising to new heights of bluntness.

'I have plenty,' Annaliese replied. She had yet to tell Gwen about the Falkenberg emeralds. 'That's the least of my worries.'

'You're thinking of the boys?' Gwen asked.

'Very much so. How will they take to being deprived of a father?'

'Douglas won't like it – at first,' Gwen said thoughtfully. 'George will be all right.' Conscious of Annaliese's searching look, she added, 'He isn't too bothered about his father.'

'He doesn't dislike him?' Annaliese asked anxiously.

'No, I wouldn't say that.' For once, Gwen seemed to be at a loss for words – but not for long. 'If you ask me, George thinks that Mr Edward is a bit of an idiot.'

Annaliese made no attempt to contain her laughter. 'Lord Douglas was right about that boy,' she gurgled. 'He said he'd got a good brain.' Serious once more, she asked, 'Would George help Douglas get over it?'

'Definitely,' Gwen replied confidently. 'Douglas makes all the noise, but George decides what's what.'

Annaliese nodded thoughtfully. 'Like he did when we heard that their grandfather had died?'

'That's right. Douglas wouldn't take any notice of me when I told him about going to heaven, but once George got it sorted out, everything was all right.' Gwen was still and quiet for a few moments before asking, 'Are you expecting to be seeing more of Major Brandon?'

'Good God, am I allowed no secrets?' Annaliese cried, feigning righteous and innocent indignation.

'Not when you're so easy to read,' Gwen retorted.

'Only to you. Most people think I'm a perfectly ordinary, over-indulged woman without a care in the world.'

'More fool them. So, it's to be the Major, is it?'

'Yes, Gwen, I rather think it is.'

'He seems a nice man – you could do a lot worse.'

'Thank you, Gwen,' Annaliese laughed. 'I'm glad that you approve!'

The hint of gentle mockery drew the only sniff of the night from Gwen. 'Are we bothering to go to sleep?' she asked.

'I don't much feel like it,' Annaliese replied. 'To be honest, I'm rather nervous.'

'Me, too,' Gwen confessed with a cheeky, companionable grin. 'Shall I see if I can find some coffee?'

'What a good idea!'

Left alone with the hum of the engines and the noises of the sea against the ship's hull, Annaliese found two thoughts stealing into her mind. The first was that she was looking forward very much indeed to seeing John Brandon: soon – probably very soon – Nancy would have to arrange something for them. An afternoon at Martha's Vineyard would be a splendid way of launching a new phase in their relationship. Then, overlaying delicious anticipation, came the conviction that Edward was also wide awake and had abandoned the idea of sleep. Annaliese had no idea *how* she knew that, or why he was doing it. Ever since that miraculous day at the hospital in Berlin, their minds had drifted inexorably apart. Idly, with a detachment that was tantamount to indifference, Annaliese wondered if Edward's disturbed state could possibly result in something that would change the way she viewed their marriage. It was unlikely.

At ten o'clock, with a little more than an hour to go before a slightly early arrival in Southampton, the purser called on Annaliese.

'We've had our head office on the radio, ma'am,' he said. 'Just to confirm that your husband is waiting to meet you.'

'Thank you.' Annaliese was puzzled. 'Do you give all your passengers such attention?'

'Well, to be honest, only some of the first-class ones, ma'am.' The purser laughed nervously. 'Your husband was wondering if you'd care to stay on board for lunch,' he continued. 'We don't sail again until tomorrow evening, you see, so we could arrange that for you with the *greatest* of pleasure.'

'Yes . . . that sounds very nice.' Annaliese looked to Gwen for an opinion, receiving a look of blank incomprehension and a shrug. 'Yes, thank you.'

'If we may, ma'am, we'd like to serve the meal in your day-cabin. We're due to lay a new carpet in the dining-saloon on this turn round, so we shall need to get cracking the minute we get the other passengers off.'

'Yes, that will be all right,' Annaliese said.

'Thank you, ma'am.' Not far off bowing and scraping, the purser hesitated, then hurried away as though he had heard that the ship was on fire.

'That's odd,' Annaliese said. 'What do you think, Gwen?'

'It seems funny.'

Annaliese was frowning as she thought about it. 'Getting the head office to contact the ship by radio?' While she was being baffled by that, something else occurred to her. 'Did you get the impression that he was . . . oh, I don't know, sort of holding something back?'

'Yes, that's it.' Gwen came to life. 'He'd been told not to say too much.'

'About what?' Annaliese asked.

But there was no chance for speculation: Douglas and George, who had seen the purser leaving, came roaring in, agog with curiosity.

They were perfectly satisfied with the news that Papa was waiting and was coming on board to have lunch. In the midst of their excitement, Gwen was suddenly betraying anxiety.

'That officer didn't say anything about Matthew,' she muttered. 'Do you think Mr Edward's come without him?'

'I'm sure he hasn't,' Annaliese said. 'It needed two cars to get us here and neither us, nor our luggage has shrunk. No, Matthew will be there, you'll see.'

After the longest hour that either Annaliese or Gwen could remember, they saw Matthew. He was standing beside Edward and two men who were obviously senior officials of the Union Castle shipping line, something else that struck Annaliese as strange.

Gwen was more concerned by Matthew's subdued demeanour. 'He doesn't seem very pleased to see me,' she grumbled.

'What about Edward?' Annaliese said. 'He looks like death warmed up.' She waved as enthusiastically as Gwen, but was rewarded only with the brief acknowledgement of a raised hand. Very strikingly, although Edward and Matthew seemed bowed down by worry, the two Union Castle men were enormously pleased with themselves.

The moment the ship was made fast, a special gangway was lowered. Edward and Matthew were guided to it and the first officer went down to meet them.

'This is getting more peculiar by the minute,' Annaliese said. 'Look at that. You'd think Edward had turned into royalty.'

'Why is Matthew carrying a big bundle of newspapers?' Gwen asked, not expecting a reply.

The five men ascended the gangway and were lost to sight. The minutes began to tick by and there was no sign of Edward and Matthew. Other passengers were disembarking, Douglas was becoming restless and George was unable to calm him.

'They might have got lost,' Gwen whispered. 'Shall I go and look for them?'

'No!' Annaliese snapped, the tension making her angry. 'They know where we are . . . there must be a reason for the delay.'

Douglas, who was keeping a look-out along the passageway, let out whoops of glee as he caught sight of Edward, accompanied by the purser, with Matthew tagging along behind.

'Hello, my dear.' Edward rushed to Annaliese. He kissed her on the cheek, keeping his hands firmly by his sides. 'You're looking well. The sun suits you. Everything all right? Good trip?'

'Yes, thank you,' she said, stiffly polite.

The purser was hovering. Gwen and Matthew were holding hands and smiling.

'You won't forget about drinks with the Captain before lunch, will you?' the purser said. 'His good lady will be aboard by then, and I'm sure she'd be honoured to meet you if you could spare the time.'

'That's very kind,' Edward said, turning to smile at the man, willing him to disappear.

As soon as he did so, Annaliese's impatience got the better of her. 'Edward, what *is* going on?'

'Rather a lot, I'm afraid,' he said. 'I have a few things to tell you. We need to be alone for a while.'

'Will you take the boys to the nursery, please, Gwen,' Annaliese said. 'Go with them, Matthew.'

Before he left, Matthew put the newspapers on a table and exchanged looks with Edward. It was, Annaliese realised at once, a pre-arranged signal. Whatever she was to be told, Gwen and the boys were to hear from Matthew. Investing such trust in a servant was startlingly new and sharpened Annaliese's interest.

Edward was anxious to get it over with. To that end, he proposed copying what Montagu Ponsonby had done at Upper Overs. 'The easiest way to tell you this, is to show you how papers reported it,' he said. 'I think you'd better sit down.'

Annaliese did so while he selected *The Times* from the pile on the table. Without further comment, Edward thrust it at her, front page uppermost.

'*Um Himmels willen! Wie furchtbar!*' Annaliese gasped, shocked into using her native language by Ralph's murder and the way it was presented to her – like a slap across the face. Tight-lipped, she read on, assimilating the main details, before pausing to stare at Edward. 'I *knew* Blanche Hamilton was dangerous,' she said.

'Yes. Bee told me.'

After looking at the date at the head of the page to discover when it had happened, Annaliese continued to read. Her face was frozen and devoid of expression until she reached the paragraph at the end that spoke of Edward as the heir.

'Why is Celia's child not eligible – assuming it's a boy?' she asked.

'Stupid rules,' Edward said. 'No one really understands them so various people have been playing games. I disapproved of that piece, by the way.'

Annaliese nodded: she had no difficulty believing him. 'When is Celia's baby due to be born?' she asked. 'It must be any day now . . . so it says here.'

'She gave birth to a boy last Saturday evening,' Edward replied. 'The poor little chap died after only a few hours.'

'I see.' Annaliese put the newspaper down. She wanted time to think before she uttered another word. 'So *you* are the Duke of Lincolnshire?' she asked.

'Yes.'

'You inherit Compton Allardyce?'

'And a hell of a lot else,' Edward replied.

'What about Celia?' Annaliese asked. 'How is she?'

Edward groped for words. 'Very upset,' he said at last.

'You've seen her?'

'Yes. I was at the Castle yesterday.'

'It's unbelievable,' Annaliese whispered. 'To have your husband murdered and lose a baby in what – three days?'

'In case you hadn't realised, it was a particularly horrible business,' Edward said. 'In Hamilton's house, I mean.'

'Yes, I had appreciated that,' Annaliese said quietly. The blue eyes showed that her thoughts were momentarily elsewhere. 'Look, before we go any deeper into this, let me tell you how sorry I am about your father. He was a lovely man.'

'Mmm . . . yes.' Edward seemed confused. 'How did the boys take it?'

'They're all right now,' Annaliese replied. She returned to the newspaper, trying to put what it told her into some sort of context.

'This awful business at Compton Allardyce happened on Wednesday night – the day you buried your father?'

'Early hours of Thursday, actually,' Edward said. He saw the point she was trying to make. 'Yes, it was a terrible shaker. Bee and I were at Upper Overs, feeling sorry for ourselves, when we got the news.'

'So, you're the Duke of Lincolnshire,' Annaliese said again, as though comprehension was eluding her.

'And you are the Duchess,' Edward replied.

They stared at each other for a very long time. Bravely, Edward cut through the tense silence to begin the discussion.

'I was very much afraid that you wouldn't come back,' he said. 'It was a great relief when the people in the office told me that you were on board.'

Annaliese met his honesty with brutal frankness. 'I *did* consider staying with Mama and Father, but I don't think I could ever get used to that sort of life. And it wouldn't be fair on the boys to keep them so far away from you.'

'But you *have* decided to leave me?' Edward asked.

'Yes.'

Even though he was prepared for the worst, the sharp, uncompromising reply came as a blow. Edward recovered and nodded. 'There aren't all that many who would blame you,' he muttered. Annaliese was certain that she saw a weak surge of resistance and hope, but it faded and he turned his back, walking across the cabin to study the view of the docks. 'I didn't want this title – can you believe and understand that?' he asked.

'Yes. You must have been frightened to death.'

'I was.' Edward grimaced. '*Was?* I still am. Until Celia's baby died, I thought that I'd be able to wriggle out of it – I really did. But I'm stuck with it. Yesterday afternoon, when I got back to Upper Overs, I felt that I might be able to manage. It was a different story when I went to bed . . . I got into a terrible state.' Edward made a futile gesture. 'I can't cope with Compton Allardyce and all the rest of it, Annaliese. I'd be a worse laughing-stock than Ralph – at least he was enjoying himself while he ignored the estate and all his duties. I couldn't even do that. But you have a feeling for the place, don't you?

You were thrilled when you first saw it.'

'Yes, I was,' Annaliese said and waited.

'Look, let me tell you the God's honest truth, Annaliese. I won't be able to do this on my own. That's a fact. It will be a disaster. Everything will go wrong, I know it . . . I could see myself having to renounce the title.'

That meant Douglas, Annaliese thought. Knowing nothing of the laws that governed such cases, she could only guess at the dangers that might confront the estate and its five-year-old title-holder. They were probably formidable – ruinous, even. And what hope was there if his parents were estranged?

Annaliese rose from the chair and walked towards the verandah where she and Gwen had spent the night talking. Gazing across the busy docks in search of guidance and inspiration, she was astonished to find it. Instead of tugs, cranes, and warehouses, she saw a new perspective of the Great War – the trauma that Europe was pretending had never happened. It was the War that had toppled the Habsburgs, split them up, and set Annaliese on a new course; the War had claimed Edward's cousin, Gerald, and his brother, Alexander – both of whom would have taken precedence in the succession to the dukedom. Finally, instead of destroying Richard Hamilton, the War had spewed him out as an unstable wreck, a man capable of the murder that offered Allardyce Castle as an end to the long road from Schönbrunn. Accepting the inevitability and strange *rightness* of her journey on the dangerous flood of history, Annaliese turned back into the cabin.

'Will you stay with me and help?' Edward said, unnerved by her silence. 'You could make a success of it. *Please*, Annaliese, I need you.'

'You and I would have to organise our lives differently,' she said, steeling herself against the unexpected dignity of his pleading.

'Yes, I realise that. I'll agree to anything you like,' Edward said eagerly, believing that she was willing to reach a compromise.

Not just yet, though. Her look was shrewd as she asked, 'Will you be going to the House of Lords?'

'Yes. I get a seat in Parliament – it's the only advantage in this job.

I've had to give up the Foreign Office, by the way. They asked for my resignation.'

'That's a shame,' Annaliese said, deeply sorry. 'It must have been a wrench.' Edward pulled a face that said, yes, it had been. 'So, what are you suggesting?' Annaliese asked. 'That you occupy yourself with politics while I run Allardyce Castle?'

'It would be a start, don't you think?' Edward said hopefully. 'You'd be wonderful, my dear. You're cut out for it.'

'I shall want certain freedoms, Edward.' Annaliese stared hard at him, forcing him to understand *exactly* what she meant. 'There will be total secrecy and discretion, of course.'

'That would be very welcome.' Edward said with great depth of feeling. 'The Castle has seen enough scandal to last it for the next fifty years.'

Annaliese studied him. She had the power to make or break him: it was a distasteful position to be in, one that she would never have sought willingly. She wavered, wondering if she truly would be able to achieve protection against Edward's unpredictable moods and moralising. A mere fifteen minutes ago, she had been convinced that her marriage was beyond redemption. Now she was contemplating a pact and Ralph's words were mocking her: *I believe you'd give anything to be mistress of Allardyce.*

Annaliese made herself think of the good she would be doing – preserving tradition and stability, assuring the livelihoods of those people who depended on the estate. Then she remembered Lord Douglas: a blindingly clear vision of his wishes made up her mind. 'Very well, Edward, I'll do it,' she said. 'We must obey my rules, or it will fail.'

'Agreed,' he said and looked as though he was about to weep from sheer relief.

Remorseful at the way she had felt compelled to behave, Annaliese smiled and spread her arms. 'Come here, you fool,' she said.

Gratefully, Edward stumbled into her embrace and Annaliese kissed him with a warmth that surprised him. 'Yes,' she laughed when she drew back and saw the look on his face. 'In my own way, I *do* still love you, you peculiar individual. Where would I be now if you hadn't taken me out of Berlin? Who knows, it might be right for us again if you learn to be sensible and more relaxed.' A mischievous thought took hold of her. 'I *wondered* why you were being treated like someone important. My goodness, the Duke of Lincolnshire, eh? You'll have to get used to that, my lad.'

'Never,' he laughed.

'I must say, you organised this pretty well. It's a good start – keep it up.'

'I'll try.'

'Make sure you do!' Slipping away from him, Annaliese walked to the door and called out, 'All right, Gwen, bring them in here.'

In a flash, the boys appeared. Douglas, Marquess of Axholme, already felt a terrific swell; George had a long way to go before he made up his mind about the extraordinary things that had been going on while his back was turned.

Gwen's face was a picture as she pushed an apprehensive, dithering Matthew out of the way to get into the cabin. Fixing Annaliese with a stare like a gimlet, she confined herself to one word. 'Well?'

'It seems that we're going to live at Compton Allardyce and join the aristocracy,' was the po-faced reply.

'*Yes*, Your Grace.' Gwen produced a radiant smile and gave Annaliese Lincolnshire the most impudent curtsy she was ever likely to see. Matthew cast off his leaden foreboding with a broad grin of relief and excitement for the future.

Almost hidden by Gwen's skirts, Lord George Boothby-Graffoe, the little boy who had been conceived at what was to be his new home, had a curious, faraway expression on his face.

Epilogue

29 June 1925

Ralph and his son were buried together. The turn-out was as big as that for Uncle William. People who had avoided and denigrated Ralph during his life wanted to be seen at his funeral. It was as if they hoped to draw a line under a desperately distressing episode and make a fresh start. They also wanted to see the new owners of Allardyce Castle – particularly the Duchess.

She did not disappoint them. The wonderful hair was more golden than ever, her features firm and flawless, the cornflower-blue eyes arresting. On the breast of her black dress, she wore Maria Theresa's brooch with the double-headed eagle. Yet the stunning physical presence was outshone by her self-assurance. Lady Torksey, watchful and perceptive, realised that it came from a profound sense of affinity: Annaliese, Duchess of Lincolnshire, a foreigner who would have been stateless but for her marriage, belonged heart and soul to Wiltshire and Compton Allardyce. By comparison, her husband looked liked a fish out of water. He seemed to be doing his best, however, and was a good sort; given time, he would learn.

For the entry into the Chapel, Annaliese took Celia under her wing. The Dowager Duchess, friendless, but the object of much sympathy, was alone and dithering, trapped in the yawning gulf that lay between full membership of the most exclusive club in Britain and the outsiders, people who were vaguely undesirable and downright unacceptable. Holding her arm, Annaliese guided her into the front pew. The simple, quite natural action gave Celia a status that she could never have attained as Ralph's wife. Edward and Beatrice, following behind, were not the only ones who exchanged eloquent glances.

Afterwards, at the buffet in the Long Gallery, when everyone queued up to pay their respects to the new chatelaine of Allardyce Castle, condolences to the young Dowager were obligatory. She received them with shy gratitude and grace. Behind the façade he had adopted for the occasion, Edward saw that people were starting to think that Celia had been the victim of atrociously bad luck.

It was Lady Torksey, staring out of one of the windows, who noticed the plume of thick smoke rising from Keeper's Wood. At once curious and anxious, she turned to find Mrs Pritchard close by, checking on food supplies.

'That looks like a big fire,' Lady Torksey said. 'Is it intentional, or has something gone wrong?'

'It's the Hamiltons' house, my lady,' Mrs Pritchard replied. 'The workmen have started to demolish it. Her Grace gave orders that it was to be razed to the ground.'

'Did she, my goodness.' Lady Torksey was impressed. 'That was quick work.'

Mrs Pritchard smiled. 'We're being kept busy.'

'Have they moved in yet?' Lady Torksey asked.

'Her Grace almost has. His Grace has a great deal of business requiring his attention in London. We're expecting him very soon, though.'

'We obviously live in exciting times,' Lady Torksey said. Looking round, she saw Nancy Shenstone. 'Now there's a turn up for the book. Someone *has* been putting their foot down.'

Nancy was enjoying herself enormously. She had been bowled over by Compton Allardyce and was looking forward to spending the next two days exploring the Castle and its magnificent Park. Already, within hours of her arrival, several men had propositioned her and a very beautiful marchioness was begging to be allowed to join the Martha's Vineyard set. More importantly, Edward was driving back to London when the guests had all gone, and Annaliese, far too busy to have made contact with John Brandon, had indicated that she was dying for Nancy's bed.

It was when Edward was preparing to leave that Annaliese turned to a problem that had been worrying her since she had begun to plan the future over lunch on the *Caerphilly Castle* a week ago. There were no longer any suspicions or reservations about Celia: with her husband and son gone, there was room for nothing except compassion.

'What are you going to do now?' Annaliese asked the young Dowager Duchess.

'I don't know,' Celia replied, aware that Edward had broken off his conversation with Baskerville and was watching her nervously. 'I suppose I'm homeless.'

'Rubbish,' Annaliese retorted. 'How can you be? We have enough room here to provide luxury for half the county. *Would* you like to stay here, at Compton Allardyce?'

'Well . . . yes . . . very much so, actually,' Celia said. 'There's a lovely house up near the north-western gate . . . it's called The Chantry.'

'I know it,' Annaliese replied. 'It needs a lot doing to it, but you'd like that, would you?'

'I'd love it,' Celia said, her demure expression suffused with a glow of appreciation.

'It will be attended to,' Annaliese said. 'Until it's ready, you can have as much of the East Wing as you want.'

Gently, looking as though he was perfectly content with his lot, Edward kissed Annaliese and went. Observing it all, Nancy was very impressed; the new order at Allardyce Castle was making a good start.

Only Beatrice was uneasy. She had stumbled across the fact that, not only were Annaliese and Edward to occupy separate bedrooms, they were as far apart as the vastness of the West Wing would allow. Also, Beatrice was beginning to fear that Charles's unwillingly divulged misgivings were not as groundless as she wanted to believe: Celia *did* strike discordant resonances. Although faint, they were very disturbing.